CAULDRON

Also by Larry Bond

Red Phoenix
Vortex

CAULDRON

Larry Bond

HEADLINE

First published in Great Britain in 1993
by HEADLINE BOOK PUBLISHING PLC

10 9 8 7 6 5 4 3 2 1

British Library Cataloguing in Publication Data

Bond, Larry
Cauldron
I. Title
813.54 [F]

ISBN 0-7472-0732-1

Typeset by Avon Dataset Ltd, Bidford-on-Avon

Printed and bound in Great Britain by
Clays Ltd, St Ives PLC

HEADLINE BOOK PUBLISHING PLC
Headline House
79 Great Titchfield Street
London W1P 7FN

To our grandparents, Ruth & Dewey Bond,
Don, Sr. and Beth Larkin,
L. A. (Pete) and Mildred (Mil) Peterson,
and Lawrence and Irene Thornton

We had a lot of help with this book. We would like to thank:

Chris Carlson, Don Hill, Jason Hunter, Ferdinand Irizarri, Lt. Col. Jerzy Janas, Polish Army, Don and Marilyn Larkin, Duncan and Chris Larkin, Erin Larkin-Foster, Marshall Lee, Gary C. 'Mo' Morgan, John Moser, Bill Paley and Bridget Rivoli, Barbara Patrick, Tim Peckinpaugh and Pam McKinney-Peckinpaugh, Laurel Piippo, Steve St. Claire, Pat Slocomb, Thomas T. Thomas and Irene Moran, George Thompson and Dr. Tom Thompson (no relation), and Leonard Wong.

They all can take some of the credit, and none of the blame.

AUTHOR'S NOTE

Cauldron is the third book that Patrick Larkin and I have written in tandem – working from the faintest flicker of a glimmer of an idea to the final draft of a finished manuscript. Collaborations, especially such close collaborations, are not supposed to be easy. This one was.

Over a period that lasted nearly two years, we plotted out this story, created its characters, and worked together to bring them to life.

Although our styles sometimes differ, and continue to evolve, we both have strengths and skills that complement our work as a team. Each of us has favorite types of action and settings. Each of us has special areas of expertise.

Many people write books by themselves, but I cannot understand why anyone would want to. Pat and I spur each other on, bounce ideas around, and help each other out of tight corners. He has been not only my partner in this enterprise but a good friend as well.

For simplicity, we have used the standard Anglicized spellings and alphabet for Polish and Hungarian place and proper names. For the same reason, we have identified Russian-made military equipment in Polish service with its Russian designation, although the Poles have their own names for them.

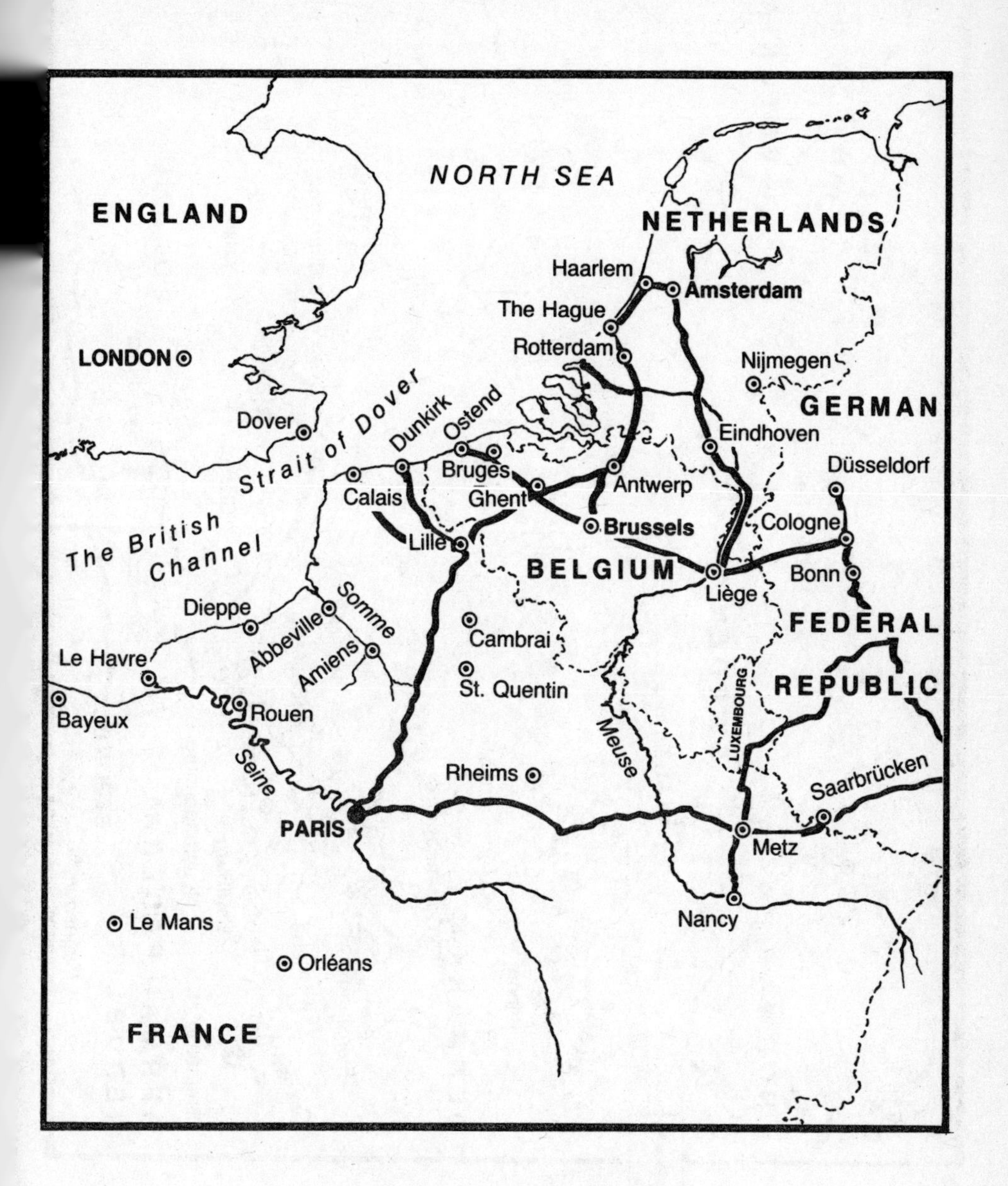

FRANCE AND GERMANY

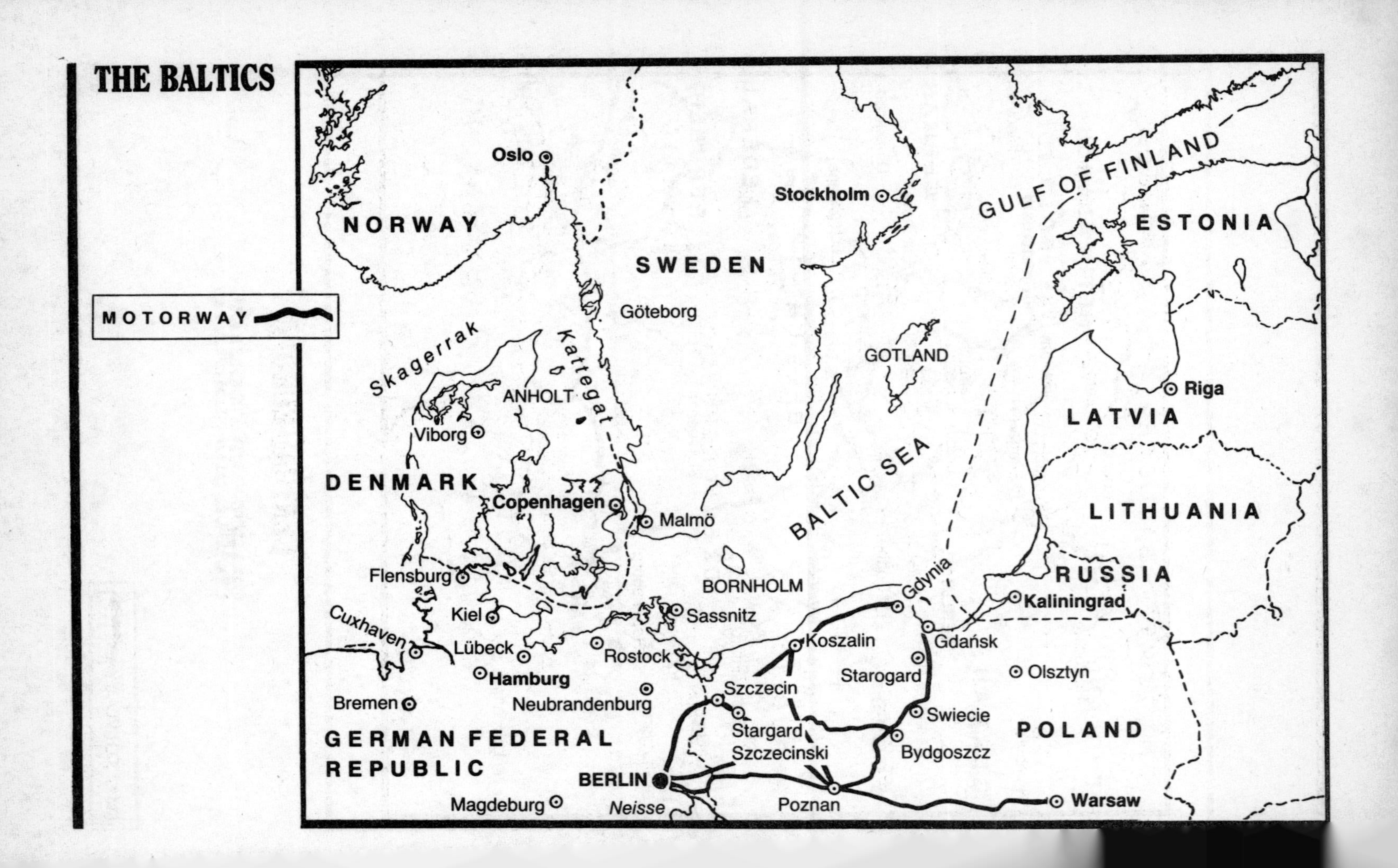
THE BALTICS
MOTORWAY
NORWAY
Oslo
SWEDEN
Stockholm
Göteborg
GOTLAND
GULF OF FINLAND
ESTONIA
Riga
LATVIA
LITHUANIA
RUSSIA
Kaliningrad
Skagerrak
Kattegat
ANHOLT
Viborg
DENMARK
Copenhagen
Malmö
BALTIC SEA
BORNHOLM
Flensburg
Kiel
Cuxhaven
Lübeck
Hamburg
Bremen
Rostock
Sassnitz
Neubrandenburg
Gdynia
Gdańsk
Koszalin
Starogard
Olsztyn
Szczecin
Stargard
Szczecinski
Swiecie
Bydgoszcz
POLAND
GERMAN FEDERAL
REPUBLIC
BERLIN
Magdeburg
Neisse
Poznan
Warsaw

CENTRAL EUROPE

MOTORWAY

DRAMATIS PERSONAE

AMERICANS

Corp. Tim Adams, U.S. Army – radiotelephone operator, Alpha Company, 3/187th Infantry, 101st Airborne Division (Air Assault)
Alex Banich, aka Nikolai Ushenko – senior field operative at the CIA's Moscow Station
Lt. Col. Jeff Colby, U.S. Army – commanding officer, 3/187th Infantry, 101st Airborne Division (Air Assault)
First Sgt. Andy 'Steady' Ford, U.S. Army – Alpha Company, 3/187th Infantry, 101st Airborne Division (Air Assault)
Gen. Reid Galloway, U.S. Army – chairman of the Joint Chiefs of Staff
Mike Hennessy – CIA field operative assigned to Moscow Station
Joseph Ross Huntington III – advisor to the President
Lt. Col. Ferdinand Irizarri, U.S. Army – liaison officer serving with the Polish 11th Mechanized Division
Col. Gunnar Iverson, U.S. Army – commanding officer, 3rd Brigade, 101st Airborne Division (Air Assault)
Len Kutner – CIA chief of station, U.S. Embassy in Moscow
John Lucier – Secretary of Defense
Erin McKenna – analyst and investigator for the U.S. Department of Commerce Office of Export Enforcement, assigned to the U.S. Embassy in Moscow
Walter Quinn – director of the Central Intelligence Agency
Capt. Michael Reynolds, U.S. Army – commanding officer, Alpha Company, 3/187th Infantry, 101st Airborne Division (Air Assault)
Clinton Scofield – Secretary of Energy
Maj. Gen. Robert J. 'Butch' Thompson, U.S. Army – commanding officer, 101st Airborne Division (Air Assault)
Harris Thurman – Secretary of State
Stuart Vance – intelligence officer assigned to the CIA's Berlin Station
Vice Adm. Jack Ward, USN – commander, U.S. Second Fleet and later commander of U.S., British and Norwegian Combined Naval Forces

GERMANS

Col. Georg Bremer – commanding officer, 19th Panzergrenadier Brigade, 7th Panzer Division
Major Feist – one of the 7th Panzer Division's staff officers
Maj. Max Lauer – commanding officer, 7th Panzer Division's reconnaissance battalion
Gen. Karl Leibnitz – commanding officer, 7th Panzer Division
Jurgen Lettow – Minister of Defense
Lt. Col. Klaus von Olden – commanding officer, 192nd Panzergrenadier Battalion, 19th Panzergrenadier Brigade
Special Commissioner Werner Rehling – European Confederation liaison officer with the Hungarian National Police
Heinz Schraeder – Chancellor
Lt. Col. Wilhelm 'Willi' von Seelow – operations officer, later commanding officer, 19th Panzergrenadier Brigade
Lt. Col. Otto Yorek – commanding officer of the 191st Panzergrenadier Battalion, 19th Panzergrenadier Brigade

FRENCH

Nicolas Desaix – director, General Directorate of External Security, or DGSE, later Minister of Foreign Affairs
Maj. Paul Duroc – DGSE special operative
Général de Corps d'Armée Claude Fabvier – commanding officer, EurCon IV Corps
Adm. Henri Gibierge – chief of staff, French Navy
Michel Guichy – Minister of Defense
Général de Corps d'Armée Etienne Montagne – commanding officer, EurCon II Corps
Jacques Morin – deputy director, later director, DGSE
Michel Woerner – DGSE special operative

HUNGARIANS

Brig. Gen. Imre Dozsa – commander, National Police
Col. Zoltan Hradetsky – police commander, Sopron District, later assigned to headquarters in Budapest
Oskar Kiraly – aide to Vladimir Kusin
Vladimir Kusin – opposition leader
Bela Silvanus – head of administration, National Police Headquarters, Budapest

POLES

Maj. Marek Malanowski – commanding officer, 411th Mechanized Battalion, 4th Mechanized Division
Maj. Gen. Jerzy Novachik – commanding officer, 5th Mechanized Division

Maj. Miroslaw Prazmo – commanding officer, remnants of the 314th Mechanized Battalion, 11th Mechanized Division
Gen. Wieslaw Staron – Minister of Defense
First Lt. Tadeusz 'Tad' Wojcik – American-born F-15 pilot, assigned to the 11th Fighter Regiment, at Wroclaw
Lt. Gen. Ignacy Zdanski – chief of staff, Polish Army

RUSSIANS

Marshal Yuri Kaminov – chief of staff, Russian Army
Col. Valentin Soloviev – senior aide to Marshal Kaminov
Pavel Sorokin – purchasing agent for the Ministry of Defense

PROLOGUE

NOVEMBER 1993 – 'EUROPE MIRED IN NEW FINANCIAL MESS,' *THE WALL STREET JOURNAL*

Torn by wildly variable interest rates and renewed pessimism about the world economy, the turmoil in Europe's financial markets intensified yesterday. Despite frantic interventions by their central banks, the British pound and the Italian lira continued their free-fall against the German mark and the French franc. Angry exchanges between government officials in London, Rome, Paris, and Berlin seemed likely to doom any hope for an early end to the chaos . . .

JANUARY 1994 – 'RACE RIOTS FLARE IN MAJOR EUROPEAN CITIES,' *WASHINGTON POST*

Angered by a new surge of economic refugees from poverty-stricken eastern Europe and North Africa, neo-Nazis, skinheads, and radical leftists went on a bloody rampage through industrial towns and cities across western Europe. In day-long rioting that left dozens dead or seriously injured . . .

JULY 1994 – ' "TRADE CRISIS LOOMING," U.S. WARNS,' *LOS ANGELES TIMES*

Recent French and German moves to protect their industries against fair international competition raise the specter of a devastating global trade war, key U.S. officials warned. On Capitol Hill, congressional leaders are already considering legislation to impose retaliatory tariffs and restrictions on goods imported from the two European countries . . .

DECEMBER 1994 – 'EASTERN EUROPE ON THE AUCTION BLOCK,' *THE ECONOMIST*

Desperate for the foreign monetary and food aid they need to stay afloat through the winter, several of eastern Europe's newly installed military regimes have signed pacts that give French- and

German-owned corporations a stranglehold over their trade and economic development. So-called Governments of National Salvation in Hungary, Croatia, Serbia, and Romania were among the first to mortgage their future to Paris and Berlin . . .

FEBRUARY 1995 – 'NATO ALLIANCE DISSOLVES,' *BALTIMORE SUN*

An era of unprecedented international defense cooperation came to an end today in rancor, bitterness, and suspicion. Outraged by French and German policies they blame for the continuing world recession, the United States, Great Britain, Italy, the Netherlands, Spain, and Norway formally withdrew from the NATO Alliance . . .

SEPTEMBER 1996 – 'WORLDWIDE SLUMP WORSENS,' *DALLAS MORNING NEWS*

With whole segments of international trade at a complete standstill, the global economic downturn worsened last month. As unemployment rose to near-record levels in all major industrialized countries and famine spread throughout the third world, many economists are now labeling this a depression . . .

COMMENTARY, ABC NEWS

'Poverty. Despair. Rising ethnic and national hatreds. Fear. This is Europe today.' Grim images flashed across the screen in time with the somber words. Pictures of miles-long unemployment lines, hollow-cheeked, hungry children and twisted corpses scattered through burning villages. 'A Europe in shambles, bleak, bitter, and adrift.

'A divided continent where old and dangerous ambitions the world thought safely buried are on the march again.' More pictures told the story. National flags of different designs and colors waved above a dozen different, strutting crowds in a dozen interwoven news clips.

The veteran journalist's voice took on a sad, wistful edge. 'When we won the cold war against communism, the world's democracies had a fleeting opportunity to secure a lasting peace founded on free trade and prosperity. We did not lose this historic opening by chance or simple bad luck. We threw it away.'

CHAPTER 1
Provocation

AUGUST 1, 1997 – EUROCOPTER ROTOR-FABRICATION PLANT, NEAR SOPRON, HUNGARY

The two men lay quietly on a thinly wooded hillside overlooking their target. Clouds covered the night sky above them, rolling slowly eastward in an ever-thickening band that promised rain before morning.

Down in the valley below, dim yellow lights outlined vague shapes in the darkness – huge aluminum-sided warehouses and factory buildings, a concrete and glass administration center, and boxcars waiting empty on a railroad siding. Other lights were strung at widely spaced intervals along a wire fence enclosing the whole compound. A single wooden guardhouse blocked an access road leading to the Budapest-Vienna highway and the Austrian border.

Nothing moved. Money and energy were both too scarce in the wreckage of Europe's economy to warrant around-the-clock manufacturing. Too scarce even for the high-tech tilt-rotor assemblies built by the French-owned Sopron plant.

Maj. Paul Duroc glanced at his companion. 'Ready, Michel?'

'Yes.' The big man's guttural French tagged him as an Alsatian – a man born in one of the twin provinces torn back and forth between France and Germany for centuries. He was half a head taller and massed at least ten kilos more than Duroc, extra weight and extra height that often came in handy for the physical side of their work. He slipped a pair of night-vision goggles over his eyes and quickly scanned the darkened factory compound. 'Still clear.'

Duroc tapped the transmit button on the tiny walkie-talkie clipped to his web gear. Two soft clicks sounded in his earphones. The other members of his team were in place and alert. Perfect.

He flipped his goggles down, rose to his feet, and moved downhill. Michel Woerner followed close behind – cat-quiet despite his size. Neither man had any trouble avoiding the trees, thorn-crowned clumps of underbrush, and moss-covered stumps in their path. Their goggles magnified all available light, turning the nighttime world into an eerie array of sharp-edged blue-green images.

Duroc paused at the edge of the woods, carefully studying the narrow band of open ground separating them from the factory's wire fence.

There weren't any signs that Sopron's security personnel had set up new motion sensors, video cameras, or other detection devices to cover this part of the perimeter. The single camera assigned to monitor this stretch of fence scanned slowly back and forth in a regular, dependable pattern. Men who knew the pattern in advance and who moved quickly enough could avoid its unblinking gaze. He allowed himself a quick, cold grin that flitted across a narrow face quite unused to smiling. For once the mission planners had been right. The Eurocopter complex was wide open. The fence, the lights, and the rest would keep out thieves, but not professionals with access to detailed information on the factory's security systems and routines.

A few TV cameras covered avenues of approach, but their regular scans were easily avoided.

He nodded once to Woerner and loped across the open ground, dropping prone next to the fence. The other man slid into place beside him a second later, already reaching for the wire cutters he carried in a pocket of his equipment vest. Duroc slipped the razor-edged jaws of his own cutters over the lowest strand of barbed wire and waited for his subordinate to do the same. Six short, powerful snips cut through three strands in rapid succession, opening a gap just wide enough for them to wriggle through. They were past the first barrier.

The two men scrambled upright and headed deeper into the darkened factory complex. Despite the continued silence, they moved cautiously, skirting pools of light and staying out of sight of the main gate guardhouse. Both men were veterans of more than a dozen 'special' operations conducted in half a dozen countries around the world. And professionals never took unnecessary chances.

Duroc led the way, picking a roundabout path through the man-made maze of warehouses, assembly lines, and loading docks. The hours he'd spent studying detailed maps and photographs were repaid with every surefooted step. Ten minutes after they'd cut through the security fence, he crouched beside the waist-high rear wheels of a tractor-trailer truck – surveying the deserted parking lot and empty lawn surrounding the plant's administration center an adjacent staff canteen. Near the main walkway, a large, floodlit billboard proclaimed 'Safety Comes First' in French, German, and Hungarian. His lips twitched upward at the irony. That might almost be his own motto.

A low rumbling and the distant, mournful blast of a train horn drifted down the valley – the sounds of the midnight freight express lumbering toward Vienna. They were still on schedule.

Duroc tapped his radio's transmit button again. His hands were already busy with a final equipment check when the response came. Three clicks this time. The others were ready for Phase Two. He looked at Woerner and found the big man's expressionless, pale blue eyes staring back. There were enough lights on around the factory headquarters to make their vision gear unnecessary.

Duroc pushed his own goggles further up his forehead and lowered his hand, frowning at the sight of the black camouflage paint smeared on his fingertips. Annoyed, he wiped them off on his sleeve. It was a cool night. He shouldn't be sweating.

He drew in a quick breath, held it briefly, and then breathed out. 'Now.'

They scuttled out from behind the truck and sped across the grass, angling away from the lighted walkway and toward concealing shadows at the base of the administration building. Duroc felt his heart speeding up, racing in time with his feet. Every noise they made seemed a hundred times too loud. Each footfall on the soft, dew-soaked grass sounded like an elephant crashing through dead brush. And every hushed, panting breath echoed dangerously through the quiet night air.

They merged with the shadows and stood still, waiting uneasily for the shout or clanging alarm klaxon that would tell them they'd been spotted. None came. Just the fading thunder of the freight train vanishing in the distance.

Duroc's pulse slowed and he swallowed hard to clear the sour taste in his mouth. The Frenchman shook his head, coldly irritated by the lingering remnants of his own fear. Maybe he was getting too old for this sort of caper. He'd seen it happen to others in the secret services. Every field operative had only a limited reservoir of courage. When it was used up, you were finished, fit only for a sterile, useless desk job.

He snorted in self-contempt as Woerner touched his arm. Precious seconds were slipping away while he wasted time in absurd self-analysis. Action would burn through the fear. It always did.

Bent low to stay below eye level of anybody inside looking out onto the grounds, they edged round the corner of the building. Duroc counted windows silently. Three. Four. There. He stopped. The architects who'd designed the Sopron plant's ultramodern headquarters had been thinking of esthetics, not security. Waist-to-ceiling picture windows made every outside room and hallway seem larger and lighter on sunny days. But they also left them exposed and unguarded.

According to the blueprints he'd memorized, the window in front of him opened directly onto a corridor leading straight to their objective, the factory's computer center. It was almost a perfect entry point. He glanced toward the nearby staff canteen – far too near for his taste. Still . . .

He shrugged. Second-guessing a good plan was usually a certain road to disaster. Speed and convenience should outweigh any risk.

Woerner was already hard at work, his thick fingers flashing nimbly through long-practiced tasks. The big man pulled a piece of metal shaped as a flattened U out of his vest and smeared a fast-acting adhesive across both ends. Then he clamped the metal bar onto the window and held it in place for several seconds, waiting for the glue to take hold. Satisfied, he let go and stepped back, leaving room for his superior to take over.

Duroc moved forward with a diamond-edged glass cutter in his right hand. They had their door handle. Now to make the door. He dragged the glass cutter through the window in four steady strokes, two vertical and two horizontal, grunting softly at the effort it took.

When he was done, Woerner grabbed the metal handle with both hands and tugged straight outward, levering a solid piece of glass right out of the window. While the giant Alsatian carefully set his burden down on the grass, Duroc unrolled a thick sheet of black matting across their new-cut opening. The steel strands woven through both the matting and his gloves would protect his hands and legs while he climbed through the gap.

Without waiting for further orders, Woerner knelt down and put his own hands together to form a makeshift stirrup. Duroc stepped up into the other man's locked hands, reaching for the edges of the cut glass as his subordinate boosted him toward the hole. He threw one leg over the protective matting, leaning inward . . .

An outside door banged open.

Duroc almost lost his balance as he jerked his head around toward the entrance to the factory's cafeteria. A blue-uniformed security guard carrying a steaming cup of coffee stood there staring back at him. Shock and surprise combined to stretch time itself, turning a single second into an endless, frozen pause.

Sudden motion shattered the illusion as the security guard tossed his coffee cup away and fumbled for the pistol holstered at his side. 'Halt!'

Duroc swore inwardly, unable to reach for his own weapons while he teetered practically spread-eagle against the window. For all his size and strength Michel Woerner was even more helpless. Neither could move without disastrously unbalancing the other.

With his pistol out and steadied in a two-hand grip, the guard edged closer, visibly more confident as his eyes sorted out the spectacle in front of him. Duroc forced himself to look beyond the muzzle aimed at his stomach. The other man was young, and young-looking despite the thick mustache curling above his upper lip. An ex-conscript perhaps, fresh from his military service and still eager for action. That was unfortunate. An older man might have been more reasonable or more worried about his own survival. But younger men prized glory above all else.

'Do not move or I will shoot.'

Duroc's mouth twisted at the clumsy, phrase-book Hungarian. Nevertheless, he obeyed and stood motionless, still perched in Woerner's cupped hands, silently willing the guard to keep walking. A little further, he thought. Just a little further.

The young man stepped away from the open cafeteria door, moving out onto the lawn to give himself a clearer field of fire. He lowered one hand from his pistol toward the radio clipped to his belt. Duroc felt his jaw muscles clench. An alert now would ruin everything.

Crack.

The security guard's chest exploded in a red rain of blood and broken bone – torn open by a 7.62mm bullet that hit him squarely in the back and threw him forward onto the grass. He shuddered once and then lay still.

Duroc scrambled down from the window and knelt beside the body, feeling for a pulse. Nothing. He glanced toward the wooded hills three hundred meters away and punched the transmit key on his own radio. 'Confirmed.'

Two answering clicks sounded in his earphones as the sniper he'd placed there on overwatch acknowledged the kill.

He pulled the pistol out of the dead man's hand and rose to his feet. 'Who was he?'

'Monnet, Jacques.' Woerner read the guard's bloodied name tag aloud.

Duroc recognized the name and shook his head slowly and sadly from side to side. Monnet had been the sentry stationed at the main door. He ought to have been safely on duty and out of the way. But he evidently couldn't wait for his shift change to get his coffee. So now the young fool was dead. A pity. His death would complicate matters.

He nodded toward the window. 'Bring him.'

Woerner grunted his assent and bent to his task. Together they manhandled the guard's body through the gap and dumped it into the corridor beyond.

Nose wrinkling at the smell of blood and voided bowels, Duroc wiped his gloves clean on the grass and checked his watch. They were behind their timetable – but still well within the planned margin for error. 'Right, Michel. Let's finish this and get home to our beds, eh?'

'*Oui, m'sieu.*' A humorless smile ghosted across the big man's face. 'I've had enough excitement for this night.'

Thirty seconds later, Duroc glided down the dark hallway alone while Woerner waited outside to guard his retreat. The Frenchman was tired of unpleasant surprises.

A thick, fireproof steel door blocked access to the computer center. And a tiny red light blinked steadily on a nearby ten-key panel controlling the door's electronic lock. Security might be lax everywhere else, but the Sopron plant's data banks held information that Eurocopter's Japanese and American competitors would dearly love to see – production schedules and costs, precise formulas for rotor metal and plastic composites, reports on advanced RD projects, and all the thousands of other facts and figures generated by any major industrial concern.

Duroc focused a small penlight on the keypad and carefully punched in the six-digit security code he'd memorized. Yesterday's security code. As he'd expected, the massive steel door stayed obstinately shut. Good. He tried the code again. This time the panel's tiny red light stopped blinking. Even better. The simpleminded computer controlling the lock would now have a record of two failed attempts using a code that would have worked just a few hours before.

He snapped the penlight off and clipped it back in place on his web gear. Now to arrange a big but relatively harmless bang. Moving quickly, he molded an ounce of pliable plastic explosive around the lock control panel. More ounces covered the door's hinges. When he was finished, the Frenchman stepped back and eyed his work appreciatively. Wires ran from igniters buried inside each piece of plastic explosive to a small, inexpensive, and old-fashioned wristwatch set for a two-hour delay. He nodded to himself. It had the right feel to it. Effective but amateurish. Even the type of explosive he'd used was appropriate. Czechoslovakia's old communist government had doled out odorless, colorless Semtex to terrorists around the world.

Duroc moved back up the corridor. Time for the finishing touches to this night's work. He uncapped a small can of red paint, shook it, and sprayed. 'Death to French pigs!' and 'Liberty, not slavery!' in meter-high letters across one wall. Duroc had been careful to memorize the nationalist slogans in Hungarian, and even used the characteristic lettering. Even the smallest details were important in a job of this kind. All of the signs would point to Hungarian terrorists, angry with French 'economic colonialism.'

Woerner was waiting for him at the window. 'It's still quiet.'

'Not for long.' Duroc dropped onto the grass and stood waiting while the big man rerolled their black steel mat and carefully set the cut-out piece of glass back in place. Then the two men turned and trotted back toward the hills rising above the factory complex.

The watch-driven bomb they'd left behind clicked another minute closer to detonation.

Duroc and his team were forty kilometers away when the timer reached zero.

The Sopron factory administration building rocked on its foundation, torn by a powerful explosion. A searing white light flared behind every ground-floor window milliseconds before the shock wave blew them apart. Behind that first shock wave, a wall of fire and superheated air roared outward from the detonation point, killing five Hungarian maintenance workers who had just come on-shift and setting everything flammable ablaze.

Even before the first emergency sirens wailed over the Eurocopter complex, flames could be seen dancing eerily through the shattered building.

AUGUST 2 – EUROCOPTER ROTOR-FABRICATION PLANT, NEAR SOPRON

Pale sunshine streamed over a scene of barely contained chaos. Fire trucks and other emergency vehicles surrounded the bomb-damaged administration center – parked seemingly at random on its scarred, wreckage-strewn lawn. Workers carrying salvaged office equipment and furniture outside mingled with weary firemen, structural engineers, and worried-looking company officials. Restless security guards armed with automatic weapons instead of their standard-issue pistols stood watch at the main gate and near the explosion site.

A thin, acrid smell of smoke and charred paper lingered in the muggy, windless air. The computer room's halon fire extinguishers and steel doors had saved the factory's data processing systems, but they hadn't stopped blast-sparked fires from roaring through the rest of the ground floor.

Fifty meters from the building, a short, round-faced man fought hard to control his temper. Even during the best of times, Col. Zoltan Hradetsky had never much liked Francois Gellard, the Eurocopter factory's general manager. The Frenchman had always been officious, arrogant, and all too ready to look down a long, thin nose at everything and everybody Hungarian. At the moment, the man's worst traits were magnified a thousandfold.

'For the last time, Colonel, I must refuse your request to investigate this affair.' The manager folded his arms. 'Your presence here is unnecessary . . . and disruptive.'

'Disruptive? You . . .' Hradetsky swallowed the string of curses that rose in his throat. 'You misunderstand me, M. Gellard.'

He jabbed a finger toward the wrecked administration center. 'That is a police matter. So is the cold-blooded murder of five of my countrymen. As the ranking police officer for this district, I am not making a "request." I'm issuing an order.'

'Impossible,' Gellard sneered. 'Your orders carry no weight within this compound, Colonel. I suggest you reread the terms of the contract between your government and my company. For all practical purposes, this is French soil. This terrorist crime has been committed against a French corporation. And it will be investigated under French authority.'

That damned contract! Hradetsky ground his teeth together. He didn't need to peruse the fine print to know that the factory manager was on safe ground. When the Sopron plant was being built, Hungary's shaky military junta had been desperate for French and German financial assistance. To the generals in Budapest, meeting Eurocopter's demands for tax-free status and complete control over its facilities had appeared a small price to pay for the jobs and low-interest loans its factory would provide. And they'd granted the same special privileges to dozens of other Franco-German business interests.

The police colonel shook his head. He'd supported the two-year-old Government of National Salvation as a regrettable but necessary emergency measure. Hungary's weak, faction-riddled, postcommunist democracy couldn't cope with economic chaos and failing harvests. Heavy-handed rule by soldiers had seemed better than misrule by inept, quarreling politicians. Now he was starting to have second thoughts about that. In effect, the generals had mortgaged their nation's sovereignty to feed the hungry, unruly people who had put them in power. After forty-five years of military and political domination by the Soviets, his poor country had staggered into the grasp of a new set of masters – France and Germany, Europe's new economic and military superpowers.

'Well, Colonel?'

Hradetsky looked up. 'What you say may be legally correct, but I do not think it is especially wise.' He tried to keep his voice dispassionate. 'If there are terrorists operating in this region, surely you can see that it will take all our combined efforts to hunt them down?'

'What do you mean, "if there are terrorists"?' Gellard demanded. 'There's no "if" about it! What's more, it's obvious that they were aided by traitors inside our own work force. By some of your lazy, shiftless countrymen!'

The factory manager frowned. 'Given that fact, Colonel, even an idiot should be able to understand why my company can't trust this investigation to you or your men. Hungarians hunting Hungarians? The very idea is ludicrous.'

Hradetsky's irritation flared into open rage. He could stomach arrogance, but he'd be damned if he'd put up with deliberate insults. He stepped closer to Gellard – a move that wiped the easy assurance off the Frenchman's long, aristocratic face. 'I think you should reconsider your choice of words, monsieur. Some of my countrymen might say that you have a tongue so sharp that it must wish for the touch of a knife. Do I make myself clear?'

The manager paled, evidently aware that he'd gone too far. 'I didn't mean . . . that is, what I said was . . .'

A helicopter roared low overhead, drowning out his stuttered apology. Both men turned to stare as it circled, flared out, and clattered in to land in the administration center's parking lot. Hradetsky scowled at the blue, white, and red tricolor emblazoned on the helicopter's tail-rotor pylon. Clearly the French government wasn't wasting any time before poking its own nose into this matter.

Three men climbed out of the aircraft, ducking under its slowing rotor blades. Two were big men, mere muscle. The third wore a dark gray civilian suit, carried a bulging leather briefcase, and walked with the easy assurance of a man used to command.

When Hradetsky turned back to face Gellard, the Frenchman had regained his poise. 'That will be the security specialist dispatched by my embassy, Colonel. An expert on terrorism and counterterrorist tactics. You can deal with him in future.'

The Hungarian police colonel eyed the short, grim-faced man striding briskly toward them. Something told him this wasn't going to be a pleasant or productive meeting. 'What's his name?'

Gellard smiled coldly. 'Major Paul Duroc.'

CHAPTER 2
Minuet

AUGUST 4 – PLACE DU PALAIS-ROYAL, PARIS

Paris lay oddly quiet beneath a cloudless blue sky – its wide, tree-lined boulevards and parasol-shaded outdoor cafés empty and deserted. For most Parisians, August was a time for vacations, for a month-long flight from their government jobs, factory floors, and schools. But now the tourists who would ordinarily have taken their places were gone, too – discouraged by the visa restrictions, high prices, and official harassment that were part of the world's ongoing trade war. Only the growing armies of the unemployed and the homeless were left in the capital. And they were too busy looking for work or food to saunter through the abandoned fashionable districts.

The Place du Palais-Royal showed its own signs of abandonment. The shops and kiosks that normally catered to foreigners eager for postcards and subway maps were padlocked. Instead of block-long lines of sightseers and chattering schoolchildren, only a few scattered art lovers wandered in and out through the Louvre's north gate, dwarfed by the museum's gray bulk. A handful of bored cabdrivers loitered near the Métro stop's escalators, exchanging gibes and the latest gossip through a thin haze of cigarette smoke.

Across the square, the Palais-Royal seemed wrapped in the same kind of August inertia. Soldiers in full dress uniform stood motionless behind the tall iron gates that blocked access to its inner courtyard and main entrance. Others, clothed more comfortably in camouflaged battle dress and fully armed, manned rooftop observation posts. Pairs of hard-faced policemen patrolled the pavement along the fence, looking for beggars or street Arabs to muscle.

Most of the massive building's windows were either shuttered or blocked by heavy drapes. Few official cars were parked in the inner courtyard, and most of those were covered by tarpaulins to keep the dust and city grime off while their usual passengers and assigned drivers were away on vacation. Despite the tight security, the Palais-Royal appeared as deserted as its surroundings.

But appearances were, as usual, deceiving.

Built during the 1600s, the Palais-Royal had first served as the residence of the Red Eminence, the Cardinal Richelieu. As the twentieth century drew to a close, it contained offices for several high-ranking French officials.

Nicolas Desaix's private office had its own aura, one matched perfectly to its master – an air of close-held power and restrained elegance. A carpet worn thin by a hundred years of use and embroidered in rich tones of royal blue and scarlet covered the floor. A tapestry commissioned by Richelieu himself graced the wall behind a massive oak desk, and paintings of famous French military victories filled the other walls, on permanent loan from the Louvre. As head of the French intelligence service, the DGSE, Desaix had two other suites – one at the Élysée Palace itself, close to that of the republic's President, and another at his directorate's headquarters. But this history-filled sanctuary was the place he preferred for important work.

Now the late afternoon sun slanted through its tall windows, filling half the room with rectangles of red-tinged gold and leaving the rest in shadow.

Alexandre Marchant paused by the door, momentarily dazzled by the sharp contrast between light and dark.

'My dear Marchant! Come in. Come in.' Desaix rose from behind his desk and strode forward, motioning him toward a pair of high-back armchairs off to one side of the room. 'You're looking well.'

'As are you, Director.' Marchant sat down gladly. Years of devotion to good food, good wine, and desk work had saddled him with increasing weight and an expanding waistline. Few of his old schoolmates would have recognized him as the same short, skinny young aeronautical engineer who had once dreamed only of designing the world's most advanced aircraft. Now those dreams were dead – crushed by the day-to-day considerations of profit margins, costs, and personalities involved in managing the huge industrial conglomerate called Eurocopter.

The man who took the chair across from him couldn't have been any more different in physical appearance. Nicolas Desaix had the same tall, slender build and prominent, jutting nose his countrymen still associated with France's last great leader, Charles de Gaulle. It was a resemblance Marchant was sure the intelligence chief valued.

'You've seen Major Duroc's preliminary report?'

Marchant nodded, remembering the blank-faced motorcycle courier who'd hand-carried the document to his home, stood waiting while he read it, and then retrieved it for immediate shredding at the DGSE's headquarters. That, more than the report's cold, factual words themselves, had rammed home the dreadful seriousness and secrecy of this matter. What had been planned as a fairly simple act of self-inflicted sabotage had escalated into gunfire and sudden killing.

Desaix seemed to read his mind. 'I regret the unfortunate . . . complications, Alexandre. Especially your security guard's death.' He shook his head sadly. 'He had a wife, I understand?'

'Yes. In Lyons.'

Desaix sighed. 'A great pity.' He looked up. 'She will be provided for?'

'Of course.' Marchant folded his hands across his lap. 'We carry life insurance policies on all our employees, and in this instance my personnel people are organizing a special compensation fund.'

'Good.' Desaix nodded his approval. 'France must care for all her fallen sons. No matter how they fall.'

Eurocopter's chief executive was struck by the evident sincerity in his voice. A few simple words transformed young Monnet's death into an act of patriotic sacrifice. It was astonishing. This man had more charisma and command presence than the President and the rest of the cabinet combined. Half his talents were wasted in his present position.

Desaix sighed again and then shrugged. 'Still, such tragedies are probably unavoidable. We live in an imperfect world and we must use imperfect tools to achieve our ends.' He looked up. 'And those ends were achieved, true?'

'Yes.' Marchant felt himself on firmer ground now. Work force changes, production schedules, and profit margins could be managed and controlled. Mental images of grieving widows could not. He sat forward in his chair. 'Your major's bomb caused only minor damage – as promised. Nothing that significantly affected our rotor output. Nevertheless, my directors are appalled by just how close this "Hungarian" terrorist group came to wrecking our Sopron operation.'

Both men smiled at that.

'Then you foresee no serious opposition to our proposals at tomorrow's board meeting? No second-guessing?'

Marchant shook his head. 'None. I already have all the votes we need in my pocket.'

Desaix looked pleased. He'd approved Major Duroc's 'special action' as a means of solving two serious problems with one small bang. And Nicolas Desaix was a man who fully enjoyed being proved right.

Despite the favorable tax and wage agreements offered by Hungary's military government, Eurocopter's Sopron plant was still a money-losing proposition for France. Government protection ensured a steady stream of European aircraft industry orders for its rotors. Overseas sales were a different story. Fierce competition from America's Boeing and the Japanese meant a need for continuing and expensive government subsidies. With the world mired in what seemed a perpetual economic slump, French companies like Eurocopter desperately needed ways to cut their costs. Naturally, cutting wages for their foreign workers in eastern Europe was far more politically palatable than slashing pay packets at home.

Unfortunately Sopron's Hungarian work force was showing signs of increasing militancy over French control and supervision. Work stoppages, 'sickouts,' and muttered strike threats were already raising tensions along its rotor assembly lines. Further wage reductions were bound to be violently opposed – at a high cost in factory downtime and lost orders. Other companies operating in Hungary, Croatia, and Slovenia faced the same kinds of labor force unrest.

That was the first problem.

The second also involved foreigners. To be more precise, foreigners living in France. During the past four decades, hundreds of thousands of 'guest' workers and their families had swarmed into the country from Algeria, Tunisia, Turkey, Portugal, and half a dozen other poor nations. Lured by a severe labor shortage during the 1950s and 1970s, they were now unnecessary. With millions of native-born Frenchmen out of work, the 'Arabs' were seen as a dirty, dangerous, and shiftless source of social friction and political trouble. Public opinion blamed them for every increase in the crime rate and for diseases like AIDS. Bloody skinhead rampages through their shabby, poverty-stricken neighborhoods were becoming commonplace.

To put it bluntly, France wanted the foreigners out.

And so Nicolas Desaix had seen a golden opportunity to aid his nation, benefit its powerful industrial conglomerates, and boost his own political career – all in one fell swoop.

Replacing their troublesome eastern European workers with low-wage 'guest' laborers would help Eurocopter and other French companies cut their manufacturing costs. It would also reduce the government subsidies now used to keep their prices below market levels. Even better, as documented aliens with French work permits, the new factory workers would pay their taxes directly into Paris' revenue-starved coffers. They would also be off French soil and under strict control in guarded, fenced-off, and isolated compounds.

On paper, it was the perfect solution. And Sopron was the first step toward putting it into practice.

Frightened by the first signs of a 'terrorist' campaign against French-owned facilities, other manufacturers were sure to quickly imitate Eurocopter's worker replacement program. The Germans would probably fall in line as well, Marchant thought. The *Boche* had their own problems with unwanted immigrants.

The Hungarians and the other client-state governments would undoubtedly protest these moves, but their protests would be futile. They needed continued French and German financial aid, backing, and goodwill far more than France or Germany needed them. Any threat to end that aid or close the factories should be enough to cow them. Or so Marchant hoped.

He cleared his throat. 'One thing still troubles me, though.'

Desaix frowned slightly. 'And what is that?'

'This Hungarian policeman Duroc mentioned. Hrad . . .' Marchant stopped, unable to fit his tongue around the police colonel's unmanageable name.

'Him?' The DGSE director snorted. He waved a hand in airy dismissal. 'He's nothing. A provincial nobody without influence in Budapest. Don't waste time worrying about that fellow, Alexandre. If he causes too much trouble, I'll have him suppressed.'

Marchant nodded his understanding. The French security services had poured a great deal of time, money, and training into their Hungarian counterparts. As a result, they exercised a great deal of both overt and covert control. Hungary's current rulers owed their power to Paris – something Desaix and his colleagues never let them forget. An official who offended the military government's chief sponsors wouldn't last long in his job.

He stood up, surprised as always at the effort it took to lift himself upright. 'In that case, I'll take my leave, Director. I'm sure that I've already taken up too much of your valuable time.'

Desaix stood up with him, an easy, companionable smile on his lips. 'Not at all, Alexandre. Not at all. My door is always open to you. Remember that.'

Eurocopter's chief executive officer looked up at the taller man. 'You have my thanks, monsieur. And those of others as well.'

Neither man felt a need to say more.

Everyone knew that France's aging and ineffectual President was on the verge of one of his periodic cabinet reshuffles. Backing by some of the nation's largest industrial firms would help Nicolas Desaix win whatever ministry he wanted to head. It was a quid pro quo Marchant offered gladly. With Europe and the world in economic and political turmoil, France needed more leaders courageous and cunning enough to seize every opening fortune held out to them.

Empires were won by bold action, not cringing caution.

AUGUST 21 – 'EURO-EXODUS,' *THE ECONOMIST*

With the ink barely dry on Eurocopter's press release, more than a dozen French-owned companies have announced similar plans to replace workers at their eastern European manufacturing sites. What began as a surprise move at one factory is fast becoming a trend.

The latest figures show more than 50,000 jobs affected by these announcements, and one senior official in Paris estimated that figure will grow rapidly in the days and weeks ahead as fresh French and German firms join the race to cut labor costs. Other experts put the numbers of Algerians, Turks, and Tunisians slated to be shipped out of France at more than a quarter of a million – with men, women, and children all being uprooted in a modern-day Exodus.

Heated protests have erupted all across Hungary, Croatia, and Romania – the nations most affected. In the most severe attack, workers in Brasov, north of Bucharest, stormed a foreign worker's hostel, killing thirteen Arabs and wounding scores more. Four Romanians and several police were also killed.

But the protests are not confined to those whose livelihoods are threatened. Nationalist beliefs drive many of the actions. One French trade union leader stalked out of a recent meeting in evident rage, growling that 'these jobs should go to true Frenchmen, not bastard Arabs.'

The public outcry in France took a violent turn on Wednesday as neo-Nazi skinheads and leftist union workers poured into Marseilles' immigrant neighborhoods. Several hours of street fighting, beatings, and arson left six people dead and dozens more injured. Onlookers have complained that the police did little to contain the violence or to arrest those responsible.

Despite these warning signs, France's top-ranking corporate and governmental leaders show no evidence of any intention to reverse course. Whether driven by racial arrogance or economic necessity, this forced mass migration seems likely to continue . . .

AUGUST 30 – MOBILE POLICE COMMAND POST, SOPRON, HUNGARY

Col. Zoltan Hradetsky stood on a grassy hill overlooking the Budapest-Vienna highway, glowering down at a scene that was every policeman's worst nightmare come to life – a riot spiraling out of control. Static and frantic voices crackled over his command vehicle's radios as his junior officers fought to regain some measure of control over their own men.

The highway looked like a battlefield. A kilometer-long column of buses sat stalled bumper-to-bumper, each packed with replacement workers and their families headed for the Sopron rotor-fabrication factory. Frightened faces stared out through steel mesh screens welded over shattered glass windows.

Thick, black smoke hung over the whole area, billowing from truck tires stacked and set afire as makeshift barricades. The smoke mingled with gray wisps of tear gas rising over rock-throwing rioters surging back and forth across the road. Policemen wearing gas masks and carrying nightsticks and Plexiglas shields raced from trouble spot to trouble spot, clubbing protesters away from the buses before they could pry doors or windows open. Trucks waiting to cart off prisoners to the city jail stood empty. Nobody had any time to make arrests. They were too busy fending off total disaster.

Hradetsky swore under his breath. Damn that idiot Gellard and his arrogant masters in Paris! They hadn't bothered to inform him of their plans until earlier this morning, far too late to put together any kind of coherent crowd control plan. As a result, his first police units hadn't been in time to stop Eurocopter's enraged workers from blocking the bus convoy.

Angry shouts, screams, and the muffled thump of more tear gas launchers being fired drifted uphill on the wind. More smoke stained the sky, rising from behind the stalled column now. Rioters had cut off the convoy's line of retreat.

He turned on his heel and stalked toward the worried-looking officers clustered around his command vehicle. 'Radio Kapuvar and tell them we need reinforcements now, not next week! And find out where those bloody water cannon are! We're running out of other options fast.'

'Your panic may not be necessary, Colonel.' Francois Gellard, the factory's general manager, folded his arms across his chest. Somehow he managed to look bored despite the confusion spilling over the highway only a few hundred meters away. Two of his own security guards stood nearby, cradling short, compact FA MAS assault rifles.

'And just what the hell do you mean by that?'

The Frenchman smiled thinly and pointed at the western sky. 'I've already taken steps that should bring this farce to a quick end.'

Hradetsky followed his outstretched arm and saw three black specks on the horizon, specks that took on shape and size as they closed at high speed. Helicopters with Eurocopter corporate markings.

Moments later the helicopters flashed by low overhead and slid downhill toward the highway, rotors howling as they decelerated. Each had its side doors open and men leaning outward over the struggling throngs only fifty meters below.

Moving slowly now, the Eurocopter aircraft flew eastward along the highway, trailing bright white flashes and a rattling, thumping series of ear-splitting bangs as the stun grenades their crews were lobbing exploded on the ground and in the air. High-pitched screams rose in their wake. Policemen and rioters alike were knocked down by the blasts and then trampled as the panicked mob broke and scattered away from the road.

Turbines whining, the helicopters spun through a tight turn and made another pass. More explosions hammered at Hradetsky's ears. And more men and women were left lying broken and bleeding on the highway.

He whirled round to face Gellard. 'You fucking bastard! How dare you order this . . . aerial massacre!' He stabbed a finger toward the bodies littering the pavement and roadside.

'Calm down, Colonel. Most of those people aren't seriously hurt at all – simply breathless and stunned.' The French factory manager nodded toward his orbiting helicopters. 'In any event, your vaunted police were losing this battle. And my men and machines have won it. I doubt you'll find very many of your superiors willing to second-guess my actions.'

Hradetsky felt his face grow red with barely suppressed rage. 'I don't give a damn what those toadies in Budapest say or don't say. You're operating on my territory now – not your precious factory grounds.'

He moved closer to Gellard, watching as the manager and his bodyguards tensed, obviously unsure of what to expect from this short-tempered Hungarian. 'I'm putting you under arrest, monsieur. The charges will include murderous assault on my police officers down there and on other citizens of this district. I will not allow anyone – no matter how powerful – to take the law into his own hands. Not while I command this post.'

Gellard shrugged. 'Then you may not command here for long, Colonel.' The Frenchman turned away, more interested in watching the buses carrying his new workers edging their way past abandoned barricades.

Col. Zoltan Hradetsky swore again and moved downhill, already issuing the instructions needed to bring some kind of order out of the bloody chaos along the highway.

SEPTEMBER 2 – FAX TRANSMISSION, SOPRON POLICE HEADQUARTERS

FROM: Ministry of the Interior
TO: Col. Zoltan Hradetsky, Commander, Sopron Police District

1. Effective immediately you are relieved of all duties at your current post. All special pay allowances and cost-of-living adjustments are also revoked.

2. Effective immediately you will suspend all extraordinary investigations or operations, pending arrival of your designated successor.

3. You are strongly reprimanded for your conduct on 30 August. Despite recent worker-related changes, Eurocopter's Sopron facility remains an important contributor to our nation's economy. Your unprofessional behavior has jeopardized this vital relationship, and this reprimand will become a part of your permanent service record.

4. Effective 05 September you are ordered to report for duty in the Office of Criminal Records, Budapest. For the purposes of pay and office organization, you will carry the nominal rank of captain – while retaining your existing grade should future assignments warrant it.

Imre Dozsa
Brigadier General, commanding

CHAPTER 3
Sentinels

SEPTEMBER 11 – DULLES INTERNATIONAL AIRPORT, WASHINGTON, D.C.

Hydraulics whining, the huge 747 rolled out of its turn and slid downward, thundering low over the green, wooded Virginia countryside. Four thousand miles and nearly seven hours after leaving Great Britain, American Airlines Flight 128 was on final approach to Dulles. Row after row of houses, steepled churches, and flat-roofed shopping malls slipped past beneath the plane's wings. Many stood empty or unfinished. The world recession had brought even Washington's suburban sprawl to a grinding halt.

Joseph Ross Huntington III pulled his gaze away from the narrow cabin window and frowned. He saw signs of economic gloom everywhere he looked these days – even on this morning flight from London. More of the airliner's seats were empty than were occupied, and most of his fellow passengers were weary-looking businessmen. Several years of global trade war had taken their toll. With the nation's unemployment level locked near twelve percent, few American families had the money or inclination to vacation overseas. Public contempt for 'foreigners' was at an all-time high.

Huntington shook his head at that. At least Americans could still put food on their family tables. That made them fortunate compared to most of the world's population. Africa and both Central and South America lay mired in unpaid debts, deadly disease, utter poverty, and political upheaval. Asia, except for Japan, South Korea, and a few others, wasn't in much better shape. Even Europe's proud, industrialized nations teetered on the brink of economic collapse, kept afloat only by frantic government spending, subsidized production, and wishful thinking.

A jarring bounce and the sudden roar of reversed engines interrupted his own depressing thoughts. They were down.

Overhead speakers crackled to life. 'Ladies and gentlemen, welcome to Washington's Dulles International Airport. On behalf of the captain and your entire flight crew . . .'

Huntington tuned out the standard announcement he'd heard several hundred times before, waiting patiently while the 747 taxied off the runway toward the soaring steel and glass terminal building that was the airport's trademark. Patience was a virtue he'd been forced to acquire in late middle age, and he still found his willingness to sit calmly somewhat surprising.

Certainly none of his former employees or shareholders would have described him as a patient man. Far from it. They'd have said he was hard-charging, aggressive, and often painfully blunt. And they would have been right. *Business Week* had once called him 'the CEO with a linebacker's body, a first-rate mind, and a sailor's mouth.' Those characteristics had helped him transform his family's aging, tradition-riddled machine-tools firm into one of the country's most profitable small corporations. They'd also nearly killed him.

At forty-nine, he'd been a driving, dynamic businessman. But he'd celebrated his fiftieth birthday in intensive care, felled by a massive heart attack brought on by stress and overwork. His recovery had been slow and painful, and his doctors hadn't given him many choices. Retire immediately or face a likely sudden death. The frightened look on his wife's face left him with only one real alternative. He'd turned the CEO slot over to his oldest daughter and settled into what he considered slower, quieter pursuits.

Other men in his position played golf or bridge or took up painting. Ross Huntington had other interests. Political interests.

He was one of the first passengers out the jumbo jet's forward cabin door. Flying first-class had its compensations, and beating the mad rush through carry-on-bag-choked aisles was the one he prized most. That and the extra legroom it offered. At six feet two inches tall, Huntington believed coach seats could only have been designed with midgets and screaming children in mind. Personal wealth let him indulge his height.

As he left the jetway and headed for customs, a middle-aged man in a dark gray suit intercepted him.

'Mr. Huntington?'

'That's right.' He slowed his pace, looking down at the man out the corner of his eye. 'What can I do for you, Mr. . . . ?'

'Rawlins, sir. Secret Service.' The man fished a wallet-shaped identity card out of his jacket, flipped it open, and showed it to him.

Huntington stopped in the middle of the hallway, standing still while other travelers flowed past him like water around a well-worn rock.

The card showed Rawlins' picture and looked real enough. He handed it back. 'Well?'

The Secret Service agent nodded toward an unmarked exit. 'No need to go through customs, sir. We've already cleared you. And there's a car waiting downstairs.'

They wanted him in a hurry, then. Damn. He'd been looking forward to a nap and hot shower at his hotel first. Twenty hours of practically nonstop traveling left their mark on anyone. 'What about my bags?'

'All arranged, sir. Our people will deliver them for you.' Rawlins paused. 'Was there anything in them you need this afternoon?'

Huntington shook his head. Everything he'd need for this meeting was already crammed into his overtired brain or his scuffed leather briefcase. Unfortunately. He'd left for Europe with high hopes and expectations.

And he was coming back with a fat lot of nothing.

The sour knowledge of failure stayed with him all the way to the waiting official car and the White House.

THE WHITE HOUSE

The antechamber outside the Oval Office looked oddly empty. The room was usually crowded – packed with important political contributors, a championship sports team, or a scouting troop waiting their turn for a quick picture with the nation's chief executive. Now it contained only the President's personal secretary, busy behind her desk, and his military aide, stiff and formal in full uniform. It took Huntington several seconds to realize what that meant. The President must have cleared his normal afternoon schedule just to hear what he had to say.

Wonderful.

He squared his shoulders and walked straight through the door. Old friend or not, these next few moments weren't likely to be pleasant.

The President looked up from a mass of paperwork. Two years into his first term, the optimistic, 'can do' attitude that had first attracted the American electorate was still there, but it was beginning to look a little frayed around the edges. And the broad shoulders and thick, muscled neck that had served him well as a younger man on the football field were hunched now – bowed down by the weight of constant battles with the same isolationist special interests that had wrecked the economy and sent his predecessor packing. The United States had already had two one-term presidents in this decade. If things didn't improve soon, he would be the third. Despite that, an easy smile formed on a square-jawed face that still looked boyish beneath his gray hair. 'Ross! How was your flight?'

'Long.' Huntington dropped into a chair in front of the desk.

'Yeah. Sorry about the rush. But you may have guessed that I'm kinda curious to hear how things went.' The President stabbed a button on his phone. 'Marla? Would you call State for me and ask Thurman to step around later this evening? Nothing formal. Just for a drink or two. Tell him Ross Huntington's back in town. He'll know what I mean.'

Huntington eyed him curiously. 'You sure that's wise?'

Harris Thurman, the Secretary of State, was a stickler for protocol and established diplomatic procedure. He hadn't liked anything about the President's plan to use a longtime family friend as an unofficial, off-the-record envoy. In fact, Huntington remembered one memo that opened with the phrase 'ill-considered' and ended with the dire prediction that 'amateur meddling will only make matters worse.'

Straight white teeth flashed as the President grinned. 'My esteemed Secretary of State has long since seen the error of his ways. He's one of your biggest fans now.'

'Oh?'

The President nodded. 'I showed him copies of the letters I sent with you. Took the starch right out of him.'

Huntington could understand that. Communications between heads of state were usually wrapped in gauzy, vague phrases of mutual respect and warm admiration. The handwritten note to the French President hadn't contained anything remotely resembling diplomatic language. Neither had the missive addressed to Germany's Chancellor. Thurman, undoubtedly horrified by their tone, was probably grateful that they'd been delivered outside official channels and without his sanction.

He grimaced. 'I'm not so sure he wasn't right the first time around. I didn't get very far.'

'I didn't really think you would, Ross.' The President cocked his head slightly to one side and nodded toward an antique globe in the Oval Office's far corner. 'We've all painted ourselves into corners with this tit-for-tat protectionist crap. We've got so many restrictions and retaliatory tariffs on our stuff that it's amazing anything sells. Nobody's willing to listen anymore. The major governments are now in power because they promise to "protect trade." The French. The Germans. The Japanese. Every mother-loving one of us. We're stuck with a trade war *nobody* can win.'

He shook his head in disgust. 'But nobody wants to back down first. World leaders, hell! We're all like a bunch of little kids screaming that the other fella threw the first punch.'

'Including you?'

The President snorted. 'Especially me! If I even so much as think about relaxing our tariffs or import quotas, I'm gonna have Congress and big labor jumping down my throat with boots on and fangs out! That's one reason I sent you over to Paris and Berlin, and not somebody carrying a passport stamped "U.S. Government Employee." If anybody had raised a stink, you'd have just been some overeager private citizen trying a little private diplomacy.'

Huntington arched an eyebrow. 'But you still didn't expect much from my mission?'

'Not really. The trade war's gone too far for quiet words behind the scenes to have much effect.' The President jabbed a finger at him. 'But I did want you to meet my counterparts. I need your firsthand impressions of these men. And your best guesses as to what their next moves might be.'

'Why me?'

'Because you're the kind of shrewd, hard-eyed bastard I can trust to give me the straight scoop . . . without any punches pulled.' The President frowned. 'Look, Ross, every other piece of analysis I get is skewed in some damned way. The CIA hems and haws and tries to cover every base from every angle. State's too busy crawling on its belly to Congress to give me a clear reading. And the rest of my so-called experts can't make up their minds about what they want for lunch – let alone where Europe's headed!'

Huntington nodded slowly. Bureaucracies rarely produced anything more than a muddied consensus. The man sitting across from him wouldn't be the first American president who'd decided to make an end run around the 'normal' channels. Or to use a friend and political advisor to do it, either. Woodrow Wilson's trust in Col. Edward House and

FDR's use of Harry Hopkins came immediately to mind.

His thoughts twisted away from the comparison. Despite his years of experience in both the domestic and international business arenas, it seemed presumptuous to equate himself with either man. House and Hopkins had helped mold history during two world wars. He only wanted to help his country muddle through its current economic woes. History could look after itself.

He shrugged. 'Guesses are about all I can offer, Mr. President. Where would you like me to start?'

'With France.'

The President's interest in his French counterpart was very keen. Everything both men knew about the European situation pointed to France emerging as the continent's leading political power. On the surface that seemed illogical. Germany was richer and had a bigger population. It also had Europe's most powerful army. But the Germans were still stepping somewhat warily – with their economy and industry still weak, they were reluctant to awaken old memories of German military power. While both had economic problems, France had not had the crushing expense of rebuilding half its industry. Their treasury was in better shape, and their industry better established.

Even more important, the French possessed both a substantial nuclear arsenal and a U.N. Security Council veto. That gave them room to maneuver without much fear of foreign interference. And for the moment, at least, Berlin found itself forced to follow the course charted by Paris.

Huntington summoned up a mental image of the French President as he'd last seen him. 'Bonnard's more a figurehead than anything else. He's too sick and too old to exercise effective control over his own household officials – let alone the country. They say he's only made ceremonial appearances for the past several months.' He grimaced. 'His aides practically had to read your letter to him three or four times before he understood it all.'

The President seemed surprised. 'He's that bad off? I'd read he's been ill but I hadn't heard anything like that before.'

'Not many people have, outside the Élysée.'

'Why?'

'Two reasons. One, most of the government's scared to death of showing any signs of weakness. They don't want the opposition calling for new elections – not right now.'

'Understandable.' No politician with the brains God gave a snail would want to campaign behind a sickly, senile old man. Especially not at a time of growing civil unrest. 'And the second reason?'

Huntington leaned forward. 'Let's just say that certain cabinet ministers enjoy operating pretty much on their own.'

The President nodded. Again, that made perfect sense. Ever since the time of Louis XIV, the Sun King, the French had shown a taste for being ruled by powerful, domineering men. Even under the republic, its presidents functioned more like elected kings than public servants. He could understand why the ambitious officials who often surrounded such leaders would jump at the chance to run their own ministries without interference. 'Which ones?'

Huntington ticked them off on his fingers. 'The defense chief, Minister of the Interior, head of intelligence, you name it. Practically everyone who controls a powerful department. Bonnard's Prime Minister is almost as much a nonentity as he is right now.'

'So who's top dog now? Or are they all still snarling for the honor?'

'Still snarling mostly.' Huntington laughed briefly at the image conjured up by the President's choice of words. Then he stopped laughing. 'But the word is that the intelligence boss seems to be emerging as the first among equals. A man named Nicolas Desaix.'

He remembered the hushed tones his French friends and former business associates had used when discussing Desaix. Their attitude toward the DGSE director had been a strange mixture of unspoken fear and uncomfortable admiration. And if just half the stories they'd told him were true, the man was charming, intelligent, supremely self-confident, and utterly ruthless.

'Will he replace Bonnard?'

'I doubt it.' Huntington shook his head quickly. Everything he'd heard about Desaix suggested the man enjoyed being the eminence *behind* the throne. He'd be surprised if the French President's chief puppeteer opted to wear strings around his own arms. 'But I do think he's the man we'll ultimately have to deal with.'

'Wonderful.' The President looked troubled. 'I don't like the idea of negotiating with somebody I can't see or talk to directly. Damn it, when I horse-trade with a man, I want to look him right in the eye!'

Huntington agreed with that sentiment. Even in this day of computerized analysis and instantaneous telecommunication, there wasn't any substitute for the personal touch. Half his success in the business world had come from an ability to size up his competitors, his employees, and his customers: to judge their strengths and weaknesses and to discern their needs and their desires, all in face-to-face meetings.

He rocked back in his chair. 'I'd be surprised if Desaix's interested in real trade talks anyway, Mr. President.'

'Oh?'

'He's a nationalist to the core. The kind who says "France for the French" and means it. The word is that he's the driving force behind this crazy foreign worker relocation program of theirs.'

'Great.' The President looked even more worried. News reports from Europe were full of horrific images these days – trainloads of frightened people guarded by soldiers and growling dogs, bloody riots in burning neighborhoods, and all the other warning signs of a rising tide of racism and xenophobia spreading across the continent. Trying to deal with someone who thought all that was a good idea seemed likely to be an exercise in futility.

He glanced out the window toward the White House Rose Garden, almost as though he were seeking solace in its quiet, sun-drenched beauty. Then he sighed heavily and turned back to face his friend. 'What about the Germans?'

'Not much better.' Huntington brushed a hand across his overtired eyes and swung into a detailed account of his meetings in Berlin. None had been any more productive than those he'd held in Paris. More of Germany's business and political leaders wanted an end to the disastrous trade war with the United States, Japan, and Great Britain, but their hands were just as tied by domestic politics and by a need for short-term profits from their captive markets in eastern Europe. Germany's eyes and full attention were focused on her growing internal problems, not on the need for fair competition with onetime allies now turned sour trading rivals. Until she could control her massive unemployment, bitter nationalism, and fragmented political spectrum, Germany would be a weak actor on the international stage.

In the western half of the country, high taxes and the loss of overseas markets were slowly strangling key old industries and vital new ones. Protected by strict labor laws, few existing jobs were being lost, but no new ones were being created. As a result, more and more young people were trapped in boredom and state-supported idleness – either on the dole or as 'professional' students endlessly pursuing meaningless degrees. They were growing increasingly radical and restless.

The eastern states were in even worse shape. Despite the huge sums invested after reunification, the easterners, the 'ossies,' were still poor relations – plagued by continuing high unemployment and by the environmental disasters left by forty-five years of communist misrule. Old tensions were rising as growing numbers of those who'd escaped one form of totalitarianism clamored for another. Though still only a small percentage of the population, neo-Nazi groups were turning bolder and ever more violent. Swastika flags were often openly displayed in smaller villages and in the east's run-down inner cities.

Attacked from both the right and the left, Germany's coalition government stood on increasingly shaky ground. The Chancellor and his cabinet were too busy trying to survive almost weekly crises to spend the time, effort, and political capital needed to drop their nation's protective tariffs and trade barriers.

With all that in mind, Huntington didn't see any realistic prospect of successful negotiations with either nation. Too many of Europe's most powerful politicians had too much prestige wrapped up in half-baked economic nationalism and in appeals to growing anti-American sentiment. His dour analysis left the President visibly shaken. Nobody wanted to go down in history as the chief executive who'd held the reins while America and its old allies bickered and squabbled their way into a global depression.

The two men were still talking when the President's secretary brought coffee in for them an hour later, and neither noticed when she took the empty pot away an hour after that. They were too busy trying to find some way out before the civilized world plunged itself into irreversible economic catastrophe.

SEPTEMBER 16 – MINISTRY OF DEFENSE, RUSSIAN REPUBLIC, MOSCOW

Pavel Sorokin stared in consternation at the brown-haired man sitting comfortably across from him. '*Fifty thousand* rubles? Per truckload? Have you gone mad?'

The man he knew as Nikolai Ushenko shrugged. 'You want the food. I have the food. The price is what we call a marketing decision, Pavel Ilych.'

'Bugger the market!' Sorokin spat out the distasteful word. Despite nearly six years of stunning economic reforms, he still had trouble dealing with the new capitalist reality. 'Look, be reasonable, will you? I've got a strict budget limit here. Meeting your price would run me out of money long before year's end.'

Ushenko shrugged again in studied disinterest. 'So get your precious marshals to up your budget. The charge is fifty thousand per – not a kopek less. If you don't want my wheat and beef, I can assure you the boys over at your Foreign Ministry will. They've already offered me forty thousand – sight unseen.'

'*Those* bastards? You know they don't have that kind of money. Not unless they've got a printing press in their basement.' Sorokin ground his teeth in frustration. The way the Ukrainian slurred crisp-edged Russian words into a soft mush was almost as irritating as his tough bargaining stance. Pavel Sorokin had taken the job as general supply manager for the Ministry of Defense because of the endless opportunities it seemed to offer for a little lucrative graft and corruption. After all, *everyone* knew how slipshod the military was about minding its money. Unfortunately all that had changed when the old Soviet Union shattered into the Commonwealth and its confusing array of semi-independent republics. The soldiers whose careers had survived the transition were notoriously tightfisted with their limited resources. Now the kind of 'private appropriation of state property' that used to be winked at if you were a party member in good standing could land you in prison – all after a fair trial, of course. And the government-owned foodstuffs he sold for private gain had to be carefully hidden in a paperwork maze of 'transportation spoilage' reports and falsified inventories. It was all a lot more work than he'd ever bargained for.

He spread his hands. 'Come on, Nikolai. This is your old friend Pavel you're talking to. The diplomats talk a good game, but they're fickle. They'll take your goods one week and dump you the next for some other supplier. But you and me, we've been doing business for what, almost six months? We can trust each other, true? I'm a guaranteed customer, also true? And that ought to be worth something . . . say, a five-thousand discount from the forty you've been offered.'

Ushenko's brown eyes brightened as he laughed. 'Nice try. But no deal. I couldn't possibly take anything under forty-five. Not and make a profit.'

Sorokin winced. He needed this shipment badly. Marshals and generals and colonels wouldn't react well to missing their midday meals because the ministry canteen didn't have any food to fix. And new jobs for overweight and out-of-date ex-bureaucrats were few and far between.

He tugged at the knot of his gray wool necktie, loosening it. 'What you're asking for is impossible. I just don't have the money to pay more than forty thousand. Not and keep my job.'

'Too bad, Pavel. It's been nice chatting with you.' The other man stood up, reaching for his fur-lined jacket. An ice-cold wind already howled down Moscow's wide avenues, an alarming portent of the winter to come.

'Wait. Wait. Don't be hasty.' Sorokin half rose, inwardly furious at himself for buckling to this Ukrainian bandit. 'There are others in this building who owe me some favors I could call in. So maybe we can make another kind of deal. Cash plus a swap.'

For a long minute, Ushenko stood motionless – as if still undecided about whether to stay or go. Then, with a sigh, he sat down. 'What kind of swap? I'm not about to go into the gun-running business, so don't bother offering me a used tank or two.'

'No, nothing like that.' Sorokin smiled weakly at what he hoped was the other man's joke. 'I'm talking about information.'

'What kind of information?'

Sorokin spread his hands. 'How about the relocation timetables and sites for three motor rifle divisions?'

Ushenko snorted. 'And what good are those to me? What am I supposed to do, sell them to the Americans? Or the Germans? I'm no traitor.'

'No, no. Of course not.' Sorokin lowered his voice. 'But you could find other buyers – some of those entrepreneur friends of yours, for example. Moving that many soldiers means big transportation and big construction contracts. Surely a little advance word of that in the right ears could be worth quite a lot.'

The Ukrainian's own ears seemed to perk up at that. 'Go on.'

And so Sorokin did. In the end it took nearly an hour of heated argument and furious bargaining, but he got his truckloads of food. And all for only forty thousand rubles apiece. Plus a few photocopied folders of Ministry of Defense documents.

Alex Banich strode briskly out of the mammoth ministry building and climbed straight into a blue Mercedes waiting for him at the curb. A parking permit prominently displayed on its dashboard identified it as belonging to the New Kiev Trading Company. His driver, a fair-haired young man named Mike Hennessy, tipped his cigarette out the car window and pulled out onto the New Arbat Road, narrowly dodging an oncoming truck. Both men ignored the blaring horns behind them. Russian drivers were used to living dangerously and driving badly. Defensive driving would have been out of character.

'So how'd it go, boss?'

Banich grinned. 'Not bad. We'll clear a cool ten thousand per load, plus . . .' He pulled the papers he'd been given out of his jacket. 'Sorokin gave me a little present that'll keep some of Langley's gophers happy and busy for a few more weeks.'

The information on Russian troop movements would help keep Washington's picture of the still-strong Russian Army up to date. Best of all, the documents represented a chink in Pavel Sorokin's armor. His decision to trade one package of relatively low-grade state secrets now would make it that much easier to persuade him to sell more important data later on.

Hennessy matched his smile. 'So this guy still thinks you're plain old Nikolai Ushenko, purveyor of fine foodstuffs?'

'Not a chance.' Banich stuffed the papers back inside his jacket. 'He's convinced I'm Nikolai Ushenko, a spy on the side. But since he thinks I'm only working for a bunch of get-rich-quick Ukrainian businessmen, trading me a few secrets doesn't bother him much.'

Hennessy nodded. Most Russians still thought of their Commonwealth partners like Ukraine as partly owned subsidiaries of their own republic. Even men in the security services and the armed forces viewed their sister states' efforts to build independent military and intelligence units with something approaching paternal amusement. That made Banich's choice of a cover identity positively inspired. Many postcommunist Russians still viewed American CIA agents as potential villains for spy thrillers or suspense films – crafty, dangerous, and devious. But Ukrainian spies? Well, they made perfect cutup characters for the new sitcoms pouring out of Moscow's film and TV studios. Nobody really took them seriously.

And that was a weakness Alex Banich was fully prepared to exploit.

A childhood spent with émigré Ukrainian grandparents and years in the CIA's intensive language training program let him shift fluidly and easily from English to colloquial Russian to flawless Ukrainian – all in the same sentence. He could pass himself off as anyone from a greedy wheeler-dealer to a stern, self-righteous soldier or policeman. Ten years of successful assignments throughout eastern Europe had honed his acting and language abilities to a razor's edge. There were nights when he even dreamed in Russian. All in preparation for what should have been the pinnacle of his active-duty career: assignment as the senior field operative for the CIA's Moscow Station.

Banich's grin slipped to one side, becoming a wry smile aimed at his own misplaced ambition. Driven by an unrelenting need to be 'the best,' he'd worked hard, sweated blood, and wrecked his marriage to get to Moscow. And for what? The hard-line communists he'd grown up hating were gone – in prison, dead, or learning how to be good little capitalists. The once-mighty USSR was just as dead. Its successor states seemed too busy trying to survive to cause much trouble for the world. And Moscow Station, once viewed as the CIA's most challenging posting, was now seen by many as little more than a dirty and cold backwater.

The real action was supposed to be somewhere else to the east or west – in Europe's great capital cities or in bustling Tokyo. The Agency's congressional minders were constantly pushing for more data on the French, the Germans, and the Japanese, not the Russians. For Washington's trendy power elite, nuclear missiles and tank divisions were out. Trade balances and subsidy levels were in.

The effects showed up whenever Langley allocated its annual operations budget and made personnel assignments. Year by year, Moscow Station's share of both got smaller and smaller.

Banich shook his head. He didn't see how much further the Agency could shrink its operations here. Not and expect his networks to gather significant amounts of useful information. The Soviet Union's self-destruction may have made spying inside its former territories easier, but it certainly hadn't made it any cheaper. These days Russians didn't pass military or political secrets to America because they hated communism. Communism was dead. Now they *sold* them – sold them for the money to buy extra food, more heat, or to cover gambling debts or stock market losses.

The shortsighted nature of the continuing cutbacks mandated by Congress gnawed at him every time he risked losing a valuable source by haggling too hard over a price. For all their internal problems, Russia and its partner republics still possessed a formidable stockpile of nuclear warheads, accurate ICBMs, and huge arsenals of conventional weapons. And behind the array of fledgling parliaments and elected presidents, Banich knew there were still dangerous men in high places who harbored imperial ambitions for their nations. Such men should be *watched*, not ignored.

Unfortunately most of Washington's policymakers were shortsighted by their very nature. Nations they didn't view as a near-term threat to America's security and issues that didn't threaten their electoral prospects tended to drop off their screens. The usual rule of thumb was: out of congressional sight and interest, out of budget.

Hennessy's voice summoned him back to more immediate concerns. 'I checked your messages while you were inside taking Sorokin to the cleaners.'

'Oh?' Banich leaned forward from the backseat, unable to resist the opening even in his somber mood. 'Anything pressing?'

The younger man winced. His boss rarely punned, but when he did they were always awful.

'Sorry.'

'Uh-huh.' Hennessy floored the Mercedes, flashing through a crowded intersection narrowly ahead of a surge of oncoming traffic. 'Seriously, Kutner wants to see you back at the embassy, yesterday and not tomorrow . . . if you get my drift.'

'Yeah.' Banich pondered that in silence. The chief of station, Len Kutner, rarely interfered with field operations in progress. Instead, he passed judgment on proposed ops and then ran interference for them against second-guessing by the 'goody two-shoes' – the embassy's State Department regulars. Something fairly important must be in the wind. Something Banich was suddenly sure he wouldn't like at all.

THE U.S. EMBASSY, PRESNYA DISTRICT, MOSCOW

The two uniformed Russian militiamen standing close to the embassy compound's main entrance weren't there on any kind of guard duty.

They were just trying to cadge whatever warmth they could from the heated U.S. Marine sentry box right behind the gate. It had been chilly even with the sun high overhead. Now, with night drawing closer and thick black storm clouds piling up in the east, the outside temperature was slipping toward the freezing mark. Some pessimistic forecasters were even predicting Moscow's first brief snowfall by early morning.

Banich was still crossing the street when one of the Marine guards recognized him and opened the gate.

The tallest of the two Russian cops stopped blowing on his ungloved hands long enough to sketch a quick wave. 'Hello, Mr. Banich.' His English was pretty good.

'Hi, Pyotr. What'd you and Mischa do to wind up on night duty this close to the river? Screw your sergeant's grandmother?'

Both men laughed. They were part of the crime-prevention detail assigned to patrol streets near the embassy. Russia's capital needed all the U.S. aid and investment it could attract, and having American diplomats routinely mugged didn't strike anyone in Moscow as a particularly good advertisement for the city's charms.

Banich stepped through the gate and headed for the huge red brick chancery building.

'Hey, Mr. Banich?'

He half turned. 'Yes?'

'Got any investment advice for us?'

Banich paused for a moment, pretending to fumble for the right, poorly pronounced Russian words. 'Of course. Buy low . . . and sell high.'

He left them chuckling behind him.

The whole incident had been recorded, of course. Probably by a hidden mike monitored in one of the apartment houses across the street from the embassy. Russia's Federal Investigative Service didn't have all the resources or powers of the old KGB, but it still existed to protect the new state from foreign spies. And foreign spies tended to work out of foreign embassies.

FIS surveillance was one of the reasons Banich always carefully changed his outward appearance before coming back from a stint as Nikolai Ushenko. It usually only took a quick stop at the downtown apartment he rented under Ushenko's name. The Ukrainian's thick, fur-lined jacket, brown sweater, and American-made blue jeans were gone, replaced by a blue London Fog raincoat, dark gray suit, white shirt, and red silk tie. The stylish pair of horn-rimmed glasses perched on his nose, a splash of after-shave, and a dab of Jack Daniel's or wine completed the transformation from plain-spoken, shrewd rustic to lazy, fun-loving, junior-grade diplomat.

When he first arrived in Moscow, Banich had spent more than a month thoroughly playing his part as a mediocre deputy assistant economic attaché firmly committed to doing as little real work as possible. While apparently evaluating sales and investment opportunities for U.S. firms, he'd led FIS watchers on a dizzying round of factory tours, boring business conferences, and marathon pub crawls. The whole booze-tinged process had been well worth it. Day by day, the team of agents tailing him had dwindled, with man after man pulled off to follow more promising suspects – or to nurse long-term hangovers. Now they hardly bothered to keep tabs on him at all.

That technique wouldn't have worked six or seven years before. The KGB would never have allowed a foreign official, especially an American, to wander at will though Moscow and the surrounding countryside. But the KGB had been torn apart for its complicity in the August 1991 coup. And the fragment tasked with counterespionage, the FIS, spent a lot of its time and resources spying on itself, trying to sniff out the faintest whiff of a renewed hard-line threat to Russia's elected government. Rumor said the splintered agency's morale and effectiveness were still at an all-time low.

Of course, that robbed Banich's own job of some of its challenge. He shrugged the thought off. He'd welcome anything that made intelligence-gathering in this crazy country easier. His own nation's changing priorities made the job tough enough as it was.

Len Kutner was waiting for him in his cramped, sixth-floor interior office. That was something else Banich liked about the tall, balding chief of station. The man never played phony power games such as holding every meeting on his own turf.

'Alex. Sorry to break in on you like this. Everything okay?'

Banich shook Kutner's outstretched hand and nodded. 'Fine. Hennessy's faxing shipping orders down to Kiev right now. And I picked up this for our troubles.' He held out the sheaf of Ministry of Defense documents.

The station chief flipped through them rapidly, his forehead wrinkling with effort as he translated technical terms into their English equivalents. 'They're moving three full divisions? Rather expensive, isn't it?'

'Sure is.' Banich pointed to the last few pages in Kutner's hands. 'And they're moving them back into Belarus from up near the St. Petersburg Military District.'

'Closer to the Polish border? Curioser and curioser.' Kutner looked up from the documents. 'Have you heard anything else about this? From your sources in the Parliament, say?'

Banich shook his head. 'Not a whisper. Which I find very interesting indeed.'

'Very. Maybe some of the generals are falling back into some bad old habits, eh?'

'Exactly.'

'Right. Put some time in on this one, Alex . . .' Kutner paused, looking troubled. 'Or at least, as much time as you can afford. We've received some new marching orders from D.C., through Langley.'

Banich waited for the other man to explain. Now they were getting to why he'd been called out of the field so soon.

Kutner laid the documents down on his subordinate's file-strewn desk and looked him right in the eye. 'It seems there's a new push on from some damned interagency working group. The Joint Trade Task Force. Whatever in God's name that is.

'Anyway, they're complaining that most of our product focuses too much on military and political matters . . . and not enough on trade and commerce. Stuff they call "the real measure of a nation's strength." '

'Jesus Christ!'

Kutner nodded but kept going. 'Whatever you or I may think about it, Alex, these folks have real pull with the Congress. And they've got backing inside the Agency, too.' He handed Banich a message flimsy. 'That came down the satellite link this morning. It lists our new priorities in order of importance.'

Banich scanned the list in growing disbelief. Sales figures and prices for French and German industrial tools and pharmaceuticals? For Japanese automobiles? Evidence of 'payoffs' for Russian buyers or government officials? It went on for ten or fifteen more categories, each one growing more obscure and more difficult to dig up. He looked up angrily. 'These assholes can't be serious! We're trying to keep tabs on a dozen republics spread across eleven time zones and they want us to waste time on this kind of crap?'

Kutner held up a hand to slow him down. 'Yes, they do. Look, Alex, I'm pulling in every chit I've got to get this reversed or at least trimmed down. But for right now, those are your new targets.'

'Great.' Banich tried unsuccessfully to tone down the bitterness in his voice. 'Can you tell me which of my contacts I'm supposed to cut off while I chase down this garbage? The Ministry of Defense? Or maybe my recruits inside the Foreign Ministry?'

Kutner shook his head. 'Just do what you can. Nobody's expecting miracles from you, Alex.'

'Well, that's good, because I'm fresh out of loaves and fishes.' Banich took a deep breath, fighting to calm down. It wouldn't do any good to piss Kutner off. He needed all the upper-echelon backing he could get. 'Look, Len. I can't even begin to track half of this junk. Not with the resources we've got now. We're going to need more bodies around here just to get the necessary legwork off the ground.'

'Agreed. I'll see what I can do.' The taller man patted his shoulder kindly and edged past him out the narrow office door.

Banich sat staring down at his crowded desk till far past midnight, trying to work out how to spin a finely tuned intelligence apparatus onto a completely new tack – all without irretrievably wrecking it.

He was still at it when the first delicate snowflakes began falling on Moscow's empty streets.

CHAPTER 4
Cataract

SEPTEMBER 21 – NEAR THE RUE DE FLANDRE, PARIS

Paris lay shrouded in darkness. The lights were out all over the city, cut off by a day-long wildcat strike that had crippled regional power plants. Only those government ministries and corporate buildings with backup generators were lit by electricity.

Others across the blacked-out capital fell back on older, more primitive means.

Flames licked the night sky above the 19th Arrondissement, dancing eerily among the district's decaying houses and shabby tenements. Silhouetted against the fires they'd set earlier, crowds of howling men and women surged back and forth through streets strewn with wrecked cars, bodies, and smoldering barricades. Some waved bloodied knives and makeshift clubs over their heads. Many were drunk, hopped up on a lethal mix of cheap wine and unleashed violence. All of them were poor and out of work and ready to settle scores with those they blamed for their troubles.

They blamed *les Arabes*. The Arabs. The Algerians, Tunisians, Senegalese, and all the other diseased, job-stealing African immigrants packed into dirty, foul-smelling apartments in the northern and eastern districts.

No one knew exactly how the trouble started once the lights went out. Maybe with a fistfight on the Rue de Flandre. Or with a shouted racial slur in the Place du Maroc. It didn't really matter much. What mattered now was that the riot was spreading through the immigrant slums, spilling through unlit streets in an orgy of arson, theft, and murder.

At the southern end of the Arab quarter, two armored riot-control vehicles and a thin line of security police in green combat fatigues and gas masks guarded the entrance to the Place de Stalingrad and its elevated Métro stop. The troops were members of the CRS, the government's mobile antiriot force. Their armament reflected the unit's well-deserved reputation for brutal efficiency. Some of the men were armed only with clear plastic shields and nightsticks, but others carried loaded shotguns and assault rifles. And turrets on both their armored cars mounted launchers equipped to lob tear gas and concussion grenades into unruly crowds.

So far, though, the CRS troopers hadn't needed to use their weapons. The mobs running amok through the burning slums north of the square hadn't tried forcing their way past them into the city's more fashionable districts. They were too busy butchering anyone who looked 'Arab' and looting neighborhood grocery stores, wine shops, and pharmacies.

And in turn, the security police had been too busy establishing a defensive perimeter to interfere. Now that was about to change.

'Yes, sir. I understand.' Lt. Charles Guyon swore in disbelief and lowered his walkie-talkie. He turned to the short, sour-faced sergeant at his side. 'We have new orders. We're to advance, clearing the streets as we go.'

An angry voice spoke up out of the darkness, mirroring his own unspoken thoughts. 'That's fucking crazy! We'll all get killed in there!'

Guyon looked up sharply. 'Who said that?' He waited, scanning the cluster of suddenly blank faces around him.

No one answered.

The lieutenant glared at his men for a moment longer before shifting his gaze back to the sergeant. 'We move out in five minutes. Other units will parallel us, advancing along the canal and the Rue de Tanger. We're free to use "all necessary force." Questions?'

The sergeant shook his head slowly.

'Good. Get the men ready. I want masks on and live rounds in every chamber.' He paused, knowing his words could be heard by every man in the platoon. 'But no one, and I mean no one, will open fire without a direct order from me! Clear?'

'Clear.' The sergeant spat it out, sounding as though he wanted to say a lot more.

Guyon spun on his heel without waiting to find out what that might be and headed for the two armored cars. He wanted to make sure their crews were ready to follow his troopers into the flame-lit streets in front of them. Having their steel-sided bulk and heavy firepower on tap would be vital if the rioters tried to fight back.

When he returned his platoon stood at attention in ranks – nightstick-armed men in front, and those with shotguns and assault rifles in the back. Their uniforms, gas masks, and helmets robbed them of all individuality.

The lieutenant stepped out in front of the formation. He left his own mask dangling around his neck. The bulky rubber masks kept you safe from tear gas, but they also left you nearly blind – especially at night. And he would need to see what was going on around them as long as possible.

Almost time. Guyon licked lips that suddenly felt cracked and bone-dry. He stared at the street straight ahead. Smoke from dozens of burning apartment houses and automobiles drifted across the square, growing thicker now that the wind had died down. Shapes moved inside the smoke, rioters carrying away stolen television sets, stereos, and furniture or simply prowling for new victims. Several corpses littered the street. Two more dangled from lampposts.

He bit his lower lip. This *was* madness. He and his men would be swallowed up inside the maelstrom ahead. Crushing peaceful political protests was one thing. Street fighting against a crazed mob was something else entirely. He was beginning to wish he'd never transferred to the CRS. All the extra pay and privileges he'd been so proud of just weren't worth dying for.

His walkie-talkie crackled. 'All units will advance.'

Christ. Guyon swallowed hard. He snapped open the flap on his holster and drew his pistol. 'Right. This is it. Platoon, follow me!'

He went forward at a slow walk, hoping his measured pace showed determination and not fear.

No one followed him.

The lieutenant turned around in disbelief. His troops still stood along the edge of the square. Not a man had moved.

'Damn it! You heard me! I'm ordering you to advance. Now!'

Silence. In the sudden stillness, Guyon could hear agonized screams rising from the slums behind him. Oh, Jesus. He could feel the hand holding his pistol starting to shake.

'Sergeant Pasant!'

The sour-faced sergeant stepped forward smartly and came to attention. 'Sir!'

Guyon lowered his voice. 'All right. Just what the hell are you idiots playing at?'

'The boys won't go in there . . . sir,' Pasant growled, nodding toward the immigrant quarter. 'Not to save black-asses and ragheads.'

A low murmur swept through the platoon as each man muttered his agreement with what their sergeant had just said.

Guyon tried an appeal to reason. 'Look, I don't like this any better than you lads do, but refusing orders is a criminal offense. This is a very serious situation, Sergeant.'

'So's dying . . . Lieutenant.'

Guyon leaned closer and dropped his own voice to a soft, barely audible murmur. 'You know, Pasant, I could make you obey my orders.' He thumbed his pistol's safety catch to the off position.

The sergeant stared back, unblinking. 'Maybe.' He shrugged. 'But then maybe you should think about how dangerous a city fight can be. You never know where the next bullet could come from . . . Lieutenant.'

Guyon's blood ran cold. The sergeant's soft-spoken threat was crystal-clear. He might be able to force his men into action against the mob, but he probably wouldn't come out of it alive. His hands shook harder.

Hell. Nothing in his training had prepared him for this. Not for the prospect of being murdered by his own men. And for what? A bunch of useless foreigners. For stinking Arabs and Africans. He shook his head. Risk his life for them? Not him. Not now. Not ever.

The lieutenant reset his pistol's safety catch and sighed. 'Very well. I'll call the command post and report our inability to go forward . . . under the present circumstances.' He looked angrily into his sergeant's expressionless eyes. 'Satisfied?'

'Yes, sir.'

'Then redeploy the men for a perimeter defense.' Guyon holstered his weapon. 'If we can't put an end to this madness, we can at least make sure it doesn't spread any further!'

Pasant saluted and strode back to the waiting security troops. They broke ranks, spreading out across the square in response to his shouted commands.

Guyon watched them for a moment, swore to himself again, and lifted the walkie-talkie to his cheek. He hesitated, reluctant to make a report that would undoubtedly end his police career. The force didn't need officers who couldn't control their own men. His thumb hovered over the transmit button and then stopped. There were other voices already crowding the circuit.

'I say again, Bravo Two, you are ordered to advance! Get moving!'

'Unable to comply, Echo Foxtrot. My men won't budge. I request reinforcements.'

Another voice crackled over the radio. 'Echo Foxtrot, this is Bravo Four. We can't go any further south. The fires in this sector are out of control. I'm establishing a police line and firebreak at the church here . . .'

Guyon kept listening in growing shock as more and more of his counterparts called in with similar stories. His platoon wasn't the only unit on the edge of mutiny. Others inside the CRS were just as willing to let the riot run its wild, bloody course.

SEPTEMBER 22 – BBC WORLD SERVICE

Satellites and powerful ground transmitters spread the BBC's evening broadcast around the world. 'Good evening. Here is the news.

'In Paris, French police and fire crews continued their rescue efforts in the aftermath of last night's disastrous rioting. Officials at the Ministry of the Interior put the death toll at more than two hundred, with hundreds more injured and in hospital. Doctors at area hospitals report that almost all the dead and wounded appear to be Algerian or other North African immigrants.

'Thousands more have been left homeless by fires that have leveled fifteen square blocks of the city. For the moment, they are being housed in nearby schools and vacant warehouses. Unconfirmed but authoritative speculation suggests they may soon be moved to what are being labeled "refugee holding camps" outside Paris.

'In related developments, a statement issued by the presidential palace blames, quote, "hooligan and criminal elements" for what it terms "this regrettable incident." One high-ranking official went further, arguing that the violence pointed out once again the importance of ridding France of what he called "troublesome alien enclaves." Meanwhile, French government sources continued to deny persistent reports that police units refused orders to end the rioting. The delays observed by onlookers are said to have been caused by unspecified tactical considerations.'

The BBC's newsreader paused, shifting from the broadcast's lead story to the next. 'In other European developments, a neo-Nazi rally in the eastern German city of Dresden drew an estimated seven thousand participants. Several policemen monitoring the demonstration were severely beaten when they tried to stop swastika banners from being unfurled . . .'

SEPTEMBER 25 – ROISSY CHARLES-DE-GAULLE INTERNATIONAL AIRPORT, PARIS

The first signs of trouble were electronic.

Video screens showing arriving and departing flights began flickering and then went blank. Passengers hurrying through the airport's gleaming, ultramodern terminal buildings gathered in small dismayed groups around the darkened monitors. Most were sure it was only another minor power failure or cutback – a product of the continuing agitation for higher wages by the nation's technical workers' unions.

They were wrong.

A sharp chime echoed over the airport's public address system. 'Ladies and gentlemen, your attention, please. We regret to inform you that all incoming and outgoing flights have been canceled. This unfortunate action is made necessary by a twenty-four-hour strike just announced by the national air traffic controllers' union. All inbound flights are being diverted to either their point of origin or the closest open airfield . . .'

Within an hour, passenger air travel, a hallmark of the modern age, had come to a complete stop all across France.

SEPTEMBER 29 – ON THE UNTER DEN LINDEN, BERLIN, FEDERAL REPUBLIC OF GERMANY

Ten thousand leather-clad skinheads and brownshirt fanatics packed Berlin's wide central avenue, spilling over its shade-tree-lined sidewalks. Black, red, and white swastika banners bobbed above the crowd, and their coarse, guttural voices blended into a rhythmic, almost hypnotic, marching song – the 'Horst Wessel.'

Under the disapproving eyes of several hundred heavily armed riot police, some of Germany's unemployed and undereducated were turning to an old master for new inspiration.

Three hundred meters up the avenue, a small, dark-haired man stood watching the neo-Nazi march come closer. His own pale blue eyes were half-closed in concentration. It was difficult to judge precise distances this far away.

But Joachim Speh, action leader for the Red Army Faction's Berlin commando, was a master of timing. One hand slipped into his coat pocket, delicately caressing a tiny radio transmitter. Soon, he thought coldly, very soon.

The marching column crossed the Charlotten Strasse, passing close by a rusting, dented Trabant parked on the side of the road. The flat tire and broken jack propped up against the Trabant's rear end showed its owner's reason for abandoning his unfashionable vehicle.

Some of the leading skinheads took time out from their singing to hammer their fists along the parked car's hood and roof, shouting and hollering in glee. The uniformed policemen paralleling the march stirred uneasily, reluctant to let such obvious vandalism go unchecked.

Now. Speh activated the transmitter hidden in his coat pocket.

The bomb he'd planted under the Trabant's gasoline tank detonated – exploding outward in an expanding ball of orange-red flame, smoke, and razor-sharp steel fragments. Those closest to the car were either blown to pieces or incinerated by flaming gasoline. Outside the fireball, dozens of other marchers and policemen were shredded by white-hot shrapnel or smashed to the pavement by the shock wave.

When the last echoes of the explosion faded away, the street and sidewalk looked like a slaughterhouse. Bodies and parts of bodies dotted the Unter den Linden's scorched pavement. Those who'd been wounded writhed in agony, screaming for help. Some were still on fire.

Moving calmly, Joachim Speh turned his back on the carnage and walked away. He had other punishment missions to plan.

OCTOBER 2 – OUTSIDE THE PALAIS DE L'EUROPE, STRASBOURG, FRANCE

Nearly four hundred miles from Germany's strife-torn capital, five grimly determined men faced a battery of television news cameras and microphones.

Behind them cold sunlight glinted off a vast modernistic structure of red concrete, bronze-colored glass, and gleaming steel. During earlier, more optimistic times, the Palace of Europe had contained chambers for the European Parliament – one of the first, tentative steps toward a politically united continent. Now the huge building stood empty, almost completely deserted. Cynics pointed to it as the visible symbol of a faded and foolish dream.

The palace served as a different kind of symbol for the men grouped in front of its main doors. They'd chosen the Strasbourg site as a sign of renewed labor radicalism and unity in Europe's two most powerful nations. Two of them headed France's largest trade union confederations. The other three ran organizations representing millions of German laborers, assembly-line workers, and white-collar professionals.

'Fellow citizens and fellow workers, we stand at an historic crossroads.' Markus Kaltenbrunner, the tall, black-haired leader of Germany's Scientists and Technical Workers Union, had been elected to speak for them all. He paused, knowing his words were being carried live into fifty million homes across the continent. 'Down one road, down the path pursued by those in power, lie poverty and degradation for German and French workers. The corporate giants and their government lackeys have one aim, one purpose: to boost their obscene profits by cutting our collective throats! They strip us of our wages and our jobs and hand them over to foreign slaves! And they have the audacity, the utter gall, to ask for our patience and cooperation while this "restructuring," this cruel robbery, unfolds!'

Kaltenbrunner shook his head angrily. 'But we will not stand for it! We will not cooperate in our own destruction.' He nodded toward the other union leaders standing around him. 'That is why we have come here today. To join in common cause against those who would reverse the progress of fifty years.

'Accordingly, we have agreed to the following nonnegotiable demands – demands that apply to the corporations and governments of both our great nations.' He pulled a pair of wire-frame glasses from his pocket, flipped them open, and slipped them onto his nose. Then he cleared his throat and began reading from a document handed to him by an aide. 'First, we call for an immediate end to the shipments of foreign workers to French- and German-owned factories in central and eastern Europe. All available positions in these facilities must be reserved for true French and German laborers, not for Turks or Algerians!'

The German labor leader scowled. 'Second, there must be an immediate and across-the-board moratorium on all layoffs and firings during this time of economic crisis. And finally we call on the politicians in Paris and Berlin to fund massive new public works programs to put our fellow workers back to work. Profits, earnings, and budgets must bow to more important human needs!'

He stopped reading and stared directly into the cameras. 'We have no illusions that the politicians and the fat-cat businessmen will agree to do these things simply because they are the *right* things to do. We are not that naïve. Not at all. If necessary, we are prepared to compel them to meet these just and reasonable demands.'

Kaltenbrunner paused again, letting the tension build. 'The bureaucrats and plutocrats have until October 7. That gives them five days to accept our terms – without condition and without compromise. If they fail, we will take our people, *all* our people, off the job and into the streets.'

The assembled journalists and camera crews stirred in astonishment. The five trade unionists in front of them represented a sizable fraction of the Franco-German labor force. Any job action involving all of them would have almost unimaginable economic consequences.

Kaltenbrunner nodded. 'That is right. This is an ultimatum. The governments and corporations must either meet our demands or face a general strike!' He held his right hand up with all five fingers extended. 'If our warnings are ignored, in five days' time no trains will run. No planes will fly. No trucks will bring food to the markets. No factories will operate. And no ships will sail with goods bound for foreign shores!'

No one listening to him could doubt that Markus Kaltenbrunner and his colleagues were in deadly earnest.

OCTOBER 3 – PALAIS DE L'ÉLYSÉE, PARIS

The eight men meeting in the presidential palace's Cabinet Room were dwarfed by the chamber's high ceiling and massive furniture. Each of the eight ran one of the republic's most powerful ministries. They represented a self-selected inner circle, and for all practical purposes they controlled the French government. The chair reserved for France's ailing President was empty.

'A general strike? Now? Can they be serious?' Henri Navarre, the Minister of the Interior, seemed stunned.

Other faces around the table mirrored his bewilderment. For more than a decade, support from the trade unions had helped keep their political party in power. The votes the labor confederations controlled were the margin of victory in any close election. And every recent election had been close.

'They are quite serious.' Jacques Morin, the new director of the DGSE, said it plainly, without emotion. 'All reports from our informers point in the same direction. The preparations for a general strike are well under way. Our German allies are seeing the same signs. Isn't that right, Foreign Minister?'

France's new Foreign Minister, Nicolas Desaix, nodded in agreement and approval. He'd secured the appointment of his former deputy to head the intelligence service. It was an arrangement that guaranteed him de facto control over the DGSE and its associated security agencies.

He leaned forward, eyeing each of his cabinet colleagues in turn. 'What Morin says is true. I do not think there is anything to be gained by hiding our heads in the sand. These radicals are not making idle threats.'

'Perhaps we should negotiate with them . . . come to some arrangement . . .' Navarre's voice trailed off as Desaix frowned. The small, stoop-shouldered Interior Minister's prestige had fallen precipitously in the past several weeks – a product of his growing inability to control the police and special riot troops.

'Negotiate? Impossible!' Desaix shook his head in contempt. 'Their demands are absurd – an insult. Meeting even the least costly of them would bankrupt our largest and most profitable companies. Nor do I see any merit in surrendering effective control of this government to a band of mechanics and shop stewards!'

'Then what, precisely, do you propose, Nicolas?' Barrel-chested Michel Guichy, the Minister of Defense, tapped the table for emphasis. 'If the gendarmes and the CRS can't keep order now, how can we depend on them during such a strike? My God, most of the bastards are in the unions themselves!'

Others around the room echoed Guichy's sharp-edged question. Even at the best of times cabinet meetings could be contentious. Now they were all on edge, worn down by the last month's steady stream of strikes, riots, and worsening economic indicators, and they were frightened by what was coming. France simply could not afford either the threatened nationwide walkout or the exorbitant demands being made by her trade unions. Her heavily subsidized industries were already on the edge of bankruptcy.

Desaix kept his face still, careful not to show his irritation. He'd worked too hard for too long to build his influence with these men to risk losing his temper now. Besides, he scented opportunity in this crisis – even in a crisis partly of his own making.

He shrugged mentally. It was becoming all too apparent that he'd miscalculated the effects of the foreign worker relocations. He'd anticipated widespread anger in eastern Europe – not this rage at home.

Still, there were positive aspects to the situation. This confrontation with organized labor had been building for years. So had public hatred for the immigrant population. His first attempt to solve those twin problems, the Sopron covert action, had partially backfired. Perhaps it was time to bring both disputes to a head. To kill two birds with one presidential decree. Especially if it could be done in a way that would advance his vision of a more powerful, more united France.

Desaix fixed his gaze on the Minister of Defense. Guichy's support for his plan would be critical. 'What I propose, my friend, are measures equal to the dangers we face.' He narrowed his eyes. 'Drastic measures.'

Then, speaking with utter conviction and iron determination, he outlined the steps he believed would save France from ruin.

The argument he sparked lasted half the night.

OCTOBER 4 – LE BOURGET AIRPORT, PARIS

Regular army soldiers in full combat gear ringed the small executive jet parked just off Le Bourget's main runway. They were the innermost element of an airtight security cordon surrounding the airport. The authorities were taking every possible precaution against trouble. Nothing could be allowed to delay this plane's scheduled departure.

'Attention!'

The soldiers snapped rigidly upright, presenting arms as a sleek Citroën limousine swung off an access road and purred up to the waiting aircraft. Tricolor flags fluttered from the Citroën's black hood.

The limousine's rear doors popped open, and a tall, hawk-nosed man emerged, carrying a leather briefcase. A single aide climbed out the other side, clutching a suit bag and a rolled-up umbrella. Clouds pushed west by a new high-pressure system rolling out of Russia carried the threat of rain over the next several days.

As the captain commanding the guard detachment saluted, both men hurried up a folding staircase and disappeared into the plane's dimly lit but plush interior. Its twin turbofan engines whined into action, howling louder and louder as they spun up toward full power.

Five minutes later, its navigation lights blinking against a pitch-black sky, the jet carrying Nicolas Desaix roared off the tarmac and climbed at a steep angle. The ranking member of the still-secret Emergency Committee for the Preservation of the Republic was flying east – toward Germany.

CHAPTER 5
Peacekeepers

OCTOBER 6 – HEADQUARTERS, 19TH PANZERGRENADIER BRIGADE, AHLEN, GERMANY

Lt. Col. Wilhelm 'Willi' von Seelow glanced out a headquarters building window at the brigade *Kaserne*. The area was alive with men and vehicles. Detachments of soldiers in gray-green field uniforms milled around open armory doors collecting weapons and ammunition. Other parties stood in line, waiting their turn. All wore the dark green beret and silver crossed-rifles badge of Germany's mechanized infantry, the panzergrenadiers.

The afternoon light, dimming as the sun set, was made grayer by a solid overcast sky. It fell on but did not illuminate the steel sides of tracked Marder APCs and the crumbling concrete walls of the brigade's barracks and garages. The outside lights were already on, but it was still too early for them to do much to brighten a scene of military confusion.

The chaos outside was matched inside the brigade's crowded operations room. Every phone was in use, and he could hear more than one officer demanding instant action in a strident tone, as if shouting made things work better. Von Seelow noticed one young captain who seemed to be doing most of the yelling. At least he could put a stop to that.

He called the man over, spoke softly and sharply to him, and then sent him on an errand out of the building. A little trip into the cold afternoon air should cool him off. More important, it would send a signal to the rest of the staff. Good soldiers stayed calm, even in the midst of crisis.

His reprimand had the desired effect. In the resulting quiet, von Seelow turned to his own work, trying hard to organize both his thoughts and the brigade. There was a lot to be done in an unreasonably short time.

They'd been galvanized into action by a sudden, hurry-up order from 7th Panzer Division's headquarters in Munster: mobilize the entire brigade immediately for civil peacekeeping duties. Von Seelow had taken the call himself once the duty officer convinced him it wasn't a joke.

He frowned at the memory. Major Feist, at division headquarters, had managed to sound arrogant and worried at the same time. He'd also peremptorily brushed aside every one of Willi's objections.

'No, Herr Oberstleutnant, I do mean the entire brigade. Yes, Herr Oberstleutnant, we are aware of your fuel situation. Yes, we know you are short of gear and men. I'm sorry, Herr Oberstleutnant, but we can't spare you any troops ourselves. We've problems here as well. We need your brigade on the road to Dortmund by midnight. The situation is very bad. The anarchists are holed up in several vacant buildings.' Willi knew the ones he meant. Unemployed youths had taken them over several months ago, turning them into graffiti-sprayed fortresses. 'They're using them as bases for looting and burning much of the surrounding area, as well as fighting with rival gangs. The police are doing their best, but they're outclassed.'

On that encouraging note, Feist had wished him luck and hung up.

Von Seelow knew the situation in Germany's towns and cities was grim, but he hadn't thought it was bad enough to warrant calling up regular army units.

A small chill ran down his back. Years ago, he'd served with Germany's U.N. peacekeeping forces in Yugoslavia and had watched with horror as civil strife wrecked a nation. Separating the warring factions had cost the U.N. force hundreds of lives and billions of marks. It had been a months-long nightmare of frustrating patrolling, sudden, bloody ambushes, and the horrid experience of being hated and shot at by both sides. Now he was being told his own country might stand on the brink of a similar nightmare.

His combat experience had been useful to him, though. In any peacetime army, promotions were rare. He'd moved up from major to lieutenant colonel because he'd shown himself cool and utterly reliable under fire. And von Seelow knew that he couldn't have gained promotion in any other way. His experience and training in the East German Army before the unification more than qualified him for his current rank, but ossies, those born in the East, were not popular in the unified Bundeswehr, the Federal German Army. Most of Willi's former colleagues were back in civilian clothes or stuck in dead-end posts. The odds were that he'd join them in a few years. The 'wessies' didn't want too many tainted soldiers from the East in their army's upper echelons.

Still, that might not be so bad. Soldiering wasn't the honorable career it had once seemed. With the Russian bear apparently declawed, peacekeeping was turning into the Bundeswehr's main job. At least half their training was devoted to 'civil affairs,' and tactics learned the hard way in Zagreb and Sarajevo were spreading fast through the entire army. This emergency deployment to Dortmund was probably only a taste of things to come.

Riots and clashes with police were now almost routine in every city in Germany. Unemployment hovered near the twenty percent mark, climbing steadily as the economy wound down. The figures were even higher among the young. But unemployment wasn't the only problem. Racial tensions were also rising rapidly as more and more eastern European refugees evaded the border patrols – all fleeing economies that were in even worse shape.

Von Seelow shook his head. It was difficult to imagine anything that could be worse. Germany's urban centers were the scene of daily pitched battles as a dangerous mix of right-wing fanatics, left-wing anarchists, and unemployed workers fought with each other, with police, and with shopkeepers. They wanted work and food, and both were scarce.

And he knew that food and work were bound to grow even more impossible to find if the nation's trade unions carried out their insane threat to call a general strike. Even his country's recent problems would pale in comparison during a wholesale work stoppage.

That seemed hard to believe. On his few excursions into Hamm, the nearest city, or to the Essen-Dortmund area, he had been shocked by the sight of ragged civilians wandering aimlessly or begging for small change or employment. Idle men and boarded-up shops lined the streets. Police barricades were commonplace, and the normal bustle of city life seemed weaker, more sullen. Certainly the government's strict gasoline rationing program had something to do with that, but the real reason was the continent-wide recession.

Von Seelow had never seen it this bad back in Leipzig – even before the Wall fell. East Germany's communist masters had known how to control things, he thought wryly. They'd kept the cost of bread low and made sure there'd been plenty to drink. Bread and circuses, Russian style. He pulled himself up short. Thinking about the past was a waste of time. Especially when East Germany's 'peace' had been purchased at such a high price. The newly unified federal republic might be wild and unruly, but at least it was still a democracy, still a nation one could be proud to serve.

He looked out the window again. It was darker, and a cold, swirling wind rattled the window glass. Temperatures were below average, with rain and wind that chilled the spirit as well as the body. Everyone predicted a cold winter. Willi knew it was going to be a hard one.

With difficulty, he turned his attention from his nation's larger problems to more immediate concerns. He had less than six hours to turn a formation of 3,500 men and three hundred combat vehicles into a police force that could control a population instead of destroying it. The brigade had enough riot gear for only one of its two active-duty panzergrenadier battalions. Now division wanted the entire brigade on the line – including its armored battalion and antitank company. How in God's name are we supposed to arm them for police work? he thought. And what orders should they be given?

A sudden flurry at the door caught his eye, and von Seelow jumped to attention as Col. Georg Bremer strode in. He had been called away from dinner at a friend's house, twenty kilometers outside Ahlen.

Bremer, the 19th Panzergrenadier Brigade's commanding officer, looked like a tanker. His dark hair belied his fifty-six years. Short, thick, solidly built, he moved quickly, and his officers had discovered that if you didn't move just as fast, he rolled right over you.

The physical contrast between the colonel and von Seelow couldn't have been any sharper. Willi was tall, almost too tall to serve in armored vehicles. His lean body was matched by a lean, square-jawed face. High cheekbones, deep blue eyes, and short blond hair just starting to go gray made him a living reminder of an aristocratic past that Germany had tried to leave behind.

Bremer headed straight for von Seelow, nodding to the rest of his staff. 'Seats, gentlemen.'

Von Seelow remained standing. As the 19th's operations officer, he was responsible for the brigade's readiness. It was now being put to a sore test.

'Any word on Oberstleutnant Greif?' Greif was the brigade's executive officer, and normally would run things in Bremer's absence. Tonight, though, he was on leave, moving his family out of Essen to the countryside.

'We think he's on the road, sir. We've asked the police to watch for him, but he isn't supposed to even check in until tomorrow morning.'

The colonel sighed and said, 'All right, that makes you acting executive officer.' Bremer looked him squarely in the eye. 'Where do we stand, Willi?'

Von Seelow knew each battalion's status by heart. 'The 191st will be ready to move by midnight, but it's only at fifty percent strength. The 192nd is about the same. We are having some problems with the 194th's fuel supply, but we're getting that sorted out. The tanks should be ready to roll in time. The 195th Artillery has been co-opted by Division in Munster. Apparently their own military police units have already been committed to police duties and they need men to provide security for the headquarters.'

Bremer listened closely and then nodded, a quick movement. 'That's unfortunate, but we shouldn't need the guns tonight. What are you doing about our missing men?'

That was a good question.

All of the brigade's battalions were badly understrength. Ending conscription had helped reconcile Germany's neighbors to its reunification, but it had played hell with its armed forces. Budget cuts made recruiting difficult. Military pay was poor, the living conditions awful. None of their units were at more than seventy-five percent of authorized manning.

Hard times had also caused many of the soldiers to take second jobs, working nights, or looking for work, after their duties were finished in the afternoon. Many of the men now needed for action were fanned out across a wide area, from Essen to Dortmund to Gütersloh, trying to augment their anemic paychecks. It was against regulations, but Bremer and von Seelow had both turned a blind eye to the practice. Their men had families to care for.

Von Seelow had also authorized a lot of emergency leaves for soldiers in the brigade. Those men were trying to move their families out of Dortmund or Essen or cities further away. The large cities offered a better chance for work, but the smaller villages had food and were safer.

With a little warning from Division, just a few hours more, he could have had virtually every man in the brigade ready to move. The alert, though, hadn't come until five-thirty, when too many men had already left the post. Put simply, the late afternoon call had caught them completely off guard.

'We have detachments from each company making sweeps through the local villages, rounding up stragglers. I've also passed word to the police to send any soldiers they find back to us.' He cleared his throat. 'In addition, I've called the local TV and radio stations, but they're unwilling to air the request unless we tell them why we're mobilizing.'

Bremer made a face. The last thing he was willing to do was tell a civilian his orders or intentions. He waited for von Seelow to finish.

'To make up some of the shortfall, I recommend stripping all personnel from the headquarters and tank-hunter companies. Putting them in the grenadier battalions will help bring us closer to full strength. We need men for riot duty, not logistical support or antitank missiles.'

Bremer agreed. 'True. Also, take men out of two of the tank companies. We shouldn't need more than one company of armor for this kind of work. Call the commanders and tell them what's going on while S-1 figures out how to apportion the extra troops.'

Von Seelow nodded in acknowledgment as Bremer glanced at the clock. It was six forty-five. 'Give me a status report at 2100 hours. I'm calling Division. I'm going to find out what's behind this business, and it better not be some kind of drill.' He grinned suddenly, including the staff in his gaze. 'Maybe we can find out what idiot came up with this order and put him in the lead vehicle.'

After the colonel disappeared into his office, von Seelow started making calls. Most of the battalion commanders, trying to solve their own problems, simply took the new personnel assignments in stride and rang off. The commanding officer of the 192nd, though, made it clear that he liked his new orders about as much as he liked foreigners, which included former East Germans. In other words, not at all.

'I need trained infantrymen. What the hell am I supposed to do with tank gunners and vehicle drivers?' argued Lt. Col. Klaus von Olden.

Willi wanted to tell him exactly what he could do with them, but held his temper. 'Use them as you see fit, Herr Oberstleutnant.'

Like von Seelow's, Klaus von Olden's ancestors had been Prussian nobles, but his family had escaped to the West when Germany was divided at the end of World War II. Willi was proud of his heritage, but a lifetime in the 'classless' East had taught him to keep a low profile. His father, once a colonel in the Wehrmacht, had even dropped the aristocratic 'von' from the family's name – becoming plain Hans Seelow, day laborer.

Von Olden, on the other hand, was as arrogant as if his obsolete title still held meaning. He'd even gone so far as to paint his family's ancestral crest on his command vehicle. He was proud of his 'Germanic' blood, and very vocal about his dislike of immigrants or anything smacking of the political left.

Von Olden's arrogant voice taunted him. 'With your broad experience in suppressing civilians at home and abroad, I was hoping you would have some suggestions.'

Controlling his temper, Willi ignored the remark. He'd heard worse. 'With these additions, how many men will you be able to field by midnight?'

'We should be close to seventy percent.' The other man sounded faintly disappointed. He'd obviously hoped his insult would draw a less temperate reaction.

'Very well. Good evening.' Willi hung up, trying not to slam the phone down. In truth, von Olden's remark had hit a little too close to home. In the GDR, army units had been used to suppress civil disturbances, often brutally. The federal republic's Justice Ministry was still trying to sort out criminal cases against border guards who'd shot their own countrymen as they tried to climb the Wall.

Several hours later, Willi von Seelow and Bremer stood next to their command vehicle. They were parked near the main gate to the *Kaserne*, watching trucks and Marder armored fighting vehicles roll out into the night. Bright lights now banished the darkness, spotlighting each vehicle as it roared out of the compound and turned onto the main road. It was eleven forty-five, and the first elements of the 19th Panzergrenadier Brigade were on the road for Dortmund.

A cold, damp wind gusted around them, carrying the stink of diesel exhaust. Even in their winter-weather gear they could feel it. It might rain or even sleet tonight. Driving conditions would be bad, but maybe the foul weather would dampen any disturbances.

'Good work, Willi, very good.' Bremer smiled as the vehicles roared by. Von Seelow appreciated the remark, but it didn't lift his black mood. Even a glowing fitness report from Bremer would never get him another promotion. Skill and experience would only carry him so far up the ladder. After that his East German birth would stop him cold.

Besides, did he want to serve in an army that operated only against its own citizens? He loved the outdoors, being in the field. No soldier loved urban combat, and a near civil war would be the dirtiest of fighting. He missed field maneuvers, where the enemy was well defined. That reminded him of something.

'Sir, you know what this deployment is doing to our fuel allowance. We were cutting back on exercises before this. I'll have to look at the figures when we're done, but we may have to restructure Cold Dragon.' Held each winter, after the crops were harvested and the ground had frozen, the exercise was the culmination of months of planning and smaller training exercises. It was the only chance the brigade got to exercise as a unit during the year.

'Tear up the training plan, Willi, and throw it away.' Bremer met von Seelow's surprised look with a secretive gaze. He glanced at his watch. 'In twelve minutes the government is going to declare martial law throughout Germany. The French are doing the same thing. I think we're going to be busy in the streets for a long time to come.'

Von Seelow nodded numbly. He'd been afraid of that. Germany's army was going to war – a war waged against fellow Germans.

Following Bremer's lead, he climbed into a jeep, eschewing the warmer but clumsier tracked command vehicle. It would bring up the rear, collecting vehicles that broke down or were lost.

Willi would much rather be in the lead jeep. Its radios crackled with last-minute orders and reports, keeping von Seelow so busy that he hardly noticed the convoy pulling onto Bundestrasse 58. A thin, cold rain started falling, spattering in wind-driven sheets against headlights and windshields.

They reached Dortmund's outskirts at two-thirty in the morning, but they'd seen the orange glow of fires flickering against the pitch-black sky for the past half hour. It would be a long night and an even longer day.

OCTOBER 8 – 5th MECHANIZED DIVISION, SWIECKO, POLAND, NEAR THE GERMAN BORDER

The Oder River valley lay shrouded in a thick, slowly swirling mist. Trees and houses on the far bank were almost invisible. Even the twin railroad and highway bridges spanning the river seemed to hang suspended in midair – massive structures of steel and concrete floating above the gray, obscuring fog.

Maj. Gen. Jerzy Novachik lowered his binoculars, thick, bushy eyebrows crinkling as he frowned. This weather was damned odd. Poland's autumn months were usually marked by a steady succession of cool, crisp, and clear days. But not this year. They were getting late November's freezing rains and bone-chilling fogs a month early. He shivered and pulled his brown uniform greatcoat tighter around his shoulders.

The sound of a hastily stifled sneeze made him turn around. 'God bless you, Andrzej.'

'Thank you, sir.' The colonel commanding his mechanized infantry regiment wiped his nose quickly and stuffed a handkerchief away out of sight.

Novachik studied him for a moment. The man looked cold, wet, and thoroughly miserable. That wasn't particularly surprising. After all, the colonel and his troops had spent the better part of the last two days out in the open – huddled in shallow fighting positions by day and trying to sleep inside their cramped, unheated vehicles by night.

He glanced toward the woods stretching north and south along low hills rising above the valley. Even this close, it was difficult to see the bulky, menacing shapes of BMP-1s and T-72 tanks waiting motionless beneath autumn-colored camouflage netting. The regiment's antitank missile teams, machine gunners, and riflemen were completely concealed. Still, a trained observer would eventually spot them all, and know that Poland's defenders were awake, alert, and ready for battle.

Novachik smiled grimly. That was exactly the message he wanted to send the Germans across the river.

The Bundeswehr's powerful divisions might be busy knocking heads together in Germany's restive cities right now, but only a fool would think that guaranteed Poland's peace. Throughout human history, too many governments had tried to blind their citizens to troubles at home with promises of quick, almost bloodless foreign conquests.

So Maj. Gen. Jerzy Novachik and his shivering but determined soldiers waited on the river's edge – deployed as a powerful sign to Germany's problem-plagued rulers that a new war with Poland would be bloody, not bloodless.

He only hoped they would heed the warning.

CHAPTER 6
Purge

OCTOBER 9 – U.S. EMBASSY, MOSCOW

Moscow's gray morning skies mirrored Alex Banich's mood as he crossed the open ground between the embassy's living quarters and the red brick chancery building. Nightly frosts, scattered snow showers, and weeks of freezing rains had turned the compound lawn into a brown, withered quagmire. The city's fall and winter months were always bleak and barren, but this year the weather was the worst in recent memory.

Somehow that seemed appropriate.

In the weeks since Len Kutner had given him Langley's new list of intelligence priorities, Banich and his team of field operatives had been working overtime to make the new contacts they needed – with very little measurable success. It took time and a great deal of effort to find the right kind of Russian trade bureaucrats and corporate officers: the kind who could be bought. Even then, every new 'recruiting' approach, however subtle, piled risk atop risk. They never knew who might get cold feet at the last minute or suddenly turn into an outraged patriot. And no matter how careful Banich and his agents were, the arrest of any one of them would help the FIS unravel their whole, painstakingly constructed network.

To make matters even worse, the Agency's Kiev-based cover company was having trouble acquiring the foodstuffs it sold. Crop yields in Ukraine and the other republics had been dismal. That was partly a product of the year's freak weather and partly because the Commonwealth's farms and transportation networks were still half-mired in socialist sloth. Breaking the bad economic habits built up over seventy years was proving an almost impossible task. Too much grain still rotted in unharvested fields and too much beef and pork spoiled in railroad cars left sitting on isolated side spurs.

The chronic supply shortages were starting to put a crimp in the CIA's Moscow operations. Profits from food sales covered a lot of the network's day-to-day expenses: bribes, safe-house rents, and the like. Even more important, having food to sell gave Banich and his agents power and the freedom to wheel and deal almost at will inside the Russian Republic's governing circles. The capital's generals, bureaucrats, and politicians were willing to overlook a lot for those who could put hot food on their plates.

Banich was tempted to make up the shortfall with imports from overseas, but he'd been fighting the temptation. Except for its original funding – ostensibly from a wealthy, expatriate Ukrainian – almost everything about the New Kiev Trading Company was exactly as it appeared to be. Ukrainian buyers bought Ukrainian products with Ukrainian money and then resold them for a profit to Russians, Belarussians, Armenians, and others. Going abroad for food would only increase the odds of Russia's counterintelligence service poking its nose into the company's lucrative and door-opening business.

Instead, it might be better to send Hennessy and some of the others down south to see if they could shake more food loose from tightfisted farmers or other hoarders. Of course, doing that would leave him even more short-handed here. Despite Kutner's best efforts, Langley had refused every request for more personnel. Apparently Congress was busy again, cutting the defense and intelligence budgets to fund extra unemployment insurance and federal make-work programs. Idiots.

He entered the chancery through the rear door, signed in with a brisk nod to the Marine sergeant on desk duty, and took the stairs to the sixth floor. Most embassy staffers rode the elevators from floor to floor. Climbing the stairs was one of the ways he dodged the mix of inbred speculation and gossip that passed for conversation in this isolated diplomatic posting. Besides, he thought, it helped him stay in shape.

Banich shook his head at that. Rationalizing wouldn't get him anywhere. The truth was that his temper was so short right now, he'd have scaled the chancery's outside walls to avoid unnecessary contact with the embassy's regular staff. Days filled with too much work and nights with too little sleep were starting to take a serious toll on both his endurance and his good humor.

Coming in early paid off. The corridors and cubicles on the way to his office were still empty. Then he stopped, frowning at the pink message sheet taped to his door. Len Kutner wanted to see him again – in his office this time.

The chief of station wasn't alone. A young woman sat comfortably in the chair facing his desk. 'Alex, come on in. There's someone I'd like you to meet.'

Kutner stood up, an action imitated by his visitor. 'Miss McKenna, this is Alex Banich, my senior field agent. He's the man you'll be working with for the next several months.' He nodded toward her. 'Alex, meet Erin McKenna. She's been assigned to us as a trade intelligence expert.'

Banich studied the woman with greater interest. She was taller than he'd first thought, with long legs and a slender, almost boyish figure. A mass of auburn hair framed her face. He was suddenly aware that she was studying him just as intently, frank curiosity clear in her bright green eyes. For some reason it was an uncomfortable sensation. He wished he'd shaved closer that morning.

With an effort he focused on more important matters. Now that the Agency's stateside, penny-pinching paper pushers had finally answered his request for more personnel, he'd better find out just what he had to work with. Starting with her background. Was she an agent or just an analyst? He smiled politely. 'Glad you're here, Miss McKenna. Where'd you work at Langley? Intel or ops?'

She shook her head. 'Neither. I'm not with the CIA, Mr. Banich.'

What?

Kutner cleared his throat. 'That's right, Alex. Miss McKenna works for the Commerce Department.'

'For the Office of Export Enforcement. Specifically the intelligence division.'

Banich felt himself starting to frown. A civilian. They'd sent him a goddamned civilian. And probably one with dreams of being some kind of female James Bond. Just fucking great.

'Do you speak Russian?' He spoke rapidly, the way a real Muscovite would.

'I'm fairly fluent. Enough to handle most conversations.' She answered him in the same language and then switched back to English. 'I've also got a pretty good grasp of French and German.' She smiled thinly. 'I even know enough Italian to read menus.'

The frown stayed on his face. Her vocabulary was good, but that accent would mark her as a foreigner no matter where she went inside the Commonwealth. Time to nip this thing in the bud and bundle her back to Washington where she belonged. He turned to Kutner. 'I can't use her, Len. Not out on the streets. I need trained field personnel.'

He had an instant feeling he'd been too blunt for his own good. He was right.

Erin McKenna's eyes flashed fire at him. 'Look, Mr. Banich, I've read the memos and message traffic from this station. All you've been doing is bitching about the new emphasis on trade intelligence. Well, that's why I'm here.' She took a step closer. 'I've got the knowledge and the experience to analyze the raw data you and your people collect. I can help point you in the right direction and call you off false scents. I am *not* here to play covert-action cowboys and Indians. Got it?'

Banich had the momentary feeling that he'd stuck his head into a buzz saw. He tried changing tack. 'It's not personal, Miss McKenna. It's just that we've been pushing hard to get this crap . . . this information . . . Washington wants, and—'

She interrupted him icily. 'This *crap*, as you call it, happens to be considered vital by the people we both work for. You have some kind of problem with that?'

Banich picked up the verbal gauntlet she'd thrown down. 'Yeah, I do. While we're busy tracking down garbage like who bribed who to get some frigging import license, we're losing track of other things. Like who's really got control of the Russian military. Or what kinds of weapons they're putting into production.'

Her voice was scathing. 'Maybe you didn't notice, but the cold war's been over for six years now, Mr. Banich. We're in a new kind of war now. One that's being fought with weapons like imports and exports, subsidies and tariffs. Maybe you ought to wake up and get with the program before the next century arrives.'

'Subsidies don't kill people and conquer countries. Tanks and missiles do. Maybe you should remember that—'

'There, there, children.' Kutner broke in, not even bothering to hide his amusement now. 'No more fighting. You're both stuck with each other no matter how much you squawk.'

Banich saw McKenna roll her eyes upward in disgust at the situation. He nodded to himself. At least they could agree on that much. And maybe he really could find some use for her. At least until he could convince somebody higher up the ladder to pull the plug on this half-assed idea. Besides, coping with all the red tape Washington tossed their way might even cool her down. He turned back to Kutner. 'All right, I give. She's on the team. For now.'

'Thank you so much, O Tsar of all the Russias.'

Ouch. Sarcasm, too. And in textbook Russian. He sighed. 'What kind of cover did Langley give her? What's her embassy rank?'

The chief of station's toothy grin grew even wider. 'That's another reason to be nice to her, Alex. On the books, Miss McKenna's a deputy economic attaché. Your *boss*.'

Banich felt a headache coming on fast. This was not starting out to be one of his better days.

OCTOBER 11 – FAST FREIGHT EXPRESS, ON THE MOSCOW-ST. PETERSBURG RAILROAD, OUTSIDE TVER

Lt. Vladimir Chuikov staggered upright as the train slowed abruptly, air brakes squealing over the roar of its diesel engine as it shuddered and slid to a stop. He stuck his head out a nearby window, his breath steaming in the ice-cold air. Why had they stopped?

Nothing he could see answered that question. They were on a siding off the main track, deep inside a forest of birch, fir, and pine. A rutted dirt track paralleled the tracks for several hundred meters before vanishing among the trees. Shadows and tangled undergrowth made it impossible to see very far into the still, silent forest. He shivered. In the stories his grandmother used to tell, woods like these were always the haunt of ghosts and evil witches.

Chuikov yanked his head back inside the passenger compartment.

'Trouble, sir?' The bandy-legged little sergeant who was second-in-command of the train guard detail was on his feet, one hand on the Makarov 9mm automatic at his belt. Most of the other soldiers were still sleeping, propped up on the car's hard wood benches. One or two were awake and had their Kalashnikov assault rifles close by.

'Maybe.' Chuikov moved toward a wall phone. He picked it up and jiggled the hook. The men driving the train should have some answers.

'Chief engineer.'

'This is Lieutenant Chuikov. What's going on up there?'

'Who can say? Central routed us off onto this spur and now we've got a stop signal showing. Perhaps there's a snarl up ahead . . . or they need the tracks for higher-priority traffic.'

Chuikov could practically hear the trainman's uninterested shrug. Of course, he thought angrily, these lazy swine were being paid by the hour, not the trip. Delays put rubles in their pockets. That wasn't all. The man was starting to slur his words together. They were drinking up there. 'I'm coming forward.'

'Suit yourself, Lieutenant.' The engineer yawned noisily. 'But we're likely to be stuck here a long while. You'll stay warmer inside.'

The young army officer hung up without offering any parting pleasantry. Sod the buggers. In the old days, they'd have shown more respect. He glanced at his sergeant. 'Some kind of traffic foul-up. Stay here. You're in charge until I get back.'

'Want me to wake the boys up?'

Chuikov shook his head. 'No point in that right now. But we'll post some sentries if we're going to be here much longer.'

He went through the forward door of the passenger car onto the platform between it and the freight car ahead. His teeth were already chattering. Mother of God, the trainman had been right. It felt cold enough to freeze fire.

The lieutenant dropped down onto the railroad roadbed, swearing as his brand-new boots sank into a mix of gravel and half-frozen mud. He looked both ways, scanning the length of the freight train. Everything seemed all right – from the single rust-stained diesel engine at the front to the caboose at the back. In between were twenty freight cars full of food and military hardware and the lone passenger car carrying his ten-man guard unit.

Chuikov understood his orders to protect this shipment from St. Petersburg's supply center to the army garrisons near the capital. In a land racked by growing shortages and ethnic violence, small arms, ammunition, light antitank weapons, and luxury goods were worth their weight in gold. Still, he was more worried about the danger posed by thieving cargo handlers at the Moscow freight yard. Lone trucks often vanished somewhere on the highway between the two cities – easy prey for bandits and black marketeers who were growing bolder. But trains were a different matter.

He started slogging his way toward the engine, increasingly irritated at this unforeseen delay. He'd wanted to be in Moscow before nightfall. Darkness would only make it easier for workers at the yard to 'lose' valuable crates.

His irritation turned to open anger when he swung himself up and into the engine's crew compartment. The two trainmen manning the big diesel were both bundled up against the cold, and both were well on the way to being blind drunk.

'Hey, General! Welcome aboard!' The bigger of the two men waved a flask at him. 'Want a snort? Only the finest for one of our motherland's brave defenders, eh?'

Chuikov wrinkled his nose in disgust. The stuff smelled more like brake fluid than vodka. He scowled. 'Get that out of my face!'

The big engineer pouted. 'All right. All right. No need to get stuffy. Right, Andrei?'

His coworker nodded once or twice, already so glassy-eyed that Chuikov wasn't sure he'd even understood what the big man had said.

'What the hell are you two playing at? Pull yourselves together, damn it!' The lieutenant brushed past both drunks. 'Where's your radio?'

The first trainman pointed with his flask, sloshing liquid out onto the steel floor. Chuikov glanced at the boxy wireless set. Its dials were dark. Idiots! They'd switched it off. What the devil was happening around here?

His speculations were cut short by a sharp buzz from the intercom phone. He picked it up. 'Chuikov.'

It was his sergeant. 'Sorry to interrupt, sir. But we have company. Vehicles moving up the road.'

'On my way.' Chuikov dropped the phone, feeling more and more bewildered. It was just one damned thing after another on this trip. He pushed past the two engineers again on his way outside. 'Get this train ready to move. And turn that bloody radio back on!'

His first fears were soothed by the sight of an army jeep leading a long column of canvas-sided URAL trucks up the muddy track. Maybe competent higher authorities were bringing some order out of this sudden chaos. He hurried toward the jeep, slipping and sliding down the embankment onto the dirt road.

'Lieutenant Chuikov, train guard commander, reporting.' He snapped a salute to the captain riding in the jeep's backseat. 'It's good to see you, sir.'

'Thank you, Lieutenant.' The captain returned his salute, stood up, and hopped out onto the road, landing lightly on his feet. He was a tall man with a narrow face and a thin-lipped, cruel mouth. 'Danilov. 55th Motor Rifles. I take it the dispatchers passed on our warning?'

Puzzled, Chuikov shook his head. 'No, sir. Not a word.'

The captain muttered a curse under his breath. Then he calmed down. 'One of my patrols spotted some suspicious activity about ten kilometers down the main line. Bandits, I think. We've been hearing rumors that some of the local criminal gangs were gathering for a big hit. This train could be it.'

Chuikov sucked his breath in, amazed. 'So some of these sneak thieves really have the balls to take the army on?'

Danilov seemed amused. He smiled dryly. 'So it appears, Lieutenant.' Then he turned serious. 'Your men are all in that passenger car?'

The young army officer nodded.

'Excellent.' Danilov lifted a silver command whistle to his lips and blew three short, sharp, loud notes.

Before the whistle blasts faded, men began boiling out of the first three trucks. All were armed. But none were in uniform. Instead, they were clothed in a motley assortment of leather jackets, jeans, and cloth caps. Some were bearded, others clean-shaven. In seconds most of them were fanning out along the length of the train while one group of ten or so scrambled up the embankment toward the passenger car.

For what seemed an eternity Chuikov stood rooted in shock. Then he fumbled with the flap of his holster, trying desperately to free his service automatic.

'I wouldn't do that, young sir.' Danilov's quiet voice was accompanied by a soft *click*. 'I can assure you it would be a fatal mistake.'

Chuikov turned slowly. The taller man already had his own pistol out and it was pointed straight at him. My God. He raised his arms above his head, careful to keep his palms out and open.

The crackling rattle of an AK-74 burst broke the silence. Both men swung round to face the passenger car. The bandits who'd been charging forward were down, in cover beneath the boxcars to either side or lying prone near the tracks with their rifles aimed and ready to fire.

Seconds dragged by, each one seeming longer than the last.

Suddenly Chuikov's sergeant appeared on the platform between the two cars. He was lugging a bloody corpse wearing army brown. 'Hey, don't shoot, you bastards. It's only me, Vanya!' He threw the dead man off the train and straightened up. Then he unslung his AK-74 and patted the assault rifle's folding metal stock fondly. 'Unfortunately Private Kaminsky just tried to become a hero of the republic! Maybe they'll bury him with a medal, eh?'

The bandits laughed.

Danilov seemed to relax. He waved one gloved hand toward the sergeant. 'Vanya, you old son-of-a-bitch! For a second there you scared the shit out of me!'

The bandy-legged little man grinned from ear to ear, jumped down to the tracks, and came over to them. 'So sorry, Comrade Danilov.' He nodded toward Chuikov. 'I see you've already met my gallant leader.'

'Indeed. He's been the perfect gentleman. A rare credit to our glorious armed forces.' Danilov holstered his pistol. 'Well, I'd better get the lads to work. We've got a lot to unload and not a lot of time to do it in.'

'You won't . . .' Chuikov choked off the rest of his sentence.

'Won't what, my dear fellow?' Danilov asked politely. 'Get away with it?' He smiled again. 'Of course we will. By the time anyone realizes this train hasn't just suffered a routine breakdown, my friends and I and the goods you've been guarding so efficiently will be halfway to Moscow. And Moscow is a very big city. You'd be surprised at how easy it is for people and merchandise to disappear there.'

The bandit chief glanced down at the bandy-legged sergeant. 'Look after the lieutenant, Vanya.' Something bleak and cold appeared in his eyes. 'Take care of him for me, won't you?' He strode off toward the waiting line of trucks.

'Why, Sergeant? Why?' Chuikov asked bitterly.

'Money, why else?' The sergeant laughed, a harsh, braying sound. 'My cut of this one job will be worth a year's pay. And I don't have to kiss any ass wearing an officer's shoulder straps to get it, either.'

There wasn't any good answer to that.

Chuikov watched his surviving troops being herded out of the passenger car at gunpoint. They stumbled down the embankment, hands clasped to their heads, pale with shock and shame. He could feel his own anger growing. By God, he'd make sure these bandits didn't escape justice. He'd help the military police hunt Danilov and this bastard sergeant down wherever they tried to hide. Their smirking faces were burned into his memory.

Their faces . . . Chuikov suddenly shivered. They'd let him see their faces.

The little sergeant read his mind. 'That's right, Lieutenant. This is as far as you're going.' He raised the assault rifle he'd been cradling so casually.

Chuikov whirled in a panic, running for the forest.

The other man let him get just ten feet before he fired.

Three burning hammerblows threw Chuikov facedown into the mud. His fingers scrabbled vainly in the dirt as he struggled to lever himself upright, trying desperately to breathe. He was still gasping when a final crashing blow sent him spiraling down into darkness.

OCTOBER 14 – YAROSLAVL

One hundred and fifty miles northeast of Moscow, the mighty Volga River meandered past Yaroslavl's domed churches and silent smokestacks. Pollution-stained chunks of ice swirled southward with the current – visible signs of a winter arriving weeks before its normal time. Patches of black ice and sudden, blinding snowstorms were already making travel along the Moscow highway a dangerous and uncertain enterprise.

There were other signs of trouble in Yaroslavl.

The line of weary men, women, and children clutching empty shopping bags wound past all the Government Milk Store's bare shelves and stretched far out into the main city square. Dour workers in stained white smocks and hair nets stood behind a wooden counter at one end of the store, dispensing small ration packets of powdered milk and moldy cheese at a glacial pace.

The tired faces of those at the front of the line tightened as a worried-looking worker emerged from the store's back room and went into a whispered conference with the store's portly, bearded manager. Just to get this far, they'd already been shuffling forward an inch or two at a time for hours. Supplies of even the most basic goods were running low as the oddly early winter closed its icy grasp around the city.

'Friends, friends! Please listen to me!' The manager waved his hands, seeking their attention. 'I have a most unfortunate announcement to make.'

He shook his head sorrowfully. 'Because of unexpectedly high demand, our stocks have fallen below emergency reserve levels. Accordingly, I am forced to close this store until new supplies arrive . . . perhaps tomorrow.'

Muttered curses rose from the waiting crowd. Some of the younger children, frightened by their parents' anger, began crying.

One of the men closest to the counter, a big ironworker, stepped out of line and glared at the manager. 'Stuff this "emergency reserve" garbage! You've got milk and cheese left back there. Now, start handing it out!'

'I'd like to oblige you, friend. Honestly, I would.' The manager's plump fingers plucked nervously at his beard. 'But regulations require me to keep—'

'Regulations, hell!' an angry voice shouted from near the back. 'These bastards are hoarding the milk for themselves!'

Others in the crowd growled their agreement with that outraged assessment. They began pushing and shoving their way forward. A rack of empty shelves toppled over with a thunderous crash.

The manager paled and backed away from his counter. 'Hold on! Hold on, friends! Don't make this a police matter.'

Jeers greeted his plea. 'Fat pig! Bloodsucker! Exploiter!'

Led by the big ironworker, shouting men and women climbed over the counter, urged on by those behind them. Others even further back began smashing the store's plate-glass windows, hurling shelves and signs they'd torn down out onto the pavement. Some started chanting, 'Food! Food! Food! We want food!'

As the crowd surged over the counter several clerks tried to block the stockroom door with their bodies. That was a mistake. In seconds, heated words turned to violent acts. The clerks went down under a sudden barrage of flying fists and boots. Pieces of wood torn from splintered shelves and now used as clubs rose and fell, thudding into skulls and smashing ribs. Blood stained the store's tile floor and splattered across its yellowing white walls.

Shaking with fear, the milk store manager turned to flee. But powerful hands dug into his plump shoulders and yanked him backward.

'No, pig. You don't get away so easily!' The ironworker's face was a hate-filled mask.

The manager screamed in terror. He was still screaming when the big man hurled him into the midst of the howling mob.

OCTOBER 17 – THE KREMLIN, MOSCOW

The big black ZIL limousine swept past the guards manning the Borovitskaya Tower gate without stopping. Command flags flying from its hood identified the car, and no soldier with any sense delayed Marshal Yuri Kaminov on his way to a meeting with the Russian Republic's President. Plenty of the dirt-poor and isolated border outposts near Kazakhstan were full of officers and men who'd done something to annoy the notoriously bad-tempered chief of the general staff.

Gearshift grinding, the ZIL followed the steeply rising road, roaring uphill past the elegant nineteenth-century façade of the State Armory building and into the main Kremlin compound. Still moving at high speed, the black limousine flashed past the domed palaces, cathedrals, the old headquarters of the Supreme Soviet, and the Russian Senate building. Flocks of startled birds and well-dressed bureaucrats scattered out of its path.

Kaminov's staff car stopped in front of the massive yellow brick Arsenal – once an army museum and now used as an office building by the President and his advisors. The driver, a young sergeant in full dress uniform, climbed out quickly and opened the rear driver's-side door. Then he stiffened to rigid attention, still holding the door open.

The marshal, stocky and squarely built with a rough-hewn peasant's face, nodded to the young man as he emerged from the ZIL. 'Wait here, Ivanovskiy. I won't be inside long.'

'Yes, sir.'

Another officer followed the marshal out of the limousine. The three stars on Valentin Soloviev's shoulder boards identified him as a full colonel in the Russian Army. Everything else about him, from his straw-colored hair, ice-cold gray eyes, and high, aristocratic cheekbones down to his immaculately tailored uniform and brightly polished boots, seemed to separate him from the older, plainer Kaminov.

A waiting functionary hurried forward from inside the Arsenal. 'The President is ready to see you, Marshal. In his private office, as you requested.'

'Good.' Kaminov pointed at Soloviev. 'The colonel is my military aide. He'll accompany me.'

'Of course, sir.' The bureaucrat's eyes flicked nervously in Soloviev's direction. Last-minute additions to presidential meetings were rare. That made this officer someone to be watched. And possibly someone to be feared. He nodded toward the Arsenal's main door. 'If you'll follow me, gentlemen?'

The inner office of Russia's President was a relatively small room more cluttered than decorated. A large marble-topped writing desk, several plush chairs, and a more modern and utilitarian computer desk all competed for the limited floor space on a hand-woven Armenian rug. Thick drapes cloaked a large, arched window overlooking the Arsenal's inner courtyard. Pictures of the republic's leader, smiling, white-haired, and boisterous in summit meetings with other heads of state, filled the other three walls.

Only close examination showed that the room's current occupant was the same man shown in the photographs. The President was starting to show the tremendous strain involved in governing an almost ungovernable nation. His thick white hair was thinning and his eyes were shadowed and bloodshot. New lines across his broad forehead and around his mouth gave him a haggard, worn appearance.

'Yuri, it's good to see you.' The President's words were more enthusiastic than his tone. He'd had to pay a continuing price to keep Kaminov's support for his political and economic reforms, and he was a man who disliked owing anybody for anything.

'Mr. President.' Kaminov gestured toward Soloviev. 'I don't believe you've met Colonel Valentin Soloviev.'

'No, I haven't had the pleasure.' The President paused, visibly searching his memory. His eyes narrowed. 'But I have heard many . . . interesting . . . things about this young officer. You were ranked first among your class at the Frunze Military Academy, yes?'

Soloviev shook his head. 'Second, Mr. President.' He smiled tightly. 'But the man who was first died in Afghanistan. I survived.' He pushed away mental pictures of the dead, the maimed, and burning, broken villages. Years of constant combat, ambush, and atrocity. And all for nothing.

The President watched him closely, as though waiting for him to say more. Then he nodded in understanding. Few veterans of the Afghan War ever said much about their experiences. All memories of that debacle were bad. He pointed to two chairs in front of his desk. 'Sit down, gentlemen. To business, eh?'

They sat.

'Now, Marshal, exactly what is so urgent that it could not wait until our next Defense Council meeting?'

'The fate of our nation, Mr. President,' Kaminov said bluntly. 'That is the urgent matter we must discuss. And decide.'

'Oh?' The President raised a single eyebrow. His hand drifted closer to the phone on his desk. The chief of the general staff was hardly likely to try launching a coup with just one officer by his side. But then stranger things had happened in Russia over the past several years. 'Perhaps you'll explain what you mean by that.'

'Of course.' Kaminov frowned. 'Anyone with his eyes open can see the dangers we face this winter.' He ticked them off one by one on his thick fingers anyway. 'Starvation and anarchy in our cities. Chaos and banditry in the countryside. Our farmers hoarding needed food. Our factories idled and rusting away.'

'All problems we've faced before and survived, Yuri. What precisely is your point?'

'Teeter on the brink long enough, Mr. President, and eventually you're bound to fall in.' Kaminov leaned forward in his chair. 'Things are different this year. For a start, we won't be getting much more emergency aid from the French or the Germans, and certainly not from the Americans. They've got too many problems of their own to do much for us. True?'

'True.' The President looked troubled. 'I've spoken to them all. They're polite enough, God knows, but also empty-handed.'

'Just so.' Kaminov seemed satisfied by the other man's admission. 'So we can't beg our way out of these troubles any longer. We must maintain order with our own resources. With all the forces at the state's disposal.'

He rapped the desk to hammer home his point. 'And yet those forces are falling apart before our very eyes.' He glanced at Soloviev. 'You have those reports, Colonel?'

Soloviev silently opened his briefcase and handed a thick sheaf of papers to his superior.

Kaminov fanned them out across the desk. 'Look at these! Police strikes in St. Petersburg, Volgograd, and Yekaterinburg. Mutinies for higher pay in two motor rifle divisions! Officers murdered by their own men in half a dozen more units!'

The President brushed the papers back toward the marshal. 'I've seen the reports, Yuri.'

Kaminov glowered back at him. 'Then you must also realize the need to regain full control over the security forces. And over the railroads and other transportation networks. For our country to survive the coming winter we must take strong action. Action unencumbered by absurd legal niceties.' He paused briefly to let that sink in and then went on. 'That is why we insist that you declare an immediate state of emergency.'

'We, Marshal Kaminov? You and the colonel here? Or are there others supporting this . . .' The President fumbled for a neutral term. 'This *proposal* of yours?'

The marshal nodded grimly. 'There are others. Many others.' He slid a single-page document across the desk. 'You'll find this document interesting reading, Mr. President. It contains an outline of the measures you must take to maintain order over the next several months. All you have to do is sign it.'

Soloviev watched the President scan the sheet of paper, racing through its bland phrases for brutal deeds with growing anger. The older man's hands were shaking by the time he reached the end. A dozen high-ranking officers had already signed at the bottom, including all five commanders in chief of Russia's armed forces. Kaminov's preparations had been thorough.

The President finished reading and looked up. When he spoke, his voice was flat, carefully devoid of any emotion. 'And if I don't approve this plan? If I refuse to declare martial law?'

Kaminov sat back, clearly confident. 'Then I would have to remind you that my loyalties to Mother Russia supersede those to any individual, Mr. President.'

'I see.' The President's face darkened. He'd forgotten a basic lesson of power politics. Not all coup d'états were signaled by tanks in the streets. Some were far more subtle. He sighed. The generals had left him with only one real, survivable choice. More important still, he had little doubt that they'd correctly read the public mood. The people were weary of chaos and disorder. They were ready to follow the men on horseback. He reached for a pen.

For the time being at least, Russia's fragile experiment with democracy was coming to an end.

OCTOBER 19 – MINISTRY OF DEFENSE, MOSCOW

Pavel Sorokin looked like he'd been losing weight in a hurry. He also looked worried and more than a little frightened.

'Nikolai! Good! You're finally here.' The bureaucrat forced a lopsided smile as Banich ambled out of the elevator, passing between two unsmiling air force majors who were waiting to get on. 'I was afraid you might be late.'

Banich looked at him curiously. Sorokin had never struck him as being either particularly energetic or a stickler for protocol. Something odd was going on. Something connected with this ridiculous last-minute demand for more deliveries to army installations around Moscow? It seemed likely. 'Well, I'm not. What's up?'

The Russian shook his head. 'There's no time for that now, Nikolai.' He glanced quickly down at his watch and bit his lip. 'Come on, there's someone you have to meet.'

Still curious, Banich followed the fat man at a fast walk down the hall. They were moving through parts of the Defense Ministry he'd never seen before. Paintings depicting famous Russian battles hung at regular intervals along the hallway, and high-ranking officers bustled in and out of busy offices. All the uniforms and gold braid made the CIA agent acutely aware that he and the supply manager were the only civilians in sight.

'This way.' Sorokin led him into an office near the end of the corridor.

Inside the room, a desk topped by a small personal computer and two telephones guarded the doorway to yet another office. A fresh-faced army lieutenant occupied the chair behind the desk. Other, older officers from different service branches filled chairs lining the walls, each obviously waiting his turn for an appointment.

Sorokin approached the lieutenant with surprising deference. 'Excuse me, sir. Could you please tell the colonel that we're here? Pavel Sorokin and Nikolai Ushenko? He wanted to see us.'

The lieutenant eyed him suspiciously, checked his watch and a thick, leather-bound appointment book, and then lifted one of the phones. 'Colonel? The supply manager and the merchant you wanted are here.' He listened to the reply, put the phone down, and nodded toward the door. 'Go on.'

Banich went through the door feeling warier than he had for a long while. Maybe he'd grown too used to manipulating puffed-up, greedy administrators like Sorokin. Something told him he was moving into a very different league right now. A much more dangerous league.

His first glimpse of the man waiting for them confirmed that. The pressures he'd used to bend Sorokin to his will wouldn't mean spit to this grim-looking bastard.

'You are the Ukrainian commodities trader, Ushenko?' The colonel's arrogant tone left little doubt that he expected an answer and expected it immediately. He stayed seated as they came to a halt in front of his desk.

'Yes, I am.' Banich made a split-second decision and kept his own tone light, almost airily unconcerned. He had to stay in character, and as Ushenko he'd never given a damn about rank or power. 'And who the devil are you?'

He heard Sorokin draw a quick, nervous breath.

The army officer studied him for a moment with cold gray eyes that looked out from under pale, almost invisible eyebrows. He seemed almost amused. 'My name is Colonel Valentin Soloviev, Mr. Ushenko.'

'And just what can I do for you, Colonel?' Banich glanced to either side, looking for a chair to sit down in. There weren't any.

'You can start by explaining this.' Soloviev handed him a piece of paper.

Banich recognized the New Kiev Trading Company's letterhead. It was his own politely worded notification that the company could not sell additional food supplies to the Ministry of Defense. He looked up. 'I don't see that there's anything to explain. You can't get milk from a dry cow, and I can't obtain the goods you're looking for. Certainly not in those quantities. And certainly not at those prices.'

Pavel Sorokin was sweating now. He mopped his brow and laughed weakly. 'Nikolai! Surely you don't mean that. You've always come through for us in the past and . . .'

Soloviev cut him off with a single irritated glance. Then he turned his attention back to Banich. 'It would be most unwise to try bargaining with *me*, Mr. Ushenko. I can promise that you would not find it a profitable experience.'

'Look, Colonel, I'm not interested in haggling with you.' Banich shrugged. 'But you're asking for the impossible. There's simply not that much food readily available. Not this winter.'

'I am acquainted with both the market conditions and the weather, Ushenko.' The Russian army officer frowned. 'Let me make myself even clearer. We need these extra supplies. We need them delivered over the next several days. And I will obtain them by any means necessary.'

Banich didn't try to conceal his confusion. 'But why the big rush? Why the need for so much so soon? Why not wait for the spring? Supplies will be up and prices down by March or April, at the latest.'

'Because we don't have until the spring!' The colonel's eyes flashed angrily. He paused. When he spoke again, he sounded like he was rattling off a prepared statement – one that he wasn't especially interested in. 'The government has scheduled an emergency exercise to test its ability to keep order during the coming months. Our part of this readiness exercise involves the rapid rail movement of an additional division to the capital from one of the outlying districts. Once here, the troops will take part in maneuvers designed to evaluate their ability to reinforce the police should the need arise.'

Soloviev smiled wryly. 'Given the current situation, I'm sure you can understand my reluctance to dump thousands of half-starved soldiers on the streets of Moscow. If nothing else, it would mean the end of a career I rather enjoy.'

Banich felt his brain moving into high gear. Readiness exercise, hell! Nobody, especially not the near-bankrupt Russian government, moved ten to fifteen thousand soldiers around on a whim or for some half-assed riot control practice. The military brass were up to something, all right. He wondered whether any of the republic's political leaders knew what it was.

In the meantime, he'd better find a way to meet the army's demands. Getting shut out now would mean losing a crucial inside track to information on military planning and personnel. He spread his hands in resignation. 'Okay, Colonel, you've made your point. I'll see what I can do.'

Beside him, Pavel Sorokin breathed a huge sigh of not-so-silent relief. It was short-lived.

'But the price per ton has to come up. I can't swing the deal for what you're offering.'

'No haggling, Ushenko. Remember? You'll meet our needs and our price, or I'll make sure you lose your licenses for doing business inside this republic. Clear enough?'

'Yes.' Banich grimaced. 'And just how in God's name am I supposed to explain this to my bosses? Doing business at a loss, I mean.'

'Simple.' Soloviev smiled again, looking more than ever like a tiger toying with its prey. 'Tell them that you're buying my continued goodwill.' He nodded toward the door in an abrupt dismissal.

OCTOBER 21 – NEAR GORKY PARK, MOSCOW

In the first hour after sunrise, Russia's capital city lay wrapped in a deep, deceptively peaceful silence.

Erin McKenna ran southward beside the gray-tinted Moskva River, long legs eating up distance with every easy stride. Her long auburn hair streamed out behind her, tied into a bobbing ponytail with a length of black ribbon. There weren't any other people in sight. For the moment at least, she moved alone in splendid isolation.

She shook her head irritably as the watch on her wrist chimed suddenly in an unwelcome reminder. It was time to head back for the start of another working day. She turned left, circling deeper into Gorky Park.

Fallen leaves in rich autumn colors littered the park's winding paths and lay heaped below bare-limbed trees. For the first time in weeks, the sky overhead was a deep cloudless blue, although temperatures still hovered near the freezing mark. Despite the pale sunshine, the tree-covered grounds were completely deserted. Few of Moscow's hungry citizens had the time or physical energy for jogging during these hard times.

Erin hoped she would never find herself in the same state. Running recharged her mind. It helped her clear away the cobwebs accumulated by hours spent reading densely written reports or searching through packed computer data bases. It also gave her time to herself – time she'd always treasured. Time for her own thoughts, or time for her mind to go blank, absorbed by the comforting rhythm of her legs covering ground at high speed. She'd proven her ability and competitive edge by winning a string of long-distance medals in high school and college. Now she ran for pure pleasure.

Not that she'd had much pleasure lately.

So far her assignment to the CIA's Moscow Station had been one big bust. Despite their best efforts, Banich's field operatives were still only able to gather the information she needed in dribs and drabs – small nuggets of fact and fancy that were barely worth analyzing and not worth reporting back to Washington. Her own moves to make contacts in the city's foreign business community were going somewhat better, but they were still painfully slow. She couldn't push too hard without raising unnecessary suspicions among the businessmen and women who managed Western trade with Russia and the other Commonwealth republics.

And now both Alex Banich and Len Kutner were busy with some hush-hush project of their own. For the past two days, they'd been closeted together in one of the embassy's secure sections – emerging only long enough to send coded reports to Washington or to grab a quick bite in the staff canteen. The field agents who'd been working with her were being sent away on other rushed assignments. Something big was happening. And they'd shut her out of whatever it was.

Just the thought of that made her angry. She was tired of being labeled an amateur, interfering busybody. Her security clearances were just as good as Banich's, and it was past time that he and his people started treating her like a full partner. She frowned at her thoughts. Winning his respect wouldn't be easy. Not when they could only seem to agree on two things. One was that Moscow *was* the capital of Russia. The other was that most politicians needed help to tie their own shoes.

Erin pushed down the beginnings of a smile as she considered that last point of agreement. She'd developed her own cynical attitude toward Washington's pontificating power brokers during a stint as an analyst for the Senate Commerce Committee. Too many senators who preached about their devotion to equal rights by day tried to grope their female staffers by night. Fending off their unwanted advances had been far more difficult than doing her assigned work. She suspected that Banich's disdain for politicians had a very different origin.

She came out of the park and turned north onto a stretch of pavement paralleling a wide, multilane avenue. Once known as Lenin Prospekt, the street had long since reverted to its prerevolutionary name – Kaluga Road. It was one of Moscow's principal thoroughfares and usually one of its busiest. But not today.

Only a few cars and taxis zoomed down the deserted street, racing over the speed limit along a road normally choked with bumper-to-bumper traffic. That was strange. Maybe the gasoline shortages she'd been reading about in the newspapers were finally starting to pinch the capital. Or maybe the government's underpaid workers were staging another wildcat strike.

The deep roar of diesel engines moving up the street behind her ripped those idle speculations to shreds.

Wheeled armored personnel carriers thundered past at high speed, rumbling northward toward the river, the Kremlin, and the two-level Grand Boulevard that ringed the city center. Soldiers armed with assault rifles rode standing up, scanning the buildings to either side through open roof hatches. Wolf whistles and leers drifted her way as they sped by.

'Hey, pretty lady! Need a real man?'

'Nice tits, baby!'

Erin flushed angrily but she kept running. She had to get back to the embassy and find out what the hell was happening. Whatever it was, the Russian Army was certainly out in force, she thought, counting vehicles as they rumbled past. She stopped counting at thirty.

The long armored column split up as it entered October Square. Some of the turreted APCs turned left or right along the Grand Boulevard. Others roared straight ahead, advancing toward the Kammenyj Bridge and the Kremlin. Three vehicles bringing up the rear slowed down and wheeled in line to block the Kaluga Road.

Troops tumbled out of the APCs, urged on by shrill blasts from a high-pitched command whistle. Several took up firing positions near the entrance to the Hotel Warsaw while others trotted across the street. Still more men followed them, uncoiling twisted, razor-sharp strands of concertina wire.

Despite herself, Erin was impressed. These soldiers were putting together a very solid roadblock very quickly. Unfortunately they were also cutting her off from the nearest Metro station.

She slowed to a walk. Running headlong into a platoon of overexcited Russian infantrymen didn't seem like a particularly good idea. Her hand slipped into the travel pack she wore around her waist, reaching for her passport and diplomatic identity card. With luck, they'd see that she wasn't any threat and simply wave her through.

'Halt!'

Damn. She stopped, feeling her heartbeat starting to speed up. More than a dozen pairs of eyes and rifles were pointed in her direction.

The officer who'd yelled at her marched closer, backed by two of his soldiers. He had a narrow, arrogant face and he didn't look friendly. Wonderful. She had the sinking feeling that getting past this checkpoint wasn't going to be easy.

'You! Show me your papers! And be quick about it.' The officer snapped his fingers at her impatiently, but he seemed far more interested in studying her breasts. The two privates behind him were openly smirking.

'I'm an American diplomat. You have no authority over me.' Erin spoke carefully, in Russian, holding out the documents he'd demanded. 'You see?'

The soldier snatched them out of her hand. 'American, you say?' He stroked his chin with one hand, thumbed through her papers for a second, and then snorted. 'But maybe these are forgeries, eh?'

Her temper flared. 'Don't be ridiculous! Now, cut the bullshit and let me pass!'

That was a mistake. She'd given this creep a perfect opening.

The Russian officer smiled lazily. 'Perhaps you should learn to show more respect, woman.' He turned to the two privates behind him. 'This so-called American could be a dangerous spy. Or a criminal. I think we should search her for concealed contraband. Thoroughly, eh?'

Both men nodded eagerly. One even licked his lips in anticipation.

Oh, God. Erin's hands balled into fists. She glanced to either side, already knowing she had nowhere to run. All the soldiers manning the checkpoint had stopped to watch.

'Let's go, bitch! We'll see just what you're carrying under that tight sweater of yours.' The officer spun on his heel, striding toward the nearest personnel carrier. He didn't even bother to look back to see if she was following.

'Captain!' The sudden shout came from down the street, on the other side of the roadblock.

Erin could see a big black car pulling up to the barrier. It was a Lincoln

Continental with diplomatic license plates. Her hands started trembling, this time in relief and not in fear. The cavalry had arrived. For the first time, she appreciated Banich's earlier irritating insistence that she leave a detailed description of the route she planned to take whenever she signed out of the embassy compound. Her eyes narrowed in speculation. He had been standing by to pull her out of trouble. That could only mean that he and Kutner had had some advance warning of what was in the wind.

Erin frowned, still not sure whether she should be touched by his readiness to rescue her, or irked that he'd kept her in the dark for so long.

One of the Lincoln's rear doors popped open and Alex Banich climbed out, his face tight with anger as he took in the scene in front of him. Without stopping, he pushed through the knot of soldiers standing in his way, flashing his identity card from side to side as though it were some kind of religious talisman. He came to a halt right in front of the Russian captain.

'You'd better just be escorting Miss McKenna through your lines, Captain.' Banich slid the card into his jacket and put both hands on his hips. 'If not, I can promise you one hell of a lot of trouble.'

'We were simply . . .'

'Don't bother lying to me. I can guess what you were planning.' Banich glared up at the taller man, openly daring him to disagree.

The army officer scowled but kept his mouth shut. He'd obviously been looking forward to humiliating a lone American woman, not provoking a full-fledged diplomatic incident.

'Are you okay?'

Erin nodded, not trusting herself to speak yet. She'd be damned if she'd show these soldiers any more weaknesses than she already had.

'Good.' Banich reached out and took her papers out of the captain's unresisting hand. 'We've got a lot to get done today. As you may have gathered, the government's declared martial law. So there's no more time for screwing around with tin-pot, mincing morons like this guy.' He jerked a thumb at the Russian.

This time it was the captain who turned red with impotent rage. Erin smiled sweetly at him and followed Banich back to the waiting Lincoln. Inside she was busy trying to sort out a world that seemed suddenly turned upside down.

OCTOBER 23 – THE PLACE OF SKULLS, IN RED SQUARE, MOSCOW

Before the Bolshevik Revolution, the circular stone platform called the Lobnoye Mesto, the Place of Skulls, had served as a site for public executions. Since the communists had preferred to carry out most of their murders in secret, the platform had fallen into disuse – becoming instead a place where tourists posed for pictures against the scenic backdrop provided by the old GUM department store and St. Basil's Cathedral. Now, under Marshal Kaminov's emergency decrees, the Place of Skulls was again a place for swift and sure punishments.

Several thousand people crowded Red Square, craning their heads for a better look at the raised platform. Excited murmurs swept through the waiting crowd as five blindfolded men were dragged down from a canvas-sided army truck and shoved up the stone steps. Their hands were tied behind their backs, and signs hung around their necks identified them as thieves and black market speculators.

Soldiers wearing heavy winter overcoats turned the blindfolded men around to face the square and forced them to kneel on the top step. When they were in place, five army officers marched smartly up the stairs and took their posts – one behind each kneeling prisoner.

'Citizens of Mother Russia!' a deep, harsh voice blared through the loudspeakers ringing the square. 'For years these criminals have stolen bread from your mouths and profited by your miseries! But no more. No more. Now you will see justice done.'

Scattered clapping greeted this announcement, but most of those watching were silent.

'These men have been tried, convicted, and sentenced to death by the Special Military Tribunal for Moscow. Their appeals have been considered and rejected by the highest authorities.'

The people jamming the square stirred in confusion at that. Most of them were unsure of precisely who the 'highest authorities' were right now. Although they'd seen the President's televised speech declaring martial law, almost all public announcements since then had come from men in uniform. With the republic's newspapers, radio programs, and television news shows all operating under restrictive censorship decrees, reliable information was a rare and valuable commodity.

'Soldiers of the Russian Republic, are you ready to perform your sacred duty to the motherland?' The waiting army officers came to attention and then, one by one, nodded. 'Very well. Proceed with the executions.'

Five pistol shots rang out one after the other, echoing off the massive stone buildings surrounding Red Square. Spilling bright red blood, five corpses slumped forward – tumbling down the steps to the cobblestones below. A soft sigh rippled through the crowd as the last body sprawled at the foot of the Place of Skulls.

The loudspeakers spoke again. 'Thus perish all who would rob and exploit the people of Holy Mother Russia! Return to your homes and factories, fellow countrymen – confident in those who guard and defend you.'

The spectators dispersed slowly, filtering out of the square under the watchful eyes of a crack infantry battalion and a small cluster of white-haired senior officers – each man a bright spectacle of gold braid, service ribbons, and medals. Wheeled BTR-80 APCs and big-gunned T-80 tanks lined the nearby streets as a steel-sided reminder of military power.

'A most impressive display, Colonel.' Marshal Yuri Kaminov clapped Soloviev on the shoulder.

'Thank you, sir.' Soloviev smiled woodenly at Kaminov's praise. The marshal himself had drawn up the plans for this afternoon's executions. All he'd had to do was follow them to the last letter.

'We Russians are a simple people. We understand simple, direct lessons. That is why the people respect power. They appreciate a firm hand.' Kaminov pointed to where the dead men were being piled on stretchers and hauled away. 'And that is what we shall give them, correct?'

Soloviev nodded.

'Good.' Kaminov motioned to another of his aides – a dark-haired major. The man came forward carrying a thick, stapled sheaf of papers. 'Nikolskii has the details for your next assignment.' He lowered his voice. 'This is a crucial job, Valentin. Executions like these will help cleanse our society. But we must also purify the armed forces by weeding out the weak and the incompetent. Russia must have a sword and shield she can rely on in these dangerous times.'

The marshal took the documents from the major and handed them to Soloviev. 'This is a preliminary list of junior and senior officers we consider unreliable. I want you to organize a series of roving courts-martial ready for immediate action. Instruct the tribunals that I want these vermin expelled from the service in disgrace.' He scowled. 'I want them starving in the streets as object lessons for any others who might forget where their loyalties should lie.'

The colonel nodded again, more slowly this time. 'As you command, sir'

Kaminov stared hard at him. 'Do not fail me in this matter, Colonel.'

'No, sir.' Soloviev met his gaze coolly. 'I know my duty.'

'Very good.' The marshal seemed satisfied. 'You are dismissed.'

Soloviev straightened to attention, saluted, and strode toward the staff car waiting to take him back to the Ministry of Defense. He ignored the soldiers already hard at work, washing blood off the Place of Skulls' gray stone steps.

Once back in his office, he skimmed rapidly through the single-spaced list of names, ranks, and serial numbers. Most of those on it were officers with a reputation for independent thinking or democratic political beliefs. Some, however, seemed there only because their last names sounded Jewish or Moslem or non-Russian in some vague, almost undefinable, way.

He picked up his phone, dialed a four-digit number, and waited for his call to go through. 'Soloviev here.'

The colonel listened to the voice on the other end for a few moments, flipping through the list all the while. Finally he nodded. 'Yes. It's begun. As we expected.'

He replaced the receiver and sat silently for several minutes more before issuing the orders that would set Marshal Kaminov's purge in motion.

CHAPTER 7
Countermeasures

OCTOBER 25 – ABC NEWS SPECIAL 'EUROPE IN CRISIS'

Viewers tuning in to the network's late news program were met by a fast-paced introduction blending dramatic footage and subdued off-camera narration.

The images were familiar but still chilling. Soldiers wearing dark scarlet berets, and olive-drab combat fatigues and carrying short, compact assault rifles advanced down both sides of a wide, empty avenue. Two men in each unit watched the rear, eyes wary, while the others scanned the buildings and sidewalks to the front and either side. Frightened-looking civilians caught in their path were stopped, frisked, and then pushed out of the way.

For a moment it looked like Belfast, San Salvador, or one of the world's other perpetually war-torn cities and towns. But then the camera view pulled back, revealing the chestnut trees and withered flower gardens lining the Champs-Élysées. The great stone mass of the Arc de Triomphe loomed in the distance.

'Paris, under martial law.'

New images flickered across the screen, grainier than the others. Superimposed captions identified the scenes as amateur video footage shot during the past week and smuggled out past German censors. It was easy to see why Berlin didn't want these pictures aired.

Armored personnel carriers clattered down a Hamburg street, moving fast toward a makeshift barricade manned by shouting protesters. When the vehicles were within a few meters, small groups of masked men popped into view, hurling Molotov cocktails. Most of their incendiaries fell short, smashing across the pavement in bursts of bright orange fire and oily black smoke. One gasoline-filled bottle hit a Marder's gun turret and exploded, spewing flame across the welded steel deck without much effect. Flashes stabbed from firing ports as the APCs surged through the smoke and plowed into the barricades. The soldiers inside were shooting back.

Several rioters were hit at point-blank range and thrown backward like bloodied rag dolls. Others were caught in the ruined barricade and pulped by spinning treads. Panicked screams rang out above the staccato rattle of automatic weapons fire. Engines roaring, the APCs bulled their way through the barrier and kept going, leaving an ugly trail of smashed furniture, crushed automobiles, and dead and wounded demonstrators in their wake.

'In Germany increasingly violent clashes with left- and right-wing militants have turned many of the country's largest cities into deadly battlefields.'

The images from Hamburg vanished, replaced by film clips released by Russian state television showing more public executions in Moscow's Red Square. 'In Russia the army continues to tighten its grip on daily life. Rail transport, air traffic, and most of the nation's industry are now under complete military control. Other former Soviet Republics, including Kazakhstan and Belarus, have taken similar steps. Wary of the chaos in its closest neighbors, Ukraine has put its self-defense forces on a higher state of alert.'

A computer-drawn map covered the screen. More than half the European continent glowed red, indicating countries under some form of 'temporary' martial law. Other symbols blinked above both Italy and Spain. Though still under civilian rule, both nations had dramatically strengthened their border defenses in recent weeks, fearing a wave of political refugees from their northern neighbors.

As the twentieth century limped to a close, Europe was sliding back, away from the light and into her violent, divided past.

OCTOBER 27 – CHEQUERS COURT, GREAT BRITAIN.

Chequers, the Prime Minister's country estate, lay at the foot of the densely wooded Chiltern Hills. Clear crisp sunlight filtered down through tall, gray-barked beech trees, burning away a few stray patches of early morning mist lingering near the ground. Coombe Hill towered a mile to the north, a sharp-edged outline in autumn yellow, red, and brown against a rich blue sky.

Three men strolled through the quiet grounds and gardens surrounding a centuries-old Tudor manor house. Two were tall, lean men. The third was slightly shorter and considerably heavier. All of them wore heavy coats, scarves, and gloves for protection against a brisk north wind.

Joseph Ross Huntington III took a deep breath, inwardly rejoicing in the morning air's cold, clean taste. He'd spent too much time lately in small, stuffy meeting rooms or breathing recirculated air in pressurized plane cabins. 'It's good of you to see me on such short notice, sir.'

'Not at all Ross.' The Prime Minister shook his head. His bright blue eyes gleamed behind thick lenses. 'It's simple self-interest, really. I've always found it a wise policy to cultivate friends in high places. Even when they don't come swathed in fancy job titles.'

Huntington grinned at that. Britain's top politician had a well-earned reputation for charm and calculated candor. Both traits had helped him ride out a tidal wave of bad economic news that would have long since sunk other British governments.

'Besides, I've been looking for the chance to sort a few things out before next month's conference with your President.' The Prime Minister glanced at the shorter, stouter man walking to his left. 'Isn't that right, Andy?'

'Definitely, Prime Minister.' Like his leader, Andrew Bryce, the Minister of Defence, had come up through Conservative Party politics the hard way – by merit and not by birth. When he spoke, his voice still bore traces of the broad Yorkshire accent of his youth. 'We don't have time to waste in Foreign Office chitchat and mummery. Not with things going from bad to worse across the bloody Channel.'

Huntington nodded. Meetings between heads of state were only rarely more than formalities – settings for state dinners and photo opportunities. The real work was usually handled on the telephone or behind closed doors and between trusted subordinates. The planned November summit between Britain's Prime Minister and America's President would be no exception. If anything, it was now more important than ever that the two allies spoke with one voice and acted with a common purpose.

They turned down a gravel path and walked in silence for several moments. Finally the Prime Minister spoke again. 'I suppose your senior officials are especially worried by the Russian situation?'

'Yes, sir. Most of them anyway.' Huntington eyed the Prime Minister carefully. The President had told him not to hold anything back. 'The Joint Chiefs have been pushing for permission to retarget our remaining ICBMs and to put Air Combat Command's bomber force on alert.'

Both Englishmen whistled softly. America's earlier decision to take its strategic nuclear forces off continuous alert had been one of the strongest signals that the cold war really was over. Reversing course now would send shock waves around the world.

'So far the President's refused to okay their requests. He doesn't want to start another dangerous, expensive nuclear buildup. Not until he's got a clearer picture of what's happening inside Russia. And in France and Germany, for that matter.' Huntington shook his head. 'But he's under a lot of pressure. A lot.'

He frowned. 'Most of the people he trusts are telling him to man the battlements – that the Russian generals will turn their missiles west any day now.'

'I take it you're not one of them?'

'Not exactly.' Huntington nodded toward the woods surrounding the estate's gardens and lawns. 'I'd trust Kaminov and his crowd about as far as I could throw one of those trees over there. But I don't think they're in any shape right now to seriously threaten us. Besides, we've still got enough nukes to blow Russia to hell and gone. They know it. And we know it. Plus, the President has told the Pentagon to push our missile defense deployments forward. SDI's prototypes are coming off the drawing board and going into production.'

The Prime Minister looked surprised by that piece of news. America's plans for a limited defense against ballistic missiles had been delayed year after year – the victim of a skeptical Congress and tight budgets. As the old Soviet Union crumbled, only the continuing proliferation of long-range missile technology around the globe had kept the program alive. Challenged to find ways to destroy ICBMs before they could hit their targets, the West's scientists and engineers had come through with flying colors. But Washington had lacked both the political will and the resources needed to field a working ABM system. Now it appeared the President was ready to supply both.

'When?'

'I've been told we can launch a first group of space-based interceptors by early next year. The rest of the system will take a lot longer to put in place.' Huntington shrugged. 'Still, any defense is better than none.'

The Prime Minister nodded. Coupling America's remaining offensive weapons with even limited space-based defenses would create a powerful deterrent to nuclear attack. With a screen of missile killers orbiting the globe, no enemy nation would ever know how many of its warheads would reach their targets. That would help make sure that not even Kaminov and his fellow marshals were mad enough to risk a direct confrontation with the United States or its allies.

'What about conventional war? Moscow's still got masses of tanks and artillery parked round the countryside.' Andrew Bryce broke back into the conversation. Britain's Minister of Defence sounded more interested than skeptical. Huntington had the feeling he was simply curious about how far Washington's fears went. 'Since NATO's pulled a vanishing act, what would stop them from pushing back into Poland or the other old Warsaw Pact states? Say, to distract the Russian people from troubles at home? You can't expect strategic weapons to deter that. No one would believe we'll go nuclear in a fight for the Poles.'

'Still too risky for them, Andy.' The Prime Minister was quietly confident. 'The Russians must know anything like that would unite the whole West against them all over again. And quite possibly pull Ukraine and the other republics in on our side. I seriously doubt they're that stupid.'

'They're too busy anyway.' Huntington remembered the intelligence reports he'd been shown. 'CIA says they're conducting a massive purge throughout their armed forces. Show trials. Predetermined verdicts. The works.'

'Our SIS confirms that.'

'Uh-huh. And everything I've ever read about Russian history tells me that will tie their armies up in knots for months – maybe even longer. Anyhow, Kaminov and his pals have some popular support for a crackdown at home. They don't have much backing for expensive military adventures abroad.' Huntington stuck his hands in his pockets. Gloves or not, they were still getting damned cold. He looked at the two Englishmen and shook his head again. 'No, I'm not that worried by Russia. Not right now anyway. I think we've got worse problems a lot closer to home.'

He hesitated. What he was about to say might strike these men as foolish or pig-ignorant. Several of the State Department's European affairs experts had already told him as much. But they were schooled in a more comfortable, more predictable Europe, one whose nations fell on one side or the other of a neat dividing line. Allies on one side. Enemies on the other.

The problem was, that Europe no longer existed.

'Go on, Ross.' Both the Prime Minister and the Minister of Defence were watching him closely.

Right. It was time to put his cards on the table. He squared his shoulders and spoke plainly. 'Frankly I'm a lot more worried by what's happening in France and Germany. In the short run, I'm afraid they're far more likely to cause trouble – in Europe or somewhere else around the world.'

'Why?'

Huntington breathed out. The Prime Minister hadn't laughed at him or told him he'd gone mad. Had the British already come to the same conclusions? He felt his confidence rising as he outlined the analysis surrounding what had started out as a pure gut feeling.

With its economy collapsing and chaos growing inside its own borders, Russia's martial law declaration made some sense. It still wasn't justified, but it was understandable. Democratic government had been a new and fragile experiment for the heartland of the old Soviet empire – one without the strength to withstand prolonged crisis.

The French and German moves to emergency rule made a lot less sense – on the surface. Their economic and political troubles were mostly self-inflicted, and though serious, they were nowhere near a level that could justify dictatorial rule by decree. True, the general strike threatened by their trade unions could have been devastating. But neither government had made any real effort to avoid it through negotiation. They hadn't even tried to just tough it out – waiting for the strike to collapse under its own weight and increasing public anger.

Instead, both Paris and Berlin had resorted to the most extreme measures imaginable. Both governments claimed they were acting only to maintain public order. Huntington suspected far less noble motives. Governing through military means to save a nation was one thing. Imposing martial law to preserve a particular political party's grip on power was quite another. Men who would do that were shortsighted, greedy, and completely unprincipled. They were also a potential threat. Once you'd turned guns on your own people, it was easier still to turn them outward.

When he'd finished, the Prime Minister nodded. 'That's something we agree on, Ross. Using force to solve political disputes . . .' He grimaced. 'It's damned stupid and damned dangerous.'

'Frightening for our friends on the continent, too,' Bryce added.

'Yeah.' Before arriving in England, Huntington had seen the urgent requests from Warsaw, Prague, and Bratislava for more economic and military aid. Poland and its Czech and Slovak neighbors to the south had sided with the free trade forces against the Franco-German push for protectionism. Now they were being hemmed in on all sides by hostile regimes. Spain and Italy were equally nervous, but less dependent on aid from London or Washington.

Britain's leader sighed. 'All of which brings us back to the reason you're here, doesn't it? To help decide what we're going to do about all this nonsense?'

'I guess so, Mr. Prime Minister.' Huntington still wasn't completely comfortable with his expanding role. He'd been happy to act as an unofficial presidential messenger or fact-finder. Deciding U.S. foreign policy seemed a bit out of his league. It was also risky for the President. He could imagine any number of journalists and political second-guessers ready to squawk about 'amateur' diplomacy.

Huntington's long friendship with the President made him better suited for some tasks than any official emissary. He served out of friendship, not to promote a career or some political agenda. In a time when official channels were full of arguments and public posturing, Huntington also represented one of the only ways a quiet message could reach a head of state. He was the President's eyes and ears, and his judgment was trusted.

'Well, as I see it, our first task is fairly straightforward. We must issue a joint communiqué opposing these foolish moves to military rule.' Britain's leader set his jaw. 'Something blunt and bold. Something that can't be misinterpreted or misunderstood by those idiots in Paris, Berlin, and Moscow.'

'That's all very well, sir, but . . .'

'But talk is cheap, Ross?' The Prime Minister laughed. 'True enough. Still, one has to start somewhere.'

Huntington had the grace to look sheepish. He'd jumped the gun. The other man obviously had more in mind.

'What comes next is a rather sticky question, though.' The Prime Minister's sardonic smile turned downward into a worried frown. 'We're somewhat short on practical options. I fear we may wind up with a lot of bark and very little bite.'

The American nodded somberly. There were really only two ways to pressure any foreign government – with trade sanctions or with stern warnings backed by military force. Sanctimonious speeches had never toppled a dictatorship or defeated an aggressor.

Unfortunately sanctions wouldn't do squat in this instance. The French, the Germans, and their client states weren't buying much that Britain or America made anyway. And the Russians didn't have the money to buy anything from anyone.

Saber-rattling seemed almost as impractical. When the cold war ended, Congress had gone to town on the defense budget – hacking away to funnel more money into already bloated social programs. Successive presidents and secretaries of defense had fought hard to preserve a core conventional force able to safeguard U.S. interests around the world. They'd won a few victories. But not many. American defense spending stood at its lowest level since 1939.

Most of the armored divisions once stationed in Europe as part of NATO were gone – either deactivated or reduced to training cadres scattered around pork-barrel military bases in the continental United States. The navy was down to twelve carrier groups and barely four hundred warships. The air force could field just two-thirds of the airpower available during the Persian Gulf War. America's armed forces were still the most capable in the world, but meeting a crisis in one region would leave them weak everywhere else.

Great Britain's military forces weren't in any better shape. Continuing cutbacks made necessary by shrinking revenues left the Royal Navy and the RAF able only to exert limited control over the Channel, parts of the North Sea, and local airspace. And, after meeting its commitments in Northern Ireland, the Falklands, and other overseas posts, the British Army had little more than a single reinforced brigade available for emergency service.

No, Huntington thought, saber-rattling is more likely to show off our own weaknesses than it is to frighten France and Germany back to democratic rule. He said as much aloud.

'Perhaps.' The Prime Minister cupped his hands and blew on them. 'But maybe we can tinker about on the edges.'

This time Huntington waited for him to elaborate.

'I believe we're both training Polish, Czech and Slovak officers in our tactics and on our equipment?'

'Yes.'

Once the Warsaw Pact crumbled, the eastern European countries had begun turning to the West for arms and military advice. After Iraq's crushing defeat, Soviet-manufactured weapons were widely regarded as second-rate. Both the United States and Great Britain had supplied the eastern European democracies with tanks, artillery, other pieces of military hardware, and the training to use them properly. Ironically, much of the gear they'd shipped east had come from stockpiles originally held in Germany to help deter a Warsaw Pact invasion.

It was a long, complicated process, retarded even more by tight budgets and congressional constraints on foreign military aid. Most Polish and Czech soldiers still used old East Bloc weapons. But slowly and surely that was changing.

'Then I suggest that we accelerate and expand those military aid programs.' The Prime Minister smiled thinly. 'And that we make sure the news is spread far and wide.'

Now, that made sense. Strengthening the three smaller countries' armies should help deter any French, German, or Russian aggression. New weapons shipments and more advisors would serve as a visible sign of the U.S. and British determination to support Europe's few remaining free trade democracies. At the same time, the moves couldn't realistically be viewed as provocative by the protectionist states. Even a larger force modernization program than the allies could afford wouldn't give Warsaw or Prague the means to act aggressively against their larger neighbors.

It would also be cheaper and safer than one of the only other alternatives – permanently stationing U.S. troops in the three countries.

'I suspect the President will be happy to go along with that, Mr. Prime Minister.'

'Good.' The tall, slender Englishman looked gratified. Then his expression changed, turning thoughtful. 'You know, Ross, all posturing aside, it might still be worthwhile to arrange some sort of joint military exercise for next year. If nothing else, it would be another concrete signal of our resolve to protect our common interests in Europe.'

Before the American could reply, the Prime Minister held up a hand to forestall any hasty comment. 'Nothing very grand, mind you. But perhaps a brigade or two of your Central Command troops could participate in our army's summer maneuvers on the Salisbury Plain.'

Huntington thought that over carefully. On the one hand, it would cost more money. Moving troops and gear over long distances was always expensive. On the other hand, the Joint Chiefs of Staff might consider such a rapid deployment exercise valuable – even without considering the intangible political benefits. When NATO collapsed, it took the Reforger exercise with it. As a result, America's armed forces had been limited to running small-scale practice mobilizations and troop movements for the past several years. Sending one or two brigades from the 82nd Airborne or the 101st Air Assault to Great Britain would help preserve logistics and planning skills the Pentagon might need someday to meet a faraway crisis.

He decided to stay noncommittal. If he was sure of anything, he was sure that promising U.S. troop movements went way beyond his vague and extralegal negotiating authority. 'I'll have to buck your proposal on up to the President, sir.' He shrugged. 'That kind of decision is pretty far over my head.'

'Fair enough, Ross.' The Prime Minister turned to his Minister of Defence. 'Put your staff lads to work roughing that out, won't you, Andy? I'd like our American friend to have details he can take back to Washington.'

'Never you fear. I'll stir 'em up, Prime Minister.' Bryce wore an enigmatic expression. 'But you know that bringing American soldiers back onto British soil, even temporarily, will bloody well drive the Labor Party's radicals stark raving mad.'

'Yes.' The Prime Minister showed his teeth. 'It would almost be worth approving on those grounds alone.'

The three men shared a quick, brittle laugh at that, eager to find something, anything, funny during a time of growing tension.

NOVEMBER 2 – PALAIS DE L'ÉLYSÉE, PARIS

Angry and alone, Nicolas Desaix paced around the ornate chamber now used for meetings of the cabinet's all-powerful Emergency Committee. Empty coffeepots, dirty china cups, and full ashtrays were the only signs of a meeting that had droned on for four hours without deciding much of anything.

Few of his colleagues understood his irritation and impatience. From a purely mechanical standpoint, the republic's martial law regime was running smoothly. Loyal troops, police, and officials controlled every major French city and administrative region. Government-appointed censors manned the editors' desks at every television studio, newspaper, and magazine. Several hundred political opponents and union bosses who had resisted martial law were under arrest. A few, regrettably, were dead. And without leadership, publicity, or legality, the threatened general strike had collapsed in its infancy. Even better, recent polls showed a majority of native-born French citizens backing the government's efforts to restore order and discipline. Nobody bothered asking Arab or African immigrants what they thought.

But Desaix wasn't satisfied.

For the moment the Emergency Committee held absolute power throughout the republic – power tempered only by the need for consensus among its members. In his view, such power should be used for dramatic action, not merely frittered away in a temporary holding action. Martial law freed them from the twin straitjackets of the constitution and politics. Why not use that freedom to reshape both the state and the continent? To redirect Europe's energies and resources in a way that would guarantee French prosperity and power?

The need for that was clear. France could not prosper in a Europe torn between rival trading blocs. Nor could it tolerate the so-called free trade babbled about by so many bubble-headed economists. A nation that allowed its fate to be determined by unrestrained competition between private companies was a nation of fools. France had always had a strong partnership between its industry and government and had used its industry as a tool of statecraft on many occasions.

Failure to protect and manage its vital industries would inevitably mean surrendering French prosperity and sovereignty to larger, stronger, richer countries – the United States, Japan, and Germany. And that was intolerable.

Absolutely intolerable. Desaix scowled. Even the thought that his country might find itself in such a state of affairs was repulsive.

There was only one real way to avoid such ignominious crawling. France must build a European alliance strong enough to fend off outside economic competition and political pressure. A league of nations where France could use its status as a nuclear power and U.N. Security Council member to manage its weaker neighbors and keep German interests closely tied to French interests.

But his colleagues were almost entirely uninterested in the larger issues confronting their nation. Instead, they were wrapped up in purely parochial concerns – each seemingly more interested in securing his own power than in the longer-term safety of the state. Desaix found their sluggish indifference infuriating.

A clock chimed the hour. Time and opportunity were both slipping through his fingers.

He shook his head angrily. If the Emergency Committee could not or would not act, he would have to take the necessary first steps toward a new continental alliance on his own. And if that meant presenting his laggard confederates with a virtual fait accompli, so be it.

Desaix spun on his heel and left the chamber. His aides clustered anxiously in the hallway outside, waiting for new instructions and demands. He would not disappoint them.

'Girault! Initiate a thorough economic and military analysis of Poland

and the Czech and Slovak republics! I want to know their weaknesses. The points where we can exert pressure if necessary!' The three countries were resisting French and German influence – breeding bad examples in the other eastern European nations. That would have to stop. He turned to another assistant without waiting for a reply. 'Radet! Arrange a private meeting with the German Chancellor. For next week. In Berlin.'

Desaix stalked down the hallway, still trailed by his aides. Their feet rang on marble tiles as he rattled out more orders. 'Bisson! Invite the Russian ambassador to my apartment for dinner, tomorrow evening. And bring me the secret file on him this afternoon! Lassere! I need to know how much money we have available in the discretionary accounts. Prepare a report . . .'

Nicolas Desaix controlled the Foreign Ministry and the intelligence services. That was enough for now. He would use his power and influence to begin bending Europe's quarreling nation-states to his will – to the will of France.

CHAPTER 8
Assignments

NOVEMBER 3 – OVER LUKE AIR FORCE BASE, ARIZONA

Four F-15 Eagles flew straight and level ten thousand feet over the rugged Arizona desert. Camouflaged in shades of light gray, they seemed to loaf through the air effortlessly, all the time hurtling along at 500 knots – more than 570 miles an hour.

The letters 'LA' on each plane's twin tails revealed they were from the 405th Tactical Training Wing, at Luke Air Force Base, near Phoenix, Arizona. Standard air force markings included the Star and Bars on the wings and tails in a muted gray color, serial numbers, the words 'U.S. Air Force,' and so on. These appeared to be standard F-15 Eagles except for two things. The first was a painted crest – a white eagle on a red shield that adorned the air intakes on each jet's side. The second was that anyone listening to the radio circuit would hear fluent Polish, not English.

The four pilots were Polish Air Force officers, full of anticipation. Soon three months of hard training would be behind them. For three of them, they would be leaving the USA and its abundance, but they would be going home. The fourth would be leaving the land of his birth.

It had been a successful training sortie, an air-to-ground mission. Nobody had been hit by the phony air defenses, and they had all scored well on the bombing runs. Pawel Blazynski, the number two pilot in the flight, had done particularly well. Everyone could hear the thin, blond, outgoing young man's excitement and pride. 'Did you see that? Did you? With each bomb I took out a Russian armored company.'

Nobody commented on the irony of his simulated enemy's nationality. All of the older pilots had received their first training from the Russians.

Stefan Michalak, not as good a pilot, but a bigger braggart, was quick to top him. 'You get much better results with cluster weapons, Pawel. Give me a load of Rockeyes and I will take out a Russian tank division – one bomblet per tank.' He was flying in the number four position. 'What about you, Tad?'

First Lt. Tadeusz Wojcik flew in the number three spot. As second element leader, he was the second-most capable pilot in the flight, after Major Sokolowicz.

Wojcik didn't reply immediately, and Pawel answered for him. 'Tad only bombs Germans,' he joked. 'He combines business with pleasure.' Laughter filled the circuit.

Silently Tad agreed.

Though he had been born in America, his Polish heritage showed in his looks. Sandy brown hair framed a round, pale face and light blue eyes. Of only average height, he was solidly built, almost stocky, but he was also in superb physical condition. Flying a supersonic fighter required that.

Where his attitude toward the Germans was concerned, he was all Polish. His father had good reason to hate the Germans, and Tad, with all the fervor of a convert, had taken the older man's attitudes for his own.

Over fifty years later, cities in his adopted country still bore scars of their coming. During the 1939 invasion, the Nazis had killed both his mother's and his father's parents, leaving them each orphaned at an early age. They'd survived somehow, only to find themselves trapped by a new form of tyranny when the Russians imposed communism on Poland after the war ended. Neither found life easy in the decades that followed. Finally, after years of trying, they'd won permission to emigrate to the United States. There they had settled into a new, more prosperous life. Tad had been born in 1976, crowning the joy his parents found in their new freedom.

Neither his mother nor his father had ever forgotten their beloved Poland. And neither had ever forgotten the first source of their homeland's misery: the Germans who'd crushed Poland, stripped her bare, and left her defenseless before the resurgent Soviets.

After much soul-searching, they'd decided to return home in 1992, bringing with them skills and financial resources desperately needed by their now free but impoverished homeland. Tad had gone with them, still more American than Polish. But now, five years later, here he was, flying jet fighters for an adoptive homeland he'd come to cherish deeply.

Poland, though free of Soviet control, was in a precarious position. Since the first months after the Warsaw Pact collapsed, Polish officers had worked to modernize their country's armed forces, but that was next to impossible while her economy made the difficult transition to a free market. Unfortunately her strategic position made that modernization necessary – no matter how much it cost. To the east, Russia, Belarus, Ukraine, and the other former Soviet Republics seemed busy with their own internal wrangles. But no Pole could doubt that there were Russians who still longed for renewed economic and military control over eastern Europe. The Warsaw Pact might be dead, but the idea behind it could still come alive at any moment. That was especially true now that Russia was under de facto military rule.

Poland's western border was menaced by a reunified Germany. Although the Germans also seemed more interested in their own economic problems than military expansion, there were still right-wing groups in Germany trumpeting historic claims to portions of Polish territory. And most of the former Soviet Bloc states had signed so many economic agreements with Germany and France that their industries and governments were all but run directly by Berlin and Paris. Only Poland and her southern neighbors had steadfastly refused any such relationship.

Instead they'd turned to the United States and the United Kingdom for help. And both countries had responded – moved by historic ties and a growing desire to counterbalance French and German influence in the rest of eastern Europe. They'd provided weapons, mostly out of now-useless NATO stockpiles, and training in Western tactics. German and Russian complaints were answered by pointing to the limited, strictly defensive nature of the American and British military aid program.

The Eagle fighters Wojcik and his comrades were flying were part of that plan. Although there were newer fighters flying, the F-15 was still a formidable opponent. Tad was openly in love with his aircraft. His American birth and upbringing might have biased him, but the other Poles in the program, some with thousands of hours in Russian aircraft types, seemed equally pleased.

Before the Eagle arrived last year, the best fighter in the Polish inventory had been the MiG-29 Fulcrum. Tad had done well in primary and advanced training, quickly graduating to the MiG-29s, a choice assignment.

The Russian-built fighters were similar to the F-15 in basic layout – twin vertical tails, two engines, and armed with radar-guided missiles. The Fulcrum was smaller, though, and couldn't carry as many weapons. Its radar was also primitive in comparison to the set in its American counterpart. The MiG did have some advantages in a dogfight, though, like the helmet-mounted sight and an infrared sensor that wouldn't warn an enemy aircraft that it had been detected and was under attack. Still, Tad preferred the Eagle.

It was the dream of every Polish aviator to fly 'the starship' – a nickname earned for the Eagle by its advanced electronics. Wojcik's perfect American English and excellent flying skills had been his ticket into the Polish Air Force's newest regiment.

'Five miles out.' Major Sokolowicz's mark was all the well-trained flight needed to hear. The four fighters neatly peeled off, changing from finger-four formation into line as they began their approach to the runway.

This landing was routine, and precise. Tad congratulated himself on another successful mission. As much as he loved to fly, he never fully relaxed until he was back on the ground again.

The major's voice filled his earphones again. 'A good flight. Debrief in ten minutes.'

Tad heard the ground controller give them clearance to taxi, then followed the first two planes. Turning onto a taxiway paralleling the runway, the four planes wound their way past rows of parked aircraft bustling with mechanics, hangars, and other buildings. Luke Air Force Base was the largest fighter training center in the world. All U.S. Air Force pilots and many from America's allies got their basic flight and air combat training high above the Arizona desert. All of the foreign pilots training in the F-15 were grouped under the 405th Tactical Training Wing. The Poles rubbed shoulders with Japanese and Saudi fighter jocks. It made for interesting conversations at the Officers' Club.

As Tad cut his throttle and cracked the canopy, he could hear the descending whine of other jet engines spooling down. The biting, familiar smell of kerosene and hot metal filled the air.

He waited quietly while a puffing ground crewman hung an access ladder on the F-15's cockpit edge, then gratefully unstrapped and climbed out of the cockpit and down the ladder. It felt good to stretch.

The debriefing was held under the eye of an American air force instructor, Major Kendall. His Polish was almost as bad as some of the trainees' English, so Tad was often called in as an interpreter. Each cockpit videotape was reviewed, critiqued, and compared with scores provided by the range operators.

As the debrief ended, Tad's mind was already far away. He had a few errands to run, then he was going to get together with Michalak, his wingman, for tomorrow's 'graduation' exercise. They had some plans to make.

NOVEMBER 8

The squadron's mass briefing was held at 0700 hours, in both Polish and English, led by Major Sokolowicz. Every man sat or stood in the packed amphitheater, even the ground crews, since this was the last mission and, according to dependable rumor, a 'ball-buster.' Chatter filled the air, mixed with laughter. Every pilot enjoyed ACM, or air combat maneuvering missions, and the fact that this one would be tough only whetted their appetite. Add that they were going home soon, the atmosphere was almost partylike.

The major's run-through was quick, almost terse. The only information they'd been given was that today's mission was to be a 'maximum effort.' Simulating a fighter sweep in hostile airspace, all eight Polish pilots completing the course were to launch in two flights of four each, Blue and Green. They were to clear the way for an imaginary strike coming in behind their Eagles.

Tad sat off to one side near the front with Stefan Michalak. He wanted to hear the brief, of course, but already knew the mission plan by heart. The two lieutenants had spent half the night studying details of the range topography and going over possible tactics. They were slated to fly with Sokolowicz again, as Blue Three and Four.

Michalak, a tall, thin, black-haired pilot, waited quietly, masking nervousness with inactivity. Because of Tad's obvious skill and his own inexperience, he was more than willing to follow the lieutenant's lead. They were going to be taking a definite risk.

The major quickly ran through the particulars. All eight aircraft carried simulators that mimicked an AIM-9M Sidewinder and an AMRAAM, as well as telemetry pods that transmitted its position and course. The equipment would allow the ground observers to follow the fight and score kills. Backed up by HUD videotapes from both sides, a few minutes of whirling air combat could be dissected and examined in embarrassing detail.

Sokolowicz's English was accented but understandable. 'This will be a tough one,' he said. 'As long as we play by the book, and remember our lessons, we will win.'

Tad nodded to himself. The major gave almost the same speech at the start of every brief. He was right, of course, but there wasn't a lot of fire in it.

Sokolowicz glanced over at Kendall, sitting quietly in a corner of the stage. Nodding toward the American officer, he said, 'Our hosts have promised to present us with a real challenge, a test to see just how much we really have learned.'

An American-accented voice in the audience muttered, 'Kobiyashi Maru,' and scattered laughter filled the air. Most of the Poles, except the major, looked a little puzzled, and only Tad laughed. He suspected that Sokolowicz didn't know anything about *Star Trek*, either, but was too cool a customer to let his ignorance show.

Sokolowicz brushed past the remark and finished up. 'Engine start in fifteen minutes.' The major finished what he was doing and strolled casually over to the end of the stage. Bending down on one knee, he spoke quietly, in Polish, with Wojcik.

'Are your aircraft ready?'

'Yes, sir. We inspected them both just before the brief.'

'Good. After we are cleared to taxi, fall into line in the first flight's number three and four slots.'

'As you wish, sir.' Tad already knew all that, but if the major wanted to review it, that was fine with him. Sokolowicz was being pretty ballsy to even let them try this. If his scheme worked, though . . .

Ten minutes later, the Polish pilots and their ground crews streamed out to the ramp. Almost immediately the whine of turbines rose into the air.

Tad sprinted for his hangar, feeling his excitement grow. Michalak pounded after him, and the two entered through a side door guarded by a Polish staff sergeant. He saw the pilots coming, saluted, and wished them good luck.

The dimly lit hangar interior seemed even darker after the bright desert sun outside, already starting to climb high above the horizon. The sun heated the building, and in the warm, stuffy darkness two F-15s sat silent, all shadows and angles as they waited to fly.

Their appearance had been altered. Both planes had been painted from top to bottom in water-washable shades of tan and brown. Only the red and white eagle crest had been left uncovered.

Tad and his wingman split up, each to preflight his own aircraft. With a good ground crew, the walk-around was a formality, but a good aviator always double-checked. Even though this was a training flight, Tad was betting his life on his plane.

He carefully examined the ordnance under the wings. In addition to the two missile simulators and telemetry pod, a white shape hung from the port underwing pylon. It also looked like a missile, but one without fins or a rocket motor. Its nose was fitted with a clear glass circle, and Tad knelt down to inspect the infrared sensor underneath.

His plan, approved by Sokolowicz, was simple: hug the earth, keeping his radar off while he and his wingman searched the sky with the infrared sensors. With the rest of the squadron yanking and banking at high altitude, two Eagles wouldn't be noticed until it was too late, until they'd popped up behind an oncoming adversary. It wasn't standard doctrine, but in air combat it was wise to deviate from doctrine once in a while.

With everything in order, he climbed in and started his preflight checks. A few moments after hooking up his radio leads, he heard 'Engines' in his earphones and pressed his starter button, simultaneously waving to the ground crew in the hangar. Even with ear protection, they deserved a little warning.

Four massive jet engines howled to life, raw sound and power reverberating off the hangar walls, and a vertical sliver of bright light widened as the front doors slid open.

'Blue and Green flights, you're clear to taxi.' The ground controller's voice sounded bored. Of course, he'd probably seen a thousand similar jets off on a hundred similar missions.

Releasing his brakes, Tad pushed his own throttles forward, just a little more than he normally used for taxiing. The F-15 leapt forward, and as the hangar's sides fell away, he saw that he'd guessed right. The major was setting a fast pace, with the first two planes of Blue flight already a hundred meters down the taxiway and accelerating. They were cleared directly onto the runway, and they were in the air a minute later, roaring higher into a clear morning sky.

It would be a wonderful fight.

CHAPTER 9
Tidal Race

NOVEMBER 15 – TEGEL INTERNATIONAL AIRPORT, BERLIN

Outlined by blinking beacons, passenger jets orbited slowly through Berlin's gray, overcast skies – conserving fuel while traffic controllers held Tegel's main runway open for an unscheduled, priority departure. The planes circled low over a city gripped hard by winter.

Below them, a freezing north wind rippled across the whitecapped Tegeler See and whined through trees planted between the lake and the airport. Driven by the wind, snow flurries whirled across concrete runways, spattering against passenger terminals and flat-roofed warehouses. Snowflakes carried far enough south vanished in the black, oily waters of the Hohenzollern Canal.

The wind tugged at camouflage netting rigged over the tanks, personnel carriers, and antiaircraft guns deployed at intervals around Tegel. Some were stationed on the tarmac itself. Other armored vehicles occupied the landscaped grounds of nearby Rehberge Park – their turrets and guns aimed at high-rise apartment buildings and shops lining the field's eastern fringe.

The airport, like the rest of Germany, was still under martial law.

More white and gray camouflage netting covered military helicopters parked around a maintenance hangar far away from the main terminal building. Their rotors were tied down against the wind. Several were shark-nosed PAH-2 tank killers, a joint French and German design manufactured by the Eurocopter consortium. The rest were troop carriers, UH-1D Hueys built by Dornier for the German Army. The Hueys were starting to show their age, but the ultramodern Eurocopter tilt-rotor troop transports that were supposed to replace them had been delayed by production and budget problems. Despite their country's professed desire for all-European manufactures, Germany's airborne troops and commandos were stuck using antiquated, American-designed helicopters. Few of them appreciated the irony in that.

One other thing was certain. None of the soldiers waiting in ranks outside the hangar appreciated being kept out in the cold as an honor guard for dignitaries who were already late. Light gray service tunics, shirts and ties, black trousers, and red berets were no match for winter temperatures.

Three Mercedes sedans drove across the tarmac and pulled up next to the hangar. Weapons rattled as the soldiers presented arms.

Several officials got out of the cars and strode briskly past the shivering honor guard, walking fast toward a twin-engine executive jet visible just inside the hangar's half-open doors. Two men led the way, talking intently. Plainclothes security men formed a protective phalanx around them.

Nicolas Desaix was on his way back to France – homeward bound after his second quick trip to Germany in as many weeks.

'You agree, then, Herr Chancellor? That the economic measures I've proposed are a necessary first step to closer, more formal cooperation between our two nations?' Desaix was insistent, eager for some sign of progress he could take back to Paris. He found the slow-motion processes of normal diplomacy maddening at a time when events were moving so fast.

Heinz Schraeder turned his head toward the Frenchman. Germany's Chancellor was tall enough to stand eye-to-eye with Desaix, but he carried far more weight on a much broader frame. Thinning black hair and a dour, fleshy face with massive jowls gave him a bulldog look. He nodded. 'I agree, monsieur. My cabinet must concur, of course, but . . .' He shrugged. 'They will fall in line.'

He had reason to be confident. Brought to power by Germany's prolonged economic woes and by a growing hatred of foreign refugees and immigrants, Schraeder's control over the Bundestag, the Parliament, had rested on a paper-thin majority – a majority threatened by rising public discontent. But now martial law made public opinion immaterial.

'Good. That's very good. Then we shall have an agreement to sign the next time I see you.' Desaix sounded certain.

The two men crossed into the neon-lit hangar, followed closely by their aides and bodyguards. Airport workers pushed the hangar doors all the way open behind them. A ground crewman wearing ear protectors already stood waiting on the tarmac outside, ready to guide Desaix's aircraft out onto the runway. With traffic stacking up over the field, Tegel's managers wanted to get their government's guests into the air as quickly as possible.

'A great pleasure, Herr Chancellor. As always. I look forward to our next meeting.' Desaix shook hands with the German leader and then hurried up a set of folding stairs into the jet. He turned and waved a final time before disappearing inside. His retinue of aides and guards followed him.

Schraeder stood watching impassively as crewmen closed the French plane's hatch.

'An interesting man, Herr Chancellor. I can understand why you find him so charming.'

'Charming?' Schraeder glanced sharply at the aide standing by his side. 'On the contrary, Werner. I think he's a smooth-tongued, manipulating swine.' He smiled at the younger man's shocked expression. 'But what I think of Desaix personally doesn't matter. His ideas make sense. For us, not just for the French. And that is what matters.'

He spoke with conviction. In his judgment, closer ties with France offered the best hope of creating a unified European political and military superpower – a superpower with German industrial might as its driving engine. Earlier attempts to unite the continent had foundered in a sea of conflicting national economic policies, currencies, and cultures. And, in retrospect, the whole idea of trying to create a closer-knit union under such circumstances had been ludicrous – doomed from the very beginning.

The Chancellor snorted. Germany and France, powerhouses in their own right, should never have been expected to bend to whims of smaller, poorer countries. It was unnatural. No, he thought, the weak must follow the lead set by the strong. That was the only rational way to organize the continent. For all his faults, Nicolas Desaix shared the same vision.

Torn by feuding ethnic groups and rival trading blocs, Europe needed order, stability, and discipline to take its rightful place in the world. And only France and Germany could provide the strong leadership Europe needed.

Naturally Schraeder would have preferred that Germany alone occupy center stage in a united Europe. He was not a fool, though. The world's memories of German militarism and the Third Reich were still too painful for that. Even the comparatively hesitant diplomatic and financial moves his country had made to regain its old influence in central and eastern Europe were viewed with strong suspicion. Working hand in glove with France, even letting Paris appear to take the lead, would help hold those suspicions in check.

Heinz Schraeder nodded to himself. Since the end of World War II, a series of leaders from both nations had toiled fairly successfully to cool the long-standing antagonisms between their two countries. High-level contacts, joint military exercises, and continual affirmations of new friendship had all been employed by French presidents and German chancellors to accustom their peoples to working together. Now he and Desaix would reap the rewards of their hard labor.

NOVEMBER 27 – 'EUROCURRENCY ON THE MOVE,' *THE WALL STREET JOURNAL*

Financial and foreign policy experts were stunned by the announcement yesterday of French and German plans for rapid movement toward a single currency. Although details are still being worked out by central bank representatives from the two nations, French Foreign Minister Nicolas Desaix and German Chancellor Heinz Schraeder promised that the new franc-mark, or FM, would be in active circulation 'by early next year.' The two men also hailed the accord as a crucial step toward a long-overdue European monetary union. Their optimism seemed justified by reports that officials in Belgium, Austria, Hungary, Croatia, Slovenia, and other Balkan states are all interested in the new currency.

Earlier efforts to develop a common continental monetary system collapsed when the old European Community splintered over trade tariffs and subsidies . . .

DECEMBER 1 – 'SCREAMING EAGLES TO STONEHENGE,' *INTERNATIONAL DEFENSE REVIEW*

Highly placed Pentagon sources have confirmed that elements of the 101st Airborne Division will participate in next year's British Army summer maneuvers on Salisbury Plain. Reportedly the rapid deployment exercise, code-named Operation Atlantic Surge, will involve two of the division's three airmobile infantry brigades and a substantial portion of its attack helicopter, troop transport, and artillery assets. With more than thirty thousand U.S. Army and Air Force personnel taking part in the June exercise, Atlantic Surge will represent the largest American military effort in recent years.

Congressional critics of the Defense Department are already decrying what one calls 'a titanic waste of time and money . . .'

DECEMBER 11 – PALAIS ROYAL, PARIS

Nicolas Desaix listened to his special ambassador's report without interrupting. Only the tight, angry frown on his face revealed his growing agitation. Professional diplomats never seemed able to say anything plainly – especially when they knew their news wasn't welcome.

He waited impatiently for the man to run out of steam.

'To summarize, sir, the Polish government has expressed an interest in further talks, although it is disinclined at this time to proceed with formal negotiations on the subject. Apparently Warsaw believes that internal political considerations must temporarily take precedence over other, broader concerns.'

'They've turned us down.'

The ambassador shifted uncomfortably in his chair. Admitting failure was not often a good career move in the foreign service. He forced an optimistic tone. 'Not in so many words, Minister. And complicated matters of this kind often require prolonged consideration. I'm sure that further discussions will produce . . .' His voice trailed away under his superior's icy glare.

'Cut the crap, Bourcet. I know hot air when I hear it. Poland has rejected our offer out of hand.' Desaix's fingers drummed on his desk as he waited for a reply. 'Well? Am I right?'

The other man nodded reluctantly. 'Yes, Minister.'

'Very well. You may go. But I'll expect your written report on my desk by tomorrow morning. Make sure that it is complete and clear. I don't have any more time to waste on fluff and nonsense.' Desaix turned his attention to the documents piled high in front of him, ignoring the special ambassador's abrupt, red-faced departure.

He made a mental note to have the man assigned to the next undesirable diplomatic posting that opened up. Somewhere as far from France as possible.

Desaix didn't mind the ambassador's failure in Poland so much. After all, he'd more than half expected it. The Poles were too stiff-necked and too stupid to join the Franco-German monetary union voluntarily. What irked him most was Bourcet's pointless attempt to disguise the truth by spouting a lot of meaningless gibberish.

He could forgive a man who failed. He would not forgive a man who mistook him for a fool.

Nicolas Desaix dismissed the matter from his mind in favor of a more immediate and important concern. Specifically the mulish resistance to the new European order he was trying to create.

In the weeks since France and Germany reached agreement on a common currency, his emissaries had fanned out across the continent. Nations with economies in hock to either Paris or Berlin were reminded of that sad fact and urged to join the new monetary union. So far all were bowing to the inevitable. Other countries, those aligned with the 'free trade' bloc, had proved far less cooperative. One by one they'd rejected the chance to change sides in the world's ongoing trade war.

Every refusal angered Desaix, but he found the Polish, Czech, and Slovak stance especially infuriating. Their stubborn adherence to national sovereignty and open markets encouraged agitators in other eastern European countries who opposed closer ties with France. With American backing, they were becoming a rallying point for the anti-French sentiment slowly spreading through the region. And that made them dangerous.

No one knew better than he how fragile the coalition he envisioned would be – at least during the first few months of its existence. The slightest setback or unexpected check might shatter it, leaving France even more isolated in a sea of hostile neighbors. It would take time to weld a confederation of unpopular, unelected governments into a strong, united whole. Polish, Czech, and Slovak intransigence threatened to rob him of that time.

Desaix's frown deepened. He could not allow that to happen. If political leaders in the three countries would not join a new European alliance voluntarily, they would have to be coerced. They'd either fold under pressure or find themselves abandoned by their own people.

His sour expression disappeared, replaced by a narrow, unpleasant smile. The ignorant Poles and their southernmost neighbors might feel themselves secure behind their thin screen of American and British military aid. But he knew differently.

He picked up a secure phone. 'Put me through to the Russian Embassy. I want to speak with the ambassador himself.'

JANUARY 21, 1998 – SECURE SECTION, U.S. EMBASSY, MOSCOW

Alex Banich stuck his head inside the lioness's den at her request. 'You rang?'

'Yep. Wait one, okay?' Erin McKenna spoke without looking away from her glowing computer monitor. Her fingers flashed across the keyboard parked in her lap, entering new data or making new demands on an already overtaxed system.

'Sure.' Banich leaned against the doorjamb, folded his arms, and watched her work. He fought off a yawn.

The Commerce Department analyst looked as tired as he felt. Her eyes were shadowed and bloodshot, the product of too many hours spent staring at tiny print and endless columns of figures. Even her long, auburn hair looked mussed. She sometimes wrapped her ponytail around her fingers when she thought no one was looking. He'd even caught her chewing isolated strands while she sat lost in thought, trying hard to piece together a coherent picture from fragments of fact, rumor, and pure guesswork.

The months since Russia declared martial law had flown by in a dizzying, exhausting cycle of busy days and work-filled nights. The CIA's Moscow Station had been understaffed and overworked even before Marshal Kaminov and his cronies made their move. Now, with personnel restrictions in place on all foreign embassies, and with all freedoms greatly restricted, things were even worse. Neither of them could waste time or energy arguing for the sheer, cussed joy of it.

So, partly out of necessity and partly out of sheer fatigue, they'd negotiated an uneasy truce and a practical division of labor. Banich focused his efforts on the military and political side of the spectrum, while McKenna concentrated on trade and economic developments.

So far at least, she had been more successful. Her contacts inside the Russian Ministries of Trade and Finance were civilians with a reformist streak who weren't happy under military rule. They fed her a fairly steady stream of raw trade and economic data – some classified, some unclassified, and some just hard to find without help.

Banich wasn't as fortunate. He was being run ragged just trying to maintain his cover as Nikolai Ushenko without being bankrupted in the process. Backed by army decrees, the government ministries he supplied made constant demands for more food at below-market prices. These new price controls made it impossible for him to bargain for sensitive information. By wiping out his profit margins, they were also siphoning away the resources he needed to buy secrets from a corrupt few still willing to sell them.

Still, he'd had a little luck recently. Like Erin, he'd made several promising contacts on the civilian side of the Russian government. Even inside the Defense Ministry there were officials who despised the army's heavy-handed attempt to reimpose Stalinist discipline and central planning. And there were persistent rumors that Russia's President – now only a figurehead under constant GRU surveillance – still hoped he could regain effective control over his country.

Banich dismissed those rumors as simple wishful thinking. Kaminov had relearned an old lesson of Russian politics: the one with the biggest guns governs. He and his fellow marshals were too firmly dug in to be ousted easily or bloodlessly. And with the West hopelessly divided against itself, there wasn't any realistic prospect of sustained outside pressure for a return to democratic rule.

Erin finished her typing with a final, triumphant stab at the keyboard, punched the print key, and slewed her chair around to face him. 'Thanks. I needed to get some ideas down before they wandered off in a gray fog somewhere up here.' She tapped her forehead.

'No problem.' He thought about straightening up and then decided against it. Leaning up against the door felt too good. 'Now, what can I do for you? Kidnap the Minister of Trade? Swipe the Czar's crown jewels? Or did you have something tougher in mind? Like talking Kutner into buying you a bigger computer?'

The corners of her mouth tilted upward in a quick, amused smile. 'Not exactly. Though those aren't bad ideas.'

She turned serious. 'What I really need is your brain.'

'Shoot.'

Her tired eyes twinkled at that. 'Sorry, I haven't got a gun.' She ignored his groan. He wasn't the only one allowed to make bad jokes. 'Anyway, I think I'm starting to see a pattern in some of the data we're collecting, but I need to bounce it off somebody to see if it makes any sense. Especially somebody who was born cynical.'

'Meaning me, I suppose.'

Erin nodded. 'Meaning you.'

'Okay.' Banich approved of her instincts. In this business it was all too easy to fall blindly in love with your own theories. That was dangerous, because those theories rested on evidence that was, almost by definition, piecemeal, uncertain, and often contradictory. A good intelligence officer was always willing to give someone else the chance to punch holes in a piece of prized analysis.

He left the doorway and perched on a corner of her desk. 'Show me.'

'All right. But it's a pretty tangled web.' She leaned back in her chair, clearly considering where she should begin. 'I'll give you the punch line first: the French have significantly upped the amount of foreign aid they're sending to the Russians. Both on a government-to-government level and on a corporate basis. What I don't know is why they're doing it.'

Her voice changed subtly as she started retracing her reasoning, always highlighting the differences between what she knew and what she could only guess at. Banich listened intently, more and more impressed by her abilities.

There were dozens of pieces to the puzzle she'd put together, some so small and so obscure that he was amazed anyone had ever spotted them, let alone recognized their significance. Some were tiny, cryptic notations on copies of shipping manifests. Others were coded transactions buried inside the State Central Bank's computer data base. Still other clues came from conversations she'd had with friendly Russian officials and business leaders or from radio and wire intercepts passed on by the NSA.

By itself none of the information she'd collected seemed particularly meaningful. It was like looking too closely at an impressionist painting. Until you stepped back far enough all you saw were tiny dots of different-colored paint. But Erin McKenna had a talent for seeing the patterns behind bits of apparently unconnected data.

Banich sat still, waiting until she was finished. Then he leaned forward. 'Let me get this straight. What we're looking at is a massive flow of new French aid to the government and to state-run industries. Things like no-interest loans and outright grants. Massive shipments of high-tech industrial machinery, spare parts, and computer software. A lot of it has both military and civilian uses. And it's all been showing up over the past several weeks. Right?'

'Right.'

'Any ideas on how much this stuff is worth?'

Erin nodded. 'From what I've seen so far . . . at least two billion dollars. That's just a ballpark guess, but I think it'll hold up over time.'

Banich whistled softly in astonishment. Two billion dollars' worth of foreign aid in five or six weeks was an extraordinary effort. The whole U.S. foreign aid budget didn't amount to more than fifteen or sixteen billion dollars spread out over a whole year. 'What the hell are the French up to?'

She shook her head. 'That I don't know. All the money and goods are coming in under the table, so they're sure as heck not trying to win brownie points with the Russian people.'

'True.' Banich rubbed the sore muscles at the back of his neck. 'But nobody throws that kind of funding around on a whim. The Frogs want something from Kaminov and his pals and they want it bad. The only question is, what?'

'Nothing good, I'm sure.'

'Yeah.' He stood up. 'I'm going down the hall for a talk with Kutner. If he sees it my way, we'll send your report off to D.C. by special diplomatic pouch tomorrow morning. I don't think we should sit on this until we've crossed every *t* and dotted every *i*.'

Erin nodded wearily and turned back to her keyboard. He knew she'd be working all night and regretted the need for it. Sleep was tough to come by at Moscow Station.

Banich paused by her open door. 'Oh, McKenna?'

She looked back over her shoulder.

'Good work.'

The smile she gave him would have launched a thousand special couriers.

JANUARY 23 – PRZEMYSL COMPRESSOR STATION, DRUZHBA II ('FRIENDSHIP II') GAS PIPELINE, POLAND

The natural gas pipeline compressor station sprawled over several acres near the Polish-Ukrainian border. Machine shops, chemical labs, fire-fighting stations, and administrative offices surrounded a long metal-roofed shed and an adjacent cooling tower. Steam rose from the cooling tower, white against a clear blue sky.

Although nearly a foot of new-fallen snow covered the empty fields around the station, very little was left inside the compound. Work crews with shovels, the passage of wheeled and tracked heavy equipment, and the heat produced by dozens of massive machines running around the clock were more than a match for nature.

Inside the compressor shed, two men knelt beside an enormous reciprocating engine – a gas-fired monstrosity three meters high and ten meters long. Each of its sixteen cylinders was as big as a beer keg. The engine was one of eighteen mounted in pairs down the shed's long axis. Color-coded pipes wove in and out of each compressor assembly.

Chief engineer Tomasz Rozek clapped his coworker on the shoulder. 'Nice job, Stanislaw! Now, tighten it down and you're done!' He had to yell to be heard over the constant, deafening roar.

The younger man flashed him a thumbs-up and then went back to work replacing an inspection hatch near the engine's gas intake valve.

Rozek stood up slowly, silently cursing his aching back and knees. As a young man, he'd have been able to scamper through the tangle of piping and machinery around him like a chimpanzee. Well, not anymore. Thirty-five years spent toiling in Poland's labor-intensive energy industry had left their mark.

He limped toward a thick metal door at the far end of the shed, performing a quick visual inspection on each pair of gigantic compressors he passed. That was standard operating procedure for any engineer moving through the shed. When his subordinates bitched about the time they wasted in such routine inspections, he ignored them. In Rozek's view, anything that cut the chances of a major mechanical failure was worth doing. As the station's chief engineer he set high standards for his crews, but he also made damned sure that he lived up to them himself.

You didn't screw around with high-pressure natural gas. Not and live to regret it.

Przemysl was one of several similar stations strung out along the Druzhba II Pipeline as it stretched from Russia through Belarus and Ukraine, into southeastern Poland, and on to Germany. Sited roughly two hundred miles apart, their massive compressors kept natural gas flowing through the network's twin meter-wide pipelines at the required pressure – around eleven hundred pounds per square inch, roughly seventy-five times the force in earth's atmosphere.

And high pressure meant high temperature. You couldn't pack that many gas molecules into that small a space at that speed without generating heat. A lot of heat. The natural gas moving through the station's compressors and piping ran at close to seven hundred degrees Fahrenheit. Even a pinhole rupture in the pipeline could create a deadly fireball twenty meters or more wide – a fireball that would burn until it ran out of fuel.

Rozek had seen the charred corpses of those who'd found that out the hard way. He didn't want to see any more.

The control room at the end of the compressor shed was a blessed haven of relative peace and quiet. Thick insulation reduced the shed's steady, pounding roar to background noise. Four technicians sat facing a dial-studded console, continuously monitoring readings from the flow meters laid every twenty miles or so up the line to the next pumping station.

The engineer took his earplugs out as he closed the door. 'Everything okay here?'

'Smooth as a pretty woman's behind, chief.'

Rozek snorted. 'That's good. Because this is as close to a pretty woman as any of you lot are likely to get.'

He dropped behind a battered steel desk parked next to a window overlooking the rest of the complex. Although his rank entitled him to an office in the administration building, he'd never used it. He preferred being closer to the action. The one concession to comfort he allowed himself was a cushioned swivel chair.

With a small sigh, Rozek settled in to wade through the pile of maintenance reports, time sheets, and union grievances waiting for him. Paperwork was the one constant in his working day. And he loathed it.

Alarm bells shattered his concentration.

'We've got gas pressure falling rapidly on both One and Two! Down to one thousand p.s.i.!'

Mother of God. Rozek whirled toward the window, fully expecting to see a pillar of flame streaming skyward somewhere close by. Nothing. 'The break must be further up the pipeline. But how the hell had anyone cut through both lines simultaneously? They were buried several meters apart as a precaution against just that kind of accident.

'Pressure at nine hundred and still falling!'

The chief engineer jumped to his feet and ran for the control console. Suddenly his back didn't hurt at all.

He leaned over the senior technician's shoulder, squinting to read the old-fashioned dial meters. They'd been hoping to put in more modern digital readout equipment, but the government hadn't been able to afford it yet. The indicators were still plunging, plummeting past 850 pounds per square inch.

In the shed outside the control room door, the regular, chugging roar from the compressors was changing, speeding up as they ran faster with less natural gas flowing through them. The sound sent a chill down Rozek's spine. The engines were overrevving. Much more of that and they were likely to tear themselves apart, slashing through piping still filled with highly flammable gas.

He reached past the technician and slapped down switches controlling the first pair of compressors, turning them off. 'Knock 'em down! Shut everything down! Now!'

His men hurried to obey the order while he grabbed the phone connecting Przemysl to the next station up the pipeline – two hundred miles to the northeast, on the border between Belarus and Ukraine.

A technician, an ethnic Russian by his clear diction, answered on the first ring. 'Compressor Station Six.'

'This is the chief engineer at Przemysl.' Rozek fumbled for the right Russian words. He'd learned the language out of necessity, not because he liked it. 'I think we've got a line break somewhere between us. We're closing down right away.'

'There is no accident, chief engineer.' The Russian technician's voice was guarded.

'No? Then what in God's name is going on?'

'Please hold for a moment.'

Rozek could hear clicking sounds as the man switched him to another line.

A new voice came on, colder and more precise. 'You are the engineer in charge at Przemysl?'

'Yes.'

'My name is Colonel Viktor Polyakov. As the Commonwealth military representative for this district, I now command this station. I suggest you put your facility on permanent standby.' The Russian Army officer delivered his next bombshell bluntly. 'My orders are to inform you that all oil and gas deliveries to your country are being stopped. Effective immediately.'

Rozek gripped the phone tighter. 'Orders? From where?'

'From Moscow, chief engineer.' The phone line went dead.

Rozek stood clutching the phone for several seconds as his mind sorted through the implications of what he'd just been told. 'Oh, shit.'

He slammed the red emergency phone down and reached for the black phone next to it. This one was a dedicated line to Poland's Ministry of Mining and Power. 'This is Rozek. I need to speak with the minister. We have a problem.'

JANUARY 25 – THE WHITE HOUSE, WASHINGTON, D.C.

The senior members of the National Security Council filled the White House Cabinet Room. They were meeting here because the basement Situation Room they ordinarily used was being given a multimillion-dollar face-lift. Work crews were busy installing the latest computer-driven displays and secure communications gear, including equipment intended to allow real-time teleconferences with military commanders and other leaders around the globe during some hypothetical future emergency. Naturally, now that they were facing a real crisis, the timing couldn't possibly have been any worse.

It was the first time Ross Huntington had ever been invited to sit in on such a high-level administration gathering. He felt distinctly uncomfortable.

The men and women seated around the long rectangular table eyed him from time to time, some with frank curiosity, others with open envy. His reputation as the President's unofficial right-hand man was spreading. Huntington tried not to let their stares bother him. There were plenty of top officials who resented his easy access to the Oval Office. Nothing would bring their PR knives and malicious press leaks out sooner than any sign of uncertainty on his part. Politicians, like other finned scavengers, homed in on the first taste of blood in the water.

He forced himself to pay close attention to the handsome, red-haired man giving the preliminary briefing.

'Basically, Mr. President, the Poles are up shit's creek, and the Czechs and Slovaks aren't much better.' Clinton Scofield, the Secretary of Energy, was a former South Carolina governor who lived up to his tough-talking reputation. The Washington rumor mill said the forty-five-year-old widower liked betting on fast horses and dating even faster women. He was also known as a knowledgeable, hardworking, and completely loyal cabinet officer. In Huntington's eyes that made up for a multitude of real and imagined sins. 'Poland imports better than ninety-eight percent of its crude oil – ninety percent from one source, Russia. They're a little better off when it comes to natural gas supplies, but not by much. Siberian gas met sixty percent of their needs last year. The two other countries are in pretty much the same position.'

'What about stockpiles?' Harris Thurman, the Secretary of State, asked his question around the stem of a pipe he wasn't allowed to light. 'Don't they have strategic reserves?'

Scofield shook his head. 'They do. But not a lot. Two weeks at normal consumption. Maybe thirty days' worth under the emergency rationing program they're implementing. If they're lucky. They sure won't make it through the winter without suffering a complete economic collapse.'

Most of those around the table looked astonished by the Energy Secretary's dire assessment. The United States held enough oil in its SPR, the Strategic Petroleum Reserve, to meet all domestic needs for at least three full months. Sometimes it was difficult to remember that other, poorer nations operated closer to the margin.

'Can't they just find other suppliers?' The dark-haired woman who headed the Treasury had done some homework. She held up one of the weekly reports prepared by DOE's Energy Information Administration. 'Your own department keeps saying there's no worldwide shortage of oil or natural gas. If that's true, I think we should simply urge them to look elsewhere and be done with it.'

Several cabinet officers murmured their agreement. Even inside the administration there were deep divisions over fundamental policy. A strong minority opposed any moves to increase America's overseas commitments. Domestic initiatives were closer to their hearts and departmental budgets. They were backed by isolationist sentiment in the Congress.

'It's not that simple.' Scofield cleared his throat. 'You can't buy on the spot market without hard currency – real dollars – and that's something else the Poles, Czechs, and Slovaks are short on. They were paying the Russians in kind, trading iron, steel, chemicals, computers, and the like for crude oil and gas. No OPEC country's going to cut the same kinds of deals with them.'

Nobody could dispute that. The world's oil powers weren't famous for their disinterested charity.

For the first time, the President spoke up. He looked down the table toward Walter Quinn, the director of Central Intelligence. 'There's no doubt that the French are behind this oil embargo?'

'None at all, sir.'

The Secretary of State added his own two cents to the discussion. 'Paris wants all of eastern Europe inside this new monetary union – or else too bankrupt to give it much trouble.'

The President acknowledged Thurman's point with a quick nod before turning back to the DCI. 'One thing still puzzles me about this, Walt. What about the Germans? Weren't they pulling oil and gas through those pipelines, too?'

'Yes, sir. Mostly for refineries and factories in the east. Replacing those supplies on the open market will cost them a pretty penny.'

Huntington mentally chalked one up for the nation's chief executive. He'd overlooked the German angle during his own hasty boning up for this meeting.

'Well, we know the French are covering Russia's out-of-pocket expenses for this thing. Are they doing the same for the Germans?'

The DCI looked troubled. He'd been riding high on the credit the CIA had gained for its heads-up warnings of Kaminov's putsch and the secret French subsidies to Russia. Now he had to admit ignorance. 'If they are, we haven't seen any signs of it. But I can't be sure about that, Mr. President. We don't have any sources high enough in the Schraeder regime to tell us, one way or the other.'

Huntington wasn't particularly surprised by that. Germany had been a trusted American ally for decades – a close partner in the long struggle against Soviet communism. It took time to successfully shift the CIA's German operations from open cooperation to covert competition. Still, even the faint possibility that the French hadn't bothered telling Berlin what they were up to inside Russia was intriguing. Maybe their fledgling friendship wasn't as solid as all their joint press releases made it seem. That was worth closer study.

The President evidently agreed. He jabbed a finger toward the CIA chief. 'Keep digging, Walt. I'd like to know exactly who's orchestrating this damned embargo.'

He ran his gaze around the crowded table. 'All right, folks, let's move this along. The problem our Polish, Czech and Slovak friends are facing is pretty damn clear. What I need to hear are some workable solutions.'

'Is that even necessary, Mr. President?' The Treasury Secretary didn't mince her words. She had been in the cabinet long enough to know that the nation's chief executive valued candor more than consensus.

'I still don't see that we have any compelling interest at stake here. Who really cares whether they pay their bills with zlotys or with franc-marks?' She shrugged. 'After all, every dollar American-owned companies make in those two countries wouldn't keep this government in pocket change for half an hour.'

'What exactly are you proposing, Katherine? That we walk away and wash our hands of this whole mess?'

'Exactly. For two simple reasons.' She outlined her position with the same sure precision she used when lecturing congressmen about basic economics. 'One. Guaranteeing oil and gas supplies to these countries could mean an open-ended drain on our treasury. One we can't afford. And let's face it, the American people aren't going to like being asked to pay other people's energy bills. They're having a tough enough time meeting ends themselves. Two. This is an artificial oil shortage. Sooner or later the Russians will want to sell their resources, so sooner or later the embargo will end.

'If Warsaw, Prague, and Bratislava have to bend a little to get them to do that, well, so what? We're not looking at the end of the world.'

One or two of those seated around the table nodded. Several others looked less sure of themselves. Doing nothing was often the best course in foreign affairs.

Huntington surprised himself by stepping into the debate. He'd intended to sit back and listen quietly. 'With all due respect, Mr. President, the secretary is dead wrong. We can't walk away from this.'

Heads turned his way. 'This is a classic test of wills. The French are betting we won't have the balls to back our friends with cold, hard cash. Our friends in Europe are betting that we will. If we fail them, if we flinch now, we can kiss free trade with Europe good-bye for years. The Italians, the Dutch, and the Spanish will all know that we'll fold the first time the French or the Germans put pressure on them. So every European government with any sense will make tracks for Paris as fast as it can. By definition, anyone who joins this monetary union accepts the Franco-German position on tariffs and subsidies. And that means we'll lose our last realistic chance to shake the world out of this goddamned trade war before it bankrupts us all.'

He stared across at the Treasury Secretary. 'This is one instance where we don't have the luxury of letting events take their own course. We have to act.'

The President's firm, determined voice cut through the stunned silence that followed his outburst. 'Ross is absolutely right. I will not abandon people who've put their trust in us.'

He turned toward the Secretary of State. 'Harris, I'd like you to arrange a meeting for me. I want to talk with the British and Norwegian prime ministers, pronto. By satellite hookup if possible, but I'll fly if I have to.'

'Of course, Mr. President.' Thurman's own earlier misgivings were nowhere in sight. He was an old hand at reading the way the White House winds were blowing.

Clinton Scofield leaned forward. 'You're planning to ask them for North Sea oil and gas?'

'The thought had crossed my mind.'

Scofield nodded. 'Makes sense.' Hoping to import supplies from the Arabs, the Poles had built an oil and gas port at Gdansk way back in the 1970s. Pipelines already ran to Warsaw, the other big cities, and south to the Czech and Slovak republics. Better still, the North Sea's vast oil and natural gas reserves lay just a few hundred miles west of Poland. Shorter tanker round trips would mean lower transportation costs.

'And how will we pay for all this petro-largess?' The Treasury Secretary's skepticism was undiminished.

'The Poles and the Czechs will pay us what they can – in hard money or in kind. The rest?' He shrugged. 'We'll have to pick up the rest ourselves. First we'll try squeezing some new money into a supplementary appropriation. Maybe we can buy Congress off by backing a few more pork-barrel projects here at home.' The President's mouth turned down as he spoke. He'd fought hard against wasteful spending for years. The fact that he would even consider reversing himself on that score showed how committed he was to aiding the eastern Europeans.

He went on. 'If we can't get new funding, we'll have to try reprogramming money that's already appropriated for foreign aid.'

Harris Thurman's face fell a bit at that. As Secretary of State, he'd be the one explaining to various governments why their promised assistance packages failed to materialize.

'Congress won't like it, Mr. President,' the Treasury Secretary warned.

'Congress? Congress, Madame Secretary, can go to . . .' He paused and smiled sardonically. 'Gdansk.'

Huntington nodded to himself. The President was committed now. America would stand by her friends in eastern Europe.

CHAPTER 10
Combustion

FEBRUARY 4 – CNN HEADLINE NEWS

The televised images were gripping and strangely beautiful.

A giant, red-hulled oil tanker slid quietly through the narrow waters between Denmark and Sweden, gliding past Copenhagen's stone jetties, houses, and somber church spires at a steady ten knots. The tanker dwarfed its nearest companions – the two tugs and pilot boat shepherding it through the channel to the Baltic Sea. A ragtag swarm of tiny sailboats draped with protest banners lined the tanker's route, kept at bay by police patrol craft steaming back and forth along the sound. Chants and blaring air horns carried faintly across the water.

'Our top story this hour: rescue on the way for Poland's oil-starved economy.

'With Polish refineries running almost on empty, the first tanker carrying North Sea oil crossed into the Baltic – dogged by radical environmentalists most of the way. No arrests were reported by the Danish police, despite earlier rumors that a Greenpeace-led coalition would try to block the ship's passage before it reached Gdansk.'

The cool, collected features of the network's Atlanta-based anchor appeared, replacing the footage shot earlier that morning several thousand miles away. 'In other news from the region, French Minister for the Environment, Jean-Claude Martineau, expressed his grave concerns about the massive oil shipments destined for the Polish port. He pointed out that meeting Poland's needs would require nearly two hundred tanker trips a year – even without counting the oil being shipped for the Czech and Slovak republics. With the area's sea lanes already overcrowded, he predicted a catastrophe that could 'utterly destroy the fragile Baltic ecosystem.'

'In Washington, State Department spokeswoman Millicent Fanon delivered a blistering response to the French official's remarks, labeling them "a calculated attempt to mislead and panic" people in the nations bordering on the Baltic Sea . . .'

FEBRUARY 6 – THE HOUSE FLOOR, WASHINGTON, D.C.

The U.S. House of Representatives was in session, and common sense was out of fashion.

'Mr. Speaker, this President is out of control and out of touch!' The tall, silver-haired congressman from Missouri pounded the lectern in front of him, ignoring scattered boos from the seats to his left. 'This Baltic boondoggle is just another example of an administration that cares more about foreigners and foreign politics than it does about the American people!'

Majority Leader James Richard 'Dick' Pendleton was in fine form, playing perfectly to the cameras focused on his rugged, All-American profile. He was a master of the one-minute speech, the congressional contribution to the age of television politics. Dozens of House members routinely took the floor at the beginning of each legislative day, speaking for sixty seconds or so on any and every subject that might win them national or local airtime. Used intelligently, it was a potent political weapon.

'Ten billion dollars, Mr. Speaker! That's billion with a capital *B*! That's how much we'll pay to fill Polish gas tanks and heat Czech homes! Ten billion taxpayer dollars down an overseas drain instead of feeding American families, clothing American children, and creating American jobs!

'Well, I say that's wrong. Downright wrong. In hard times like these, we should be looking after our own people first – not squandering billions like some kind of global Santa Claus! America deserves more, not less, Mr. Speaker. And America deserves a president who understands that.'

The majority leader was confident that very few American voters would realize that the 'huge' energy aid program he'd attacked so vigorously represented just one-half of one percent of the total federal budget. When government spending soared into the trillions, it soared beyond comprehension for most people.

Pendleton left the House floor wearing a satisfied smile. He'd done a good day's work. Millions of Americans would see sound bites from his speech on the evening news, and their support for the President and his party would slip a little bit more. Not much. Just a percentage point or two in the polls. But that would be enough for the congressman's tastes. Undermining an incumbent president was always a long-term process. Although the next presidential contest was still more than two years off, Pendleton was already planning to win that election.

Like most of his colleagues, he never considered the impressions his intemperate, ill-chosen words might create outside the United States.

FEBRUARY 10 – FRANCO-GERMAN SUMMIT, PALAIS DE L'EUROPE, STRASBOURG, FRANCE

For the better part of five days Nicolas Desaix, Schraeder, and other would-be architects of a new European order had been meeting inside the lavishly appointed conference rooms of the old Parliament building. After weeks of preliminary discussions by lower-level officials, the French and German leaders were in Strasbourg to finish hammering out the basic military, economic, and political mechanisms needed to make a new continent-wide alliance work. Once they were satisfied, the array of related treaties would be presented to Europe's smaller countries as accomplished facts open to acceptance but not to amendment.

With the talks recessed for the afternoon, two men, Nicolas Desaix and Michel Guichy, the French Minister of Defense, trudged through the snow-shrouded Orangerie – a park adjacent to the towering red, bronze, and silver Palace of Europe. Aides and assistants trailed them at a discreet distance – out of earshot but close enough to run errands.

'I'm still not sure about this scheme of yours, Nicolas.' Michel Guichy shook his head slowly. 'So much change so fast. It seems unwise.'

'When you're on a tiger's back, my friend . . .' Nicolas Desaix left the rest unsaid. The other man knew the risks they were running. The French people seemed willing to endure martial law for the moment, but that could change quickly enough once the weather warmed up. Political unrest and spring sunshine were a familiar and unwelcome pairing in France. Even worse, Bonnard, the republic's half-senile President, was in failing health. If he died, he'd take the Emergency Committee's paper-thin veneer of legality with him.

No, Desaix thought, they didn't have time for second-guessing. That was why he'd buttonholed the barrel-chested Defense Minister before the evening negotiating sessions began. He was determined to win Guichy's support for the treaties he and Schraeder were crafting. Jacques Morin, his handpicked successor at the DGSE, was already on board. Together the three of them controlled the most important functions of the French government – the military, foreign policy, and espionage. Under the emergency decrees now governing France, they held most of the war-making and diplomatic powers ordinarily reserved for the head of state and commander in chief. Once they joined hands, the rest of the rump cabinet would trip all over itself falling into line.

On the surface, executive power in the European Confederation they were proposing would rest with a Council of Nations made up of officials from all member states. But the council would meet only two or three times a year. That and its very size ensured that it could never be anything more than a glorified debating society. In practice, real day-to-day decision-making would lie in the hands of permanent secretariats. And the leaders for those secretariats would be appointed by France and Germany.

Military matters would be handled through a NATO-like command structure. The Germans were prepared to accept French candidates for the top military and foreign policy slots. They were even willing to integrate their armed forces all the way down to the divisional level.

Those arrangements at least had Guichy's unhesitating approval. Combining French and German troops in a unified army would act as a powerful check on any future German territorial ambitions. An existing Franco-German corps showed that creating such an army was possible, if not easy. Better yet, he would be the logical choice to head the new confederation's forces.

'But what do the *Boche* get out of this?' The Defense Minister's pleased look faded to a frown. 'Germans don't even piss without asking for a receipt.'

'You're right about that.' Desaix allowed himself a smile. Bored by anything not directly connected with defense policy, Guichy had absented himself from the talks concerned with other matters. 'They want us to guarantee their control over the finance and industry posts.'

'And you've agreed?'

'Of course.' Desaix shrugged. 'We each have our spheres of influence in eastern Europe and our own vital industries. The Germans know better than to interfere with those. If they want to play at printing pretty new bank notes and setting interest rates for our junior "allies," I for one see no reason to stop them.'

'True.' Guichy stroked his chin. Awarding Germany the nominal responsibility for making economic policy meant very little. France had long ago learned how to ignore policies and agreements it disliked. In any event, these days the Germans were better businessmen and bankers than they were soldiers and statesmen. 'I begin to see why you want this new alliance so badly.' He shook his head in undisguised admiration. 'You are a sly one, Nicolas.'

'Merely careful, my friend. I gamble, but only when I know what cards the other players are holding.'

The Defense Minister nodded. 'So I've seen.' He hesitated. 'But what about the wild card? The United States, I mean. I doubt the Americans will want to see Europe unified under our banner.'

'The Americans?' Desaix grimaced. 'They're nothing. All wind and no backbone.'

'But this Polish venture of theirs . . .'

'Means nothing, Michel.' Desaix contemptuously waved away the U.S. oil and gas supply effort. True, he'd been stunned by the first reports. He'd never expected Washington to break the energy embargo he'd engineered. Since then, however, he'd seen American public and political opinion starting to crack. Americans liked quick, easy victories like the Persian Gulf War. They didn't have the stomach these days for open-ended, expensive commitments.

That was a weakness – one he planned to exploit.

Desaix laughed sourly. 'Even their own Congress is trying to stop these shipments. One small setback and the whole ridiculous thing will come to an end. Like that!' He snapped his fingers. 'And when it does, we'll have the Poles and the Czechs begging at our doorstep.'

He could tell that Guichy liked that image. The Defense Minister was a proud man, and several failed attempts to sell the two countries French military hardware and expertise still burned in his memory. Reports he'd seen suggested that they'd all but laughed at Guichy's offers before turning to the Americans and British for weapons and advice. Seeing them come crawling for admission to a new European alliance would avenge that insult.

Equally important, Guichy was a patriot. Desaix's vision of a continent subject to French authority – no matter how indirect or disguised – was bound to stir his spirit. The twentieth century had not been kind to their beloved country. Bled white by World War I and crushed underfoot during World War II, she had been largely ignored by the two superpowers during the cold war years that followed. Now, for the first time in a hundred years, France had a real chance to regain its glory and its rightful place in the sun.

'Well, Michel? Will you stand with me?' Desaix stood waiting while his colleague came to a decision. Though it irked him to plead with any man, he concealed his irritation. For the time being, humility best served his ends.

Slowly, ponderously, the Defense Minister nodded.

Nicolas Desaix had his ally. France would pursue its old imperial ambitions in a new guise.

Heinz Schraeder and Jurgen Lettow, Germany's Defense Minister, stood at a window overlooking the Orangerie, watching the two Frenchmen take their walk.

Lettow, shorter and leaner than his leader, nodded toward Desaix's distant figure. 'I do not trust that man, Chancellor.' He grimaced. 'Was it wise to award the French so much?'

He had reason to be displeased. The treaties they were finalizing would make the ministry he headed only an adjunct to a French-dominated Confederation Defense Secretariat. French generals would command German troops. The Defense Minister's scowl grew deeper.

Schraeder shrugged, unconcerned. 'Let the French strut about in uniform for a time, Lettow. This is a modern age. Who will go to war now?' He smiled thinly. 'The rest of these agreements are very much in our favor. We give Desaix and his colleagues a slight measure of authority over the trappings of power – the soldiers and the diplomats – and they give us control of the real *levers* of power – industry, banking, and trade.'

Germany's Chancellor shook his head. 'No, Lettow. We will allow France to bask in its artificial glory while we reshape the continent to our advantage.'

For their own wildly contradictory reasons, Europe's two strongest powers were coming to the same conclusions.

FEBRUARY 15 – NATIONAL POLICE COMMAND, MINISTRY OF THE INTERIOR, BUDAPEST, HUNGARY

Col. Zoltan Hradetsky folded his newspaper and took his feet off the desk. He glanced at the clock hanging on his wall. Only two-thirty in the afternoon. Another hour and a half before he could leave the office, and even that would be an hour earlier than everyone else who worked in the ministry.

Of course, his peers had real work to do. He didn't. After being yanked out of Sopron for offending the French-owned Eurocopter conglomerate, he'd been shunted from dead-end department to dead-end department.

Now stuck in a windowless office, with flaking green paint so old it was starting to look gray, he pushed papers all day. It was bad enough to go from an active, challenging post to a desk job, but what a job!

Oh, his title sounded impressive enough. He was the Ministry of the Interior's 'academy training supervisor.' Hradetsky smiled wryly. Less impressive was the fact that his only task involved monitoring the number of students enrolled in each of the nation's police training academies. Each day he filled out the proper form and gave it to his immediate superior's secretary. And each day, he was sure, Brigadier General Dozsa signed the report without reading it – promptly filing it into oblivion.

Whenever he'd tried to make his post anything more than a waste of time and space, he'd been slapped down. Dozsa, the National Police commander, hadn't even bothered to hide his disdain. During his first and only meeting with the precise, perfectly uniformed officer, he'd been told, 'Be grateful for what you still have, Colonel. Especially after all the trouble you've caused me. Rock the boat just once more, and I'll see that you're drummed out of the service in disgrace.'

Hradetsky's hands curled into fists, crumpling the newspaper he still held. Remembering Dozsa's insults brought all his repressed rage roaring to the surface. In the old days, he could have erased the stain on his honor with a well-timed saber cut. But dueling was out of place in this modern world. In any case, honor meant nothing to the government he still served – however unwillingly.

The simple truth was that he had nowhere else to go. He was a policeman, first and last. With the whole world mired in what seemed a perpetual recession, work of any kind was hard to get. And with work came ration cards for heat and food. Not a lot, but enough. Enough to survive a winter that had been the worst in decades. Subzero temperatures and the food shortages produced by autumn crop failures made life almost unbearable for all Hungarians. Those who were unemployed were even worse off. Priority for scarce foodstuffs went to those who still had jobs.

Of course, Zoltan Hradetsky had another important reason for staying at his post. An old-fashioned reason. Duty. He'd sworn an oath to uphold the law and to protect his fellow countrymen. And even though his superiors seemed determined to chain him down inside the Interior Ministry's idle bureaucracy, the oath remained.

So, torn between his anger, his duty, and the need to eat, he'd rotted uselessly at his desk, watching his poor country endure the winter's bitter cold like a man in a threadbare coat. Draconian security measures and international relief efforts had kept mass starvation at bay, but the past few months had been one long, dark nightmare. Curfews, rationing, and peremptory curbside executions for thieves and looters made it feel like wartime, even if the only obvious enemies were hunger and cold.

Those were bad enough. The very old, the very young, and the sick all suffered as rations were cut and cut again. Despair was spreading as parents saw their children's faces pinched by the cold and malnutrition.

Deaths from bronchitis, pneumonia, and influenza stood at all-time highs. So did public unrest.

Hradetsky frowned. You wouldn't know that from reading the tightly controlled government press. But he'd seen enough unvarnished crime statistics to know that only very careful juggling could make them sound good. Murder, muggings, and child abuse were all up. And, for the first time since the fall of the nation's postcommunist democracy, there were signs of organized political resistance to military rule. 'Subversive' newspapers were beginning to appear on Budapest's streets – taped to lampposts or slipped under doors. Some of the civilians who had led the old government were said to be forming clandestine opposition groups.

Hungarians were angry, and they were looking for a focus for their anger.

Hradetsky knew where his countrymen should look.

French and German emergency aid shipments were keeping Hungary afloat, but only by a narrow margin. And every shipment carried a price tag in lost national sovereignty. With every passing week, Hradetsky saw his country sliding closer to being a wholly owned French and German client state.

He had several old friends in the building, some of whom would still talk to him, despite his pariah status. Certainly his job left him with plenty of time to read and think, and to listen and learn. Even from his lowly post the Interior Ministry was still a good place to pick up information that contradicted the 'official' line.

Or to see interesting things. Like the nameless, arrogant visitors who dropped by the minister's private office. They came, stayed for a few hours, and then flew back to Paris or Berlin. Rumor had it that they were checking up on police activities, reporting to their governments on the 'behavior' of Hungary's law enforcement apparatus.

If that were true, their visits were having an unsettling effect. From Major General Racz on down, high-level ministry officials were taking an increasing interest in routine personnel assignments – even in the outlying police districts. To limit contact with the 'free trade' states, border crossings were being either closed or put under army control. Every report had to be forwarded to Budapest for approval. Racz, Dozsa, and their cronies were also aggressively collecting information on anyone even remotely connected with what passed for the political opposition. It didn't matter if it was a food riot, a labor demonstration, or just a coffeehouse gathering. The generals wanted to know who 'the troublemakers' were.

As support for the military Government of National Salvation sagged, old tyrannical habits were gaining new strength.

Hradetsky found this renewed emphasis on political intelligence-gathering especially troubling. During Hungary's first heady years of freedom, he and other junior officers had worked hard to make the National Police a professional crime-fighting force. One that was free of the corruption, inefficiency, and brutal misconduct so common under communism.

Now, with foreign backing, his country's rulers were reversing course, undoing reforms that had made Hradetsky proud to wear his police uniform. Toadyism and unquestioning deference to French and German interests were valued more than competence.

He grimaced. There wasn't much chance that would change any time soon. The generals were in too deep to back out now. Like their counterparts in the rest of eastern Europe, they were signing any agreement the two European superpowers put before them. Treaties to adopt a single currency. Treaties to blend existing national legal systems and economic regulation into a continent-wide monolith. Arms sales and joint military exercises. And on and on and on. The pace was dizzying – deliberately so, he suspected.

Hradetsky could read the handwriting on the wall. If the generals were allowed free reign, Hungary would be absorbed. She would be swallowed whole by bigger nations that preached the common interest while working for their own selfish ends. He bit his lip. The prospect of working under orders issued in Paris or Berlin made him feel sick.

FEBRUARY 18 – HOLDING AREA, OFF THE NORTH PORT, GDANSK, POLAND

Running lights outlined several huge ships moored several miles off the wind-swept Baltic coast – oil and liquid natural gas tankers waiting their turn to off-load at Gdansk's overcrowded docks. Snatches of music and canned laughter rose above the steady slap of small waves against steel hulls. Sounds carried far across the sea at night.

Five miles outside the offshore anchorage, a rusting, storm-battered fishing trawler drifted silently with the tide and currents. Crewmen in winter coats and gloves clustered on the tiny vessel's stern, grunting softly as they wrestled a heavy Zodiac inflatable raft back on board.

Four shivering men stood near the trawler's darkened wheelhouse, stripping off dry suits and scuba gear. Their features were almost invisible under layers of black camouflage paint, but all of them were young men in perfect physical condition.

The trawler's short, fair-haired captain, older but just as fit, stepped down out of the wheelhouse. 'Any problems?'

One of the divers shook his head. 'None. Everything went just as planned.'

The captain clapped him on the shoulder and leaned back inside to speak to the helmsman. 'Right. Let's get out of here. All ahead one-quarter.'

'All ahead one-quarter. Aye, sir.'

The fishing vessel's diesel engine coughed to life with a stuttering, muffled roar and its single screw started turning, churning the sea to foam. Still sailing without lights, the trawler headed west, hugging the Polish coastline.

ABOARD THE SEATRANS *NORTH STAR*

The *North Star* rode easily at anchor.

Capt. Frank Calabrese leaned on the bridge railing, his hands cupped around a steaming coffee mug for warmth. His ship, an LNG tanker, stretched forward almost as far as his eyes could see. Nine hundred and fifty feet long and with a 140-foot beam, she was as big as an aircraft carrier and almost as massive. The top halves of four heavily insulated domes rose above the *North Star*'s hull like giant white golf balls – refrigerated tanks holding 786,000 barrels of natural gas kept liquid at 323 degrees below zero.

'You wanted to see me, Skipper?' Charles MacLeod, his first officer, stepped out onto the open bridge wing.

Calabrese sipped his coffee and then nodded. 'Sure do, Charlie. I just got the word from the harbormaster. We're cleared to off-load starting at 0900 hours tomorrow.'

'About bloody time.'

'Amen to that.' The American tanker captain chuckled, amused by his first officer's impatience.

He could also understand the younger man's irritation. MacLeod had a pregnant wife waiting for him in Stavanger, *North Star*'s home port. Every day they were delayed multiplied the Scot's already staggering radiotelephone bill.

So far they'd been anchored off the Polish port for more than forty-eight hours, kept waiting while other tankers pumped their precious cargoes ashore. Despite working around the clock, Gdansk's refinery teams and pipeline crews were falling further and further behind. Trying to funnel all the oil and gas Poland needed through one medium-sized port facility was like trying to irrigate the Sahara through a single garden hose.

Calabrese stood up straight, taking his weight off the railing. 'The Poles are sending a harbor pilot aboard at first light, so I'd like you to make sure everybody's awake and ready to go by 0500.'

'You can count on me.' MacLeod grinned. 'Sooner in, sooner out. And it's certain that none of the boys will be sad to see the back of this place'

The tanker's mixed American, British, and Norwegian crew had been on this run once before. With the city under a strict dusk-to-dawn curfew to save energy, Gdansk's nightlife could best be described as nonexistent. Not that it really mattered. No one aboard would have a spare moment to go skirt-chasing once *North Star* docked.

'Need anything else, Skipper?'

The captain shook his head. 'Nope. Not right now.' He waved the other man back inside. 'Get out of the cold, Charlie. And get some rest. You'll need it.'

He raised the mug to his lips for another sip of hot coffee.

Four hundred feet forward, the limpet mine magnetically clipped below *North Star*'s waterline detonated, rupturing her hull. Salt water, superheated air, and burning shards of steel blew inward, ripping through one of the huge refrigerated LNG storage tanks.

Whump. The tanker shuddered once, rocked from side to side as though she'd struck something below the surface.

Frank Calabrese's eyes widened in surprise. 'What the hell?' He grabbed the bridge railing. 'Charlie, find out what's happen . . .'

His last words were drowned out by blaring collision alarms.

Deep inside *North Star*'s wounded hull, liquid natural gas jetted out of the torn storage tank, pouring out under high pressure. As soon as it hit the warm, oxygen-rich air it began changing back to its natural state – boiling into a diffuse, highly flammable gas. Seconds later, the gas cloud touched a live electrical wire left dangling by the limpet mine blast.

The tanker exploded.

Calabrese, MacLeod, and the forty-seven other men aboard *North Star* died instantly – incinerated by an expanding ball of flame that lit the night sky for hundreds of miles around. They didn't die alone.

Driven by enormous pressures and temperatures, a blast wave raced outward from the blinding pillar of fire shooting up through the lower atmosphere. It smashed into two oil tankers anchored close by and left them both sinking and ablaze – torn by 190-knot winds and flying debris. Sailors who had been on deck were either blown overboard or pulped against steel bulkheads and heavy machinery. Those trapped below drowned or burned to death.

Eight miles from *North Star*, the shock wave slammed into Gdansk with hurricane force, toppling trees all over the city. Windows facing the blast suddenly blew inward, sending shards of glass sleeting through homes and offices with deadly force. Those hit by the hail of flying glass, men, women, and children – anyone caught facing the wrong way at the wrong time – went down screaming, disfigured or dying. Still others burned to death in fires sparked by fallen electric power lines. Exposed to the full force of the shock wave, several old or poorly constructed buildings near the waterfront collapsed, crushing their inhabitants beneath tons of brick and broken concrete.

When the first deafening echoes faded, thousands of stunned Poles stumbled out of their damaged homes to stare in horror at the eerie, flickering orange glow on the northern horizon.

FEBRUARY 20 – NEAR GDANSK

Ross Huntington trudged grimly along the shore. His escort, a short, stocky man, wore the blue uniform jacket of the Polish Navy. Four stripes on his shoulder boards identified him as a *Komandor*, a captain. They were accompanied by four soldiers in full battle gear and armed with AKM assault rifles. Blue shield and white anchor shoulder patches marked them as members of the elite 7th Coastal Defense Brigade. More soldiers from the same unit manned artillery pieces and antiaircraft guns scattered up and down the waterfront.

Thick black crude oil coated the sea and coastline for miles in all directions. Its sickly sweet smell hung over everything. Several miles offshore, flames and heavy smoke still billowed above one of the tankers set afire when *North Star* exploded. The other lay on its side closer in, sunk in shallow water and leaking oil from ruptured cargo holds. Smaller craft swarmed around the two wrecks – fighting fires or deploying floating booms in a desperate effort to contain the oil spill.

Oil and gas tankers that had survived the blast were anchored further out, barely visible through a thin gray haze of smoke and early morning fog. Warships surrounded them, steaming slowly back and forth on patrol around the anchorage. Helicopters prowled out to sea and along the coast.

Four-man teams moved slowly down the oil-smeared beach, kneeling from time to time to study pieces of unidentified debris scattered among the dead fish and dying seabirds. Surgical masks, gloves, and nylon protective suits gave them an unearthly, almost inhuman appearance.

Huntington stopped walking for a moment to watch them work. He glanced toward the Polish Navy captain waiting silently by his side. 'What are they looking for? Evidence?'

The shorter man shook his head. 'Remains, Mr. Huntington. Some parts of those who were killed are still being washed ashore.'

Huntington's stomach knotted. He'd seen the preliminary numbers before flying out of Washington on this emergency fact-finding mission. The explosion had reached far beyond the harbor, flinging debris into the city itself. Forty-two men, women, and children were confirmed dead. Another sixty-one sailors were still missing and also presumed dead. Eyewitness accounts made it clear that no one aboard *North Star* or near it could possibly have survived the explosion. Somehow, though, those casualty figures had been unreal, comfortingly abstract. Seeing the soldiers and medical personnel combing this blackened beach for corpses made the disaster sickeningly real.

He looked away, staring out to sea. He'd fought hard to win approval for the oil and gas shipments to Gdansk. At the time, it had seemed the next logical move in the bloodless tit-for-tat trade war they were waging against the French and Germans. Now more than one hundred people were dead. No matter how hard he tried, he couldn't stop feeling somehow responsible for their deaths.

He'd miscalculated. The men in Paris and Berlin were far more ruthless than he'd ever imagined.

Huntington turned back to face the Polish naval officer. 'We still don't have any hard evidence of sabotage?'

'No, sir.' The Pole shook his head in frustration. 'And we're not likely to find any, either. Not after a blast like that.'

Huntington nodded. Preliminary estimates were that the natural gas carried aboard *North Star* had exploded with a force equal to roughly sixteen thousand tons of TNT – nearly the punch packed by the atomic bombs dropped on Hiroshima and Nagasaki. All that was left of the LNG tanker were several million tiny metal fragments scattered far and wide across the Baltic seabed.

Still, it didn't take a genius to imagine what must have happened. Or who was responsible.

Huntington shivered as the wind gusted, swirling loose sand into the air. Just to the east lay the Westerplatte, a headland guarding the harbor entrance. The promontory had already earned a grim place in the world's history books. A German battleship, the *Schleswig-Holstein*, had fired the first shots of World War II there – trying to bombard Gdansk's small Polish garrison into submission. The war that followed had submerged the entire globe in blood and fire for six long years.

He looked out across the wreck-strewn sea, suddenly afraid that history was repeating itself.

FEBRUARY 21 – PARIS

Nicolas Desaix almost never watched television. This evening he was making an exception. He sat alone in his private office, transfixed by the images being broadcast from just off the Polish coast.

'No one knows what went wrong aboard this floating bomb, the SeaTrans *North Star*. A careless accident? Sabotage by environmental extremists? Who can say? But one thing is very clear according to the experts. This disaster could have been worse. Much worse.'

Desaix was delighted. The TV journalist's commentary might almost have been written by his own staff.

'If *North Star* had been in port when she blew up, Gdansk itself would have been utterly destroyed. Tens of thousands would lie dead or dying in the rubble – far more than the hundred or so who died three days ago. And a hellish firestorm fed by natural gas and oil would be sweeping across northern Poland – blackening the skies above all Europe.

'One thing more is clear. Poland and the Czech and Slovak republics cannot be allowed to put us all at risk for their own selfish aims. The time for nationalism is over. Europe must stand united as a single, strong force for peace and prosperity. Or else surrender in shame to those who would exploit us for their own profit.

'This is Raoul Peree, reporting live from Gdansk . . .'

Desaix used a remote control to turn off the small television. After checking his watch, he punched a special code into his secure phone.

The head of the DGSE was still in his own office. He answered immediately. 'Yes, Minister?'

'Fine work, Morin. A most satisfying operation. Congratulate Commander Regier and his men for me.'

'Of course, Minister.'

Desaix hung up, confident that Poland and eastern Europe would soon submit and join the new European order. Their vaunted independence had fallen prey to a single, well-timed explosive charge.

CHAPTER 11
Confederation

FEBRUARY 23 – CAMP DAVID, MARYLAND

Falling snow blanketed the steep, wooded Maryland hills surrounding Camp David, drifting down out of a slate-gray sky. Soft white flakes settled gently across the mountainside presidential retreat. Wisps of steam rose from an outdoor heated swimming pool, glowing brightly in the light thrown by floodlamps dotting the compound. Beyond the shining mists, men moved in the darkness growing beneath the nearest trees – Secret Service agents on guard duty.

Dogs barked in the distance – faint and far off. The snow hushed all sounds and made all the world seem at peace.

'Ross? Are you all right?'

Huntington turned away from the window. The President, Harris Thurman, and the others crowded into Aspen Cottage's small wood-paneled parlor were staring at him. Damn. He'd let his mind wander when he should have been paying attention. The President needed an advisor who could give cogent advice. Not a daydreamer wrapped in his own weariness.

He forced a tired smile. 'I'm fine, Mr. President. Just a little short on sleep is all.'

That was a half-truth hovering on the edge of being a full-fledged lie. Constant travel, stress, and gnawing worry over what he saw happening in Europe were taking a serious toll on his health. For the first time since he'd left the hospital two years ago, Huntington felt warning signs from his heart – warning signs he couldn't easily ignore. An aching right arm and jaw. Trouble breathing after almost any unexpected exertion. Even climbing a single flight of stairs too fast left him winded.

He knew it showed. His wife was starting to look scared again. She wanted him to go in for a checkup, but he'd been putting her off.

A doctor would probably order him to slow down, to take some time for himself. And he couldn't. His time belonged to the United States and to the President. As long as the nation's chief executive found his efforts and counsel valuable, personal considerations had to be put on the back burner.

Crap, Huntington told himself. He reined his ego in before it soared out of control. The real truth was that he didn't want to quit. He'd felt lost and useless after that first heart attack shoved him into early retirement. Gaining the President's trust had helped him regain his own confidence. Settling for enforced idleness at home or on a golf course somewhere would mean surrendering to boredom and quiet despair all over again.

Besides, he couldn't give up. Not now. Not when a crucial part of the foreign policy he'd helped shape seemed close to total collapse.

Political shock waves from the LNG tanker explosion were still echoing around the globe. Aided and abetted by the French, environmental extremists were using the *North Star* disaster as a rallying point for further, more radical opposition to tanker traffic in the Baltic. Even the region's moderate, unaligned governments – Denmark, Sweden, Finland, and the Baltic republics – were under increasing pressure to openly oppose the U.S.- and British-led energy supply effort.

The administration itself was sharply divided over the wisdom of continued oil and gas shipments to eastern Europe. An uneasy coalition formed by the Secretaries of Energy, Defense, and State still backed the program. But its cabinet-level critics were growing bolder, buoyed by polls that showed public opinion sliding their way. So far the President's clear determination to help the Poles, Czechs, and Slovaks had kept a lid on the debate. Policymakers sparring over the shipments were keeping their disputes out of public view. All that could change overnight if any of them sensed their leader's resolution weakening.

Huntington knew how easily actions could be misinterpreted. Rightly or wrongly, the officials who opposed the President's energy aid program saw him, Huntington, as the 'evil genius' behind it. So if he threw in the towel and went home, even for medical reasons, he might take the cabinet's shaky consensus with him. All their bickering and bitterness could break out into the open and onto the front page. And isolationist vultures in both Congress and the media were already circling – ready to pounce the first time the administration wavered.

That was the deciding factor.

France and Germany were waiting in the wings. Waiting for a cold-war-weary America to abandon the eastern European countries to their tender mercies. Well, Ross Huntington would be damned before he'd walk away and watch that happen. Not without one hell of a fight. This wasn't just another memo-riddled skirmish between factions scrapping for control over the administration's agenda. There were bodies in the Gdansk morgue to prove that. For all practical purposes, whoever had planted the bomb aboard the SeaTrans *North Star* had declared war on the United States.

The President shared his view of the situation. Which explained this emergency meeting at Camp David.

Huntington studied the men grouped together near the parlor's stone fireplace. As always, Harris Thurman stood closest to the President, wreathed in the smooth-smelling tobacco smoke curling from his favorite pipe. Despite that, his lean, patrician features were tense. As the Secretary of State, a lot of the political flak lobbed at the oil supply effort was coming his way. In contrast, Clinton Scofield, the Secretary of

Energy, looked considerably calmer. He leaned against a wall with his arms folded comfortably in front of him. The Secretary of Defense, John Lucier, stood beside Scofield, shorter by several inches than anyone else in the room. His intelligent brown eyes gleamed behind thick horn-rimmed glasses. The final member of the group, Walter Quinn, head of the CIA, perched on an armchair pulled up next to the fireplace. From time to time the CIA chief mopped sweat off his high, balding forehead, but he stayed right where he was. Caught between a desk job, a slow metabolism, and an aversion to exercise, Quinn carried enough extra weight to be far more comfortable sitting down than standing up. He'd learned how to cope with heat during half a lifetime spent suffering through Washington's sweltering summers.

All of them were dressed casually, sporting a mix of jeans and corduroy trousers, sweaters, open hunting vests, and unzipped ski jackets. And all of them supported the President's decision to aid the eastern European republics.

The White House press office was telling reporters they were at Camp David for a day's cross-country skiing, but every one of them knew that was pure bullshit. Calling the day-long gathering a ski trip gave the cabinet officers who hadn't been invited up the mountainside a way to save face. In reality, the President wanted to reassess events in Europe without sparking another clash between those who wanted to help the countries and those who'd just as soon ignore them.

Huntington moved closer to the fire and away from the window. He didn't see any point in giving his exhausted mind more chances to roam free. He was here to explore policy options, not to stare out at the falling snow.

They had already been at it for hours.

Scofield made room for him by the fireplace and kept talking. 'What I'm saying, Mr. President, is that unless we take some pretty dramatic steps pretty damned quick, the whole Gdansk operation is dead in the water. Finished.'

'Insurance problems?'

'Sure.' The Energy Secretary ran a hand through his unruly red hair. 'Lloyd's and the other maritime insurers have jacked Baltic tanker rates up three or four hundred percent in just the last two days. That's pushing costs way beyond what the Poles can afford and way beyond what we'd budgeted.'

He frowned. 'Plus, I've been getting calls from every shipping firm and oil company we've been able to rope into this thing. They want out. Now, not later. Nobody bargained for what happened to the *North Star*.'

'Shit.' The President rubbed his jaw, thinking hard. 'What's the supply situation like over there?'

'Still not good.' Scofield looked grim. 'Even operating nonstop, we were barely able to move in enough oil and gas. My people tell me all three countries are down to a ten-day margin. Maybe less if the weather stays bad.'

Christ. Huntington's mouth went dry. The Poles, Czechs, and Slovaks had almost unimaginably rigid conservation programs in place. No one with a private automobile could get any gasoline to keep it running. All cities were under strict, energy-saving curfews. And dozens of factories were operating only sporadically, idling tens of thousands of trained workers. Citizens in the three nations already faced lives that were increasingly dark, dreary, gloomy, and cold. He doubted their governments could survive for very long if matters got much worse.

He knew Scofield, Thurman, and the others shared the same somber conviction. He could see it on their faces.

The President stared into the fire, obviously making the same depressing calculations. For just an instant, sagging shoulders and a haggard, careworn look showed his true age. But when he looked up again, his aides saw only the same firm, youthful expression he was careful to show the public. 'All right, gentlemen. We tried to help our friends out of a jam, and now we've been suckerpunched. The question is, what should we do about it?'

'Giving up isn't an option?' Scofield asked quietly.

'No.'

The Energy Secretary nodded, satisfied. 'Then we roll with the punch, Mr. President. We roll with it and shake it off.' He straightened up. 'First we have to keep the oil and gas flowing. To do that, we're going to have to insure the tankers ourselves. Provide total coverage against any losses.'

'And where do we find the money?' Harris Thurman didn't conceal his skepticism. 'Good God, man, they're saying the bill for the *North Star* explosion will run close to a billion dollars by the time all the lawyers are through. What if there's another disaster on the same scale? We couldn't begin to scrape that much extra funding together – not without going to the Congress.'

'Exactly.' Scofield smiled tightly. 'That's why we have to make sure there aren't any more so-called disasters.'

He glanced at the shorter man standing by his side. 'And that's where the navy comes in. Right, John?'

The Secretary of Defense stepped forward into the flickering firelight. 'Precisely.' He turned to the President. 'I've talked to the chief of naval operations, sir. We could have an escort force on station in a week. Sooner if the British will join us. Put enough ships and surveillance aircraft around any tanker and you can be pretty sure she'll arrive safely.'

'A carrier battle group?'

'Not necessarily, Mr. President. A carrier operating in the North Sea could prove useful, but most of the real work would have to be done by smaller stuff – frigates and destroyers. The Baltic is too confined for anything bigger.' Lucier adjusted his glasses, pushing them tighter across his nose. 'I think we'd also be wise to deploy a few Patriot and Hawk missile batteries around the harbor perimeter.'

The Defense Secretary's lips tightened in a quick, thin smile. 'Just in case some troubled maniac decides to take a bomb-loaded Cessna for a spin over Poland.'

'Sensible.' The President stood quietly for a moment with his hands in his pockets. Then he nodded. 'Okay, John. Work up your plan and have it ready for me to look over. By tomorrow morning, if possible.'

'Sir, you're not seriously considering this?' Harris Thurman sounded more and more agitated. 'Sending U.S. forces in harm's way for somebody else's oil is practically guaranteed to set Congress off like a Roman candle. Pendleton and the rest of them will crucify you for risking American lives overseas.'

The President swung round to face his Secretary of State. 'They can try, Harris. But I'm the commander in chief. I'm the one the people elected to watch over this country's vital interests. Not Jack Pendleton or the Senate majority leader. Hell, if the people don't like the job I'm doing, they can always throw me out on my ear in the next election. Clear?'

'Of course, Mr. President.' Thurman backed off and tried another tack. 'But I still think we might be jumping the gun a bit. All this protection against terrorists or commandos could be completely unnecessary. How do we know what happened to the *North Star* wasn't just a freak accident?'

'Because there's almost no chance that it was.' Scofield stepped into the argument again. 'I've had DOE and gas industry experts going over every detail they can get their hands on. The weather that night. The ship's position. Crew experience. Maintenance records. The whole kit and caboodle. And not one of them can concoct a scenario that would result in that kind of explosion. Not without more warning.'

The President turned to Huntington. 'You were just there, Ross. Are the Poles still convinced this was a deliberate case of sabotage?'

'They are.' Huntington nodded. 'They're still digging hard for evidence, any evidence, to confirm their suspicions. Their police and military intelligence people are questioning anyone who might have seen anything suspicious out near the anchorage.' He frowned. 'But so far nothing's turned up.'

'I'm not surprised.' Walter Quinn spoke up suddenly. 'I don't think there's anything for them to find.'

'Oh?'

'Waiting until the tanker was anchored right off the Polish coast seems too risky. Anyone caught snooping around that mooring area would have been damned hard-pressed to explain what they were doing there.' The CIA director shook his head. 'Professionals don't like working without a safety net. They'd pick somewhere busier, with more ships of all types coming and going. Somewhere they could slip into without being noticed and still get out of fast if anything went wrong.'

Quinn wiped his forehead again and this time pushed his chair back a foot or so from the fire. 'That's why we're fairly sure whoever sabotaged the *North Star* did it long before she ever reached Gdansk. Maybe while she was still loading in Stavanger. Maybe sometime during her transit through the Skagerrak or the Kattegat.'

He shrugged. 'Trouble is, there are just too many bases to cover. I've got officers spread through the region and so do both the British and the Norwegians, but it's like hunting for a needle that's not only hidden but invisible as well.'

The President, Thurman, and the others nodded their understanding.

Without any physical evidence to narrow down the type of explosive device or even its location aboard the ship, Quinn's agents faced a Herculean challenge. They didn't know whether to look for a turncoat dockworker, bearded Green lunatics aboard a sailboat, or a highly trained commando team sent in by minisub.

Suddenly Huntington's mind came alive as he remembered what he'd seen and been told at the Polish port. He lifted a hand, interrupting the CIA chief. 'Hold on, Walt. It's likely this mine or bomb or whatever it was, was set to go off at a particular time, right?'

Quinn nodded. 'Probably. Command detonation would be chancy – especially through the water or a metal hull. Radio waves don't travel too well through either medium. Given that, using a timed device of some sort would be the best method.'

'And that's exactly why we know the explosives were planted sometime *after* the *North Star* arrived off Gdansk.' Huntington looked around the parlor. 'The tanker didn't off-load on schedule. We all know that now. But who could have known that *before* she got there?'

He answered his own question. 'Nobody. By the time she showed up, Gdansk was taking ships in on almost a catch-as-catch-can basis. Some tankers were in and out of the port on schedule. Others wound up days late.'

Quinn looked puzzled. 'I don't see your point.'

'Think about it.' Huntington felt excitement rising inside. It was the same feeling he used to get when he spotted the solution to a stubborn production problem or when he held a winning poker hand. 'If the explosives were planted aboard any earlier, they'd have been timed to go off while the *North Star* was in port. Anchored smack-dab in the middle of Gdansk instead of sitting several miles offshore.'

Scofield saw it first. 'Of course. Not even those bastards in Paris or Berlin would destroy a whole city just to cut off Polish oil imports.'

The President turned his gaze on the CIA director. 'I think your invisible needle just turned visible, Walt. And the Poles are looking in exactly the right place.'

'So it seems, Mr. President,' Quinn said stiffly, obviously irked and embarrassed at being one-upped by an amateur. Huntington had a feeling that the director's senior advisors were in for a tongue-lashing when he got back to Langley.

Fortunately for the CIA chief, the President seemed more interested in the next move than in finding fault for past errors. 'Okay, Walt. I want a full-court press from every intelligence organization and asset we've got, focusing on the area around Gdansk. Satellite photos. SIGINT. Everything. Get your field people in touch with the Poles and coordinate with them. Somewhere, somehow, there's evidence that connects the goddamned French or the Germans to what happened. And I want it. Understand?'

'Yes, sir.'

'Good.' The President paced to the window and stood staring out into the fading afternoon. 'Then, when Pendleton or any other congressional son-of-a-bitch starts moaning about our support for Poland, I'll be ready to fire back.'

'That could be very risky, Mr. President,' Thurman warned. 'Telling the American people that French or German agents murdered the *North Star*'s crew could rouse a fire storm of public fury – one we couldn't control.'

'You think we should just look the other way?'

Thurman paused to relight his pipe, then nodded slowly. 'There are precedents.'

Huntington knew that was true. During the cold war, the Soviets had shot down several U.S. reconnaissance aircraft – some over the Sea of Japan, others closer to the Russian coast. And Israeli jets had turned a U.S. intelligence ship, the *Liberty*, into a flaming, bombed-out wreck during the 1967 Six-Day War. In each case, the United States had ruled out direct retaliation or even immediate public disclosure. At the time no one in power had wanted to provoke a crisis or escalate existing tensions.

'After all, a quiet, unofficial approach to Paris with the information could . . .'

The President turned his head. The cold, grim expression on his face choked Thurman off in midsentence. 'First we find the evidence, Mr. Secretary. Then I will decide what we do with it.'

He turned back to the window. More lights were coming on around Camp David as the day gave way to another long winter night.

FEBRUARY 25 – COUNCIL OF NATIONS, PALAIS DE L'EUROPE, STRASBOURG, FRANCE

Nicolas Desaix stood near the entrance to the old European Parliament's debating chamber, watching government officials from half the continent mingle with one another, each surrounded by a gaggle of junior aides and translators. The vast hall was one great sea of gray – gray hair, gray suits, and dull, gray faces.

What a gathering of apes in fancy dress, he thought sourly.

The prospect of spending the next several days in close contact with these bumpkins from a dozen different countries was anything but pleasing. Nevertheless, it was the price he would have to pay to see his dreams for a Europe united under Franco-German influence take final shape. This conference was a necessary formality. The little nations must have their chance to babble and fume and fuss before they signed agreements already reached by their powerful patrons. International diplomacy was a game more of form than of substance.

Well, so be it.

Desaix donned a pleasant smile suited to the occasion and sauntered through the crowd, exchanging friendly words with those he knew and polite nods with those he didn't. It was an exhausting charade. Delegates from Austria, Belgium, Croatia, and Hungary approached him one after the other, each seeking some special concession or sign of French favor. Each went away dazzled by his charm and completely empty-handed.

Their Serbian, Romanian, and Bulgarian neighbors followed close behind, and received the same polite attention.

He moved on, paying careful heed to several of the neutral observers attending the conference. Russia, Ukraine, and Denmark were all nations he had set his sights on. Bringing them into the emerging European Confederation would greatly increase its size and power. The new alliance would then run unchecked from the Atlantic to the Urals and beyond.

Or almost unchecked, he reminded himself.

There were still no representatives in Strasbourg from Warsaw, Prague, or Bratislava. Desaix pondered that irritably while swapping meaningless courtesies with one of the Russians. The eastern Europeans were proving far more recalcitrant than he'd imagined possible. What else would it take to bring them to heel?

'Minister!'

Desaix glanced toward the voice, frowning as he recognized one of his own aides. He drew away to a quieter corner. 'What is it, Girault?'

The younger man handed him a wire service printout. 'It's the Americans, Minister. And the British. They're going to keep shipping oil and gas to Gdansk. And they're sending warships to escort each tanker from now on!'

Desaix was stunned. 'What? Impossible!'

'The American Secretary of Defense made the announcement an hour ago.' Girault pointed to the crumpled piece of paper still clutched in his superior's hands. 'He called it Operation Safe Passage.'

The Foreign Minister skimmed through the report, his jaw tightening as he realized that his aide was right. Against every expectation, the Americans and their British lapdogs were not abandoning their attempt to break the Russian oil embargo. If anything, they were upping the ante. Committing military forces to the Baltic was a clear signal that the two English-speaking countries planned to reinvolve themselves in Europe's internal affairs.

That spelled trouble. Trouble because the Poles, Czechs, and Slovaks would be even more likely to spurn his latest diplomatic overtures. And trouble because a strengthened Anglo-American presence could only encourage the irresponsible elements already resisting Franco-German influence throughout Europe.

He shoved the printout into his pocket and grabbed Girault by the arm. 'Find Chancellor Schraeder and bring him to me. Immediately. Tell him we have important matters to discuss. In private.'

The younger man nodded and hurried away into the milling crowd.

Desaix watched him disappear and then swung away on his heel. His mind was already busy exploring ways to hurry this insufferable conference along. With luck, the Americans and British would soon see their paltry naval venture overshadowed by the power of a newly united Europe.

FEBRUARY 26 – NATIONAL PHOTO INTERPRETATION CENTER, BUILDING 213, WASHINGTON NAVY YARD

The National Photo Interpretation Center occupied a large, nondescript office building deep inside Washington's Navy Yard. Managed by the CIA for the country's other intelligence services, the NPIC's several thousand specialists were responsible for analyzing the pictures obtained by America's orbiting spy satellites. Every president since John F. Kennedy had relied on their skills and expert knowledge during times of crisis.

This President was no different.

Bill Reilly was the senior photo interpreter assigned to the center's northern Europe section. He'd spent years analyzing satellite pictures covering the old Warsaw Pact's major naval bases, airfields, and army installations all the way from the Baltic to the Kola Peninsula. So many years, in fact, that he often joked he could find his way around Murmansk better than he could around his own hometown – at least from two hundred miles straight up.

His coworkers called him the KH Gnome. He stood just an inch or so over five feet tall, and even on a good day his short-sleeved shirts, wide ties, and brown or blue slacks looked like he'd slept in them. A surprisingly deep, gravelly voice and tufts of white hair that stuck up despite his best efforts to comb them down only reinforced the nickname.

Now he sat hunched over the wide-screen computer monitor on his desk, studying pictures taken days earlier over Gdansk. The pictures, stored on high-capacity CD-ROM disks, were from a KH-11 satellite pass requested in the hours immediately following the *North Star* explosion. Storing them on computer saved time and space. It also made them easier to enhance and call back.

The pictures Reilly was scanning were thermal infrared images – images produced by the heat given off by different objects and surfaces. Thermal imaging was a capability only recently added to the KH-11 series satellites to allow night surveillance missions. In the Gnome's expert view it was a redesign that had been long overdue. The bad guys never seemed to work in broad daylight.

'Hello.' His right hand suddenly stopped moving the mouse he was using to scroll through the series of computer-enhanced images. He'd gone over them once before, right after they'd been shot, downloaded off the MILSTAR network to the Mission Ground Site at Fort Belvoir, Virginia, and then uploaded into his computer. But the first lesson in photo interpretation was that you usually only saw what you were looking for. And he'd been studying those first satellite photos to get a handle on the disaster's size and scope – not its cause.

Even then he'd barely been able to make out anything interesting. The enormous heat 'bloom' caused by fires aboard the sinking oil tankers had blotted out an equally enormous amount of detail.

These pictures were different. They'd been broken down, digitized, and 'washed' pixel by pixel to produce cleaner, sharper images. More important still, he knew what he was supposed to be looking for this time. Anything odd. Anything that looked out of place near the Gdansk oil port holding area.

And that was exactly what he'd just found.

Reilly used the mouse to draw a quick, ragged circle around the object centered on his computer screen. Several seconds later, NPIC staffers were treated to a rare and startling sight – the KH Gnome sprinting down the corridor to his supervisor's office in his stocking feet.

MARCH 2 – U.S. EMBASSY, BERLIN

'You want me to do what?' Stuart Vance stared down at the artist's sketch he'd just been handed. It showed what looked like a small, dilapidated fishing trawler from several different angles.

His boss, the CIA's chief of station in Berlin, said it again, slower this time. 'I want you to go looking for that trawler.'

'But why?' Vance saw the older man starting to glower and hastily rephrased his question. 'I mean, why this particular trawler?'

'Because the director thinks there's a good chance the people on board that boat were the ones who blew that LNG tanker to hell and gone.' The station chief held up his own copy of the sketch. 'Apparently it showed up on a satellite photo taken right after the explosion.'

Vance chewed on his lower lip and then shrugged, still puzzled. 'I guess I still don't see what the big deal is. What's so surprising about a fishing trawler steaming around the Baltic? There must be a thousand or so running around up there or out in the North Sea.'

'Maybe. But there are several very strange things about this one.' Berlin's chief of station started holding up fingers. 'First, Gdansk Bay is too polluted for fishing. Seems the old communist government never invested much in sewage treatment plants and the new guys don't have the money to build them. Second, that boat was spotted way out of the normal channel. Right up against the coast in real shallow water. Pretty stupid if you're just a law-abiding sailor on your way past Gdansk. But pretty smart if you're trying to avoid radar detection by mixing in with the coastal clutter.'

He stopped and held up a third finger. 'Third? Well, the third one's the charm in this case. The Poles say nobody, and I mean *nobody*, saw that trawler. It sailed in that night without lights and it left that night without lights.

'Now, I don't know what they taught you down at Yale Law School, Vance, but when I was learning how to add two and two to make four, that's what we'd have called suspicious behavior.'

Vance reddened. The chief of station was a Harvard man and it showed. 'Yeah, okay.' Then the tall, fair-haired CIA officer spread his hands helplessly. 'But those photos were taken more than ten days ago. That trawler could be almost anywhere by now!'

'Right.' The older man grinned unsympathetically. 'That's why every junior intelligence officer from here to Oslo is going to be very busy for the next couple of weeks or so.'

He walked over to the map pinned on his office wall. 'You, Mr. Vance, start at Heringsdorf.' He tapped a tiny dot near the Polish border. 'And work your way west toward Kiel.

'I want you to visit every town that's got so much as a single rotting wharf. Talk to the locals. Find out if any strangers bought or leased a boat like that recently. And if they did, see if you can dig up who they were or claimed to be.' The chief of station showed his teeth again. 'Technology can only take us so far, fella. Now we're down to pure, slogging legwork. In this case, using your legs.'

Great, Vance thought gloomily, join the CIA and get to see a dozen stinking German fishing villages. He folded the sketch in half and left, inwardly fuming at an assignment that seemed certain to be tedious, demeaning, and futile. He passed other young officers waiting outside the station chief's office for their own orders.

The lambs were going forth to stalk lions.

MARCH 4 – *WASHINGTON POST*

STRASBOURG, FRANCE – European foreign ministers meeting here stunned the world today by signing a series of sweeping agreements designed to produce a new, continent-wide alliance – the European Confederation. If ratified by the respective national governments, these treaties would establish a common currency, a single, multinational army, closer links between national police forces and judicial systems, and unified trade and foreign policies.

As a first step, France and Germany announced their own plans to fully integrate their armed forces, intelligence services, and police units. Other nations joining the confederation are expected to follow suit in the coming weeks . . .

CHAPTER 12
Threat Warning

MARCH 9 – HEADQUARTERS, 19TH PANZERGRENADIER BRIGADE, AHLEN, GERMANY

The first unmistakable signs of the new European order were already reaching Germany's armed forces – right on the heels of a fast-moving rainstorm.

A cool, damp breeze ruffled Lt. Col. Willi von Seelow's uniform coat as he stood waiting near the headquarters helipad. The brigade staff, a little knot of officers and senior noncoms, stood at ease around him, chatting softly as though worried that they might be overheard by their august visitor even before his arrival.

He shifted his weight, frowning slightly as he felt the ground give under his feet.

The brigade's parade ground stretched for several hundred meters to either side, still a little muddy from yesterday's rains. More mud-filled ruts had been 'plowed' by the 191st Panzergrenadier Battalion's tracked armored vehicles. Forty-two Marder APCs were lined up by companies and platoons, with two command tracks out front. Self-propelled 120mm mortars, trucks, and other 'soft-skinned' vehicles were drawn up in neat rows behind them. Bundled against the cold and fitted with full combat gear, the battalion's five hundred men and officers milled around their vehicles, waiting like the brigade staff.

Von Seelow was especially proud of the 191st. He'd served with the battalion as a company commander for several months after transferring over from the defunct East German Army. His old comrades had done well during the winter troubles. Despite being underpaid, outnumbered, and loathed by many of their fellow countrymen, they had kept the peace all winter long. Of course, several months spent enforcing the government's martial law decrees had eroded their 'conventional' combat skills, but at least these men were now battle-hardened. They had seen a few of their comrades die and many others injured. They were veterans.

He glanced at the officer standing beside him.

'You wait and see, Willi. A Frenchman commanding German troops. It will be a disaster.' Lt. Col. Otto Yorck shook his head. Only a little shorter than von Seelow, his bleached blond hair and faded blue eyes made him look more like a ski instructor than an army officer.

Von Seelow smiled. As CO of the 191st, Yorck had a reputation for straight talk, even when it might be more politic to keep silent. He had also been a ready friend in the brigade's hierarchy, one of the few fellow officers who didn't seem to care about Willi's eastern birth.

Privately, of course, he shared Yorck's feelings. Under the newly signed Articles of the European Confederation, the French and German armed forces were being joined at the hip, blended together to form a new multinational army. This new EurCon II Corps, for instance, would include not only the German 7th Panzer and 2nd Panzergrenadier divisions but also the French 5th Armored.

Close military cooperation between the two former NATO allies was nothing new. In just one example, German and French airborne divisions had worked together during annual *Colibri*, or Hummingbird, exercises since 1963. One combined Franco-German army corps already existed. Formed during the early 1990s, it had symbolized a 'European' approach to security issues. As a military unit, though, the corps had never been much more than an experimental unit.

What was happening now, though, was a very different and vastly more complex process. The two nations were trying to merge their military command, communications, intelligence, and logistics functions into a single seamless whole. And all in a matter of months. The language barrier alone was formidable, but there were also significant differences in operating procedures, even basic organizations. For example, at full wartime strength, the 7th Panzer Division could field more than three hundred Leopard 2 tanks, nearly two hundred Marder APCs, and seventeen thousand fighting men. Its closest French counterpart, the 5th Armored, was only a little over half that size.

But this new drive for unity was going forward, even at breakneck speed. Moreover, it was a curious merging. Most of the corps and higher joint commands were being given to French officers, some newly promoted for their billets. Even the new II Corps, with its two German divisions, now had a French commander.

There'd been a lot of grumbling against Schraeder and the rest of the German leadership. Many of the more conservative officers were complaining about being sold out by their own leadership. The idea of allying with the French, recent partners but longtime enemies, made Willi uneasy as well. The French certainly seemed to be well in charge.

Willi winced inside. His father, Col. Hans von Seelow, and his grandfather, the old general, were certainly spinning in their graves.

The radio on his belt crackled. 'Private Neumann to brigade. Helicopters in sight.' Even as he looked for Colonel Bremer and nodded, shouts rang out across the parade ground, '*Stand auf!*'

The once-quiet compound burst into activity. Equipment rattled and boots thudded into the soft, rain-soaked ground as the panzergrenadiers shook themselves into close formation.

Von Seelow acknowledged the transmission, then took his own place in line. Silence settled over the compound. Some men were shivering. The late winter wind had a sharper bite when you couldn't move to stay warm.

Their wait was mercifully short. Only moments after the brigade staff and the battalion took their places, a dark dot appeared just over the skyline, quickly growing into a clattering gray-green helicopter. It flew low overhead and then circled, sliding downward toward the marked landing area.

Even though the brigade staff stood a discreet distance away, Willi had to brace himself against the Puma's rotor blast.

The troop carrier settled heavily onto the helipad, kicking up a fine, cold gray mist. A descending whine matched the slowing rotor blades. When they stopped turning, the Puma's door slid to one side, and Général de Corps d'Armée Etienne Montagne alighted.

As Montagne's foot touched the ground, shouts of '*Achtung!*' echoed across the parade ground. Out of the corner of his eye, von Seelow watched the 191st snap to attention.

He studied the new corps commander. Montagne was tall, so tall that he had to crouch to get out of the helicopter. Once on the ground, he carried himself carefully erect, ramrod-straight. In his late fifties, his hair was almost completely gray, with just a few streaks of brown poking out from under his service kepi.

Seeing the general's distinctive headgear sent a strange feeling through von Seelow. The French kepi was an almost perfect flat-topped cylinder, about six inches high, with a small straight visor. In Montagne's case it was dark blue, generously decorated with two gold rings of oak leaves, his four-star rank in a wreath on the front, and a red stripe around the crown. In various forms, it had been worn by the Army of France for a hundred years. Nothing else was so distinctly French.

Another officer stepped down, not as tall and much darker. Willi recognized Gen. Alfred Wismar, a German and another tanker. Assigned as deputy commander for the new II Corps, Wismar did not look particularly happy with his new assignment. Gen. Karl Leibnitz, commanding officer of the 7th Panzer Division, trailed along behind his two superiors.

Colonel Bremer braced and saluted the group. The two German generals hung back while Montagne cheerfully returned Bremer's salute.

The two chatted briefly, in passable German, Willi noted, before Bremer guided the tall Frenchman down the line of brigade staff officers. Greeting each one warmly, the corps commander seemed careful to pronounce each man's name properly.

It was his turn. The Frenchman had a firm handshake and his dark brown eyes seemed as friendly as his manner. Von Seelow let himself feel a little more optimistic. Maybe this won't be such a disaster, after all, he thought.

With the senior officers following and a burly-looking German sergeant taking notes, Montagne moved on to conduct a quick, perfunctory inspection of the 191st. The general strode confidently, almost arrogantly, past the assembled battalion, stopping only occasionally to exchange a few words with one of the officers or for a closer look at the soldiers or their gear.

Von Seelow's first favorable impression faded slightly as he watched the French general examine a panzergrenadier's weapon. The G3A3 assault rifle was older, longer, and heavier than the ultramodern MAS rifle used by French forces. Everyone in the Bundeswehr knew it was outdated, but budget cuts in the early 1990s had slowed production of the army's high-tech replacement, the Heckler Koch G11. Even so, the G3 was still a rugged, reliable firearm, perfectly capable in the hands of a well-trained soldier. So there seemed little justification for Montagne's contemptuous glance when he tossed the rifle back to the blank-faced grenadier. Or for a later comment that some of their Marder personnel carriers seemed 'a little long in the tooth.' Considering that the comparable French APC, the AMX-10P, was almost as old, the remark seemed unnecessarily snide.

His inspection apparently over, Montagne marched back to a small raised platform and microphone near his grounded helicopter – trailed by a frowning group of German officers.

'Soldiers of the 19th Panzergrenadier Brigade, I greet you! Today marks an historic moment, a moment of glory for all Europe! For France! And for Germany!'

Von Seelow stirred uneasily. The general's words were spoken in accented German, but the underlying posturing seemed all too French. With old customs and forms tainted by Nazism's absurd melodrama, the Bundeswehr cultivated a deliberately low-key professionalism.

'I look forward with great eagerness to the coming years. You and the other men of this division show great promise. And I am sure that, with hard training and constant devotion to duty, you will all become fine troops – soldiers for the future.'

From his position behind the Frenchman, Willi could see the carefully concealed resentment rippling through the ranks. He felt it himself. Who did this general think he was dealing with? These men were seasoned volunteers, not callow conscripts.

'In the coming months, my staff and I will institute a series of refinements to your tactical doctrines. New thinking is always hard, but I promise you that the advantages of these reforms will be readily apparent to each and every one of you – even to the lowliest private! And with these new tactics will come greatly increased fighting efficiency and combat power.'

No wonder Wismar looks unhappy, Willi thought. We are schoolmasters being taken to task by the students. As if the French could teach Germans anything about armor doctrine . . . My God, Rommel himself had once commanded the 7th Panzer!

Von Seelow's unspoken concerns crystallized into certain dismay while Montagne thundered on about the bright future waiting for the combined Franco-German armed forces. Otto Yorck was right. This man was a disaster. The kicker came when the French general spoke about what he termed 'simple administrative matters.' His language, so falsely dramatic before, suddenly turned vague and bureaucratic.

'Naturally, new force structures and new defense commitments require new dispositions. Accordingly, the Confederation's Council of Nations has approved the redeployment of certain units. Including this one.

When our II Corps becomes fully operational early next month, it will begin assuming key defense responsibilities for the region around Cottbus.

'To prepare for that, the 7th Panzer Division will send advance parties to that area next week. Your division's leading elements will transfer during the last half of this month. I expect this entire corps to be at its new posts within six months.'

Willi was thunderstruck. Redeploy three divisions all the way to the other side of Germany in six months? Certainly it was possible to march units further in just a fraction of that time, but this was a permanent move. Ammo dumps, fuel depots, and spare-parts stockpiles would all have to be packed up, shipped, and then unloaded by the corps's supply troops. Several thousand armored vehicles would need special maintenance support. And nearly fifty thousand soldiers and their families would have to find barracks and housing in and around the eastern German town. Better than most, he remembered what those old Soviet-built facilities were like. Bad when they were built, they must be almost unlivable now. The men were going to need careful handling. Who was . . .

Von Seelow suddenly noticed that both Leibnitz and Bremer looked as stunned as he did. Was this a total surprise to everyone? He studied Wismar's face. Montagne must have told his deputy, but the German general looked even unhappier.

And why move them in the first place? The Bundeswehr only had three corps in its entire army. Stretched thinly, I Corps, the 7th Panzer's present parent organization, was responsible for maintaining order over much of central and western Germany. Now, less than a week after this new European Confederation took shape, its leaders were apparently planning to cram almost the same firepower into a single narrow sector on the Polish border.

Von Seelow had seen the news reports of rising unrest inside Poland as oil supplies ran short. But that hardly seemed a justification for this massive troop transfer. The Poles weren't a military threat. Nor were there any signs that the Russians were emerging from their self-imposed cycle of martial law and military purges.

He shook his head slowly. Whatever was going on, it didn't look good.

MARCH 13 – 11th FIGHTER REGIMENT OPERATIONS CENTER, WROCLAW, POLAND

First Lt. Tadeusz Wojcik noticed the change as soon as he walked inside out of the damp, chilly morning. An air of quiet concern and steady purpose filled the regimental operations building.

The long concrete building was the nerve center for the 11th's three fighter squadrons. Not only were the regiment's administrative offices here, but downstairs in the specially hardened basement, radio and radar operators managed a slice of Polish airspace stretching from the Czech republic in the south to the border with Germany in the west. The camouflaged headquarters bunkers and buildings housing the 3rd

National Air Defense Corps were right across the airfield. Responsible for all of southwestern Poland, the 3rd's staff officers and senior commanders controlled the 11th Fighter Regiment, several other aircraft units, and a mixed bag of missile units – some using American-made anti-aircraft missiles, others still equipped with old Soviet-manufactured SA-2 and SA-3 missiles.

Normally the ops center was a cheerful, busy place. Today everyone's expression was grim. Tad stopped the first pilot he saw, Lt. Stanislaw Gawlik. The thin, hawk-nosed pilot looked worried.

'Stan, what's wrong? Somebody have an incident?' Nobody used the word 'crash,' as if avoiding the word could avoid the actual event.

Gawlik shook his head. 'No. Take a look at the intel board. More Confederation units are moving into eastern Germany. Ground forces, aircraft, the works. The French and Germans claim it's just part of a routine "redeployment." '

Wojcik half grinned. 'Yeah, right. That's so absurd it's insulting. It's all pressure to get us to knuckle under.'

The other lieutenant shook his head decisively. 'Never. Look at what they've done to Hungary and Romania and the others. Economic colonies, with their people working in foreign-owned factories for pitiful wages. Puppet governments, secret police. We were under the Soviet boot too long to want someone else's foot on our necks.' There was a grim light in his eyes when he spoke about the Russians.

Gawlik's worried look returned as he continued. 'First this damned oil embargo and now these troop movements. It's like we're being hemmed in on all sides. The government's already protested, and the President and Prime Minister are both going to speak on television tonight. But I don't see what else we can do. Any chance we're getting more aid from the Americans? Or from Britain? Have you heard anything?'

Everyone assumed that Tad's American birth somehow gave him an inside track on developments in the West.

He shrugged. 'Nothing new. Not that I've heard about anyway.'

Tad wasn't really sure what more Poland's two faraway allies could do. Protected by USN and Royal Navy warships, their tankers were already pumping oil and gas ashore as fast as they could. Beyond that, several dozen weapons experts and training teams were already busy helping his country's armed forces make the difficult transition away from old-style Soviet equipment and tactics. Short of actually stationing U.S. troops on Polish soil, there weren't many other options open.

Gawlik seemed briefly disappointed, but he rallied fast. 'Better check the board. You're flying today. In fact, most of us are.'

The older man glanced at his watch. 'I'll be up in an hour. Good luck.' The lieutenant put real meaning into the trite expression.

The assignments board told the story. Pairs of F-15 Eagles were flying along the border on a twenty-four hour basis. A map showed the new patrol zones. The 11th's area of responsibility was a two-hundred-kilometer section of the frontier, running from Kostryzn south to the southwest corner of Poland.

Tad noticed with interest that the border patrol track ran right next to the frontier, not back a few dozen kilometers as standard tactics and peacetime procedures might suggest. Any turn west would put them in German territory. The lack of maneuvering room meant this was a 'fence' exercise, intended to tell these German and French bastards that the Polish Air Force was ready to block any movement into its territory.

Wojcik smiled at his own eagerness to climb inside the cockpit. With money and aviation fuel so tight, he'd only been able to fly once every two or three days. Now he'd fly at least daily, and with the German border right in his face. In an odd sort of way, things were looking up at the same time they were looking down.

Tad hooked up with his wingman, Lt. Sylwester Zawadzki after lunch. After a routine physical check, they both collected their maps and charts and then walked briskly down the hall to the regiment's ready room.

Pilots and a full complement of staff officers packed the ready room – sitting in battered wooden chairs facing a map-filled wall or standing along the other walls. The regiment's operations, intelligence, and meteorology officers sat off to one side, each waiting his turn to give a quick briefing. Even the 11th's short, cherub-faced commander was there, standing with a knot of pilots just back from a mission.

Colonel Kadlubowski spotted them in the doorway and motioned them over. He looked tired, and Zawadzki whispered that the colonel had already flown two missions that morning himself.

'You boys are up next?'

'Yes, sir.'

The colonel clapped Tad on the shoulder and nodded toward Zawadzki. 'Be careful up there, gentlemen. There's a lot of activity on the western side of the border. Don't start a war, but,' and his voice grew hard, 'don't give them an inch of our airspace.'

'Yes, sir.'

As the colonel turned away, the 11th's operations officer took his place, flanked by two strangers. The two Eagle pilots introduced themselves to a major and captain who were the pilot and copilot of a 'special electronics' An-26. Wojcik noticed that their flight suits did not have name tags, or any unit insignia. The two men were friendly enough, but their monosyllabic answers soon got the message across: 'Don't ask questions, because we won't answer them.'

The nameless major was their mission commander, and would fly his aircraft as required. The two Eagles were going along to make sure he wasn't bothered.

The operations officer gave them the correct radio frequencies, call signs, and other routine information. Their CAP station was Yellow Station, and they were Yellow Five and Six. They were set to relieve Yellow Seven and Eight. If they needed to communicate with the Curl, it was 'Black flight.'

All the intelligence officer would say was that there had been sightings of German aircraft very close to the border. 'Expect them to pay attention to you.'

He also emphasized the correct setting for their IFF equipment.

Polish-manned Patriot and Hawk SAM batteries were now deploying along the nation's frontiers almost as fast as they could be unloaded, and surface-to-air missiles travel too fast to allow time for explanations.

Tad and Zawadzki left the ops building with the major and his copilot and walked to the flight line, just a short distance away. The Curl was parked close by, so the two Eagle drivers stopped for a moment to look over the elderly 'bus.'

Painted in drab green and brown colors, the twin-engine, turboprop transport plane had long, straight wings and a tall tail. It normally carried forty paratroops or a six-ton cargo load, but the cargo compartment on this one was filled with electronic equipment and seats for operators. Odd-shaped dielectric patches covered its surface. A long metal 'canoe' ran half the length of the plane's belly, and even its nose looked subtly different. Some of the gray insulation patches looked recent, and Tad suspected that some of America's latest military aid shipments had included Western electronics upgrades for these 'ferret' aircraft.

Their two companions headed for the top-secret plane without saying another word. Tad and his wingman exchanged a quick grin at that. Habits of perpetual silence must be hard to break. The two Eagle drivers trotted over to their F-15s.

They taxied to the end of the thousand-meter concrete strip, the Curl leading.

It was a cold, gusty day, with scattered low clouds a few thousand meters high. Drenched by the remnants of an overnight storm, the runway was still wet in spots. A hexagonal pattern stood out clearly on the damp concrete, showing the joints between the massive blocks making up the Russian-style runway. They were laid so that if the surface was cratered by enemy air attacks, any damaged sections could be quickly lifted out and replaced by spares. Of course, all those joints made for a rough ride on takeoff and landing.

The An-26 turned onto the runway and stopped, its brakes set. Its engines increased their pitch, shaking the wings at full power. After a few moments, even the fuselage started to vibrate, and the Curl's pilot released his brakes. Rolling forward, the big turboprop thundered down the long concrete strip, quickly gathering speed. It soared aloft with half the runway left.

Even fully loaded with fuel and missiles, the two Eagles used less runway than their larger, slower companion. Tad's airspeed rose quickly once contact with the earth was broken.

There beneath him was the An-26, its brown and green camouflage blending with the drab gray-brown landscape below. The lumbering plane cruised at half the normal speed of its two nimbler companions, no more than 240 knots or so. Chopping his throttle almost to idle, Tad extended his Eagle's flaps and tried to think slow thoughts.

The flight from Wroclaw to the border took about twenty minutes, with Wojcik and Zawadzki scissoring and circling over the ferret plane, trying to keep it and each other in sight.

Tad tried to sort out the mass of information blanketing his cockpit display. Right now his RWR was tuned to receive only fire control and weapons radars, immediate threats to an Eagle in flight. Even so, there were so many signals showing that he was sure some of them must be coming from other airborne friendlies. No such luck. All the bearings and identifications flickering across his scope matched hostile radars.

Christ, he thought, there were so many sets sweeping the sky through this sector, you could almost get out and walk on the radio waves. Great. The Germans had to know right where he and Zawadzki were.

He broke radio silence. 'Yellow patrol, this is Yellow Five.'

'Roger, we hold you at fifty kilometers one two five.' Tad recognized Lieutenant Gawlik's voice. The two Eagles now on patrol were thirty miles off to the northwest.

It was time to turn on his own radar. Turning to face the other F-15s, he hit the radar mode button, changing it from standby to air. Instantly the screen lit up, showing two small dots, both with symbols showing them to have friendly IFF. As the APG-70 locked onto the nearest friendly, his HUD displayed a small lit box showing its position in the sky in front of him, even though the Polish plane was still too far away to see. A straight line ending in the box gave Tad the correct intercept course, while figures glowing on his radar screen showed him the other F-15's course, speed, altitude, and closing velocity. Normally used to help close on and kill enemy aircraft, the data also made rendezvous and CAP relief almost child's play.

Glancing down at the radar screen also let him check the RWR display again. There were even more radars showing now. So far, though, they were limited to radars tracking him. None were locked onto him, and the ominous launch warning light was still dark.

Climbing, Tad burst through fragments of low clouds and emerged into a pale blue, sunlit sky. 'Yellow Seven, closing on your position.'

The range dropped to six kilometers before he spotted a gray dot in the center of the cueing box on his HUD. The F-15 was a large plane. A smaller fighter like a Fulcrum might not be seen until it was even closer. Even so, Tad had needed the box to know where to look. At first glance he wasn't even sure it was real, so he continued his regular scan: instruments, HUD, far left, craning his neck to look behind him, and then carefully working his way around to far right.

On his next glance the dot was a distinctive twin-tailed shape. 'Tally.' Contact in sight.

Yellow Seven, Lieutenant Gawlik's plane, was heading north, away from him, loafing along at 250 knots. Yellow Eight, Gawlik's wingman, flew a little to the right and below him.

Moving the stick gently, Wojcik eased the Eagle's nose down just as he came level with the two patrolling F-15s. 'Yellow Five is in position.'

The pair of Eagles in front quickly turned, changing in appearance from rear to side views for half a second before they flashed by to the right, diving and heading east.

The An-26 following in Tad's wake still hadn't made a transmission, but it didn't need to. It simply took up position at the highest altitude comfortable for its turboprop engines, about eight thousand meters. As they flew parallel to the border, the Curl would stay near the center of the

Eagles' crisscrossing racetrack pattern, at a slightly lower altitude.

The plane was there to listen to radar, radio, and even microwave relay signals. By analyzing them, the Curl's intelligence specialists could identify radar types, locations, and capabilities. A good operator could even tell when a radar set had received new parts. And radio and microwave relay intercepts could help pinpoint the new Confederation ground and air units shifting closer to the border.

At this altitude, the Neisse River seemed to be directly below him, but as long as he checked the nav display frequently, he could stay on his own side of the line.

The landscape on either side of the river was identical. Through the scattered gray clouds below him, he could see isolated patches of woods dotting smooth, flat terrain. This was farming country. From this high up, only major highways and cities were easily visible in the fuzzy patchwork of browns, yellows, and greens.

It took about forty-five minutes to make a complete circuit on the racetrack and return to their starting point. After only twenty minutes, Tad knew that the major and his crew were very busy people. His radar warning receiver was still alive with symbols, appearing and disappearing almost at random. If there was a pattern there, he couldn't see it.

They turned the corner, heading south. The Curl, slower, was still north-bound, about two thousand meters below them and thirty kilometers to the south.

The major's voice interrupted Tad's scan of the horizon. 'Yellow flight! We have a fire control radar, strength eight, and getting stronger! Bearing two eight zero.'

Tad looked down at his radar scope. In his blind spot, damn it!

'Syl, swing wide, now!' He turned his own plane's nose to the west. The radar scanner could only train sixty degrees to either side of dead ahead. Luckily he could see the radar on his warning receiver, labeled 'UNK' next to it. That meant the signal's characteristics did not match anything in the receiver's library of known transmitters.

This close to the border, Tad had very little maneuvering room to the west. He was really counting on Zawadzki, who was heading east to get some elbowroom, to back him up. Tad's low speed gave him a fairly tight turning radius, so he planned to make a tight circle, lock up the bogey, and classify it as a threat or benign. By that time his wingman should be in position, far enough back, if they had to shoot.

His hands moved rapidly, dropping the range scale on the radar. This fellow had popped up suddenly, with enough signal strength to make him real close. His F-15's nose was turning, swinging right. Why hadn't they spotted the bogey on their northbound leg?

There. The signal should be within his radar scanner's arc. He checked the screen but saw nothing. He waited two more sweeps, and the screen was still blank. All right, Tad thought. He changed the range scale. Still nothing. As if to confirm that whatever the problem was, it wasn't just his radar, Zawadzki radioed, 'Negative lock, Seven.'

Tad clicked twice in acknowledgment, almost absentmindedly.

'Yellow flight. Signal strength is nine. Signal has shifted to high PRF.'

The major's voice sounded calmer, but his initial surprise had been replaced by clear concern. The hostile radar had changed to ranging mode, which could be a precursor to launching an air-to-air missile.

'Turning east.' The major was taking his ELINT plane deeper into Polish territory, probably diving and firewalling his throttles, too. But the Curl was too big and slow for agile maneuvering. It would be some time before they were out of danger.

Tad still had nothing. Shit. He needed help from the An-26. 'Black, Yellow Seven. Interrogative elevation.'

'Target is slightly down, Seven, steady azimuth, two seven five.'

Rolling his aircraft inverted, Tad yanked back hard on the stick. Throttling back even more, he popped his speed brakes as well. The energy-wasting maneuvers went against his grain, but he didn't need speed, he just wanted to dump some altitude.

Tad watched his altimeter unwind, at the same time keeping an eye on the horizon and the warning receiver and its mysterious signal. He knew exactly where to look. Almost due west. Eight thousand meters, seven, six . . .

A small gray dot rose from the landscape, silhouetted as it crossed the horizon line. The bogey was now slightly higher than his F-15, and easier to spot against the lighter sky. In a heartbeat it swelled from a dot to a shape, and then into a jet fighter, suddenly turning from a head-on to a side view as it banked sharply to the south, paralleling his course.

'Tallyho your signal, Black. Source is a fighter.' Tad fought a near-overwhelming urge to break hard left into the bogey. Instincts ingrained by long, hard air combat training ran deep.

'Roger, Seven, confirm lock.'

Tad clicked his microphone switch twice, all the time watching the bogey. He couldn't type it. The other plane was still at least five or six kilometers away.

What he could see was a raked vertical fin and what appeared to be a delta wing, without any horizontal tail surfaces. It looked like a French Mirage of some sort, but he just could not make a precise identification.

Holding the stick with his right hand, he reached down with his left and opened a compartment containing a pair of light 7 × 35 binoculars. They were useless in a dogfight, but against aircraft flying straight and level, they gave him a set of long-range eyes.

Tad checked his course and position one more time before raising the binoculars to scan the narrow sector holding the stranger. He caught a glimpse of its nose, overcompensated back, and then steadied his view on the strange plane.

Obligingly the other pilot kept his craft straight and level, pacing Tad's Eagle. The bogey's nose was sharply pointed, and he could see a set of small fins, called canards, high on the fuselage, just behind and under the canopy. Instead of side-mounted intakes like a French Mirage, its intakes were smaller, and half under the fuselage.

There was only one fighter with that configuration: the Rafale. Tad whistled softly to himself. None of the intelligence briefings had warned him about this.

Every fighter pilot knew about the Rafale, although few had seen them. Now here he was flying side by side with one painted in shades of gray and carrying what looked like live missiles under its wings. That was a tricolor roundel on its fuselage, not the Maltese cross, so it was a French aircraft. Tad was a little disappointed. He would rather face a German opponent.

The Rafale shadowing him was brand-new, which made it sexy, and in foreign hands, which made it dangerous. The plane also had a reduced radar cross section, which explained how it had popped up so unexpectedly and unnervingly. Reports said it could engage several targets simultaneously with launch-and-leave air-to-air missiles. The French-made warplane was also supposed to be very maneuverable, more than a match for either the Eagle or the Fulcrum. Again, Tad fought the urge to yank his stick over, to maneuver and pit his machine against this potential enemy.

He beat back the urge and then thought again. By roaring right up to the frontier and radar-pinging the hell out of the An-26, this bastard had already shown that he wanted to screw around. Why not indulge him?

Tad pressed his mike switch. 'Yellow Eight, this is Seven. Cover Black flight. I am maneuvering.'

'Let's see what this bastard is made of,' Tad muttered to himself. He stowed the binoculars, then settled himself in his seat, tightening his harness.

As quickly as he could, he chopped the throttles to idle and popped his speed brake. He waited a beat for his plane to slow. As soon as he saw the Rafale start to slide ahead, he yo-yoed the F-15's nose up and down sharply, killing even more speed. At the same time, he slewed one of the Sidewinder seekers to the right as far as it would go.

Turning to the west as far as he could dare, he kept one eye on the nav display while waiting for a tone from the Sidewinder's infrared seeker. Letting the Rafale pull ahead allowed his missile to see its tailpipe, setting up a missile launch. Tad grinned. He wouldn't fire, of course, but the other pilot would know that he had been set up.

He watched the Rafale as it came into view through his HUD. The Frenchman was reacting now, pulling his nose up. Too late. The enemy fighter was at his Eagle's one o'clock, well within its missile arc. So where was the tone? Nothing, just a hissing noise in his headphones.

Wojcik swung the F-15's nose a bit more to the right, still waiting for the familiar sound. A bad missile? Quickly he selected another Sidewinder. Still nothing. Son-of-a-bitch. The Rafale's engines must be shielded, reducing its IR signature.

His nav display showed him crowding the border a little too closely. Damn. This was getting tricky. He turned back east a bit, opening the distance between the two planes.

The Rafale's nose was climbing smoothly. Tad expected a loop, but instead of gaining altitude, the French fighter flew forward straight and level while its nose rose past the vertical and actually tipped backward.

It was the 'cobra' maneuver, invented by the Russians, and it was the first time Tad had ever seen a plane do it in a maneuvering situation. Not only did it look odd, but it was effective. The Rafale was dumping speed in a hurry.

Tad saw his opponent quickly slide back, first even with his Eagle, then behind him. When the other fighter reached his five o'clock, its nose tipped forward as smoothly as if the Rafale were mounted on a pivot. Now its own nose turned slightly toward him.

The other pilot was setting up his own heat-seeking missile shot. And the Eagle's engines weren't IR-suppressed like the Rafale's. If he didn't get out of this, he'd be the grape who got peeled, not the Frenchman. Yanking back hard on the stick, Tad pulled his Eagle into a smooth loop. The horizon disappeared, instantly replaced by an elevation ladder on the HUD showing his altitude and pitch angle.

Tad concentrated on keeping the F-15's nose parallel with the imaginary border. With so many hostile eyes and radars watching, crossing over into German airspace, even accidentally, was unthinkable. His superiors would be interested in his report about the Rafale and its capabilities, but only if he didn't screw up and create an international incident.

He neared the top of the loop, a thousand meters higher than when he started, pointed north. Now where was that Frenchman?

He scanned the landscape below and to the west, forcing himself to ignore the upside-down world and the fact that he was hanging in his seat. There was no sign of motion, no wing flashes below him. He widened his search, looking above the horizon.

There. The bastard was abreast of him now, also inverted and heading north. The other pilot must have waited a second and then followed him into a parallel loop on his side of the border. Good stick, Tad thought.

At least he'd broken the Rafale's missile lock. Flying side by side like this meant neither of them would be in position to get a shot off when this maneuver ended.

Both planes were now on the downward leg of the loop. Tad was planning his next move, all the while monitoring his own plane's status and his opponent's position. Suddenly, out of the corner of his eye, he spotted the Rafale's nose moving, not changing in pitch, but swinging sharply over in his direction!

It turned a full forty-five degrees off its original heading, pointing straight at his F-15. Was this guy crazy? He'd be over the border in seconds at these speeds. Wojcik braced himself, certain that the Frenchman now intended to enter Polish airspace, which meant what? A personal grudge? A test of the border defenses? War?

He jammed the throttles forward, pulling out of the loop early. G-forces pushed him down in his seat. For an instant the corners of the cockpit grayed out as his HUD's g-meter showed over five gravities of acceleration.

He glanced to the right, over at the bogey, ready to break into him with a quick Sidewinder or cannon shot, but the Rafale's position was all wrong. Instead of coming closer, the French fighter was still distant, still moving south, and still on its own side of the border. Even worse, the enemy jet still had its nose pointed at him! Those canard fins really worked!

Tad knew when he was licked. Any plane that could fly in one direction while keeping its nose pointed in another was going to take some careful thought and planning to beat.

Turning south, he ignored the hostile fighter and concentrated on restoring his CAP racetrack position. The Rafale wasn't out to get him. If the Frenchman had wanted to nail him, he could have done it when he first popped up, or twice since then.

Unsure of how well he could actually protect the An-26, he called the major and recommended a new position well inside Polish airspace. That would significantly reduce the ferret plane's effectiveness but it was the only sure way to keep it safe.

Wojcik knew the Frenchman was laughing his ass off. He could feel a burning lump in his chest. No fighter pilot likes to lose, even in a mock dogfight. That clown would be bragging for a week about the Eagle driver he foxed, and there wasn't a damn thing he could do about it.

He tried to concentrate on flying his fighter and watching the radar screen, futile though that might now be. He had a lot to think about, but most of it would have to wait until he landed and debriefed Two questions wouldn't leave him alone, though: how did you beat a Rafale, and how many of the damn things did EurCon have?

MINISTRY OF THE INTERIOR, BUDAPEST, HUNGARY

Reading the newspaper was like hearing about the death of a friend.

'Hungary Joins the European Confederation!' it trumpeted in a bold, banner headline. Sick at heart, Col. Zoltan Hradetsky read the state-controlled paper thoroughly, forcing himself to learn all he could.

Articles on page after page were filled with glowing praise for the new political, economic, and military union. According to official opinion, the only kind permitted, joining the Confederation would bring abundance, employment, and no loss of Hungarian sovereignty or liberties. It was the best of both worlds, close cooperation between neighbors toward a brighter future . . .

Hradetsky threw the paper down in disgust. He'd already seen the results of close cooperation with the French and Germans. It was strictly a one-way street. Those idiots in the National Salvation Government had to know what they were doing. But did they have any real choice? In the carefully structured agreements already in force, Hungary's debt to France and Germany was growing. Like miners in a company store, his country could never seem to get clear.

An office messenger came by, scowling as he dropped off a memo on Hradetsky's desk. The young police corporal sniffed contemptuously at him and left without a word. Evidently, disgraced colonels were considered fair game by the rank and file. One more sign of my own weakness, he thought wearily. In the not-so-distant past, that self-important young pup wouldn't have left his office with either his stripes or an unbroken nose.

More out of boredom than interest, he skimmed through the memo.

> As part of the integration of Hungary into the European Confederation, Special Commissioner Werner Rehling, formerly of the German Federal Office for the Protection of the Constitution (BfV), will be arriving tomorrow, to serve as a liaison between our National Police and the EurCon Interior Secretariat. He will be directly responsible for any matters not strictly national. I am sure you will all welcome him to the force.

It was signed by the National Police commander, Brigadier General Dozsa. An attached sheet showed a new organizational diagram. Rehling and Dozsa occupied identical boxes at the top of the page. Every other line on the chart ran upward toward these two, joined, then split into two lines. One said 'local' and led to Dozsa. The second line was labeled 'all others' and went to Rehling.

Hradetsky stared down at the memo in shock. This was worse than before! Instead of simply interfering in Hungarian affairs, the French and Germans were installing a duplicate chain of command. More ominous still, this Rehling wasn't even a real policeman. The BfV was Germany's state security service.

His country had been conquered, sold for bread and jobs.

MARCH 16

Rehling's arrival had done nothing to soothe Hradetsky's growing fears. If anything, it brought them closer to the surface.

The Hungarian frowned, remembering his first glimpse of the new EurCon 'liaison' at a special ceremony three days earlier. The German was a colorless man, with close-cropped gray hair and a bland, round face. He seemed unimpressed by everything and everyone around him, including Dozsa and the other ministry officials there to welcome him. Their tide of effusive speeches had washed right over the German security service officer and left him unmoved and unsmiling.

Hradetsky's stomach tightened when he thought back over the scene. Despite Rehling's cold, contemptuous manner, Dozsa and the rest had still crowded around him. Like all good lackeys, they were ready to lick any master's boots in the hope that he might toss a few crumbs their way. He grimaced. Their opportunity was his purgatory.

He'd had to spend the rest of that morning down at the police pistol range, squeezing rounds into anonymous targets just to regain a semblance of control.

Today, still torn by what he was seeing, he'd wandered upstairs from his windowless cubbyhole for a short visit with Bela Silvanus, one of his few remaining friends inside the ministry.

An unashamed bureaucrat, Silvanus smoked incessantly and looked older than his years. The two men had gone through the police academy together, but their different temperaments had led one to the streets, the other to a desk.

With their careers running on different, though parallel courses, they had bumped into each other from time to time, but never frequently – at least not until recently. Although they had never been particularly close, at least the bureaucrat wasn't afraid to talk to him. Hradetsky occasionally tried to get the administrator out from behind his desk and into the gym or the pistol range, but right now he just wanted to blow off some pent-up steam.

Silvanus had an office on the ministry's top floor – one that was well appointed, especially for austere times like these. It wasn't luxurious, because luxury bred resentment. The administrator believed in making friends, not enemies. Instead, the room was neat, with freshly painted walls and a good carpet. His office equipment was new, including a very impressive-looking computer. Prints and photos on each wall and rich wood furniture gave the room the look of a private, comfortable den. Visitors invariably came away with an impression of efficiency and quiet, unobtrusive personal power. In fact, the office had only one flaw – the constant, acrid reek of cigarette smoke.

Silvanus was hunched over a computer keyboard, a cigarette dangling from his mouth, swearing, when Hradetsky knocked on the doorjamb. The small, pudgy man turned, his scowl changing to a smile when he saw who his visitor was. 'Zoltan! Come in and have a seat. It's good to see someone I can complain to.'

Smiling almost against his will, Hradetsky eased himself into a well-upholstered leather chair. 'Everything screwed up as usual, Bela?'

The little bureaucrat threw his hands up in the air, almost knocking over an ashtray in the process. 'No, not like usual, ten times the usual!' He leaned forward, looking Hradetsky in the eye. 'Today, my friend, I wish I was on the streets, chasing thugs and robbers and all the other wonderful people a policeman meets.'

Suddenly all the anger seemed to flow out of him, like air leaving a balloon. His expression softened to one of sadness. 'I like my job, Zoltan. I'm good at it. I made the system work, first under the communists, then under this National Salvation Government. I know where the bodies are buried, which wheels turn and which ones just spin, and I've done well for myself.'

Curious, Hradetsky waited. Silvanus was a cheerfully contentious individual, an able and powerful administrator. He had excelled in making connections, storing up favors. He'd survived three separate changes of governments and won promotion each time. He was well liked, by those who hadn't tried to cross him anyway. So what could be bothering him?

'I can talk to you about this, Zoltan, no one else. Everyone else around here is wearing a happy mask, afraid of losing their ration book.' The bureaucrat paused and sighed. 'I am, too.' He motioned toward the door. Hradetsky quietly pushed it closed.

Once the latch snicked shut, Silvanus took a deep drag on his cigarette before going on. 'This German, Rehling, is starting to give orders. Troubling orders.

'Not only are all cases involving foreigners being routed to his office, he's also making major personnel shifts. Our police and plainclothes detectives are being pulled from other cases to protect French or German executives and businesses. Here in Budapest, for example, almost half our people are being assigned to look for what are being called "subversive elements" in the work force.'

'My God!' Hradetsky didn't hide his surprise. Shut away down in the training command, he hadn't heard about any of this. 'That's crazy!'

'It gets worse. The budget is being altered, too.' Silvanus screwed up his face and adopted a mock German accent. 'Never mind the regulations! Never mind efficiency! Take money away from enforcement and operations! Push it into little holes labeled "Intelligence" and "Security." ' Nodding toward his friend, he said, 'Even the training allocations are being cut back. Pretty soon you'll have fewer cadets to count.'

'How much of a cut?' Hradetsky asked.

Silvanus waved his hand in the air. 'Ah, what does it matter how much? What matters is that more criminals will go free because some German industrialist wants to know how many of our people hate him.'

Hradetsky frowned. 'But none of this makes any sense. Why put so much extra effort into looking for so-called subversives? Since the Sopron raid there's been no major terrorist action against foreign interests. Is some new group targeting them?'

Silvanus shook his head. 'I haven't heard anything.' A small smile crept onto his face. 'And you can bet, my friend, that if I haven't heard about it, it hasn't happened.'

He continued, 'One more thing, Zoltan.' He leaned forward conspiratorially. 'There are going to be some personnel cutbacks. A real shake-up.'

'How do you know?' Hradetsky felt suddenly cold. He was the deadest of deadwood. And where could an out-of-work police colonel get a job?

'Because the printshop just got a rush order for a batch of end-of-service forms. We had a year's supply.'

'And I suppose you already know who they're going to dismiss.'

Silvanus nodded calmly and handed him several sheets off his desk. 'I have a list. Don't ask me where it came from. Don't worry. Your name isn't on it.'

That was strange. His face must have shown his mixed relief and confusion, because the other man shrugged. 'Don't ask me why. Maybe they still want you where they can keep track of you, eh?'

Hradetsky snorted. If they were afraid of him, Dozsa and the other ministry monkey masters certainly didn't show any sign of it. Probably they'd simply forgotten he'd ever existed.

He took the list and paged through it. Names he knew kept popping out at him. Emil Kornai, in homicide. Imre Zarek, in fraud. Was there a pattern? Not that he could see, but he knew that many of these men were damned fine policemen. If he wasn't on this hit list, what the hell were they using as a criterion?

Silvanus saw the question on his face. 'I don't know how those names were picked, either, except that the order will be signed by Rehling, not Dozsa, and that there are a lot of good people on that list.' A touch of anger crept into his voice.

There were two raps on the door, and it opened. A thin, blond man with an angular face leaned in, saw Hradetsky in the office with Silvanus, and said in accented Hungarian, 'Excuse me, please. I will come back later.'

The door closed behind him.

Hradetsky raised an eyebrow. He nodded toward the door. 'A German?'

Silvanus nodded. 'One of Rehling's people, one of his spies. But he won't be back. He probably just wanted to see who I was talking to.'

'I'm getting you in trouble, Bela. I'd better leave.'

Silvanus waved his hand airily. 'Don't worry about it. The special commissioner and I have already crossed swords. He can't touch me. Not yet anyway. He knows he needs me to keep this place running.'

But Hradetsky could hear the uncertainty in the other man's voice. He didn't know which worried him more: the sudden, radical changes the EurCon appointee was making or the fact that even Silvanus – Silvanus the Survivor, people called him – was growing fearful.

Something had to be done. And fast. This new Confederation was like a cancer cell growing inside Hungary. The time to deal with it was now – before it spread too far for simple treatment and required radical surgery.

Hradetsky made a decision. One of the options he'd been exploring seemed worth pursuing further. Perhaps reform could still come from within the system. He lowered his voice. 'Look, Bela, I need proof of what you're telling me. Documentation on these cutbacks and firings. And on anything else you think is strange. Something I can show people.'

Silvanus sat forward. 'Why?'

'Because I think I may know a way to get Rehling's orders retracted.'

MARCH 17 – NEAR FREEDOM SQUARE, BUDAPEST

The church domes and spires dotting Budapest's graceful skyline gleamed in the pale, cool sunlight. That same sunlight sparkled off the Danube and cast long shadows down Pest's broad nineteenth-century avenues and Buda's narrow, hilly medieval streets. Green leaves were budding on trees that had escaped being cut down for firewood. Hungary's capital was coming alive again after a long, bitter winter.

Its people were out in force, too. Some were the unemployed, moving from district to district in search of work. Others were shopping, hunting from store to store for the food, clothing, and other necessities their government promised them. Soldiers and policemen were visible on every street corner. The military government wanted to be sure its citizens knew they were being watched.

Hradetsky moved through the crowds with ease. Even years spent working in provincial cities and towns couldn't erase the skills he'd learned as a young boy growing up in the twin cities. But he couldn't help noticing the hard looks and angry stares turned his way by some he passed. Clearly many of his fellow Hungarians again regarded the blue and gray police uniform as a visible sign of tyranny.

Normally he enjoyed walking the city streets for exercise. Today was different. Today he was taking the morning off to run an errand. A dangerous errand.

His errand was at the Prosecutor General's Office, a few blocks away from the Ministry of the Interior.

Several years ago, he had worked with someone in the Prosecutor General's Office. Anthal Bartha had impressed him as competent, energetic, and dedicated. If he, too, had favorable memories of Hradetsky, he might be able to give him an entry to someone higher up – maybe someone with access to the prosecutor general himself.

Unlike the Justice Department in the United States, the prosecutor general and his subordinates controlled all criminal prosecutions in Hungary. Under the constitution, they were also responsible for reviewing the legality of all government actions. He was hoping that would give them enough power to stop Rehling before EurCon's special commissioner rode roughshod over the whole police force.

The Prosecutor General's building stood out like a sore thumb among its more graceful, elegant neighbors. It was a drab, featureless concrete structure originally erected by Russian engineers hastily repairing bomb damage after World War II. Hradetsky suspected Hungary's old communist puppet government had housed its lawyers in such a place to foster the notion of grim, faceless state authority. Bureaucratic inertia kept them there even after the communists fell from power.

Still, the foyer was bustling – crowded with attorneys and legal clerks coming and going on court business. Feeling out of place and conspicuous in his uniform, he brushed past them to an information desk where a lone, harried clerk reluctantly provided a building directory for his use.

Finding Bartha's office number, he rode the creaking, manually operated elevator up to the right floor, got off, and walked down a hall painted a fading tan. To save electricity, every other light fixture was empty, creating pockets of shadow. The dingy gloom made Hradetsky faintly uneasy, almost as though he were committing a treasonous act in coming here. He squared his shoulders, rejecting the notion. Certainly he was going outside the normal channels of communication, but the idea of appealing to that drone Dozsa was ludicrous.

He stopped in front of an old-fashioned frosted-glass door. Black lettering told him the office belonged to 'Anthal Bartha, Assistant to Budapest Prosecutor.' He knocked, waited a moment, and then went in.

The room's only occupant sat at a desk facing the door, surrounded by piles of folders and bound documents. More paper filled the bookshelves on either side. The impression was not one of disorder, but of a tremendous work load.

The man at the desk was younger than Hradetsky by several years, but his black hair was already more than half gray. He was taller, too, but Hradetsky was used to that. He had a narrow face that looked up at his visitor in mixed puzzlement and expectation. 'Yes? What can I do for you' – keen dark eyes took in the three silver stars on his shoulder boards – 'Colonel?'

'Solicitor Bartha, I'm Zoltan Hradetsky. We worked together a few years ago in Sopron – on the Andorka case.'

'That's right.' Recognition and pleasure replaced Bartha's previous expression.

Hradetsky nodded toward the only other chair in the room. 'May I?'

'Please.' The lawyer waited for him to get settled. 'So what brings you here today? I assume you have more on your mind than pleasant reminiscences.'

Hradetsky cleared his throat. This was where things got tricky. 'I must ask you a question before I tell you my business, Solicitor.'

'Certainly.'

'Will you swear to keep this meeting private, until I say otherwise?' Even in Hradetsky's ears that sounded melodramatic. Nevertheless, he couldn't see any other way to proceed. With eyes-only documents that could be traced back to Silvanus in his attaché case, his wasn't the only career at stake.

'Of course,' Bartha answered, his curiosity evidently piqued. 'I am quite used to sensitive matters.'

'Not like this, I am afraid.' Hradetsky shook his head. 'I'm here to ask your help. I have information, some documents, that I must get into the right hands. I believe this new EurCon liaison, Rehling, has plans to turn my service into another secret police force, another AVO!'

Bartha's eyes opened wide at his mention of the hated Stalinist-era security service. Used to smash all dissent during the first years of communist rule, AVO troops had even fired on their own people in the 1956 revolution.

'Brigadier General Dozsa is doing nothing to stop him, and my own situation inside the ministry is so tenuous that I cannot take any action myself.'

'What? But you're full colonel. A man with years of honored service. How can this be?'

Hradetsky sketched in the details of his clash with the French in Sopron and his subsequent exile to the ministry's bureaucratic depths. Reliving the humiliating events of the past few months ate away at his self-control. By the time he finished, his voice was tight with anger.

'So now this Rehling appears and suddenly rules us by fiat. If he has his way, real criminals will wander unchecked while we become just guards protecting French and German businesses! Just another group of thugs hunting down our own people who object to all of this!' The memory of Sopron leapt into his mind again.

His face full of concern, Bartha nodded his understanding. 'You mentioned some documentation of these charges?'

Hradetsky passed him the printouts he'd been given and waited in silence while the lawyer perused them, carefully scanning each page.

When he'd finished, Bartha handed them back, shaking his head unhappily. 'Is this all you have? There is nothing else you can show me?'

'Isn't this enough?'

'Not for my superiors or me to take action.' Seeing Hradetsky's puzzled look, he hastened to explain. 'Yes, a few regulations have undoubtedly been broken, but these are all internal police organizational matters. They aren't even misdemeanors.'

'I wasn't looking for an indictment,' said Hradetsky. 'I just wanted to show these to someone who could cancel them, or stand up to this German. Dozsa certainly won't.'

'Nor will anyone in this building. I can tell you right now that my superiors would throw you out of their offices.' Bartha jerked a thumb toward the ceiling. 'Your commander isn't the only one who's running scared of our new "allies." '

Zoltan spread his hands. 'I have nothing to lose.'

Bartha's tone hardened. 'Yes, you do. Your freedom.' He leaned forward and lowered his voice. 'We have our own problems here in the Prosecutor General's Office. The government has been quietly issuing new decrees for the past several weeks. They allow the arrest of anyone labeled a subversive – on very shaky legal grounds. As a lawyer, I would challenge these laws if I were ever asked to enforce them.'

His shoulders slumped. 'But in this day and age I don't think our Supreme Court will ever get to hear such a case.'

'So we are losing the last vestige of our rights.'

'Perhaps. In any case, it would be well to lie low for a while and see how things develop. Getting yourself in trouble won't help anything.' Bartha suddenly stood up, ending the interview. He went to the door, opened it, and looked left and right down the hall.

We've become prisoners in our own country, Hradetsky thought sadly. Even our best officials are afraid.

He took his leave quickly and left the building. Silvanus' documents were still in his briefcase. Walking back to his own office gave him time to think. He didn't even feel the cold wind still blowing off the Danube.

Things were as bad at the Prosecutor General's Office as they were inside the Interior Ministry. Maybe even worse. Watching existing laws flouted or ignored under emergency military rule had been troubling enough. But he'd be damned if he'd enforce a whole new set of laws designed to make Hungary's serfdom a permanent condition.

So nobody in higher authority would talk to him. Very well. He grimaced. Bartha's advice to 'lay low' left a bad taste in his mouth. He'd laid low long enough.

Changing direction, Hradetsky lengthened his stride. He had a long way to go, but he needed the time to plan. He knew someone who would look at the evidence he carried. Someone who might be able to do something about it.

CHAPTER 13
Revelations

MARCH 21 – WISMAR, GERMANY

Vance could smell the sea as soon as he climbed out of his rented Audi. He was beginning to hate that smell.

Nothing in his privileged childhood in one of Connecticut's wealthy suburbs, his Ivy League schooling, or his initial CIA training had prepared him for this. Germany was his first operational posting and this was his first assignment. For nearly three weeks now, the young intelligence officer had been working his way west along the Baltic coast, trying to visit two or three tiny villages or larger towns a day. It hadn't been easy. Poorly maintained and poorly marked roads turned even the shortest drive into a grueling, time-consuming chore.

The abysmal weather made it worse. Stretches of dark, gnarled trees, saltwater lagoons, beaches, and rugged cliffs were blurred by rain and fog until the whole bleak countryside seemed one vast, flat, waterlogged mess. Sandwiched between the winter snows and spring rains, March was supposed to be a relatively dry month, especially in a part of Germany that was usually drier than the rest. But not this year. One storm after another had lashed unpaved roads into muddy quagmires and left paved highways slick and deadly.

If anything, trying to worm useful information out of the locals was even more difficult than finding them in the first place. Decades under communist tyranny gave the region's inhabitants an ingrained dislike for nosy, prying strangers – especially strangers who had trouble following their slow, slurred local dialect. To them, his fluent High German was either the mark of an arrogant, Berlin-bred twit or, worse, a snooping, sneaking official. With high tariffs and import restrictions on foreign goods, smuggling was making a comeback in northern Germany, and smugglers survived by keeping their mouths shut. Few people were willing to even talk to him, let alone help him find one particular fishing trawler out of the hundreds berthed up and down the coast.

Still, he was learning. In the beginning, he'd tried visiting every waterfront *Gasthaus* and bar, hoping to pick up some local gossip and make useful contacts. Instead, he'd earned nothing but hard, flat stares, hangovers from drinking too much beer, and an abiding hatred for pickled herring in sour cream. Now he made a sweep through each harbor first, looking for the right boat or one that looked something like it. Then, armed with a specific trawler's name, he went looking for its owner, ostensibly with an unspecified 'business proposition.' He'd also stopped trying to pretend he was German. Ironically the Baltic coast seamen and fisherfolk trusted shady foreigners with ready cash and illegal goods more than their own inland countrymen did.

Of course, Vance thought sourly, the final results had all been the same. *Nada*. A big fat goose egg. He'd seen big boats and small boats, old tubs that would barely float, and brand-new 'fishing' craft packed with high-powered engines and navigational gear. None of them had been the trawler spotted off Gdansk by the KH-11.

He sighed, straightened his aching back, and made sure the Audi was locked. Wismar's nearly sixty thousand citizens made it a much larger town than most of those he'd been scouting through. And with more people came more crime. He didn't want to call police attention to himself by filing a theft report. He certainly didn't want to present the Agency's notoriously unsympathetic accountants with the bill for a stolen rental car.

With his camera slung over one shoulder, Vance set out along the waterfront. On one side, fishing trawlers and sailboats were moored at rotting piers, rocked gently from side to side by small waves. On the other, old warehouses stood empty. Some still showed bomb scars from Allied raids during the closing weeks of World War II.

He had the area almost all to himself. Apparently, few of Wismar's seamen had any business pressing enough to make them brave the bone-chilling, late afternoon drizzle. Even the shipyard, the town's only important business, was deserted, padlocked and abandoned to a few stray cats who roamed over and under unfinished hulls.

Vance stopped a hundred meters or so from his car and stood close to the water's edge, scanning the anchored small craft. It took real mental effort to make more than a cursory inspection. He'd studied so many boats in the past few days that he was starting to see them at night in his dreams. His eyes fell on one of the trawlers, stopped, moved on, and then came back. Something about her seemed familiar somehow. The boxy shape of the wheelhouse? Or the way old truck tires were strung along her hull as makeshift fenders? Had he seen this boat before in one of the other fishing ports? Or . . .

The CIA officer held his breath as he stared out at the old, rust-streaked vessel. It couldn't be! He fumbled inside one of his windbreaker pockets for the drawings he'd been given. Holding the artist's sketch in front of him, he walked further along the quay, trying to duplicate one of the views it showed.

They matched. Even in the fading light the resemblance was perfect. He squinted through his camera's zoom lens, looking for a name or number on the trawler's stern. He found one painted in yellowing white across her black hull. *Hexmadchen*. Witchmaiden. Ugly, he thought. Like the boat itself.

Vance snapped several pictures from different spots up and down the waterfront. Comparing his shots to those taken by the satellite should give the Agency's photo interpreters enough to make a positive identification. Not that he had the slightest doubt. He'd found the mysterious trawler last seen hovering off Gdansk.

Suddenly scarcely able to contain his excitement, the American turned on his heel and hurried away from the harbor, looking for the first sailor's haunt he could find. Somebody had to know what the *Witchmaiden* had been up to lately . . . and who owned her.

Compared to its decaying and desolate wharf area, the rest of Wismar looked considerably more appealing. One massive, red brick church spire towered off to the east, poking high above gabled rooftops. The bombed-out remnants of two other great brick churches stood south of that, near the town's large marketplace.

Vance found the pub he was looking for there – inside Wismar's oldest building. The 'Old Swede' had been built nearly six centuries before and its age showed in low ceilings, narrow doors, and soot-blackened wood beams. The sound of clinking steins and rough-edged, booming voices led him straight to the bar itself.

He stopped in the doorway. The Old Swede was packed.

Sailors, trawler captains, and townsmen occupied practically every booth, table, barstool, and square centimeter of open space. A thick haze of cigarette and pipe smoke hid the far corners of the tiny room. Vance's eyes started watering right away.

Those inside turned to stare at him as he crossed the threshold. In seconds, the whole crowded, noisy place fell silent. Hard expressionless eyes followed him as he came down a pair of stone stairs and made his way to the bar.

'A beer, please.' Vance forced an American accent into his ordinarily flawless German.

The barman glared back at him for several seconds before shoving a full glass under his nose. He knew that look very well. Strangers, especially foreigners, are not welcome, it said. He ignored it and sipped his beer.

'You have some business here, perhaps, *mein Herr*?'

Vance looked up. The speaker was a stout, red-faced man. Grease stains down the broad front of his brown wool sweater suggested he was a mechanic, a sloppy eater, or both.

'I'm looking for a man who owns a boat.'

'Really.' The fat man's piggy eyes almost disappeared as he grinned broadly. 'Well, you've certainly come to the right place, friend. Hasn't he, boys?'

The room exploded in laughter.

Vance waited for them to quiet down, smiling faintly. When he had their attention again, he went on. 'I meant a particular trawler. The *Witchmaiden*. I'd like to speak to her captain about a quick . . . charter . . . I have in mind.'

The other man had obviously elected himself spokesman for everyone present. He chuckled again. 'Old Hummel's boat? Then you're too late.'

'I am?'

'*Ja*. Somebody else already beat you to it. Put cold cash right in that sour fart's hot palm.' The big man gestured with his own beer. 'Naturally old Hummel legged it off that floating wreck before they could think twice. And nobody around here has seen him since!'

'Bastard owed me money, too,' one of the other sailors muttered.

'Half the town, more like. But it would have cost the buyers more than the boat cost to settle all his debts.' The fat man drained the rest of his beer and then glanced at the American. 'Maybe they were some of your competitors, eh?' he asked shrewdly.

'Maybe.' Vance said it as casually as he could. He shrugged. 'Those damned Swedes are always fast off the mark.'

The fat man shook his head in amusement. 'They weren't Swedes, friend.' He pointed to the bar around them. 'We know them very well here.'

The CIA agent nodded his understanding. One of the guidebooks he'd consulted had said Wismar was once a Swedish foothold on German soil – all the way up to the early 1900s, if he remembered right. He'd mentioned Sweden deliberately to turn the conversation toward nationalities.

He wanted to forge ahead faster, to ask outright who had bought the boat, but he pulled back at the last second. Dragging useful data from these clannish fishermen was like making your way through a minefield. You couldn't move too fast. 'You look thirsty. Another?' He raised his own glass.

The German smiled contentedly. 'My thanks.'

Vance looked around for the barman and frowned. He wasn't there. The man had vanished sometime during the conversation, leaving a harried-looking assistant in his place. He'd probably dodged out to avoid being forced to sell another drink to an American. Well, screw him. He tapped his glass on the bar to get the assistant's attention. 'More beers, please. One for me. And the rest for these good gentlemen here.'

That earned him several more smiles.

In the end it took him several drinks and nearly half an hour to bring the conversation back around to the *Witchmaiden*'s new owners.

'Who, them? They're French. Not that they want us to know that. Secrets, eh?' The big German tapped his own nose and winked. Then he wiped his mouth with the back of his hand and took another swig. 'Standoffish bunch, aren't they, boys?'

His companions nodded their agreement.

'You're sure of that? That they're French, I mean.'

'Very sure.' The fat man snorted. 'Snail-eaters with too much money and too little sense, if you ask me.'

'Oh? Why?'

'Who else would be stupid enough to pay Hummel all that money for a boat and then leave her sitting after just one trip?'

Vance sipped his own beer to buy time and stay calm. This was what he'd been waiting for. 'A trip?'

'*Ja*. Last month.' The German grinned. 'I thought that would interest you. Maybe they were on a little jaunt across the water to bring back a few crates of untaxed whiskey? Or some other luxury goods, eh?'

The CIA officer nodded vaguely, listening with only one ear while the sailors batted back and forth their own ideas about the *Witchmaiden*'s illicit cargo. He was busy trying to evaluate his next move. Should he keep digging or head back to Berlin?

Berlin, he decided. Although all the evidence he'd gathered was only circumstantial, it was strong enough to warrant further investigation by more experienced personnel. He'd narrowed the field down to one trawler in one small German town. That should be good enough. Once America and Great Britain flooded Wismar with trained criminal investigators, there would be too much international publicity for the French to sweep things under the rug.

But first he'd better phone in a preliminary report. Berlin was a long drive away, and his superiors would need time to assemble the right team. He disengaged himself from the small circle still arguing the relative profits to be made from smuggled liquor or other products.

The barman was back, still with the same angry look and sullen disposition.

'Is there a telephone here?' Vance asked.

'Down the hall.' The man jerked a thumb toward the door he'd just come in. 'By the bathroom.'

The American nodded. He tossed a wad of newly issued franc-marks on the bar. 'Another round for my friends there, please.' With a cheerful wave toward the sailors, he headed toward the phone.

As he'd expected, the chief of station wanted him back in Berlin that same night, if not sooner. His photos of the fishing trawler were about to become a very hot commodity in Washington and London.

It took him longer than he expected to say his good-byes. The Old Swede's customers were reluctant to let their newfound source of free drinks make a quick escape. He finally broke lose with the promise to come back after conferring with his 'business partners.'

Night had come to Wismar by the time Vance stepped outside, shivering in the sudden cold. At least, the rain had stopped falling while he'd been inside the bar. He zipped his windbreaker up, stuck both hands in his pockets, and walked briskly toward his car – awash on a small tide of beer and general contentment. Despite all the obstacles he'd faced, he'd finished his first assignment with flying colors.

He never saw the two men closing in behind him from a darkened alley.

One of the two French agents knelt beside the American, going through his pockets with practiced hands. The other put two fingers to his mouth and whistled softly, signaling an unmarked van waiting around the corner. That done, he looked down. 'Is he dead?'

'No. I only gave him a quick tap on the back of the skull.' The kneeling man straightened up. 'Here we go.' He held out Vance's rental car keys.

'Good.'

The van pulled up beside them. Two more men hopped out through its open side door. Working fast, they picked the unconscious CIA agent off the pavement and bundled him inside. The van was moving almost before they'd climbed back aboard and slammed the door shut.

As the vehicle's taillights disappeared from view, the team leader turned to his subordinate. 'Right. You know the drill. Pay the bartender what we promised. Then bring the American's car to the rendezvous point. We'll search it there.'

'And you?'

'I'll be along. First, I've got to call the director and tell him about our little problem here.' He frowned, anticipating his likely orders from Paris. The head of the DGSE never liked leaving loose ends lying around.

MARCH 23 – BERLIN

Richard Strozier, the CIA's chief of station for Berlin, took a long look before he nodded grimly. 'Yes. That's him. That's Vance.' He dragged his gaze away from the mangled corpse on the mortuary slab, fighting the urge to vomit.

'You are sure? The features are so badly damaged.'

The American glared at the burly German police captain standing beside him. 'Yes, I'm sure, goddamn it.'

'Very well, Herr Strozier. I believe you.' Another German, thinner and in civilian clothes, motioned to white-coated morgue attendants waiting close by. 'Cover him.'

'What happened?'

'A car crash near Wismar. Two days ago. The roads were very bad that night. Very wet.' The police captain shrugged, obviously bored by what seemed a routine traffic accident. 'And he was intoxicated.'

'Bullshit.'

The second German sighed. 'Believe what you wish, Herr Strozier. But the autopsy report was conclusive. Your man Vance had enough alcohol in his bloodstream to knock a young elephant over. And witnesses in the town saw him drinking not long before the accident.' He spread his hands. 'What else could have happened?'

Strozier scowled at the BfV liaison officer. He'd known Helmut Ziegler long enough to know when he was being willfully obtuse. Somebody higher up must have told him to play dumb. 'What about his personal effects?'

The policeman answered that. 'We have them here.' He handed the American a sealed plastic bag. 'If you'll sign for them, you can take them back to the embassy with you.'

Strozier dumped the bag's contents out onto a nearby table. A wallet. Comb. Passport. Pocketknife. No camera. Naturally. He looked up at Ziegler. 'I'll want to see the crash site.'

'I'm afraid that is impossible.'

'Why?'

Ziegler smiled apologetically. 'The Baltic coast is now a restricted travel area, Herr Strozier. We've had more trouble up there recently. Riots. Strikes. General unrest. In view of the circumstances, my government has decided to keep all foreign nationals out until we can guarantee their safety.'

Sure. Strozier stood rigid with anger. 'My ambassador will protest this, Helmut. Vigorously.'

'Of course.' Ziegler turned to the watching policeman. 'I think we're done here, Captain. Would you please make sure my driver is ready?'

'At once, sir.'

The two men watched him leave. When the doors swung shut, Strozier turned on the BfV officer angrily. 'All right, just what the fuck is going on around here? Jesus Christ, Helmut, that kid was murdered and you know it!'

Ziegler nodded sadly. 'I know it.' He pointed to Vance's body. 'Believe me, Richard. This was not our work.'

The German lowered his voice. 'I don't know exactly what your people have stumbled into, but I do know that it's very dangerous. The orders to seal off the Wismar region did not come from my government. They came from somewhere even higher.'

'EurCon?'

A look of distaste crossed Ziegler's lean face. 'The Interior Secretariat.' He shook his head. 'Be very careful, Richard. And keep your people away from that town if you want to keep them alive. These French bastards don't give a damn who gets in their way.'

When Strozier got back to the embassy, he found Maj. Kasimir Malinowska waiting for him.

The short, thin Polish intelligence officer was acting as his government's watchdog for the German end of the *North Star* investigation. 'Well? Was it as you feared?'

'Yes. Maybe even worse.' Strozier filled him in on the afternoon's events.

'I see.' Malinowska frowned. 'What will you do next?'

'I don't know.' The Berlin chief of station shook his head wearily. 'I'm not sure where we go from here. We know that the French planted that bomb. We know the name of the fishing trawler they used for the job. Hell, we even know they killed poor Vance to cover it up. But we've got no proof.'

'Perhaps the satellite photographs are enough?' Malinowska suggested.

'Unlikely.' Strozier shrugged. 'Besides, I doubt that Washington will risk releasing those pictures without other hard evidence. On their own, all they do is show the bad guys just how good our coverage is.'

'Then your superiors may do nothing?' The Pole sounded angry.

'No. Yes. Possibly.' Strozier rubbed his forehead. 'Jesus, I really don't see what they can do. Without Vance's pictures or access to this Wismar place, we've reached a dead end.'

Malinowska's pale blue eyes turned hard. 'Perhaps that is true. And perhaps it is not.' He didn't bother explaining what he meant by that.

MARCH 28 – MINISTRY OF TRADE, MOSCOW

Erin McKenna was making her routine rounds through the Russian bureaucracy when she caught the first whiff of impending trouble.

'Speaking bluntly, Deputy Minister, Honeywell isn't going to spend the money needed to retool the Tula plant until they're sure your government isn't planning to renationalize it.' She smiled to take the sting out of her words. 'After all, nobody puts their best silver out when they know a thief is on the way.'

'That is true.' Russia's deputy minister for trade looked troubled. The martial law regime's on-again, off-again attitude toward the private sector was wreaking havoc with her efforts to encourage foreign investment and foreign trade. Kaminov and his fellow soldiers didn't seem to understand that their capricious seizures had very real and very predictable economic effects. Businessmen could not and would not make long-term financial commitments without some assurances that their investments were safe from arbitrary government action.

Erin watched the other woman carefully. Getting a handle on Russia's intentions toward the Tula electronics factory was important for two reasons. First, an American firm now owned a forty-nine percent stake in the place – a multimillion-dollar investment. And an important part of her cover involved helping U.S. companies navigate their way through the convoluted, peculiarly Russian web of regulation, intrigue, and competing ministerial interests. The second reason was much more important. The personal computer components produced at Tula could be used for either civilian or military purposes. Government plans to seize the factory would be a clear warning that Russia was rearming.

The deputy minister made up her mind. 'I can assure you, Miss McKenna, that—' A sharp knock on the door interrupted whatever she was going to say. 'Yes, what is it?'

Her special assistant poked his head into the office. 'Galinia Ostrokova, may I see you for a moment? It's very urgent.'

'All right, Viktor.' The deputy minister rose from behind her desk. Erin noticed again that she was a lot shorter than she looked sitting down. 'Will you excuse me, please?'

'Oh, of course.'

The door shut behind the two Russians, leaving Erin alone inside the office. She glanced at the side table where the Trade Ministry official kept her computer. Her fingers practically itched at the chance to go dancing through secret files, but she fought off the impulse. She'd promised Banich that she'd stay out of the operational side of the intelligence game. That was the price he'd exacted for letting even an admittedly talented 'amateur' roam through Moscow's streets and government ministries.

The deputy minister came back in looking strained and very frightened. 'Miss McKenna, I must ask you to leave. Immediately. I am afraid this interview is concluded.'

Erin felt cold suddenly. Was another purge under way? Or something much worse? She stood up. 'Can I see you tomorrow, then? Or would another time be more convenient?'

'No. I . . .' The Russian woman visibly hesitated. 'I am not sure when it will be possible for me to meet with you again. Please check with my assistant later.'

It had to be a purge. Kaminov must be making another sweep through the ministries, ridding them of reformers and other 'undesirables.' Erin had a very strange feeling, though. The deputy minister was scared, all right, but she seemed more frightened of *her* than of anything else.

Her sense that something was very wrong intensified when she came out of the Trade Ministry building and saw Mike Hennessy standing beside one of the embassy cars. She always rode the Metro whenever possible. Using the subway for her visits to government officials was usually easier, faster, and certainly more discreet.

Hennessy already had the Lincoln's passenger door open and its motor purring by the time she cleared the ministry's revolving doors.

'What's up?'

He shook his head. 'I'm not sure. I just got a hurry-up call from Alex to pick you up and bring you straight back.'

'And he's the boss?'

'That's right. He's the boss.' Hennessy nodded and put the car in gear.

They made the short drive to the embassy in shared silence.

Alex Banich looked both relieved and surprised to see her back so soon.

'I thought you might give Hennessy more trouble,' he confessed, scrambling out of the only other chair in her office.

'I might have if I hadn't already had a pretty weird meeting with one of my best contacts.' Erin frowned. 'Something's going on, right?'

'Yeah.' He glanced at her, obviously still concerned.

'Another purge?'

Banich shook his head. 'No.' He checked his watch. 'Come on. There's a news story you should see, and it ought to be on again right about now.'

He led her fuming down the hall to a small conference room equipped with its own television set.

CNN's hourly news roundup came on in midsentence. '. . . accused the French and German governments of criminal involvement in last month's devastating natural gas tanker explosion. The Polish government spokesman went on to claim that an American CIA agent had recently been murdered near the tiny German town of Wismar as part of an ongoing Franco-German effort to block the *North Star* investigation.'

Erin whistled in amazement. This was big news. But how did it connect up with her experience at the Trade Ministry? She turned toward Banich. 'What . . .'

He nodded toward the TV. 'There's more.'

'When pressed for evidence to back up Poland's charges, Mr. Wiatr responded by revealing that U.S. intelligence reports from Moscow showed a direct link between French economic subsidies and the Russian oil and gas embargo aimed at his country. Highly placed sources inside Poland's own spy agency confirmed his account . . .'

Oh, hell. Hell and damn. No wonder Ostrokova and her assistant had looked at her so suspiciously. The Poles had unwittingly blown her cover.

'. . . Apparently in reaction to the news, angry mobs attacked EurCon consulates in Warsaw, Gdansk, and Kraków. Police armed with tear gas and water cannon turned them back in bitter street fighting that left several dozen people injured – some seriously. In a bid to restore public order, Poland's Roman Catholic primate and other church authorities have appealed for calm . . .'

With her mind in turmoil Erin looked away from the violent pictures flashing across the screen. She felt ill. Just when all her work was really starting to pay off, this had to happen. She saw Banich watching her sympathetically. 'Now what happens? Will the Russians expel me?'

He shook his head. 'I doubt it. Kicking you out would only give us the chance to bring in someone they don't know about. Why risk that when they can just keep closer tabs on you?'

She nodded. Given the way Russians thought, that made sense. But then another, darker thought struck her. 'What about the people I've been getting information from? What happens to them?'

As always, Banich gave it to her straight. He reserved deception for his country's enemies. 'They're in trouble. The Russian government's goons will be backtracking every move you've made since you came to Moscow. Anybody you've made contact with is automatically suspect. And if the FIS finds hard evidence that they fed you data?' His mouth turned downward. 'Espionage and treason are still capital crimes in this country.'

Erin choked back tears. This was worse than her worst nightmare. She'd put people who had trusted her in mortal danger.

Banich took her face gently between his hands. 'This is not your fault, McKenna. You haven't done anything wrong.' He sighed. 'This comes with the territory. Sometimes the information we gather leaks out. Sometimes accidentally. Sometimes deliberately. Sometimes because it's necessary. And sometimes because someone higher up the ladder screwed up. But people always get hurt.'

He brushed away a single tear trickling down her cheek. 'Blaming yourself won't change that.'

Erin breathed out softly. Did he know the effect he was having on her? 'Then where do I go from here?'

Banich gave her a small, sad smile. 'You keep your head down. Stay inside the embassy compound as much as possible.'

'But . . .'

He laid a finger across her lips. 'You have to. The FIS isn't yet what the KGB used to be, but some of its agents are still thugs. They could try to set you up or use you to set someone else up – say, a prominent reformer Kaminov wants out of the way.'

'What about my work?'

Banich nodded. 'That's a problem. Hennessy, the others, and I will try our best to cover some of the same ground, but we're going to be stretched pretty thin. You still have your taps into the state computer system?'

'I think so. At least until they change the passwords and access codes.' Erin felt calmer now, better able to think clearly and plan ahead. 'And even then their security people might leave some holes I can burrow in through.'

'Good.' He stepped back, visibly turning more professional and more formal. 'All right, McKenna, we'll take a hit on this, but we're still in business. Find out how much access you still have and let me know as soon as you can. I'll have to report to Langley. Okay?'

'Okay.'

Erin watched Alex Banich walk away, again armored in polite indifference. But she'd seen him drop his guard. The workaholic CIA agent had a human side, after all. And she liked it.

MARCH 29 – BUDAPEST

The ten-story, prefabricated apartment building had been shabby when Hungary's old communist government first constructed it. Now, after decades of neglect and overcrowding, it could only be called squalid.

On the seventh floor, Col. Zoltan Hradetsky squeezed past the bicycles chained to the banister and made his way down a cramped, dimly lit hallway. Cracked, unpainted concrete walls and the sour, unwashed smell of too many people living with too little running water spoke volumes about the miserable existence endured by Budapest's poorest citizens.

He paused outside Apartment 7-E and checked the hallway to either side. All the doors were shut. Even though he had come wearing civilian clothes, the building's inhabitants were nowhere in sight. They must have a nose for policemen, he thought wryly. Well, perhaps he would soon need to learn their instincts.

Despite all his bold thoughts after leaving Solicitor Bartha's office, it had taken Hradetsky a long time to find the right man. Although Vladimir Kusin was well known in the city, no current directory listed his phone number or address. And even a famous man could vanish among the capital's two million people – especially with help from his many friends and supporters.

So, after spending nearly two weeks beating his head against a brick wall of feigned ignorance and outright evasion, Hradetsky had decided on a riskier, more direct approach. That was why he'd come here, to the apartment occupied by Kusin's wife. Officially she and her husband were separated and in the midst of a messy divorce. Well, he had a hunch that the separation and the divorce were both a smoke screen – one designed to protect the woman from excessive police scrutiny and harassment. He was here to play that hunch.

He knocked once. 'Mrs. Kusin?'

The door opened immediately. 'I am Mara Kusin.'

Hradetsky nodded. The photo he'd seen in her police file matched the woman in front of him: a young-looking, thickly built woman with two teenage children.

He saw no point in hiding his identity. 'I am Colonel Zoltan Hradetsky, of the National Police.'

Kusin's wife blanched, then steeled herself. She nodded quietly, guardedly. She must be used to trouble.

'May I come in?'

For an instant, a surprised look flickered across her face. Policemen were rarely so polite. She stepped back into the dingy apartment and stood waiting, her arms folded across her chest.

Hradetsky stepped across the threshold and shut the door behind him. He didn't want prying ears to hear what he had to say.

He did not bother asking her where her husband was. Even if she did know, the last person she would tell was a police colonel. 'I am not here in an official capacity. But I do have a message and important information for Vladimir Kusin. It is essential that I speak with him.'

'But I don't know . . .'

'Of course you don't.' Hradetsky shook his head. 'All I ask is that you get this to him – wherever he is.'

He handed the woman an envelope containing a brief summary of the information he'd been given by Bela Silvanus, along with a schedule of public places where he would wait for contact over the next three days. When she took it, he felt his neck muscles tightening. He'd done it. He was committed now. Going to Solicitor Bartha with his concerns could be passed off as misguided bureaucratic maneuvering. Contacting an active member of Hungary's banned political opposition could not.

APRIL 1 – HEROES' SQUARE, BUDAPEST

Hradetsky sat on a park bench with his eyes slitted against the welcome spring sunshine, trying hard not to let his nerves get to him. That wasn't easy. This noontime rendezvous outside the sprawling, neoclassical Museum of Fine Arts was the last of the three options he'd given Mara Kusin. Had the opposition decided to ignore him as a possible *agent provocateur*? Or worse, had his message fallen into the wrong hands? The European Confederation's German liaison, Rehling, and his Hungarian subordinates were strengthening the nation's internal security apparatus with every passing day. They might have been paying more attention to his activities than he'd imagined.

He studied the office workers crowding the square more closely, wondering if any of them were agents assigned to watch him. Then he shrugged, almost amused at his own developing paranoia. How could he tell? There had to be several thousand people eating lunch in the vast open space dominated by the winged statue of the archangel Gabriel mounted atop a thirty-six-meter-high column. When he'd picked this spot as a possible rendezvous, he'd been thinking too much like a policeman and not enough like a conspirator. Mentally he was still on the other side of the surveillance camera.

He was on the edge of rising to go when a young, powerfully built man with blond hair sat down next to him. Without looking up, he opened a lunch pail and laid something on the bench between them. 'I think you dropped this, Colonel.'

Hradetsky glanced down. It was the manila envelope he'd given Kusin's wife. He picked it up. 'Yes, I did.'

'Good.' The young man smiled thinly and offered him an apple. 'Then let us begin.'

Hradetsky took a bite and listened intently as his nameless companion started asking a series of difficult questions. What were his attitudes toward the various regimes that had ruled Hungary? What had he done in past assignments? What did his current job entail? And most important of all, why did he want to see Vladimir Kusin?

To anyone passing by, they were just two friends sharing a rare treat of fruit on a delightful spring day. The police colonel knew differently. He was being vetted – checked – by the opposition before they let him get close to Kusin.

Hradetsky had conducted enough interrogations to know what the man was looking for, and why he wanted it. His questioner was intelligent and suspicious. The only way to deal with him was to answer every question as quickly and plainly as possible.

Although interrogators often revealed much about themselves by the kinds of questions they asked, these were so limited, or so straightforward, that Hradetsky learned little about the man or his group. From his build, his haircut, and some of the expressions he used, the colonel suspected the younger man might be an ex-army officer.

Abruptly the man closed his lunch pail, stood up, and said, 'That's enough for now. I must report to my superiors.'

Hradetsky stood also and they strolled casually toward the nearest Metro stop, mingling with the other workers streaming back to their offices. He had questions of his own, but he knew this man would not answer them. Still, he volunteered, 'Please tell Kus—'

The other man gave him a sharp look, and shushed him sharply.

Hradetsky corrected himself. 'Please tell your superiors that there is not much time.'

The younger man smiled grimly. 'We have been trying to tell you and your kind that for a long time.' Then he seemed to loosen up a little. 'If you are what you claim to be, you can be a great help to us, Colonel. Still, a man can say anything and sound sincere. Actions always speak louder than words.'

He handed Hradetsky a piece of paper with a single name written on it. 'Obtain the police file on this person and then come to the Central Etterem Cafeteria in two days' time. At noon again. Is that sufficient?'

Momentarily nonplussed, Hradetsky muttered an affirmative.

'Good.' The man stood still for a moment, watching the crowds pouring down the stairs to the underground subway line. Then he glanced back at Hradetsky. 'And be more careful in the future. I followed you all the way from your ministry as easily as a wolf tracking a wounded deer. Next time it might not be someone so friendly.' He showed his teeth at his own small joke.

Hradetsky flushed but nodded. However obnoxious the younger man's manner, his warning was valid. He would have to learn the caution so necessary to those living outside the law.

Two days later, he sat at a table in the packed Central Etterem Cafeteria sipping a cup of strong black espresso. His elbow rested on the same manila envelope, this time containing the police file his contact had requested.

Hradetsky frowned. Copying the confidential file had proved almost ludicrously easy. An overworked staff and sloppy office procedures saw to that. After all, any ranking police official had routine access to that kind of information. The trick had been to do it without attracting attention or leaving a paper trail.

Now that he had the file, he had the time to wonder why exactly Kusin's people wanted it. From what he'd seen, the man they were interested in was a democratic activist – a longtime opponent of both the old communist regime and the current military government. Perhaps they needed to know how closely the police were watching the fellow. Or maybe the opposition already had a copy of this particular file and only wanted to see if he brought them the right one.

Whatever else it was, this job was certainly a test of his loyalty and resourcefulness. Until he delivered the information they'd asked him for, Kusin and his allies would view him as little more than a big talker. If he delivered the wrong information, they'd write him off as a police plant. And if he'd been caught while trying to get it, they'd have known he wasn't cut out for covert work.

Hradetsky stirred restlessly. He felt soiled somehow. He'd spent his life enforcing the law and keeping the peace. Now it seemed almost too easy to break both, even in a good cause.

Then he shook his head. His own feelings were unimportant in this case. And his first loyalty had to be to Hungary – not to any particular ruling clique. Especially not to a group of generals in French and German pay. Freeing the nation from their incompetent grasp was not a task for the fainthearted. It was time to act.

The same blond-haired man he'd first met slid into the empty chair across from him. 'Good afternoon, Colonel. Do you have what I asked for?'

Hradetsky shoved the envelope across the table and waited while the man glanced inside it briefly and handed it back. He seemed satisfied. 'Follow me.'

Without saying anything more, the younger man got up and left the cafeteria. With Hradetsky in tow, he took a circuitous route through Budapest's crowded streets – a route that ended at a small apartment building in one of the more fashionable districts.

They went in through a back entrance, climbed two flights of stairs, and halted in front of an unmarked door. The blond-haired man turned for one last look down the stairs and then knocked three times. When the door opened, he motioned the police colonel through ahead of him.

Two men were waiting for them in a tastefully furnished living room. One of them, markedly older than the other, stood up and said quietly, 'I am Vladimir Kusin.'

The man in front of Hradetsky was pale and thin, almost anemic. His clothes were shabby, although this appeared to be more from long use than lack of care. Although he was only in his fifties, his hair was snow-white, and a deeply lined face added ten years to his apparent age. A winter spent in prison had clearly been hard on him.

During Hungary's brief postcommunist flirtation with democratic rule, Kusin had been the elected leader of one of Budapest's district councils. When the military-dominated Government of National Salvation took power, he'd been jailed for unspecified acts of 'agitation.' What that meant, the colonel knew, was that he'd complained too vehemently and too vocally about the new regime's emergency decrees.

And even though Kusin was articulate enough to have acquired some following in the Western media, that hadn't protected him from a trumped-up charge and six months in prison. The generals had only released him when they were sure he was a spent force – a weak and ailing reed unable to challenge their hold on power.

They had miscalculated.

Even illness and imprisonment hadn't stopped him. Kusin's ability to smuggle out statements on human rights, French and German economic and political influence, and other forbidden topics was one of the reasons Hradetsky had sought him out.

In the month since Hungary had joined the European Confederation, Kusin had become even more vocal. Pamphlets and underground newspaper articles bearing his signature called for an end to military rule and immediate withdrawal from the Confederation. He was the closest thing to a national leader that Hungary's growing opposition had.

Kusin turned toward Hradetsky's escort. 'Any problems?'

The blond man shook his head. 'No, sir. I saw no warning signals, and my boys are still in place.'

Kusin saw Hradetsky's puzzled look and explained. 'This is Oskar Kiraly, Colonel. He and a few of his friends watch over me.'

So that was it. The police colonel studied his escort with greater interest. For all practical purposes, Kiraly was Vladimir Kusin's chief of security. Maybe these people were better organized than he had thought.

The older man motioned him into an adjacent room – from the look of it a small bedroom temporarily converted into an office and library. Kusin sat down and indicated a second chair for Hradetsky. Kiraly stood behind them, near the door.

'May I see the file you showed Oskar?'

Hradetsky gave him the manila envelope, along with a separate packet containing all the documents he'd been given by Bela Silvanus. He nodded toward the photocopied police file. 'Aren't you worried that may be false?'

Kusin shook his head. 'If it is, your future is short, I'm afraid.' His eyes flickered toward Kiraly. Suddenly the colonel's shoulder blades itched. He forced himself to sit calmly. If they wanted him dead, there wasn't much he could do about it. The opposition leader scanned the copied file quickly, smiled, and then opened the other envelope.

Kusin's white, tufted eyebrows rose as he realized what it contained. 'This is fascinating, Colonel Hradetsky. You would make a first-class spy.'

He winced inwardly, and some of it must have shown on his face, because the older man quickly added, 'That is not why we need you, though.'

Kusin leaned back in his chair. 'So, Colonel, what is it that you want? Why did you seek me out?' He flicked the pile of reassignment orders and termination lists in his lap. 'Only to show me these? Or for something more?'

Hradetsky sighed, knowing this was a moment of truth – a turning point from would-be reformer to revolutionary. 'I started out wanting to stop this man Rehling's orders, to bring some sanity back to the National Police. Now I don't think that can happen. Not under this government.'

'It can't,' Kusin agreed firmly. 'Rehling and the others like him are merely symptoms of a greater illness. These French and German satraps infect our country because the generals believe they need this Confederation's support to maintain their power. What the soldiers do not seem to realize is that their onetime allies are very rapidly becoming their masters. And our masters as well.'

'Yes. I understand that.' Hradetsky stifled his impatience. For all his eloquence, Kusin was still a politician. And politicians liked to talk. 'But what can we do to stop this?'

'Beside printing futile complaints, you mean?' The older man laughed softly. 'There are a lot of people like you, Colonel, who were willing to accept a Government of National Salvation, but not this supposed European Confederation. We are going to mobilize those newly dissatisfied people. We are going to expand our own organization. Recruiting some of the police officers on this list you gave us will be very useful.'

Kusin's voice grew harder, even more determined. 'And if the French and the Germans push us too far, we will fight.'

There was a fire in his eyes and his voice that Hradetsky felt warming his own blood. He wanted to act, not sit here in this study. 'Then what do you want me to do?'.

'You are a trained leader, Colonel. An expert in the art of managing men and controlling crowds. We will use that expertise for our own purposes.' Kusin leaned closer to him. 'Very soon, we will mass ten thousand people or more for a march on the Parliament building to demand reforms. You are going to help us organize this protest.'

The opposition leader sat back. His eyes were colder now, fixed on some distant horizon beyond Hradetsky's view. 'And then?' He smiled sadly. 'Then we shall see just how far these madmen in Paris and Berlin can be pushed.'

APRIL 5 – NATIONAL SECURITY COUNCIL MEETING, SITUATION ROOM, THE WHITE HOUSE

The news from Europe was grim.

'Essentially the French and German military buildup along the Polish and Czech borders is continuing, Mr. President. In fact, it may even be accelerating. The whole border area is rapidly becoming a powder keg.' Gen. Reid Galloway, chairman of the Joint Chiefs, stood behind a podium next to a wall-sized video monitor. The fact that America's top-ranked soldier was delivering this briefing in person emphasized how seriously he viewed the events piling up across the Atlantic. The creases across a normally optimistic, good-humored face were another clear indication.

Ross Huntington shared the general's pessimistic view. Outraged by the French-funded oil embargo and the attack on *North Star*, Poland and the Czech and Slovak republics had broken all diplomatic ties with the European Confederation. And with France stonewalling demands for a full investigation, Britain and Norway had recalled their ambassadors from Paris for 'consultation.' Public pressure in the United States was building for similar moves. What had begun as a political and economic crisis was rapidly taking on a military aspect as well. He clenched his left fist repeatedly, hoping it would ease the pressure in his chest.

Galloway clicked through several images in rapid succession, using a hand-held controller to circle the parts of each image he considered particularly important. Some of the photos he highlighted showed jet aircraft parked out in the open near hardened shelters. Others featured row after row of tanks and other armored vehicles lined up in cleared fields near small villages and larger towns. 'As these satellite photos show, EurCon is in the process of moving substantial air and ground forces to new bases in eastern Germany. Significantly, they aren't making any real effort to hide this redeployment.'

'Could they?' The President sat forward in his chair.

Galloway nodded vigorously. 'Yes, sir. My EurCon counterparts know the orbital data for every recon satellite we have. If they wanted to, they could be moving this hardware around when we're blind – and concealing it under camouflage netting or in shelters when we're not. We'd still pick up signs of movement, but not anywhere near this fast or this easily.'

'So this is primarily a political maneuver to step up the pressure on the Poles and Czechs – and not a preliminary move toward deliberate military action?'

'Exactly, Mr. President.' The chairman of the Joint Chiefs keyed the monitor off and raised the room lights to full brightness. 'But our allies can't take that chance, so they're being forced to respond in kind.

'Although they're still worried about Russia, the Poles are more worried about EurCon. So far they've deployed four of their nine active-duty divisions along the German frontier, with another two close behind in reserve. And when I talked to General Staron, their Defense Minister, this morning, he informed me that his President is considering reactivating one of their reserve divisions. The Czechs and Slovaks are taking similar steps.'

Huntington felt the band around his chest tighten even more. This was very bad news. Calling reservists from their civilian jobs back to the colors was always a costly proposition. The fact that the eastern European countries were even considering it in a time of great economic hardship indicated just how concerned they were.

Galloway shook his head somberly. 'With tens of thousands of troops on full alert and aircraft flying combat air patrols in close proximity to each other, the place is just one hell of an accident waiting to happen.'

'Swell.' The President swiveled his chair toward Harris Thurman. 'Any recent diplomatic developments I should know about?'

'No, sir.' The Secretary of State sounded apologetic. 'Nobody's budged so much as an inch.'

'All right, people. I need your input. What exactly are my options here?' The President tapped the table with his pen. 'General? John? Any ideas on your end of things?'

The Secretary of Defense looked thoughtful. 'The Joint Chiefs and I believe we should boost our military aid to Poland and the others even further, Mr. President. By drawing down some of our reserve forces equipment we could—'

'Send more tanks?' Thurman looked aghast. 'General Galloway is right. The whole region is an armed camp now. How can shipping in more weapons possibly help?'

Lucier kept his attention locked on the President. 'Weapons by themselves don't provoke wars. Perceptions and intentions are far more important.'

Huntington nodded to himself. The short, bookish Secretary of Defense was right there. Too many arms control pundits focused only on the hardware side of the equation. By their bizarre set of rules, both Adolf Hitler's massive program to rearm for conquest and the belated Allied efforts to thwart the Nazi dictator would have been judged equally destabilizing.

'EurCon evidently views the Poles and the rest as militarily weak, and thus susceptible to military pressure. In turn, they know that much of their equipment is outdated. To make up for that, they've had to bring their armed forces to higher and higher states of alert. When you're outgunned and outnumbered, you must make sure every available tank, plane, and soldier is ready for battle.'

Lucier looked over his thick, horn-rimmed glasses at the Secretary of State. 'Perceived weakness is exacerbating this crisis, Harris. Not strength. So we can accomplish two very important aims by increasing our military aid now. First, we put EurCon's leaders on notice that we're calling their bluff. And second, we'll build Polish and Czech confidence. The more certain they are that they can withstand a sudden EurCon attack, the more likely they are to pull their forces back from the border and ratchet down their alert state.'

In the momentary silence that followed, the President sat frowning, evidently still somewhat unsure of which course to follow. He scanned the assembled group. 'If I okay this extra military aid, what's the likely EurCon reaction?'

'Paris and Berlin will be furious.' Thurman sounded unhappy. 'They regard all of eastern Europe as their own backyard, so they're bound to regard further arms shipments as a deliberate provocation.'

The President nodded slowly, still frowning. 'But how far will they go, Harris?' He glanced around the table. 'Take the worst case. Would EurCon risk a military confrontation over this issue?'

'Unlikely, sir.' Galloway shook his head. 'They're trying to intimidate the Poles and the rest – not start an open war with us.'

'EurCon won't roll over, though,' Huntington warned. 'The French and Germans want Poland and the others inside their orbit too badly to give up so easily. We can expect heated protests.' He paused. 'Probably coupled with additional covert attacks against us or against our allies.'

The President and the rest of the NSC nodded. Though they didn't have enough proof to go public with their suspicions, everybody in the room knew EurCon agents were responsible for the destruction of the LNG tanker and for the murder of an American intelligence officer. Nobody would be particularly surprised by more EurCon sabotage attempts. He looked down the table at the head of the CIA. 'What about it, Walt? Can your antiterrorism people handle the threat?'

'Yes, Mr. President,' Quinn said confidently. 'I know there's no such thing as a leakproof defense, but now that we know what we're up against, we've got a much better chance to thwart any covert operations aimed our way.'

Galloway backed Quinn up. 'Besides the warships we send as escorts, we can put special teams from Delta Force and SEAL Team Six on every freighter and tanker going into the Baltic.' The general's eyes flashed fire. 'And with those guys in place, I'll guarantee any son-of-a-bitch who tries to plant another limpet mine a short ride to hell.'

Huntington watched his old friend sit silently, weighing his options. Putting more U.S.-flagged ships, citizens, and soldiers at risk wasn't an appealing prospect, but the alternatives – accidental war as border tensions rose, or Franco-German control over the whole European continent – seemed far worse.

The President straightened up. 'All right, we'll send the equipment, and back it up if need be.' He glanced around the table. 'Any other objections or comments?'

'Yes, Mr. President.' Apparently Thurman wasn't quite ready to surrender completely. 'Before we send more war matériel to Poland, we should at least make sure the other European states understand our intentions. Substantial arms shipments without full notification could provoke a dreadful misunderstanding. Surely that's a risk we don't want to run.'

'Agreed. What do you have in mind?'

'Well . . .' The Secretary of State fiddled with his pipe, obviously at something of a loss. 'A public statement would be helpful. Or perhaps you could talk to the French ambassador. He represents EurCon interests here.'

'No.' The President's eyes narrowed. 'I will not meet with any representative of a government that has murdered American citizens and destroyed American property.'

Other NSC members growled their agreement.

'Then perhaps I could call the ambassador in to . . .'

The President shook his head again. 'I don't want any official, high-level contacts, Harris. Not while these people are essentially waging a covert war against us.'

'Then how are we supposed to communicate with EurCon, Mr. President?'

'Unofficially. Unofficially and through the back door, Mr. Secretary.'

The irritated took on Thurman's face confirmed what Huntington had half suspected all along. The State Department's patrician chief often cared more about his own prestige inside the cabinet and the Beltway than he did about effective policy. But if the President didn't want to use the diplomats to convey his message, that left only one other route and one other messenger.

Huntington sat up straighter as the President turned toward him, hoping he could mask his fatigue.

'How about it, Ross?'

'Yes, sir.' He nodded firmly. 'I can make another trip.'

APRIL 10 – TRAINING AREA, 5TH MECHANIZED DIVISION, NEAR GAJEC, POLAND

Maj. Gen. Jerzy Novachik stood still facing east, watching the western edge of a small patch of forest near the German border. He shaded his eyes with an open hand, squinting against the rising sun. He resisted the temptation to check his watch again. Predawn maneuvers were always tough to coordinate. Showing his impatience would only make his staff nervous without achieving anything useful.

Startled by a sudden noise from deeper inside the woods, birds exploded into the air in a mass of black, fluttering wings. Now.

Fourteen M1 tanks howled out of the forest, moving in line abreast at high speed. Mud sprayed out behind them, thrown high by their clattering tracks. Novachik could see helmets silhouetted in open hatches on top of each tank's low, squat turret.

Good, he thought. The company's tank commanders were on the ball, risking shell fragments and sniper bullets while they scanned the terrain around them for signs of the enemy. The temptation to sit snug and secure inside a buttoned-up armored vehicle was always strong. It was also almost always dangerous.

With the hatches closed, tank crews were almost blind and deaf – especially when moving through woods. And what they didn't see could very often kill them.

As the M1s cleared the treeline, Novachik heard one of his staff officers snap out an order. 'Activate!'

Five hundred meters north of the charging tanks, several rows of cardboard targets popped up off the ground. Some bore Leopard 2 silhouettes. Others showed Marder APCs. Like other officers in Poland's army, the general didn't believe in screwing around with generic labels. He knew his likely enemies.

Almost before the last target flipped up, the M1s were reacting. Turrets whined right, slewing around to bring their 105mm guns to bear. The whole line wheeled north – still moving at close to sixty kilometers an hour.

Crack! An M1 fired – disappearing for just an instant as it thundered through the smoke from its own gun. As it reappeared, more tanks opened up, pumping shell after shell into the mass of pop-up targets.

They stopped shooting almost before the sounds of the first volley finished echoing across the open field. The M1s changed front again, sliding back into a line headed west.

Novachik raised his binoculars, zeroing in on the target area. Fantastic. The silhouettes were gone – every one knocked back down onto the torn, shell-churned ground.

'Exercise complete, sir.'

He smiled genially at the young officer who had organized this display. 'So I see, Henryk. Very impressive.' He meant it. The M1's ability to fire accurately while on the move put it light-years ahead of the T-72s and T-55s that equipped the rest of his division. Unfortunately the 5th Mechanized still only had enough of the American armored vehicles to outfit one of its five reorganized tank battalions. There were reports that more U.S. equipment was on the way, but the Polish general knew he couldn't count on getting it. If war came, whether deliberately or accidentally, he would have to fight his battles with a mix of disparate weapons and tactics.

Novachik turned to the short, black-haired American officer standing next to him. 'And what did you think, Major?'

After nearly six months in Poland, Maj. Bill Takei was picking up the language fast. 'A solid performance, sir. Your troops are learning how to use their new equipment almost faster than I can teach them.'

'I'm very glad to hear it.' Novachik studied the Japanese-American closer. He'd worked with Novachik and his men closely, certain that they would have to use this equipment and their training, somewhere, sometime.

The 'Hell on Wheels' armored division combat patch on the younger man's shoulder showed that he had seen action during the Desert Storm campaign. And whenever he smiled, a thin, faint tracery of scar tissue showed on the right side of his face, climbing from his cheek almost all the way up to his eye. It was a strange feeling to command a man who had actually fought in a war while all he'd ever done was practice for one.

Americans like Takei were working throughout the Polish Army and Air Force, trying to blend American equipment and tactics with their Soviet predecessors into something that would meet uniquely Polish needs.

Followed by a gaggle of staff officers and other observers, the two men walked back across the muddy, rutted field toward a parked column of GAZ jeeps and Humvees. As his boots sank into the soft ground, Maj. Gen. Jerzy Novachik wondered how Takei's lightning-swift war of sweeping movement, blinding sandstorms, and burning oil might compare with one fought in this soft, green, confining landscape. It would be bloodier here, he thought grimly. Much bloodier.

CHAPTER 14
Narrow Margin

APRIL 15 – CNN HEADLINE NEWS

European developments dominated CNN's afternoon news wrap-up.

'Furious at Washington's plans to ship more arms to Poland and the Czech Republic, the European Confederation's fledgling Foreign Secretariat issued a stinging condemnation at a hastily called press conference in Paris.'

The camera view cut away from the Atlanta anchor desk to a prerecorded clip taped hours earlier outside the French Foreign Ministry. Sheltered from a spring drizzle by umbrellas held aloft by his aides, an unidentified official stood reading a prepared statement in French. An English-accented voice translated his angry words for American viewers. 'The Confederation utterly rejects this latest cynical attempt by the United States to inject itself in Europe's internal affairs. At a time of unfortunate rising tensions, it is an act of madness to ship more weapons to a region already bristling with arms. If this regrettable confrontation explodes out of hand, it will be the United States itself which has furnished the gasoline and lit the match . . .'

The scene shifted to a military airfield identified by caption only as being somewhere in 'Northern Germany.' Crewmen could be seen working on several camouflaged warplanes, while other jets taxied past them in the background. Patrolling soldiers and guard dogs were visible near a barbed-wire fence in the distance. An off-camera reporter narrated this segment. 'While its diplomats express their outrage at the administration's actions, the EurCon Defense Secretariat is taking sterner measures. CNN has learned that several squadrons of German and French combat aircraft have been placed on a higher state of alert. A high-ranking Secretariat official characterizes this as a "sound precautionary move, given the large number of American warships now operating so close to our northern coast." '

APRIL 24 – ABOARD USS *LEYTE GULF*, IN THE NORTH SEA

Eight ships raced southeast at high speed, slicing through long, gray-green waves rolling steadily eastward. A long line of low-lying dark clouds stretched across the western horizon behind them – the leading edge of a slow-moving storm they'd punched through while rounding the northern tip of Scotland.

Four of the vessels were massive SL-7 container ships, each nearly a thousand feet long but still able to move at thirty-three knots. Together the freighters carried enough M1 Abrams tanks, M2 Bradley infantry fighting vehicles, artillery pieces, helicopters, spare parts, and ammunition to completely refit a Polish mechanized brigade. They were ringed by four sleek, antenna-studded U.S. Navy warships – two Aegis-class guided-missile cruisers, *Leyte Gulf* and *Monterey*; *John Barry*, a *Burke*-class guided-missile destroyer; and an improved *Spruance*-class destroyer, *Conolly*.

Task Group 22.1 was a powerful force to guard just four cargo ships, far more powerful than standard naval doctrine would have dictated. With tensions in Europe still climbing, Washington was using this arms convoy to send a strong signal to the leaders in Paris and Berlin: America would not back away from its Polish and Czech allies. Not even under growing EurCon pressure.

Vice Adm. Jack Ward lowered his binoculars, satisfied by what he could see from *Leyte Gulf*'s bridge wing. He'd been working the whole group incessantly since their mid-Atlantic rendezvous, running drill after drill against every imaginable threat. Now all that hard work was starting to pay off. Even the civilian-manned container ships were keeping station with almost military precision.

The admiral was a middling-tall man with broad shoulders and a long reach that had served him well as a boxer at the Naval Academy. Snow-white hair topped a tanned, square-jawed face that only turned red when he was ready to jump down somebody's throat. That didn't happen often. Just often enough to keep his subordinates on their toes.

Since joining the fleet during the mid-sixties, Ward had seen steady, if not spectacular, promotion. Along the way he'd attended all the right staff and command schools, held several commands both ashore and afloat, and managed to finagle more sea duty than any of his contemporaries. For the admiral, being a sailor meant being aboard a warship at sea – not confined to sailing a desk or navigating the Pentagon's labyrinthine corridors.

Now he commanded Task Force 22, the collection of American warships assigned to provide escorts for the oil and LNG tankers keeping Poland and the Czech and Slovak republics alive. Task Group 22.1 and their charges was only one of several similar formations under his control.

His cruisers, destroyers, and frigates had been hard at work for more than six weeks now, shepherding the mammoth floating bombs from Scotland and Norway through the narrow straits to Gdansk. At first, their biggest problems had come when Greenpeace demonstrators tried chaining themselves to the tankers or forming small boat blockades. Lately, though, his captains had been reporting increasing Franco-German air and naval activity – barely disguised harassment, really – along the sea approaches to the Baltic.

Ward was expecting even more trouble this time. Egged on by their political leaders, EurCon's military commanders were taking more serious measures to turn their anger into action. Over the past several days, they'd stepped up their air patrols over the Atlantic and the North Sea, put several squadrons of maritime attack aircraft on higher states of alert, and sortied an unusually large number of diesel and nuclear submarines. But it was all part of the same dangerous game of intimidation they'd been playing with his oil and gas convoys. Probably.

The admiral frowned. He didn't scare easily. Of course, he also didn't plan on making his opposing numbers' lives any easier. That was why he'd brought this convoy around Scotland rather than through the English Channel. The SL-7s were so fast that going the extra distance cost very little time. And taking the northern route avoided the bulk of the French coast – making it that much more difficult for EurCon's search planes to find them.

Ward looked up as a bright light began flashing from the closest destroyer, *John Barry*. He checked his watch. Probably the noon position report.

All communications between his ships were being passed the old-fashioned way, either by signal flags or by blinker light. Task Group 22.1 was operating in EMCON, or emission control. Traveling in radio and radar silence would make the convoy harder for the French or Germans to find. The less they knew about his position, course, and speed, the happier he was.

Naturally the closer the group got to the funnel called the Skagerrak, the easier it would be to find. But then it wouldn't matter so much. With their own trade lifelines at risk, Denmark and Sweden were enforcing strict operating restrictions on ships and aircraft near the straits. And with both EurCon and U.S. diplomats wooing the two countries, neither side wanted trouble there. No, the only place with enough room for real monkey business was the North Sea. Here.

Ward took one last breath of crisp, clean salt air and left the bridge wing, headed for *Leyte Gulf*'s CIC. It was time to settle down to business. The boatswain's announcement 'Admiral's left the bridge' followed him as he headed for the ship's brain.

The days when opposing ships met yardarm-to-yardarm were long gone. Modern naval battles were fought at long range by men hunched over computer displays in darkened, air-conditioned compartments.

CIC was one deck down, behind a door with a cipher-key lock on it. A brass plaque proudly proclaimed the ship's name, builder, and dates of launching and commissioning. As he punched the combination and pushed the door open, he stepped into a different world.

The darkened space was crammed with equipment, its huge size hidden by row after row of displays and panels. Two 'alleys,' lined with consoles on either side, ran almost the full length of the space. Capping the alleys at one end were four special consoles for Ward and *Leyte*'s captain in the center, and their watch officers on the sides.

Equipment didn't just cover the deck. Overhead, TV screens replaced the old Plexiglas and grease-pencil status boards, displaying ship's status, contacts, the Aegis computer's health, and other vital information. TV cameras mounted fore and aft showed views of the bow and stern, while any spot on the overhead not already used held pencil-beam lights, air-conditioning equipment, or mysterious gray boxes filled with electronics. While the space was neatly laid out, it was so jammed with gear that Ward's first impression was that he had somehow stepped inside a piece of electronic equipment.

He nodded to his staff watch officer, Commander Miller, and the ship's tactical action officer. These two posts were always manned, and they would have to 'fight the ship' if a threat suddenly appeared. Before sitting in his own chair, he scanned the displays, trying to understand their situation.

Laid out in front of the command consoles were four huge computer screens, each four feet square and able to show any part of the world that an operator desired. Right now they seemed almost blank – robbed of input by the group's EMCON status.

They showed a computer-generated map of the North Sea, overlaid with symbols showing the estimated positions of reported air, surface, and subsurface contacts. A cluster of eight symbols in the center of each screen showed 'TG22.1.' Several officers and men were busy constantly updating the display from the sources they did have – visual sighting reports and even long-range sonar contacts.

Some of the data they were using came from the Task Group's passive sensors. While Ward's ships were electronically silent, they were still listening with every antenna they had. Emissions from EurCon's search planes and ships could be analyzed and dissected to reveal their bearings and their identities. The information gathered by passive sensors was never very precise, but it was better than nothing.

John Barry even mounted a special intelligence-collection van on her fantail. The admiral wasn't privy to exactly what went on in there, but he knew the van carried enough electronics equipment to spy on the little green men on Mars, if the operators wanted to. Most of the data they gathered would go straight back to the Joint Chiefs. The Pentagon wanted to know just how well the French and the Germans were working together. How closely did they cooperate? How did they manage tactical communications? Were EurCon's armed forces still using standard NATO tactics or were they developing new methods?

Other pieces of the information came from the British. Royal Navy and RAF units were scouring the region – shadowing their French and German counterparts, or complicating matters for the EurCon searchers by giving them more potential targets to track and identify.

He settled into the chair and put on his headset. As he listened to the calm, businesslike interplay, Ward studied the screen, trying to see the pattern behind what appeared at first to be a random scattering of EurCon planes, ships, and submarines. There was a pattern, he was sure. There must be. It took careful planning to mount an efficient sea search – to formulate a precise, synchronized ballet that took into account varying scouting platform speeds, endurances, sensor ranges, and the weather. Guessing the next moves in that intricately choreographed dance might help him spot a gap big enough for Task Group 22.1 and its four valuable charges to slip through undetected. Or, failing that, he might be able to tear open the hole he needed – using British vessels as decoys to lure the hunters off target.

Pieces of the puzzle started falling slowly into place. Most of EurCon's assets seemed to be concentrated further south, along the approaches to the English Channel. They were mounting an aerial sweep northward to cover the waters between Britain and Norway, but the coverage seemed tentative, almost incomplete. Odd . . .

An enlisted man operating the electronic warfare console sat bolt upright. His voice betrayed a little excitement, but he still kept his report precise. 'Racket bearing one six five. Evaluated as Iguane airborne radar. Strong signal. Time one two one nine.' A symbol appeared on the display, and selecting it, Ward saw a line of bearing appear, running from *Leyte Gulf* out in the direction the radar had been detected. There was no telling exactly how far away the plane carrying that radar was, but a strong signal meant it was probably close – too close.

Miller, seated to his left, scanned his own console and nodded. 'An Atlantique, sir.'

Damn. The French Atlantique was a long-range patrol plane similar to the U.S. Navy's P-3C Orion. Ward checked the display. Nothing showed. No earlier sightings or distant radar emissions that correlated. For all practical purposes this guy had materialized out of nowhere. Hell, that EurCon pilot out there must have been hugging wave tops since takeoff. He suppressed a quick flash of admiration for the flying skill that showed, and asked a single question. 'Does he have us spotted?'

'Probably, sir. Signal strength is still increasing.'

Another operator passed word over the circuit. 'We're picking up a high-frequency radio transmission, sir. Same bearing as the radar.'

Ward scowled. The Atlantique must be radioing in a contact report. Terrific. They'd been tagged. He looked at the plot again. The French plane had to be close. And it was flying in from a direction he'd picked out earlier as a possible gap in the EurCon search pattern. Either French sensors were better than the navy's intelligence community thought they were, or some Frog staff officer had practically read his mind.

Well, that was something to ponder later. Right now he had bigger fish to fry, or at least to illuminate. He caught the TAO's eye and nodded. 'Okay, Jerry, light 'em off. Tell the Task Group to energize all radars and data links. Let's see just what we're up against.'

'Aye, aye, sir.' The lieutenant commander spoke softly into his microphone, passing orders to his own ship and the others in the formation. Ward also heard him inform *Leyte*'s captain of the change in the ship's status.

The tempo picked up in CIC as screen after screen came to life. The main display suddenly filled with hundreds of air and sea contacts, quickly sorted out by the Aegis system's computers. Most commercial aircraft carried radar transponders that identified them as such, while friendly military aircraft could be identified down to type and side number. EurCon military aircraft also carried transponders, but they would only answer to their own coded transmissions.

Task Group 22.1's data links were as important as its radars. The links allowed computers on each ship to communicate with each other, sharing information on targets and weapons status. Since they required the use of radio, they had been shut down to avoid detection. Once the data links were active, the group's cruisers and destroyers could fight welded into a single, integrated unit instead of operating as a loosely knit team.

Ward focused on the main screen, looking for the snooper who'd picked them up. A small inverted vee shape showed the position of the EurCon Atlantique, while a line from it showed its course and speed. The patrol plane was sixty miles out, orbiting at medium altitude. In wartime, he could have had that aircraft shot from the sky in moments. Now all he could do was watch it pace his convoy, counting, classifying, and reporting.

He glanced toward his staff watch officer again. 'We need more information, so let's go out and get it. Throw a picket line of helos out in front of us.'

Within minutes, three SH-60 Seahawk helicopters – half the group's total strength – were clattering away to the east, southeast, and south. Once on station, they would form a picket line sweeping eighty miles out in front of the formation before turning back to refuel. Although *Leyte Gulf*'s SPY-1 radar could pick out large targets at high altitude up to several hundred miles away, it couldn't spot smaller warplanes or missiles flying low until they came over the horizon, just fifty miles away. Not even a phased array radar could see through the earth itself. Deploying the Seahawks with their own data-linked radars, ESM gear, and sharp-eyed crews gave the group that much more warning time.

'Advise CINCLANTFLT that we expect company shortly. And contact the British. See if they can rustle up some kind of top cover for us.'

Ward would have preferred having U.S. Navy fighters flying overhead on combat air patrol. They were used to working with Aegis-equipped ships. But there weren't any F-14 Tomcats or F-18 Hornets available. The nearest American aircraft carrier was still far out in the North Atlantic – nearly a thousand miles away. Reluctant to escalate tensions any further, Washington had ruled out committing a carrier battle group to the North Sea. He understood the politics involved. He just didn't like the naked feeling he got operating without the aviators backing him up.

He had one more order for Commander Miller. 'Have the formation go to general quarters.' Moments later, he heard the shrill boatswain's pipe and the klaxon.

SEAHAWK 202

Lt. Dan Maguire, Seahawk 202's sensor operator, yawned loudly, glad that the noise he made was swallowed up by the helicopter's own rattling, pounding roar. Even when you were expecting trouble, flying a long patrol over the ocean could be boring. They were seventy miles and one hour out from Task Group 22.1.

Maguire was a short, wiry man, full of energy, in his mid-twenties and with two years of navy experience already under his belt, who found the Seahawk's comfortable cockpit absolutely roomy. His black hair and dark, Irish looks were well hidden behind a flight helmet and visor.

He scanned the glowing displays in front of him in a rapid, practiced sequence. The Seahawk was a sensor platform as much as anything else – a long-range and mobile pair of eyes and ears for U.S. Navy formations. It carried a surface search radar, magnetic anomaly detection gear, or MAD, to spot the metal in a submerged submarine's hull, and ESM, electronic intercept equipment, which told them the direction and type of any hostile radars.

'Anything interesting?'

Maguire glanced up from his instruments. The pilot of 202, Lt. Peter Chen, was busy with his own checks – keeping an eye on his flight instruments and periodically sweeping the sky and sea around them. 'Nope. Plenty of surface contacts, but they're all fishing trawlers or merchants. ESM shows nothing but low-power nav radars out there.'

'How about the Atlantique?'

'Still orbiting.' Maguire jerked his head to the left. 'Over there. Off to port about ten miles.'

At that distance the twin-engine French aircraft was just a barely visible dot. Sunlight winked off its wings as it made another slow, lazy turn.

Maguire and Chen had flown together for six months now, and were a good match. Maguire knew his gear inside and out, while Chen was incessantly curious. In another time Maguire could easily imagine Chen, also short and wiry, on horseback, scouting for the enemy, riding the same way he flew the Seahawk, darting, probing, searching. Chen even bragged about being half-Mongol, on his mother's side.

Maguire studied his sensors again. The radar display still showed the same scattered array of slow-moving ships. He froze. No, it didn't. There were new blips near the edge of the screen – blips that were coming closer fast. He clicked his radio mike. '*Leyte Gulf*, this is Seahawk 202. Many high-speed bogies bearing one seven six, forty miles, level zero!'

He heard the cruiser's antiair warfare coordinator acknowledge the contact report and made sure the helo's data link was working properly. It was. The men waiting in the Task Group's darkened CICs were seeing everything he was.

'Bogies still bearing one seven six. Range now three five. Speed six hundred.'

The Seahawk turned and lost altitude, sliding down toward the ocean. The incoming planes would have to pass right by it on their way to the convoy. With luck, the helicopter's two crewmen might be able to make a visual identification.

Maguire kept his eyes glued to the radar screen, still calling out rapidly decreasing ranges and a steady bearing. Chen leveled out five hundred feet above the water and watched the southern horizon.

'Range six. See 'em yet?'

'No . . . yes!' Chen saw three groups of four aircraft straight ahead. They were flying lower than the helo and growing larger every second. 'Jesus, Dan, they're coming in right on the deck.'

'Can you identify them, 202?' *Leyte Gulf*'s antiair coordinator asked.

'Negative. Hold on. Bogies are climbing . . . Christ!'

Engines roaring at full thrust, the EurCon jets screamed right over them – rocketing past with barely one hundred feet to spare. Eight were big-tailed, two-seater aircraft with German crosses painted on their fuselages and white missiles hung beneath their swept-back wings. The four trailing aircraft were marked with the tricolor roundel. Chen fought to regain control as the Seahawk, caught in their wake, rocked violently up and down before plunging toward the sea below.

Maguire grabbed his shoulder straps with one hand and keyed his mike with the other. 'Bogies are Tornados and Rafales! Tornados are armed! Repeat, the Tornados are armed.'

Maguire hung on, ignoring the information dancing across his display screens. Attacking German aircraft were something you saw in old war movies. Were they really going to do it all over again?

LEYTE GULF

Twelve arrowhead shapes appeared on the CIC's main display. The incoming German attack jets and their French fighter escorts had finally been detected by the Aegis system as they climbed above the radar horizon. They were just sixty-six miles out and still closing. Ward felt the hairs rise on the back of his neck.

'ESM warning! Multiple Ku-band radars bearing one seven six!' Even as they matched the bearing with the arrowhead symbols, the electronic warfare operator announced, 'Transmissions ceased.' Simultaneously the SPY radar operator reported, 'We've lost height data. They've gone below my horizon.'

Shit. Ward glanced at a smaller side screen, one showing the data-linked radar picture still being broadcast by Seahawk 202. The EurCon aircraft were still boring in. They'd dived back down to the deck, flying close to Mach 1 just above the waves. Because the Seahawk still tracked the aircraft, the computer could continue to show their positions accurately on the display.

He knew exactly what it meant. The Tornados had popped up and turned on their radars just long enough to find the convoy and feed targeting information into the antiship missiles they were carrying. From now on they could fly in low enough to launch an attack in near-perfect safety.

Ward kept his eyes on the Tornados' symbols. He had the lead plane 'hooked,' so that its speed, course, and most important, range were displayed on a small screen in front of him. A small line across the top marked each plane as 'engaged.' The Aegis system had locked on and assigned missiles to each aircraft.

Before Task Group 22.1 linked up with the four SL-7 container ships, Washington had issued a warning notice, an 'exclusion zone,' consistent with international law. Any aircraft approaching the convoy closer than fifty nautical miles would be fired on.

The Tornados were only sixty miles away now. They were closing at roughly ten miles a minute. He was running out of time to make decisions.

On a long-range, low-altitude mission, each of the eight German attack jets still barreling in could carry two Kormoran 2 antiship missiles. Sixteen missiles launched from close range might be enough to saturate even an Aegis cruiser's defenses.

The Kormoran 2 had a thirty-nautical-mile range. It would take the *Leyte Gulf*, *Monterey*, or *John Barry*'s SM-2 antiaircraft missiles a minute to cover that distance, and it would take another half a minute to launch enough missiles to destroy the German aircraft carrying the Kormorans. That means that once the Tornados crossed the fifty-mile line, Ward would have just thirty seconds to decide whether or not to start a war.

Fifty-five miles. His mouth felt dry. Turning his head, he could see his missile engagement controller's hand hovering over the console, waiting for a command.

Fifty-three miles. Any second now.

On the main display, the lines showing the Tornados' course and speed suddenly shortened, then started to turn. In one moment they were definitely pointing away from the formation. In the next they were ninety degrees off of their original course. He glanced at the small screen in front of him. They were definitely slowing and turning, and the SPY radar held them again. The Tornados and their Rafale escorts were climbing. They were turning away!

Ward breathed out. He'd been granted a reprieve. The EurCon planes had only been conducting a 'live' exercise. It was harassment, but also training in its purest form, for both sides. The men in Paris and Berlin didn't want a shooting war – at least not yet.

APRIL 28

The map and radar displays in *Leyte Gulf*'s CIC showed the Polish coast just ninety miles ahead. Task Group 22.1 and its four laden charges were four hours away from Gdansk.

Ward sipped a scalding-hot cup of coffee, his fifth in as many hours, and pondered the situation. Since that first mock air attack, EurCon's commanders had thrown everything they had at his convoy – more aircraft, diesel submarines, small missile attack boats, armed helicopters, even surface groups of German destroyers and frigates. It reminded him of the sixties and early seventies. He had been a junior officer then, serving in the Mediterranean. For years the U.S. Sixth Fleet and the Soviet Fifth Eskadra had played hardball, seeing just how far each could push the other. Now old allies were playing the same dangerous game with each other. EurCon played the game well, even better than the Russians.

At least the confrontations were useful training for his bleary-eyed crews. With the fragments of the Russian Navy now staying very close to home, America's warships had the world's oceans pretty much to themselves during the past several years. Each nerve-racking brush with a potentially hostile force lent new urgency and new impetus to the group's combat and damage control drills.

The four-day-long simulated 'battle' had taught him to regard submarines as the biggest EurCon threat. With enough warning and enough sea room for maneuvering, his three Aegis-armed ships could fend off most air or missile attacks. Finding and sinking enemy subs in these confined waters was a very different story.

By definition, modern submarines were designed to be unseen and unheard killing machines. Anyone trying to hunt them had to sort out the soft sounds made by their propellers and machinery from a confusing mix of background, or ambient, noise. Since both the North Sea and the Baltic were so shallow, even a little chop on the surface could raise the ambient noise level significantly. Add to that the engine sounds made by all the other military and civilian ships operating in the area and the weird sounds of marine life and you had a real mess. Without deep water for their towed arrays, his sonar crews were like deaf men straining to hear serpents slithering through a boiler factory.

And an undetected submarine attacking from close range could smash the convoy with a spread of wire-guided torpedoes or submerged-launched missiles.

As a result, every time his antisubmarine warfare coordinator reported a half-reliable sonar contact, Ward had been forced to turn the entire Task Group away from it – zigzagging back and forth at high speed. They'd lost several hours that way, but he considered the time well spent. The key to defeating torpedo attacks was to stop subs from ever getting close enough to launch them.

He'd also had the antisubmarine air controller, the ASAC, drive his overworked helicopter pilots all over the area, dropping strings of active sonar buoys. Pinging the hell out of a detected submarine was a good way to keep its skipper more worried about survival than about conducting any attacks.

As far as Ward could tell, the combination of maneuver and aggressive ASW patrolling had worked. No French or German sub had been able to get within firing range of his ships.

'New air contacts, Admiral. Bearing two five five. Range eight zero and closing.' After four days under almost constant pressure, his chief of staff's voice was strained and hoarse.

Ward downed the rest of his coffee in one swift gulp and focused on the display. Symbols showed the new EurCon aircraft. Others showed aircraft identified as Polish MiG-29s moving to intercept. 'Go on.'

'Sierra Foxtrot evaluates the bogies as Mirage 2000s mixed with more Luftwaffe Tornados. He's vectoring the Poles in to chase them away.'

The admiral nodded. Sierra Foxtrot was the call sign for an American E-3 Sentry orbiting over Gdansk. The AWACS plane had been dispatched from its base in Great Britain to coordinate air cover for the convoy once it crossed into the Baltic. He glanced at the young, brown-haired officer standing somewhat uncertainly in the one relatively clear corner of the crowded CIC. Clad in the unfamiliar steel-blue uniform of the Polish Air Force, the major had been helicoptered aboard *Leyte Gulf* to act as a liaison during Task Group 22.1's approach to the Polish port city.

Ward and his subordinates monitored the intercept by watching it on radar and listening to it over radio circuits assigned to the Poles and their controllers aboard the circling American E-3. Voices crackled over loudspeakers, distorted by high g-forces as the opposing jets turned and turned tighter still – caught in a swirling, tangled fur ball just above the Baltic.

The admiral frowned. The Polish pilots were doing an effective job, forcing the EurCon strike aircraft and their escorts further and further away from his convoy. But they were taking big risks to do it. His displays showed planes crisscrossing back and forth across each other's flight paths

– often with very little room to spare. Normal safety restrictions were being ignored by both sides. He waved the antiair warfare coordinator over.

'Oh, shit.' The soft, shocked exclamation came from several officers at the same moment.

Ward spun back to the display. Two of the aircraft symbols, one for a Polish MiG, the other for a French Mirage, had just merged – colliding at four hundred knots. Now both were tumbling toward the sea below.

The voices on the radio circuit took on a new urgency. Some were in Polish. Others, emanating from the E-3, were in English.

'Green Two, this is Sierra Foxtrot! Eject! Eject! Get the hell out!'

Both of the stricken aircraft disappeared off *Leyte Gulf*'s radar.

'Green flight, this is Sierra Foxtrot.' The airborne controller's voice sounded shaken. 'Can anyone see Green Two?'

An angry, accented voice answered. 'Negative, Foxtrot. He hit the water. No parachute.'

'What about the Mirage?'

'It's down, too. No chute, either.'

Ward felt cold. EurCon's 'mock' attacks had just turned deadly.

A new voice came on the radio circuit, furiously demanding something.

Ward saw the Polish liaison officer turn pale. 'What the hell's going on, Major?'

The younger man swallowed hard before replying. 'Green Leader is asking for permission to fire!'

'Jesus Christ.' Ward grabbed the antiair coordinator. 'Get Sierra Foxtrot on the horn! Tell them to pull the MiGs back! Now!'

'Aye, aye, sir.'

No midair collision was worth a full-scale conflict.

The Mirages and Tornados were changing course, turning back toward Germany. His EurCon counterpart must have come to the same conclusion.

Four hours later, Task Group 22.1 crossed into Polish territorial waters.

Standing on *Leyte Gulf*'s bridge wing and leaning wearily on the railing, Jack Ward thought that the rust-streaked cranes and shipyards of Gdansk were one of the most beautiful sights in the world. He had accomplished his mission without having to shoot anyone. This time.

CHAPTER 15
Death Warrant

MAY 1 – PUBLIC BROADCASTING SERVICE *NEWSHOUR*

After the usual, quick-paced recitation of the day's major events, *NewsHour* cut to its Washington-based co-anchor. 'Now we turn to our top story for this Friday: First Flowers of a Budapest Spring. Paul Hamilton of Britain's Independent Television News narrates this report smuggled out past Hungarian censors.'

The camera view shifted – moving in the blink of an eye from the program's Washington, D.C., studio to scenes videotaped in Budapest much earlier that same day. The images were a far cry from earlier amateur videos hurriedly shipped across the Czech border and beamed by satellite around the world. These pictures were steady, focused, and professionally edited. Hungary's blossoming opposition movement clearly had allies in the state-run television network.

Against a dramatic backdrop formed by the soaring, neo-Gothic spires, arches, and the great dome of the Parliament building, thousands of people packed a vast cobblestoned square. Hundreds of red, white, and green Hungarian flags fluttered above the crowd. Deep-voiced, angry chants rippled through the square, echoing back and forth and growing ever louder.

'Hungary's political opposition emerged from hiding today – taking to the capital city's streets in numbers not seen since the elections in 1990 swept the old communist regime from power. In a move that clearly took the military government by surprise, more than twenty thousand demonstrators converged on Kossuth Lajos Square for a Labor Day rally demanding an end to martial law and a return to democratic rule.'

The camera zoomed in for a close-up of the thin, white-haired man speaking from the Parliament building's broad stone steps. Commandeered police sound trucks amplified his voice.

'In a stirring, twenty-minute-long address, Vladimir Kusin, leader of the outlawed Democratic Forum, called for the immediate restoration of civil rights, free and fair elections, and for an end to Hungary's membership in the French- and German-dominated European Confederation.' The camera panned outward again, sweeping across a sea of shouting, cheering faces.

Another crowd shot – this time profoundly moving – showed

thousands of men and women swaying from side to side as they sang their nation's proud, melodic anthem.

'Although the entire hour-long rally took place in defiance of martial law regulations, the government's security forces remained strangely passive. No officers tried to make any arrests.' The camera cut to small groups of policemen stationed at intervals around the growing crowd. Most looked uneasy or frightened. A few even seemed ashamed of their own uniforms. 'Some went further than that.' The pictures showed many police officers joining the crowd in singing the anthem – some with tears streaming down their cheeks.

'Where Hungary's rejuvenated political opposition goes from here is uncertain. But one thing does seem certain: its campaign to bring democracy back to this country is just beginning . . .'

MAY 6 – BUDAPEST

They were meeting in Kusin's third new apartment in three weeks. This one was small and cramped and smelled as though its tenants were often forced to dine on rotting fish.

Col. Zoltan Hradetsky missed their previous host – an industrialist run out of business by a German chemicals firm. The man had actually had a separate conference room and a well-equipped office in his house.

Now they were back in a working-class flat in one of the city's poorest neighborhoods. A single bedroom, a tiny kitchen, and a small, sparsely furnished sitting room made up the whole place. The bathroom – shared by all tenants on the same floor – was down the hall. With living and working space at a premium, the couple that had loaned Kusin the apartment were away, staying with friends and family members.

Despite the inconvenience, the frequent moves were necessary. Staying mobile and staying inconspicuous were the opposition's best defenses against Rehling's EurCon agents and the Hungarian officials they'd corrupted.

Hradetsky stared at the shut bedroom door in unconcealed impatience. It was nearly dark outside. He'd arrived at the flat nearly an hour ago, only to find Kusin closeted with unnamed men he didn't know. His police identity card would get him past any curfew checkpoints on the way back home, but he didn't like the idea of making his movements so easy to trace. 'So just how much longer is this "vital meeting" going to take?'

Oskar Kiraly, Kusin's security chief, smiled, a smile that didn't quite reach his eyes. 'It will last however long it lasts, Colonel. Kusin has his reasons.'

He didn't volunteer any more information about the men meeting in the bedroom. Nor did Hradetsky really expect more. Rebels and outlaws who wanted to survive soon learned the value of compartmentalization. What he didn't know couldn't be torn out of him if Rehling or General Dozsa got their hands on him.

Kiraly offered him some coffee, strong and bitter, and they sat together at the kitchen table with two other members of the opposition's inner circle. Kusin's secretary perched on a nearby chair, tapping away on a humming laptop computer.

It was a familiar scene to Hradetsky, almost comforting. Certainly the comradeship he'd found with these men and women was something he'd missed since his abrupt demotion and transfer to Budapest. Since losing his command at Sopron, he'd also missed having a sense of purpose – something he now possessed in abundance.

He found the work invigorating. The chance to influence events on a national level acted like a tonic on him, washing away all the fatigue and frustration he'd felt piling up over the winter. He had always had a policeman's contempt for politicians, but he was beginning to admit that this was a time when the only thing that really mattered was politics.

Kiraly looked at him over the edge of his coffee cup. 'You know, Colonel, you're still making problems for us.' He said it with mock seriousness.

'How so?'

'We've got twice as many new recruits as we can handle. And more are approaching us all the time.'

Hradetsky nodded. The first major rally he'd helped organize had been remarkably successful. More so than he had ever dared hope. The news of their defiance of the government's edicts had spread like wildfire, passed by word of mouth, underground papers, and broadcasts over clandestine radio and TV networks based in the Polish, Czech, and Slovak republics. Since then spontaneous, unplanned protests had flared in Gyor, Debrecen, Pecs, and half a dozen other cities and towns. And in almost every case, the local police authorities had carefully looked the other way. The generals must know that their hold on power was shakier than it had ever been.

The bedroom door opened. Finally.

Hradetsky and the others rose to their feet as Kusin ushered his anonymous guests out. There were four of them. All of them were middle-aged, and all were trim and physically fit. The colonel's eyes narrowed. Whoever these men were, they looked as uncomfortable and out of place in civilian clothes as he did. He suspected that when they walked they had a tendency to fall into step. They had to be soldiers.

After they were gone, Kusin returned to the kitchen. His eyes flashed with excitement, and years seemed to have dropped from his lined face. 'My friends, the time has come for us to act, and to act decisively!'

Kiraly and Hradetsky exchanged puzzled glances. The security chief spoke for them all. 'Sir?'

'The momentum lies with us. We must make use of it!' Kusin straightened to his full height. 'The winter was a time of despair – a time when the generals had the edge. Our people were hungry. They were cold. They were afraid. They wanted food and security – whatever the price. But now it is spring. And in the spring our countrymen's thoughts turn toward freedom!'

He looked at their stunned faces and smiled. 'Don't worry, my friends. I haven't lost my mind. There is method in my madness.' His manner changed as he became businesslike, transforming himself from prophet to practical politician. 'We must march again, in even larger numbers this time. In numbers that no one can ignore. And I want this city paralyzed by a general strike before we begin. This must be a march of those who have work as well as those who have none.'

Hradetsky shook his head. 'We were lucky the last time. But organizing a mass strike and an even larger demonstration? It can't be done.' He frowned. 'Not covertly.'

'Exactly!' Kusin smiled at him. 'Our plans should be public. The time. The place. Everything. I want maximum coverage by our friends in the world press.'

Kiraly nodded sagely, then added grimly, 'Easy enough to arrange. But it will also be easy for EurCon and government security forces to provide their own form of full coverage.'

'Yes. This will be a test of strength,' Kusin agreed. 'A gauntlet thrown down before the generals and their French and German masters.'

Hradetsky felt his fingers flex as though they were curling around the hilt of a saber. He fought to keep a cool head. The images conjured up by Kusin's confident words were pleasing, but were they realistic? 'Are we ready to throw down such a gauntlet?'

'I believe we are.' Kusin sounded certain. 'The people are with us. The press is with us. And this government is weaker than we first imagined.' He smiled grimly. 'Perhaps even weaker than it knows.'

MAY 8 – PALAIS ROYAL, PARIS

'You're sure about this?' Nicolas Desaix tapped the red-tagged Most Secret report in front of him. 'This isn't just a case of panic brought on by the sight of a few bearded fools with painted signs?'

'No, Minister.' Although Jacques Morin now headed both the French DGSE and the Confederation's Interior Secretariat, he never forgot his place or his patron. 'I believe the information is accurate.'

Desaix grimaced. The rising tide of Hungarian resistance to their own military government and to French and German influence there had taken him by surprise. His attention had been focused almost exclusively on the growing dispute with Poland, the Czech and Slovak republics, Britain, and the United States. A few petty protests in one small country had seemed utterly insignificant when compared to the larger, more serious game being played out in the North Sea and along Germany's eastern border. He was starting to regret not paying heed to Hungary sooner. The trouble there should have been nipped in the bud – not allowed to spread virtually unchecked.

Of course, he thought, this is all part of the same struggle. The Poles and their neighbors are stirring up trouble for us in Hungary to hit back for the energy embargo. It was something like a flea trying to bite an elephant, but even a fleabite could be annoying if left untended.

Like this. Desaix paged through the report, glancing briefly at its headings and conclusions. Hungary's police force was falling apart. Although no police units had yet openly sided with the opposition, illegal demonstrations were allowed to go untamed. And raids launched against reported 'safe houses' or outlawed printing presses netted little. Opposition sympathizers inside the force saw to that.

Even worse, there were persistent rumors of growing dissatisfaction in the army – especially among junior officers and in the ranks. Hungary's rulers were becoming increasingly nervy. He frowned as one particular piece of information caught his eye. Some of the generals were moving their money out of Budapest banks and into Swiss safe havens. The cowards! And the fools! If he could find that out, so could the rebels. Knowing that some of the junta were already preparing for possible flight would only make this Kusin and his fellows that much bolder.

Desaix flipped the report shut and pushed it away. 'So now these hotheaded scum are planning an even bigger demonstration?'

Morin nodded. Worry lines furrowed his high pale forehead. 'Kusin and their other leaders have called for a general strike, a protest march through Budapest, and another mass rally – all starting on the sixteenth.'

'A shrewd maneuver,' Desaix conceded. By openly declaring its intentions, the opposition was challenging the military regime to a fight the generals could easily lose. Allowing the threatened strike and rally to go ahead would only encourage more trouble. But using unreliable Hungarian police units in an attempt to crush the protest might be disastrous – especially if it failed.

He swiveled his chair to look out across Paris. Army aviation helicopters clattered low over rooftops and monuments, flying slowly over the city on patrol. Despite months of relative calm, the capital was still under limited martial law.

French troops guarded every major intersection, and a dusk-to-dawn curfew kept all but essential people off the streets. The City of Lights was a dark, frightening place at night. In the daytime sullen groups of unemployed, some French and some foreign, clashed, or demonstrated, or raided some luckless shop owner for food. Most citizens had enough to eat, barely, and a job, but unemployment was far too high and growing. More and more angry people were being added to the near-explosive idle population.

What the economy needed could not be provided. Tariffs and other restrictions had crippled the trade and commerce Europe depended on for prosperity. The French and German economies, the strongest in Europe, had shrunk last year, and would shrink even faster this year. And now the eastern Europeans and their U.S. and British backers were thwarting the French- and German-led effort to build a unified, self-sufficient continental market.

Desaix scowled. He and his colleagues on the French Republic's Emergency Committee still found it easier to govern their unruly countrymen with the aid of the army's 'big stick.' Seeing the patrolling helicopters was an unwelcome reminder of just how tenuous all his recent achievements really were.

France held the dominant position in this new European Confederation, but the Confederation itself was still a relatively weak and fragile instrument. For all their governments' promises that joining

EurCon would bring them peace and prosperity, few people in the smaller member states were reconciled to their loss of sovereignty. If Hungary's pro-Confederation regime collapsed, it could easily drag other friendly governments down with it.

Desaix shook his head angrily. He would not risk that. He spun away from the window. 'Very well, Morin, listen closely. If the Hungarians cannot put an end to this nonsense on their own, then we must help them. Clear?'

'Yes, Minister.' Morin nodded again. 'Do you want Special Commissioner Rehling to handle the matter?'

'No.' Desaix slapped his hand down on the desk. 'Not the Germans. They're too soft. Too prissy about following proper procedure. Rehling has had his chance and he's muffed it.'

He rapped the desktop. 'I want someone tougher – more ruthless. Someone willing to take risks to get results. Somebody who won't shirk from a little "wet" work, if that proves necessary. You understand?'

'Perhaps Major Duroc . . . ?'

Desaix smiled slowly and unpleasantly. 'Yes. Paul Duroc. He would be the perfect choice.'

MAY 12 – MINISTRY OF THE INTERIOR, BUDAPEST

The door to Bela Silvanus' office was half-open when Col. Zoltan Hradetsky knocked on it. The short, pudgy bureaucrat looked up irritably from his work, then smiled wearily when he recognized his caller. He motioned the colonel inside.

Hradetsky shut the door behind him. 'I got your note. What's up?'

'Nothing good.' Silvanus lit a cigarette, inhaled deeply, and nodded toward the chair in front of his desk. 'Take a seat.'

Curious, Hradetsky sat down. Although the other man had never asked him where all the documents he'd been feeding him were going, Silvanus had to know he had contacts in the resistance. Discretion had always been one of the administrator's most prized traits.

Silvanus spoke quietly, earnestly. 'There's trouble brewing, my friend. Trouble I think you need to know about.'

'What kind – personal or professional?' Hradetsky grinned tightly. Were Dozsa and his toadies finally catching on to him?

'The EurCon kind. Connected to this upcoming demonstration I keep hearing about.'

Hradetsky sat back in his chair. He'd been wondering when Rehling would step in to play a more active part in the ministry's somewhat disjointed preparations for the May 16 rally. General Dozsa and the other high-ranking officials were in a dither, moving riot control troops in from outlying cities almost as fast as they could find transport for them. But the colonel found the attitudes of those below the upper echelons extremely interesting. Heartened by the reappearance of a viable political opposition, fellow officers who had once seemed prepared to go alone with EurCon were increasingly willing to show their true feelings. And men who had once shunned him in the corridors now went out of their way to shake his hand.

He spread his hands. 'So what have you got?'

Silvanus shrugged. 'Bits and pieces, and none of them reassuring, I fear.' He stubbed his cigarette out in an overflowing ashtray and rubbed his eyes. 'I've been kept busy running errands the last few days – playing travel agent for our lords and masters.'

Hradetsky waited patiently for him to come to the point. Silvanus had a pleasant voice, but sometimes he liked to listen to himself talk just a bit too much.

'Most of my work has come in making arrangements for several groups of special visitors to our fair city. Airport pickups, rental cars, and hotel reservations. That sort of thing. Curious thing about these men, though: they're all young and they're all flying direct from Paris. I've also been ordered to issue them special identity cards and weapons permits. Interesting, eh?'

'How many?'

'Around fifty.'

Hradetsky pondered that. Fifty Frenchmen, even fifty security agents, didn't sound like much of an invasion. Still, they could cause a lot of trouble by being in the wrong place at the wrong time. He frowned. 'Who commands them? The German?'

Silvanus shook his head. 'Rehling isn't in charge. This Interior Secretariat of theirs is flying in someone special. A Frenchman. A man named Duroc. You know him, I think?'

Hradetsky nodded grimly. 'I know him.' He felt cold. First Sopron, now here in Budapest. And everywhere this Duroc went he seemed to bring death with him. Maybe EurCon was getting ready to take the gloves off. If so, he would have to warn Kusin and the others – tonight, if possible.

He rose to go. 'My thanks, Bela. You've done me a great service. I'm only sorry I have no way to repay you.'

Silvanus waved a hand. 'Never mind. I am owed enough favors.'

Hradetsky frowned. 'Still, giving me this information is dangerous . . .'

'I've already decided to take an "early retirement," my friend. The Germans have been sniffing around too much, and I'm getting tired of being Rehling's stooge.' Silvanus grinned. 'So I'm going to strike my own blow for Hungarian independence by letting them try to run this place without me!'

Hradetsky had to smile at that. 'When do you leave?'

'My letter will be on the generals' desks tomorrow morning, and by dawn my wife and I will be halfway to a little place we have northeast of here – up in the Matra Mountains. No television, no telephone. Just a little fishing and a little reading. You see, that's the other reason I wanted to see you. We just held my going-away party.' The administrator's grin faded. 'I have a feeling that Budapest could become a very unhealthy place to live in the near future.'

The colonel nodded. 'You're probably right.' He shook the other

man's outstretched hand and turned away.
'Oh, Zoltan?'
Hradetsky paused with his hand on the door.
Silvanus reached into one of his desk drawers and tossed him an armband – one dyed in Hungary's red, white, and green national colors. 'Tell your friends to be a bit more careful when handing these out. After all, some of the people in this building still work for the generals.'
Hradetsky nodded somberly and stuffed the armband in a coat pocket. 'I will remind them of that.'
Evidently Kusin and the others were casting their nets further and faster than he had imagined.

MAY 16 – ON THE RADIAL AVENUE, NEAR HEROES' SQUARE, BUDAPEST

They were lucky in the weather. May was usually one of the wettest months in Hungary's capital, but this day dawned clear and sunny with the promise of moderate temperatures later on.
Col. Zoltan Hradetsky stood with Kusin and Kiraly, watching his countrymen streaming in from every direction – tens of thousands of them, maybe more. The general strike they'd called was holding. Most businesses and factories were shut down, either voluntarily by patriotic owners or because all their employees were on their way here. The only parts of the public transit system still operating were the buses and Metro subway trains ferrying people to the march. As they arrived, opposition workers assigned as parade marshals shepherded the men, women, and children into places along the wide, tree-lined avenue. Others circulated through the crowds, handing out flags and placards.
Hradetsky idly fingered the armband around his blue uniform jacket. Appearing like this, in full uniform and at the head of the march, had been Kusin's suggestion. It was one way to show the people they were not alone – that some of the government's own officials were turning against it. Of course, if the military regime stood firm against the combination of this march and the general strike, showing up among the demonstrators would make him a hunted man.
He shrugged. So be it. He was tired of playing a double game.
The colonel ran his eyes over the swelling crowd. At least he would have plenty of company on the run. There were several other policemen and even a few army officers scattered in the front ranks – all of them in uniform. Most of them looked very nervous. Well, that was understandable. He'd had more time to come to terms with betraying an oath for the love of his country.
They weren't the only uniformed men present. Small groups of patrolmen were stationed at nearby intersections, hanging well back. From time to time, demonstrators walked right up to them, trying to talk them into joining the march. Sometimes it worked. Hradetsky could see several police squads already wearing the tricolored armbands that showed they were siding with the opposition.
There were still no signs of the government's riot control troops or

Duroc's French security men, though. They had to be further ahead – hidden somewhere among the buildings lining the avenue. Waiting for a signal. But waiting for a signal to do what?

He turned to Kusin. 'I'll say it again, sir. If you must march, at least march further back in the column. Let Oskar and me and more of his men go first.'

Kiraly nodded. 'The colonel is right, Vladimir. This insistence on staying so close to the front is not sound. It's too . . .'

'Dangerous?' Kusin finished for him. 'Perhaps it is.' He nodded toward the milling crowds behind them. 'But it is dangerous for all of us. And the people have a right to see those who would lead them taking the biggest risks.'

He saw their frustrated looks and laughed gently. 'Come, my friends. You cannot protect me from myself or others forever. Besides, I've already agreed to carry more than my fair weight today, eh?' He patted his shirtfront.

At Kiraly's insistence, Kusin was wearing a bulletproof vest under his suit. With luck it might stop a shot fired by a sniper or other assassin. But that was the only compromise Hradetsky and the security chief had been able to persuade him to make. When they'd pressed him on the need to play it safer, he'd only smiled and clapped them both on the shoulder. 'When you match your strength against a foe, gentlemen, you can't afford a show of weakness. We go forward, not back.'

To Hradetsky, this march was taking on a whole new aspect. It was changing rapidly from a 'test of strength' to the kind of crazy game called Chicken he'd seen played out in American movies. The kind of game where two automobiles raced straight toward each other – with each driver betting the other would chicken out first.

Kusin looked at his watch, took a deep breath, and looked up with a confident smile on his careworn face. 'It's time, gentlemen. Oskar? Will you do the honors?'

Kiraly nodded. He started relaying orders to the marshals scattered up and down the still-growing crowd, using a hand-held portable phone. The phones and dedicated cellular circuits were the gift of opposition sympathizers inside the city's telephone center.

Slowly, with several fits and starts, their march got under way – picking up speed and support as they tramped down the avenue. Within minutes, more than 100,000 Hungarians were heading for the Danube and the government offices around the Parliament building. Thousands of colorful banners and flags waved above the crowd, streaming proudly in a light, westerly breeze.

They were led by a thin line of Kiraly's toughest men, all army or National Police veterans, holding large Hungarian flags spread out on poles between them. Kusin, Kiraly, Hradetsky, and other opposition leaders followed right behind. Many sought actively by the security services wore placards that said simply, 'Outlawed – For Loving Hungary.'

Rank after rank of Budapest's citizens came after them, sometimes organized and sometimes not organized at all. Men in business suits mingled with laborers in hard hats and dungarees. Policemen, some wearing opposition armbands, paced them. Mothers pushing infants in strollers walked side by side with their next-door neighbors or with people they'd never seen before. Bands deployed at regular intervals played a mix of stirring marching songs that set a brisk, purposeful pace and lifted people's hearts.

Striding along beside Kusin, Hradetsky carefully scanned the faces of his fellows. He saw determination, fierce joy, and very little uncontrolled anger. They were off to a good start.

SPECIAL OPERATIONS COMMAND POST

Another watcher saw the same crowd, but with a very different set of emotions.

Maj. Paul Duroc leaned forward, almost touching the glass window in a third-floor office overlooking the Radial Avenue. He'd 'borrowed' the office from the aging, homesick manager of a French-owned firm. Now it served as his command post.

The command post was small, just himself, a radioman, and one assistant to answer the phones and run any errands. That was enough, though, to manage the platoons of Hungarian riot police and French security agents under his immediate control. And if he needed more men, he could get them with a single phone call. The head of the DGSE had made it clear that the Hungarian government itself would answer to Duroc's orders if he wished it. Dismayed by their own inability to control events, the generals were ready to grasp at straws.

He would have preferred making a preemptive strike by arresting Kusin and the other opposition leaders before they could organize this protest march. Unfortunately the Hungarian regime's incompetence and sloth had made that impossible. You couldn't capture people you couldn't find.

Duroc sneered at the sight of the massive, ragtag mob coming down the street. Numbers meant nothing. He had sufficient strength in hand to crush this demonstration, and more important, the minds behind it. Any fool could use force to break up a rally. The key was to move so quickly and so violently that those you hit were left stunned, unable to defend themselves or strike back. But he had bigger plans. His orders from Paris were clear: His superiors wanted him to do more than just temporarily restore order to Budapest's streets. They wanted him to smash Hungary's political opposition once and for all.

Well, he thought, that should be simple enough. Kusin and the others on his list were positioned close to the front – out in the open and out of hiding at last. That was brave, but foolish. They would be easy pickings.

Still, years of experience had taught him to plan for the unexpected. That was why he'd stationed Michel Woerner and five men armed with automatic weapons in the building's central stairwell. They would provide security against any unwelcome intruders if things went wrong.

He leaned closer to the window to get a better view.

The first rows of marching morons were almost in the noose he'd fashioned. Kusin and his followers were just moving into Kodaly Circle – a major intersection surrounded by ornately decorated buildings whose façades curved to follow the circle. The other streets feeding into the circle were a maze of businesses, small hotels, and apartment blocks.

Small knots of tough-looking men loitered near the intersection. They weren't hiding, but they kept to the corners and to the early morning shadows. Although they were dressed in plain, workingmen's clothes, no one could possibly mistake them for civilians. They were too quiet, too disciplined.

Beyond them, out of sight, were trucks and armored cars full of riot police. Once his men had the king and other important pieces in hand, the Hungarians could clear the board of the pawns. With their leaders gone, the mob out there would run like sheep – not roar like lions.

Duroc watched the approaching crowd draw nearer, noting the individuals in it but not really seeing them as people. They were simply obstacles he had to overcome to complete this mission. Three stories below, the line of Hungarian flags crossed into the circle. Now. He turned to his radioman. 'Proceed with Phase One.'

KODALY CIRCLE

Hradetsky swore suddenly as the men he'd been watching suspiciously sprang into action. Long-handled nightsticks and blackjacks came out from under windbreakers and long coats as thirty to forty of them formed into three squad-sized wedges and charged. Others hung back, apparently armed with short-barreled grenade launchers. Without waiting for further orders, they aimed and fired.

He whirled to shout a warning. Too late.

Tear gas grenades whirred overhead and exploded in the crowds further back – bursting in puffs of white, choking smoke. Panic spread backward along the avenue as the CS gas drifted east on the wind. Marchers stumbled and fell, overcome by acrid fumes that left them retching on the ground or crawling away with tears streaming down their faces. In seconds, Hradetsky, Kusin, Kiraly, and several hundred others at the front of the march were isolated – cut off from their supporters by a rising wall of tear gas.

Nightsticks rose and fell as the first wave of plainclothes security agents smashed into the flag bearers at the front. Men spun away from the melee, clutching bloodied faces, fractured ribs, and broken arms and legs. Torn Hungarian flags fluttered to the pavement. Shouts, curses, and guttural snarls echoed above the fray – some in Hungarian, others in French.

The first Frenchmen broke past, breathing hard as they sprinted toward Kusin. Two of Kiraly's marshals tried to tackle them and went down – clubbed brutally to the ground. Bastards!

Hradetsky moved to intercept Duroc's men, sensing others running with him.

One of the Frenchmen saw him coming. Hradetsky dodged a quick, flickering jab from a nightstick, grabbed the agent's outstretched arm, and whirled, pulling the man off his feet. As the Frenchman's head slammed into the pavement, the colonel kicked him hard in the ribs and turned away, looking for a new opponent.

Kodaly Circle had turned into a battlefield. Bodies sprawled on the street, some moving and others unmoving. Blunt-nosed Csepel lorries appeared at the far end of the intersection, crammed with helmeted riot police.

Hradetsky caught a glimpse of Kusin's white hair through a tangle of struggling, swearing men and headed that way. He could see Kiraly pulling the older man back, trying to shield him from blows raining down on all sides.

A taller, heavier Frenchman blocked his path, teeth bared in sharp defiance and blood-slick stick at the ready.

The colonel ducked under the man's first vicious swing, struck at his exposed stomach, missed, and backed away. They circled, each looking for an opening.

Duroc looked sourly at the melee developing below him. He'd underestimated the ability of the Hungarians to defend themselves, and now he was running out of time. Bands of enraged protesters were already streaming back down the avenue to the intersection, braving the tear gas to close with his struggling plainclothesmen.

Damn it, where were Kusin and his top lieutenants? With the opposition's leaders in custody, his men could pull back, clearing the field for the riot squads already deploying in several of the surrounding streets. Without them, he had nothing.

'Major! Captain Miklos wants permission to advance!'

Duroc spun away from the window, his face dark with anger. 'No! Tell him to wait!'

He remembered Miklos. The young, black-haired captain was one of the Hungarian police officers under his command for this operation. He was also a man the French security agent viewed with some suspicion – one with several black marks in his dossier for allegedly criticizing both the government and the new Confederation. Confronted by Vladimir Kusin's unexpected ability to mobilize the people, the generals were being forced to rely on even their most unreliable officers.

Duroc scowled. He had the uncomfortable sensation that events were sliding beyond his control.

Down in the street, Hradetsky blocked a wild swing with his left forearm and got inside the tall Frenchman's reach. Ignoring the pain rocketing all the way up to his shoulder, he rabbit-punched the security agent in the throat. The big man dropped to his knees, choking on a broken larynx.

Now what? He looked wildly around, trying to spot Kusin or Kiraly. He doubted it would do any good to shout for them. Not in a confused mess like this. More and more protesters were flooding into Kodaly Circle, intent on getting to grips with the men who had turned a peaceful march into a bloody free-for-all. With their comrades locked in a confused melee, the Frenchmen armed with tear gas launchers had stopped firing and joined the fight.

'Colonel!'

Hradetsky half turned toward the yell, just in time to see Oskar Kiraly knocked off his feet by several club-wielding men. My God. He took a step in that direction and felt the back of his head explode.

The agony drove him down to his hands and knees as the security agent who had hit him from behind struck again, this time slamming the nightstick into his side. His awareness danced away toward a world of darkness and shrieking pain. Dimly, through half-closed eyes, he saw his attacker tackled by one of Kiraly's marshals. Five or six protesters crowded in, jostling each other as they kicked and pummeled the Frenchman senseless. Some of them were policemen wearing opposition armbands.

Still groggy, Hradetsky pushed himself up off the pavement, fighting to stop the world spinning around him. Each breath stabbed his side as sharp as any dagger. A broken rib, or maybe just badly bruised, he thought clinically – amazed at the mind's ability to stay detached under stress.

'They have Kusin!' The panicked, sorrowing cry tore through both his pain and his adrenaline-enforced calm. He opened his eyes wide.

Those few Frenchmen still able to walk or run were falling back. But they weren't alone. They had a small number of captives with them. Most were opposition leaders who had been wearing the placards proclaiming their status as wanted men. Two plainclothes agents were dragging the lean, white-haired opposition leader between them. Kusin's head lolled, rolling from side to side, as his captors hurried away, staggering under their burden. He was either dead or unconscious.

Hradetsky's long-suppressed rage exploded, burning white-hot. He stood up straight, balancing precariously on wobbly legs for a moment. First one breath and then another cleaned the worst of the pain out of his lungs. He started running toward the retreating French. Others followed him.

As they shoved and clubbed their way toward safety, Duroc's men were forced to fight through an ever-thickening crowd. More and more Hungarians were swinging wide around the tiny phalanx of security agents to block their path and slow them down. The colonel saw his countrymen surrounding the Frenchmen linking arms, trying to form a barrier to movement. Wherever the two groups came in contact, they fought tooth and nail – clawing and tearing at each other in a mindless fury.

Hradetsky was only meters away now, dodging through the ring surrounding Duroc's men. Several of the Frenchmen raised their arms, frantically beckoning for help from the riot police waiting barely a block away. The Hungarian colonel could sense their growing desperation. Although their goal was in sight, they were now too weak and too few in number to reach it.

One of Kiraly's biggest men, a burly, bearlike ex-army sergeant, bulled his way deep into the French phalanx. He backhanded one of the men holding Kusin and reached for the other, shouting aloud in triumph.

Hradetsky, just a few steps behind, saw everything that followed as though it happened in slow motion.

Instead of backing away from his attacker or dropping Kusin, the Frenchman's hand darted inside his windbreaker and reappeared holding a weapon. As the barrel cleared his jacket, he fired twice, pumping two rounds into the ex-sergeant's chest. The big man flew backward, punched off his feet in a spray of blood.

'Down! Down! Everybody down!' Hradetsky clawed for the pistol holstered at his side.

Other Frenchmen, also sensing defeat, were pulling their own weapons. The colonel recognized them as German-made MP5K submachine guns – special, shortened variants designed to be carried concealed under clothing.

Without warning they opened fire, carefully aiming into the crowd in front of them. They weren't shooting to frighten. They were shooting to kill, deliberately clearing a path with bullets. People went down in droves under the hail of gunfire – either ripped open by 9mm rounds or throwing themselves prone behind the dead and dying to escape the slaughter.

Hradetsky dropped to one knee, with his service automatic extended in his right hand and braced by his left. He aimed quickly at the security agent who had fired first, and squeezed off two shots. The first caught the Frenchman in the shoulder and spun him around. The second blew a red-rimmed hole in his forehead.

The colonel searched rapidly for another target, cursing under his breath as panicked demonstrators stumbled into his line of fire. He swiveled back and forth, still holding his pistol braced. A clear space opened up in front of him. He had only a split second to decide. Should he fire at one of the men dragging Kusin toward the riot police? Or take out a Frenchman murdering his compatriots?

One of Duroc's men leveled his submachine gun and fired a series of walking bursts into the screaming men and women ahead of him. More people crumpled, cut down by bullets fired at point-blank range.

Hradetsky squeezed off another shot. Blood spurted from the gunman's back as he staggered and fell facedown onto the street.

The dead man's comrades were already on the move, stepping over bodies while they fired at anyone still standing ahead of them. Two turned and began shooting at the crowds pouring into Kodaly Circle from the Radial Avenues to hold them back.

Bullets whipcracked through the air over Hradetsky's head. He threw himself flat, taking cover behind one of the Frenchmen he had killed. High-pitched screams and low, muffled groans rose from the people behind him.

He raised his head, risking a quick glance ahead. Duroc's agents were close to safety – a line of helmeted riot troops, most of them ashen at the butchery they were seeing, and rows of trucks and armored cars waiting to carry them away. The Frenchmen were too far away for him to risk another shot. At this range, he could easily hit Kusin or one of the policemen by accident.

Hradetsky wanted to roar in anger and frustration. They'd been beaten.

In that instant, the universe turned upside down.

Capt. Ferenc Miklos watched in stunned disbelief as the Frenchmen approached with their handful of battered and bruised prisoners. Did they really think he would shelter them after what he had seen? After watching them massacre his own people?

He bit his lip hard enough to draw blood. Kodaly Circle looked like a slaughterhouse. The dead and wounded lay heaped where bullets or billy clubs had thrown them. He could hear a baby wailing inside a stroller lying on its side next to a young woman who stared up at the sky with open, unmoving eyes.

The captain could also hear the outraged murmurs rising from the formed ranks of his own men. None of them had signed on for something like this. Nor had he. As a young police cadet, he'd sworn to uphold law and order, but whose law and which order? Those of Hungary? Or those of France and Germany? The laws that made a simple protest march illegal? Or those that made outright murder a crime?

The French agents came closer, dragging or shoving their captives along at gunpoint. One of those in the lead, a tall, hard-faced man, arrogantly waved Miklos and his men out of the way with his snub-nosed submachine gun.

Something snapped inside the short, black-haired police officer. He had to do something – even if that meant taking Kusin and the other opposition prisoners into his own custody. He stepped into the French security agent's path. 'Halt!'

Miklos saw the taller man's arrogance change to fear. He had only a second to feel satisfied by that before the Frenchman stuck the submachine gun in his stomach and pulled the trigger.

The young Hungarian captain died a martyr without ever really deciding whose side he was on.

Hradetsky scrambled to his feet before the echoes of the latest shots faded. Had Duroc's men gone mad?

Fifty meters ahead of him, the policemen stared from the group of French agents to their captain's sprawled corpse and back again. Then they charged. More submachine guns stuttered, spreading chaos and carnage. Uniformed Hungarians went down, torn in half by concentrated bursts. But Frenchmen were falling, too, beaten to the ground by flailing nightsticks and Plexiglas shields.

As Hradetsky sprinted toward the battle he could see other police units moving into the circle, closing in on the French. They were ignoring the demonstrators.

The surviving agents were retreating, hobbling away from the trucks that were supposed to ferry them to safety. Instead, they were falling back toward a small, three-story stone office building overlooking Kodaly Circle. Still carrying Kusin, they disappeared inside.

Several helmeted riot troopers followed them all the way to the door and then crumpled suddenly, mowed down by automatic weapons fire from inside. Other policemen close by scattered for cover behind the armored cars and trucks parked next to the building. Protesters raced to join them.

Bent low to stay out of the line of fire, Hradetsky worked his way through the crouching men, looking for the highest-ranking officer he could find. He came face-to-face with a major kneeling beside a badly wounded police corporal. 'Are these your men?'

The man looked up, staring at him with shocked and wild eyes. 'Yes, they are, damn you!' Then he saw Hradetsky's shoulder boards. 'Sir.'

'Will you obey my orders, Major?'

The man's eyes focused and slid down to the red, white, and green band over Hradetsky's uniform jacket. He stiffened instinctively, then glanced down at the injured man gasping for air by his side. When the major looked up again, his expression had changed. It was harder and more determined. 'Yes, Colonel, I will. And so will my men.'

'Good.'

'Colonel?'

Hradetsky turned to see Oskar Kiraly limping toward him. The big, blond-haired man looked dazed and in tremendous pain. Blood streaked the side of his face, dripping from an open gash over one cheekbone.

'Where is Kusin?'

Hradetsky nodded toward the office building. 'In there. The French have him.'

'No! Oh, God.' Kiraly slammed his fist against the steel side of a truck. Tears mingled with the blood running down his face. 'I failed him. I couldn't stop them!'

The colonel grabbed his wrist before he could pound the truck again. When Hradetsky spoke, he kept his voice low. 'None of us could stop them. But this isn't over. Not yet. Fall apart later, when it doesn't matter. Right now we need you. So pull yourself together, man.' He released Kiraly's wrist and turned away to give the big man time to recover his composure.

Thousands of protesters were still flooding into the circle. Some were ministering to the wounded or staring in horror at the carnage. Most were streaming past on their way toward the city center and the government buildings there. They were angry now, ready for revenge against those responsible for the nightmarish scenes all around them.

Members of Kiraly's security team stood watchfully around small bands of riot police – shielding them from the mob. Others moved among the policemen handing out opposition armbands. What had been planned as a protest was rapidly becoming a full-scale rebellion. Hradetsky stood silent for a few moments, weighing the odds in their favor. Then he shrugged. There were times when you could control events, and there were others where events controlled you. The people were taking matters into their own hands. His job now was to make that as swift and sure and peaceful as possible.

He glanced at the officer still waiting by his side. 'I want you to get on your radio, Major. Get in touch with all major police and military commands throughout this city and tell them what's happened here. Everything that has happened here! Understand?'

The major nodded vigorously, obviously relieved to have orders he could follow with a clear conscience. He hurried away, heading for his command car.

The colonel turned back to Kiraly. Though still somewhat dazed, the man looked calmer and more in control of his emotions. Good. 'Oskar, I want you to take command here. Organize a force and surround those bastards in there.' He jerked a thumb toward the office building and ducked involuntarily as gunfire rattled somewhere not far off.

'Should I attack them?'

Hradetsky shook his head. 'Not without more weapons. They're too heavily armed.' As though to emphasize his point, more automatic weapons fire from inside hammered the sidewalk next to the building's entrance. Several policemen and protesters who had been readying themselves for another charge dropped back into cover.

'And what about you, Colonel? What will you be doing?'

'I'm going on to the Parliament,' Hradetsky growled. 'While you keep these swine penned here, I want the cowardly scum behind this butchery brought to justice. Our justice.'

Kiraly nodded grimly. Hungary's military rulers were about to pay a blood price for selling their nation to foreign powers.

SPECIAL OPERATIONS COMMAND POST

Maj. Paul Duroc glowered at his closest subordinates. He and his surviving agents had been trapped in this godforsaken building for more than an hour – trapped while Budapest crumbled into riot and ruin.

Shots rang out in the stairwell. Woerner and his men must be dealing with another attempt by the mob to break in.

'Major! We've lost contact with the Interior Ministry! And with the Houses of Parliament! All the phone lines are dead.'

Duroc sighed, staring out across the Budapest skyline. He could see smoke rising from near the city center – both the white wisps of tear gas and dense black columns spiraling upward from burning buildings. On the street below, police riot vehicles roared by, crowded with helmeted troops and protesters waving clenched fists. Each armored car now had a Hungarian flag flying from its radio antenna. He had lost – betrayed by his own agents' cowardice and incompetence, and by the treacherous Hungarian police.

One of the office windows blew inward in a torrent of flying glass, shattered by gunfire from across the street. The rebels were growing bolder. It was time to leave. He turned to his radioman. 'Signal the ambassador. Tell him I advise immediate evacuation.'

As the frightened young man keyed his microphone, Duroc added one more order. 'Then contact Captain Gille. I want those helicopters now!'

KODALY CIRCLE

With the bitter taste of defeat in his mouth, Oskar Kiraly watched the second of two overloaded Puma helicopters climb heavily away from the office building and fly southeast – toward the airport and safe passage out of the country. Matching his hastily gathered force against a group of trained commandos had proved futile. Police-issue pistols, shotguns, and a few hunting rifles were no match for high-powered assault rifles in the hands of men who knew how to use them. There were plenty of dead policemen and protesters heaped on the street and inside the building to show that.

Now Duroc and his men were making their escape. And Vladimir Kusin was going with them – taken captive to France.

PRIME MINISTER'S OFFICE, HOUSES OF PARLIAMENT

Col. Zoltan Hradetsky leaned over a map of the city, marking key positions with one hand while cradling a phone against his ear with the other. 'That's right, Captain. I want you to push patrols out along the M1 Highway. If they spot anything – a convoy of tanks and troop carriers, or even just a single army truck – I want to know about it immediately. Is that clear? It is? Excellent. Good luck, then.'

He hung up and jotted another quick note on the map. The M1 ran west out of Budapest toward Gyor, Sopron, and the Austrian border. It also ran through Tata, a small city just seventy kilometers away. And Tata was the headquarters for the Hungarian Army's most powerful armored corps. If the army decided to crush this rebellion, its tanks and guns were sure to come trundling down that highway.

He hoped that would not happen. For the last several hours, Hungary's Budapest-based television networks had been airing footage shot during the French attack – including pictures showing the EurCon security agents killing uniformed policemen without provocation. Surely no one who saw those images could fail to understand why the capital's citizenry had taken both the law and the reins of government into their own hands.

The colonel finished his map work and looked around the crowded room. Other police officers worked side by side with civilians in business suits and blue jeans, trying hard to restore order. All of them wore armbands in the national colors and all of them were exhausted.

Hradetsky's eyes watered. He could still smell traces of tear gas and smoke lingering in the air – evidence of the brief battles that had raged earlier in the day. Backed by his hastily organized police and opposition forces, the mobs had overrun the Parliament building and government ministries with relative ease. Most of the very few police and security troops who had stayed loyal to the generals were either dead or in hiding. Most of their masters, panicked by the first reports of the disaster at Kodaly Circle, had fled along with EurCon's special commissioner, the French and German ambassadors, and a host of lesser functionaries.

Of course, not all of them had escaped the deluge. A few terrified prisoners waited in the hallway under armed guard. They included a middling-tall man whose once immaculate police uniform was now rumpled and torn. To the colonel's immense, if unspoken, satisfaction, Brig. Gen. Imre Dozsa was one of those who had been captured while trying to flee.

Hradetsky crossed the room to where Kiraly sat alone, silent and dejected. His reckoning with Dozsa would have to wait. He had far more important and immediate problems to sort out. 'Oskar, I must ask you and your men to do one thing more for me tonight.'

Kiraly looked up, wincing as a gash on his forehead tore open again. 'Of course, Colonel. But what?'

'Find every leader in our organization who is still alive and still free. Bring them here as quickly as you can.'

'Why?'

'Why?' Hradetsky pointed out the window. Whole sections of Budapest were pitch-black – knocked off the electric grid by the fires or by confusion in the capital's power plants. Against the darkness the sky glowed red, lit by dozens of fires burning out of control across the city. 'Because when Hungary wakes up tomorrow morning, she must have a new government.'

CHAPTER 16
Collision Course

MAY 18 – PARIS

Nicolas Desaix watched with unconcealed contempt as the Hungarian generals filed into his private office. Aides ushered them into chairs in front of his desk. He didn't bother getting up to greet them. Beggars and incompetents weren't entitled to anything – even the normal courtesies. By fleeing their capital after only a token resistance, they had betrayed his trust and saddled the European Confederation with a crisis it should not have to face.

He made them wait for nearly a minute before beginning. 'I will be blunt, gentlemen. Many of my colleagues have argued that we should abandon you to your enemies. That we should seek accommodation with the rebels controlling Budapest.' He paused to let their translator catch up. Apparently few of them spoke French. Idiots!

Alarmed by his harsh tone and even harsher words, the military men turned instinctively to their leader, Gen. Laśzló Bruk. Over the years, the tall, white-haired man had been a communist, a reforming democrat, the first among equals in a military dictatorship, and now a refugee. The one constant in his long career was opportunism. The general sat forward hastily. 'Sir, I can assure you . . .'

'I don't want your assurances, General. I want results.'

Bruk nodded stiffly. 'Of course, Minister. I . . .'

'You've told my subordinates that most of your soldiers remain loyal. Is that true?'

'Yes.' Bruk glanced quickly at his fellow officers. None seemed willing to contradict him. At least not in front of an angry French official. 'I've spoken with the commander of our I Corps. He is confident that he can crush this rebellion in a matter of days. A week at most.'

'Really?' Desaix arched an eyebrow in disbelief.

'Once Budapest falls, the other cities will submit themselves to lawful authority.' Bruk sounded very sure of that.

Desaix nodded. Budapest had always been modern Hungary's nerve center – a focal point for the country's industry, government, and culture. Recapturing the capital would undoubtedly break the back and spirit of the rebel movement.

He leaned forward. 'Very well, gentlemen. You have one week to restore order on your own terms. One week. If you fail, my government will explore other, less pleasant alternatives. Do I make myself clear?'

He stared hard at Bruk until the Hungarian looked down. 'Well?'

'Your terms are clear, Minister.'

'Good.' Desaix pressed a button on his desk. In answer to his summons, an aide entered and held the door open. 'Then we have nothing further to discuss. For now. So I bid you good day, gentlemen.' He turned his attention to routine paperwork, ignoring the embarrassed soldiers filing out of his office.

When they were gone, he picked up the telephone. 'Put me through to the Defense Secretariat. I want to speak with Guichy himself.'

Hungary's ousted rulers had failed him once. A second failure would not surprise him at all.

MAY 19 – HOUSES OF PARLIAMENT

Col. Zoltan Hradetsky watched the green-and-brown-painted helicopter gunships orbiting the city like prowling beasts. His eyes narrowed.

Three days after the rebellion broke out, Budapest had begun returning to normal. Most of the fires were out. Power and routine government operations – mail and telephone service, and the like – were all being restored at a rapid pace. Businesses, at least those owned by Hungarians, were reopening. After all the confusion and violence, the capital's inhabitants were ready to get back to their lives.

The respite, however, was unlikely to last for very much longer.

The army was outside the city.

Armored vehicles blocked every road – deployed in platoon-sized outposts. Their parent units, three brigades of the I Combined Arms Corps, were dug in out of sight in the western hills above Budapest. So far, they'd rebuffed every peaceful overture and appeal made by the provisional government.

Hradetsky knew the forces arrayed outside the city could easily smash through their hastily organized defenses. Lightly armed policemen, troops from an artillery brigade that had defected earlier, and a surface-to-air missile battery from the capital's air defense force were no match for tanks and trained infantry.

If the army had truly decided to move against its own citizens, Hungary's new democratic experiment was doomed.

FORWARD HEADQUARTERS, I COMBINED ARMS CORPS, OUTSIDE BUDAPEST

The command post followed the dictates of the army manual, right down to the height of the poles supporting its camouflage netting. It was dug into the military crest of a hill overlooking the city. The camouflage netting and cut foliage were there to conceal it from the air. Of course, with the air force still sitting on the fence, the rebels didn't have any combat aircraft, but that was beside the point.

Lt. Gen. Emil Lakos, commander of I Corps, had arrived by helicopter half an hour before dawn. He was a round-faced, black-haired man of average build – blessed or cursed with boundless energy and a martinet's eye for detail. Since arriving he'd made his presence felt throughout the compound. At any moment he might materialize behind a staff officer or clerk, outwardly affable, but quick to spot any flaw. He was a stickler for correct procedure.

For what was supposed to be a forward position, the headquarters complex was elaborate. It included a radio command center, an artillery observer's position, bunkers for the aircraft and special weapons coordinators, as well as quarters for all the staff and bombproofs in case of attack by 'the enemy.'

The forward-most dugout served as the artillery observer's position. With overhead cover for shade and concealment, Lakos found it a pleasant place from which to make war.

From it he could see the outskirts of the city, with the rest fading onto the haze beyond. The silver ribbon of the Danube River cut through the city from left to right.

He and his corps artillery commander occupied a considerable amount of space, cramping the forward observer and his two assistants, but Lakos wanted to review his bombardment plans here, with the city in full view.

His voice, even in the open-sided dugout, seemed to boom. 'The rebel guns are their only force of any significance. I want them hammered and hammered hard before we send the assault force in. I also want that damned SAM battery suppressed so our gunships can operate freely.'

Lakos tapped several spots on a map of Budapest. 'Since we know where their batteries are sited, I expect you to pour counterbattery fire onto their positions during the first phase. A mix of airburst and point-detonating rounds should do the job nicely.'

Colonel Kemeny, the corps artillery commander, was an experienced gunner. He was taller and darker than Lakos, and younger by ten years. He also did not share his superior's carefree attitude toward throwing massive firepower into populated areas.

'General, the rebels have extremely limited combat power. Their ammo stocks are low, and without a fire direction net, even their guns will have to depend on untrained observers.' Lakos seemed unimpressed, and started to respond, but the colonel risked interrupting him to make one more point. 'Their fields of fire will be extremely limited by buildings along the shells' trajectory. We can plot the dead ground and use it for our attacks. And once our troops are inside the city, they'll quickly be inside minimum range—'

'Colonel.' Lakos cut him off abruptly. 'I do not want any gun, even at reduced effectiveness, left intact to menace my men. I do not intend to commit troops to the attack until *after* the defenders are completely suppressed by artillery and gunships.'

Kemeny tried one more time. 'Sir, the barrage you ask for will cause many civilian deaths. It will wreck the city. Think of the damage even one errant shell would inflict on St. Stephen's or the Roman ruins. In my professional opinion, the police troops entrenched along the outskirts represent a bigger threat, but even they are no match for our forces. If we lay a mixture of smoke and—'

Lakos' face turned hard and remote, his words sharper. 'Colonel. If you say one more word, I will have you relieved.' The general's hand rested on his sidearm, and his chief of staff, hovering in the background with two enlisted escorts, took one step forward.

Kemeny stopped speaking, fighting to control himself.

Lakos pressed his point. 'I understand your arguments, but I want these rebels obliterated and quickly. The government is depending on me to restore order here, and I cannot do it without absolute obedience from all in this command.

'A long fight in the city will give the rebels time they do not deserve. When we enter Budapest, it should be as conquerors, not combatants. Now, do I have your word as an officer that you will obey my orders?'

Kemeny swallowed hard. 'Yes, sir.'

'Then let's get on with it. No more delays, Colonel. You will open fire in one hour.'

'Sir.'

Lakos glared at him for a moment longer, then nodded, apparently satisfied that he had quenched the colonel's momentary spark of mutiny. He turned away and left the dugout, heading for the communications tent to report back to Bruk and the others waiting in Paris.

Behind him Kemeny shook his head in disbelief. He gazed toward the city's graceful skyline and then down at the fire plot he still held in his hands. With more than one hundred artillery pieces under his command, the day-long pounding Lakos envisioned would leave much of Budapest in burning ruins. Hundreds, maybe even thousands, of innocents would be killed. Their deaths would be on his conscience, their blood on his hands. He shivered.

The colonel looked up and found the forward observer and his assistants staring back at him. Something in their carefully blank faces unnerved him. 'Listen carefully, Captain. You will not call for any fire without a direct order from me. *Only* from me, understand?'

'Yes, Colonel.'

Kemeny folded the artillery fire plan and slid it into his pocket. He had a few critical and dangerous visits to make in the next hour.

Lt. Gen. Emil Lakos sat in his tent, meticulously scrutinizing details of the assault plan before presenting them in a final briefing to his tank and motor rifle commanders.

He was still working when he heard diesel engines rumbling in the distance. The sound was familiar, armored vehicles repositioning most likely, but the noise grew louder and louder.

It finally intruded on his consciousness. There were too many engines running out there – enough for an entire company of tanks. He looked up from the city map, concerned. There shouldn't be any troop movements in daylight, not this close to the enemy, and especially not this close to his headquarters. Somebody would have to catch hell for breaking his standing orders.

Lakos grabbed his steel helmet, opened the tent flap, and stood blinking in the bright afternoon sunshine. He was surprised to see men jumping out the rear of wheeled troop carriers. They were fanning out through the compound, with their weapons at the ready. What the devil? He hadn't ordered the deployment of any additional security troops. Whose ridiculous idea was this? He called for his chief of staff. 'Colonel Fenrec!'

He spotted one group of officers, striding quickly toward his tent. Fenrec was among them, plainly distressed. Kemeny was also in the group, carrying an AKM assault rifle in one hand. The others were also from his command, each of them a brigade or battalion leader – almost twenty in all.

He strode out to meet them, fighting the urge to run and shout questions. As they drew close, the group stopped at a respectful distance and saluted. But one of them held a pistol with its muzzle digging into Fenrec's ribs.

Treason! Despite the cool breeze, Lakos could feel sweat beading on his forehead. He swayed, suddenly dizzy.

The most senior officer, one of his brigade commanders, spoke. 'General Lakos, I am relieving you of command. I'm afraid that you are out of touch. Unlike you, we will not murder our fellow Hungarians for the simple crime of longing to be free. Those on your staff who wish to join us, may. Those that do not' – he made a face – 'will be removed to a place of safety.'

Lakos looked around him. Most of his staff officers were already gathered together out in the open. A few sat dejectedly with their hands on their heads, under guard. Most, though, appeared friendly to the new rebels. As if to reinforce the point, a pair of helicopters, their gun barrels tracking, made a low, slow pass overhead.

'The National Salvation Government is finished, General. And so are you.'

Lakos sputtered, and fixed his gaze on Kemeny. 'You gave your word. You swore loyalty to me and to the government!'

Kemeny smiled thinly. 'I lied.'

Hungary's armed forces were making their choice.

MAY 21 – MOVEMENT CONTROL POST, EURCON IV CORPS, RAILROAD FREIGHT YARD, VIENNA, AUSTRIA

'Attention!'

Boots crashed on the concrete floor as the officers and enlisted men occupying the hastily converted warehouse leapt to their feet and stood at rigid attention. In the sudden silence, the soft humming made by their desktop computers seemed very loud.

Général de Corps d'Armée Claude Fabvier swept into the room, trailed by an array of French and German military aides. All of them were armed and wore battle dress.

Fabvier was a short, lean man turned brown by long service in Chad and the Middle East. He waved the startled staff officers back into their seats and smiled. 'At ease, gentlemen. At ease. You have a lot of work to do, if I'm not much mistaken.'

That earned him a quick, nervous laugh.

Still smiling indulgently, the general turned to the German colonel commanding the movement control post. 'Well, Joachim? Any problems?'

'None, Herr General.' The German led him over to a series of detailed topographical maps pinned to freestanding temporary partitions. Each showed a portion of the Austro-Hungarian border near Sopron – approximately forty kilometers south of Vienna. 'All divisional, brigade, and battalion quartering parties have selected and marked assembly areas for their formations.' Using a red grease pencil, he circled them one by one.

Fabvier studied them for a short time. At first glance, at least, the sites were good – offering adequate concealment from prying Hungarian eyes, protection from ground or air attack, and good routes forward to the border itself. 'And the movement schedule itself?'

'Nearly complete.' The colonel nodded toward a thick stack of printouts on his own desk. Coordinating the rail movement of three divisions, thousands of pieces of heavy equipment, and tens of thousands of tons of supplies from several different locations in France and Germany was an enormously complicated process, especially on such short notice. 'The first trains roll later today.'

Fabvier squinted down at the first page of the printouts. Codes and abbreviations made it virtually indecipherable to anyone but a staff specialist. He looked up. 'And the whole corps will be in position by the twenty-seventh?'

'Yes, Herr General.'

'Excellent. Splendid work, Colonel.' Fabvier believed in being generous with his praise, when praise was due.

Spurred on by Nicolas Desaix, the European Confederation was massing a powerful force on the Hungarian border. Dozens of combat aircraft and forty thousand heavily armed troops were converging on Austria. Their looming presence should make Hungary's rebels less eager to renege on solemn treaties and economic commitments.

MAY 25 – THE WHITE HOUSE, WASHINGTON, D.C.

Lightning flashed outside the Oval Office windows, streaking down out of a coal-black sky. The low, booming rumble of thunder echoed eerily across Washington's city streets and public buildings. Torrential rains followed close behind, sheets of solid water that pummeled the White House gardens, ripping blossoms off trees and petals off flowers.

The President stared moodily out into the gray-green half-light. 'Was I right to recognize this new Budapest regime, Ross? Or just so eager to hit back at the French that I've put us in a box?'

Ross Huntington shrugged. 'I don't see that you had any choice. You've seen the reports. This revolution's about as genuine and democratic as they come.' He winced when he tried to breathe, glad the President's back was turned. The tightness in his chest was getting worse and harder to conceal. 'Besides, it's the first crack in EurCon. Something to encourage, I'd say.'

'Yeah.' The President turned from the window. 'Easier to kill a cub than a full-grown wolf, I guess.'

Huntington nodded. 'Not as sporting, but sure easier.'

The President snorted. The ghost of a grin flickered across his face and vanished. 'I'd feel a helluva lot better about all this, though, if the French and Germans didn't have all those troops piling up across the Austrian border. Every satellite pass shows more and more troops.'

In Huntington's view, the Franco-German saber-rattling was another good reason that American and British backing for Hungary's new government made sense. Together with Polish, Czech, and Slovak offers of military assistance and free trade accords, it put France and Germany on notice that their bullying dare not cross over into active interference.

One of the phones on the desk rang. The President scooped it up in the one fluid motion. 'Yes?' His voice faded as he listened to the man on the other end. When he hung up, his face was bleak. 'That was Thurman. Our new ambassador to Hungary just reported in.'

Huntington was surprised. The envoy could only just have reached Budapest. Whatever was happening had to be pretty urgent.

'It seems the Hungarian government has just been handed a real hot potato. The French and Germans have offered their diplomatic recognition, but only under certain stringent conditions.'

'Impossible conditions?' Huntington guessed.

The President nodded. 'On the nose, Ross. They get recognized as a legitimate regime *if* they remain inside EurCon, and *if* they agree to honor all treaty commitments made by the military government.' He frowned. 'So all they have to do is act like the old government, kowtow like the old government, and the French and Germans will graciously *treat* them like the old government.'

'And if they refuse?'

'Various but unspecified "dire consequences." '

'Shit.'

The President nodded unhappily. 'My sentiments exactly.' He punched a button on his phone. 'Marla? I need you to make a few calls for me. I want Thurman, John Lucier, Galloway, and Quinn here on the double.'

MAY 26 – PARIS

Paris by night was as lovely and elegant as ever, but Nicolas Desaix was in no mood for beauty or elegance. He kept his chair faced away from the windows in his private office. He scowled. 'So they've refused our generous offer?'

'Yes, Minister.' The career diplomat he'd dispatched as a special envoy to Budapest shrank back in his own chair. He'd taken the full force of the brooding temper beneath the Foreign Minister's surface charm once before. He had no desire to experience it again.

'Get out.'

'Yes, Minister.'

Desaix waited until the other man had scuttled out before swearing once, sharply and violently. Then he got up and began pacing across his office, walking off some of his irritation.

He'd agreed to offer Hungary's new government a way out only at Germany's urging. He had always suspected the Germans were gutless. Now he knew it.

Their so-called compromise had proved a useless and dangerous gesture. French and German control over their economy was the primary Hungarian grievance, but it was also the keystone of French and German foreign policy. Given those two realities, no real compromise was possible.

Desaix clasped his hands behind his back. Once the news spread, Hungary's stubborn stand against the Confederation would only encourage others to do the same. It was inevitable.

He shook his head. There was only one real way to prevent that. Hungary still had a legitimate government – a government-in-exile. And France and Germany had three divisions moving into positions on the Austro-Hungarian border.

The Hungarian rebels had called the tune. Now they and their misguided followers would have to pay the piper.

MAY 27 – SCOUT PLATOON, 1ST HUNGARIAN TANK BRIGADE, NEAR SOPRON

Lt. Stefan Tereny lay propped up on his elbows, watching the enemy armor deploy through binoculars. Through a minor miracle, he'd managed to find the one dry spot in the still-muddy field, so he was relatively comfortable. The other members of his detail weren't quite so fortunate. They squatted nearby, monotonously and softly cursing all officers, all sergeants, the French, the Germans, and the wet weather.

Tereny smiled slightly. He would only be worried if he didn't hear his enlisted men grumbling.

He was within one kilometer of the border itself, just a line of fence posts linked by some old wire. There hadn't been any need for anything stronger, since Austria and Hungary were at peace. Now, though, Austria was part of the European Confederation and an accomplice to its plans.

Tereny was worried about those plans. Only a few kilometers away, he could see dark, square shapes moving off the highway, picking their way through unplowed fields and patches of woods.

French, all right. Frontline gear, too – LeClerc tanks and AMX-10 armored personnel carriers – and they weren't being shy about it, either. Tereny was careful to stay concealed, but only out of professional pride.

The French bastards over there obviously wanted to be seen.

Taking his time, he carefully counted thirteen tanks, then another group of thirteen, and then another – all neatly arrayed in line. Two more tanks and six jeeps brought up the rear – a command group. He was looking at a full French armored regiment – a battalion-equivalent in other armies – deployed right across the border on a very narrow front. Other units, tanks and mechanized infantry formations, were moving up beside them. He ordered his corporal to take some photos while he scouted the detachment's next hide.

The move to another concealed position gave Tereny more time to think than he would have liked. Sopron, the nearest road junction and an obvious target if war broke out, was defended by little more than the 1st Tank Brigade itself. He thought of his own men – well motivated and, he liked to think, well led. But the Hungarian Army had no depth, no reserves of ammunition or equipment.

He loved his land, and he would fight if the French and Germans crossed the border but he wasn't sure of the outcome. Not at all.

MAY 28 – HEADQUARTERS, EURCON IV CORPS, NEAR GROSSHOFLEIN, AUSTRIA

Général de Corps d'Armée Claude Fabvier tilted his head, listening to the steady rain drumming on the welded aluminum deck of his armored command vehicle. The weather could certainly be better, he thought. Then he smiled wryly, amused by his own sudden fastidiousness. Wars were fought as often in the mud and rain as in bright sunshine and on firm, dry ground. Perhaps he had spent too much time as a young officer in Africa. His eyes fell again on the decoded message clipped to his map table.

WARNING ORDER

TO: Commander, IV Corps
FROM: Defense Secretariat
SUBJECT: Military Operations in Hungary

The Confederation Defense Committee has authorized military intervention to restore order and a legitimate government to Hungary. Accordingly, you will prepare for imminent military operations against the rebel forces inside Hungary. Your objective is Budapest.

CHAPTER 17
Offensive

MAY 29 – SCOUT PLATOON, 1ST HUNGARIAN TANK BRIGADE, NEAR SOPRON, HUNGARY

It was raining again, soaking the wooded hills near the Austrian border. Lt. Stefan Tereny huddled miserably under a plastic sheet, trying unsuccessfully to stay warm and dry in the shallow, muddy hole he and his crew had scraped out of a hillside overlooking the highway from Vienna. Local farmers might welcome this nighttime storm, but he didn't. The rain and darkness reduced visibility to practically nil, right when he desperately needed to see as far as possible.

His platoon's three BRDM-2 scout cars and twelve men were deployed in widely scattered and well-camouflaged positions along a two-kilometer stretch of the frontier. Other scout platoons flanked them. The 1st Brigade's tank and motorized rifle battalions were deployed far to the rear – in Sopron's outlying suburbs and along the forested Karoly Heights overlooking the city.

Tereny raised his starlight scope for another quick look, careful to keep the precious device dry. The green and black images were fuzzy, distorted by a myriad of small flecks – falling raindrops. He wished in vain for a portable infrared scope, a thermal imaging system like those used by their potential enemies. But even the most sophisticated night-vision gear couldn't see far through a heavy spring downpour like this.

Damn. The word from headquarters was that EurCon's forces might cross the border anytime. Like tonight. Now. And it was Tereny's job to raise the alarm if they did.

Frustrated, the Hungarian lieutenant lowered his starlight scope. He could barely make out the main highway from here, let alone the frontier line. They would have to get closer. He glanced at the two men huddled under the tarpaulin with him – his gunner and radioman. The scout car's driver waited a few meters further back, inside the four-wheeled vehicle. 'Right. Grab your gear. We're moving up.'

Suddenly his gunner, a corporal, grabbed his shoulder and whispered fiercely. 'Lieutenant, wait! I hear something.'

Tereny froze, trying hard to listen but at first only hearing the patter of rain on leaves and his own racing heartbeat. Then he heard it – the low muffled sound of a diesel engine somewhere very close by.

He raised the scope again, scanning in what he thought was the right direction. The damned rain was interfering with sounds as well as sight. One thing was certain. Whoever was out there wasn't friendly. There were no other Hungarian Army units this close to the border, and absolutely no civilian traffic allowed in this sector.

Now that he knew what to listen for, he heard the engine noises again. There were at least two enemy vehicles out there – feeling their way slowly through the rain-soaked woods. He nudged his radioman. 'Contact Brigade HQ. Tell them we hear movement to our front.'

The engine noises were growing louder. Tereny stiffened. The enemy must be almost right on top of them. He cocked his Soviet made AKR, a carbine version of the AK-74 assault rifle. The radioman did the same while the gunner readied an RPG-16 antitank rocket launcher.

Then the three soldiers flattened themselves, burrowing deeper into the mud. Something clanked out to the front and the lieutenant swiveled his scope toward the sound. There! A six-wheeled, turreted shape loomed out of the darkness and falling rain. He could make out a gun as well, a big one. Another shape materialized off to the right, trundling in the same direction.

As the first vehicle turned, maneuvering between two trees, Tereny recognized its distinctive silhouette. It was a French AMX-10RC, a reconnaissance vehicle armed with a powerful 105mm cannon. EurCon had its own scouts out, probing for the first signs of Hungarian resistance.

The lieutenant put his mouth to the radioman's ear and whispered. 'Send "Two AMX-10s moving east! Am engaging." ' While the private relayed his message, he turned to his RPG-armed gunner. 'We're going to have to take these bastards here. We're too close to bug out now. Right?'

The corporal nodded vigorously. Their briefing on the AMX-10 had included the unwelcome news that its fire control system was one of the most sophisticated ever installed in a light recon vehicle. Trying to run away from a gun system equipped with a laser range finder, ballistic computer, and low-light TV cameras would be suicide. Even in the rain they wouldn't get fifty meters before being spotted, engaged, and destroyed.

'Good. Give me thirty seconds and then take the one on the right.'

The corporal acknowledged the order 'Sir!' through clenched teeth.

Tereny slithered out from under the tarpaulin and got to his feet, careful to keep a tree trunk between himself and the French vehicles. Then he scrambled uphill to their own camouflaged scout car. The little BRDM only mounted a single heavy machine gun, but at this range it might be able to penetrate the side armor on the French armored cars.

He clambered up onto the BRDM's deck and lowered himself in through the open commander's hatch. The wide-eyed, pale face of his driver turned toward him. 'Christ, Lieutenant! What do we do now?'

'We fight,' Tereny said brusquely, worming his way into the scout car's cramped turret. He settled in behind the grips of the 14.5mm machine gun and frantically cranked the gun turret around. Any second now . . .

A streak of fire tore through the night. The sudden burst of light illuminated the two French vehicles, both caught broadside. He had only a fleeting glance before the corporal's RPG-16 rocket slammed into one of the AMX-10s, tore through the light armor at the base of its turret, and exploded.

The French armored car fireballed. Sheets of flame poured out through open hatches as its ammunition and fuel ignited. Shadows fled in all directions, eerily flickering in time with the crackling flames.

Without waiting Tereny centered his sights on the remaining AMX and fired. The heavy machine gun chattered, spraying glowing tracer rounds toward the enemy vehicle. Sparks flew as bullets slapped into its hull and turret, punching holes through aluminum armor designed to fend off shell fragments and lighter infantry weapons. The French armored car ground to a halt, lifeless.

Elated, the Hungarian lieutenant let go of the machine gun and clambered back into his commander's seat. He stuck his head out the open roof hatch. 'Corporal! Take Markos and check out those AMXs for prisoners!'

Obeying those orders, his gunner and radioman abandoned their hiding place and moved cautiously toward the wrecked vehicles. Both men held their weapons at the ready.

A shell screamed overhead and burst higher up the hill. The explosion took away his sense of victory. Now that they were detected, the French were abandoning stealth in favor of firepower.

More shells rained down along the slope, splintering trees and sending deadly fragments sleeting in all directions. Tereny had the sudden horrified feeling that he'd kicked open a hornet's nest. It was time to get his platoon to safety. He grabbed the BRDM's radio mike. 'All Sierra units! This is Sierra Alpha! Withdraw to Phase Line Bravo! Repeat, withdraw to Phase Line Bravo!'

Hurried acknowledgements crackled over radio circuits flooded with other urgent sighting reports and calls for fire support. From what he could hear, French recon forces were advancing across the border at several widely separated points.

Tereny ducked beneath the hatch coaming as a shell slammed into the ground only fifty meters away. Splinters whined overhead and clanged off the BRDM's side armor. He raised his head cautiously, looking for his gunner and radioman. Why the hell were they taking so long?

A parachute flare burst high overhead, lighting the tree covered hillside and valley below with its harsh white glare. As it drifted downward through sheets of falling rain, the lieutenant saw his two missing crewmen staggering up the muddy slope toward him. They were supporting a wounded Frenchman between them. He waved them on and leaned out of the hatch, ready to help hoist their prisoner aboard.

'My God.' Tereny froze again, staring into the valley. There were tanks and armored personnel carriers moving down there. Dozens of them. This wasn't a skirmish. EurCon was invading in force.

He hauled the injured, bleeding man through the BRDM's open hatch and then scrambled out of the way as his gunner and radioman tumbled inside. They slammed the hatch shut behind them and stared wild-eyed as Tereny leaned over the driver's shoulder shouting, 'Crank it up! Let's get out of here!'

With the teeth-rattling roar of incoming artillery fire urging them on, the Hungarian scouts raced for the dubious safety of their own lines.

TOKOL MILITARY AIRFIELD, NEAR BUDAPEST

It had taken the EurCon warplanes just twenty minutes to hammer Tokol into oblivion. Protected by fighters, three separate waves of Mirages and Tornados loaded for ground attack had roamed across the Hungarian airfield, bombing and strafing practically at will. Only two antiquated MiG-21s had managed to get airborne before the raiding force arrived. Both had been bounced and blown out of the sky without ever seeing their attackers.

When the French and German jets turned for home, they left nothing but wreckage behind them. Every runway was cratered, torn apart by French-made Durandals. Laser-guided one-thousand-kilogram bombs had turned rows of heavily reinforced shelters into mounds of twisted steel and shattered concrete. Burned-out wrecks littering the scorched and bullet-pocked tarmac showed where aircraft had been caught out in the open. And dense columns of black smoke in a ring around the horizon marked destroyed SAM sites and radar installations.

Col. Zoltan Hradetsky climbed out of his car and walked over to the tiny knot of grim-faced air force officers surveying the destruction. Four of Oskar Kiraly's best bodyguards moved with him, each carefully watching in a different direction. Having already lost one of the democratic revolution's top leaders, Kiraly had no intention of losing another.

The air force officers stiffened to attention as he approached. Although he held no place in the formal military hierarchy, his position as national security advisor to the provisional government commanded respect.

'Is this as bad as it looks?' Hradetsky saw no point in beating around the bush. The new government's ministers had crucial decisions to make and they were waiting for his first hand report.

'It's worse.' The brigadier general now commanding Hungary's air force spoke bluntly and bitterly. 'They hit every one of our active airfields within a single hour last night. Aided by picture-perfect intelligence, no doubt.'

Hradetsky understood the other man's anger. Four of the nation's top-ranked air force officers were among those who had fled to join the EurCon-supported 'government-in-exile.' Their inside information on Hungary's bases, radar and SAM systems, and tactics must have proved invaluable to the French and Germans. 'What about our losses?'

'Crippling.' The air force commander nodded toward the devastation in front of them. 'This field is typical. Our preliminary estimates show that we've lost well over half of our interceptor and ground attack aircraft. Plus thirty to forty percent of our attack and transport helicopters. Our ordnance stores were hit, as were our maintenance facilities. Those that fly won't be able to fight very well.'

Hradetsky whistled softly in dismay. In just sixty minutes, the French and Germans had destroyed at least eighty MiG-21s and MiG-23s, and maybe another fifteen Hind-A helicopter gunships. For all practical purposes the Hungarian Air Force had been destroyed before it could get off the ground. Now enemies controlled the skies over his native land.

With its embattled troops naked to EurCon air attack and in full retreat, Hungary would need every scrap of help its new friends to the north could provide, and soon.

MAY 30 – BLUE FLIGHT, OVER VESZPREM, HUNGARY

Four twin-tailed aircraft slid through the cold night air. Navigation lights that would have been left on in peacetime for flight safety were off now. Poland's F-15 Eagles were going to war.

Inside the lead Eagle, 1st Lt. Tadeusz Wojcik kept wanting to shove his throttles forward, to hurry and catch the EurCon aircraft he was after before they could make their strike. But the geometry was all wrong.

The battered Hungarian air defense system hadn't detected the incoming raid until it was halfway to its target – the helicopter base at Veszprem, a city nestled in the Bakony Mountains near Lake Balaton. More precious minutes were wasted while the information passed down the chain of command to where Tad and his three flightmates had been sitting in their cockpits for half the night. By the time they'd got the news and scrambled off the airfield and into the air, it was too late to catch the strike aircraft before they dropped their bombs. They'd have to settle for jumping the bastards on their way home.

Within hours of Poland's decision to aid Hungary's democratic government, Wojcik's squadron had moved south – to the Czech air base at Brno. That put them only a hundred klicks north of Vienna and the EurCon airfields around the Austrian capital. Right now, the Polish and Czech planes were operating under strict, defensive rules of engagement. They could only attack French and German planes in Hungarian airspace and only conduct strike missions against EurCon ground forces inside Hungary itself. If those rules changed, though, they'd be perfectly placed to attack right down the enemy's throat.

Wojcik glanced down at the map board strapped to one knee, mentally tracking his position as ground controllers fed them course changes. The men controlling this intercept had first swung them east, then almost straight south. They were trying to bring the four F-15s in from the enemy's two o'clock, so that the Eagles wouldn't have a tail chase. Careful positioning was vital, but it all took more time and fuel than he liked.

At least coming in from slightly to the side would help them detect the enemy aircraft. German Tornados had radar-absorbent material on their engine intakes and gold-coated canopies to make them tougher to see on radar, but those stealth modifications would only help from the front.

Tad glanced at his fuel gauges. Even with drop tanks, they were going to have to be careful if they wanted to make it back to Brno. Any Hungarian air base could refuel them, but landing at one would put him smack in the middle of a shooting gallery. It was dangerous enough up here.

He returned to his careful scan of the sky, the symbols on his HUD, and back down to his cockpit instruments again. Even when racing to an intercept and certain air combat, attention to detail was vital. He forced himself to follow procedure, to think ahead. 'Buck fever' was a real threat, especially on his first combat mission.

His four F-15s were each armed with four Sparrow and four Sidewinder missiles, along with a centerline drop tank. Although the Eagles could carry the new and better AMRAAM missile, there were only a few of those 'silver bullets' in the Polish inventory at the moment. And the brass had ordered them retained for the defense of Polish territory. Their decision made sense, Tad guessed, but right now he was more worried about the piece of Polish territory inside his cockpit.

The flight moved south at 750 knots. They were flying at ten thousand meters, well above a solid cloud layer. Below the clouds, rain and low visibility made it a dirty night for flying, but that was perfect intruder weather. The Polish planes had their radars off, to avoid alerting the enemy to their presence. Part of Wojcik wanted his fighter's 'eyes' on, but he knew they were too far away to pick out fleeting contacts flying only a few dozen meters above the rolling landscape.

'Blue flight, raid is seventy kilometers, bearing one seven five.' The intercept controller's voice was perfectly calm.

Tad felt his own heartbeat starting to speed up. It was almost time to energize their radars. His four aircraft would be in radar guided missile range in another thirty kilometers – only minutes at their present closing speed. The idea was to turn on the radar, lock up quickly, and fire Sparrows before the Tornados could react. Although they'd be firing at extreme range, the first salvo should break up the EurCon formation and force them to maneuver, wasting precious fuel. Right now the enemy pilots were outbound and tired, anxious to escape unfriendly territory, maybe even damaged or short on fuel. In other words, vulnerable. The fact that they were Germans was icing on the cake.

Minutes passed, seeming slower now as adrenaline pulsed through his bloodstream and altered his time sense. He glanced down at the clock on the F-15's control panel. They should be within range. But his threat receiver was still quiet, so Tad continued on silently. The closer to the enemy, the better. He risked a glance aft, but the other three Eagles, spaced out at half-kilometer intervals and staggered altitudes, were invisible in the darkness.

Another minute brought him a dozen kilometers closer to the enemy's estimated position, close enough for his tastes. He keyed his mike. 'Blue flight, energize.' Microphone clicks acknowledged his order.

The first few radar sweeps showed only a hash of dots as the F-15's computer tried to sort out ground clutter and weather effects. On the third sweep, though, Wojcik saw a cluster of dots in a regular pattern. There they were – three pairs of enemy aircraft and one singleton trailing slightly behind.

In a long-range, radar-guided attack like this the trick was to avoid wasting missiles by having two aircraft engage the same target. Believing that the simplest methods were always best, he'd briefed the other pilots before takeoff to engage their opposite numbers, left to right. Tad's wingman for this hop, a young rookie pilot named Milan Rozek, was flying to his left and slightly back, so he would take the leftmost German jet. Wojcik would fire on the Tornado just to the right of that. Training made target selection automatic, and it could be done without time-consuming radio chatter.

He thumbed a button on his stick, designating one of the distant EurCon aircraft as his target. A box appeared around the symbol on his radar screen. The enemy plane was too far below him for any kind of a cueing box to appear on his HUD, but he was ready to shoot. Wojcik waited one beat for the rest of his flight to finish locking up, then squeezed the trigger on his stick.

A *whoosh* and the sudden bright flare of missile exhaust from under his starboard wing told him he had a good launch. His peripheral vision caught the glare as his number three launched at almost the same time. The small, gleeful boy inside Tad who had always loved Fourth of July fireworks wanted to watch the missiles flashing away and down into the night, but he forced himself to concentrate on the scope. It was just as well. The German planes were already starting to maneuver – alerted by their own threat receivers.

The Eagle's weapons computer had already selected and tested another Sparrow and Tad pulled the trigger again. Firing two missiles against a long-range target like this was standard doctrine, to increase the chance of a hit. An alert and skillful enemy pilot might dodge the first incoming missile, but he might not even see the second one.

Ahead, the missiles arced up, climbing to thinner air where they could fly at almost four times the speed of sound. When their motors burned out, they vanished into the darkness, coasting through the rest of their trajectory. They would dive on their targets from above, at blinding speed.

Tad clicked his mike again. 'Go to cruise.' He throttled back, not only to save fuel but also to slow his rate of closure with the enemy aircraft. The otherwise excellent Sparrow had one major flaw – the attacker had to keep his radar pointed squarely at his target, 'illuminating' it for the missiles in flight. Sparrows needed to 'see' those reflected radar beams to home in on their target. Even at this range, missile flight time was only a minute, but that was an eternity under combat conditions. And for that relative eternity, the four Polish F-15s had to fly a relatively straight and level course. Only the absence of EurCon fighter escorts allowed them to attack this way.

The radar display was getting mushy again. The Tornados were using jammers and bundles of chaff as they maneuvered, trying to break the radar lock. Tad's own target acquisition box flickered, then disappeared.

He swore, then swallowed his string of curses a half second later when his target vanished, too. Unguided but still ballistic, his missile must have gotten close enough for its proximity fuse to detonate before the Tornado could change course. A wave of satisfaction washed over him, and again he forced himself to concentrate on the job at hand. He had his first kill, against an old enemy.

They were close to the frantically maneuvering EurCon jets now, only a dozen kilometers away. The Tornados, flying in pairs, reacted differently to the attack. One pair turned away, trying to outrun the ambush. Four more were turning toward their attackers – attempting to increase the closure rate and break past the Poles before they could fire again. This was going to get down and dirty real fast.

Tad was already selecting his Sidewinder missiles when two more radar contacts disappeared. Yes! At this range, loss of detection meant almost a sure kill. Three German strike planes down and only four more to go. He grinned under his oxygen mask. They were cleaning up!

Wojcik continued to scan the sky around him, but he could see neither his friends nor his enemies. Still, his radar showed German aircraft in front of him. That was good enough.

'Break into pairs, turning left.' He banked the fighter left and pushed down on the stick. They would have to dive under the clouds before his Sidewinders could lock . . .

A line of fire past his right side. Shit. He slammed the stick to starboard, straining against his harness, craning his neck around to see aft. Nothing. 'Fighters aft! Break right!'

In that same instant, another missile sliced through the darkness, off to the left this time. This one exploded. Tad caught one brief glimpse of an F-15 in flames and tumbling out of control toward the ground. 'The second missile had hit his wingman. 'Blue Two! Eject!'

Only static answered him as the burning Eagle fell. Oh, Christ. Wojcik swallowed convulsively, fighting down the burning taste of vomit creeping up his throat. Milan Rozek was gone.

He continued his own tight, diving turn, now seeing the clouds as cover instead of a barrier. One hand chopped his throttles still further, instinctively reducing the F-15's infrared signature. Then he stabbed the chaff and flare release, spewing decoys out behind him in case there were other missiles closing in.

Urgent calls from Blue Three and Four indicated that they didn't hold any other contacts, but were also maneuvering frantically while searching for the enemy planes that had sneaked up behind them.

His Eagle continued to corkscrew down, the clouds a dark gray mass below him. Tad's mind worked fast, trying to get the measure of his unseen opponents. He hadn't heard a peep out of his own radar warning gear. They must have been using an infrared scanner then, after being cued by Blue flight's own radar emissions. A totally passive attack. Understanding dawned. The MiG-29 mounted such a device. And the Germans had Fulcrums – two full squadrons they'd inherited during the reunification.

It was wildly, almost insanely, ironic. Here he was, serving in a former

Warsaw Pact air force and flying an American-made fighter in battle against a former NATO ally flying Soviet-made Fulcrums. He controlled a sudden, maddening urge to laugh and concentrated on staying alive.

His threat receiver was still blank, so the Germans weren't using their radars yet.

The clouds engulfed him, and Tad let his fighter descend another five hundred meters before leveling out. Inside the mass, he was screened from infrared detection. They'd have to turn on their radars if they wanted to find him.

His plane raced northeast through almost total darkness, toward the origin point for the missiles that had narrowly missed him and killed Rozek. The F-15 rattled and shook, buffeted by turbulence inside the storm clouds.

There. Two blips appeared on his radar screen, out in front and turning toward him. Neither showed friendly IFF and both were inside Sparrow range. Even as he locked up, his threat receiver came on, showing a Slot Back radar on a bearing that matched with the bogeys. They *were* Fulcrums, then, activating their radars now that they had lost him on their IR scanners. They were too late.

Tad's finger squeezed the trigger on his stick. His third Sparrow dropped off his starboard wing and ignited. It vanished, leaving a glowing trail through the clouds.

He advanced the throttle, closing on the German MiG coming at him head-on, and selected Sidewinder. As his missile streaked out of the clouds, the enemy plane suddenly turned hard and climbed. Perfect.

Wojcik pulled back on his stick, climbing himself. Suddenly the F-15 broke out into clear air. A growling tone in his headphones indicated that the missile he'd selected could see its prey. The Fulcrum, trying desperately to evade the Sparrow he'd fired, was using full power – maybe even its afterburners.

Tad pulled the trigger again.

The heat-seeker leapt off its rail, racing toward the enemy fighter now just two miles ahead of him. A cueing box appeared on his HUD, centered on the fleeing MiG. The Sidewinder's bright exhaust merged with the box and then vanished in a bright orange fireball. A hit! Glowing shards and pieces of debris cartwheeled out of the explosion, already spinning downward.

Wojcik circled, checking for the second German Fulcrum without success. It was gone – nowhere in sight and nowhere on radar. So were the four surviving Tornados. Worse, Blue Three and Four were also missing. And his increasingly frantic radio calls to them went unanswered.

Alone in a black sky, over a battlefield, Tadeusz Wojcik decided it was time to head for home. What had started out as a turkey shoot had all too quickly turned into a fight for his own personal survival. He didn't like being ambushed. It was time for a change in tactics. Even his own two kills couldn't balance the guilt he felt for losing his inexperienced wingman.

SITUATION ROOM, WASHINGTON, D.C.

Huddled for their second emergency session in two days, the men and women who served on America's National Security Council still looked stunned to Ross Huntington. He shared their dismay. Despite all of EurCon's threats and menacing troop movements, none of them had really expected an armed invasion of Hungary.

Gen. Reid Galloway put down the phone he'd been using and looked straight at the President. 'That was Tom Foss, sir. Our liaison with the Polish Air Force. He confirms those early reports. Polish aircraft flying from Czech and Slovak bases *have* engaged EurCon planes over Hungary.'

'My God.' Harris Thurman turned pale. 'Do we have airmen stationed at those bases?'

'No, Mr. Secretary.' Galloway shrugged. 'But we do have training groups at some of the Polish airfields being used as staging and repair areas for the squadrons they're sending south.'

Openly appalled, the Secretary of State faced the President. 'We have to get our air force people out of there! Right away!'

'Why?' the President asked quietly. Of all those in the room, he seemed the least surprised by recent events.

Thurman stared back at him, trying to calm down. 'Isn't it obvious? If they stay, the French and Germans can accuse us of playing a part in this war.'

'A war they started,' Huntington felt compelled to point out. The pompous Secretary of State never failed to irritate him.

The other man ignored him, focusing instead on the man he wanted to sway. 'Mr. President, there is only one prudent course. We must immediately and publicly withdraw all U.S. military personnel from Poland and the Czech and Slovak Republics. It's the only way to make sure that we aren't dragged into this thing.'

'And just how do you suppose EurCon would interpret a move like that, Harris?' the President asked flatly. 'Not to mention the rest of our allies?' He answered his own question. 'They'd believe we were abandoning the Poles. That we were cutting and running at the first sign of trouble.

'And I believe that would be the worst imaginable signal we could send.' The President shook his head decisively. 'The best deterrent against even more EurCon aggression is a strong, visible American presence on the ground in Poland.' He turned to Galloway. 'Tell Brigadier General Foss and the others to stay put.'

Huntington nodded slowly. The President's decisions made sense. He just hoped the men in Paris and Berlin were still able to think rationally.

MAY 31 – FORWARD HEADQUARTERS, EURCON IV CORPS, NEAR FERTOD, HUNGARY

Two centuries before, the elegant, horseshoe-shaped Esterházy Palace had been the summer home of a Hungarian princely family and their court composer, Joseph Haydn. Now, tracked and wheeled armored vehicles festooned with radio antennas crowded the cobblestoned courtyard and neatly landscaped gardens. Staff officers in French and German battle dress conferred in small groups against the backdrop of the building's elaborate yellow and white Baroque façade. EurCon's IV Corps, its invasion force, had established its forward headquarters at this chateau popularly known as the Hungarian Versailles.

Near the palace's wrought-iron main gate, Général de Corps d'Armée Claude Fabvier stood looking down an access road leading to the main highway. More armored vehicles were parked in the tall, uncut grass to either side – squat, powerful-looking LeClerc main battle tanks of the 2nd Dragoons and tracked AMX-10P APCs belonging to the 51st Infantry. Soldiers, stripped to the waist in the late spring heat, lounged in the shade provided by their vehicles and by the tall trees that lined the road. Both French regiments were resting after spearheading the EurCon drive across the border.

Fabvier's new leading elements, German panzer and panzergrenadier battalions from the 10th Panzer Division, were fighting on the outskirts of the tiny village of Szarfold, twenty kilometers to the east. Smoke from burning houses and tanks stained the eastern horizon. The general could hear a steady, muffled thumping in the distance as his corps and divisional artillery softened up Hungarian positions along Highway 85.

He shook his head, irritated by the signs of continued heavy fighting. Two days after storming across the frontier, the four divisions under his command were already fifty kilometers inside Hungary. But even though his troops and tanks were advancing at a fair clip, this campaign was already proving far more difficult than he'd anticipated. The Hungarian Army's antiquated T-55 tanks and PSZH-IV personnel carriers were no real match for his four hundred LeClercs and Leopard 2s – especially at long range. God only knew, there were enough smoldering wrecks strung out along the roadside from Sopron on to prove that. Still, the Hungarians were putting up fierce resistance wherever and whenever they could. Clearing their dismounted infantrymen out of the woodlots and small villages along the highway usually meant close-quarters combat. And that meant taking casualties.

From the moment they'd crossed the frontier, the French corps commander had watched a steady stream of ambulances heading west – carrying his dead and wounded. Maintenance units were swamped with salvage and repair work on damaged or destroyed tanks and APCs.

Fabvier gritted his teeth. Very little of this heavy fighting would have been necessary if the flyboys had achieved air supremacy over the battlefield – as they had promised. After dealing the first night's death blow to the enemy air force, French and German warplanes were supposed to be ranging overhead on call, swooping in to smash the Hungarian tank and motor rifle battalions hurrying to block the IV Corps' path. Other planes were supposed to be busy escorting French airmobile regiments on raiding missions deep into the enemy's vulnerable rear areas.

Polish and Czech aerial intervention had put all those plans on hold.

Fearful of being bounced by marauding F-15s and MiGs, EurCon Air Force commanders were refusing to mount strike missions without heavy escort and thorough preparation. As a result, the air units stationed in Austria were flying fewer sorties and had slower reaction times when they were presented with fleeting targets of opportunity. Hungarian columns that should have been obliterated by cluster bombs and strafing cannon were reaching the front almost unscathed.

There were also worrying signs that Poland and its allies might be considering entering the conflict on the ground. Fabvier had seen signals intelligence intercepts that suggested at least two Czech tank divisions were massing near the Slovak capital, Bratislava – just north of the Hungarian border. His brow furrowed as he frowned. If the Czech Army moved south to face him, he would need substantial reinforcements to continue the attack. And even if their tanks and APCs stayed on the right side of the line, they could cause him significant problems. He'd be forced to keep one eye perpetually peeled over his left shoulder as he pushed closer to Budapest. The need to guard his northern flank against possible attack would force him to divert large numbers of badly needed troops from his spearheads.

'General!' Boots rang on the cobblestones behind him.

Fabvier turned. His aide, Maj. Castellane, hurried closer. 'What is it, Major?'

'Rochonvillers wants us to move faster. They claim we're already several hours behind schedule and falling further behind all the time. I tried to explain the situation, but they want to talk to you directly.' Castellane was apologetic. Rochonvillers, near Metz, was the site of the French Army's underground war headquarters.

The IV Corps commander turned purple with rage. He loathed the rear-area slackers and civilian ninnies who infested the headquarters' neon-lit corridors. Not one of them knew what real soldiering was all about. He stabbed a finger at his aide. 'You tell Minister Guichy and the rest of his bootlickers that I'm busy fighting a war here. And tell them that we'll be able to advance faster when *they* clear the goddamned Poles and Czechs out of the sky and out of our way! Not before!'

'Yes, sir.' The major saluted and headed for the command vehicle carrying their secure communications channels. Fabvier's ill-tempered words were about to stir up more trouble than he'd imagined.

JUNE 1 – CONFEDERATION DEFENSE COMMITTEE, ROCHONVILLERS, FRANCE

Eleven men sat around the large circular table that nearly filled the underground War Room. Aides occupied chairs behind them, ready to run errands or to translate. Six of the men at the table, the service chiefs of the French and German armed forces, wore uniforms. The rest were in civilian clothes. Although the ventilation system was running on high, a haze of cigarette smoke hung near the low ceiling. The high-ranking members of the European Confederation's Defense Committee had been meeting in urgent session since early that morning.

'Clearly, gentlemen, we can no longer operate under the delusion that this action will be swift and painless.' Jürgen Lettow, Germany's Defense Minister, sounded exhausted. 'Perhaps we should consider the possibility of a negotiated end to this crisis – before it worsens. As I see, the Swiss offer to mediate could yield . . .'

Nicolas Desaix listened with mounting irritation. With the Confederation already at war, it was far too late for any timid misgivings about the use of force to restore Hungary's military government to power. Now that the shooting had actually started, the only thing that mattered was to win, and win quickly. Anything short of unmistakable victory would shatter the Confederation he had so painstakingly forged.

Several of the smaller countries, Austria included, were already increasingly reluctant to honor their treaty commitments. Austrian troops that should have been guarding IV Corps supply lines were being held inside their own country – ostensibly for 'national security' reasons.

The French Foreign Minister shifted restlessly in his chair. He abhorred this necessity to wage war by committee. By their very nature, deliberation and compromise were the enemies of swift and decisive action. If it were possible to *talk* one's way to victory, French and German tanks would have been in Budapest two days ago.

In any event, Lettow was right about one thing. Their initial timetables and casualty estimates had been wildly optimistic. The invasion planners had believed the Hungarian government-in-exile's claims that their soldiers wouldn't fight hard for the new regime. Of course, the Hungarian generals had been wrong – and not for the first time. According to intelligence reports, nearly all of Hungary's tank and motor rifle brigades were actively siding with the revolutionaries in Budapest.

But the appearance of Polish and Czech aircraft over the battlefield had been the biggest and most unpleasant surprise so far. Operating from sanctuaries inside their own territory, their fighters and fighter-bombers were proving a serious annoyance. More than that, in fact, if General Fabvier's reports could be believed. Desaix had to admit that he had never imagined that the eastern European 'free trade' states would offer Hungary more than moral support. American and British backing must be making them bolder than prudence would otherwise dictate.

Desaix glanced down the table toward Schraeder. Did the German Chancellor share Lettow's belated misgivings? He couldn't tell. The Chancellor just sat there, saying little and showing even less.

Still, Schraeder had studied history. Whether or not he had misgivings, he must know that generals and politicians who led their nations into unsuccessful wars never held power for long afterward. It was too late to back away now.

Desaix leaned forward in his chair, interrupting Lettow. 'The Swiss offer may be kindly meant, Herr Lettow. But I really do not see that we have anything to talk about!'

He aimed his words toward the German Chancellor's end of the table. 'We support the legitimate government of Hungary – a fellow member of this Confederation. All our actions to restore that government and good order are in accordance with international law and our own treaty obligations.' Desaix put steel in his voice. 'If anyone backs away from this crisis, it must be Poland and its friends – not us!'

Several of the others muttered their agreement with his hawkish stance. Schraeder nodded reluctantly. Lettow merely looked appalled.

'And how do you think we should persuade them of that, Nicolas? With a diplomatic communiqué?' Michel Guichy asked sharply. His position as head of the Defense Secretariat made him the most vulnerable of all if their attack on Hungary's rebel government ended in failure or even a bloody, Pyrrhic victory.

Desaix shook his head. 'No. Words mean nothing when bombs are falling. I have a somewhat more *practical* form of communication in mind. A way to put Warsaw and the rest on notice that we will not let them meddle in Hungary – not without paying a very high price.'

He turned toward the short, sallow-faced commander of the French Air Force. 'General Vichery is better qualified to brief you on the military aspects. General?'

'Of course, Minister.' Vichery rose and strode to a wall map at one end of the War Room. Symbols showed the location of all known friendly and enemy ground and air units along the Confederation's eastern border. One after the other, he pointed to three airfields, two in Poland and one in the Czech Republic. 'These are the linchpins of the enemy air campaign against us. But all of them are vulnerable to attack. One swift, coordinated strike could cripple these facilities.'

Lettow broke in suddenly. 'You cannot be serious, Minister Desaix! There are American Air Force technicians and advisors stationed at those bases!'

'What of it?' Desaix said coldly. 'With or without an official declaration, Poland and the others are making war against us, Herr Lettow! The air bases General Vichery has identified are being used to mount attacks that are killing Confederation pilots and ground troops. By remaining there, by continuing to work with the Poles, these Americans have become combatants. And as combatants, they are at risk.' He scowled. 'It is time to make the American people and their Congress aware of the dangerous games their President is playing with American lives!'

Lettow swallowed visibly. 'But the risk of war with the United States . . .'

'Is minimal,' Desaix finished for him. 'Except for a few hundred technicians and trainers, the Americans have no significant military presence in Europe. And no easy way to get any more soldiers to Poland in time to matter.' He shrugged. 'They would also be fighting a war on our ground and at the far end of a very long line of communications. Given that, I believe Washington will very quickly see reason. They will not fight a war they cannot win.'

He looked expectantly at Schraeder and the rest of the Confederation Defense Committee. 'So the question remains, gentlemen. Do we allow the Poles and Czechs to attack us with impunity? Or will we strike back and put an end to this nonsense once and for all?'

One after the other they nodded their approval for the retaliatory air raids he proposed. Only Lettow grimly shook his head.

Nicolas Desaix paid little attention to the rest of General Vichery's briefing. He found details on ordnance loads, mission parameters, and flight paths utterly uninteresting. Only the effects mattered. Poland and its partners were about to learn that defying the European Confederation could be an extremely expensive proposition.

JUNE 2 – OVER GERMANY

Six pairs of swept-wing, single-tailed Mirage F1E fighters roared off the main runway of the old Soviet air base at Jüterbog, leaving one after the other at precisely timed intervals. None climbed higher than five hundred meters above a gently rolling landscape of forests and farmland.

Originally intended primarily as an interceptor, software and radar system upgrades were supposed to make the F1 a capable all-weather strike aircraft. The pilots flying this mission intended to prove that beyond any doubt. Each Mirage carried two long, angular shapes slung under its wings – Apache cruise missiles. The Apache was one of the newest French weapons, a stealthy, ground-hugging cruise missile specifically designed to evade enemy radars and air defenses.

Formed up in three four-plane flights, the Fls dove even lower and turned toward the rising sun. Their shadows rippled across a patchwork of fields and woodlands as they flew east at five hundred knots.

WROCLAW AIR FORCE BASE, POLAND

Staff Sgt. Jim Frewer, USAF, stood near the hardened aircraft shelter's open doors, watching carefully as a Polish Air Force captain realigned the APG-70 radar antenna on an F-15. Quick, efficient work was critical because this fighter would leave for Brno in a few hours and from there for Hungary and combat. To get at the radar system, they had the Eagle's pointed nose unlatched and hinged all the way back. Technical manuals stuffed full of Polish-language crib sheets were stacked on a wheeled parts and tool trolley nearby.

Frewer smiled. Capt. Aleksander Giertych was good, but he still had trouble with some English technical terms. Even after some months spent as part of the U.S. Military Assistance Advisory Group in Poland, the sergeant found it strange to see officers doing maintenance work that would have been handled by enlisted men back in the States. Different systems, different ways of doing things, he reminded himself. It was a reminder he'd used many times while watching the Polish fliers and their ground crews make the faltering leap from Russian MiGs to American F-15s.

In the Russian system, which the Poles had inherited, officers handled all the technical work, while their conscript enlisted personnel did little more than sweep up. Eventually that would have to change, but it couldn't possibly happen overnight. To their credit, the Polish maintenance officers hadn't stood on rank, they'd listened to his lectures like rapt schoolboys.

They had done more than that, of course. Despite the differences in their ranks, his 'students' had taken him into their homes and families. They'd made him part of the 11th Fighter Regiment. He thought of them as his 'boys' and their planes as his 'birds.'

Poland was a long way from Minnesota, where he'd grown up, and Langley Air Force Base, in Virginia, his last duty station, but he could easily relate to the men here and what they were doing.

Right now Frewer's formal classes were on hold. The entire regiment was on a war footing, working almost around the clock readying a second squadron for service over Hungary. He spent all his time on the line with them, performing systems tests and making final adjustments. Six months of MAAG training just wasn't enough to teach the 11th's maintenance crews everything, and he'd be damned if he let men go into battle with planes that weren't ready.

Like this one. Red 201 couldn't fly south – not with an out-of-whack radar. The sergeant moved a little closer, ready to offer advice if Giertych asked for it. He stayed near the doors, though. They'd left them open to let in much-needed light and fresh air, and he wanted to take full advantage of both. After a long, cold winter it felt good to stand in the sunlight with a cool morning breeze on his back. The only thing he'd disliked about serving in Poland had been the long spell of wet weather they'd endured. Maybe he'd spent too much time in the hot, bone-dry air at Nellis Air Force Base, deep in the Nevada desert north of Las Vegas . . .

Warbling, high-pitched sirens went off all around the airfield. An air-raid warning! Frewer and Giertych stared at each other in shock for a single instant and then reacted. The captain shouted something in rapid-fire Polish to one of his men near the door controls. Nodding rapidly, the corporal whirled round and hit a switch on the panel. Smoothly and quickly, with a roar like a volcano rumbling to life, the massive armored doors slid into place, sealing the shelter in dimly lit darkness. The solid slam as they came together was almost loud enough to mask the sound of the first explosion outside.

Frewer followed Giertych toward the personnel exit on the side of the reinforced aircraft shelter. Standing regulations be damned. He needed to see what was happening.

Smoke billowed up from one side of the base – right where the operations center was located. Just as they tumbled out the shelter door, another low rumble and a shock wave rattling through the pavement carried more bad news.

They turned to see a flaming cloud and debris arcing through the air. A small shape, no more than a black streak, flashed into view and dove into the same area. A second blast shook the ground. Oh, Jesus, Frewer realized, those were the repair shops. The other members of his training team were on duty there. Without pausing for further thought, he started running. Giertych took off after him.

The repair shops were at least a quarter mile away, but they could already see red and orange flames dancing through the rising smoke.

Another streak, identifiable this time as a cruise missile, skimmed over the rooftops at blinding speed. It had to be French or German, he thought. It was coming from the wrong direction to be Russian.

The missile came apart in midair, suddenly dissolving into near-invisible black specks. Bomblets, Frewer thought dully. Sounding like firecrackers popping off in one long, crackling string, they smothered the maintenance sheds in hundreds of individual explosions. Unlike the aircraft shelters, Wroclaw's repair facilities weren't armored or protected in any way. Thousands of white-hot fragments sliced through thin aluminum roofs and walls and into the rooms and corridors inside.

Frewer knew what they could do. The U.S. Air Force had its own bomblet dispensers, spewing out softball-sized devices by the hundreds. Each weighed a few pounds, and was equally capable of penetrating armor, scything down exposed personnel, and even starting a good-sized fire. He was sure the EurCon weapons were just as advanced.

Even as he neared the burning buildings, he cursed himself for knowing so much about what those weapons could do to the men trapped inside. Then he cursed the enemy who'd used them, struggling to breathe in with lungs that were laboring under the strain of running so far so fast.

The two men pulled up short of the building, about a hundred meters away. Thick, greasy smoke and the heat coming off the fire made it impossible to get any closer.

Fire crews, some in shiny, asbestos hot suits, were making some headway against the flames, but there was nothing left to save. Frewer looked frantically for survivors. He couldn't see any – only corpses lying silent on the grass nearby, not yet covered. Some wore Polish uniforms, but many, too many, wore U.S. Air Force blue.

Anger and grief flowed through the sergeant. They'd all speculated on how EurCon might react to the Polish intervention in Hungary, but the idea that the French and Germans would attack Polish bases, especially without some sort of ultimatum, had been dismissed as insane by everybody.

Everybody had been wrong, Frewer realized. The cruise missiles, weapons capable of incredible precision, had to have been deliberately targeted on buildings full of American personnel. EurCon knew that, he thought angrily. They just don't give a shit. Well, he did, and as far as he was concerned, America was in the war now, all the way.

Almost against his will, his weary feet carried him over to the bodies. He recognized one, Mike Cummings, and thought he knew another, but the rest were too torn or burned to identify. He could hear Giertych muttering and choking back sobs.

His own eyes full of tears, Frewer looked away from the mangled bodies of his friends and coworkers. The EurCon attack had plastered the whole base. Fires raged out of control on all sides. Besides the operations center and repair sheds, cruise missiles had hit fuel and ammo storage areas. More smoke curled from the air traffic control center.

Only the aircraft shelters and flight line looked untouched. The American sergeant nodded somberly. Why waste hits on single aircraft when you could knock out the control, resupply, and maintenance capabilities that kept them flying? For the time being at least, the 11th Fighter Regiment and its American advisors were completely out of action.

THE WHITE HOUSE, WASHINGTON, D.C.

The first reports of EurCon missile attacks woke official Washington in the predawn dark. Reporters hastily despatched to the White House could see lights burning behind closed curtains in both the East and West wings. The lights were also coming on at the Pentagon and at the State Department. By five a.m., black government limousines were pulling up in front of the tall, graceful columns of the White House portico, depositing grim-faced men and women arriving for an emergency meeting of the National Security Council.

Despite the air of tension and grave concern pervading the basement Situation Room, Ross Huntington felt oddly detached, almost light-headed. In a strange sense, he felt as though his body and brain were separated from each other by some vast, uncrossable gulf. He made yet another mental resolution to see his doctor – a resolution that he knew he would not keep. Events were moving too fast to allow poor health to put him on the sidelines.

He pulled his chair closer to the table, listening intently while the chairman of the Joint Chiefs brought the NSC up to date.

So far, there had been three separate cruise missile attacks on three separate airfields – two in Poland and one in the Czech republic. All had been launched at more or less the same time by planes operating from bases in Germany. All had inflicted heavy casualties and damage. That was bad enough. What was worse was that at least twenty-five American servicemen were among those killed or seriously wounded. The numbers were still climbing as more detailed reports came in.

Gen. Reid Galloway's ordinarily good-humored face was brick-red with barely suppressed anger. 'These attacks were clearly planned to kill as many people as possible, Mr. President. Our people included.'

'You're sure?'

Galloway nodded abruptly. 'Yes, sir. If EurCon's only goal was to inflict damage on those base facilities, they could just as easily have attacked at night, when fewer people were on duty. In fact, from a strictly military point of view, that would have been a better time. Less risk that anyone might spot those cruise missiles visually.'

Harris Thurman put his own oar in the water. 'It's obviously intended to send a very strong message to the Poles and Czechs, Mr. President. And through them to us.'

'Message, hell! It's a goddamned declaration of war.' Galloway was outraged. 'You don't fire twenty-plus high-explosive warheads into critical targets as part of some diplomatic game.'

'I remind you, General, that this attack came only *after* Polish and Czech aircraft fired on French and German planes over Hungary . . .'

'Gentlemen.' All heads turned toward the President. He sat alone at one end of the table. His eyes were cold and angry. 'I don't particularly care what prompted these attacks. Our policy on Hungary stands: Our allies are fully within their rights in helping the Hungarian people resist this unjust French and German aggression. And we are fully within our rights in providing those allies with technical and military assistance. Clear?'

Thurman's face fell. 'Of course, Mr. President.'

The President looked toward Galloway again. 'Are they planning to retaliate?'

'Yes. We've had requests from the Polish Air Force HQ for updated satellite photos of German airfields. They've also asked for a special AWACS sortie.'

'When?'

'June 4, two days from now.' Galloway frowned. 'It'll take them at least that long to unscramble the mess at Wroclaw and their other airfields.'

'What about their air support missions over Hungary?'

'On hold, sir. Their losses were already pretty high. Close to crippling for the first squadrons committed. And with EurCon showing its teeth over their own territory now?' Galloway shrugged. 'The Poles will need every plane they've got just to hit back and to ride out any EurCon counterpunch.'

The general's gloomy assessment cast a pall over the room. Without friendly air cover, Hungary would fall – crushed by superior firepower and brute force. A EurCon victory over Budapest's fledgling democracy would be an unmitigated disaster for American economic and foreign policy. In the short term, it would solidify the protectionist grip on European trade practices, prolonging the trade war ravaging the world's economy. With the handwriting on the wall, other small countries like Denmark and the Netherlands were bound to fall into line. In the long term, letting EurCon ride roughshod over one small country would set a terrible precedent. The rule of international law and the rights of self-determination, however tenuous and often impractical, would be supplanted by an older and deadlier precept: might makes right. That could spawn a whole new cycle of war and aggression around the globe.

The President spoke into the sudden silence. 'As I see it, we've got one last chance to stop this thing before all hell breaks loose in Europe. One last chance to shake these clowns awake. Agreed?'

Huntington nodded, and noticed others around the table do the same. But what more could they do? Trying to impose a peaceful resolution through the United Nations would go nowhere. The French Security Council veto made that impossible. So what was left? Then he saw it. 'You intend to issue an ultimatum to the EurCon governments, Mr. President?'

'Yes, I do. I've spoken to both the Senate majority leader and the Speaker of the House and they agree that we have to act, and act now.' America's chief executive set his jaw, plainly determined. 'We've pussyfooted around with these people long enough. I want them to know once and for all that they're looking right down the barrel of a mighty big gun.'

ASSOCIATED PRESS DISPATCH

WASHINGTON, D.C. (AP) – The full text of a statement released by the White House at 7:00 p.m., Eastern Standard Time:

'At 3:30 this morning, French and German warplanes conducted a series of missile attacks on airfields inside Poland and the Czech and Slovak Republics – killing and wounding several hundred people. Tragically, more than thirty American military personnel were among those who lost their lives.

'Like the invasion of Hungary itself, this latest aggression by France and Germany further demonstrates their intention to control all of Europe by threats, by violence, and by armed occupation.

'The United States cannot and will not allow these attacks to go unchallenged and unpunished. We urge the French and German governments to end their aggressions against their neighbors before it is too late – for France, for Germany, for Europe, and indeed, for the whole world.

'Accordingly, the United States, in concert with Great Britain, Poland, the Czech and Slovak republics, and Hungary, calls on the governments of both France and Germany to immediately and unconditionally withdraw all military forces from Hungary by midnight, Greenwich Mean Time, on June 3. If this demand is not met, we reserve the right to restore a just and lasting peace by any and all means necessary – up to and including the possible use of American and British military power.'

White House Press Secretary Michael Kennett has announced that the President will speak to the nation at 9:00 tonight. His address will be carried live on all major radio and television networks.

CHAPTER 18
Thunderclap

JUNE 3 – USS *LEYTE GULF*, NEAR ANHOLT ISLAND, IN THE KATTEGAT, BETWEEN DENMARK AND SWEDEN

Vice Adm. Jack Ward kept remembering an old movie, one of his favorites. In it, the heroes, searching for treasure in a ruined temple, had entered a room and unknowingly triggered a deadly trap. Suddenly the door slammed shut on them, walls on either side rumbled inward, and rows of poisoned, needle-sharp spikes popped out.

His ships were in a similar situation.

It was easier on film, of course. A native guide, separated from the party earlier, found them in the nick of time and disabled the trap's mechanism – just as the intrepid, if clumsy, heroes were about to be ventilated.

Unfortunately he didn't have any native guides right now. The door could close anytime, and there wasn't a damn thing he could do about it.

Checking the computer-driven display down in the CIC wouldn't help, either. The situation hadn't changed in the last fifteen minutes, and if he hovered over them long enough, some of his nervousness might rub off on his staff. This was one time when he earned his admiral's pay by trying to be the calm, laid-back 'Old Man' of navy legend.

He leaned on the rail of the port bridge wing. In the fading light Kobbergrund's flashing light marked the westernmost extension of Anholt Island, a shallow sandbar with only ten feet of water over it. Anholt itself lay just a few miles away, a dark mass already blending with the horizon.

The island marked the halfway point in their rapid trip northward through the Kattegat, a narrow body of water lying between Denmark and Sweden. The only ways in or out of the Kattegat were through exits to the north and south. His convoy was still three hours away from entering even the dubious safety of the Skagerrak.

Anholt was Danish territory, and he was sure there were observers watching with great interest as his ships steamed past. Although Denmark had declared itself neutral, the fact that Germany lay only a few short miles beyond meant he had to consider the island a hostile shore. At least Sweden was a true neutral, jealously guarding her own territorial waters and fiercely determined to avoid being drawn in on either side. Of course, that just meant only one wall of the trap had spikes.

Ward turned and paced the narrow confines of the bridge wing. Damn it, he needed sea room and deep water! The Baltic was bad enough, with shallow water and uneven salinity and lousy underwater acoustics. The Kattegat was worse – even smaller and shallower. With a water depth of twenty, sometimes only ten fathoms, you could forget towed arrays and long-range sonar detection. It was also a major shipping channel, so there were dozens of surface contacts to track and classify. The air picture was even more nightmarish. This close to Germany, enemy air bases practically sat in his back pocket, reducing warning time to nil. Right now his Task Group's radars showed hundreds of air contacts. How many were hostile?

He couldn't know, and hopefully wouldn't until the American ultimatum to EurCon expired at midnight, GMT, just four hours away.

Damn Washington for issuing that twenty-four-hour ultimatum! Ward understood the reasons for it, and even approved of them – in a detached way. But it would have been nice if the politicians had checked with the Pentagon before making that demand. Some of their promises might be hard to keep.

When EurCon had fired its air-launched cruise missiles at Poland and the Czech republic, Task Group 22.1 was not ready for a major sea battle. Three separate convoys, with two or three merchant ships apiece, were headed south for Gdansk, each loaded with essential military supplies, crude oil, or natural gas. To escort each convoy, Ward had been forced to spread his warships too thinly for comfort or sound defense. One or two frigates, destroyers, or cruisers were enough to show the flag. They weren't enough to fend off a massive missile or torpedo attack.

The rest of Task Force 22 was spread even further afield, from the North Sea to the Atlantic. The admiral had elected to remain embarked on *Leyte Gulf* because the cruiser's Aegis display systems allowed him to keep tabs on the entire region. At Washington's urging, he had tried to keep arms and oil convoys moving through until the last possible moment. The fighting in Hungary was burning up supplies at a frightening pace. Poland and its partners needed the material aboard those ships right away, not when it was safe. Nevertheless, although no rational person could have anticipated EurCon's apparent willingness to widen the Hungarian conflict into general war, Ward was beginning to believe he'd cut things a little too fine.

One convoy should reach Gdansk about 2300 hours, a full hour before he expected to clear Skagen, the cape at Denmark's northernmost tip. Another was almost out of the Skagerrak, heading north up the Norwegian coast. It was already under carrier-based fighter cover. Unfortunately the four ships under his direct command, *Leyte Gulf*, the *Perry*-class frigate *Simpson*, and two merchantmen, were caught dead center in the bull's-eye.

There was no way his two northernmost formations could reach Gdansk before the ultimatum expired. If the French and Germans refused to withdraw their forces from Hungary and started shooting, the two convoys would both still be hours away from safety. Even if they could fight their way to the Polish harbor, his warships would be exhausted, isolated, vulnerable, and difficult to resupply. Presented with that fact, he had made the difficult decision to have both groups turn tail and head back north at full speed.

Every move he made in the Baltic was under heavy EurCon surveillance. Since the war in Hungary erupted, all mock attacks on his ships had stopped, probably so the French and Germans could rest their forces and prepare their own plans. Instead, shore-based radars and patrol aircraft tracked his convoys. He wasn't helpless, but he was in EurCon's front yard, and they were holding all the high cards.

His biggest problem was the lack of support. Warships operating alone could rarely handle every threat imaginable – one lucky hit by an enemy attacker, or an unlucky malfunction, could cripple even the most powerful ship. Two or three ships can cover each other, combining strengths and canceling out weaknesses. But they're still limited to whatever ammunition they have on board, to their own sensors, and to their own helicopters. Add replenishment ships and you gained a more powerful group that could fight a battle, rearm, and fight again. Tossing in an aircraft carrier created a powerful formation that could detect its enemies hundreds of miles further out – and fight under a protective umbrella of fighters and attack jets.

His nearest carrier, though, was *George Washington*, far away in the North Sea. A 'bird farm' needed sea room, both for launching and recovering aircraft and to hide from enemy attack. Carriers were too valuable to risk in confined waters.

Georgie's aircraft wouldn't be able to help him here – not at first anyway. As part of their declared neutrality, the Danes had closed their airspace to all armed planes. If and when the shooting started, that wouldn't mean much. He doubted that the small Danish Air Force would do much to stop either side from overflying its territory. Nobody expected the armed forces of the tiny neutral country to commit suicide for the sake of a principle. So his carrier's interceptors and attack aircraft should have a free hand. But that could very easily be too late to save his isolated ships and tired men.

And they were tired.

Once the President announced his ultimatum, the admiral had set Condition II in all units under his control. Condition I was general quarters – full battle readiness. In Condition II, half the crew manned their general-quarters stations, while the rest tried to eat, catch up on sleep, and perform the most vital maintenance tasks. You could keep it up for a lot longer than general quarters, but 'port and starboard' was still hard on sailors.

Fighting a yawn himself, Ward turned to look aft at the two merchants, trailing in *Leyte Gulf*'s wake. He groaned inside. *Dallas Star* was a tanker, loaded with jet fuel. *Tartu* was a container ship, carrying Patriot missiles, radar parts, and tank ammunition, all desperately needed in Poland and to the south. It still galled him to fail – to turn tail and run.

But the percentages were against any other course, and the cargoes aboard two merchant ships would never reach port if they were lying on the bottom of the Baltic.

When he looked away from the ships he was supposed to protect, the sun had vanished – its passage marked only by a fading red glow in the west. The Kattegat's choppy waters were slowly blending with the darkening sky and darkened land to either side. Stars were already visible, pale against the eastern horizon. There would be a quarter-moon tonight and clear weather.

Blacked out, his ships would soon be invisible, but only to the naked eye. Shore-based and airborne radars tracked him, and his own ships' radars were all lit off, searching for the first signs of impending trouble.

A tall, angular officer leaned out through the open portside bridge door. Even with night falling, Ward could recognize the worried face of Capt. Jerry Shapiro, his chief of staff. 'Sir, we're getting a message from the Poles.' His tone made it clear the news was serious.

Stepping into the cruiser's enclosed bridge, Ward heard an accented voice crackling over the radio speaker. '. . . listing badly. Tugs are coming, but I don't think we can save her.'

Shapiro nodded toward the speaker. 'There's been an explosion on board *Canyon*. Probably a mine. No known submarines in the area.'

Ward's chest tightened. *Canyon* was a container ship loaded with air-to-air missiles, computers, and spare parts. A battery of self-propelled artillery was strapped to her deck as well. Part of the southernmost convoy, she had been under Polish naval escort, and only a few hours from safety. Her two American protectors had broken off earlier. Free of the slower merchant ships, the *Kidd*-class destroyer *Scott* and the *Perry*-class frigate *Aubrey Fitch* were racing north at thirty-plus knots.

The voice continued. ' . . . continuing sonar search. No contacts yet. We think this is a mine attack. Recommend you take extra precautions as well.'

As *Leyte Gulf*'s radio talker acknowledged and signed off, Ward thought it was past time for simple precautions. He turned to the cruiser's commanding officer. 'Put the ship at general quarters, Captain.' He had instructions for Shapiro as well. 'Relay that order to the rest of the force, and pass the information on to CINCLANTFLT. Flash priority, Jerry.'

The sharp, blaring sound of *Leyte*'s klaxon followed Ward down to the CIC.

The electronics-packed space was filled with quiet, purposeful activity. With half the crew already at their general-quarters stations, much of the bustle associated with going to battle stations was missing. Men wearing headsets hunched over glowing screens and consoles, speaking quietly over radio and intercom circuits.

Ward slipped into his chair, followed moments later by *Leyte Gulf*'s skipper, sitting on his right.

The command display directly in front of him showed a map of the Kattegat and every detected air, sea, and submarine unit in the immediate area. One to the left covered the entire Baltic. The electronic displays gave the impression of omniscience, of having a godlike 'eye in the sky.' It was a false impression, the admiral often reminded himself. Small circles and boxes and triangles marked friendly, unknown, and known EurCon contacts.

As he studied the screen, Shapiro approached. 'CINCLANTFLT has the word, Admiral. They wanted to know if we were going to change our plans. I said no.'

'Good work, Jerry.' A good chief of staff knew the commander's intentions and could often speak for him, especially when their course of action was this clear. No, Ward thought, if he had any Last Best Moves, he would have already used them.

One thing, though. 'Call *Scott* and *Fitch*. Have them run for the Polish coast. There's no way they'll get out of the Baltic in time.' He paused, then explained. 'I think the balloon's going to go up real soon now.'

'Sir, it'll be at least an hour before they're in range of Polish air cover.'

Ward sighed. 'I know that, Jerry, but Gdansk is the closest friendly territory. Tell them to run like hell. Tell them to burn out their engines.'

Shapiro left in a hurry. Ward pondered all the information laid out in front of him. There was one vital fact missing. How long did he have before EurCon tried to hammer his convoy? He couldn't attack on his own – not without orders from above. Besides, he really didn't want to. Every minute of peace brought his ships half a mile closer to safety.

By now word of the attack on *Canyon* would have flashed up the chain from commander in chief, Atlantic Fleet, to commander in chief, Atlantic, to the National Command Authority – a fancy name for the President. Modern communications would put his message in the President's lap in minutes. But how long would it take to get a decision back down the chain of command?

'Don't just sit here, Jack,' he muttered to himself. Although the American ultimatum hadn't yet expired, somebody somewhere had started shooting. For all practical purposes, he was already in a battle. 'Don't let the enemy make the first move.'

All right, think. So far EurCon had hit one container ship. Where were the planes, missiles, and submarines that should be barreling in on this convoy? *Leyte Gulf* was too valuable a target to be ignored or bypassed, even if its firepower made it a tough target. Just the political value of taking out one of the U.S. Navy's Aegis cruisers early in a war would make the attempt worthwhile.

Making piecemeal attacks, though, was worse than foolish. If the French and Germans really were going to war right now, they'd already given him precious time to alert his forces, to warn Washington, and to do all the things you really don't want an enemy to do.

Ward frowned. No matter what the Poles said, he didn't believe *Canyon* had struck a mine. Mines were very precise creatures. Any mines laid by EurCon forces would be equipped with timers ready to activate them in concert with a set-piece surprise attack. Instead, he was willing to bet that some German or French sub skipper had seen *Canyon*, a little ahead of schedule, plowing past him. Knowing that the merchant's supplies were vital, the man had opted to send her to the bottom rather than let such a fat prize get away.

He nodded. That hypothesis fit the facts.

So somebody had jumped the gun. If that was the case, EurCon's senior commanders would be almost as flummoxed as he was. Once a decision came down from Paris and Berlin, they would move quickly enough, but they weren't ready to launch a massive strike – not just yet. And that meant he had a few precious minutes to make some final crucial preparations.

Ward started at the top – reacting to what he believed to be the most immediate threat. A submarine had attacked his southernmost convoy. Well, submarines were also the best way to sink an Aegis cruiser, especially one steaming in restricted waters and crappy sonar conditions.

He punched keys on the pad to his left. The image on his primary display shifted as numbers and curved lines, representing depths and bottom contours, glowed to life. The screen also showed his own group's planned track. It ran slightly east of straight north.

At twenty-two knots, an hour's travel would put them abreast of the Groves Flak and Fladen banks, two shallow spots on the seafloor that would make perfect hiding places for small diesel submarines. And the already narrow channel narrowed even further near there. That was bad. Very bad.

Ward called his helicopter coordinator on the intercom. 'Mike, I want somebody up checking both those two banks for lurkers. Stick to a passive search only for now. If there are French or German subs up there, let's see if we can find them without tipping anybody off.'

'Aye, aye, sir.'

He listened as the lieutenant quickly issued orders to launch one helicopter each from *Leyte Gulf* and *Simpson*. Working in tandem, the two SH-60 Seahawks would sweep back and forth across the areas he'd tagged, using their MAD and dropping dozens of LOFAR sonobuoys to hunt for EurCon subs lying doggo. The only trouble was that he still wasn't sure what he could do if they actually found any. Under the existing rules of engagement, he could only fire if fired upon. The Kattegat wasn't wide enough to enforce a declared exclusion zone.

While listening to the radio chatter in his headset, he checked the display more closely. *Simpson*'s other helicopter, 401, was out on surface search duty – patrolling to the south. He issued another order. 'Get 401 down as soon as the other birds are off. I want her refueled and rearmed for ASW. I think we'll need her.'

Symbols crawled across the screen as his units responded to their new instructions. The minutes passed slowly while Ward ran through his limited options over and over again. Waiting like this was the hardest part of any naval commander's job. In battle, supersonic missile speeds left very little time for thought – and no time at all for worry.

Shapiro came up and stood quietly behind Ward's chair, waiting. His news wasn't urgent, then. The admiral took another moment to examine the display before swiveling around.

'Washington says stand by. No changes to the rules of engagement.'

The chief of staff saw Ward's reaction and added, 'Admiral Macmillan said to shoot when you have to, and he'd sort it out later.'

Ward sighed. It was nice to have CINCLANT's support, but now was the moment to strike, while EurCon was still trying to—

'Sir!' The lieutenant coordinating his helicopters broke in, his voice climbing rapidly. '401 reports several streaks of light moving from west to east, heading straight for us!'

Too late. We've missed our chance, Ward realized. EurCon had decided to throw the first punch.

SH-60 SEAHAWK 401

Lt. (jg.) Bill Alvarez, piloting Seahawk 401, looked over at his sensor operator in shock. Lt. Tom Calhoun was on his fifth cruise. He had over five hundred hours in Seahawks. This was Alvarez's first deployment, and things were moving a little too fast for him. 'What will *Leyte* do?'

'Open up, my friend.' Calhoun's eyes never left his instrument console. 'Turn port, new course three three zero, speed seventy knots. Take us down.' Even though Alvarez was the pilot, Calhoun was the mission commander. He had the sensor displays, and the experience to know what he was looking at. Alvarez, like any other helicopter pilot, was kept busy enough just keeping the Seahawk in the air.

Wheeling the big machine to the left, Alvarez juggled his cyclic stick, collective, and throttle, smoothly losing altitude and slowing until Seahawk 401 clattered only thirty feet above the Kattegat's dark waters.

As Alvarez maneuvered, Calhoun amplified his initial report. 'Negative radar contact on vampires. Visual and FLIR only. Estimate ten plus, low altitude. Negative ESM.'

EurCon's stealth missile technologies were getting another battlefield test – a successful one. The Seahawk's APS-124 radar wasn't powerful enough to spot the incoming missiles against all the clutter created by the Kattegat's short, choppy waves.

Calhoun broke radio contact with *Leyte Gulf*. 'They'll find out the rest for themselves. We've done our bit for Uncle Sam, we're on our own time now. Turn port again, new course two two five.'

Automatically Alvarez complied. He was trained to obey orders immediately, and Calhoun's orders were eminently sensible. The planes that had launched those missiles at the convoy could still be somewhere close by. And the best way to avoid attracting their unwanted attention was to throttle the Seahawk's engines back, lay low, and pretend to be nothing more than night air. Throttling back would also conserve fuel – giving them up to an extra hour of flying time. With their parent ship under attack, it might be a long while before 401 could land. Just as important, the new course kept them well clear of both *Leyte Gulf* and *Simpson*. Neither man wanted to be shot down by their own side in all the confusion.

Repeated flashes shattered the darkness off to the right. He automatically closed one eye trying to preserve his night vision. *Leyte Gulf* carried over a hundred antiaircraft missiles, loaded in vertical launchers fore and aft. She was firing from both launchers.

A blinding flare signaled the first launches. For a moment, the ship's bulky shape was outlined in a flickering orange-red light. Then rocket exhaust covered her bow and stem in billowing smoke clouds, lit from within.

The first pair of SAMs leapt up out of the roiling smoke clouds, their own smoke trails also glowing. Even from twenty miles away, their exhausts looked like giant-sized highway warning flares soaring high overhead, almost too bright to look at. It was a spectacular and frightening sight.

A second later, with the first two missiles already high overhead and starting to arc over, a second pair thundered out of the expanding clouds. Then another pair and yet another roared skyward, until the cruiser, moving through the water, had built a towering arch of missile smoke trails.

Looking aft, Alvarez waited for their own ship to launch. Nothing. 'Where's *Simpson*?'

Calhoun shook his head. 'She doesn't have a fancy radar like the Aegis.' He sucked in his breath a little, figuring. 'Against stealthy missiles, it's going to be close. There,' he said finally. 'She's firing now.'

A new pair of fiery streaks leapt up from the horizon and leveled out, seemingly headed straight toward them. After a few seconds, *Simpson*'s missiles started drifting to the right, then flashed past their starboard side.

Leyte Gulf's SAMs, now invisible, started to reach the incoming EurCon missiles. In the dark middle distance, well off to starboard, flashes suddenly erupted, burning away the night in blinding white pulses as proximity-fused warheads went off. But the flashes marched closer as the waves of enemy missiles bored in.

Then it happened.

An enormous explosion lit the sea between the two American warships. An image flashed against the darkness, so quickly and so blindingly bright that Alvarez realized what he had seen only after the flash faded. He'd seen a merchant ship's hull, dark against a brilliant white and yellow and orange light that backlit but also enveloped its victim.

Blinking away the dazzling afterimages, Alvarez scanned the horizon. A dull orange glow remained. On the FLIR, the gray-white image of the merchant ship, warm against the cold sea, grew whiter and whiter toward the bow until the display shimmered and sparkled with the heat of the flames. A ship was on fire. Oh, God. He felt chilled to the bone, despite the sweat staining his flight suit.

'Turn right, new course two seven zero,' Calhoun ordered. 'I'm going to take a peek with the radar.'

Turning, Alvarez carefully watched the altimeter. He could almost hear the waves outside and feel the mass of the water below him. Helicopters were nimble, but this close to the surface, he wouldn't get a second chance to correct any mistakes.

Calhoun hunched over his multifunction display. His shoulders stiffened and he keyed his radio mike. 'Echo Five, this is 401. Ten contacts, five zero miles, at three zero zero, speed six zero zero. Negative ESM.'

There were enemy aircraft out there, still closing on the embattled convoy with their own radars shut down.

Calhoun quickly flicked a switch. 'Radar off. Turn us to zero three zero, now!' The urgency in his voice almost spun the helicopter by itself. 'Increase speed a little'

Alvarez steadied on the new course – nudging his collective forward until they were up to a hundred knots. While Calhoun anxiously scanned the sky to the northwest, they were too close to the sea for him to do much more than watch his flight instruments. The few glances he could spare were for the battle out ahead of them now.

More glowing sparks streaked low over the water toward the convoy – coming from the south now. Jesus, they were being hit from two sides.

It was impossible to see details at this range, but the patterns of light told the story. He knew what it had to look like, with missiles flashing in. He also knew what the men on those ships were doing, hunched over their displays, sweating, each man doing his assigned job and fearing the first mistake. Any mistake, even the smallest, could bring death and failure for them all.

Simpson and *Leyte Gulf* were both firing now, launching SAM after SAM in an almost continuous stream.

'There! Ten o'clock, Bill!'

Alvarez snapped his head over to the left and followed Calhoun's arm. A narrow arrowhead shape, silhouetted against the night sky, passed quickly from left to right. Turning on the Seahawk's radar, even for that brief instant, had been like waving a red flag in front of a maddened bull. Now they were being hunted. The enemy pilot must have run down their radar bearing. He had to be searching for them with his bare eyes. Radar couldn't pick them out this close to the surface.

Calhoun slewed the helicopter's thermal imaging sensor, its FLIR, over, and they were rewarded with the black-and-white image of a French Mirage screaming low over the water – flying hundreds of knots faster than they were.

Both men held their breath. If the enemy pilot spotted them, they were goners. Then, after a thirty-second eternity, the predator banked left and headed north. He was giving up, going after more profitable or more visible targets.

Alvarez looked back at the formation. New missile flashes were backlighting smoke trails made by previous launches. Only a few of the SAMs appeared to be headed in their direction. Some went to the west or south, and some even seemed to be headed straight north. Was the EurCon strike force attacking from that direction, too? In addition to the SAMs, rapid-fire, rhythmic flashes from both ships showed that their guns and Phalanx systems were in action as well. The enemy missiles and aircraft had punched through the convoy's outer defenses.

On this course, the helicopter was closing the formation rapidly. One of the cargo ships was clearly visible, enveloped in flame and thickening black smoke. Suddenly and irrationally, Alvarez wished for a weapon –

some sort of missile or gun, any sort of missile or gun. He wanted to chase down that enemy fighter they'd seen and splash the bastard.

A ripple of light, almost a sheet of flame, to the north caught his eye. The EurCon aircraft they'd spotted earlier were firing a new salvo of air-to-surface missiles.

Using binoculars, Calhoun studied the display for a moment, then radioed in another warning. Breaking contact with *Leyte Gulf*, he said, 'All right, Bill. New course three five zero. And slow us down again.'

Alvarez complied, now almost unmindful of the water below. Out the helicopter's right window, the formation was hidden in a mass of smoke. Flickering lights inside the cloud showed when missiles or guns fired. The burning ship had drifted outside the smoke, dead in the water.

A bigger, brighter flash near where *Simpson* should be alarmed him for a moment, but Calhoun, listening in on the radio circuit, announced, 'Got one with the Phalanx!'

The frigate's automated, six-barrel Gatling gun had knocked down a EurCon missile just a few hundred yards from impact.

Calhoun heard another report passed over the radio and paused, listening intently. When he spoke again, his voice was somber. '*Tartu*'s burning.'

More glowing lights streaked low across the sky. The next missile wave had arrived. Alvarez couldn't see the displays, but knew the American warships' defenses were already pressed to the limit.

'Change course. Due north.'

He followed Calhoun's order without thinking, keeping his eyes riveted on the formation.

The smoke cloud now hid the ships completely. Inside, explosions rippled like chain lightning, but he couldn't see any detail at all. Calhoun, studying the Seahawk's ESM display, could tell part of the story. '*Simpson*'s MK92 radar is gone,' he announced quietly.

Shit. If *Simpson*'s missile fire control radar was off the line, she'd been hit, and worse, the hit made her vulnerable to the next wave.

'How about using the radar?' Alvarez asked.

Calhoun shook his head. 'Negative. It won't tell us if she's a hulk or just dinged. Don't sweat it yet, Bill. Might be nothing but a scratch.'

Both men knew he was lying. Any hit on a frigate-sized ship by a modern antiship missile would wreak havoc – killing dozens of men in a searing, shrapnel-laced blast, dozens of their friends and shipmates. The older, more experienced Calhoun was doing his best to steady his younger, greener pilot, and maybe himself as well.

More flashes lit the cloud's interior. Large flashes. Missile impacts. Before they had time to make sense out of the pattern, the still-burning *Tartu* vanished in a giant white fireball. Alvarez glanced at a digital clock on the Seahawk's instrument panel, instinctively marking the instant the big container ship died.

'*Tartu* was loaded with Patriots,' Alvarez said shakily. He crossed himself in horror.

'Yah.' Calhoun nodded, but kept his eyes on the displays, trying to wring more data out of them.

A sound came over the water, barely audible over the helicopter's engines. Alvarez had braced himself for a shock wave, but at fifteen miles all that was left of *Tartu*'s death was a low rumble.

The sea and sky were dark again – lit only by the strange, flickering glow of ships on fire.

Calhoun straightened as he received new instructions from the Aegis cruiser's helo coordinator. He keyed his mike. 'Three zero minutes. Understood. Roger.' He turned to his pilot. 'They think the attack's over – at least for right now. Take us up to two hundred feet and head for *Tartu*'s last reported position. We're supposed to search for survivors, then go to *Leyte Gulf* for an in-flight refuel.'

'Any news on *Simpson*?' Alvarez asked.

'Yeah. She's hit bad. At least one fire. Maybe more.' The sensor operator saved the worst news, at least from their perspective, for last. 'And she's got a foul deck. It'll be a half hour before they even know if they can clear it. *Leyte*'s hit, too – fore and aft.' His businesslike tone and the work at hand pushed away the questions they had about their friends and their ships.

Alvarez pushed his throttle forward and pointed the helo's nose toward the drifting, burning wreck. Maybe her crew had abandoned ship before the final blast, or maybe someone had been blown clear. Even as he hoped for survivors, Alvarez knew it was probably wishful thinking.

Clattering low over the choppy Kattegat at seventy knots, they quickly closed in on the battered convoy. Just five miles from *Tartu* they flew over the first sign that the battle hadn't been wholly one-sided. There below, the waterlogged wreckage of an enemy fighter bobbed lazily up and down as waves sloshed over its mangled fuselage. Tangled shrouds and a ripped parachute canopy trailed backward from the aircraft's submerged cockpit. Its ejection system must have gone off on impact.

Calhoun swung the Seahawk's FLIR up to cover the sinking merchant ship. He found the burning hulk and steadied the black-and-white image in the center of the screen.

They both gasped. The container ship's clean lines were gone. *Tartu*'s deck was twisted and torn open in places. Fires burned everywhere, flashing to superheated steam as seawater hit them. A huge hole gaped in her side, just as though some sea monster had taken a bite out of her. The freighter was down by the stern and listing heavily to port – visibly rolling further and further over as the Kattegat poured in through her shattered hull.

'Jesus, Tom. She's going down real soon,' Alvarez volunteered. They roared low over the doomed merchantman, bucketing up and down in the hot air currents rising from her fires. He spun the Seahawk around in a tight turn, headed back west.

Calhoun nodded. 'Let's make one more pass to see if anyone's still on board. After that, we'll do an expanding search . . .'

Suddenly a brilliant, searing white flash filled the whole right side of the cockpit window. For half a second, Alvarez thought they had been hit by something, but the helicopter's engine sound didn't waver.

Momentarily blinded, he heard Calhoun yell, 'It's *Simpson*!'

Simpson had been struck by three missiles, the first an ARMAT antiradar missile, one of four fired at the frigate. Detonating a hundred feet directly overhead, it had sprayed the ship with high-velocity fragments, shredding her radars and killing or wounding the few crewmen on her weather decks.

The second wave of aircraft had fired antiship missiles. While *Simpson* was not the primary target of the attack, pressure on her increased the chances of the other attackers getting through. Four ANL supersonic missiles, hugging the water, streaked toward the frigate. The crippled ship, unable to launch her surface-to-air missiles without her fire control radar, had fired a cloud of shells from her 76mm gun at them, but none of the shell bursts came close enough to knock the ANLs and their armored warheads into the sea.

In the last seconds, chaff blossomed from launchers on either side of the ship. Only the bursting charges were visible in the darkness, but to guidance radars the air over the ship was suddenly filled with bright, reflective targets, larger and more attractive than the ship below them.

With the incoming missiles only hundreds of meters away, *Simpson*'s Phalanx radar-guided rotary cannon had fired one tearing burst, then another, and a third, finally clipping one of the ANLs. In an eyeblink, the missile spiraled into the sea and exploded – close enough to shower the ship with seawater.

The other three missiles were too close for the Phalanx to engage. One, seduced by the chaff, flew harmlessly past, searching for the ephemeral target created by the silvered plastic.

But the two remaining missiles, already locked onto *Simpson* by the time the chaff deployed, had stayed on target. Moving at just under the speed of sound, both slammed into the frigate, one forward of her bridge near the Standard missile launcher, the other in the middle of her superstructure, right above engineering.

The sheer force of the two missiles' impact had heeled her over, throwing everyone aboard to the deck. Their warheads, delay-fused so that they would only explode after they penetrated the skin of the ship, went off together. Each carried 360 pounds of explosive, surrounded by a shell of incendiary zirconium. This metal case, shattered and then ignited by the detonation, turned into hundreds of lethal fragments, driving through the ship. Wherever a fragment passed, it left a trail of flame. Only a few of the frigate's vital compartments, protected by Kevlar armor, were proof against the deadly projectiles. Elsewhere, scores of men were killed by the blast, by secondary fragments, or in the fires that followed.

Simpson's captain had known his ship was doomed the instant the fireballs blossomed. Even as choking, toxic smoke filled the bridge, he ordered Abandon Ship, then did his best to get anyone he could find over the side.

By the time Alvarez and Calhoun arrived at *Tartu*, only thirty or so of their shipmates had received the order and recovered enough to go over the side. Even the bitterly cold waters of the Baltic were a welcome relief from the blazing inferno that was once a warship. They struggled and swam away as best they could, their onetime home now an enemy.

Simpson's end came suddenly and violently when the fires on board the stricken frigate finally reached her missile and gun magazines. She disintegrated in the blink of an eye – torn apart by a rippling series of smaller explosions too close together in time and space to be distinguished as separate blasts. When the frigate's shattered hulk slid beneath the Kattegat minutes later, she carried more than three-quarters of her 215-man crew with her.

JUNE 4 – USS *LEYTE GULF*

Ward watched the half-circles creep closer and closer to what was left of his formation. The little computer-displayed symbols, each with a line pointing straight at his ship, represented F-14 Tomcats from *George Washington.* To Jack Ward, they might as well have been angels.

Even though the Aegis cruiser could only make twenty knots, a night's travel had brought them 150 miles closer to the powerful carrier.

He grimaced. He'd have to call this battle a draw. EurCon had sunk two of his four ships and damaged a third, but they'd been trying for a knockout blow – trying to make the most of their early advantage in catching Task Force 22 strung out across the Baltic. Their own losses had been heavy. He knew there were a lot of French and German aircraft that hadn't made it home.

Ward thought about all the sea battles he'd read about and studied. He'd fought before, in the Persian Gulf, and he and his colleagues had greedily devoured the lessons to be learned from it and every other modern conflict. But the Gulf had been nothing like this.

Nothing could have prepared him for the speed, the violence, and the confusion of last night's battle. He'd been scared, so scared that he'd almost been afraid to act, lest he do something wrong. He'd seen the same look on the officers and men as well, and only the fear of letting them down had kept him thinking, and fighting, until his fears had been drowned by his actions.

He coughed, a long, dry spasm that left him gasping for air. The smoke had gotten pretty thick last night. He was sure some of that junk was still in his lungs. Add fatigue, no food, and the pain caused by losing both *Simpson* and *Tartu*, and he became very grateful for the support provided by his command chair.

He hated to admit it, but if the Tomcats hadn't arrived when they did, he and the rest of his force could very easily have been on the bottom of the Baltic. As it was, *Leyte Gulf* was hurt. A missile hit close to her bridge had rocked the CIC, damaged one face of the SPY-1 radar, and wrecked her forward missile launcher. Ward silently thanked God the launcher had been nearly empty when they took the hit.

The second missile had been even worse, starting a fire in *Leyte*'s engineering spaces that killed twelve men and damn near finished her. Only good damage control had stopped the flames from spreading.

So here they were. He was short on missiles, running on half engines, and overcrowded with his own wounded and a few, badly burned survivors plucked from the water near where *Simpson* and the *Tartu* had gone down. One of his helicopters, another survivor from the frigate, was camping out on *Dallas Star*'s helipad. He was still two hundred miles from the relative safety of *George Washington*'s formation. Beyond that, he knew, *Leyte Gulf* had a longer trip to the yards for badly needed repairs.

In the meantime, though, she was still a fleet unit. Most of her weapons systems still worked, and the all-important SPY-1 radar and Aegis computers were back on the line. She could still fight.

'We're ready, Admiral.'

Capt. Ralph Gunston, *Leyte Gulf*'s skipper, had taken over as Ward's chief of staff. Jerry Shapiro was in sick bay with a broken leg and a chest full of missile fragments. Gunston looked more like a marine than a ship's captain, stocky with a blond crew cut.

'No signs of damage?'

'We found a few rattled circuit boards, but everything's been checked, and we've reloaded all the target packs, just as you ordered.'

'Very well, Captain. We'll launch on schedule.'

'Aye, aye, sir.'

Ward stood up slowly, leaning heavily on his chair for support at first. It took him a while to climb one level to the bridge and step out onto the bridge wing, but he wanted to be there when the cruiser showed these French and German bastards her teeth.

The fresh air on the bridge wing woke him up. Their own course and speed turned a cool breeze into a chilling gale. It was already slackening as *Leyte Gulf* slowed and turned. Even though the wind was within tolerances, Ward didn't want anything risked. Not for this.

Deep inside the ship's superstructure, Gunston issued the final orders.

An amplified voice declared, 'Now hear this. All hands on the weather decks, remain clear of the fantail.' It was the third, and last, warning – really only a formality. Ward heard a shrill *beep, beep* over the speakers before all sounds merged in a single, deafening roll of thunder.

It was different, being outside when a missile was fired. *Leyte Gulf*'s launchers had roared last night, but, with the ship at general quarters, the CIC had been tightly sealed. And Ward had been too busy thinking about other things to pay much attention to the noise. Things like fending off the sudden, surprise attacks that seemed to come from every compass point. Like the men who had been dying. The men he'd hoped to keep safe.

Now he had time to watch. Every ten seconds, a twenty-one-foot-long, finned gray shape thundered into the clear blue sky above the Aegis cruiser's fantail, riding high on a pillar of fire before turning and heading south. Twenty Tomahawk missiles, his entire load, were carrying the fight to EurCon's north German airfields. It would exact a small measure of vengeance for his murdered men and lost ships.

The last Tomahawk roared off, skimming southward past a long thick pall of white exhaust smoke curling behind *Leyte Gulf*.

Ward stepped back inside. His body cried out for sleep, but he had work to do and priority signals to send. The paybacks had just started.

U.S. SPACE DEFENSE OPERATIONS CENTER

Brig. Gen. Howard Noonan, USAF, occupied the watch officer's desk – overlooking a room filled with row after row of consoles crowded with control keyboards, communications gear, and display screens. Soft, subdued lighting and the quiet, ever-present hum of air-conditioning created the illusion of a calm, restful working environment. Space ops center duty officers and noncoms sat in comfortable chairs behind each console, monitoring space surveillance data flowing in from radar and optical telescope networks scattered around the globe, in low earth orbit, and in geosynchronous orbit.

All duty stations faced an enormous, wall-sized computer-generated display showing the world and man-made objects in orbit around it. Although the men and women working in the operations center routinely tracked nearly six thousand objects, right now the main screen showed only a few specific satellites that were of extraordinary interest. Bright lines showed the predicted orbital path for each satellite, and small vector arrows showed their current, plotted positions.

Noonan, a trim, dapper man, nodded gravely to himself – satisfied by what he could see. As a young man he'd been fascinated by outer space and the possibility of space travel. As a young officer he'd narrowly missed qualifying for astronaut training. He'd taken the setback in stride and buckled down to do his best for the country. Now, at forty-five, he commanded the world's most advanced space defense force.

After years spent in research and development and after bitter congressional funding battles, the first elements of the G-PALS system were in orbit and operational. G-PALS stood for 'Global Protection Against Limited Strikes.'

One of the red phone symbols on his computer monitor flashed. He had an incoming call – direct from the Joint Chiefs of Staff. Finally.

Noonan tapped the appropriate key on his board, noted the lights verifying that he was receiving scrambled audio and video communication, and punched the receive control on his console.

A familiar face appeared on his monitor. Gen. Reid Galloway, chairman of the Joint Chiefs, looked tired. He'd been locked up in a nonstop National Security Council meeting since the first reports of EurCon attacks on U.S. and British shipping began pouring in.

'Yes, sir?'

'I'll make this short and sweet, Howard. The President has approved your plan. "Blackout" is a go. When can you initiate?'

'Right away, sir. My people finished rewriting and testing the necessary sections of battle management code about an hour ago.'

Reid nodded, pleased. Then he turned deadly serious. 'Take 'em out for us, Howard. We're going to need every edge we can get.'

'Yes. sir. You can count on it.' Noonan had seen the navy's preliminary casualty estimates. The French and Germans had pretty clearly won the war's opening round. He planned to help them lose the second.

* * *

Five minutes later, Noonan sat with his headset on, ready and alert. A blank inset box on the main display screen suddenly filled with a jumbled string of numbers and letters. They were receiving a system release authorization code from the President. Almost as soon as the code appeared, it vanished – replaced by a blinking notification in large, bold letters: LAUNCH ENABLED.

Noonan switched to the G-PALS command circuit. 'You ready, Zack?'

The colonel manning the space defense system duty station answered immediately. 'Yes, sir. My boards confirm selective release authorization.'

'Good.' Noonan swept his eyes over his own monitor and the main display one last time for a final check on weapons status and target positions. Everything looked set. He sat up straighter. 'Okay, Colonel, let's do it. Commence firing.'

G-PALS CONSTELLATION BRAVO ONE, IN ORBIT

Four hundred miles above the blue-green, white-flecked earth, a cloud of fifty tiny bullet-shaped interceptors orbited together – circling the globe at seventeen thousand miles an hour.

Each 'Brilliant Pebble' was barely three feet long, a foot in diameter, and weighed just a little more than one hundred pounds. Inside the casing, advanced microminiaturization techniques packed enormous computing power into a few tiny silicon chips. Each fist-sized supercomputer drew its tracking data from a nose-mounted, miniaturized television camera equipped with a wide-angle, fish-eye lens. Maneuvering rockets and their propellant filled the rest of the remaining space.

The order relayed through the G-PALS command net activated five of the interceptors, triggering a new engagement program uploaded less than sixty minutes before. Minute clouds of vapor puffed into space as maneuvering thrusters fired in a preset sequence. Slowly, inexorably, the five Brilliant Pebbles drifted out of the main cloud – moving into a new orbit. Seeker heads that had been focused on the earth below were now locked on an empty point several hundred miles above the surface.

A tiny shape appeared there, rising quite suddenly above the earth's curvature and closing rapidly. Sunlight sparkled off solar panels deployed on either side of a two-ton, box-shaped satellite. HELIOS was a French military reconnaissance platform. Its sophisticated cameras could take detailed pictures of objects smaller than a baseball bat – even from orbit.

It was dawn over eastern Europe, and the low sun would make the long shadows so loved by photo interpreters.

With their prey in sight, the tracking and guidance systems aboard each Brilliant Pebble went into high gear. On-board supercomputers took the images supplied by their TV cameras, matched them against an approved target set, and cycled into attack mode.

More vapor puffed into space as each Brilliant Pebble's main motor fired. All five darted forward, racing toward the oncoming photo recon satellite. They covered the distance in sixty-eight seconds.

The HELIOS satellite vanished in a single, blinding flash – hit head-on by an interceptor at a relative speed of more than thirty thousand miles an hour. Millions of metal fragments spread over dozens of square miles. Two Brilliant Pebbles a microsecond behind the first plunged right into the heart of the expanding debris cloud and disintegrated. The last two missed by somewhat wider margins and plunged toward the atmosphere, where they would burn up harmlessly.

Deep within the G-PALS constellation, five more Brilliant Pebbles went active. A new shape rose above the distant horizon – a new target. The Franco-German Radar SAR satellite came rushing toward its own destruction. Within an hour, every French and German reconnaissance platform in low earth orbit met that same fate.

Even as its first tank columns rumbled toward the Polish frontier, EurCon's sophisticated orbital 'eyes' had been blinded.

CHAPTER 19

Movement to Contact

JUNE 5 – HEADQUARTERS, 19TH PANZERGRENADIER BRIGADE, COTTBUS, GERMANY

Lights were on all across the compound, bright against a pale black, starlit sky. Although it was already past midnight, the officers and men of the 19th Panzergrenadier Brigade were still up, readying their weapons and vehicles for war. Work details crowded around canvas-sided trucks, hurriedly off-loading crates containing ammunition, rations, and spare parts. Company and platoon officers and NCOs circulated through the stacked crates, ready to pounce on supplies their units still lacked. Shortages were the rule rather than the exception.

When the shooting started at sea on June 3, the brigade was strung out across Germany, caught right in the middle of its accelerated redeployment to Cottbus. Some units had already been moving into their new quarters, though 'new' was definitely the wrong word to use for ramshackle barracks built in 1945 to house Soviet occupation forces. Other battalions had still been stuck in their old cantonments around Ahlen, waiting for their turn on Germany's clogged rail lines and autobahns. They'd reached Cottbus the day before, spurred by a preliminary war warning order from II Corps headquarters. Moving the hundreds of tons of stores they would need for sustained combat was proving considerably more difficult.

Lt. Col. Willi von Seelow frowned as he stood looking out a window in the brigade commander's spartan office. He and the rest of the staff had been working hard for several days to remedy the chaotic supply situation. Now they were out of time. Despite their best efforts, the 19th would go into battle with barely fifty percent of the ammo, food, and fuel stocks he considered essential.

From what he'd heard, few units in the Confederation's newly integrated army were in better shape. A logistical system already showing the strain of the army's hasty redeployment to the Polish border and the heavy fighting in Hungary was starting to fall apart.

Von Seelow shook his head angrily. It was one thing for senior officers and government leaders to talk blithely about conducting a 'come as you are' war. It was quite another to actually fight one – especially with half your supplies still locked up in warehouses four hundred kilometers behind the likely front line.

He turned away from the window when the phone on Col. Georg Bremer's desk rang.

'Bremer here.'

Von Seelow watched his short, dark-haired commander sit up straighter.

'Yes, Herr General.' Bremer listened intently to the voice on the other end for a few moments, jotting down notes all the while. When he put the pencil down, his face was more serious than von Seelow had ever seen it. 'Yes, sir. I understand completely. You can count on us. Thank you, Herr General. And good luck to you, too.'

He replaced the receiver and then looked up. 'That was Leibnitz.'

Von Seelow nodded. Gen. Karl Leibnitz commanded the 7th Panzer Division, the brigade's parent formation.

'It's official.' Bremer stood up from behind his desk and tugged his uniform jacket straight. 'We cross into Poland at 0400 hours today. The plan is "Summer Lightning." '

Von Seelow felt cold. As relations with Poland and the Czech Republic worsened, the army's general staff had prepared several contingency plans for operations along Germany's eastern border. Summer Lightning was the most ambitious of them all. Naturally, as the brigade's operations officer, he'd studied each plan in detail. But he'd never really expected to see any of them put into practice – not even when the crisis began heating up. Somehow, he'd always believed cooler heads and common sense would ultimately prevail.

Under Summer Lightning, two full EurCon corps, the II and III, would attack across the Neisse River south of the city of Frankfurt. Together, the two corps could mass fourteen hundred main battle tanks, nearly a thousand armored personnel carriers, and six hundred artillery pieces – all manned by 120,000 tough, highly trained soldiers. They would be supported by fighter-bombers and more than one hundred attack helicopters.

Three more French and German divisions, EurCon's I Corps, would feint along the Oder River north of Frankfurt. With luck, they would tie down the Polish troops deployed there. At the same time, the VI Corps and several Austrian units would conduct probing attacks to pin the small but formidable Czech Army in place. EurCon's V Corps, with two German panzer divisions, would remain in reserve in central Germany.

If all went well, the six divisions in II and III Corps would easily punch a hole through the two Polish mechanized divisions they faced. But to what end?

He put the question into words. 'And our strategic objective?'

'To "punish" the Polish armed forces.' Bremer shrugged. 'Whatever the devil that means.'

Von Seelow didn't like the sound of that at all. Without a clear military or political goal, they could easily wind up flailing wildly about inside Poland, wasting precious strength and time pursuing an elusive victory nobody could define.

Bremer saw his uncertainty and nodded. 'I don't like it much, either. But at least our part in all this is clear enough.' He smiled thinly. 'So now we try putting this wild-eyed scheme of yours into practice, Willi.'

Army-level plans like Summer Lightning laid out only the broad outlines of a campaign. Operations officers like von Seelow were responsible for crafting the detailed brigade-, division-, and corps-level plans needed to implement their superiors' grand schemes. II Corps' current ops plan was largely based on concepts he had evolved during staff exercises earlier in the year.

The knowledge that his bold ideas were about to be tested under fire stirred contradictory emotions. As a soldier, he felt proud that his abilities were finally being recognized by his comrades and by his superiors. At the same time, he couldn't shake a nagging belief that this war was fundamentally unjust. He'd read and heard enough unfiltered news to know the kinds of pressure the French and many Germans had been applying against Poland and the other small countries in eastern Europe.

Bremer must have been thinking along somewhat the same lines. 'At least we have one consolation. We are soldiers, not politicians. We need only do our duty and let the vote-buyers sort out the rest, eh?'

But Willi von Seelow was not so sure of that. The professional soldiers who had served the Third Reich had also held firm to their duty. They had been wrong. Duty must always be measured against the demands of individual conscience, he thought. Ultimately all soldiers, especially those in command positions, are called on to decide whether or not they are fighting a just or an unjust war.

His superiors, both in the army and in the government, were entitled to the presumption that their decisions met those tests, but he couldn't help feeling uneasy. The Chancellor's declaration of martial law had seemed a necessary, though harsh emergency measure at first. As the months passed, though, Willi couldn't help noticing that laws and methods of governing enacted as temporary seemed increasingly regarded as permanent. That worried him. As a young officer, he'd served one dictatorship, however unwillingly. He did not want to serve another.

Two hours later, the 19th Panzergrenadier Brigade was on the road, a long, blacked-out column of tanks and APCs slowly clanking east toward the border town of Forst. Their route took them through tiny, run-down villages and patches of dead or dying forest. The vast, open-pit brown coal mines that pockmarked the surrounding countryside had wreaked havoc on the local environment.

Other tank and mechanized infantry units filled the roads behind them, funneling into Cottbus in columns that stretched for kilometer after kilometer. Most of EurCon's II Corps was massing near the city, preparing for the lunge into Poland after a chosen few cleared the way.

NEAR FORST, ON THE POLISH BORDER

It was daybreak.

Although the woods on the Polish side of the Neisse River were still cloaked in shadow, the sun had already climbed above the horizon – a ball of fire rising in a cloudless sky. Red-tinged sunlight touched the rusting steel girders of the Forst railroad bridge and set them aglow. Light winds from the south and southeast promised warm and dry weather later in the day.

Men in camouflage-pattern fatigues, combat engineers, swarmed over the railroad bridge, laying wood planking across its tracks and ties so that armored vehicles could use it safely. Other engineers, attached to the brigade by the 7th Panzer Division and II Corps, were busy deploying two ribbon bridges across the Neisse. They worked as fast as their self-propelled pontoon sections arrived and splashed into the water, bolting them together to form floating roadways reaching across the river.

Clusters of armored vehicles dotted an open park just west of the bridging site. Gepard flakpanzers mounting radar-directed, 35mm guns were on watch in case the Polish Air Force made an unwelcome appearance over Forst. Longer-range Roland SAM batteries stood guard further back, outside the town.

In the narrow streets of Forst itself, the 19th Panzergrenadier's Marder APCs and Leopard tanks were lined up nose-to-tail, waiting to cross into Poland. Infantrymen wearing helmets and camouflage battle dress lay curled up beside their Marders. They were making use of the delay by trying to catch up on some of the sleep they'd lost during the previous night. Tank crewmen wearing olive-drab fatigues and black berets stood on top of their vehicles, using binoculars to scan the silent, wooded enemy shore.

Several staff officers and NCOs chatted together near an American-made M577 command vehicle parked in a street overlooking the railway bridge. The boxy tracked vehicle served as the brigade's TOC, its tactical operations center. Bent low to clear the M577's low roof, Lt. Col. Willi von Seelow walked down the rear ramp and joined his subordinates. He stood blinking in sunshine that was painfully bright after a night spent cooped up inside the TOC's map- and radio-filled compartment.

'Any news, sir?'

Von Seelow nodded. 'Major Hauser assures me that his bridges will be completed on schedule, and that we'll be crossing in half an hour. Since he is a punctual and punctilious man, I think we can count on his assurances.'

His mild jest drew a laugh from those in earshot. A louder and longer laugh than it deserved, he noticed. Beneath their carefully assumed nonchalance, these young men were all nerves, frightened by the very real prospect of killing or being killed. No amount of riot control duty or street patrolling could compare with the sheer frightfulness of modern war.

Von Seelow knew he should be feeling the same grating anxieties. Certainly he'd been scared enough under fire in the Balkans – caught between the warring Serbs, Croats and Muslims. For some reason, though, this was different. He was still conscious of being afraid of death or failure, but his fears were buried deeper than he remembered them. Maybe it was because he had more control over events now than he'd had as a junior officer obeying other men's orders. Maybe he was just too busy.

Movement near the far end of the railway bridge caught his eye. With their hands held high in surrender, a steady trickle of disconsolate Polish infantrymen in their distinctive 'worm' camouflage-pattern field uniforms came walking across, prodded at riflepoint by German soldiers whose faces and hands were daubed black.

The Poles had been captured during the first and most dangerous phase of this river crossing. Crammed into flimsy rubber rafts, an infantry company from the 7th Panzer's reconnaissance battalion had paddled silently across the Neisse before dawn. Once ashore, they'd overwhelmed a tiny Polish garrison posted in the little village of Zasieki to keep an eye on the railroad bridge. Together with a light infantry company from one of the division's Jaeger battalions, the recon troops were now spread in a semicircle through the woods, guarding the bridgehead until the brigade's heavy tanks and vehicles could relieve them.

Willi had bet that this crossing point would be only weakly garrisoned, and he had won his bet. With just four divisions deployed along a border nearly four hundred kilometers long, the Poles were too thin on the ground to defend everywhere at once. In this sector, they'd concentrated their troops opposite the highway bridge at Olszyna, ten kilometers south. A German assault at Zasieki, with only a rudimentary road net and surrounded by forest, must not have seemed a significant threat.

Von Seelow planned to show them they were wrong. Once across the Neisse, the 19th Panzergrenadier would sweep southeast along the railroad embankment and the woods themselves. The forest wasn't old-growth. It lacked the dense, tangled undergrowth that would have rendered it impassable to vehicles. Movement would be made even easier by using some of the dirt logging tracks that crisscrossed the area. Most of them fed onto the highway near Olszyna. The brigade's Leopards and Marders should hit the reinforced Polish battalion guarding the bridge from the flank and rear before its commander knew they were coming.

7TH PANZER AUFKLARUNGS (RECONNAISSANCE) BATTALION, NEAR TUPLICE

The 7th Panzer Division's reconnaissance battalion prowled onward through the woods, advancing in a kilometer-wide wedge. Sunlight streamed down through the trees, splintered by gently swaying green leaves and branches into patches of light and shadow rippling over camouflaged hulls and gun turrets. Eight-wheeled Luchs scout cars roved ahead, probing for the first signs of stiffening Polish resistance. Tanks and six-wheeled Fuchs troop carriers followed a few hundred meters behind.

Maj. Max Lauer rode proudly erect in the unbuttoned turret hatch of his Leopard 1 headquarters tank. Although they mounted smaller-caliber main guns and had less armor protection than the newer Leopard 2s, the thirty-six tanks under his command still gave his recon battalion a powerful punch. He and his men could fight most enemy forces they encountered on equal terms and outmaneuver most of those who outnumbered them.

Thunder rumbled to the southwest – the sound of heavy shelling muffled by distance and by the trees. Lauer brushed his radio headphones back for a moment to listen and then nodded grimly. The Poles holding the highway bridge were catching hell from at least twelve artillery batteries. He didn't envy them the experience.

He slipped his headphones back on. The battle for the bridge wasn't his concern. Not directly anyway. The 19th Panzergrenadier would deal with the enemy troops there. His battalion had its own mission. They were supposed to seize and hold the road junction at Jaglowice, six kilometers further down the highway.

From there, Lauer's tanks and infantry could block or delay any reaction force speeding toward the battle. They would also tighten the noose around any Polish units that survived the attack at Olszyna and tried to flee east down the road.

HEADQUARTERS, POLISH 411TH MECHANIZED BATTALION, OLSZYNA

Maj. Marek Malanowski was knocked off his feet as another near miss rocked his command bunker. Dust and smoke from the explosion boiled in through observation and firing slits beneath the bunker's timber and sandbag roof. One of his sergeants helped him up.

The major bent down and scooped his helmet off the earth floor. Then he clapped it back on over his close-cropped black hair. 'I don't think they like us very much, Jan.'

The sergeant grinned, a quick flash of tobacco-stained teeth across a dirt-smeared face. 'No, sir.'

Malanowski took another look outside. It was like staring into a whirling, roaring maelstrom – only one made up of smoke and fire instead of water and foam. More shells churned the riverbank and nearby woods. Airbursts shredded treetops, sending wood and steel splinters whining earthward. Shock waves from the explosions tore the leaves from those trees left standing and sent them swirling wildly through the air. Plumes of oily black smoke curled into the air from several vehicles smashed and set on fire by direct hits.

Nevertheless, despite the pounding they were taking, his defenses appeared mostly intact. If their nerves held out under the constant, shattering noise, troops in well-prepared positions could usually ride out even the worst artillery bombardment. So far, at least, the men of the 411th Mechanized Battalion were standing firm. If they could just hold on a little longer, he was confident that they would tear to shreds any EurCon attempt to cross the river.

Malanowski's battalion was organized along American lines, but it was still using Soviet-style equipment. He had three companies of BMP-1s dug into the woods along the riverbanks, sited to cover the bridge and other potential crossing points with their 73mm smoothbore cannon and wire-guided antitank missiles. Their infantry squads were all dismounted and in firing positions with overhead cover to protect them from shell fragments. He even had a T-72 tank company in support.

With that much firepower on tap, any first German tanks that tried storming across the highway bridge wouldn't get more than a hundred meters. And if they tried sending infantry across in rubber rafts or assault boats? The Polish major shrugged. Mortars and machine guns should deal pretty handily with those poor bastards. Even a smoke screen couldn't stop converging automatic weapons fire. Put enough bullets into an area fast enough and you were bound to hit someone.

Of course, it would have been a lot easier if they could have just blown the bridge and been done with it. But rigging enough demolitions to bring down a major structure took time. It was also obvious. Even with a strike and counterstrike air war in progress, Warsaw hadn't wanted to give EurCon any more excuses to escalate the conflict.

He turned to the lieutenant manning the command bunker's communications gear. 'Any word from the Zasieki OP yet?' He had to shout to be heard over the constant, deafening barrage.

'No, sir.'

'What about Lieutenant Lesniak?'

'Nothing, Major.'

Malanowski chewed his lower lip. That worried him. They'd lost contact with the tiny observation post more than an hour ago – shortly after the enemy artillery barrage began. Maybe the shelling had cut the telephone wires his signals troops had laid. And maybe not.

Concerned by the ominous silence on his flank, he'd sent Lesniak and a small patrol north along the river. They were under orders to make contact with the OP and report back. Now they were missing, too. Were they pinned down by the artillery? Silenced by German radio jamming? Or had the lieutenant and his men run into more trouble than they could handle?

After Malanowski's first reports of increased enemy activity across the river, his regimental commander had promised him the first available reinforcements. But the major knew they would be a long time coming. With so much ground to cover, the 4th Mechanized Division had very few reserves held back.

Essentially the 411th was on its own.

Faced with that reality, he'd deployed his own tactical reserve, D Company, at right angles to the river, covering his northern flank. It wasn't much, just fourteen BMPs and a hundred infantrymen, but it was all he had.

The shelling changed tempo suddenly, slowing and growing softer.

Malanowski scanned the ground sloping down toward the Neisse again. He could see shells bursting along the shoreline, exploding in puffs of grayish-white smoke. The Germans were building a smoke screen to cover their assault! He showed his teeth in a quick tigerish grin. His battalion had suffered under the enemy's artillery fire for long enough. Now they would have a chance to pay the Germans back in full.

'Thermal sight!'

His senior sergeant handed him a thermal imaging sight they'd stripped from one of their American-supplied Dragon antitank missile launchers. He cradled the bulky sight in both hands and hoisted it up to the bunker's observation slit.

The sight 'saw' temperature variations among different objects – leaves, the water, men, and vehicles – and turned them into a clear, monochrome view of the world outside. Hotter objects showed up in shades of white and cooler ones in shades of black.

Malanowski panned back and forth between the highway bridge and the opposite shore, looking closely for the first signs of enemy movement. Nothing yet. But they wouldn't wait much longer. He glanced at the lieutenant manning his commo gear. 'Order all companies to stand to!'

'Sir.'

The major checked the river again. Still nothing. What the devil were the EurCon commanders playing at? Every minute they delayed gave his soldiers more time to scramble into their fighting positions and to clear away blast-heaped dirt or shattered tree limbs that blocked their fields of fire.

Gunfire exploded on his right flank and quickly spread down the line – first a single shot, then a crackling, ear-splitting roar as assault rifles, machine guns, and tank cannon opened up.

'Major! D Company is under attack!' Obviously stunned by what he was reporting, the young lieutenant stood shaking, with one hand still pressing the field telephone against his ear. 'They're being hit by enemy tanks and infantry! Battalion strength at least!'

Malanowski dashed to a firing slit looking north. The gray haze was thicker there. More shells burst among the shattered trees, blending with the dense, black smoke pouring out of burning APCs. Flames stabbed out of the murk – marking both his firing line and the wave of German tanks and panzergrenadiers smashing into his battalion's flank and rear.

Christ. He spun toward the ashen-faced lieutenant, rattling off new orders as fast as they popped into his head. 'Tell A Company to reinforce the right flank! And tell Captain Stachniak to swing his T-72s north!'

If D Company could just hold for a few more minutes, they might buy him enough time to reorient his defenses.

It was too late. Malanowski could see men falling back through the smoke, pausing just long enough to fire a burst or two in the direction they'd come before retreating again. One cartwheeled backward, knocked off his feet by return fire. Another lay bloody and broken, sprawled across a fallen tree trunk. Rounds whipcracked. overhead. A T-72 clanked forward through the fleeing infantry, still trailing torn camouflage netting from its turret and rear deck. Its turret whined, slewing from side to side as it looked for targets.

Whanngg. The T-72 disappeared inside a bright orange flash – hit by a

German armor-piercing round. Its rounded turret blew off and fell beside the burning tank. Secondary explosions rocked the hull as stored fuel and ammunition cooked off.

The smoke thinned for an instant, giving Malanowski a brief glimpse of men in 'Fritz' Kevlar helmets moving closer – advancing in short rushes through the woods. They were tossing grenades and firing bursts into Polish foxholes and bunkers. His flank was collapsing. The Germans were inside the battalion's defensive perimeter.

He made an instant decision. His soldiers were being overrun too fast to put up any effective resistance. Staying here meant dying here. But maybe he could save something from the wreckage. He pulled his head away from the firing slit. 'Order all companies to withdraw! We'll fall back south to the alternate rally point and regroup!'

While the lieutenant relayed his instructions to anyone still listening on the battalion net, Malanowski handed the precious thermal sight to his sergeant. Then he grabbed his personal weapon, an AKM assault rifle, and a knapsack from one corner of the bunker. He spun round, checking the rest of his staff. They were ready. Papers, codebooks, and maps they didn't have time to pack up were heaped in a single pile, ready for destruction.

Machine-gun fire rattled somewhere outside. Stray rounds thwacked into the bunker's timber roof and shredded sandbags on its sides. The Germans were closing in, and it was high time they were gone.

Malanowski and the sergeant led the way, clearing the bunker door in a rush with their assault rifles at the ready. The rest of the staff followed, crouching low as bullets whined past. The last man out turned, pulled the pin from a grenade, and lobbed it back through the door. It went off with a dull *whummp*, blowing dirt, sand, and fragments of shredded paper through firing slits and the opening.

Still bent low, they sidled away from the bunker. Their headquarters BMP was parked just a few meters away, surrounded on three sides by raised earth embankments and covered by camouflage netting. Its crew already had the engine running and the rear troop doors open.

A German Leopard came thundering out of the smoke only a hundred meters away. Its turret and long-barreled gun pointed off to the left, aiming at a target somewhere closer to the river.

'Down!' Malanowski threw himself prone.

The BMP's gun barked once, slamming a 73mm HEAT round into the Leopard at point-blank range. The German tank rocked sideways and shuddered to a stop with smoke pouring out through the jagged hole torn in its armor. The corpse of its commander lay draped over his roof-mounted machine gun.

Before the Polish major could start to smile, another Leopard, invisible through the gray haze, avenged its fallen comrade with a single cannon round.

Whammm. The BMP exploded, spraying sharp-edged metal in all directions. Malanowski could hear its trapped crew screaming in agony as they burned to death. He scrambled to his feet, hearing shouts in

German to the north and east. The panzergrenadiers were practically right on top of them.

'On your feet! Move! Move!' He erupted into action, kicking and hauling stunned soldiers to their feet, then pushing them south – away from the burning BMP. With their commander urging them on, the battalion's headquarters team faded deeper into the woods.

Exhausted, they stopped moving several kilometers and several hours later. It was nearly noon.

Malanowski took another swallow from his field canteen and swished the water around his mouth, before letting it slide down his parched throat. Then he sloshed what was left onto a handkerchief and used it to wipe away the worst of the sweat, smoke, and dust coating his face. With the sun high overhead, the small copse of trees he and his soldiers were hiding in provided welcome shelter from the sweltering heat.

He laid the canteen aside, slumped back against the tree trunk, and studied what was left of his battalion. Besides the six survivors from his command staff, he'd found another twenty or thirty bedraggled infantrymen and footsore vehicle crewmen at the rally point. From there, they'd headed further south, intent on putting as much distance as possible between themselves and the victorious Germans.

Since they'd stopped to rest in this grove, more weary men had come stumbling in by ones and twos. Right now, he had roughly fifty soldiers under his command – armed only with small arms and a few light antitank weapons. The major grimaced. That was just ten percent of the force he'd taken into battle. The rest of his men were dead, captive, or scattered across the countryside.

Once night fell, he planned to lead this ragged, worn-out remnant of his battalion southward again, sticking close to the woods for as long as possible. With a little luck, they could commandeer enough civilian transport to rejoin their own army.

If not . . . Malanowski sat up straighter. He and his men would fight on as partisans, raiding EurCon's exposed supply lines and rear areas.

Poland had been beaten before, but her soldiers had fought on. Malanowski had heard the stories again and again as a cadet. Now they would continue that tradition, fighting the enemy any way they could. They had lost a battle, not the war.

19TH PANZERGRENADIER BRIGADE, HIGHWAY 12, NEAR LUBIESZOW

A dull red glow in the west marked the setting sun and cast long black shadows over the highway. It was already dark under the trees lining both sides of the road.

The muted roar of heavy traffic could be heard for kilometers around – a steady rumble of powerful diesel engines and the squeaking, grinding, clanking of tank treads on pavement. Thousands of tanks, APCs, and trucks were wending their way through in the gathering darkness. With the 19th Panzergrenadier Brigade still in the lead, the 7th

Panzer was pushing deeper into Poland.

Inside the dimly lit interior of his M577, Lt. Col. Willi von Seelow braced himself against the APC's motion with one hand and marked his map with the other. Led by Bremer in person, the brigade's advance guard was already thirty-two kilometers beyond the Neisse River. Strong patrols from the division's own recon battalion were probing even deeper – cutting telephone lines and setting up roadblocks to keep the news of their breakthrough from spreading. Although the 19th's losses at Olszyna had been heavier than he'd hoped, they were making good progress. Since the morning battle, opposition had been light, almost nonexistent.

So far, at least, Summer Lightning was going according to plan.

Early that morning, III Corps had attacked far to the south, near Gorlitz, where the terrain was more open – better tank country. It was also the sector where the Poles had massed most of their defending forces. Reports indicated that the Polish troops – the 11th Mechanized Division and most of the 4th – were holding their ground in very heavy fighting.

And that was just what the EurCon high command wanted.

While III Corps pinned the enemy in place, the 7th Panzer and the rest of II Corps were pouring across the Neisse, plunging southeast through Poland's western forests toward Legnica. Once there they would wheel south, trapping and annihilating the better part of two Polish mechanized divisions.

The Confederation's political leaders were confident that a defeat of that magnitude would be enough to bring Poland to its knees and to the bargaining table. Then, with their larger ally humbled, the Czech and Slovak Republics and rebel Hungary would be forced to do the same. All of Europe, from the Russian border west to the Atlantic, would be under the effective control of a single alliance. And once their eastern European allies switched sides, America and Great Britain would surely see reason. Robbed of any continental foothold, they would face only the prospect of a long, bloody, uncertain war for uncertain aims. Isolationist sentiment was still strong in both countries. Pressure from their own people, weary of war for no conceivable gain, would force Washington and London to sign their own peace with Europe's new superpower.

Willi von Seelow wasn't so sure about that. Too much of the EurCon war plan depended on their enemies reacting slowly and predictably to the military moves already under way – dancing to the Franco-German tune. But what if the men in Warsaw and Washington had another melody in mind?

JUNE 6 – MINISTRY OF NATIONAL DEFENSE, WARSAW

Gen. Wieslaw Staron, Poland's Minister of Defense, leaned over a map showing western Poland, studying the road net and terrain. Staron knew the map as well as he knew his own face in the mirror. Thirty years in uniform had given him a fine appreciation of the uses of terrain, and he now saw it not just as roads and rivers and forests, but in terms of movement rates, defensive strengths and weaknesses, and communications centers.

He'd moved troops around the Polish landscape for twenty-five of those years, starting with a platoon and working his way up to a full corps. While few in the Polish Army had engaged in combat, no one was better qualified to send it into battle.

Bushy brown eyebrows knitted together. He looked up and shook his head slowly. 'I don't like it, Ignacy.'

'No, sir.' Lt. Gen. Ignacy Zdanski, the chief of the general staff, kept his face carefully impassive.

'Not at all.' Staron looked down at the map again. He tapped the river line near Gorlitz. 'Two enemy divisions here – with a third in reserve. Yes?'

His younger, leaner subordinate nodded. 'The 5th Panzer, 4th Panzergrenadier, and the French 3rd Armored. They're across the river in several places, but not very far.'

The Defense Minister frowned. 'And why not?'

'The force ratio isn't in their favor.'

True enough, Staron thought, focusing on the map – trying to see the terrain as though he were a young tank commander again, and not a middle-aged military bureaucrat penned in a Warsaw office in the middle of the night. With only three divisions attacking against nearly two defending, the French and Germans couldn't possibly hope to achieve a breakthrough in the south. According to the latest satellite and signals intelligence provided by the Americans, EurCon still had at least three uncommitted divisions on the border. Possibly more. So what were they playing at? Then he saw it. The EurCon commanders didn't *want* to punch a hole in his lines there. They were playing a different game entirely.

He'd once heard inspiration described as 'a zigzag streak of lightning in the brain.' This wasn't like that at all. It was more like watching a curtain rise slowly, revealing a suddenly familiar stage. 'The Ardennes!'

'Sir?'

Staron stabbed a thick finger down on the map. 'The damned Ardennes! That's what they're trying to do to us. Here.' He traced the highway running from Olszyna to Legnica. 'They're coming this way. Through the forests. Cutting behind us.'

He thumped the table for emphasis. 'Look at it, Ignacy! It all adds up.'

'Mother of God.' Zdanski turned pale. It did make sense. The communications failures plaguing that region since early yesterday morning weren't random chance or the work of isolated raiding parties. They were the first warning signs of an oncoming tidal wave.

Staron put both fists on the table. He'd let misguided political considerations sway him into deploying half the Polish Army along the frontier in a show of force. But he'd be damned if he'd repeat all the mistakes of 1939 by allowing his units to be surrounded and rolled up by another German-led blitzkrieg.

The Defense Minister fired out directions. 'Order the 4th and 11th

Mechanized to withdraw. Immediately. Tell them to break contact and fall back to . . . here.' He circled a position near Wroclaw itself – seventy-five kilometers back from the Neisse. If his commanders moved fast enough, they should still be able to escape the closing jaws of the EurCon trap.

'But what about the President and Prime Minister? Will they agree to abandon so much of our country to the enemy?'

'They'll agree,' Staron growled. 'Land can always be retaken. Soldiers are harder to come by. And Poland lives so long as she has a fighting army in the field!'

While his subordinate hurried away to issue the necessary orders, the Defense Minister returned to his study of the situation map. Even a successful withdrawal would only delay the inevitable. Matching two Polish divisions against two full enemy corps was a prescription for certain defeat. He needed to put more men on the battle line. But where could he pull them from?

Not from the east. Not yet. Russia's declared neutrality in this conflict meant nothing. Marshal Kaminov and his cronies had already stabbed Poland in the back once for French gold. Who could say that he wouldn't make the same kind of bargain again?

Staron's eyes moved north, tracing the line of the Oder as it flowed toward the Baltic Sea. EurCon forces had made only a few scattered thrusts across the river there – small-scale battalion and company-sized raids that went nowhere. But were they trying to lull him into complacency before launching a bigger offensive later? No, he judged. France and Germany wanted a quick, uncomplicated war and a quick, decisive victory. They were making their main effort in the south.

He nodded to himself. He would gamble in the north.

HEADQUARTERS, POLISH 5TH MECHANIZED DIVISION, NEAR SWIECKO

The tall, rail-thin colonel in charge of the division's intelligence section finished his briefing without notes, using only a map tacked to an easel and a long thin pointer. 'In summary, at least three EurCon divisions have crossed the Neisse River at Forst and Olszyna. Our best current guess is that they're aiming for Legnica in an attempt to pocket our units withdrawing from Gorlitz.'

Maj. Gen. Jerzy Novachik watched the officers crammed into the headquarters tent react. All of them were worried by the news of the EurCon breakthrough south of them. Few were very surprised by it. As a show of force during the early stages of the crisis, Warsaw's decision to deploy half the nation's army in a thin, dispersed screen along the frontier had made some sense. Once hostilities flared, it had been an open invitation to military catastrophe.

He strode forward and faced them squarely. 'I won't mince words, gentlemen. The strategic situation is bleak.'

Heads nodded in agreement.

'But it is *not* irretrievable.' Novachik let that sink in for a moment before continuing. 'This division is being committed to battle in the south. Two regiments, the 51st and the 52nd, will leave immediately. The 53rd will stay behind until it can hand off the defense of this sector to the 20th Mechanized.'

Their eyes widened at that. Warsaw was taking an enormous risk. Pulling the 5th off the Oder line would leave only a single division and an odd assortment of poorly armed Home Guard companies behind.

'The division will proceed to Wroclaw by this route.' Novachik picked up the colonel's pointer and swept it across the map, east to Poznan first and then south to Wroclaw. Their planned line of march swung wide around the EurCon forces pouring down Highway 12. 'This will be a forced march, so speed is absolutely vital. Vehicles that break down will be left behind to follow along when they can. If necessary, we will eat and sleep on the move. This is a horse race, gentlemen, and the enemy is on the inside rail. And there are no prizes for second place.'

They nodded again, their faces solemn in the lamplight. The 5th Mechanized Division was about to enter a contest where the stakes were Poland's continued existence as a free and independent nation.

U.S. EMBASSY, MOSCOW

Erin McKenna smiled happily when Alex Banich leaned in through the open door to her office. They were both so busy these days that she rarely saw him at all – especially not during working hours. The fighting spilling through eastern Europe added a special urgency to their efforts to monitor Russia's armed forces and defense industries.

Her smile faded. Behind the poker face most people saw, he looked worried. 'What's wrong?'

'I'm afraid dinner's off. Duty calls.'

'With a shrill and unpleasant voice?'

Banich nodded. 'Very shrill and very unpleasant.' He came in and closed the door behind him. 'I just had a chat with Kutner. He's received a priority signal from Langley.'

Erin grimaced. 'What do they want now? The phone number for Kaminov's newest mistress?'

'Not exactly.' He carefully pushed a pile of printouts to one side and took his usual perch at one end of her desk. She sometimes wondered what he had against sitting in chairs.

'What, then?'

'They need to know whether or not the Russians plan to intervene against Poland.' Banich said it flatly, without evident emotion.

Erin stared at him. 'And how are you supposed to find that out? Just waltz right up to the Kremlin and ask?'

Banich shrugged. 'When the boys on the top floor want results, they really don't care what I have to do to get them.'

'Seriously.'

He shrugged again. 'Anything I can . . . up to and including twisting a few greedy little arms inside the Defense Ministry.'

Erin was aghast. 'That's crazy!' She pushed her keyboard away and turned to face him. 'You know that whole building will be crawling with FIS agents by now.'

'Probably.'

'Just waiting for the first Western spy stupid enough to come barging in with cash and miniature camera in hand.'

Banich nodded. 'Probably.' He grinned suddenly. 'Hey, risk comes with the territory. If I'd wanted a safe, boring job, I'd have gone in for circus high-wire work like my grandma wanted me to.'

She forced a smile of her own. She'd worked with him long enough to realize that being flippant was the way he dealt with stress. He knew the risks. Harping on them wouldn't help.

Banich studied her face intently, almost as though he were memorizing it. Then he checked his watch and stood up. 'Gotta run. My alter ego, Ushenko, has a very important appointment at ten.' He looked down at her. 'Wish me luck.'

'Always.' Erin kept her voice light. 'But if you stand me up one more time, Alex Banich, I'll sue you for trifling with my affections. Either that or ask my daddy to horsewhip you through the town streets.'

He laughed softly and ghosted out of the room and down the hall.

'Damn it!' Someone she was starting to care a lot about was putting himself in a lot of danger, and she couldn't do a thing to help him. She swiveled back to her computer and jabbed viciously at the enter key. It beeped in protest.

Her usefulness in Moscow was just about at an end. With the FIS breathing down her neck, she couldn't risk any personal contacts with potential sources. That left electronic espionage. But Russia's computer security teams were steadily and methodically finding and sealing the nooks and crannies she'd been using to slip in and out of confidential data bases. Pretty soon, for all the good she'd be able to do here, she might as well be back in D.C. filling out and filing meaningless Commerce Department reports.

Erin McKenna stared emptily into her computer screen. With Europe in flames, she was trapped inside the Moscow embassy compound.

CHAPTER 20

Meeting Engagement

JUNE 7 – HEADQUARTERS, 7TH PANZER DIVISION, NEAR LEGNICA, POLAND

The small village of Legnickie Pole had a troubled history stretching back over many centuries. In 1241, Duke Henryk the Pious and his Polish and Silesian knights had been defeated there by Mongol horse archers pouring out of the eastern steppes. Benedictine monks built a monastery to honor the fallen duke but were driven out by German overlords during the Protestant Reformation. They returned centuries later and built a new abbey facing the old. Unfortunately for the monks, covetous secular hands were never far behind. For nearly a century, the abbey buildings housed a Prussian military academy. One of its graduates was Paul von Hindenburg, Germany's last commander in chief during World War I and the man who named Adolf Hitler as Germany's Chancellor.

Now Legnickie Pole served as a temporary headquarters for another invading force.

The cluster of jeeps, trucks, and armored vehicles constituting the 7th Panzer Division's forward command post filled a small campground on the edge of the village. Infantrymen, Milan antitank missile teams, and air defense units stood guard around the perimeter. Polish stragglers cut off by the rapid Confederation advance were showing an irritating reluctance to accept defeat and surrender. Instead they seemed determined to fight on – attacking supply convoys, command posts, and even fighting units whenever possible. Constant vigilance was necessary – especially at night.

Lt. Col. Willi von Seelow paused before following Colonel Bremer into the central headquarters tent. Since the war began he'd been spending eighteen to twenty hours a day inside the brigade's cramped M577 headquarters vehicle – preparing and discarding or distributing new operations plans as the tactical situation changed. Now he relished this rare chance to stretch to his full height. It was also a chance to breathe fresh air only lightly tinged with diesel fumes, smoke, and sweat.

Flashes lit the night sky to the south, followed seconds later by the muffled drumbeat of heavy artillery. III Corps gunners were pounding stubborn Polish rear guards holding the road junction at Jawor. A flickering orange glow to the west marked a village set ablaze during the day's fighting.

Von Seelow could also hear the steady rumble of heavy traffic crawling south and east along the highways outside the town. He frowned. With six divisions converging on a front only fifty kilometers or so wide, the roads were clogged. Vital supplies – tank and artillery ammunition, and diesel fuel – weren't getting forward fast enough. Unless those rear-area logistical tangles could be sorted out, this offensive risked bogging down under its own weight.

He shook his head, pushing away strategic concerns beyond his scope, and went inside.

Bremer was up front, near a pair of cloth-covered map stands. The 19th Panzergrenadier's short, dark-haired commander stood in the middle of a small circle of other senior officers, chatting amicably with the men who led the division's two Panzer brigades. Willi pushed through the crowded tent to join him. Gen. Karl Leibnitz had evidently summoned all of his combat commanders and their top staff officers to this late night meeting.

That wasn't surprising. With events knocking their prewar plans further and further out of whack, the 7th Panzer and the other Confederation units inside Poland urgently needed new instructions and new objectives.

'*Achtung*.'

The assembled officers came to attention as Leibnitz pushed past the tent's blackout flap.

'At ease, gentlemen.' The general took his place at the front. 'Let's not waste time with formalities.'

He pulled the cover off the left-hand map. It showed the EurCon Army's current positions and those held by the Poles. 'Summer Lightning has failed to achieve its primary objective – the encirclement and annihilation of the Polish 4th and 11th mechanized divisions. The Poles have fallen back too far and too fast for us to get behind them.'

Von Seelow and the others nodded. Despite their best efforts, the 7th Panzer's rapid advance through the forest had netted only a few laggard enemy units – none larger than company-sized groupings of antique T-55 tanks and wheeled troop carriers. Poland's best troops had escaped the trap. The war plan's vaunted 'jaws of steel' had closed on empty air and deserted Polish farmland.

'As a result, we've been given new orders by II Corps.' The division commander turned to the map on the second stand. It showed a set of red arrows arcing north past Legnica before turning and coming south again.

'We turn northeast, pushing along these tertiary roads here and here.' Leibnitz traced them as he talked. 'Our first objective is the bridge over the Cicha Woda at Kawice.' He tapped a tiny village near the junction of the Oder River and its small tributary.

'From there we advance southeast toward Sroda Slaska and Katy Wroclawskie, using the Oder to protect our left flank.' The general saw their understanding and nodded. 'That's correct, gentlemen. If we move fast – very fast – we can swing around the Polish lines and cut them off from Wroclaw before they have time to retreat again.'

What? Willi wondered which idiot on the corps staff had come up with this half-baked half-measure? Without stopping to consider the consequences, he shook his head and took a step closer to the map.

The movement and gesture caught Leibnitz's attention. 'Something about this plan troubles you, von Seelow?'

Suddenly feeling all the eyes in the crowded tent boring into his back, Willi nodded. 'Yes, Herr General, it does.'

'Well?'

Willi swallowed the urge to retreat. His duty as an officer required him to speak up. 'This turning movement is too shallow, Herr General. Once the Poles realize what we are up to, they'll have little trouble shifting local reserves to slow us down or seal off our penetration entirely. And once that happens, we'll only find ourselves locked into a bloody, head-to-head slugging match again.'

'And what do you suggest instead?' The general's flat tone made it very clear that he had better damned well have an alternative in mind.

'That we advance north *past* Kawice and cross the Oder itself before turning east.' Von Seelow injected as much confidence in his voice as he could. 'Then, with the river protecting our *right* flank, we can swing deep around Wroclaw itself. If III Corps does the same to the south, we can still pocket a sizable portion of the Poles in and around the city.'

Leibnitz pondered the map in a silence that dragged uncomfortably. Then he shook his head. 'Our orders are clear, Colonel. They come straight from General Montagne himself. He has little patience and less time for perfect 'staff school' solutions. Do you understand?'

'Yes, sir.' Von Seelow groaned inwardly. Until now their French corps commander had seemed content to rely on his staff and his division commanders. The prospect of trying to carry out superficial plans hatched by Montagne himself sent chills down his spine.

'Good.' Leibnitz scanned his assembled officers. 'We move out at first light. I suggest you all make sure your vehicles are topped off and restocked. Once we break into the enemy's rear areas, it may be some time before we can be resupplied.'

His gaze fell on the commander of his reconnaissance battalion. 'Major Lauer's tanks and scout cars will lead the way. Your watchword, Max, is speed. Speed, speed, and still more speed!'

His ears still burning from the general's implied rebuke, Willi von Seelow listened to the rest of the briefing in silence.

JUNE 8 – 7TH PANZER RECONNAISSANCE BATTALION, NEAR KAWICE

Sixty Leopard 1 tanks, Luchs scout cars, and Fuchs infantry carriers raced east, thundering through fields of standing wheat and corn. Dust plumes marked their passage. Robbed of rain by several days of unseasonably clear weather, the roads and fields were dry.

Maj. Max Lauer spat to clear some of the dust from his mouth, and used one gloved hand to swipe at his goggles. He squinted down the dirt road ahead, trying to catch a first glimpse of the little farming village called Kawice.

It appeared as soon as his command tank crested a low rise rolling up out of the flat Polish countryside. A half-timbered church steeple rose above scattered roofs only a couple of kilometers away. Small stands of trees traced the meandering path of the narrow river that cut Kawice in half. The bridge linking the two halves was still out of sight. But at this speed his battalion would be on top of it in minutes.

A voice crackled through his headphones. 'Rover One, this is Rover Charlie One.' The commander of C Company – a mixed force of Leopards and Luchs scout cars – had something to report. 'Spot report! Vehicles moving toward the town! Across the river.'

Lauer snapped his head in that direction and raised his binoculars. At first, he could only see the yellow-brown haze of dust churned up by speeding tracks and tires. Then he could make out individual vehicles – little more than brown and light green dots at this distance. They were moving up the road from Sroda Slaska at high speed.

New reports came through his headphones, pouring in from vehicle commanders ahead of him. 'Vehicles are BRDMs, BMPs, and T-72s. Estimate enemy is in company strength at least.'

Damn it. They'd run right into a Polish recon outfit heading for Kawice on a converging course. And the Poles were closer to the town and its bridge than they were.

'This is Rover Charlie One. Enemy in range. Am engaging!'

Lauer could see C Company's tanks and Luchs scout cars veering away from the road, trying to take the speeding Polish column in the flank. He nodded to himself. If they could force the Poles to halt, to deploy for combat, his battalion might still win this race for Kawice.

He keyed his mike. 'All Rover units, this is Rover One. Push for the town! No stopping!'

Tank cannon cracked in the distance. C Company's Leopards were in action – pouring 105mm shells toward the enemy as the range wound down. Moments later, he heard a steady chattering roar. The scout cars had opened up with their 20mm rapid-fire cannon.

Smoke boiled up through the haze. His men were getting hits! One of the lead BRDMs vanished in a ball of flame. Another lay on its side on fire. Riddled by 20mm rounds, a BMP ground to a halt with smoke pouring from its engine compartment. Burning men tumbled out the back and crumpled to the ground. A T-72 sat off to one side of the road with its turret blown off.

But most of the Poles were still charging toward Kawice, swerving around the wrecked and damaged vehicles in their path.

Lauer swore fiercely. Those bastards across the river were too brave.

Something flashed past the Leopard's turret, trailing a shock wave of displaced air that slapped him in the face and tore at his black beret and headset. Startled, he ducked and then swore again. The Polish T-72s were firing back on the move. Luckily, their Soviet-made 125mm guns weren't accurate beyond fifteen hundred meters!

He'd been so busy commanding his battalion that he'd almost forgotten he was also inside a fighting vehicle.

The German major dropped back into his seat and grabbed the gun override, traversing the massive turret to the right. He pressed his face against the sight extension, searching for the enemy tank that had fired at him. There! A low-slung, turreted shape came into view, bucketing up and down as it crossed a dirt lane and ditch separating one wheat field from another.

'Gunner! Tank at two o'clock!'

'Identified!' His gunner, seated below and in front of him, had the T-72 in sight. 'Sabot!'

'Up!' The Leopard's loader confirmed they had a tank-killing, discarding sabot round in the main gun and that he was out of the way.

'Fire!'

The gun fired and recoiled, rocking the tank to the left. A tungsten-steel dart, surrounded by a metal shoe, or sabot, left the tank gun barrel. As it cleared the muzzle, the sabot fell away, transferring the punch of a large-bore round into a much smaller, superdense projectile.

A cloud of smoke and flame from the muzzle blast obscured their vision for a brief instant and then vanished – left behind by the Leopard's forward motion.

The T-72 was still rolling. They'd missed!

Lauer grimaced. 'Gunner! Reengage!'

Smoke and dust billowed up in front of the Polish tank as it fired again and missed a second time.

'Up!'

'Fire!'

Another flash and bang and another cloud of smoke and dust. But this time, Lauer's sight revealed the enemy tank swerving off to one side, cloaked in flame as its ammunition and fuel detonated. He kicked the gunner's shoulder lightly. 'Good shooting, Sergeant. Engage other targets at will.'

The major popped his head and shoulders back through the open hatch. He'd lost the bigger picture while concentrating on the necessary task of killing that one T-72. Now he had to regain his grasp of the tactical situation, and fast.

His own Leopard had almost reached Kawice – racing toward the little cluster of wood-frame houses, walled vegetable gardens, and narrow, unpaved streets. His lead companies were already there. He could see German armored vehicles and scout cars bunching up as they formed in column for a final dash toward the bridge.

Lauer mentally urged them on. Speed was crucial. They had to get across the river and into the other half of the village before the Poles could deploy.

A flash and puff of white smoke from a house across the water caught his eye. He spun around and saw a bright flame arcing toward them – only a meter or so off the ground. 'Missile! Evade!'

He stabbed frantically for the button that would fire his tank's protective smoke grenade launchers and missed as the Leopard swerved abruptly to the right, throwing him forward hard against the hatch coaming. In the next second, the tank's main gun fired, and this time the recoil threw him backward.

The enemy antitank missile screamed past and slammed into the ground just a few meters away. It left a length of control wire draped over the command tank's deck as concrete evidence of an attack that had come entirely too close for comfort. Lauer knew that only the combination of the wild evasive maneuver and a shell howling close by had spooked the Polish ATGM gunner, throwing his aim off in that last crucial second.

Other German tanks had seen the missile launch and now they opened fire, pumping HE rounds into the one-story wood house. It disintegrated, torn apart by a series of bright orange and red explosions. Pieces of burning timber tumbled lazily through the air before splashing into the river.

Dirt fountained skyward next to a Leopard on Lauer's flank. Then it blew up, hit broadside by a second 125mm round from a T-72 that had been lurking between another pair of buildings across the Cicha Woda. The Polish tank reversed out of sight before anyone could return fire.

The voice of C Company's commander came through his headphones, barely intelligible over the echoing roar of machine-gun and tank cannon fire. 'Rover One, this is Rover Charlie One. Crossing the bridge now! I'll . . .'

The transmission ceased suddenly. To his horror, Lauer saw thick black smoke climbing above Kawice's rooftops.

'Rover One, Charlie One is hit and burning! The bridge is blocked! Repeat, the bridge is blocked!'

The major cursed. Despite the trail of burning and broken vehicles they'd left behind, too many enemy tanks and APCs had made it inside Kawice for Lauer and his men to simply bull right through them. With their antitank teams and infantry dispersed among the houses and gardens, the Poles could turn their half of the little village into a hornet's nest.

The 7th Panzer's recon battalion had lost its race.

Lauer scowled and lifted his mike. 'Rover Delta, this is Rover One. Deploy your infantry to cover the bridge approaches.' D Company's foot soldiers stood a better chance out of their lightly armored troop carriers. 'All other Rover units, withdraw fifteen hundred meters west.'

Acknowledgments crackled in while he angrily reviewed his options. They were limited. Digging the Poles out of Kawice now would take the combined efforts of infantry, tanks, and heavy artillery. His battalion didn't have enough infantry. The division's artillery was still somewhere on the road behind them. And taking on those T-72s at point-blank range with his Leopard 1s was a good way to wind up with a wrecked unit.

He shook his head. No, he would have to let the 19th Panzergrenadier pass through to take the town.

While Bremer and his men fought it out, Lauer planned to scout south along the river, looking for a spot shallow enough for his snorkel-equipped tanks to ford. If that failed, they would have to wait for the division's engineers to lay another pontoon bridge across the Cicha Woda.

The 7th Panzer Division's 'lightning-fast' advance against the Polish flank had been slowed to a slogging crawl.

19TH PANZERGRENADIER BRIGADE, NEAR WILCZKOW

Lt. Col. Willi von Seelow lay prone on the lip of a small fold in the ground watching artillery pummel the Polish-held woods. Thirty-six 155mm howitzers were in action, dousing the treeline with high explosives.

The brigade's TOC and other command vehicles were parked in the shadowed hollow behind him. The sun was a huge red ball low on the western horizon.

Col. Georg Bremer came stomping up from von Seelow's M577 and dropped flat beside him. He'd been talking with both the division and corps headquarters over the TOC's radio. 'Madness! They've all gone crazy back there, Willi! Now that there's no hope of pocketing the Poles here, they've changed their minds again. Now we're supposed to push them out of Wroclaw by direct assault. The higher-ups claim *that* will end the war!'

Von Seelow frowned. Madness, indeed. Abandoning maneuver warfare in favor of a straight slugging match to take a single geographical objective violated the three basic tenets of German Army doctrine – mobility, agility, and flexibility. Attrition warfare wasted lives, supplies, and time. It was also unnecessary.

With half their army still tied down watching their eastern border, the Poles could not possibly be strong everywhere. Throwing six EurCon divisions squarely at their main line of defense was foolish. His worst fears were coming to life. Frantic to win a quick victory before the war escalated further, the Confederation's political leaders were starting to grasp at straws.

He lowered his binoculars and turned his head toward Bremer. 'So we attack as planned?'

The colonel nodded silently, too frustrated to speak out loud. Both of them had urged another end run around the Polish troops blocking the Sroda Slaska road. But General Montagne, unwilling to accept further delay, had ordered a full brigade attack on the enemy positions instead. And Leibnitz, their division commander, still seemed unable or unwilling to contradict his French superior.

The barrage lifted suddenly, leaving an unearthly quiet in its place. But the silence did not last long.

Twelve PAH-1 attack helicopters swept low overhead, flying in line as they approached the woods at high speed. Fiery-white flares streamed out behind each helo. It was a wise precaution.

Several white smoke trails arced up out of the shell-torn and splintered trees. The Poles were firing hand-held SAMs at the German helicopters – either American-made Stingers or Soviet-supplied SA-14s. Von Seelow held his breath, watching the missiles curve toward their targets.

The SAMs missed, decoyed by the falling flares.

And the PAH-ls opened fire, volleying hundreds of unguided, spin-stabilized rockets. From a distance, they looked like swarms of glowing sparks lancing down into the trees. Brown clouds of rocket exhaust coiled beneath the helicopters, caught in their rotor downwash. Explosions crackled through the woods.

Still trailing flares, the German helos veered west and lost altitude, heading for their own lines with their skids only meters above the ground.

Perfectly timed by a forward air controller, the next attack came in right on their heels. Four swept-wing Tornado attack jets screamed north along the edge of the woods. Thousand-pound bombs tumbled off their wing and fuselage racks – twelve from each plane.

The Tornados were turning away when a Polish ZSU-23-4 antiaircraft gun hammered them – spraying 23mm tracer rounds across their flight path. Staggered by multiple hits, one of the German jets rolled over and nose-dived into the ground. It exploded in a rolling, tumbling ball of flame. The other three howled past von Seelow and Bremer and disappeared.

The edge of the woods seemed to dissolve in a rippling series of blinding white flashes.

When the afterimages stopped dancing in front of Willi's eyes, he could see flames and black smoke rising from the treeline. There were burning Polish tanks and APCs in there. He nodded to Bremer. 'That was the last air strike, sir.'

'Right.' The colonel wriggled backward until he was below the rise. Then he clambered to his feet and jogged toward the little cluster of command vehicles in the hollow, already shouting the orders that would set the 19th Panzergrenadier's battalions in motion.

Von Seelow swiveled his head, watching clusters of armored vehicles break from cover and rumble toward the shattered patch of woods. Forty long-gunned Leopard 2s led the attack. Marder APCs crammed with infantry followed several hundred meters behind the tanks.

Shells began bursting inside the trees, churning the smoking earth. The German artillery batteries would 'shoot in' the assault – firing until the Leopards and panzergrenadiers were almost on top of the enemy's defensive positions.

Willi von Seelow glanced at the setting sun and shook his head in dismay. Although he was sure the brigade's attack was powerful enough to shove the Poles out of the woods and back another few kilometers toward Wroclaw, he knew it wouldn't tear a lasting hole in the Polish lines. It was too late for that. Disentangling the intermingled panzer and panzergrenadier battalions, evacuating their casualties, and refueling and rearming their surviving vehicles would take hours – especially in the confused darkness under the trees.

The German and French offensive was bogging down, blunting itself in a series of head-to-head clashes with an increasingly experienced and prepared enemy.

JUNE 9 – 5TH MECHANIZED DIVISION, NEAR SRODA SLASKA

Flashes pulsed in the black early morning sky. The Germans were shelling the Polish battalions forming a new line just west of the city.

Maj. Gen. Jerzy Novachik stood in the tall grass beside the two-lane road, watching the remnants of one of his battle groups limp by. Every vehicle showed signs of damage – scarred by shell fragments and blackened by flame. Ambulances interspersed with the retreating Bradleys and M1s carried the worst of the wounded toward Wroclaw's hospitals. Other injured men, still able to fight or just too stubborn to quit, stayed with their comrades. A third of those who had gone into battle were dead – trapped in burned-out tanks or torn apart in smoking shell craters.

More tanks and fighting vehicles lumbered past the stumbling, weaving column, heading for the front.

These gallant soldiers had held the enemy long enough for reinforcements to show up. Other units of Novachik's division were coming in piecemeal – delayed by EurCon air attacks and the refugees flooding all northern and eastern roads out of Wroclaw. Each new force joined the battle as soon as it arrived.

The general's bushy eyebrows came together as he frowned. His troops were slowing the enemy advance, but they couldn't stop it. There were too many German and too many French tanks and guns pouring across the frontier. Trying to hold them back with three battered Polish divisions was like trying to hold back the tide with a few schoolchildren armed with buckets and shovels.

EurCon's growing air superiority only made things worse.

Novachik had watched French and German warplanes and helicopters bombing and strafing his men all day – working back and forth along his lines with apparent impunity. Where the hell, he wondered bitterly, was his nation's own vaunted air force?

JUNE 10 – 11TH FIGHTER REGIMENT, WROCLAW, POLAND

'*Porucznik! Porucznik!* Lieutenant! Lieutenant!'

Someone was shaking Tadeusz Wojcik's shoulder, dragging him out of a soft, warm blackness. Awareness came flooding back, like the memory of a particularly bad nightmare. He realized he had been asleep in the pilot's quarters and that it was time to get up for another mission. The voice was still speaking, but it took him several seconds to decode the orderly's Polish.

He had to think for a moment before he could even say '*Dziekuje*,' or thank you. Normally his Polish was very good, but right now he was just too groggy. Even speaking coherent English would have been a chore. After five days of three or even four combat missions a day, four hours' crew rest didn't refresh him – it barely took the edge off his fatigue.

The corporal took a moment to make sure the *porucznik*, or first lieutenant, was fully awake, then went on to his next victim.

Tad's watch read 3:04, but he resolutely dragged himself out of bed. He had a mission scheduled for this morning. Right now, just moving took an effort. Sitting in an ejection seat and flying at high g-levels day after day had given him a sore back and behind. Lying deep in sleep for four hours allowed everything to stiffen up, so that now on waking he felt like he'd been beaten up.

The day's flying would only make that worse. He could expect to be in the cockpit for eight to twelve hours today, if he lived that long. And survival was high on Tad's priority list.

He was proving very good at that. His skills had been honed to a razor's edge since that first night battle in the sky over Hungary. He had eight kills to his credit now. Most were attack aircraft of one kind or another, but there were German Fulcrums and French Mirages hanging from his belt as well. Still, the flying, always at the edge of his skill and endurance, drained him.

A cold shower helped clear his head, but it couldn't touch the deep core of fatigue that left him aching and bone-weary.

When he came out, a TV in one corner of the deserted commons room was on, as it had been when he fell into bed. It was tuned to CNN. Tad heard the American anchorman speak of 'anguished appeals from Warsaw and Prague for immediate military aid.'

The journalist's words irritated him, although he wasn't quite sure why. They were probably a fair statement of the desperate situation his adopted homeland found itself in. Maybe he just didn't like hearing about it. Not in such dispassionate tones from a man thousands of miles away and well out of danger.

Buttoning his tunic, he stepped out of the barracks into the chilly, predawn blackness – headed for the airfield's operations center.

The building was still under repair. Ground crewmen working under dim, shielded lights were busy shoveling dirt away from one bomb-damaged side, while heavy equipment stacked concrete slabs against other parts of the bunker. Some of the damage had been inflicted by the EurCon stealth cruise missile attack more than a week before. Some was more recent.

Two nights ago, enemy planes had raided the base – this time hitting the runways with Durandals while they targeted buildings and aircraft shelters with laser-guided bombs and missiles. Four aircraft had been destroyed on the ground. Another had been shot down trying to defend the field.

Luckily the Russians who had first constructed the base had built well. The thick layer of earth covering the ops bunker had been blown off, and its outer walls had been weakened, but the officers inside were still in business, planning missions and assigning pilots to fly them. Of course, stacked runway sections and sandbags couldn't offer as much protection as reinforced concrete. One more direct hit would finish them.

The same repair crews working on the bunker had put the damaged runways back in service within hours. Even the lost shelters were not too terrible a hardship, either. There were fewer and fewer planes and pilots to fill them.

The raid had been expensive for the enemy as well. Wroclaw was well defended by American-made Hawk and Patriot missiles and Soviet-made antiaircraft guns. Tad glanced at a shadowed, angular mound of metal piled between the two runways. Only the shape of the outer wing panels and part of a Maltese cross identified the wreck as the remains of a German Fulcrum. The sight cheered him up in a grim sort of way.

The inside of the ops bunker was alive with activity. He headed for the briefing room first, which was now also doubling as a cafeteria. It was half-filled with pilots and other squadron personnel, listening as the intelligence officer briefed them on the night's developments. Most were eating, and they all had lined, drawn faces.

The smell of food made his stomach growl, and Tad spotted a side table piled high with coffee, juice, sandwiches, and *kolduny*, meat turnovers. As he loaded up a paper plate, he listened to the brief.

' . . . SAM battery at Legnica is being reinforced to battalion level, so it's dangerous to approach the place within thirty kilometers, except at low altitudes.'

'Kostomloty fell last night.' Reacting to the looks on the faces of his audience, the intelligence officer tried to reassure them. 'It's one step closer to us, but the army hadn't really expected to hold the town for long, and they made EurCon pay for it.'

Maybe so. But that put the French and German spearheads only twenty-five kilometers from the edge of the city.

'Remember, our strategy is to delay them and inflict as many casualties as we can. With luck we can hold on until Tad's old friends can make it over here.'

Wojcik, sitting down as he chewed on a *kolduny*, shrugged and tried to look hopeful. He had taken a lot of ribbing, some of it with a sharp edge, over the apparent slowness of the American and British response to the invasion. All the press statements and proclamations in the world from the White House and 10 Downing Street weren't going to stop the French and German troops surging deeper and deeper into Poland.

'The general staff confirms that we are still a major objective of the EurCon advance. If they can take Wroclaw, they cut Polish-Czech communications, take a big step toward Warsaw, and interfere with the operations of Poland's best fighter regiment.'

Scattered laughter and smiles showed there was still some spirit in the assembled pilots.

A sergeant nudged his elbow. 'Lieutenant, Major Broz is ready for you.'

Carrying his food, Wojcik left the room, with the briefer's words trailing after him into the crowded hallway. Nodding to those he knew, Tad edged through the press into a room marked 'Mission Planning.'

Broz, the first squadron's operations officer, sat at one of four desks crowded into a room meant for two. Another pilot was just standing up as Tad walked in, and the major tiredly waved him into a seat. The remains of breakfast were mixed with maps, printouts, an F-15 flight planning handbook, and rather ominously, a 9mm automatic pistol being used as a paperweight.

'It's a solo mission for you first, Wojcik,' Broz announced. 'Air-to-ground along the A4 Motorway, two-thirds of the way to Legnica.'

As he spoke, he handed Tad a packet containing the mission profile, radio code card, and the other information he would need.

Although the Eagle was designed as an air-to-air fighter, it still had a respectable ground attack capability – at least in daylight and clear weather. Thankfully the weather was clear, because the Polish Air Force was throwing every aircraft it had, even trainers and squadron hacks, against the advancing EurCon columns. There were plenty of air-to-air targets, too, but killing airplanes wouldn't stop the tanks closing on Wroclaw.

Tad remembered the intelligence officer's briefing. Wroclaw's capture would shatter Polish-Czech communications. And that would put an end to any hope that Czech troops could move north to reinforce Poland's outnumbered army.

He scanned the mission profile, noting that his Eagle would be carrying an interesting mix of ordnance. The F-15 was loaded with twelve Russian-designed KMGU cluster bombs on two MERs, multiple ejection racks, along with American-built Sidewinder and Sparrow missiles for air-to-air combat.

The old Soviet Air Force had designed all its ordnance with NATO-standard bomb lugs, just like their planes' fuel and electrical fittings. Intended to let them swiftly take over NATO airfields in time of war, it now allowed western- and eastern-bloc weapons to be used together. It was another of this war's many ironies.

Broz finished talking and nodded him toward the door. It was time to fly.

Back in the open air, Wojcik hurried toward the fragment-scarred rows of squat, concrete aircraft shelters. He passed by other pilots and other enlisted men on the way. The ground crews looked even worse than he felt.

At least standing regulations required flight personnel to get a certain amount of sleep. Maintenance techs and the other ground staff basically worked until they fell over, and they were then allowed a little rest before being wakened again.

He grimaced. The base was damaged, they were losing aircraft, and everyone was on the edge of exhaustion. Poland's ground forces were 'regrouping' to meet the unexpected EurCon invasion. If they didn't regroup soon, Tad thought, it would be too late.

He found his shelter, and was relieved to see a well-maintained, if worn, Eagle loaded and ready. The crew chief, a stocky, unshaven staff sergeant, still had enough energy to salute and report the aircraft ready.

Tad took his time going over the plane. Tired people make mistakes and mistakes kill pilots. So he looked carefully for unfastened access panels or improperly mounted bombs and missiles. He needed help from the staff sergeant as well, to check the arming wires on the unfamiliar Russian ordnance.

He climbed up into the F-15's cockpit, checking the upper wing surfaces at the same time. With a twinge in his nether regions, he settled himself into the ejector seat and ran through his checklist while he hooked up. Satisfied, he hit the starter and waited while the engines spooled up, bringing life to the plane's instrument panel.

With both engines roaring, Tad took his Eagle through the shelter's open armored doors and out onto the runway. He already had clearance for a fast taxi and takeoff as soon as he was outside. Poland's aircraft were more vulnerable on the ground than in the air.

Even fully loaded with bombs and missiles, the Eagle still seemed to leap skyward, and some of his fatigue seemed to stay behind on the ground.

Turning north, Tad cruised at low level until he picked up the Oder River valley, then turned northwest to follow it, dropping lower. By doglegging north along the valley, he planned to avoid the enemy troop concentrations deployed across the A4 Motorway. Frontline troops were never easy targets. Dug in, concealed, and ready for trouble, the odds were against him. His primary target for this mission was further back, one half hour's flying time from Wroclaw – most of it spent on this detour down the Oder.

He hugged the water, now silvered as the sun rose, constantly moving his head as he scanned his instruments and the sky. EurCon aircraft did not have complete air superiority, but the numbers were usually on the wrong side for the Poles, and the last thing Tad wanted now was a dogfight. Not only would he have to jettison his air-to-ground ordnance and abort the mission, but he might lose, and Poland needed every plane it had. Standing orders repeated by Broz this morning, were that he was to 'preserve' his aircraft, and coincidentally himself, so that they would both survive to fight tomorrow, and the day after that.

The river started to curve around to the west, as it approached Brzeg Dolny, a sleepy river town that was still in Polish hands. The waypoint cue on his HUD shifted, and Tad carefully nudged the throttles forward a little.

Banking left and climbing out of the valley, Wojcik turned southwest, skimming over alternating patches of forest and farms with freshly planted crops. The land was all thickly settled, and he could see the invasion's impact on the roads. Orderly groups of military vehicles, presumably Polish, since they weren't shooting at him, moved to the west. Refugees, dark, ragged shapes on foot or packed into heavily loaded cars, fled to the east.

He thought of his grandparents, and wondered if they had looked like that in those first terrible days of World War II, trying to flee a merciless enemy. His hand tightened on the F-15's stick. Now his mother and father faced the same dangerous, heart-wrenching trek.

His parents lived, or had lived anyway, in Wroclaw. His last communication with them had been a hurried phone call three days before. Life in the city was difficult, his father had said, but not as hard as what you are doing. Tad knew that wasn't true. Doing one's duty was easy. Especially when it meant fighting Germans.

Then they asked him if they should stay or go, a sensitive question to ask one of the city's defenders. With his mind full of bleak situation briefings, Tad had told them to go – erring on the side of caution. Now they were somewhere on the road, heading to the east and uncertain safety in Warsaw.

Anger built up, but he tried to channel it, turning it into concentration on the job at hand. Maybe he could buy his mother and father a little more time to reach a safe haven, if any place in Poland could truly be said to be safe. He only wished his parents had kept their American citizenship so he could have wangled them a place on one of the evacuation flights back to the States.

The halfway point on his southwest leg was the road from Sroda Slaska and Wroclaw. According to this morning's intelligence summary, the city was still in Polish hands, so he'd planned to pass west of the town. The summary was out of date.

As his Eagle sped past the outskirts of town, the right side of his cockpit came alive. The radar track, and launch warning lights all lit up at virtually the same moment. The enemy radar signal showed dead ahead.

Tad looked up from the panel and saw two dark shapes arrowing toward him, rising on billowing white columns. Radar-guided SAMs!

Reflexively he turned hard left – almost too hard. The F-15's nose dipped toward the ground, and he hurriedly corrected, adding more throttle. At the same time, one thumb punched both the chaff and flare buttons. He wanted chaff in the air to confuse the enemy launcher's radar, and he wanted flares spewing out behind him in case the SAMs had a backup IR tracker.

The F-15's nose spun to port, and Tad put the missiles on his right rear, about five o'clock. He couldn't outrun them, but the Eagle had a smaller radar signature from that angle, and if he could just get beyond the horizon of the ground-based radar guiding them, the missiles should lose him.

He pushed the throttles forward to full military power, and even lowered the jet's nose a little – diving lower still. Flying so low was hazardous in this built-up maze of power lines and buildings, but it beat getting his tail blown off. He fought the urge to crane his head back and see where the missiles were. At this altitude, taking his eyes off his flight path for that long would be suicide.

The Eagle built up speed quickly, although the drag and weight of the bombs prevented him from going supersonic. Hopefully it was enough. Wojcik counted the seconds, trying to figure ranges and speeds. And the threat display went dark, just as quickly as it had lit up. Pulling up a little and throttling back, he risked a glance behind him.

The Eagle's bubble canopy gave him an excellent view to the rear, and he could see the two smoke trails, curving smoothly upward, angling off to the left. He was clear. Some bastards on the ground had tried to kill him and they'd failed.

Tad let out his breath and turned back toward his target, following the steering cues on the HUD in front of him. He made a mental note to warn intelligence that EurCon's forward units were now past Sroda Slaska.

A small village loomed ahead – surrounded by fields and small orchards.

It was time. He changed his weapons settings, selecting the cluster bombs instead of the Sidewinder he always had prepped in transit. As he double-checked his settings, the cockpit threat receiver lit up again, this time warning him about a search radar probing somewhere up ahead. He knew the signal's source, the SAMs guarding the Cicha Woda River crossing.

Retreating Polish troops had dropped the highway bridge as EurCon forces approached, but enemy engineers had quickly rigged a replacement across the narrow river. But that wasn't his target. Pontoon spans were easily replaced.

Instead, Wojcik was going to hit the traffic waiting to cross that pontoon bridge. No temporary bridge could be as efficient as the original span, so the area's already-crowded roads were backed up with every type of enemy vehicle. The military term for the traffic jam was 'chokepoint.' The drivers stuck in it probably had their own, considerably more profane terms.

Tad pushed the nose down once again, taking his plane from a hundred meters high to twenty. The radar warning signal went away. Whether they'd shut down or simply lost him, he didn't know. He was now masked by the surrounding terrain, which was the only reason any sane pilot would want to fly this low. He stayed low, holding his breath but glad to have it.

Skimming over plowed fields, he shot through a gap in the treeline praying that there weren't any power lines strung in front of him. Still, he'd risk running into wires rather than exposing his plane to SAMs or flak. Now Tad ignored the landscape in front of the Eagle. Even throttled back, all he could see was a streaked blur. Instead, he gauged his height by looking out to the side, where his eyes could fix on objects in the near and middle distance.

Trees, houses, and fields flashed past and vanished astern. Flying this low was somehow exhilarating and terrifying at the same time. Not even the wildest roller-coaster ride could compare. Although he tried to look at the steering cues on his HUD occasionally, he dared not risk a look at the map display. Instead, he relied on memorized landmarks and mental calculations to plan ahead. Things were going to start happening very quickly.

Suddenly a cluster of buildings at a crossroads passed underneath and he was at the IP – the initial point for his bomb run. Gladly shedding the hair-raising safety of nap-of-the-earth flight, he throttled to full military and climbed, turning slightly to line up with the road ahead. He set the chaff and flare dispenser to automatic.

His F-15's nose had barely come up when the warning receiver lit up again, every light and warning buzzer sounding one right after the other. The EurCon air defenses were ready and waiting for him. He ignored the sounds, instead concentrating on the motion of the aircraft and his carefully planned attack maneuver.

As the fighter's nose popped up, it blocked his view of the target area. Tad gently pressed the stick to the right and rolled his airplane inverted, so that the terrain was laid out in front of and over him.

He easily spotted the Cicha Woda River and the A4 Motorway running east to west, crossing it. The wreckage of a concrete span lay to one side, and he could see the gray-green pontoon bridge next to it, with raw cuts in the earth embankment on either end where heavy engineering vehicles had bulldozed and scraped ramps down to the river.

The bridge and the road west were lined with trucks, personnel carriers, tanks, and every kind of military transportation. Tad could see soldiers jumping from truck cabs and scattering in all directions, but tracers were still rising from all along the road. Every vehicle with a machine gun was firing at him.

More tracers floated toward him from a flak battery deployed on the south side of the highway. Oddly enough, the enemy ground fire didn't seem to be bothering him too much, either. Combat had taught him to spend more time worrying about the dangers he could control, evade, or defeat. Flak was too random. If one of those glowing balls arcing skyward had his number on it, so be it. There wasn't much he could do about it.

His HUD said he was high enough, and pulling the stick hard to the left, Tad quickly rolled wings level and a little nose-down. The F-15 straightened out at two hundred meters high – just above minimum safe height for his cluster bombs. He felt his speed building up.

His concentration was completely fixed on lining up on the mass of enemy materiel in front of him. He noted the ground fire, gray puffs and tracers more intense than before. Now it was starting to worry him, and fractions of a second passed like years as symbols crawled across his HUD and the ground rippled past beneath him. He had to hold a steady course. If he jinked, he'd miss.

The bomb line shortened to a dot in the center of his windscreen and Wojcik pressed the weapons release. Cluster bombs dropped from the ejector racks at quarter-second intervals, fell a hundred meters, then split apart, showering the enemy with five-pound antitank bomblets. Over five hundred of the deadly spheres rained down onto a box fifty meters wide and three-quarters of a kilometer long.

The area below him erupted in small explosions. Dust kicked up by each blast quickly obscured his view. Small red flashes lit the inside of the dust cloud. While the bomblets were relatively small, each one could destroy a tank or any other vehicle it landed on. Each explosion also sent deadly fragments slicing in all directions.

The stores panel showed the last bomb gone, and the Eagle accelerated again, freed of their drag and three-ton weight. The road ahead of him was still full of German and French equipment, though. Deviating from the attack plan, Tad lowered the F-15's nose and pressed the gun trigger, hammering the stalled column with 20mm fire. He had to slow the enemy down, to kill as many of them as humanly possible. He held the run as long as he could, but finally had to break off as his altitude dropped dangerously low.

He banked hard right and kept his nose on the horizon. Although it was a dangerous companion, the cluttered landscape was turning into a familiar friend. Automatically he reset the gunsight and computer from air-to-ground to air-to-air mode, selecting Sidewinder. He was now ready to defend himself, though he hoped he wouldn't have to.

He ran north at high speed, then angled to the northeast, over flat farmland and small villages. Occasionally he saw a burned patch on the ground or a cluster of vehicles where none should be.

The HUD cues changed, and he throttled back to cruise, turning carefully to the southeast. A minute's run at afterburner had put him twenty-five kilometers away from the scene of his attack, and hopefully his victims had reported him fleeing to the north. Now his turn toward base should evade any pursuers. He eased up to the relatively safe altitude of one hundred meters. At economical cruise, he was only a few minutes from Wroclaw.

The symbols on the HUD were just stabilizing when the right side of the instrument panel lit up again. Sparing a glance down from the blurred landscape ahead, Tad saw two bearings on his radar warning receiver, with the legend 'RDX/Rafale' next to each one. Almost as soon as they appeared, they changed, with the track warning light illuminated. Two of EurCon's most advanced fighters were in the air and they knew right where he was.

His chest tightened, and almost without thinking he accelerated to full afterburner, pointing the F-15's nose straight at the fighters. He energized his own radar, not really expecting to see anything, and was rewarded with little more than a few flickering echoes across the scope. The Rafale was not a 'full stealth' design, but it had a reduced radar cross section. Even if anyone was lucky enough to get a lock on one, its powerful radar jammer could easily break the tenuous hold.

But Tad had expected that. Ever since that first embarrassing mock dogfight with a Rafale, he'd put a lot of mental energy into developing the tactics he'd need to take them on and win. Lining his aircraft's nose up on the enemy fighters, he also angled it down, back toward the ground. With the speed of long practice, he set up his weapons panel.

He watched the HUD cues carefully, smoothly trading altitude for airspeed. Tad knew his maximum speed in this load configuration, and he also knew the range of the French Mica missile, about fifty kilometers. He counted the seconds, hoping that the French radars would have trouble sorting him out of the ground clutter. The French pilots, not feeling threatened, might take a few extra moments to set up their attack. After all, they might reason that a plane on the deck, running fast, was probably trying to evade – its pilot too busy and too frightened to strike back effectively.

Tad was forced to divide his time between the HUD, the threat warning display, and the earth racing by below him. The track warning was still illuminated, the missile light still dark. Wojcik pressed the chaff release twice, although he was pretty sure it wouldn't help. It didn't. The French radars stayed locked on.

Now! Tad pulled back on the stick, hard. He was braced for the g-forces, but the crushing sensation grew and grew until the edges of his vision grayed out and his breathing was no more than a shallow pant. His HUD danced with squiggling lines and symbols. The g-meter showed seven point something.

A glowing box suddenly appeared on the glass in front of him. He eased off on the stick and guided the plane's nose up until the box was inside a large circle – the vulnerability cone, a visual cue showing the area where his missiles were most effective. He was now going almost straight up, using the raw power of the Eagle's big turbofans to maneuver vertically as well as horizontally. The Rafale's largest radar cross section was from above or below, and his radar had finally found enough return at that angle to get a lock.

The instant the cueing box passed into the circle, Tad pressed the trigger, and was rewarded with a roar and a plume of smoke in front of him as a Sparrow missile raced skyward, almost straight up.

Even as the instruments confirmed a valid launch, Tad thumbed the weapons selector button on his stick. Lettering on the lower left corner of his HUD changed from 'AIM-7' to 'AIM-9' and without waiting for a tone, he fired a Sidewinder. His radar was still guiding the Sparrow as it accelerated to almost Mach 4. It wouldn't be long now.

He climbed through the expanding trails of the two missiles, searching for the enemy fighters. The smoke billowed across his canopy, sometimes blocking the area in the sky enclosed by the HUD box. He concentrated on keeping it at the center of his windscreen, and risked a glance down at the radar. The two fighters were high, almost twelve thousand meters. Still, the Sparrow should be there in a few more seconds. Just a few more . . .

The box disappeared. Maneuvers, jamming, chaff, it didn't matter how the French fighter had shaken off his radar lock, but without it the chance of a Sparrow hit went way down. Tad shifted to boresight mode, centering the radar antenna and pouring radiation into the space in front of the F-15's nose. Nothing. The Rafales had vanished. He peered into the windscreen. Where were they? Had they split up? If they'd moved too far to one side . . .

The launch warning light on the threat display commanded his attention, and Tad craned his neck right. A white spear sped from his four o'clock straight for him. Shit!

Banking hard left, Tad abandoned the Sparrow. Split seconds counted now. Breathing in pants to fight the g-forces, he put the incoming enemy missile at his eleven o'clock, triggered more chaff, and sent the Eagle into a corkscrew maneuver designed to eat up the missile's energy in a series of last-minute course corrections.

The world spun around Tad's canopy, and the shifting g-forces pushed him around the cockpit. Out the corner of one eye, he saw two white lines drawn against the blue sky. One, his Sparrow from the size of the trail, went straight up until it faded from sight, but the other ended in a dirty-gray puff of smoke, with smaller trails extending downward from it.

In the midst of his jinking, Tad smiled grimly. The Sparrow had missed, but the Sidewinder he'd fired had locked onto the Rafale's engines when it maneuvered to avoid the first weapon.

A shattering explosion rocked the Eagle, almost stunning him. Tad's head rang, and a sharp pain behind his eyes made him afraid his neck had been broken. It sounded like someone was throwing rocks against the side of the plane. He'd been hit! Already violently maneuvering, the sudden shock threw his fighter out of controlled flight, tumbling toward the earth.

Fighting to keep control of the aircraft, he felt it fall out of the right bank onto its back and start to spin. Desperately Tad throttled back and tried to right the plane, unsure if his controls even functioned. The cockpit was a mass of red lights and flickering numbers. His vision blurred, and the jarring ride sent flashes of pain into his head.

Either by accident or as a result of his efforts, Tad found himself with the sky above and the ground beneath him. Quickly, lest the opportunity pass, he stomped hard on the right rudder pedal and pushed the stick forward, hoping he still had enough altitude to recover.

Wincing at the pain, he craned his neck up and back, searching for the surviving Rafale. The sky seemed clear, and his threat display was empty. Maybe the Frenchman had a more pressing engagement elsewhere. Or more likely the enemy pilot had seen the Polish F-15 spinning out of control and assumed his missile hit was a kill.

The horizon steadied, and Tad took a moment to find out where he was and where he was headed. He turned southeast, heading back for the airfield, now only twenty or so kilometers away. His Eagle's response was unusual, though, with the bank almost turning into another spin. He had to apply positive pressure to hold the nose up and keep the plane from turning to port. He'd taken the blast on that side. Drag from damaged, fragment-torn skin was certainly pulling the aircraft in that direction.

With the F-15 in moderately controlled flight, he quickly scanned his cockpit instruments. The nav system was out, as were the stores panel and the artificial horizon. Port engine rpm were down by over fifty percent, and the turbofan also had an elevated tailpipe temperature. Some of the warhead fragments must have sliced into that engine. He was lucky they hadn't connected with one of the fans. Time to shut it down, he thought, no questions asked.

As he pulled back on the port throttle with his left hand, he advanced the starboard engine power a little more. When he checked his fuel status, he saw that his port wing tank was empty. More holes.

That was bad. Even though each had been only a few minutes long, those two earlier afterburner blasts had already taken a big bite out of his fuel supply. Losing what was left in the port tank wasn't going to help. The gauge showed twelve hundred pounds remaining. If he could set the jet down fast, that should be enough. But getting the Eagle down fast might be a big if.

Intending to request a straight-in approach, he called the Wroclaw tower.

The base ground controller answered instead, using the tower frequency. 'Zebra One, divert to Lask. We are under artillery barrage.' The controller's rapid words, almost slurred in his haste, also carried fear. 'We've already lost the tower, Zebra, and now our SAM batteries are being hit. Wroclaw is closed!'

Tad felt panic rising inside, and controlled it only with effort. How had the enemy moved that close? A breakthrough? It didn't matter – certainly not to him right now. Lask was 150 kilometers to the east. He couldn't make it anywhere but the base. He was running out of both gas and airplane.

'Negative divert, Ground.' He checked his instruments one more time, making sure. 'Insufficient fuel and aircraft damage. I don't know how much longer I can stay in the air. Is the runway clear?' Tad didn't mention the pain in his head. He wasn't bleeding, and seemed to be able to fly. Besides, he thought darkly, he'd probably be killed trying to put the half-wrecked F-15 down anyway.

'Affirmative, Zebra. No damage yet. There's no other traffic, and you are cleared for a straight-in approach. Good luck.'

Tad clicked his microphone switch twice, then concentrated on flying the aircraft. He retrimmed it, since it was taking even more pressure to keep the nose up and straight.

He scanned the countryside. Tad knew the Wroclaw region well, but he couldn't see the airfield. A gray-brown haze hung over the whole area, and only long practice let him make a visual approach.

Finally, at half the normal distance, he spotted the long, friendly ribbon of runway. He dropped his landing gear, and was pleasantly surprised to see three green lights on the panel. Gear down. He started to ease down the flaps, but the Eagle almost fell out of control to the left again. Something was jammed or damaged on the port side.

There was no need to throttle back. With one engine and a port yaw, he was already at minimum flying speed.

Although his attention was on the runway, Tad could see the rest of the base. Bustling, if battered, when he'd left just over an hour ago, it was now deserted, with no sign of human life or other aircraft. Standard procedure when an air base came under ground attack was to evacuate immediately. He'd even participated in drills where they'd moved the entire regiment. But this wasn't a drill. The 11th Fighter Regiment was gone. He felt suddenly adrift.

As he watched, two shells landed near the hangars. Earth fountained up, spilling away from bright orange balls of flame. The explosions were audible even over the noise of his jet engine.

His lineup was good, and Tad nursed the damaged F-15 down gently. He had twice the runway he needed, so he took his time. He had a good descent rate. There was only a little crosswind. Nothing fancy, Tad thought, just plant this thing and taxi quickly under cover.

The runway's rough, gray surface appeared under his wheels, and he smoothly brought Eagle down. He felt the first touch of the wheels as they kissed the concrete, then pulled up gently to flare and slow the airplane.

A loud bang threw the Eagle off course, and Tad tried desperately to stop the sudden turn as his fighter spun to port. For an instant, he thought an artillery shell had landed nearby, but then he realized that his left tire had blown. Damaged by missile fragments, it had shredded itself under stress, and the port landing gear was now nothing more than a steel pipe, dragging on the ground in a shower of sparks.

Wojcik instinctively chopped the throttle and rode the right brake hard. In the half-second it had taken for him to understand what had happened, the crippled Eagle had already completed a full circle and was starting on another, with no perceptible loss in speed. A horrible scraping, grating sound fed his fear.

The F-15's main gear strut, abused and maybe damaged itself, gave way, tearing out of the wheel well and taking part of the mechanism with it. His port wing tip dropped to the ground, tipping the plane over. Praying hard, Tad reached for the ejection handle and then stopped. With the wing dragging on the ground, the aircraft was slowing more rapidly. He decided to ride it out.

After another very bumpy half-circle, the Eagle finally stopped moving, surrounded in a cloud of what Tad hoped was dust and not smoke. He hit the canopy release, but it didn't work. The backup release, driven by a battery, did.

As the dust-streaked canopy bubble whined upward, he hurriedly disconnected his harness, g-suit, and microphone leads. He remembered to grab the maps and other papers in the cockpit, then squeezed out through the opening as it widened and dropped to the ground.

Tad's only thought was to get away from the still very flammable airplane, with its jet fuel and oxygen systems and missile warheads. He scrambled upright and started to run for the nearest shelter. Then he saw a GAZ jeep hurtling across the airfield, straight toward him.

It braked just a few meters short of him, and a technical sergeant he recognized, one of the regiment's maintenance staff, jumped out – grabbing a jerrican on the way. 'You all right, sir?'

When he nodded, still a little dizzy, the sergeant pointed him toward the jeep. 'Hop in, quick.'

Leaving Tad still standing in a daze, the maintenance tech ran toward the wrecked F-15. Pulling down the Eagle's built-in access ladder, he used it to climb up to the cockpit, and opened the jerrican. He sloshed gasoline over the seat and instrument panels, then splashed more onto the upper fuselage – as far as he could reach. Then he jumped down, still holding the open can.

More shells hammered the far side of the field, setting several buildings ablaze. Tad watched the sergeant's bizarre actions for about two seconds, uncomprehending. Then, as he realized what was happening, and where he was, he scrambled into the jeep, the pain in his head completely forgotten.

The maintenance sergeant took one step under the F-15's tilted wings, set the can down and deliberately tipped it over. Gasoline poured out, spreading across the runway beneath the plane.

Satisfied, the sergeant trotted back to the jeep, slid behind the wheel, and backed up a little further, angling upwind.

He drew and loaded a flare pistol.

Tad looked at the broken Eagle, sitting just off the runway. It had probably been almost a loss anyway, but the only reason to burn a plane was to prevent it from falling into enemy hands. German and French tanks must be close.

The sergeant's flare drew a straight, bright line from the pistol's muzzle to the fighter's forward fuselage. As it burst, the gasoline, already partially in vapor form, ignited in an orange-red cloud with an explosive whooph.

The maintenance tech already had the jeep turning and speeding away. 'We're evacuating, sir. All the flyable aircraft have already left. The rest of the regiment will be gone in a few hours. You're 1st Squadron, right?'

Tad nodded, then winced as his injured neck sent what felt like a red-hot nail stabbing into his skull.

'They're still here, over at the ops building.' Once away from the burning aircraft, the sergeant slowed the jeep from flat out to a merely breakneck pace. 'So how did your mission go?'

Among the artillery explosions in the background, a slower, deeper rumble ended in a boom. Tad looked back to see a ball of thick black smoke billow upward from his shattered aircraft.

He sighed, remembering the burning trucks and supply vehicles he'd left behind him at the Cicha Woda bridge. 'Good. Just not good enough.'

CHAPTER 21
Corridors

JUNE 11 – THE WHITE HOUSE, WASHINGTON, D.C.

Ross Huntington watched White House gardeners slowly working their way from flower bed to flower bed – weeding, trimming, and watering to restore and maintain beauty and order. The sight of so much peaceful labor seemed strange to him after spending so many hours following the war burning through northern and central Europe.

Especially a war that America and her allies seemed to be losing.

Poland's armies were retreating again, driven out of Wroclaw by superior French and German numbers and firepower. The little Czech and Slovak republics, hard-pressed themselves, had not been able to provide more than token assistance to their northern ally. And Hungary's soldiers had their hands full just fending off the relentless EurCon drive toward Budapest.

They all needed help, and soon.

Unfortunately neither the United States nor Great Britain could do much yet to meet those needs.

Ever since the first French stealth missiles slammed into Polish soil, the President and Britain's Prime Minister had been waging a campaign both in public and behind the scenes to broaden the coalition against EurCon and to win clear passage to the war zone. With decidedly mixed results, Huntington knew.

The Netherlands, torn between its free trade principles and the looming Franco-German military presence on its borders, had reluctantly opted for a wary neutrality. That wasn't likely to change – not with EurCon moving from victory to victory. Spain and Italy also seemed determined to stay on the sidelines, and he couldn't blame them very much for that. Neither had much to gain and both had much to lose in any wider European war.

To the north, the Danes had proved powerless to enforce neutrality in the skies over their own country. EurCon and allied jets had repeatedly clashed in Danish airspace without any challenge from Denmark's tiny air force. Sweden seemed content to patrol its own borders and issue stern warnings that all belligerents should leave its shipping unmolested. So far those warnings had been heeded.

Only Norway had sided with its traditional allies. And its decision came only after several days spent in futile efforts to mediate a peaceful settlement. Finally convinced that France and Germany could not be brought to their senses, the Norwegians had at last opened their airfields to U.S. and British warplanes. The first squadrons, F-15s and F-16s from the United States, were due to touch down in a matter of hours.

'Of course I understand your position, Madame Prime Minister.' The faintest hint of carefully concealed exasperation tinged the President's voice. 'But surely you can understand our need to mount a fully coordinated air and sea campaign as soon as possible.'

Huntington turned away from the Oval Office windows.

Right now the President was on a secure channel with Norway's Prime Minister, sorting out last-minute glitches over command authority. A State Department translator stood by on a separate extension, ready to interpret technical language. So far the young man's services hadn't been necessary. Brigitte Petersen spoke perfect English.

Apparently her reply was satisfactory, because the tension in the President's jaw eased slightly. His voice was considerably more cordial when he spoke again. 'Yes, I see . . . that just might work. Very well, I'll have my military people get in touch with your service chiefs and Defense Ministry to fill in the details. Thank you, Madame Prime Minister. Yes, good luck to us all.'

When America's chief executive hung up, he glanced at Huntington, shook his head, and showed his teeth in a brief, wry grin. 'Jumping Jesus, Ross. Sometimes I think waging coalition warfare is a hell of a lot harder than going it alone would have been. At least then I'd only have to wrestle with the Joint Chiefs, the Congress, the press, and my own staff.'

'True. Churchill or Roosevelt would probably have said the same . . .' Something sparked in Huntington's brain – the faint flickering of an idea. He fell silent, willing it to life.

'Yeah?' The President looked up at his longtime friend and adviser. 'C'mon, Ross, I've seen that look before. The last time I watched you draw four aces, as far as I remember.'

Huntington shrugged. 'Nothing so dramatic, I'm afraid. Just a sudden grasp of the obvious.'

'Like what?'

'That EurCon's just as much a coalition effort as we are – maybe more so. But we've all been talking and thinking like it was a giant French- and German-controlled monolith.'

The President stroked his jaw. 'Sure seems to be.'

'That's the operative phrase, "seems to be," ' Huntington argued. 'But what do we really know about the decision-making process over there? Were the other, smaller member states consulted about going to war? Are they willing to commit their own troops to it? There's still a lot we don't know about how EurCon works – or doesn't work.'

'What's your point, Ross?'

'That there may be openings out there to exploit – political or military. Fracture lines we could find and pry open.'

The President sat back in his big leather chair, absorbing that. Then he rocked forward and stabbed a finger at Huntington. 'Okay, you've sold me.'

'Then you'll have the State Department—'

'Nope.' The President shook his head and smiled again – the trademark grin that made him look years younger than he really was. It had been a long time since Huntington had seen it. 'We both know the Foggy Bottom boys have a real bad case of NIH syndrome, Ross.'

Huntington nodded. 'Not Invented Here' was a classic Washington problem. Sections of the federal government's bloated bureaucracy routinely dismissed ideas, proposals, and solutions that came from outsiders – no matter how sensible, practical, or cost-effective they were. 'Then who do you want to pull the answers together? The CIA? DOD?'

'I want you to handle this, Ross. You had the right hunch about how the Frogs blew up our LNG tanker when Quinn and his cloak-and-dagger pals were still scratching their heads. Hell, you were even right about my campaign themes and TV ads,' he joked. The President turned serious. 'It's your ball now. Run with it.'

JUNE 12 – NATIONAL SECURITY AGENCY, FORT MEADE, MARYLAND

The National Security Agency was one of the largest and most powerful of all U.S. intelligence organizations. Nearly forty thousand employees crowded its Fort Meade headquarters buildings, with others deployed at facilities around the globe. Charged with managing America's signals intercepts and code-breaking efforts, and with protecting the security of America's own classified communications and information, the NSA was also one of the most secretive.

So secretive, in fact, that Ross Huntington wasn't quite sure if the bland little man sitting across from him ever used his own name. The director of the NSA's National SIGINT Operations Center seemed the personification of anonymous officialdom. He had a sudden, whimsical vision of the man's own wife referring to him as 'my husband, the director.'

Certainly the fellow had a chilly, forbidding exterior – one that was on full display as he glanced back and forth between the White House letter with Huntington's credentials and the typed list of what he wanted. When he finished perusing them, he frowned. 'I don't see how I can help you, Mr. Huntington.'

The SIGINT Operations director picked up the list. He pursed his lips and read the key sentence aloud. ' "NSOC should immediately initiate a high-priority effort to collect and analyze diplomatic and other internal communications between the Confederation's smaller member states." ' He shook his head. 'My people are already extremely busy, as I'm sure you can imagine, Mr. Huntington. This project of yours would only absorb staff resources needed for other missions.'

He didn't say 'other, more important missions,' but the implication was clear.

'I would need direct orders from my own superiors before I could even consider such a drastic reshuffling of our priorities.'

Huntington nodded. He hadn't really expected enthusiastic cooperation from the start, but he'd wanted to give the man a fair chance first. He pulled out a three-by-five index card from his suit jacket's inside pocket and handed it across the desk. 'I suggest you call that number, sir. I think you'll find I have the authority you're looking for.'

The SIGINT director's eyebrows rose slightly when he glanced down at the card. The number had a prefix identifying it as a White House secure telephone. He looked up at Huntington, shrugged as if to show that even talking to an NSC staffer wouldn't faze him, and reached for his phone.

But his pale features grayed still more when he heard the voice on the other end telling him in no uncertain terms that he would 'cooperate fully with Ross Huntington or find yourself monitoring Tibetan radio broadcasts from somewhere in the Aleutian Islands.'

Huntington hid a grin. He'd thought that this might be necessary. Sometimes it helped to have the President himself in your court.

MINISTRY OF DEFENSE, MOSCOW

Alex Banich stood in the hallway outside Pavel Sorokin's office, waiting for the elevator with mounting impatience. How the Russians had ever hoped to conquer the world when they couldn't even keep their public buildings in good repair was beyond him.

He'd just come from another meeting with the rotund general supply manager. Ostensibly angling for another food contract from the ministry, he had really been aiming to pry out more information on Russian troop movements close to the Polish frontier. They could provide a vital clue to Russia's intentions in the conflict. Unfortunately Sorokin had turned him away empty-handed.

Banich frowned. The fat man's fear of his nation's revitalized internal security services was growing fast. If he kept pressing Sorokin so hard, the bureaucrat might decide it would be safer to turn in the man he knew as Nikolai Ushenko for espionage and take his chances with accusations of corruption and bribe-taking.

'Well, well, Mr. Ushenko. Come to visit us again?' A languid, arrogant voice made Banich turn around.

He recognized the lean, aristocratic officer instantly, remembering that chilling, unnerving meeting last October. A meeting that had come only days before Russia's civilian leaders 'handed over' the reins of government to their soldiers.

Col. Valentin Soloviev was one of Marshal Kaminov's top military aides. Reportedly he was also the man the marshal relied on for 'dirty' work of almost any kind – organizing executions, purging suspect officers, and the like.

Banich forced himself to smile. 'It's good to see you, Colonel.'

'Of course.' Soloviev arched a straw-colored eyebrow. 'And what brings you here, Mr. Ushenko? Business?'

Banich nodded politely. 'That's right. I'm trying to drum up a few more government contracts.'

'A merchant who wants to sell *more* of his goods at a loss? Interesting.' Soloviev stepped closer. 'You are a very curious specimen, Mr. Ushenko. Unique, in fact.'

The American kept his mouth shut. There wasn't any safe reply to the colonel's barely disguised probe.

Soloviev looked him up and down for a long moment. Then he smiled, but the smile didn't reach his cold gray eyes. 'I think you would be most unwise to keep haunting these halls, Mr. Ushenko. If I were you, I would pursue other, more profitable endeavors instead. Endeavors that do not involve Manager Sorokin or any other ministry officials. Some men I know, very unsympathetic men, are growing very interested in Manager Sorokin's hyperactive financial dealings. They are beginning to wonder what he is selling to reap such rich rewards. You understand?'

The elevator arrived.

When the doors shut on the tall Russian colonel, Banich breathed out in relief, conscious of having escaped with his cover still intact, if only just. Then he frowned, puzzled. Had Soloviev been trying to intimidate him – or to warn him? But why would one of Kaminov's top men give a damn about a Ukrainian merchant? He was still mulling that over when the elevator reached the ground floor. Well, warning or intimidation, the colonel's words locked him out of the Defense Ministry as surely as any padlock.

ROYAL NAVY FLEET COMMAND HEADQUARTERS, NORTHWOOD, LONDON

Surrounded by a brick wall topped with barbed wire, the Royal Navy's headquarters building was made from the same pale bricks. It wasn't a particularly impressive-looking structure, but looks do not always indicate importance.

Northwood, headquarters for the shrinking Royal Navy, now also held staffs from the U.S., Norwegian, and Polish navies. Although there had been some spare office space, the place was now packed to the point where it spilled over into several rented trailers parked on the grounds.

Vice Adm. Jack Ward's offices were definitely not in a trailer. In fact, he and his personal staff had been given some of the nicest rooms in the headquarters. Only Admiral of the Fleet Sir Geoffrey Stone, the Royal Navy's operational commander in chief, could lay claim to better. Not that the American really minded the First Sea Lord's more elaborate quarters. If he'd had his druthers, he'd still be out at sea. But orchestrating a coordinated air and sea campaign across all of northern Europe required more officers and communications gear than he could effectively cram aboard an aircraft carrier or missile cruiser.

At the moment, Ward sat in Northwood's freshly painted conference room, an elegant setting with wooden wainscoting and furniture that looked older than every man in it combined. Some of the room's furnishings had to have come from the admiralty building itself. As he listened to the morning briefing, he couldn't help wondering if Admiral Howe had planned his voyage to the rebellious American colonies at this very table two centuries before. A rare sense of tact had kept him from asking one of the British sea officers.

The news was bad. Losses were still high in the North Sea, and the chance of getting anything through to the Poles and Czechs was virtually nil.

Their latest attempt to break the blockade had come to a bloody end.

Two high-speed ships, loaded to the gunwales with badly needed ammunition and spare parts, and armed with jury-rigged defenses, had tried to use night and bad weather to run the gauntlet. Combined Forces Headquarters, the organization controlling U.S., British, and Norwegian units operating in the war zone, had supported the attempt with diversions, probing attacks, and one heavy strike against the EurCon base at Wilhelmshaven.

It had all been for naught. A German U-boat had ambushed and torpedoed both merchantmen near the Skagerrak, with a heavy loss of life. And although the American air attack on Wilhelmshaven had been a success, the moderate damage they'd inflicted could be repaired in a short time. Meanwhile the rest of the EurCon military machine was still intact.

Of course those two merchant ships hadn't represented the only allied link to eastern Europe. Cargo planes, flying circuitous routes under heavy escort, were managing to keep a trickle of supplies flowing. But, heavily tanked, and flying long-range, low-altitude flights, their payloads couldn't begin to meet Polish, Czech, and Hungarian needs. The ships he'd ordered through the gauntlet had carried a hundred planeloads.

With last night's disaster fresh in mind, Ward was confident that his proposal, reluctantly approved by all three governments, was the correct military decision. Until Combined Forces strength was greater, there would be no more resupply runs.

The only comforting part of the morning's brief was news about the steady supply of matériel coming from the United States. *George Washington* and her escorts were already under his operational control. A second carrier battle group, centered on *Theodore Roosevelt*, had sailed from Norfolk two days after the shooting started. It was due in range tomorrow. *Vinson*, in the yards when the crisis broke, was being hurriedly put back together. CINCLANTFLT had promised him she'd arrive in a little over a week.

The problem was that Poland might not last a week.

The briefer finished up with a long list of air force squadrons, supplies, and personnel arriving in the next twenty-four hours. *George Washington*, as previously arranged, was now covering British and Norwegian ASW patrols, as well as adding her own planes to the effort. Special training plans were under way, and arrangements for housing and security were proceeding swiftly, if not always smoothly.

When the briefing broke up, the room began clearing out. Lieutenant Harada, his flag secretary, worked his way through the bustle. He looked worried, and he was careful to speak softly. 'Captain Zagloba is waiting for you in your office, Admiral. He says it's urgent.'

Zagloba was the Polish naval liaison to Combined Forces Headquarters. He was also the senior Polish military man outside his country right now. Harada's tone implied trouble.

'Did he tell you why he wants to see me?'

'No, sir, but he looks upset.'

Ward nodded. If Harada's face was any indication, the Pole must be near exploding. He affected a relaxed air. 'Well, the captain has a lot to be upset about. Let's see what's on his mind.'

Ward's office, even more richly appointed than the conference room, was a comfortable place to wait, but that didn't seem to have soothed Capt. Kazimierz Zagloba in the slightest.

Tall and ramrod-straight, Zagloba's slender build had been exaggerated by more than a week of incredibly hard work and emotional stress. As an official representative of the Polish government, the officer took pains with his appearance, but a well-pressed uniform could not hide his gray, lined face or the dark circles under his eyes. Nor could it conceal an expression that mixed worry, grief, and anger.

Zagloba came to attention, then sat down when the admiral waved him to a chair. Ward sat down next to him in an antique chair old enough to have been used by Queen Anne herself.

The Pole got right down to business. 'Admiral, my government has asked me to pass on to you, in the strongest terms, our distress at your decision to end all sea resupply efforts.'

Ward paused for a moment and thought carefully before replying.

Zagloba must have taken his silence as a request for an explanation, because he quickly continued, 'We are aware of the great risks you have taken for us, and the losses you have suffered. We are grateful. We share your grief. Those who have died will be heroes in Poland forever.' Zagloba fought to control himself. 'But how will we honor them if my country is lost?'

His voice took on a pleading tone. 'We have done everything we can to protect your ships. We have also suffered losses. There is little more that we can do, but if there is anything that we have missed . . .'

Ward shook his head. 'No, Captain, your forces have reached their limits and gone beyond them. This is not a matter of one nation's actions or one nation's failures. Only a trickle is reaching you now . . .'

'And that trickle may be what keeps us alive.'

Ward answered firmly. 'No, sir, it won't. We don't have the resources to waste getting that trickle in. Many of the ships on the bottom of the Baltic might have been making their second trip by now. Those merchantmen were not expendable. And some of those lost cargoes cannot be replaced.'

He leaned forward, trying to use a tone that was both friendly and firm. 'Pushing more convoys into the Baltic is a losing game, Captain. We'd only be sending our forces into a small sea ringed with hostile bases. That's playing in EurCon's backyard, where we don't even have the firepower to hold our own.'

Ward shook his head. 'It isn't enough to kill individual French and German ships and aircraft. We have to go after those bases and pound them into the dirt. But doing that right means going in strong enough to really hurt them. Piecemeal efforts will only waste our strength without helping you in the slightest. Our forces are massing fast, Captain. When we're ready, I plan to give EurCon a body blow it won't forget and won't recover from.'

Zagloba sadly shook his head. 'That will not work if your attack comes too late, Admiral. If the French and the Germans keep advancing at their present rate, you may have to make an amphibious landing in Gdansk, because it will be held by the enemy.'

The admiral paused for a moment, thinking. 'Let me show you something, Captain.' Ward stood up and went over to his desk. He picked up an envelope and carefully removed a single sheet of paper. Then he handed it to Zagloba.

'This came in the diplomatic pouch yesterday. It's in the President's own hand. As you can see, it's a private communication, supporting my decision to stop the shipments and encouraging me to do what I think is right. More important, though, is what he says about halfway down, at the third paragraph. I think that's as clear a statement of American policy and determination as your government could ask for.'

Zagloba read it aloud. ' "The key to saving Poland and the rest of eastern Europe lies in your efforts to open the North Sea and the Baltic – by breaking the back of EurCon's naval forces. Without that open door, all the armed might in the world cannot prevail. Make your plans. I know you are not wasting time. The instant you are ready to go, attack, and attack hard. Once we grab hold of the Baltic we will never let go." '

Handing the note back to Ward, the Polish officer said softly, 'Poland has never doubted the sincerity or the strength of your efforts, Admiral.' He sighed. 'But I'm sure you can understand my government's growing concern.'

'I do.'

Ward came to a decision. He'd planned to make the announcement to his own officers first, but restoring Zagloba's confidence took precedence. 'All right, Captain, you've made your points. Now, what I'm about to tell you can't go any further than these four walls. Not to your own Defense Ministry. And especially not to your politicians. You'll have to calm them down without spilling the beans. Is that clear?'

Zagloba nodded. He knew how easily crucial operational security could be shattered by flapping lips in Warsaw or in London.

'Good.' Ward stood tall, looming over the Polish naval officer. 'We're only waiting for *Roosevelt*'s battle group and two more submarines. And then I'm going to give EurCon hell, Captain. "Counterweight" starts in forty-eight hours.'

CHAPTER 22
Storm Front

JUNE 13 – CONFEDERATION DEFENSE COMMITTEE, MINISTRY OF DEFENSE, PARIS

The Defense Ministry meeting room was furnished in a Baroque splendor more appropriate to Versailles or the Élysée Palace. Crystal chandeliers scattered light onto oil paintings and antique furniture. The centerpiece of the room was an almost impossibly long mahogany table, easily big enough to seat thirty people, with space at the sides of the room for their functionaries and attendants.

The room was about half-filled now, a mixture of middle-aged and older men in expensive suits and bemedaled uniforms. Weary of the spartan discomfort of the underground war headquarters at Rochonvillers, and wary of a prolonged absence from Paris, the French members of the Defense Committee had insisted on gathering here.

Now Adm. Henri Gibierge, a solid-looking, almost stout man, prepared to brief them on the naval situation. He was uncomfortable, fidgeting with his briefing book and maps. Although he was the navy's chief of staff, many of these men wielded far more power than he did. They could make or break careers with a single word.

Some of his nervousness came from facing these exalted figures. The rest arose from the news he had to bring them. A delicate, measured chime from a Baroque clock marked the hour and the start of the meeting.

Gibierge opened briskly. 'We believe that the Americans and British will move against us soon – sometime in the next few days. As our ground forces turn north toward Poznan, the Polish government must be issuing increasingly frantic appeals for immediate assistance. And with good cause. Once we take Poznan, two of their five largest cities will be in our hands. That should give the Poles ample reason to seek peace talks on our terms. That and a shortage of fuel, spare parts, and munitions. Intelligence estimates they have only two weeks' worth of war supplies remaining.'

'We heard that same estimate three days ago, Admiral. Have the Poles found themselves some new savior who can make diesel fuel out of water and tank shells out of stones?' Nicolas Desaix spoke softly, with just enough of an edge to cut into Gibierge's briefing. His acid tone invited, almost demanded, that the admiral respond.

Gibierge shook his head doggedly, knowing that Desaix despised servile cowardice even more than he disliked being contradicted. 'No, Foreign Minister. But the bad weather moving through Poland over the past forty-eight hours has reduced the tempo of all military operations, reducing consumption of critical supplies.'

Several of the uniformed men seated at the table nodded sagely.

Gibierge had many supporters in the ministry. He was a professional, heir to centuries of French military tradition. Rumor had it that he was an arrogant bastard, sure of his abilities, but a competent one nevertheless. The admiral shared Desaix's vision for France, but he was only one of thousands that did so.

'In addition, we believe the Poles have been stripping supplies and spare parts from their divisions still stationed along the border with Belarus. Naturally those expedients can only be taken so far. Poland's armed forces will soon reach the end of their logistical rope.'

He left carefully unmentioned the fact that the German and French divisions already deep inside Poland were experiencing their own supply problems. The admiral would let the generals take the heat for their own errors.

Impatiently Desaix nodded and waved the admiral on.

Gibierge returned to his notes. 'Present enemy strength includes the entire U.K.-based Royal Navy and Air Force, minus a few planes and small ships that we have already accounted for in action. In addition, the United States has now moved four combat wings and at least two carrier battle groups into the area.' He looked up. 'Human intelligence also indicates that advance elements of the American 101st Air Assault Division have arrived in England. Other, heavier American divisions are said to be mobilizing or heading for ports of embarkation.'

The admiral frowned. 'In short, gentlemen, if the enemy succeeds in opening the surface line of communication through the Baltic to Gdansk, we can expect American ground troops and supplies to pour in. Details are on page four of your briefing books.'

Several men glanced down at the books lying open in front of them. Each of the principals at this meeting had been provided with a bound notebook, labeled 'Top Secret' – full of maps, statistics, and other supporting information. No video or computer screens would intrude on the antique splendor of this room. The printed page was much more tasteful.

The rest looked at the admiral expectantly, waiting for him to go on.

'I believe that the Americans and the British, these so-called Combined Forces, have been husbanding their strength – hoarding their ships and planes until they can mount a strong challenge to our control of the Baltic.' He paused. 'That time has arrived.

'We have already seen the opening phases of their developing attack. British antisubmarine patrols have been strengthened in the North Sea. We know that American submarines have probed along our coasts. We have also seen a marked upsurge in enemy surveillance flights.' Gibierge was into the rhythm of the briefing now. Even Desaix seemed less impatient.

'When they do attack, we don't expect anything subtle. They don't need it. Their strike aircraft outrange ours. They have a greater variety of assets, including cruise missiles and stealth aircraft, which we will find very hard to stop. In some areas, such as submarines, they outclass us in both numbers and individual unit quality.' The admiral hammered each of his points home with a forceful, certain tone. It was essential that he make these men understand the difficulties facing the Confederation's naval and air forces. Only then could they be persuaded to make the difficult and dangerous decision needed for victory.

'There is little point in further Confederation naval operations in the North Sea. With enemy bases lining both its western and eastern shores, it has become a hostile body of water. We have already lost two of our conventional submarines there, for no appreciable return.

'Our real strength, though, is in the Baltic. Our own bases in Germany and our minefields have made the narrow waters impassable to Combined Forces shipping. Their transport aircraft must use long routes to avoid our fighters. The Americans and the British know that as long as we hold both the Baltic and the North Sea approaches, they cannot effectively resupply the Poles or their other eastern European allies.'

Gibierge paused again and looked about the room. Fixing his gaze on each man in turn, he said with certainty, 'Trying to clear the Baltic by destroying our air and sea bases there and along the North Sea coast is more than the obvious move. It is their only move.'

He shook his head grimly. He had chosen the next words carefully, but there was no way to make it sound good. 'And they will succeed.'

The admiral raised his voice a little, cutting off the anticipated questions and protests. 'The outcome is almost as certain as the answer to a simple mathematical equation. We have good intelligence about the enemy's capabilities, and we know the limits of our own resources. The Americans and British have the firepower, both in numbers and technology. The battle will take time, but when it is over we will have lost control of the Baltic. And with it, we will have lost any hope of bringing this war to a swift and victorious conclusion.'

Gibierge focused on Desaix. Of all the formidable men in this room, the Foreign Minister was the most formidable. The others would follow his lead. 'Working within those parameters, the naval staff can only see a single option: a massive, concentrated air attack on a single enemy carrier, just as it comes within striking range of our coastline. Destroying one of the two American carriers would significantly weaken their offensive. More important, it would deal a severe political blow to the United States.'

Desaix and the others nodded. With five or six thousand sailors and airmen aboard each carrier, the losses suffered in any sinking would certainly shake American public opinion. They might even turn it against continued intervention in Europe.

All right, Gibierge thought, he'd given them hope. Now to dash those hopes. 'Unfortunately this plan will not work, either – not as it stands.'

He could see them sitting up, puzzled, ready to object. 'Without long-range missiles with large warheads, any attack on an American carrier battle group would only result in serious aircraft losses for us – with very little chance of success. Soviet anticarrier tactics were based around missiles with ranges of five or six hundred kilometers, equipped with one-ton explosive warheads. Our air-launched weapons are shorter-range and carry warheads only a fraction of that size. So any strike we mount using conventional missiles would require too many planes operating too far from home with too few fighter escorts. America's Tomcat and Hornet interceptors would chop our attack force to ribbons before it could even fire.'

The admiral straightened to his full height and delivered his own bombshell. 'There is one way and *only* one way to assure success. We must use nuclear weapons.'

The room erupted in a chorus of agitated exclamations all mixed together. Words like 'impossible' and 'madness' emerged from the confused babble.

Gibierge waited patiently for Defense Committee members to settle down. As he had expected, so did Desaix.

The Foreign Minister fixed Gibierge in a steady gaze, then said, 'I would like to hear your reasoning, Admiral.' His tone made it clear that what he really meant was, 'This had better be good.'

Gibierge nodded his head. 'Of course, Minister.' He'd practically lived with the relevant numbers for the last week. 'Our longest-range conventional antiship missile is the ANL, with a range of one hundred eighty kilometers. It is a stealthy, supersonic seaskimmer, and a fearsome antiship weapon. One or two hits will sink a frigate or destroyer. Unfortunately we would need dozens of hits by those same missiles to cripple something as large as a carrier. Penetrating an American battle group's defenses and achieving that many hits would require at least fifty successful launches. Factoring in likely losses from the enemy's fighter interceptors, that means we would have to commit four full squadrons of aircraft just as missile carriers. That is too much of our air strength, leaving nothing for the vital supporting roles.

'Our supersonic, nuclear-tipped ASMP nuclear missile has a longer range and mounts a three-hundred-kiloton warhead. And one hit from one missile will obliterate an American aircraft carrier.' He stopped, letting the assembled commanders and politicians savor that.

'The military implications are clear, Admiral, but what about the risk of escalation? After all, the United States has its own nuclear forces – forces that far outmatch ours.' Desaix's measured tone held no criticism or approval. Gibierge guessed that the jury was still out.

He had expected the Foreign Minister's question. 'If we limit our attacks to naval targets in the open ocean, I do not believe that America will dare use its nuclear weapons against us. The risks are too high and the rewards are too few. Our air and sea bases are largely surrounded by civilian population centers. Striking them would mean killing tens of thousands of innocents. No American or British political leader could authorize such an attack – especially not if we threaten to retaliate in kind. Although our strategic nuclear weapons cannot reach American territory, we could devastate Britain – and they know it.'

The admiral saw Desaix and most of the other committee members nodding. America's space-based missile defenses couldn't hope to block all the ballistic missiles fired at such short ranges. Even if they could, the French Air Force possessed enough aircraft-carried nuclear bombs to turn its island neighbor into a radioactive slag heap. A few of the men in the room, mostly Germans, looked horrified at the turn their planning had taken.

Gibierge ignored them. 'If the strike works, and there is no reason to think it will not, we can repeat it against the other American carrier.' The admiral felt his own enthusiasm rising again. In his professional opinion, the limited tactical use of nuclear weapons at sea was the only realistic option. Any other course doomed his beloved navy to certain destruction. 'The loss of even one battle group will break the back of the Combined Forces offensive. And the Americans and British will not have time to make another effort before Polish and Czech munitions and fuel supplies are exhausted or they come begging for peace.'

From their expressions, Gibierge could tell that his reasoning had convinced many of the assembled military and political leaders. Desaix seemed to have made the same calculation, because he asked, 'When could you mount such a strike?'

'Both carriers are in the North Sea now, but they're well out of our range. I doubt we'll have a chance to attack until they begin closing our coast to launch their own air strikes on us.'

Desaix nodded. 'Very well.' He glanced at his colleagues before continuing. 'Although I'm sure we'll need further discussion before issuing any final approval, I suggest you begin making all the necessary preparations, Admiral.'

Guichy, Morin, and the others murmured their agreement. Given the French hold over the EurCon military command structure, further discussion would be mostly for form's sake only. Despite the alliance with Germany, the French nuclear arsenal remained under unilateral French control.

Gibierge felt a mixture of relief and tension pass though him. The prospect of using nuclear weapons was frightening, even to the man who proposed their use. He was relieved, though, because he really saw no other military solution to their situation.

Desaix had agreed quickly, almost too quickly, he thought. That was fine in this case, though, since he'd agreed with Gibierge. Desaix had a reputation for fast action, and for strong, straightforward action. This certainly fitted in that category.

'We will be ready long before the carriers are in striking range, sir,' the admiral answered.

Desaix continued. 'In the meantime, I suggest we order our commanders inside Poland to step up their attacks. Let's try to break the Poles before the damned Americans can intervene.' Nicolas Desaix turned to Michel Guichy. 'Tell your commanders to turn up the heat.'

JUNE 14 – GDYNIA AIR BASE, POLAND

'Alert!'

An incredibly loud klaxon pulled Tadeusz Wojcik out of his lounge chair and a sound sleep. He awoke to find every light on and every door in the operations building opening automatically.

Habit and adrenaline propelled him down the hall and out a pair of double doors onto the flight line. It was already light outside, though the sun wouldn't be fully up for another few minutes.

Pilots spilled outside into the crisp, clear morning air, jumping into waiting jeeps. Other figures, ground crews and antiaircraft gunners, ran for their posts as well.

Gdynia's shelters were crammed with aircraft, the compressed remains of much of Poland's fighter force. One of them was Tad's. His experience, and his nine kills, had entitled him to a new aircraft, one of the precious replacement aircraft flown in from the States. The F-15's exhausted ground crew had taken the time to put five German Maltese crosses and four French roundels under its cockpit, along with his name and new rank: captain.

Once the starter turbine was running, feeding power into his Eagle, Tad hooked up his radio leads. 'Ocean Leader, checking in.'

The other three pilots in his four-plane flight were also on the circuit within moments. They were all good men, following a well-rehearsed drill.

Tad hurriedly brought the fighter to life. His start-up procedure differed from that for a normal mission. In a scramble, time is everything. The F-15's inertial navigation system took five minutes to spin up, so rather than wait for it to stabilize, Tad would fly without it, getting steering commands from ground controllers. For an intercept over home territory, that and a magnetic compass should be good enough.

More voices from other flights checked in on the same frequency. Some were voices he recognized easily. Others, less familiar, belonged to pilots from the 34th Fighter Regiment. Polish air losses had been so severe that the higher-ups had combined the 34th and the 11th into one composite unit.

He was halfway through start-up when Major Dmowski, the 34th's operations officer, came on the line. 'Ocean, Razor, and Profile flights, forty-plus bandits inbound. Heavy jamming. Steer two eight zero magnetic after takeoff.'

Tad whistled to himself, letting his hands work while his brain absorbed the size of the raid. The biggest yet. There wouldn't be any lack of targets out there. The needles on two dial gauges in the middle of his instrument panel quivered and stopped rising. His tailpipe temperatures were stable.

He signaled the shelter crew. As they pulled the chocks and swung the armored door open, Wojcik gently advanced his throttles and started to taxi.

Over the radio, Dmowski issued orders positioning the twelve Polish fighters he was sending into the sky for battle. 'Flights, step at one, two, and three thousand meters. Attack anything without positive IFF.'

Craning his neck behind him, Tad saw the three remaining aircraft of Ocean flight following him. Other F-15s swung into place behind them. Speeding up, he turned onto the runway and waited a moment while his wingman rolled up alongside him.

'All flights, new data. There is another raid behind the first. Count unknown, but many. Wait one . . .'

Tad shoved the throttles forward again and watched the runway race past beneath him. Whatever was coming, he needed to get aloft. He pulled the F-15 up steeply, accelerating fast.

Dmowksi came on the air again, concern filling his voice. 'All flights, this is Castle. College is off the air, Climax is under attack. All flights go to free search. Good luck.' He sounded like he really meant it.

The enemy was going after Poland's radar and ground control network with a vengeance – trying to blind Tad and his fellow pilots before they could close with the incoming raids.

'Ocean, this is Ocean Leader, radars on, turn left now.' Tad pressed his own radar switch and swung the F-15's nose to the west. The screen came alive, filled with dots and masses of flickering snow. His threat receiver also lit up, cluttered with so many signals that he was tempted to just shut it off.

Despite the EurCon jamming, the Eagle's radar had already locked onto a target, almost seventy miles out. Now if he could just keep himself and his flight alive long enough to close the range.

Under his oxygen mask, Tad Wojcik started sweating. This was going to be a hard day.

THE LOIRE VALLEY, NEAR SAUMUR, FRANCE

The Loire River, the longest in France, seemed designed by God to frustrate those who coveted its waters for recreation or for commerce. Quicksands, whirlpools, and swirling, strong currents made the Loire too dangerous for swimming or for shipping cargoes between the towns and cities lining its banks. The river was something to look at, not something to use.

At least not for most.

But there were a few, some of those born and bred beside its levees, for whom the Loire held few terrors. They had learned to 'read' the river and each of its capricious moods. They knew its traps and they knew the safe passages between each watery snare.

Jacques Liboge was such a man. Still supple despite his sixty-six years, he rose early almost every day to fish in the Loire. As a boy, it had been a way to help feed his family during the war. After that, he had kept on fishing – for the peace it offered as much as the food.

This Sunday morning, as he tramped down the path to the tiny boat tied to a small wooden dock, he could tell the day would be a warm one. The river coiled west toward the distant ocean, its surface as smooth and unruffled as glass. It was still dark, so he was careful of his footing as he loaded his tackle and sat down. Then, with sure, swift motions born of long habit, Liboge cast off, picked up the oars, and glided easily out onto the river.

To the south, the land rose gradually, decked with vineyards and bright yellow sunflowers. His farm, now run by his sons, and those of his neighbors were to the north. Cows grazed placidly in small pastures, cropping the grass beneath fruit trees.

The Liboge farm wasn't a large place, just a few dozen acres. The farmhouse was two hundred years old, built by his ancestors. He resembled the house, square and gray and a little weather-beaten, but strong and solid. There were thousands of farms like Liboge's in France, and thousands of farmers as well.

He fished, enjoying the soft, muted light as it crept into the Loire valley. First there were shapes where there had been only darkness, then the shapes had shadows, and finally color blossomed, spilling east with the rising sun.

Liboge sat quietly content. He'd already caught several fine fish. Now all he had to do was decide between staying out on the river while they were biting and rowing back to start his chores. Church bells pealed in the distance. The village priest was summoning his congregation to early morning mass. The old fisherman cocked his head to listen and smiled lazily, knowing his wife would be furious if he missed the service. Then he shrugged. God would understand. After all, had not Saint Peter himself been a fisherman? And had not God made this perfect day and the fish who seemed so eager to strike at his lures?

A sound, something between a roar and a whine, shattered the morning's peace. He looked up from his rod just in time to see a dark shape race past him, only a few dozen meters above his head. Surprised, he dropped his rod, fumbled for it, and gripped it tightly just as another went by. A third followed the first two only seconds later.

This time his eyes tracked the slender, finned shape as it flew down the length of the valley, neatly turning to follow the winding river as it passed over an old abandoned windmill.

A fourth made the same turn in exactly the same place, and another after that. In all, Liboge counted twelve of the missiles – because that was what they must be. He had seen enough aircraft during the war, and these were simply too small to hold a pilot.

They were flying east, up the river. France was at war again. Were these enemy weapons? If so, at least his own village was safe.

After the last missile disappeared to the east, Liboge put down his tackle and grabbed his small boat's oars. Rowing quickly, he headed for the dock. He would tell the mayor. Yes, the mayor would surely know what to do.

The Tomahawk cruise missiles flew in single file, hugging the river valley. Landmarks like the ruined windmill were useful checkpoints for each missile's guidance systems as it matched stored images of the landscape with what it actually saw.

All twelve of these missiles, fired from a single U.S. submarine a hundred miles off the Atlantic coast, followed the same route. Normally they would have been split into smaller groups – flying two or three separate paths to reduce the risk of interception. But the men who had planned this mission in London were swamped. They had only had time to lay out one track for each target.

In this case, it didn't matter. EurCon radars, even the American-built E-3s in French service, couldn't pick out the twelve tiny, RAM-coated missiles hugging the river valley. Most of France's eyes were turned east or north anyway.

When they were seen by farmer Liboge, the first Tomahawk was just four minutes from its target. It continued to use the Loire as a highway, flying just high enough to clear the occasional bridge or other structure on its banks.

Ten miles from Tours, the cruise missile banked sharply right, then climbed for a moment to fix its position one last time against the landscape. This time, the scene included its target, a Thompson-CSF factory complex. Part of a massive French defense conglomerate, this site was responsible for the manufacture and repair of fighter radars.

Each Tomahawk's specific aiming point had been picked by an American industrial expert – a man who had years of experience in building and running similar facilities. Asked to select twelve vital locations from satellite photos, he'd marked the production line, parts storage, critical machine-tools sheds, and other areas.

Carrying a thousand-pound warhead, the first missile slammed into the plant's executive offices. The explosion and fire that followed did not destroy radar components themselves. They wrecked something even more important – the computers containing the factory's design data and manufacturing records. Their loss would cripple any attempt to resume production.

One after the other, the eleven Tomahawks trailing behind it popped up and then dove into the factory complex. Successive blasts gutted the plant and shattered windows all over Tours.

By the time the twelfth warhead detonated, three of the factory's five vast buildings were reduced to piles of mangled steel and shattered concrete. The other two were burning. Dozens of highly skilled workers lay dead or badly injured in the rubble. Although it was early morning and a Sunday to boot, three shifts had been working night and day to supply EurCon's military needs.

Led by Desaix and his cronies, France had already bloodied half of Europe trying to bring it under EurCon control. The United States wanted the French people to know they would pay the price for their government's aggression.

An American reconnaissance satellite passed overhead later that morning. The images it data-linked down allowed intelligence analysts to report that Thompson-CSF's Tours facility had been eighty percent destroyed. Reconstruction time was estimated at six months for the first production line alone. Bringing the full plant back into operation would take the French at least three years and cost tens of millions of dollars.

Liboge's report of the missiles he had sighted reached the French Air Force about the same time that damage assessment photos were laid on the President's desk in Washington, D.C.

THE NORTH SEA, NEAR WILHELMSHAVEN, GERMANY

In addition to being a major commercial port and shipyard, Wilhelmshaven was Germany's largest naval base on the North Sea coast. While Germany's small missile boats functioned well in the Baltic, the wilder, rougher weather of the North Sea demanded bigger, more capable ships. For that reason most of the German Navy's frigates and destroyers were based there.

It also made the Germans very protective of this valuable port. Constant fighter and helicopter sweeps above the water were matched by patrolling submarines and minefields below the water.

Germany's naval staff was confident of Wilhelmshaven's defenses. A combination of interceptors, SAMs, and antiaircraft guns had already driven off one abortive American air raid against the base, inflicting what were reported as heavy losses on the enemy.

Now ships sheltering inside the protected port would be used to strengthen other areas along the coast. The minelayer *Sachsenwald*, escorted by two frigates and two minesweepers, had been ordered to lay a new barrier across the Elbe River mouth, near Cuxhaven and the western entrance to the strategically and economically vital Kiel Canal. The canal connected the Baltic with the North Sea. In addition, Germany's second largest city and most important port, Hamburg, lay only seventy kilometers up the Elbe.

While the shoreline hinted at easy access to the river, the actual shipping channel was long and narrow. Silt filled the rest of the bay, forming shallows barely covered with water. That narrow entrance made it easy to 'lock the front door' with a mine barrier.

With an entrance and exit route known only to Germany's own harbor pilots, a defensive minefield would make any naval attack on Hamburg or the Kiel Canal, by stealth or strength, a risky undertaking.

Defensive minefields are an important, if low-profile, part of naval warfare. Mines, even sophisticated modern ones, are cheap, never sleep, and are very hard to remove. They have been used for over a hundred years. When Farragut damned the torpedoes and ordered full speed at Mobile Bay during the American Civil War, he was actually referring to Confederate-laid mines. Farragut's Union ships had broken past those primitive mines and captured the port. Germany's naval commanders doubted the American admiral's successors would find it easy to duplicate his feat.

With the sun gleaming on their gray camouflaged superstructures, the five German warships sortied out of the Jadebusen, through the wide mouth of the bay. They were careful to stay not just in the buoyed channel, but in a special passage marked on their charts. Wilhelmshaven had its own large defensive minefield.

The minesweepers led the way. Using ultrahigh-frequency sonars, they swept the channel for enemy mines that might have been laid by submarine or aircraft during the past several days.

Sachsenwald followed, flanked on either side by guided missile frigates. With their sonars and radars energized, they would screen their charge from air, surface, or submarine attack. This was not a job for stealth or concealment. This close to home they could count on a lot of help if they came under attack.

Just to be on the safe side, an antisubmarine helicopter crisscrossed the formation's path, dipping its sonar into the water for periodic searches. Even the fighter patrols orbiting high overhead followed racetrack patterns that kept them close to the group.

Proceeding at fifteen knots, the formation steamed northeast for four hours, crossing in front of the Weser River mouth and Bremerhaven on their way to the Elbe. The German warships actually had to go out a fair distance into the North Sea to clear the shallows, before they could make the turn back toward Cuxhaven.

Nothing menaced them during the short voyage. Once they rounded the western point of the river's mouth, the covering force spread out while the minelayer went to work.

Sachsenwald was an old ship, but minelayers don't need fancy sensors or weapons systems. She was fitted with the latest navigational gear, and her capacious holds carried almost a thousand SAI moored mines. Steering a slow, straight course, her sailors planned to spend the entire day rolling the deadly devices out ports in her stern. Each would be dropped as part of a carefully predetermined pattern, weaving a deadly and nearly impenetrable web.

When the conflict started, the British submarine *Ursula* had been in port. Acting under orders issued by the admiralty, her crew had worked rapidly to off-load some of her Tigerfish and Spearfish torpedoes and to replace them with a smaller but equally deadly cargo – Stonefish mines.

Ursula had sailed from its Scottish base that same night and arrived off the Elbe four days later – intact and undetected despite a few close brushes with EurCon ASW patrols. The same shallow seas that hampered British and American sub-hunting efforts cut both ways.

Creeping in on her whisper-quiet electric motor, the small submarine had maneuvered in close to the German coast, crowded by the shallows and bucking the currents at the river's mouth. The same eddies that made it difficult to maneuver, though, helped hide her from enemy sonar. The mix of fresh and salt water where the Elbe met the North Sea further confused the sonar picture.

With her tubes loaded with mines instead of torpedoes, *Ursula* had moved along a preplanned track – firing them one after another during an hour-long, nerve-racking cruise down the main shipping channel. Then, its mission accomplished, the British submarine had crept out by the same way it had come, with no one the wiser.

One of those Stonefish mines now lay in *Sachsenwald*'s path.

Other German ships had already come near the mine as it lay half-buried in the mud on the channel floor, but each of them had been rejected as a potential target by the microchip in its brain. Most had been fishing craft or patrolling gunboats. A pressure sensor measured their wake as they passed, and spurned them as too small. Several vessels – mostly freighters and barges – were large enough, but the mine's acoustic sensor rejected them because they didn't match the sound signatures loaded in its memory.

One of the ships the Stonefish had ignored was a minesweeper towing a magnetic and acoustic sweep. Although the German vessel's minehunting sonar passed right over it, the mine lay off to one side, not directly beneath the ship. Its plastic construction and rubberized coating didn't return much of an echo, and it was missed.

Now *Sachsenwald* approached. She was on the third leg of her pattern, plowing through the river mouth's choppy waters at twelve knots. The destroyer-sized pressure wave she created fulfilled the mine's requirements, and the sounds her diesel engines made matched a set loaded into its memory. The weapon waited. There was still a chance that this enemy ship would not approach within lethal range.

The noise of *Sachsenwald*'s engines grew and grew. When the acoustic sensor's calculations said it was close enough to inflict damage on the target, the mine armed itself. But it didn't detonate yet. Although the German minelayer was only about seventy meters away, the noise level was still increasing as she drew nearer.

Sachsenwald plowed on, her twin mine chutes dropping packages at precise intervals. The mine listened, sensing but not understanding the thrum of the propellers and the clattering of her engines.

She passed ten meters to port and started to open the distance.

The Stonefish's sensors picked up the drop in noise level and triggered the fuse.

Five hundred kilograms of PBX, half a ton of modern explosive, detonated on the seabed just thirty-two meters away from *Sachsenwald*'s steel hull.

The violence of the explosion knocked the ship almost all the way onto her port side. A massive column of dirty water shot fifty meters high into the air before cascading down on the heeled-over minelayer with crashing force.

Anyone standing was instantly thrown to the deck, or into a bulkhead. The shock was hard enough to break bone. It also knocked dozens of pieces of machinery and electronic equipment out of commission as it rippled through the hull. The ship's screws, turned slightly toward the mine, were both shattered, and the propeller shafts were twisted out of true. Worst of all, both diesel engines, massive multiton blocks of steel, were torn off their foundations and slammed into bulkheads.

As the force of the explosion whipped through the minelayer it sprung the seams on several hull plates. Some of her structural members were broken and a spot on the hull nearest the blast was dished in. The ship's keel was actually bent, wrenched out of alignment. But *Sachsenwald* was still watertight. Her hull was not breached.

The worst result was fire. Diesel fuel pipes, cracked by the shock and still under pressure, spewed a fine mist into the engineering compartment. The minelayer had righted itself, and was starting a roll in the other direction, when a spark ignited the fuel-air mixture. Another explosion rumbled through the ship, killing every man in engineering instantly.

Those of the bridge crew who could stand were getting up when they heard and felt the thunder aft. A quick glance back confirmed their worst fears. A wide, dark column of black smoke billowed high above their ship. Flames licked red and orange deep in the heart of the smoke.

Sachsenwald's captain, sitting on the deck with a broken ankle, ordered damage control teams into action on the double. He had already determined to fight for his ship's life as long as she was above water. He had no choice. If the fire burned out of control, no one abandoning ship could possibly get far enough away in time.

But the fire was already out of control. Ruptured bulkheads had allowed the flames to reach the mine hold aft. Broken in a dozen places, its automatic sprinkler system couldn't put out enough water to keep the mines cool.

Only a fifth of *Sachsenwald*'s mines had been laid, so the compartment was still packed to capacity. Heated to near-red heat by the flames roaring through the hold, several of them 'cooked off,' detonating and starting a chain reaction. SAI mines were smaller than the British Stonefish, but there were eight hundred of them aboard the minelayer – more than sixty tons of high explosive crammed together in a small space.

Sachsenwald disappeared in a wall of water, fire, smoke, and hurtling debris – shredded by a stuttering series of explosions, each big enough to have wrecked the ship by itself. Separate blasts followed each other so closely that they were almost indistinguishable. It took almost forty-five seconds for all the mines to explode.

Several were blown clear and burst in midair, or in the water after they landed.

The shock wave roaring outward from the fireball and smoke cloud was strong enough to rock the furthest ship, *Koln*, a *Bremen*-class frigate nearly three kilometers away. Pieces of *Sachsenwald*'s shattered hull cascaded onto her deck, smashing radar and radio antennas and killing several sailors caught out in the open. All of the minelayer's escorts were damaged by flying debris.

There was worse to come.

While racing to the scene, *Bayern*, the other escorting frigate, fell afoul of another of *Ursula*'s Stonefish mines. Gutted by the resulting blast, she also sank. Unlike *Sachsenwald*, though, some of her crewmen survived.

MINISTRY OF DEFENSE, PARIS

Some years ago, the Defense Ministry's old basement storage areas had been gutted and replaced by a state-of-the-art situation room. Although not a true command center, the room did allow ministry officials, as well as the rest of the French national leadership, to see the big picture while still being close to their offices and the comforts of the capital.

The gleaming facility, filled with floor-to-ceiling color map displays and computer terminals, was the pride of French industry. High-ranking foreign visitors were often taken on tours, to showcase the technology that France might provide to them, for a price.

With most of the Confederation's Defense Committee there, the room was crowded to capacity. French and German officers of all services filled the space, tensely discussing the unfolding events. Nicolas Desaix, flanked by Admiral Gibierge, sat in one of the elevated seats near the center.

They were watching a battle. Gibierge had alerted his superiors the evening before that the Combined Forces were moving.

An increased number of enemy surveillance flights, a sharp rise in the amount of coded radio traffic, and unusual activity at British airfields had convinced him that the offensive he had predicted was about to begin. He was right.

Some officials, notably the Defense Minister and his closest military subordinates, arrived before dawn. They were in time to see the Tomahawk strikes raining down all over France and Germany, to hear the reports of *Sachsenwald*'s and *Bayern*'s loss, and to receive news of a commando attack on the naval base at Brest. All were bad in themselves, but the men in the situation room knew they were just the opening moves. Like the first drops of rain, these pinprick raids around the periphery would continue throughout the storm. Everyone waited for the lightning.

The center screen had been set up to show the Channel coast, the Low Countries, Germany's north coast, and the southern half of the North Sea. Data from many sources, including an American-built E-3 radar plane, was fused into a single integrated picture. As Desaix watched, a second E-3 took off from its base at Avord, reinforcing the one already aloft.

Colored symbols flowed across the display, showing aircraft and ship positions, courses, and speeds. Even an amateur could see patterns in the movement: fighters and antisub planes on their patrols, ships entering and leaving port, and, in the center, two massive groups of red symbols.

Tracking the American carrier battle groups had been easy. In the crowded North Sea, information was more important than concealment, so almost every American radar was on. EurCon surveillance units had located each radiating ship and classified them based on the types of radars they carried. Other ships, not radiating, could be seen by airborne radar.

One symbol was labeled *George Washington*, another *Theodore Roosevelt*. Each was surrounded by a cluster of red ship symbols – their escorts, tankers, and replenishment ships. Circles, centered on the carriers, showed the range of their aircraft and their escorts' land attack cruise missiles. Other circles, centered on French and German air bases, showed the range of the aircraft based there. The range circle for *George Washington* almost touched the German coast near Wilhelmshaven.

Gibierge checked the clock, then leaned over and whispered to Desaix. 'Our strike is launching now, Foreign Minister. With luck, we can catch the Americans right in the act of launching their own attacks.'

'Won't they see it coming?' asked Desaix.

The admiral shook his head confidently. 'We have jammer aircraft screening the attack formation, both standing off and providing direct escort for our strike planes. By the time the Americans can get a clear picture, our strike will be in the air and well on its way.' He smiled wolfishly. 'These Combined Forces are moving exactly as we expected them to. We will make them pay for their predictability.'

MUSTANG LEAD, COUNTERWEIGHT STRIKE, OVER USS *GEORGE WASHINGTON*

Nearly one hundred navy warplanes orbited high over the North Sea, a moving cloud of sophisticated aircraft growing steadily as more planes thundered off *George Washington* in clouds of catapult steam.

Thirty thousand feet above the wavetops, Commander Rudy Mann, USN, watched his squadron form up. So far, the launch had gone like clockwork, but that was expected. His pilots had better be able to take off and assume formation competently. A lot more would be demanded of them before lunch.

Mann's youthful face was almost completely masked by his helmet, oxygen mask, and visor. His thinning hair, close-cropped like many pilots, gave a better idea of his age than his features. In his early thirties, he was at the typical age for a squadron commander, with years of experience 'in type,' flying the Hornet.

Mann's F/A-18 Hornets, the shortest-range of the strike's aircraft, were the last to launch, but they wouldn't have any trouble catching up with the rest of the raid.

'Hatchet' Mann swept his eyes over the instrument panel one last time, then ordered, 'Mustangs, turn to zero eight five now.'

Looking over each shoulder, he watched the rest of the squadron, twelve planes in all, follow his movements. The new course would intercept the main air formation quickly. Proceeding at a stately 370 knots, his Hornets had almost a hundred-knot overtake on them.

In the clear early morning air, he could see dozens of planes from both *George Washington* and *Theodore Roosevelt* spread out below him in Alpha Strike formation. An attack against a land target was called an Alpha Strike. One against a naval target was a Sierra Strike. The size of the strike was determined by the target's value – and by how badly you wanted it to die.

This was a big one. Admiral Ward had spent half the previous day juggling the two carriers' planes so that only those actually going on the strike were on *George Washington*. Fighters from *Roosevelt*, still outside enemy strike range itself, would cover her. In turn, land-based British Tornado and American F-15 and F-16 fighters covered *Rosie*. If everything went according to plan, the air groups would unscramble automatically after the raid, each landing on its own carrier.

Mann's squadron, one of the four Hornet squadrons involved, flew ahead and to port of the main formation. Six jammer aircraft, already radiating an invisible electronic fog, flew among the F/A-18s. Lower still and even further out were two flights of A-6 Intruders, armed with

Harpoon antiship missiles. They would take out any enemy vessels that lay in the raid's path.

George Washington's air group commander, or CAG, rode in an E-2 Hawkeye, one of the two accompanying the raid. Their high-powered radars would allow the CAG to see the raid as it progressed, and make what adjustments he could.

Other aircraft orbited in the vicinity, watching. Mann could not see them, but they did not have to be close. An air force RC-135 and a navy ES-3, different aircraft with the same role, flew lazy circles at high altitude. Equipped with webs of antennas and other electronic sensors, they would listen to the signals made by both sides and learn what they could.

Radar on, Mann scanned the sky with his eyes as well. They were headed into trouble, and he wanted to see it coming.

MINISTRY OF DEFENSE

A junior officer reported, 'New airborne activity near *George Washington*.'

More aircraft symbols appeared around the closer of the two U.S. carrier groups. Desaix looked over at Gibierge and raised a single eyebrow in silent speculation.

The admiral nodded. 'This could be their opening strike, Foreign Minister. I don't think these new planes are interceptors. Our raid is still forming out of their radar observation. In any case, the Americans would not launch their fighters for some time – certainly not until they had a good idea of our numbers and destination.' He studied the display. 'Those planes are forming at high altitude, in easy view of our radars. They certainly aren't trying to conceal their movements. It's as we thought. The Americans think they can simply overwhelm our defenses.'

Desaix nodded, approving Gibierge's apparent certainty. The admiral knew his craft. Still, he had questions. 'I thought your plan anticipated attacking those carriers before they could hit us.'

The tall man's tone was calm, but the admiral thought he heard a hint of irritation beneath the measured words. He hastened to explain. 'That is true, Foreign Minister. But this situation may work even more to our advantage. This inbound American strike must be escorted, and that means fewer fighters will be available to defend that carrier. If their primary target is Wilhelmshaven, the two raids will meet almost head-on. And in that case, I believe the Americans will abandon their own attack to concentrate on their own defense.'

'Can we handle them?' queried Desaix.

'Yes, Foreign Minister, we can. We have almost half of our frontline fighter strength concentrated here.'

Desaix appeared convinced, and the admiral turned to one of the display operators. 'Any further information on the inbound strike?'

The young lieutenant nodded. 'We have identified airborne radars consistent with F/A-18 and A-6 aircraft. Plus, there appear to be two E-2

Hawkeyes accompanying the group.' He shrugged in apology. 'We don't yet have a precise raid count, Admiral. There is very heavy jamming.'

Gibierge nodded, undismayed. 'As we expected.'

Everything was still unfolding according to his earlier predictions. The Americans would never waste two of their prized E-2 radar warning and command and control planes on a mere probe. If they followed normal practice, the practice he had seen a dozen times as a NATO observer during peacetime exercises, the incoming raid would contain two squadrons of A-6 Intruder aircraft and two of Hornets, escorted by a full squadron of F-14 Tomcats and a pair of EA-6B Prowlers to jam French and German radars. Two Hawkeyes aloft could also indicate that the Americans were combining planes from both their carriers in this one strike. Well, he thought grimly, the more the merrier. He turned back to Desaix.

'Do the Americans have any other courses of action when we meet them?'

'They may choose to continue, trusting to their missile ships and the remaining fighters. That would be better for us, of course.'

'But what about the damage they might cause to Wilhelmshaven?'

Gibierge gave a very Gallic shrug. 'We will be hit, of course, but we still have our SAMs and fighter defenses.'

Desaix nodded his understanding. Both men left unsaid the thought that Wilhelmshaven was German territory anyway.

The admiral leaned forward, pressing home his point. 'Most important, sir, whichever way they move, the Americans will only be able to launch this one attack. By the time they turned for home, they will have no carrier to land on, only a patch of radioactive water.'

USS *GEORGE WASHINGTON*

'Admiral!' Lieutenant Harada had to shout to get Adm. Jack Ward's attention on the noisy bridge wing. At thirty-plus knots, the wind almost ripped the words out of your throat. Add the scream of dozens of jet engines, and you might as well use sign language.

The admiral turned to his aide. Harada thought he looked a little better than he had while he was stuck on shore. The stress of the past several days had aged his boss.

Watching the airborne phase of Counterweight get under way was a tonic, though. Nobody could watch plane after plane roar off the carrier's flight deck without being encouraged. Things were finally moving, and when those planes reached their target, EurCon was in for a rough morning.

Harada hated to call the admiral in, but it was important. He cupped his hands. 'New enemy contacts, sir! Airborne over Germany.'

Ward nodded and quickly ducked through the weather deck door.

The Tactical Flag Command Center was Ward's turf, and he loved it. Information from dozens of sensors could be displayed in as many different ways, and secure communications links put him in touch with his commanders. Unlike an army or marine officer, Ward couldn't ever expect to see much of the battlefield. The TFCC took its place. From here, he could run the war in the North Sea and the Baltic.

It was a dark, quiet place, the hum of subdued voices indicating a well-trained team. The man responsible for that, his chief of staff, approached Ward as he came in.

Capt. Harry March should have been a lawyer or a CPA, but the navy had been lucky enough to get him. Business colleges cost money, but the academy had offered a black city kid a degree for free. His passion for detail was Ward's secret weapon.

Now he didn't waste time. 'SIGINT planes are picking up a lot of airborne radio traffic over several German air bases, including Bremerhaven and Cuxhaven. Traffic is in both German and French. Some aircraft radar signals, too.' Although he spoke softly, he sounded worried.

'What's your evaluation, Harry? An air strike?'

'Probably, sir, and we're the only logical target.' He sighed. 'The problem is, we don't have a clear picture of what's going on over there. Our radar coverage is nil.'

Ward frowned. His intelligence officers' best guess had been that EurCon wouldn't come after his carriers from the air. Computer-run wargames and analyses had showed such an attack would absorb too much of French and German air strength to make it worthwhile. Apparently the enemy's own staff studies had come to a different conclusion. He said as much to March.

'I agree, Admiral. I've run the numbers, though. Based on what we do know, and their aircraft ranges, we're the only worthwhile target out here right now.'

Ward felt a small chill run through him. 'If they are going to hit us, Harry, it won't be a half-assed attempt.' What went unspoken was the obvious fact that the incoming EurCon strike force would meet their own outbound raid head-on. 'How long till we know for sure what they're up to?'

March answered instantly. 'About ten minutes or so, Admiral, based on their course and speed, plus their time in the air. I recommend tanking our outbound planes now and launching more tankers to refuel our own top cover. I've already passed our data over to *Roosevelt*.'

'As well as giving *Rosie*'s CAG a heads-up, I bet.' Ward rubbed his face, then stared at the map display for a minute. 'It means losing some range on the strike if we tank now, ahead of schedule, but I agree. Launch another E-2 and get the SAR helos alerted.' He glanced at his watch. 'We'll decide whether to abort or press on in ten minutes.'

MINISTRY OF DEFENSE

'Our strike is outbound,' announced an operator.

Gibierge studied the cluster of blue symbols just north of Cuxhaven with satisfaction. Two squadrons of Mirage 2000Ns armed with ASMP nuclear missiles. Two more squadrons of German Tornados armed with antiradar missiles and conventional antiship missiles. A squadron of

Rafales, two of Mirage 2000s, and two of German fighters accompanied the strike force as escorts. He and his fellow commanders were throwing nearly 120 aircraft into this battle – the cream of the Confederation air forces.

USS *GEORGE WASHINGTON*

'They're headed straight at us, Admiral.' March's voice was filled with suppressed excitement. 'There's some jamming but we're dealing with it. Raid count in excess of one hundred aircraft.'

Ward stood taller. Years dropped away from his face along with all the doubts and worries of the past few weeks. They were committed now. 'Tell Rancher to execute as soon as his planes have finished tanking.'

MUSTANG LEAD

Mann watched the last of the F-14s nose into the tanker's drogue and hurriedly take on fuel. Thank God they'd decided to do this in daylight. In-flight refueling was a fine art and demanded a high level of skill. Passing a baton from one car to another on a superhighway was child's play in comparison.

But they needed the fuel. The navy planes heading for the German coast had already expended a quarter of their load, and combat could drain their tanks in a few minutes. All together, almost two squadrons of A-6 Intruders had been dedicated to tanker duty.

They were just finishing up now. His Hornet squadron had already refueled.

'All Counterweight units, this is Rancher. Chuckwagons and outriders to the rear.' Captain Macmillan, the CAG, had a spread in Montana, and cowboy slang always seemed to figure in the radio codes he developed. Mann was a city boy at heart, but he had to admit that they seemed more appropriate than anything he might have dredged up out of a childhood spent in Brooklyn.

Mann knew that Macmillan would rather be flying his F-14 than riding a Hawkeye, but his job could not be performed in a fighter cockpit. Someone had to lead.

Now Rancher sent the A-6 tankers and the antishipping aircraft home, stripping the formation for action. The jammers spread out, where they would stay clear of the fight, and the E-2s' dedicated fighter escorts moved in closer to their charges.

'All units, this is Rancher. Execute.'

Mann pushed his throttle forward.

MINISTRY OF DEFENSE

Gibierge watched the two clusters of symbols move toward each other. They were still two hundred miles apart, but with both formations flying at almost four hundred knots, they would be in missile range in about fifteen minutes. The American F-14s with their Phoenix missiles would be able to fire sooner, but long-range shots were effective only against clumsy bomber aircraft.

He focused his attention on the American formation. Which way would they jump?

One of the situation room's secondary screens showed an expanded view of the two raids. The French and German planes were neatly labeled with aircraft types and call signs for each flight, along with their course, speed, and altitude.

The opposing American raid, though, simply showed up as a muddle of hostile aircraft symbols and a crisscross tracery of ESM detection lines. Where they intersected, a label marked the type of radar detected and the aircraft fitted with it. Several small groups of planes near the fringes of the raid were marked with 'APG-65/Hornet' or 'AWG-9/Tomcat.' The center of the formation was marked with 'APQ-156/Intruder.' Radar and ESM gave him a good idea of the enemy raid's composition. So far there hadn't been any surprises.

His eyes narrowed. The American commanders would have to make their decisions soon. Would they press ahead toward Wilhelmshaven or turn back to defend their own ships? The range was down to 150 nautical miles.

Some of the American symbols shifted in relation to their counterparts. Simultaneously several of the lines indicating radar signals disappeared. The signals for fighters remained, but the Intruder radars had gone away.

Desaix leaned closer to him, wanting to know what was going on, but Gibierge waited a moment more before turning to respond. 'It looks like they are sending their attack aircraft home, Foreign Minister. It was the logical course for them, and I've alerted our raid commander. We are prepared . . .'

Desaix was still watching the screen while the admiral explained. Suddenly the Foreign Minister's eyes widened in puzzlement and alarm. Gibierge checked the display again and felt his jaw drop open.

A new network of lines, thicker than a spider's web, covered the American raid. Every one of them was labeled 'APG-65' or 'AWG-9'. In addition, only a few aircraft symbols had disappeared. The bulk of the raid was not turning back, but accelerating. He watched as the speed values next to the aircraft symbols changed and changed again, always increasing. They were already well over six hundred knots, while a loaded Intruder could not even make five hundred.

'Gibierge, what is this?' Desaix demanded. The admiral was already reaching for a red command phone.

MUSTANG LEAD

With the tankers and antishipping planes gone, Mann felt like a ball and chain had been removed. Under Rancher's direction, the Counterweight raid accelerated from attack aircraft cruising speeds to fighter intercept speeds. Blips representing hostile aircraft covered his radar now, although enemy jamming still cluttered parts of the scope with fuzzy white blotches.

He could only spare a short glance at the radar screen itself. Much of the data on it was automatically fed to his Hornet's HUD anyway, and a pilot who spends too much time heads-down is sure to get surprised one day. And surprises in air-to-air combat are usually fatal. He scanned the sky and double-checked his weapons settings. It would be several more minutes before they were in Sparrow range.

But the F-14s would be in range a lot sooner than that. He looked down at them now, wings swept back and still spreading out from a close formation used by attack planes to one more suitable for high-altitude missile combat.

'Cactus, Lasso, Longhorn, you are clear to engage assigned targets. Out.' Rancher's voice ordered the three Tomcat squadrons under his command to attack. Each of the thirty F-14s carried four long-range Phoenix air-to-air missiles, two shorter-range Sparrows, and two Sidewinders for dogfighting. Like Mann's Hornet, they also carried two drop tanks. The tanks were slowing them down, but the Tomcats would hang onto them – until the fuel they carried was gone, or until the fighters were going into a close-in fight where maneuverability counted for more than endurance.

Now, almost before Rancher finished his transmission, each F-14 fired once. White lines, tipped with fire, appeared in front of the Tomcats. They shot straight out ahead of the big, twin-tailed planes for a fraction of a second, then suddenly pitched up and climbed almost out of sight.

The smoke trails flashed past the formation, but Mann's eyes followed the missile tracks as long as possible. Just as the first group of missiles disappeared, the three F-14 squadrons fired again.

Following the first wave, the second wave of Phoenix missiles climbed until they were out of the troposphere entirely. Following preset flight commands, they leveled off at over 100,000 feet. The near vacuum twenty miles up allowed each missile to reach Mach 5 and hold it, even after its rocket motor burned out. Their targets were seventy miles downrange – well within the missiles' range. They would reach the EurCon formation in a minute and a half.

MINISTRY OF DEFENSE

Stunned and panicked shouts echoed in his ears. The crowded situation room filled with questions and accusations as Gibierge tried desperately to concentrate on the voice at the other end of the command circuit.

Desaix, rising out of his chair, shook the admiral's shoulder, demanding that he explain, that he act.

Gibierge, shouting into the handset to make himself heard, yelled, 'Attack now! Push them in at full speed! Remember, we only need one hit!'

He hung up, and realized that the man demanding his attention was not some aide but the Foreign Minister of France, the controlling mind of the European Confederation.

'Explain this,' ordered Desaix in a barely controlled voice.

'It's an offensive fighter sweep, sir. Based on the information there' –

Gibierge waved an arm at the display – 'we are facing the combined fighter strength of both aircraft carriers.'

He shook his head in astonishment. 'The Americans are not conducting an attack on Wilhelmshaven or any other land target. They flew the same profile as attack aircraft, and mixed enough attack planes into their formation to fool us.' Gibierge pushed down a sneaking admiration for his American counterpart. This Admiral Ward was wilier than he had thought.

Desaix still looked lost.

The admiral hastily sketched out his deductions with one eye locked on the display. 'If we had not been launching our own strike, we would have thrown every fighter we had at them. The Americans would have met our planes with their own and outnumbered us. Then, with our air defense forces crippled, their real strikes would suffer fewer losses.'

Desaix scowled. 'So now instead of our air defenses, they are going to decimate "the cream of our air forces." We must abort the strike now, before they get in range.'

'At this stage that would be almost impossible, Foreign Minister. It would also be unnecessary.' Gibierge half argued, half pleaded with the politician. 'Our own fighters almost match theirs in numbers. While they occupy the Americans, our Mirage attack jets can accelerate to maximum speed and slip past. And they will be in launch range in just a few minutes.'

Desaix started to object, but Gibierge stopped him. 'It's too late, Foreign Minister. Events move too quickly in an air battle. The orders have already been given.'

A display operator's voice cut through the confusion. 'Strike leader reports they are under missile attack.'

OVER THE EURCON STRIKE FORCE

The Phoenix missiles, linked back to their launching aircraft, nosed over, plunging almost straight down at the enemy planes a dozen miles below them.

Both waves of American missiles flashed through the enemy formation in an eyeblink. Every EurCon plane immediately pulled up into a weaving climb, trying to force each attacking missile to waste energy turning and climbing itself.

The Mirage 2000 and Tornado crews could have jettisoned their loads and lived. With a few exceptions, they chose to keep their own missiles and trust to luck. Without those weapons, their mission would be a failure. Most managed to evade the attacking Phoenixes by jinking and dropping chaff.

The jammer aircraft suffered the worst. Six elderly Mirage F1 fighters each carried a centerline jammer pod. Weighing half a ton, the pod sent out signals that could hide a whole squadron of aircraft from radar, as long as they stayed within a few miles.

Their electronic noise served as a perfect beacon for the Phoenix's 'home-on-jam' feature. Each F1 was swarmed by several missiles.

Roughly half the pilots realized what was happening and switched them off, but it was a futile gesture.

Only one Mirage F1 survived.

The long-range American attack had stripped the EurCon strike of its jamming support. Dodging the missiles had also wasted precious time and fuel and disrupted their formation.

But their orders were clear. Nosing into a shallow dive, the EurCon planes went to full military power.

OVER THE NORTH SEA

As their radar scopes cleared, new commands vectored the U.S. Navy squadrons toward the accelerating EurCon raiding force. The opposing groups of aircraft were forty miles apart at thirty thousand feet, heading straight for each other at a combined speed of twelve hundred knots.

The EurCon side fielded about sixty fighters of three types, all equipped with long-range air-to-air missiles. A squadron of Rafales were the newest and deadliest of the three, accompanied by delta-winged Mirage 2000s, old but still effective. The German contribution was limited to the elderly F-4F Phantom II. They were still escorting more than forty French and German Tornado and Mirage attack jets.

The Americans had just over eighty planes and they launched first. Two Hornet squadrons carried the AMRAAM, a 'smart' air-to-air missile. It outranged all French and German weapons. Twenty-four white smoke trails drew arcs from one group to the other.

Diving down into the enemy's scrambled formation, the advanced AMRAAM seekers ignored the lone EurCon jammer.

The AMRAAMs were targeted on the greatest threat, the Rafale squadron. Each plane pulled up into a wild series of maneuvers. Many missiles missed, but five aircraft, the best fighters in the EurCon arsenal, were hit and disappeared in black and gray explosions. The rest were prevented from firing back for a few precious moments.

The other EurCon fighters were not maneuvering, and the Mirage 2000s fired a salvo of active radar homing Mica missiles. The German Phantoms added their own fire, American-built Sparrows. Almost fifty missiles arrowed toward the oncoming navy planes.

Simultaneously the Americans fired again. More AMRAAMs and Sparrows leapt from under gray-painted wings, speeding toward the EurCon planes still twenty-five miles away. Both sides saw each other only as blips on glowing radar screens and target designator boxes on HUDs.

That was a serious problem for the French and German aircraft. Their screens were still cluttered with American jamming. It didn't stop them from launching missiles, but it slowed them down, and in air combat, time is a weapon of its own.

Surrounding the navy fighters were six EA-6B Prowlers. Packed with antennas and electronics, their transmitters were so powerful that the signals were lethal to nearby personnel on the ground. They felt out the electronic spectrum, found the enemy radar and radio frequencies, then poured electronic radiation into them like a waterfall. Tied together by their own data links, the six jamming planes were welded into a single unit, sharing information and assigning targets.

Another missile salvo flashed out from the American planes, matched by a more ragged salvo from the EurCon side. Planes from the opposing sides were just coming into visual range. Tracks from half a dozen different missiles filled the air between the two formations. Even as the missiles struck aircraft of both sides, the two formations merged.

MINISTRY OF DEFENSE

Radar tracking of the combat was now meaningless. Gibierge could only see a hash of blue and red symbols on the left-hand screen. One thing was clear. There were fewer and fewer blue symbols.

The only sound in the room was the formation radio circuit. Like commanders half a century before, all the waiting men could do was try to pick out stray scraps of information from the frantic calls of the pilots, fighting hundreds of miles away.

'. . . three planes to port . . . launching now . . . stand by, break *now*! . . . I'm hit, my port wing's gone . . .' Each voice had its own background of warning beeps and howls, and one was accented by the roar of a rocket motor igniting as a missile launched.

On a separate frequency, emergency locator beacons sent out their *beep-beep-beep* signals, marking the locations of downed pilots. They appeared on the display, too, but there was no way to tell which side they belonged to. There were a lot of them, though, and their numbers grew steadily.

MUSTANG LEAD

Mann hoped like hell his wingman was all right. He'd lost sight of the other F/A-18 only a minute into the fight, and he'd been far too busy since then to look for him.

There were too many planes climbing, diving, and turning through too little airspace. Over half his attention was devoted to avoiding a midair collision, not to killing the enemy. He'd nearly lost it once already, when a hard break away from somebody's missile had almost slammed him into a scissoring German Phantom.

He looked around, rapidly scanning a sky full of arrowed shapes at every aspect and angle possible. Streaks of smoke marked the passage of missiles between the rival aircraft, as well as the places where planes had died. The lower edge of the dogfight was marked by colored parachutes.

It was a battle of snap shots and fleeting chances. He'd scored one gun kill early on, firing instinctively as a Mirage filled his canopy. The French jet had fireballed, rocking his Hornet. Since then, though, he'd felt like a ball in a pinball machine.

A Tomcat appeared out of nowhere, passing in front of him at high speed. Beyond it was a Rafale, facing away from him, nose-up.

With Sidewinder already selected, he brought his Hornet's nose over, waiting for a tone. Nothing. Damn it!

He switched to guns and increased the throttle, intending to close the range before firing. Instead, the track light on his radar warning receiver lit up. A frantic glance over his shoulder revealed a Mirage at his five o'clock.

Abandoning his quarry, Mann chopped the throttle and pushed the stick forward, unloading the Hornet's wings. Then he broke hard left, turning into the delta-winged French fighter. They passed within a dozen yards of each other, canopy-to-canopy.

Another Tomcat hurtled toward him, approaching almost head-on and in pursuit of the Mirage. Mann brought his nose right to clear the F-14, and had a spectacular view of the Tomcat's Sidewinder as it left the rail. He didn't see the result. He'd spotted a German Phantom above and to starboard. Increasing the throttle, he pointed the Hornet's nose up a little, risking a stall to bring the enemy aircraft into his sights. The Phantom's engines weren't as stealthy as a Rafale's and this time his heat-seeking missile's tone was clear and strong. Perfect!

Mann's thumb pressed the fire button on his stick. The Sidewinder dropped off its rail and covered the quarter mile between the two planes in an eyeblink. It scored a direct hit, slamming into the German's left wing and blowing it off.

He watched the F-4 start to spin, almost too slowly. Still in slow motion, its canopy popped off, and Mann saw a blast of smoke and flame flare in the cockpit. The Phantom's ejector seat tumbled free of the torn aircraft, carrying its pilot to the relative safety of the North Sea.

'Mustang. This is Rancher. All units, vector three one five. Bandits inbound at level ten. Buster.'

Mann recognized the CAG's voice, and the meaning of the call. Three one five degrees was a rough bearing back to *George Washington*. Some of the EurCon attackers had broken clear of the dogfight. 'Buster' meant to intercept at full power.

He keyed his mike. 'Roger, Rancher, all Mustangs to three one five. Hatchet out.'

He advanced the F/A-18's throttle. He felt his aircraft's speed build up quickly, carrying him out of the fight. He adjusted his course, then cast a quick glance at his six o'clock. At full military power, his engines made a dandy IR target. Fortunately nobody was following him.

Mann spotted several other Hornets, all on the same course, scattered above and below him. His radar showed a cluster of contacts in front and below him at twenty miles – all headed toward the carrier at high speed. They were still out of launch range but wouldn't be for long. The F/A-18 was light now, without its drop tanks and half its missile load, almost clean.

Mann noticed the 'Bingo' indicator light come on. Building up this last burst of speed had drained his fuel supply. He was going to need a tanker, and soon.

He selected his last Sparrow and locked up a target. 'Mustang Lead, engaging.'

USS *GEORGE WASHINGTON*

'Admiral, we've got ten-plus inbounds at five-fifty knots. Fighters are engaging. We've got *Dale* on that side, weapons tight. She'll be in range soon, but we have to get the fighters out of there first.'

March's report and implied recommendation was half formality, but it was Ward's decision to make. Sitting in his command chair, surrounded by displays, he felt a little superfluous. 'Clear the fighters and tell all ships to go to weapons free.'

It was the only logical thing to do. He had missile ships facing an incoming enemy attack with their hands practically tied behind their backs. Going to weapons-free status would clear them to fire SAMs more effectively. Any air target not positively identified as friendly would be fair game.

Ward nodded toward the symbols showing fighters chasing after the EurCon strike planes. 'What's their fuel state?'

'Tankers are already on the way, sir.'

Ward nodded and went back to watching the displays. It wasn't really a feeling of being superfluous, he decided. Events were just out of his hands now. His plan was in motion, and everyone else had a job to do but him.

MUSTANG LEAD

'All units, this is Rancher, break off and steer zero four five.'

Mann gauged the distance to the remaining bandits and reluctantly turned to the ordered course – heading away from *George Washington* and the enemy. The EurCon aircraft were too far ahead and too close to the battle group's SAM envelope to catch.

He added his own 'Mustangs, form on me' to the CAG's command and waggled his wings. It was time to count noses.

Behind him, the remains of four EurCon attack squadrons tucked into two tight formations. Of nearly fifty attack aircraft that had ventured out to challenge the Americans, only eight were left. Others were limping home, nursing damage that made it impossible to press on. Most were gone – blown out of the sky by guns or missiles. Three far out in front were German Tornados. The five trailing behind were Mirage 2000s carrying ASMP nuclear missiles.

Decimated by the navy fighters, the French and German pilots knew they were on borrowed time. They no longer watched their fuel gauges, but simply poured on all the speed they had. Their only hope of survival was to reach launch range and salvo their weapons. After that, each of them could evade and try to make it home while the Americans tried to deal with the missiles. Even a rubber raft looked attractive after the hell-ride they'd all gone through.

In accordance with their attack plan, the Tornados, well out in front now, fed targeting data to the Mirage pilots. The French plane's short-range radar could not see the U.S. ships at this distance, and precise targeting data was crucial. Their ASMP missiles didn't have radar seekers that could home in on moving targets. Designed to attack stationary objects on land, they mounted only a plain inertial seeker. Just before launch, each pilot would set his missile's target as a simple geographic location.

As the Mirage crews took the range and bearing supplied by the Germans, they tried to calculate flight times, the American carrier's course and speed, and come up with the proper impact point. Even with a nuclear warhead, a sure kill could only be guaranteed against a warship if it landed within a mile and a half. The damage radius was twice that. At the distance they were firing from, that worked out to a margin of error of less than two percent. But then, all they needed was one good hit.

With their target locked in, the Mirages fired. Five finned missiles dropped from centerline pylons and flew northwest, accelerating rapidly past the speed of sound.

When the French planes banked away, heading for home, the German Tornados dove for the deck, barreling in only fifty meters above the water. While the ASMP had a range of 150 nautical miles, the Kormoran antiship missiles they carried had to be launched within thirty miles of their intended target.

USS *DALE*

Dale's skipper had already decided to fire before Admiral Ward's order came over the circuit. He was not the sort to stand on formality where enemy aircraft were concerned.

The *Leahy*-class missile cruiser and *Klakring*, her *Perry*-class frigate escort, occupied a missile picket station thirty miles out in front of *George Washington*. That thirty miles could be added directly to the range of her SM-2ER missiles. She was the first line of the carrier's defense.

Dale's crew had been at general quarters for hours. Since then her well-drilled CIC team had monitored every stage in the air battle – watching carefully as the fight moved closer. Their radars had shown the surviving EurCon attack jets break out of the dogfight. Now they saw several small contacts appear in front of one group of enemy planes.

The cruiser's tight-faced captain watched the new blips just long enough to be sure they were real. His missile engagement controller reported, 'They're still climbing and accelerating, Skipper. They won't be in our SAM envelope for another minute. I count five.'

'All right, Steve. What's the threat?'

'Unknown, sir.' The lieutenant paged rapidly through a loose-leaf book with red plastic covers. 'Supersonic, high altitude, doesn't fit any French or German antiship missile. No radar signal from them yet.' Half to himself, he wondered, 'An ARM targeted on our radars?'

Still leafing, the lieutenant glanced up at his display. 'Speed's up to Mach three, Skipper.'

He looked down at the book again and stiffened. Then he carefully studied the page, comparing the data there with the numbers on his screen. The blood drained from his face.

USS *GEORGE WASHINGTON*

They were tracking the same inbound missiles in the carrier's flag command center, and Ward's staff recognized them the same instant that *Dale*'s lieutenant did.

His voice tight with control, the antiair warfare coordinator reported, 'Admiral, inbounds are probably nuclear! Evaluated as ASMPs . . . about two minutes out.'

Ward fought the impulse to panic. He had too much to do. 'It's too late to disperse the formation. Emergency turn. Put every ship stern-on to them, and order all ships to individual maximum speed. Get all exposed personnel belowdecks! And send a flash message to the NCA!'

Facing away from a nuclear detonation would offer his ships limited but still significant protection. A blast wave running down a ship's long axis would meet less resistance and hit its stronger stern first. Going to full speed might give each ship enough extra maneuverability to ride out the explosion and resulting sea surge.

He looked around and found his chief of staff. 'Anything I missed, Harry?'

'Turn off and isolate nonvital radars. It might help with EMP effects.'

'Do it,' Ward confirmed. 'That's about all we have time for.'

Under his breath, he muttered, 'Those bastards. I'll make them regret this day.' But another voice ghosted through his brain reminding him he might not live long enough to keep that promise.

'*Dale* reports she'll engage in thirty seconds.'

TORNADO FLIGHT

Under the original attack plan, Germany's Tornados were expected to attack all American missile defense ships ahead of the ASMPs – clearing a path for the nuclear-tipped missiles. Now, instead of saturating the carrier's defenses, the three surviving planes aimed for the keystone, and hoped that would be enough.

While the Germans had been passing information to the French planes, they had also used their radars to locate the picket missile cruiser. With its location, course, and speed locked into their computers, they'd plunged to the deck. Howling in only fifty meters above the waves, the Tornados were below *Dale*'s radar horizon – out of sight and out of the line of fire. Of course, they couldn't see the American cruiser, either.

Their computers knew where she was, though, and guided them toward the target. Just over thirty miles out, HUD indicators prompted the crews to fire. The Tornados popped up, climbing to five hundred feet. First one missile, then a second, left each Tornado.

Gratefully the Germans turned away, beginning a long and perilous journey back to base.

A dozen miles overhead, the five ASMPs sped on.

USS *DALE*

'New raid, bearing one six three, correlates with the Tornados we saw earlier. Probable prelaunch maneuver.' *Dale*'s tactical action officer turned toward the captain. The cruiser would launch her first pairs of Standard 2ER SAMs in a few seconds.

The captain turned his head to look at the TAO, but his attention was still concentrated on coping with the first threat they'd detected.

'If they've fired Kormorans, Skipper, we won't see them until they're twenty miles out – about one minute from now. *Klakring*'s the only other ship in range.'

'Then tell *Klakring* to unmask and engage.'

The TAO replied, 'I estimate five-plus missiles, sir. She probably can't do it alone.'

Dale's captain turned and gave him his full attention. He nodded slightly. 'Understood, Tom.'

Protecting *George Washington* took precedence over self-defense.

The lieutenant at the missile console announced, 'Birds away.' A rippling roar from fore and aft confirmed his statement.

At each end of the ship, a massive twin-armed missile launcher swung back down to near level. In the metal skin of the ship just behind them, small doors opened up and needle-nosed missiles slid out quickly, belying their ton-and-a-half weight. Now carrying a three-ton load, the launchers slewed up and out again.

It took about thirty seconds for each launcher to go through its reloading cycle. In that time, *Dale*'s first four SAMs were halfway to the rapidly closing targets.

Klakring fired as well. Her single-arm launcher fired a shorter-range, older version of *Dale*'s missile, but the smaller launcher was quicker – pumping out a missile every ten seconds. The frigate's deck and launcher were soon black with scorched paint and missile exhaust.

Her SM-1 missiles had a hard time with the sea-skimming Kormorans. The German missiles hugged the wavetops, only a man's height above the water. At that height, the water itself returned an echo to the missile's seeker.

The first salvo of *Dale*'s long-range SAMs reached the ASMPs just as the first of *Klakring*'s missiles missed one of the Kormorans. Both sets of targets were difficult. One high-flying and very fast, the other not so fast but very low.

Dale's missiles were newer and had a clearer view of their targets. Two of the four connected, shredding the ASMPs' airframes and their warheads.

Klakring's second SM-1 struck a Kormoran, slamming it into the water in an explosion of spray. The third, intended for the same target, missed and the frigate's missile director quickly shifted to another missile in the same group.

The German seaskimmers were much closer now. As *Dale*'s third group of four missiles left her launchers, chaff blossomed over both ships. At the same time, the frigate's three-inch gun opened up, pumping out round after round at one-second intervals. A puff of black-gray smoke marked each shell as it burst.

The second group of four SAMs from *Dale* intersected the ASMPs' track. Two more nuclear missiles died, leaving just a single attacker.

So far *Klakring*'s launcher had spat out eight missiles, but she'd only been graced with a single hit. Now, as the Kormorans converged on the cruiser, the frigate's last shot missed. She still carried plenty of SAMs in her magazine, but the German missiles were too close. If she fired again, she would be more likely to hit her larger companion.

The Kormorans were only seconds from impact.

Dale's starboard Phalanx fired, sending an almost solid stream of tungsten projectiles out in a quarter-second burst. As it fired, the six-barrel Gatling gun's dual radars tracked both the target and its bullet stream, bringing the two together. A mile away, a small black dot suddenly blossomed into an ugly black ball of smoke. The automated gun did not pause to admire its accuracy, but fired again – exploding another incoming missile. Both engagements took only seconds, but while the gun knocked down those two Kormorans, three others reached the ship.

Two missiles hit, slamming into her port side – one in the afterdeck house, the other near the bridge. Each carried nearly five hundred pounds of explosive moving just under the speed of sound.

Sections of *Dale*'s superstructure were torn out, while red-hot fragments slashed through her interior. In seconds, *Dale* was a pyre. The last four SAMs she had fired, deprived of their guiding hand, flew harmlessly past the remaining ASMP.

Ships in the inner screen were now in firing range. In a ragged salvo, an Aegis cruiser on the far side of the carrier, a *Perry*-class frigate, and a *Kidd*-class missile destroyer all launched SAMs.

Twenty miles out, at thirty thousand feet, one of the American missiles hit home.

Unlike the other French missiles, this ASMP had gotten close enough to arm itself. 'Salvage-fused,' it sensed its own death and detonated.

Sailors who hadn't yet taken cover belowdecks saw a bright sphere, the size of a small coin, appear in the sky – glowing like a weak red sun.

There wasn't any real danger at that distance. After averting their eyes from the initial flash, everyone stared at the angry symbol of Armageddon. Twenty seconds later, a sudden puff of warm wind swept past – the only tactile sign of temperatures and pressures that had briefly rivaled the sun itself.

Admiral Gibierge's masterstroke had failed.

USS *GEORGE WASHINGTON*

Ward was busy with the search-and-rescue efforts and the air battle's aftermath. The fireball had almost dissipated by the time he stepped outside. Off to the southeast, the sky was littered with shredded white smoke trails, while a black column of smoke closer in marked *Dale*'s demise.

They'd been damn lucky, he thought. He'd made an unexpected move, caught the enemy off guard, and come out relatively intact. They'd lost one cruiser, about twenty fighters, but they'd decimated EurCon air power. It had cost the lives of about five hundred sailors and airmen, he reflected sadly, but without the victory they could have lost many times that number.

Another missile ship was already steaming over to take *Dale*'s position. His fighter squadrons were recovering on board the two carriers. Once his pilots had time to rest and eat, each bird farm would launch the first in a long series of Alpha Strikes aimed at French and German air and naval bases. He planned to make sure EurCon paid dearly for what it had done.

Better yet, the carrier *Vinson* would arrive in the area in several more days, allowing him to keep two carriers on the line continuously while the other pulled back to replenish and rest its air crews.

In the meantime, Ward had some serious planning to do. EurCon's step across the nuclear threshold presented him with new military challenges. For a start, formations that had been closed up to offer better protection against conventional air attack would have to be dispersed to prevent multiple losses if another nuclear weapon got through.

He'd leave the bigger issues to the politicians in Washington and London. But one thing was already clear. The whole nature of this war had changed in the blink of an eye.

CHAPTER 23
Shifting Fortunes

JUNE 15 – NATIONAL SECURITY COUNCIL MEETING, THE WHITE HOUSE, WASHINGTON, D.C.

Ross Huntington sat in a chair and let the heated argument flow over and around him. This was one time he planned to let the NSC's official membership handle things without the somewhat dubious benefit of his advice. The military ramifications of the abortive French nuclear attack on *George Washington* were beyond his scope. He was a political advisor, not a defense expert. In any case, he already had more than enough on his plate. He felt worn down and about fifteen years older than he really was.

Huntington spent most of his waking hours out at Fort Meade – watching over the team of NSA analysts assigned to monitor EurCon's internal governmental and diplomatic communications. Although they'd been digging deep, looking for disagreements and disputes, his SIGINT gophers hadn't come up with much hard data.

The pandemonium in official and unofficial Washington more than made up for the European hush. For the past two days, pundits and politicians had swarmed over the nation's airwaves and newspaper op-ed columns – each with his or her own slant on what should be done, and done *now*.

Dovish liberals issued impassioned appeals for a cease-fire, a negotiated settlement, and above all for talks, talks, and more talks. Furious conservatives argued for unrestricted bombing across France and Germany. Some even urged the retaliatory use of U.S. tactical nuclear weapons against EurCon ground targets. Isolationists of both stripes contended that the incident showed the folly of American involvement in Europe's 'petty' quarrels.

The spectacle seemed absurd to Huntington whenever he surfaced from scanning decoded radio and microwave intercepts – another manifestation of the Beltway freak show in full swing. As always, it pissed him off to see journalists and news anchors paying respectful heed to 'experts' who'd been wrong so many times in the past. Why give airtime to people who had once solemnly assured anyone watching that KAL 007 had been a CIA spy flight, that the Soviets would never use chemical weapons against civilians, or that economic sanctions alone would force Saddam Hussein out of Kuwait?

Still, he had to admit that the TV talking heads seemed to represent every imaginable segment of American public opinion.

Not surprisingly, the administration's own inner circle split along somewhat the same lines. The cabinet officers who had first opposed energy aid to eastern Europe saw the nuclear attack as further proof that Poland and the others weren't worth the potential price in American lives and treasure. Lucier, Scofield, and Quinn were among those scornfully rejecting any idea of retreating under EurCon military pressure. Thurman wobbled between the two factions, trying to sit on both sides of the fence at the same time. As always, the military chiefs were among the most cautious when it came to the lives of the men and women they commanded. That didn't mean they backed withdrawal, but it did mean they wanted assurances that the nation's political leadership wouldn't leave them high and dry if the conflict escalated.

For the moment, the President seemed content to keep his own counsel.

He turned to the chairman of the Joint Chiefs. 'What's the latest word on our troop deployment, General? Are you still on schedule?'

'Yes, sir.' General Reid Galloway nodded. 'We're almost ready to start flying both the 101st and the 82nd to Gdansk. It's going to take a lot of time and a lot of planes, but we'll get there.'

Huntington had seen the figures. Moving just one brigade of the 101st Airborne and its associated aviation task force by air meant lifting 2,800 troops, over one hundred helicopters, and nearly five hundred other vehicles. During the Desert Shield buildup, more than a hundred giant C-5s and C-141s had taken thirteen days to accomplish a similar feat. Two things had helped them cut those times somewhat. First, two of the 101st's brigades were already packed and ready for movement to the U.K. for summer exercises with the British Army when the war broke out. Second, Poland was closer than Saudi Arabia and that cut flight times and wear and tear on crews. But it was still an enormous task.

'And our first two heavy divisions?'

The chief of naval operations, a slender, wiry man with salt-and-pepper hair and a pronounced Boston accent, answered that one. 'We're still assembling the transports we need, Mr. President. Once that's done, it'll take several more days to load them. Right now, our best guess is the first convoys can sail in a week to ten days.'

Carefully seated beside the President, Thurman cleared his throat.

'Yes, Harris?'

The Secretary of State folded his hands together and adopted his most serious expression. 'I believe we should hold those ships in port, sir. At least until we have a better handle on the situation.'

'Explain that.'

'Well, Mr. President, it seems foolish to put such a slow-moving, high-value target within reach of French nuclear weapons. Before we let this convoy sail, we need a firm commitment from Paris that they won't use those weapons again. Until we have their solemn pledge in hand, we would only be tempting the French and unnecessarily exposing our ships and military equipment to destruction.'

Members of the NSC's isolationist faction murmured their agreement with the Secretary of State.

'Unnecessarily?' Despite his best intentions, Huntington found he couldn't let that pass unchallenged. His pulse accelerated, driven by anger and irritation. 'You've seen the same battlefield reports I have, Mr. Secretary. Poland needs help as quick as we can send it! We should . . .' Pain tore through his chest. Oh, God. He shivered, feeling cold sweat trickling down his forehead and under his arms. Breathing was difficult. He stared down at the table, panting rapidly.

'Ross? Ross? Are you okay?'

Huntington made an effort and lifted his head. He saw the President staring down the long table at him in sudden concern.

'Jesus, Ross! You look like shit.'

'So I've been told, Mr. . . .' Huntington doubled over in his seat, fighting to pull air through lungs that felt like they were being squeezed by red-hot pincers. The room started to gray out.

Through the roaring in his ears, he heard the President snap, 'Get a medical team to the Situation Room! Now, goddamn it!'

An hour later, Huntington sat upright on a chilly examination table in the White House infirmary, acutely uncomfortable in a thin, sterile paper gown. Raw, stinging patches on his chest showed where a nurse had yanked hairs off along with a set of taped-down EKG leads.

He looked up at the trim, white-coated doctor standing close by, reviewing the EKG trace with pursed lips. 'Well?'

Francis Pardolesi, the President's personal physician, frowned down at the long, thin strip of paper. 'Your readings are normal now. But that's not unusual in angina. And your other symptoms and past medical history are indicative of the possibility.' He shook his head somberly. 'Diaphoresis. Shortness of breath. Crushing substernal pain. Those are not good signs, Mr. Huntington.'

'Cut to the chase, Doctor. Did I just have another heart attack?'

'Probably not,' the younger man admitted almost reluctantly. 'But in my best medical judgment, such a result is all but inevitable – especially if you keep pushing yourself so hard.'

Huntington started to object, but the doctor interrupted him. 'There are a few tests I'd like to have run – just to be sure of my diagnosis. A couple of days in Walter Reed certainly won't do you any harm.'

'No.'

'Mr. Huntington, you're not behaving sensibly. You have got to get some R&R.'

'I don't *have* time to rest, Doctor. We're at war, and I have a lot of work to do.' Huntington stood up, looking around for his shirt.

Pardolesi sighed. 'If you say so, but I think you're making a mistake. A big one.' Then he shrugged and turned away, rummaging in a filing cabinet. 'Before you go, I'll need you to sign this AMA form.'

Huntington raised an eyebrow. 'AMA? American Medical Association?'

The doctor shook his head. 'Against Medical Advice. It affirms that you're willfully rejecting my considered opinion.'

'So if I drop dead, my family can't sue?'

'Something like that.'

The President poked his head around the examining room door. 'How's it going in here, Frank?'

'Mr. Huntington seems determined to run himself into the ground, sir.' Pardolesi threw up his hands. 'He's refused hospitalization.'

'Well, that's his right.' The President came all the way into the room and turned to Huntington. 'Feeling better, Ross?'

'Much better.' Huntington tried for a sheepish smile. 'I'm only sorry about all the fuss earlier. Probably just a touch of indigestion.'

'Uh-huh.' The President exchanged a glance with his physician. 'Look, Ross, I don't let my friends commit suicide. So I want you to take it easy for a while. just rest and get your strength back, okay?'

Huntington felt oddly like a small child caught picking up the pieces of a broken lamp – guilty but determined to brazen it out. He shook his head stubbornly. 'With all due respect, I will not spend my time flat on my back in the hospital.'

'Not in the hospital. Here.' The President pointed toward the ceiling. The White House living quarters were above them. 'I'll have the staff fit out one of the guest rooms for you. That way the good doctor here can pop up and check in on you from time to time. That'll make *him* feel better anyway. Right, Frank?'

Pardolesi nodded.

'What about my project?' Huntington played his strongest card. Finding some way to fracture EurCon was a top priority.

The President looked at him with an unreadable expression in his eyes. 'Are those analysts at the NSA incompetent?'

'No. But . . .'

'Tell me, Ross, when you ran your own company, did you stand behind your assembly-line guys every single minute?'

'No.' Huntington saw his point and acknowledged it with a rueful grin.

'Then for God's sake, apply the same common sense to this situation,' the President argued in exasperation. 'Let the NSA sort the wheat from the chaff. I'll have a federal courier hand-deliver anything interesting to you at your bedside, poolside, or wherever. Fair enough?'

Huntington nodded slowly, accepting the inevitable. Then he looked up. 'What happened after I . . . left the room? About the troop convoys and the French nuclear threat, I mean?'

The President's face took on a new expression – one that was grim and utterly determined. He glanced quickly toward Pardolesi. 'Let's just say that I made certain critical decisions. It'll take time to pull everything together, but those ships will sail on time.'

MINISTRY OF NATIONAL DEFENSE, WARSAW

Gen. Wieslaw Staron studied the situation map in silence, ignoring the anxious officers who hovered nearby, ready to run errands or answer questions for him. He sighed softly.

Despite his best efforts and his soldiers' valor, Poland's military fortunes were still on the wane. French and German troops held Wroclaw solidly, and they were closing in on Poznan from the south. Though both sides were taking heavy casualties, the three Polish divisions trying to stem the EurCon tide were badly depleted. They were surviving only by giving ground whenever the enemy pressed them too closely.

The situation was slightly better in the air. More than two weeks of combat against long odds had cost the Polish Air Force many of its best planes and best pilots. EurCon's losses had been even higher. And now America's victory over the North Sea meant those losses could no longer be easily replaced by squadrons held in reserve in Germany and France.

Staron shrugged. The good news wasn't good enough. Even without assured air superiority, Poland's enemies had a manpower and firepower edge they could use to batter his bloodied army down before American or British reinforcements reached the battlefield. Somehow, from somewhere, he had to pull together enough troops to change that equation – to throw EurCon's invasion force off balance and buy more time.

His dark brown eyes slid east while he fumbled a cigarette out of a crumpled pack stuck in his jacket pocket. An aide stepped forward with a lit match. The Defense Minister bent his head down, puffed the cigarette into life, and then nodded his thanks – all without taking his gaze off the map in front of him.

The smoke he inhaled and blew out smelled more like a hellish concoction of burning leaves and cardboard than tobacco. As a young officer, Staron's salary wouldn't stretch far enough to buy American or even French cigarettes. He'd learned to make do with Russian dregs then. Now that he could afford to buy better, anything else seemed tasteless – too smooth to be real.

Russia. He had four divisions stuck on Poland's eastern border, warily watching Belarus, Ukraine, and their bigger brother behind them. Half his nation's armed strength was pinned down hundreds of kilometers from the real war – as useless as though they were on the far side of the moon. But there wasn't any evidence that the Russians were doing anything beyond taking normal defensive precautions against a war so close to their border. Certainly the American satellites weren't picking up any Russian military movements out of the ordinary.

Staron considered that. Satellite intelligence wasn't perfect. Their orbits were too predictable and their sensors could be spoofed by a clever opponent. He would have felt a lot more comfortable with political intelligence from inside the Kremlin itself. Then he shrugged. He'd like to be able to read his opponents' minds, too, for that matter. Making decisions and taking risks on the basis of incomplete information came with the office and with the silver stars and braid on his shoulder boards.

He turned to the officer in charge of communications between Warsaw and the army's various field headquarters. 'Get me the commander of the 8th Mechanized Division.'

JUNE 17 – ASSEMBLY AREA, 19TH PANZERGRENADIER BRIGADE, LESZNO

Parked Leopard 2 tanks and Marder APCs filled Leszno's town square and the surrounding streets. Their scarred turrets and mud-streaked tracks and side skirts looked out of place beside the brightly painted Baroque buildings around them. Dull-eyed German soldiers sat slumped on the cobblestones or sprawled on top of their vehicles. But each man kept his helmet and rifle close to hand.

The 7th Panzer's officers and men had been in combat almost continuously for twelve days and they were exhausted. Many of their vehicles were broken down or badly in need of repair. Between mechanical breakdowns and battle losses, some battalions were barely above half strength. The whole division urgently needed time to rest and regroup.

Tracks clattered and squealed across the pavement as LeClerc tanks and AMX-10 troop carriers crowded past on their way to the front. The French 5th Armored Division was moving up from reserve to take over the lead.

Lt. Col. Willi von Seelow scratched his chin, frowning at the feel of the blond stubble under his fingers. He hadn't had time to shave for two days and now he itched and stank. Baths had consisted of splashing water from his canteen over his hands and face in occasional, usually futile efforts to clear away caked-on dust or mud.

He dropped his hand and stood still, watching the French column lumbering forward.

'Pretty bunch of sluggards, aren't they?' Lt. Col. Otto Yorck muttered. 'Do you suppose our glorious allies are finally ready to get their brand-new tanks dented in combat?'

Willi shrugged. 'Maybe.' He eyed the long parade of passing vehicles angrily. 'I was beginning to think General Montagne was saving them for the victory celebration.'

'A duty the damned French would undoubtedly perform to perfection,' Yorck growled.

Willi nodded. His friend had every reason to be bitter. This relief was long overdue. Some officers openly wondered whether Montagne had secret orders from Paris to hold down French casualties in what was rapidly becoming a prolonged and unpopular war.

Now, with French armor finally out in front, II Corps, 7th Panzer's parent formation, was turning northeast against stiff opposition. They were driving hard to cross the Warta River below Poznan at a little town called Srem. Once across the river, the corps would swing northward again, advancing down the Warta's east bank toward the city. Montagne, Leibnitz, and the other generals hoped the move would outflank the Polish Army's best defensive positions.

They were supposed to link up with the III Corps' three divisions on the far side of Poznan.

And then what were they supposed to do? As far as von Seelow was concerned, the belief that capturing or isolating Poznan would somehow force the Poles to the bargaining table was a fantasy of the worst kind. The Americans were busy flattening Germany's naval and air installations along the Baltic. Once they were done, the Baltic would lie open to U.S. and British freighters and troop transports. Why should Poland surrender now when time was on its side?

Von Seelow spun abruptly on his heel and strode toward the building he'd commandeered for the staff operations center. He couldn't shake the growing feeling that he and his fellow soldiers were mired to the knees in a deadly bog and sinking fast.

JUNE 20 – GROUP MALANOWSKI, SOUTH OF THE WARTA RIVER

Artillery grumbled to the north, like distant thunder on a gray, overcast day. The dirty, ragtag band of forty Polish soldiers concealed in the band of birchwoods stiffened and then relaxed. The shelling was too far away to menace them. They settled back to their work, stripping and cleaning an oddly varied assortment of personal weapons – some Polish, some German, and some French. A few were busy performing routine maintenance on a small collection of equally varied vehicles. Two civilian cars, a Polish GAZ jeep, an American-made Humvee, and a canvas-sided German truck were parked beneath the trees.

Maj. Marek Malanowski squatted easily on his haunches in a small clearing near the center of the woods, listening respectfully to the elderly, weatherbeaten farmer who had come in that morning bearing glad tidings. He waited until the man finished speaking and then asked, 'Why are you so sure that this camp is a headquarters of some kind? Couldn't it be a field hospital or a supply dump?'

The farmer snorted. 'I served my time as a conscript, Major. Where else but a headquarters do you see enough saluting to wear arms out – not to mention enough radio antennas for a whole village? And when did you ever see doctors saluting each other?'

Malanowski grinned. 'True enough.' He rocked back on his heels and stared down at his locked hands, considering the presence of an enemy command post within striking distance. Then he looked up. 'What about their security?'

The old man hawked and spat to one side. 'Pathetic. A few foot soldiers, a machine-gun nest or two, and a few trucks.'

'Any signs that they're planning to move?'

'No.' The farmer shook his grizzled head confidently. 'If they move out today, they'll be leaving a lot of vehicles behind. I saw mechanics overhauling engines all over the place.'

Malanowski stood up, straightening to his full height. His calf muscles ached, sore from constant overuse and too little rest. He ignored the pain. 'All right, my friend, I'll come see this headquarters of yours for myself.'

He glanced round the clearing at his men and smiled coldly. 'Then we may all pay these Germans a social call later on tonight. Right, boys?'

Grim, silent nods answered him.

Malanowski was satisfied by that. His soldiers were hungry for revenge. Some were survivors from his battalion. Others were stragglers he'd picked up on the long, dangerous journey eastward from the Neisse River. They'd kept busy on the way – dodging EurCon patrols and ambushing couriers and supply trucks. But now the major was ready to hunt bigger game.

COMMAND POST, 19TH PANZERGRENADIER BRIGADE, NOCHOWO

The 19th Panzergrenadier's main command post occupied an orchard just off the road connecting Lezno and the Warta River crossings at Srem. Five hundred meters of open fields separated the orchard from Nochowo, the closest hamlet.

Von Seelow came out of his M577 TOC and waited, letting his eyes adjust to the dark. The sun had set two hours before and the moon wouldn't be up for a little while longer. In the meantime, the headquarters unit had to make do with a few shielded electric lamps.

Repeated flashes rippled along the northeastern horizon, backed up by a rhythmic, muted thumping. He frowned. Although II Corps HQ had passed very little information down the chain, it was clear that the Poles were hitting the French in strength. But what magic hat had they tapped to find the troops for a counterattack? Where had they made themselves weak to be strong here?

Von Seelow looked away and walked toward the cluster of officers huddled around a dimly lit map table. Aware that they might be called out of reserve soon to retrieve a deteriorating tactical situation across the Warta, Colonel Bremer had summoned his battalion and company commanders to the brigade CP for a quick brief.

The map taped to the table showed the broad extent of the Confederation's advance into Poland. Our vaunted invasion looks just like a ridiculously big fishhook, he realized, with the bend beginning at Wroclaw. Well, von Seelow thought wryly, maybe we're confusing the Poles almost as much as we're confusing ourselves.

A stocky shape tugged at his sleeve. 'Herr Oberstleutnant!'

He recognized Private Neumann's hoarse voice. The signalman must have followed him out of the TOC. 'What is it?'

'Division is on the line again, sir. They say it's urgent.'

Von Seelow stifled the urge to swear. He'd spoken with the 7th Panzer's operations officer only a few minutes before. What could possibly have changed in such a short span of time? He caught Bremer's eye and inclined his head toward the TOC, indicating he'd been called back.

The colonel nodded briefly and kept talking, filling his officers in on what he knew about the battle raging ahead of them.

Von Seelow headed back to his bulky, blacked-out armored vehicle. On the way he noticed again how few troops were guarding the command post. He made a mental note to raise his concerns with Lieutenant Preussner, the junior officer currently responsible for headquarters security. The men usually charged with the task, soldiers from 7th

Panzer's jaeger and security battalions, were spread across southwest Poland, guarding bridges and supply convoys. To replace them, Bremer had detailed Preussner to command a scratch force of men volunteered by each of the brigade's battalions.

Willi was beginning to believe that the colonel had made a mistake there. Naturally enough, most of the battalion COs had taken the opportunity to rid themselves of a few feckless incompetents and disciplinary hard cases. Given enough time, a tough, experienced leader might have been able to whip them into shape, but not Preussner. The thin, bookish lieutenant ordinarily ran the 19th's cryptographic cell. He was a good staff officer. He was also the last person von Seelow would have put in charge of line troops – at least under ideal circumstances. Of course, the circumstances were anything but ideal. Preussner had been chosen because two weeks of war had left the brigade with a distinct shortage of junior officers. Matching assignments and personalities was a peacetime luxury.

Von Seelow strode up his M577's rear ramp and ducked his head as he brushed through the blackout curtain into its crowded compartment. One of his subordinates handed him a headset. Preussner's troubles would have to wait. II Corps was undoubtedly about to dump a whole new load on the 19th Panzergrenadier's shoulders.

At the sandbagged guard post two hundred meters down the road to Nochowo, a match flared suddenly.

'For God's sake, Vogler!' Lt. Paul Preussner snapped. 'Put that damned cigarette out! You're on sentry duty here, not waiting for the bloody bus to Berlin!'

'Yes, sir,' the private answered sullenly. A red glow flipped through the air and landed close to his foot.

Preussner stared down for a second at the still-smoldering cigarette and then ground it out. He felt like tearing his hair out. These idiots were hopeless! He felt a moment's intense longing for the quiet competence of the enlisted men who staffed his cryptographic van.

The throbbing sound of a heavy diesel engine approaching brought him out of his reverie. A vehicle had turned off the main road and was rattling up the dirt side track that led to the orchard. His head came up. 'Report, Vogler.'

'It's a truck, Herr Leutnant.'

Preussner fought off his first impulse to throttle the private and sighed. If he reacted to every insolent remark, he'd have half the headquarters guard detachment up on charges. 'And?'

'One of ours, sir.'

The lieutenant closed his eyes in exasperation and said, with far more patience than he felt, 'Why don't you go and make sure of that, Private?'

Vogler muttered something Preussner chose to interpret as agreement. Still muttering, the sour-faced private slung his assault rifle over one shoulder and stepped out of the guard post into the road. He used a shielded flashlight to wave the canvas-sided truck to a stop.

Preussner leaned against the guard post's waist-high wall, waiting patiently for the private's next screwup.

The truck driver's door creaked open and a man clambered out from behind the wheel, dropping lightly to the ground in front of Vogler. Something about his uniform looked odd in the dim red glow from the private's flashlight. Just what kind of camouflage pattern was that?

Vogler stiffened suddenly and whirled toward Preussner, eyes wide. 'Sir, they're Pol—'

Something bright gleamed in the darkness and plunged into the private's back. Vogler moaned once and crumpled to the ground.

Preussner felt his mouth fall open. He stood rooted in shock, staring from the private's contorted body to the Polish soldiers already leaping out the back of the truck. Everything around him seemed to freeze.

Then the frozen moment passed and movement came back in a flash. The lieutenant's hand was already fumbling for the pistol at his side when a dark shape flew through the air, smacked onto the sandbags in front of him, and rolled inside the guard post – right between his feet.

Paul Preussner had just enough time to recognize the Soviet-style fragmentation grenade before it went off.

Even as the muffled burst of light and sound faded, figures were already rising up out of the tall grass and standing crops in front of the shredded, smoking guard post.

Major Malanowski and his men had come to pay their respects.

'. . . French are falling back, Willi . . . need you to plug the gap by morning . . . critical . . .'

Willi von Seelow pressed the headphones tighter against his ears, trying to make sense out of the static-filled, scrambled transmission from division HQ. Polish radio jamming was getting better, and they hadn't had time yet to lay wire communications. Two things were disastrously clear, though. First, the damned French had been beaten and were retreating fast. And second, Montagne and his underlings expected the 19th Panzergrenadier to save their bacon – again.

He clicked the transmit switch. 'Understood, sir. But . . .'

Whummp. 'Wait one.' Von Seelow pulled the headphones off and glanced at the sergeant sitting beside him. 'What the hell was that?'

Gunfire erupted outside the TOC – the chattering roar of machine guns and the higher-pitched crackling of assault rifles. Startled cries and screams rose above the noise. Realization broke past his surprise. They were under attack!

Von Seelow tossed the headset to the sergeant. 'Get help fast!' Without waiting for a reply, he reared up off his chair, undogged the commander's cupola, and poked his head through the opening.

Trucks parked around the command post perimeter were on fire, burning brightly as fuel fed the flames. Everywhere he looked men were toppling, cut down by the bullets scything through the camp. Others dove for cover behind vehicles or piles of equipment, clawing at their sidearms to return fire.

An RPG streaked through the night and exploded inside a Marder APC, gutting it. Razor-edged steel fragments blew outward, slicing two

German officers who had been sheltering beside the Marder into red ruin.

Flashes stabbed out of the darkness along the perimeter. The Poles were still outside the camp, but he could see shadowy forms scrambling upright and moving forward. They were coming in to finish the job. Another grenade went off near the overturned map table.

Von Seelow grabbed the MG3 machine gun mounted beside the cupola and opened up, sending a long, withering burst along the line of advancing enemy soldiers. Several were hit and knocked off their feet. The other Poles dropped flat, seeking shelter wherever they could find it.

One man knelt, leveling a rocket launcher.

Willi sensed more than saw him and whipped the machine gun around with his finger still locked on the trigger. Four 7.62mm rounds moving at 2,700 feet per second tore the RPG gunner to pieces before he could fire.

Heartened by his example and with the Poles pinned down, more German crews made it to their own armored vehicles and started shooting back. Tracers lit the night, floating out over the open fields around the orchard.

As quickly as it had begun, the attack ended. The Polish soldiers faded back into the darkness, dragging their own dead and wounded with them. They left the 19th Panzergrenadier Brigade's headquarters in shambles behind them.

Half an hour later, von Seelow stared down at a familiar figure sprawled beside the splintered map table. A grim-faced medical officer kneeling by the body looked up and shook his head.

Col. Georg Bremer was dead.

Willi swallowed hard and turned away. So many were dead, and so many others were badly wounded – Jurgen Greif, the brigade second-in-command, and his old friend Otto Yorck among them. The Polish commando raid had decimated the 19th's command structure.

'Sir?'

'What is it, Neumann?'

The private still sounded shaken. He'd been standing close to the colonel when the attack began. 'II Corps is calling again, Herr Oberstleutnant. They want to know when we can move up. They say things are going from bad to worse across the river.'

'And what do they think we're doing here? Cleaning up after a damned picnic?' Von Seelow instantly regretted the outburst. The private was only doing his job. He put a hand on the younger man's shoulder and felt him flinch. 'Tell Captain Weber to inform Corps that we'll have two battalions on the road within the hour. And tell them to make sure the bridges are cleared for our advance. Understand?'

Neumann nodded and hurried off.

Willi von Seelow sighed once. Then he moved into the tangle of burned-out and bullet-pocked vehicles, rounding up his surviving officers. With Bremer dead and Greif out of action, command of the brigade fell to him. Whether anyone higher up liked it or not.

JUNE 21 – 19TH PANZERGRENADIER BRIGADE, ON THE WARTA RIVER

Von Seelow squinted into the rising sun and scowled angrily. Despite all the promises made by II Corps, the three pontoon bridges across the Warta were packed with French troops and vehicles streaming back in disorder. Signs of barely contained panic were everywhere. LeClerc tanks showing clear signs of battle damage – scarred armor, jammed turrets, or smoking engines – mingled with others that seemed completely untouched. Dazed soldiers threaded their way through the slow-moving columns on foot. Trucks that stalled out in the growing heat were pushed off into the river instead of being towed to the opposite bank.

He grabbed the French military police captain who had been directing traffic and stabbed a finger toward the bridging site. 'I'm not asking you, Captain, I'm telling you! I want at least one of those pontoon bridges clear for my brigade to cross! Not later! Now!'

The MP licked dry lips and shrugged nervously. 'I'm afraid that is impossible, sir. General Belliard himself gave me my orders. All bridges are reserved for the 5th Armored.'

Von Seelow nodded. Belliard was the commander of the 5th French Armored Division.

He glanced up the road behind them. Leopard 2s and Marders were backing up, stalled in close formation while they waited to cross the Warta. They were sitting ducks while stuck like that. His men called the Leopard *Der Schimpanse* because it was so easy to drive that even a monkey could do it. But not even the Chimp could swim. Only God himself could help them if a Polish fighter-bomber broke through the air patrols overhead and the SAM defenses here below. Or if the Poles got forward observers in a position to call in artillery fire on the riverbank. 'And where is General Belliard?'

Again the same nervous shrug. 'I am not sure, sir. His command vehicle went by several hours ago.'

Shit. Willi's anger flared to white-hot rage. The cowardly son-of-a-bitch was probably already back hiding behind Gen. Etienne Montagne's dress uniform trousers. Part of him wanted to sit back and simply accept the fact that getting across the Warta into combat again was impossible. But another part of him – older, more inflexible, and still bound by honor – summoned up reminders of the oaths he had sworn and of his duty as a soldier.

He spun the French MP around and pointed to the big, 120mm main guns mounted on his Leopard 2s. 'Do you see those guns, Captain?'

'Yes, sir.'

'Good.' Von Seelow leaned forward to stare directly into the other man's frightened eyes. 'Listen to me very carefully. Either you clear a path for my men and me immediately, or my tanks will blow every single one of those damned bridges into the Warta – with or without your men on them. Do I make myself clear?'

The Frenchman's mouth dropped open and hung there while he stared back at von Seelow. Then he closed it hastily and nodded rapidly.

Von Seelow released him and walked away without looking back – striding back to his command vehicle. With Willi in the lead and in command, the 19th Panzergrenadier was heading back into battle.

CHAPTER 24
Assembly

JUNE 21 – EMBARKATION AREA, SAVANNAH, GEORGIA

Down on the Savannah waterfront, the bells pealing to signal Sunday services were drowned out – buried beneath the constant roar of diesel engines and heavy machinery. Ignoring the noise and frantic human activity, clouds of midges and biting flies drifted lazily through hot, humid air, sliding low above oil-stained water and between rusting steel hulls.

Ships crowded the harbor, taking on military cargo destined for the war in Europe. Several were RO/ROs, roll-on/roll-off vessels with stern and side ramps specially designed to speed the process of loading and unloading large numbers of vehicles. Most were breakbulk, general-purpose freighters. Cargo-handling cranes towered over the dock area, dwarfing the crates, containers, and stores pallets they were busy lifting from the piers and lowering into freighter holds.

Mike Decker put his lunch box on a crate and eased his large frame down onto the wooden surface. The seats in the pierside cranes were all right, but after eight hours in one of those steel cages even this wooden crate felt comfortable.

He mopped his rugged face and balding head with a kerchief. It had been a muggy night, and a busy one. He was still strong, still one of the bulls on these docks, but a guy his age, counting the months to retirement, had a right to feel a little stiff. He could do his job, the same one younger men did, but it took more out of him now.

He'd spent the entire night shift – on double time, he reminded himself – loading crates and vehicles and guns and everything else the U.S. Army needed. Now, in the morning light, it looked like he hadn't done a damn thing.

The port was jammed. Row after row of green and brown camouflaged tanks, trucks, self-propelled guns, and other vehicles filled parking areas near the docks. He knew others were still tied down on flatcars in the rail yards adjacent to the harbor. Crates and cases on pallets occupied every flat spot until there was hardly room to walk.

Two U.S. Army divisions were being readied for sea transport to Poland from Savannah – the 24th Mechanized and the 1st Armored. Other units were loading their gear aboard trains for transportation to

different ports along the eastern seaboard.
In addition to the civilian longshoremen, Merchant Marine sailors and Navy Sealift crews were sweating around the clock to load and stow the heavy equipment as it came rolling in by train.
Decker had been working the docks for thirty years. He'd gone out himself, on a ship like these, to Korea. After that, he'd spent his life loading ships, sometimes for war.
The papers were full of stories about the war in Europe, and his father, nearly an invalid but still clear-eyed, was full of stories about the last time Americans had fought in Europe. Like his son now, he had loaded the ships, then watched them sail off over the horizon, wishing them luck and a speedy return.
Decker wished these ships luck as well.

JUNE 22 – ALPHA COMPANY, 3/187TH INFANTRY, OVER GDANSK

The spacious compartment of the C-141 cargo plane was still dark, even with all its interior lighting on. Capt. Mike Reynolds could barely see the loadmaster standing at the forward end of the compartment.
The barrel-chested staff sergeant needed an amplifier to make himself heard over the steady roar of the transport's jet engines. Holding onto a bracket to steady himself, he shouted instructions into a microphone. 'Listen up, gentlemen. This will be a "hot landing." Not having any great ambition to get blown up by some Frog or Kraut jet jock, we want to be on the ground for the shortest time possible. So make sure you have all your gear ready to go and go fast. There ain't no lost luggage counter at this here airport.'
That earned him a low chuckle from the listening troopers.
'We'll turn off the seat belt sign early, as soon as the plane's landed and slowed a little. Stand up and head for your assigned door, then get out as soon as the doors open. Last time, we emptied this puppy in ten minutes, and we had more cargo then.'
Reynolds looked at his men. Most were nodding, accepting the challenge. Good soldiers were by nature competitive, and this was not an idle contest. While Combined Forces aircraft controlled the sky over Gdansk, a surprise EurCon raid on the airfield would pay big dividends. The enemy might risk planes for the attack, or send in a salvo of cruise missiles. They could hardly miss. The field was crammed with planes and equipment. Besides, other aircraft were stacked three deep behind them, waiting for their turn on a runway. Gdansk was one knotted end of the lifeline keeping the eastern European democracies afloat.
Unable to stay seated, he unbuckled and moved down the rows of seated soldiers, ostensibly checking over his men and their gear. He hated the confined seating of the Starlifter, folded almost double, and jammed tight against the next man. The bulky, standard-issue rucksack and equipment harness was filled with bumps and hard corners, so that no matter how you sat, some part of your anatomy was being poked by something.

Reynolds was a lean, rangy man, with straight brown hair cut short, almost a crew cut. A pair of wire-rimmed glasses sat on his nose. It was his one kick against army regulations. When they got closer to a combat zone, he should switch over to the ugly, heavy-duty, black plastic frames commonly referred to as the 'most effective birth-control device known to man.'

His command, Alpha Company of the 3rd Battalion of the 187th Infantry Regiment, occupied most of the Starlifter's cargo compartment. The space left over was filled with palletized cargo and small-arms ammunition.

Reynolds' infantry company was one of three in the battalion. Together with an antitank and a headquarters company, they gave the '3rd of the 187th' a strength of almost eight hundred men. The outfit had a long history, going back to World War II. The company's motto was 'Angels from Hell,' and that was a description its officers and men took very seriously.

The 3/187th was one of three airmobile infantry battalions making up the 3rd Brigade. In turn, there were a total of three infantry brigades and one helicopter brigade in the 101st Airborne Division (Air Assault), the famous 'Screaming Eagles.'

Alpha Company had over a hundred men in it. Reynolds had trained hard with them since joining the 101st. And he'd worked hard to get to know them – as soldiers and as individuals. Some, many of the senior sergeants, were combat veterans. He wasn't. He'd been commissioned shortly after Desert Storm. West Point and Infantry Officer Basic Course and all the other training that the army had loaded onto him had given him the skills, but not the experience of combat. Right now, he faced the same question as the rawest private: How will I do once the shooting starts?

Caught by minor turbulence, the C-141 rattled and shook briefly. Reynolds rode it out standing upright in the aisle. He felt better on his feet. He wasn't claustrophobic, but it had been a long flight, straight from Fort Campbell, Kentucky, to Poland – over ten hours in the air. The only break in the monotony had come during the in-flight refueling, west of the British Isles, but there hadn't been much to see. A few of the troops had glimpsed some escorting fighters, which had started a low-grade panic until the Starlifter's pilot confirmed the planes were friendly.

He smiled, remembering the mildly sarcastic remark from one of his sergeants. 'If those *are* enemy fighters, Private Wilson, why the hell aren't you dead?'

His men were crammed into canvas-backed metal seats fastened to the cargo bay floor. Dressed in full field gear, most of them had sat for the entire flight with their rucksacks and personal weapons in their laps. Where space allowed, soldiers had piled their personal equipment to one side or in odd corners, but those spaces were few and far between.

Knowing that it might be their last chance for quite some time, they'd all slept as much as possible. Reynolds, exhausted by the frantic preparations needed to ready his unit for an overseas move, had fallen asleep almost as soon as the plane started moving. He'd started awake after a few hours, stiff and restless. From then on he'd read, talked, eaten a box lunch, finally slept just a little more, and wished a hundred times for the interminable flight to end. He knew his body could use the rest, but his active mind wouldn't slow down.

Now, as the Starlifter approached its destination, there was a last-minute bustle as troops collected and double-checked their gear. He moved down the rows of seats yet again, finishing his inspection. He knew many of them well: Corporal Cook, curled up with a paperback horror novel, Private Khim, asleep until the last minute, and third in the row, Sergeant Ford.

First Sgt. Andy Ford was a combat veteran, and one of the key men Reynolds depended on to make Alpha Company work. He was the senior enlisted man in the unit, and his only job was to help Reynolds make things happen. His nickname was 'Steady,' a compliment to his temperament. Now he met the captain's gaze with his own. Ford smiled and nodded at the captain. Some of his confidence seemed to rub off.

Reynolds needed it. The closer they got to Poland, the more worried he was when he contemplated combat against EurCon's tanks and armored personnel carriers. The 'One-Oh-One' was strategically mobile, designed for rapid deployment to world trouble spots. But portability had a price. The division's combat battalions didn't have any M1 tanks or Bradley Fighting Vehicles of their own. They relied on antitank missiles and helicopter gunships, potent in themselves, but not always enough when matched against fully armored units. Without 'tracks' – armored vehicles – they were not terribly mobile on the battlefield, either. The division's organic helicopter brigade couldn't lift everyone at once, and they needed air superiority for the vulnerable helicopters to operate safely.

The plane pitched forward sharply, losing altitude fast. The loadmaster came over the sound system again. 'We're on final approach, gentlemen.'

Reynolds staggered back to his seat. Rank had granted him a window, and now he used it to view the city below. Old and crowded and darkened by industry, Gdansk had been darkened further by war. Through a broken layer of white clouds, the city seemed almost black beneath him.

Gdansk was a long way from Texas, where he'd been born and raised, or Fort Campbell, home of the 101st. The army had moved him around a lot in his six years since he'd earned his commission. That was one of the reasons he liked the service. As a youngster, even a trip into town had seemed like a big deal.

He could see the Baltic to the north, steel-gray but shimmering in the patches where the sun hit it. The harbor was crowded with ships. Somewhat incongruously, the countryside outside Gdansk looked peaceful – a softly rolling landscape of lakes and forests. The fighting was still well clear of the city, about two hundred kilometers out, but the word was that the enemy might be coming on strong again at any time.

Most of 3rd Brigade was already on the ground, with the balance arriving today. The 3/187th would spend the rest of the day gathering and unpacking its heavy equipment. Current plans called for them to move out that same night for an assembly area closer to the front lines. In a few days, they could be in battle.

Reynolds forced a confident grin onto his face. His soldiers were looking to him. Any doubts he had were for himself alone.

With a sharp jolt, the Starlifter's big wheels touched down and Alpha Company entered the war zone.

CHAPTER 25
Shadow War

JUNE 22 – PALAIS ROYAL, PARIS

Outside the windows of Nicolas Desaix's office, Paris was aglow. Streetlamps, neon signs, and lighted residences burned away the darkness, turning the night sky a soft orange. Low-light sensors and infrared targeting systems rendered blackouts ineffective. Given that, the French government had decided to avoid unnecessarily alarming its citizens.

But the capital's broad avenues, restaurants, and theaters were all deserted. The city was still under martial law curfew.

Three men sat in armchairs grouped around a low coffee table. A silver tray on the table held wineglasses for Desaix and for Jacques Morin, the head of the DGSE. Michel Guichy sipped Calvados – the dry apple brandy made in Normandy, his home region. Together, Desaix, Morin, and Guichy formed the triumvirate that ruled France and, through the Confederation secretariats, much of Europe. They were meeting to review progress in the war they had helped ignite.

Or perhaps the lack of progress would be a better description, Desaix thought bitterly. 'So both the Americans and British have troops in Poland now?'

Guichy nodded. 'Around Gdansk.' The dark circles and heavy bags under the man's eyes testified to the long hours he spent in the Defense Ministry's situation room and in traveling back and forth between Paris and the armed forces' war headquarters on the German border. 'Only lightly armed airborne units and Marine Commandos so far, but their heavier units cannot be very far behind. Days at best.'

Desaix scowled. Far from frightening the so-called Combined Forces away, Admiral Gibierge's ill-conceived nuclear gamble seemed only to have spurred them on. He shifted minutely in his chair to face his other companion. 'And the Poles?'

'They're transferring their forces west at a rapid pace.' Morin was atypically blunt. Usually the intelligence director preferred to hedge his assessments. 'When we attacked, four of the eight Polish divisions were in the east – watching the Russians. One of those same divisions mauled our 5th Armored two days ago. The Germans say another is already moving toward the battle area, and I see no reason to doubt them.'

Desaix received the news in silence. Though not formally trained as a military strategist, he knew how to 'count rifles.' Once those new soldiers arrived, the allies would have eight and a half divisions on the line – six Polish, two American, and one British brigade. Even committing their invasion army's reserve, the V Corps, would leave France and Germany with just eleven divisions to match against their enemies.

He supposed they could scrape together additional forces from France, Germany, and the Czech-Hungarian front, but not without grave risk. With casualties mounting, French and German civilians, already restive under prolonged martial law, were growing increasingly disillusioned. The latest troop call-ups had proved disappointing. Large numbers of reservists urgently needed to guard lines of communication and key installations had failed to report to their units.

To cover his growing dismay, Desaix took a sip of wine and rolled it around his mouth, automatically savoring the complex flavors before swallowing. Then, almost as though the wine itself had unlocked his mind, he saw the answer, a way to completely transform the bleak strategic situation they faced. He set his glass down and smiled.

'Do you see something amusing in all of this, Nicolas?' Guichy asked irritably.

'Not at all, my friend.' Desaix looked from one man to the other. 'But I do see that we've been guilty of tunnel vision. These Polish troop moves are not a disaster for us. Far from it! If we move quickly enough, they offer us the chance to secure a decisive victory!'

Both Morin and Guichy stared at him, still uncomprehending.

Desaix explained what he had in mind, rapidly sketching out the broad outlines of his proposal.

Guichy's eyes opened wide in astonishment. 'But what about the *Boche*? They'll be furious! They'll never approve such a move!'

'True, Michel.' Desaix nodded. He lowered his voice. 'And that is why the Germans must not know what we're about – not until it is too late.'

JUNE 23 – VNUKOVO AIRPORT, MOSCOW

Vnukovo Airport, one of the four major landing fields surrounding Moscow, lay twenty-nine kilometers southwest from the city center, just off the Kiev Highway. Ordinarily only domestic flights and planes from the other former Soviet Republics used the field. International carriers were supposed to fly into either Sheremetyevo One or Two to the north.

So the unscheduled arrival of a four-engine Airbus A340 with Air France markings should have generated excited speculation among Vnukovo's traffic controllers, ground crews, and mechanics. But not with hundreds of FIS agents and uniformed soldiers prowling every corridor, workshop, and office. Under Marshal Kaminov's autocratic rule, the airport workers knew very well that the old admonition 'Careless talk costs lives' meant their own lives – not those of others. They kept their mouths carefully shut.

Guided by instructions from the tower, the Airbus turned off Vnukovo's main runway and stopped beside a waiting army honor guard, military band, and a line of long black limousines. Ground crewmen hurriedly maneuvered a mobile staircase into place at the forward cabin door.

Drums rolled, a hundred gloved hands slapped rifle butts, and gleaming bayonets flashed in the summer sun as the honor guard presented arms. Two flags – one Russian, the other French – dipped slowly in a salute.

Men emerged from the Airbus and walked slowly down the staircase toward a small party of Russian Army officers waiting on the tarmac. Some of the Frenchmen wore dark, elegant, perfectly tailored suits. Several more wore military uniforms representing the three different services.

With a crash of cymbals and a blare of trumpets, the band broke into '*La Marseillaise*.' After a long, roundabout journey through Confederation and neutral airspace, Nicolas Desaix's handpicked ambassador and negotiating team were safely on Russian soil.

Maj. Paul Duroc stood at attention several paces behind Ambassador Sauret and his personal entourage, inconspicuous in civilian clothes among the other junior aides. With his hand resting over his heart for the anthem, he could feel the shoulder holster and automatic pistol hidden beneath his suit jacket. It was somehow reassuring – something solid to hang on to during his rapid fall from grace. The step down from independent special operations commander to this current posting as a glorified security chief was a long and humiliating one.

Fairly or unfairly, he'd been blamed for the Budapest fiasco. Even his capture of the chief Hungarian leader, Kusin, hadn't been enough to stem his superiors' wrath. Caught unprepared as their policies unraveled, the DGSE's top brass had needed a convenient scapegoat. Someone high enough up the chain of command to be believable, but not powerful enough to turn the blame aside. They'd picked him.

So here he was, plucked out of disgrace for an assignment that required the appointment of a senior intelligence officer as a figurehead. Paris had shunted him off to Moscow with explicit orders to keep his mouth shut, his eyes open, and above all, to do nothing that might upset his Russian hosts. His instructions gave him permission to 'liaise' with the Russian security services during the negotiations and nothing more. In short, the major knew he was supposed to be the perfect unobtrusive and inoffensive watchman.

Duroc locked his jaw against a sudden wave of anger. Very well, he would be a watchman. He would follow his orders to the letter. For now. And if he saw a chance to retrieve his reputation by breaking those rules? He shrugged inwardly. Then Paris and all its prissy bureaucrats could go hang.

JUNE 24 – U.S. EMBASSY, MOSCOW

Erin McKenna paused in the door to apply her name tag, eyeing the crowded reception hall ahead of her. It was a sea of tuxedos, dress uniforms, and evening gowns. Half of Moscow's movers and shakers were inside, clustered around tables piled high with food, wine, and hard liquor. Music stands and chairs in one corner marked out the territory set aside for the big band the U.S. ambassador had engaged for tonight's event. With the war heating up, America's diplomats were spending more time trying to win the goodwill of the Russian political and military leadership – especially those who took their orders directly from Marshal Yuri Kaminov.

Hence this official 'Gathering to Promote Peaceful Understanding Between the Great Peoples of the United States and the Russian Republic.' Yeah, right, she thought cynically. From what she'd seen since arriving in Moscow, Kaminov's preferred method of achieving 'peaceful understanding' was usually a bullet in the back of the skull.

Erin had been hoping that Alex Banich would come with her tonight, but he'd taken just one look at the guest list before shaking his head. 'Too many of those guys already know me as Nikolai Ushenko.' He'd smiled wryly. 'Why confuse them?'

His reasoning made sense, but it still robbed her of his company.

She circulated through the room, secretly enjoying the looks coming her way from the embassy staffers and guests alike. Prudence would have dictated wearing something drab and unnoticeable – anything in gray, perhaps. After all, as a suspected agent of the CIA she was basically a prisoner in the embassy and an embarrassment to the regular diplomatic functionaries. Under the circumstances, it might even have been more discreet not to show up at all. And for a time she'd seriously considered staying in her quarters, after all. But then a streak of defiance had surfaced. Why not, she'd thought, why not go out in a blaze of glory?

Glory in this context translated into a backless, emerald-green satin dress, high heels, emerald earrings, and upswept, elegantly styled hair. From the appreciative murmurs and discreet nudges she noticed in passing, it appeared she had achieved the effect she'd been aiming for. Undiplomatic, yes. Indiscreet, absolutely. But definitely stunning.

Erin took a glass of champagne from a passing waiter and turned to survey the crowd.

She found herself face-to-face with a tall, good-looking man in uniform. A Russian Army uniform. Her eyes flicked down to the name tag stuck above rows of service ribbons and decorations she couldn't recognize: 'Col. Valentin Soloviev.' The name was familiar. Then it clicked. This was the officer Alex called 'Kaminov's hit man.' Strange. He didn't look at all the way she had pictured him.

Erin was suddenly aware Soloviev had been inspecting her just as closely. 'You are Miss McKenna?' He smiled briefly. 'They tell me you're a spy.'

'And you're Colonel Soloviev. They tell me you're a tyrant.'

'We sound like a terrible pair, don't we?' the Russian colonel said dryly. 'I cannot imagine why either one of us received an invitation.'

Erin found herself smiling almost against her will. She laughed. 'Neither can I, Colonel. Perhaps we're supposed to cling together under a little black cloud.'

She'd never seen gray eyes twinkle before. 'I can think of worse fates, Miss McKenna.'

Off behind them, the band began playing Cole Porter's 'Begin the Beguine.'

Soloviev half turned toward the music and then swiveled back. He held out a hand. 'Would you care to dance?'

She surprised herself by nodding. 'I'd love to.'

He led her through the crowd to a relatively open air near the band. Two or three couples were already there, swaying and spinning in perfect time with the music. Erin noticed her colleagues' eyes widening as she and the tall Russian officer passed by. It amused her. Devil or not, Soloviev seemed to have a born aristocrat's disdain for petty convention. High-ranking members of Marshal Kaminov's inner circle were very definitely *not* supposed to hobnob with suspected American intelligence operatives.

He was also a first-rate dancer.

As they slowly spun across the floor, he murmured in her ear, 'I must say that you are a most unusual espionage agent, Miss McKenna. A refreshing change from the usual, pipe-smoking Ivy Leaguers we see here in Moscow.'

She laughed, imagining Banich with a pipe clenched between his teeth. He'd look absolutely ridiculous. 'I'm sorry to disappoint you, Colonel, but I'm really just a boring commercial attaché. The only spies I see here are those men practically padlocked to the drinks table.' She nodded toward a little knot of Russians eagerly downing the ambassador's vodka.

Soloviev smiled down at her. 'Of course.'

They danced together, moving gracefully in oddly contented silence, until the song ended in a polite patter of applause. Soloviev held her close for just a moment longer and then stepped back, bowing. 'My thanks.'

His lips brushed across the back of her outstretched hand.

Erin stiffened. Not because she was embarrassed by his oddly old-fashioned courtesy, but because he'd just slipped a folded piece of paper into her hand. The colonel straightened up. His face was quite calm, perfectly still. 'I enjoyed myself, Miss McKenna. Perhaps we shall dance again one day.'

She nodded without speaking and watched him move off into the crowd. Still bemused, she noticed that many of the women looked after him with just a hint of longing and most of the men with a mix of admiration and jealousy. She forced herself back to reality. What the hell had just happened?

For the first time that evening, Erin wished she *had* dressed grayly and inconspicuously. It took her several minutes to find a quiet corner where she could study what the Russian soldier had passed her without being observed.

It was a brief note in strong, masculine handwriting. 'I must see you again. Come running with me. Alone. At 6 a.m. on the day after tomorrow at the Novodevichy Convent. The matter is urgent.'

Erin looked up in astonishment, instinctively seeking Soloviev's distinctive features among a blur of several hundred different faces. He was gone.

She refolded the note and headed upstairs for the chancery building's Secure Section. Whatever was going on was not something she could keep to herself.

Thirty minutes later, Erin and Alex Banich sat in the Moscow Station chief's office. Len Kutner stared down at the unfolded piece of paper lying on his desk. He tugged at the tight collar of his tux, loosening it slightly, and looked up. 'What's your read on this, Alex?'

'It's a setup.' Banich was insistent. 'That son-of-a-bitch Soloviev is trouble. With a capital *T*. Or maybe with a capital *K* – for KGB.'

'The KGB doesn't exist anymore,' Erin pointed out.

'The hell it doesn't!' Banich exploded. 'They can call it the FIS, or whatever else they want, but it's still the same damned thing.'

She shook her head stubbornly. 'I don't think so. He didn't seem like one of them.'

'That's the point.' Banich frowned at her. 'Don't forget, I've dealt with this guy before. Soloviev's as smooth as silk. All smiles and easy charm right up until he plants a stiletto between your ribs!'

Kutner leaned forward and rested his elbows on the desk. 'Maybe so. But I still don't see why one of Kaminov's senior advisors would get personally involved in a sting op.'

'Because he's the perfect bait. Highly placed and well connected. They know we'll be tempted to play along just on the off chance he is genuine.' Banich shrugged. 'All the more reason to give this one a pass.'

'But why now?' Erin asked. 'The FIS has had me pegged as an intelligence agent for months. Why wait this long to come hunting me?'

'Because something's in the wind. Something they don't want us to know about. Maybe connected with Poland. Maybe not.' Banich turned to Kutner. 'You saw my report on the airport clampdown. Not even Kaminov would throw that many security personnel around on a whim.'

'Yeah.'

'Then you can see what these bastards could have in mind. They must know we've got a network here in Moscow – one they haven't been able to penetrate yet.' Banich nodded toward Erin. 'Say they lure McKenna outside the embassy, pass her a few worthless state secrets, and then grab her red-handed. The FIS gets two big pluses from that. One, they disrupt our operations and force us to commit resources arranging a swap or a buy-back. Two, they can break her wide open under interrogation.'

He lowered his voice. 'She knows too much, Len. My name. My cover. The trading company. Everything. And the frigging Russians would get it all.'

Erin flushed angrily at the implication that she would spill secrets so easily. But she had to admit that Banich was probably right. She was an analyst, not a field agent. She didn't have the training to withstand prolonged questioning – whether under torture or drugs.

Still, he seemed far too inclined to view only the worst-case situation.

Would he have been as adamant if the Russian colonel had contacted Mike Hennessy instead of her? She doubted it. Maybe somebody should point out the possibility that this particular glass might be half-full, not half-empty. 'What if Soloviev isn't setting a trap? What if he does have vital information to give us? Look, Alex, you say yourself that there's something big happening inside the Russian government. Have any of your sources been able to tell you what's up?'

He shook his head reluctantly.

'Then isn't it worth taking some risks to find out more?'

Banich shook his head again, vehemently this time. 'No, it's not. I don't care what the payoff seems to be. I don't make sucker bets.'

She turned to Kutner. 'So that's it? We just walk away from a man who could give us access to Kaminov's inner circle? Can we really afford to pass up a chance like this?'

The station chief didn't answer her right away. Instead he studied the crumpled note in front of him one more time. When he looked up, he was looking at Banich, not at her. He grimaced. 'I'm afraid Miss McKenna could be right, Alex. This may be one sucker bet we have to make.'

CHAPTER 26
Time on Target

JUNE 25 – OVER ENGLAND

Four delta-winged Mirage 2000s screamed north over the rolling, windswept Lambourn Downs, flying so low they nearly merged with the shadows rippling over long, green grass. Below them, strings of racehorses out for early morning schooling panicked, broke free from their stable lads, and scattered in a frenzied gallop – spraying across the barren landscape like pellets from a shotgun.

The pilot of the lead Mirage eased back on his stick, pulling his jet up as the ground ahead rose steadily toward a line of low chalk hills stretching east and west. One hundred meters. Two hundred. Three hundred.

Abruptly the landscape dropped away below them, falling into a wide, settled valley dotted with small villages and fields – the Vale of the White Horse.

As he dove for the valley floor, a series of low, bass beeps sounded again in the lead pilot's headphones. The sounds signaled an airborne search radar hunting for them. Either the Americans or the British had an AWACS plane orbiting over southern England. He checked the radar signal strength. High. Too high. They'd been detected.

He shook his head. The AWACS was too late. The four French warplanes were just twenty kilometers and ninety seconds from their target. He rocked the Mirage from side to side as a signal to the others and accelerated.

CNN HEADLINE NEWS, ON THE FLIGHT LINE, RAF BRIZE NORTON, NEAR OXFORD

CNN's viewers were being treated to live pictures of a massive military operation in progress. Huge U.S. Air Force C-5As, looking more like sections of gigantic pipeline than anything flyable, lumbered over the concrete tarmac. In the distance, other transports, C-141s and C-17s with their ramps extended, loaded trucks, missile launchers, and pallet after pallet of supplies. More colorful civilian airliners were intermixed with the green-painted military planes, pressed into service to carry troops. Long files of infantrymen shuffled forward to board the passenger aircraft, bowed down under rucksacks, weapons, and gear weighing up to 120 pounds.

With its three-thousand-meter long main runway, the RAF base at Brize Norton was an important center for the airlift pouring men, equipment, and supplies into Poland.

The reporter's khaki pants, shirt, and bulky flak jacket gave him a martial air that fitted his surroundings. He had to shout into his mike to make himself heard over howling jet engines and rumbling machinery. 'The British 1st Armored is only one of—'

A sudden, high-pitched wail stopped him in midsentence, rising and falling in a steady rhythm.

'What's that noise?' Alarm flashed across the reporter's face as he recognized the base air raid siren. Still looking into the camera, he stammered, 'Is this some kind of drill?' He turned to his left and repeated the question.

The view shifted, showing an ashen-faced RAF lieutenant motioning frantically toward the ground. 'Take cover! Take cover!'

Explosions drowned out the siren.

The camera image jarred, then tumbled to lie on its side, showing a cluster of buildings – aircraft hangars and living quarters. A mike picked up shocked voices in the background. 'Are you all right? . . . Jesus, look at that! Where's the camera?'

The image spun and shook, then steadied on a transformed scene. A pall of smoke hung over the flight line, fed by masses of flames below it. The fires dwarfed everything in sight – solid sheets of flame that towered over the trucks and men scrambling to control them.

Shaking again, the CNN cameraman panned left, then right, unable to capture the scope of this disaster in a single frame. The long, ordered lines of soldiers were gone, replaced by screaming clumps of wounded men and silent heaps of those who were dead. Secondary explosions threw mangled pieces of aircraft into the air as balls of orange-red flame mushroomed in the mass of wreckage.

IN THE THAMES ESTUARY

The German submarine commanded by Capt. Theodor Ritter lay bottomed on the Thames Estuary, practically hugging an old wreck left over from the last war. She was just forty kilometers east of London.

German submarines have never had names. This one was no exception. She was simply called U-32, the 'U' standing for *Unterseeboot*, undersea boat. She was small, only one-fifth the size of a *Los Angeles*-class nuclear sub. Unlike America's SSNs, Germany's U-boats didn't need a cruising range measured in tens of thousands of miles. They were built for coastal operations, close to their home ports.

As a Type 212 boat, U-32 was also brand-new, and new technology gave her an edge over the enemy. Instead of a large, expensive nuclear reactor, she carried an 'air-independent' propulsion plant. When their electric batteries ran low, older conventional submarines had to snorkel

– drawing air from the surface for their diesel engines. But snorkeling makes noise, and making noise during wartime is a sure and certain way for a submarine to get itself killed.

U-32 and the other boats in her class didn't have to snorkel. Instead, a tank of liquid oxygen supplied an advanced engine, which replaced the diesel. That meant they could charge their batteries while submerged, and then proceed silently on electric motors. The combination of ultraquiet propulsion, a small, nonmagnetic hull shaped to help scatter sonar echoes, and a first-rate sonar and fire control system made U-32 and her sisters deadly opponents.

Slipping this far through the Combined Forces ASW patrols had been difficult, but the German sub wasn't looking for a fight. U-32's submerged mobility, almost as good as a nuclear boat's, had let her sidestep or backtrack if she found herself near a prowling adversary. Her skipper and crew knew there would be time to deal with isolated enemy destroyers or frigates on the way out.

Besides, the war was almost three weeks old now. Patterns had begun to emerge in the way the Americans and British patrolled – patterns that could be exploited.

So now U-32 lay motionless in the mud. With her motors and even her air recirculation pumps shut down, she would be almost impossible to hear on passive sonar. Even nominal active sonars couldn't find her this close to the bottom – the mud and sediments blurred sound waves bouncing off it.

But the Royal Navy was used to operating in shallow water. Many of its ships carried special high-frequency sonars that could provide almost picture-quality images of whatever lay on the bottom.

The German submarine was relying on three things to safeguard her from such sonars. First, her small size – barely one thousand tons surfaced – and minimal sonar cross section. Second, her anechoic coating and special hull design should help absorb and scatter enemy sonar pulses. Last, and most important of all, U-32 lay close beside the old wreck, almost hull-to-hull – hiding in the sonar and magnetic shadow cast by the larger vessel.

Ritter and his crew resigned themselves to a long stay on the bottom, breathing air that would grow fouler as the hours passed. Like a spider in its web, the U-32 lay in wait for her prey.

HMS *Brecon* led the outbound convoy heading for Gdansk. Built with a glass-reinforced plastic hull, and equipped with a pair of unmanned submersibles and a high-frequency sonar, the *Hunt*-class minehunter had proven her worth after the Falklands war by sweeping Argentine minefields laid off Port Stanley.

Now she plodded down the estuary at a sedate ten knots, sweeping back and forth. Behind her came two Type 22-class frigates, HMS *Chatham* and HMS *London*. Three merchant ships followed the warships. A third frigate, HMS *Argyll*, a Type 23, brought up the rear.

Every warship was at action stations, expecting trouble. The three merchant ships, one bulk freighter and two container ships, held the better part of a British armored regiment, along with spare parts and ammunition.

U-32's crew, lazing at their own duty stations, sat up as the first chirp of the enemy's sonar beams came over the attack center speaker.

Ritter cocked his head toward the ceiling, listening as the British ships steaming overhead came closer.

The high-frequency chirping swelled, backed by the low, dull thrum of the minehunter's engines. New sounds over the speaker signaled another British ship moving in behind the first. *Chatham*'s active sonar made a deeper, duller noise than *Brecon*'s set.

More crewmen tensed as the sounds grew steadily louder. In theory, they were reasonably safe from detection. But theory seemed a poor substitute for certainty when the sonar pulses lashing the U-32 could be heard pinging through the hull itself.

Aboard *Brecon*, the senior petty officer manning the high-frequency sonar watched his screen carefully. He knew these waters well. The wreck, a coastal freighter sunk by Stukas in 1940, was a familiar landmark on his charts. He glanced at the digital clock above his display. They were right on time.

The wreck appeared, crawling down the screen as *Brecon* steamed toward it. He studied the bottom area around the sunken freighter closely. Nothing. Just the usual jumble of green-white shapes. Anything shaped like a submarine should have stood out clearly.

U-32's sensitive sonar gear picked up machinery sounds emanating from the oncoming convoy and fed them to her fire control computers. By comparing the noises against prerecorded data sets, the computers were able to rapidly classify each ship. As always, information obtained during peacetime exercises was proving useful in war.

Ritter hovered over the computer display, watching the results of this automated search appear. Moving blips indicated seven ships sailing east in line, centered in the channel. His fingers drummed against the console. The three warships were tempting targets, but his instructions were clear. The merchantmen were his first priority.

'Prepare for an attack,' he ordered. 'Two torpedoes at the lead merchant, three each at the other two.'

Every man in the boat held his breath as the ships drew nearer. The swishing roar of the enemy minehunter's screws passed overhead and began to fade.

Ritter kept his eyes on the display, watching the six ships behind *Brecon*. Bearing, still steady. Range, decreasing. He looked up at his diving officer. 'Lift off.'

Valves opened, and a shot of compressed air entered U-32's ballast tanks, changing her buoyancy from slightly negative to slightly positive. She lifted smoothly off the bottom. At the same time, her silent propellers spun up slowly, giving the submarine bare steerageway.

Once depth and speed were stabilized, the diving officer nodded silently to Ritter. They were in position.

The captain turned to the fire control officer. 'Ready?'

'Solutions checked and valid.'

Ritter wrapped one hand around an overhead support and took a deep breath. Now. 'Shoot!'

One after another, eight Seal 3 torpedoes, pushed out of their tubes by a pulse of water, came to life and sped toward their targets. Dual-core wires connected each torpedo to the U-32 and her fire control computer. These wires carried guidance commands from the sub to its weapons. They also allowed the sub to see everything its torpedoes saw.

With so many propellers thrashing the water, the British warships had failed to hear the German submarine as she vented her tanks and came off the bottom. But the high-pitched screw noises made by eight torpedoes screaming in at thirty-five knots were unmistakable.

In seconds, sonar plots aboard all three frigates showed their bearing and probable origin point. But it was too late.

The first torpedoes were already reaching their targets.

Van Dyck, a bulk freighter of twenty thousand tons deadweight, took one torpedo in the bow and another in the engine room. Although each Seal 3 carried a quarter ton of PBX, the vessel was only crippled, not destroyed. Within seconds she was practically dead in the water, listing to starboard. She would have to be towed back for repairs in Great Britain's already overtaxed shipyards.

Three torpedoes slammed into *Falmount Bay*, a container ship of the same size. Without decoys, at slow speed, the large ship was an easy target. Three plumes of yellow-stained water and smoke fountained high into the air. *Falmount Bay* broke in half and sank.

Behind her, only two of three incoming Seals plowed into the container ship *St. Louis*. The third missed and ran up the estuary until it ran out of fuel and drifted harmlessly into the mud. But she was smaller than the others and carried a flammable cargo. Internal explosions tore her apart in minutes – sending a huge plume of smoke high into the atmosphere.

Chatham and *London* raced for the old wreck, sonars blasting, pounding the estuary in a frenzied search. *Argyll*, in the rear, turned to assist the stricken *Van Dyck*. She also launched one of her two Westland Lynx helicopters to assist in the hunt.

Ritter didn't waste time patting backs. Celebrating could come later – once he and his crew were safely back in port. 'All ahead flank!'

U-32 was not silent now. Her only hope of escape lay in speed, and she had a lot of it in reserve – twenty-three knots submerged. She darted out from the wreck, right under *Chatham* as it charged in. That meant risking an over-the-side shot by the British ship's triple torpedo mounts, but the closing speeds were so high that the frigate didn't get a solid fix on her until it was too late.

The German sub skipper divided his attention between the sonar display and the plot. Every minute spent at full speed cost him five hours' worth of battery charge. Like all conventional submarine captains, he had to constantly weigh the advantages of speed with the risks of running out of power. 'All ahead two-thirds.'

Ritter's escape-and-evasion plan was simplicity itself. If he could break contact with these three warships, the rest of the estuary was clear all the way out into the North Sea. He had the endurance at medium speed to reach open water, where the British would have a very hard time finding him.

Argyll's helicopter was his undoing. The submarine's high-speed burst, although only a minute long, created a wake in the shallow water – a wide vee shape streaming away from the fleeing U-boat. Even as U-32 slowed, the Lynx flashed over *Chatham* at masthead height and dropped two depth charges just in front of the point of the vee.

The depth charges splashed into the water, sank rapidly, and detonated a fraction of a second later. One was just ten meters away from the German submarine's hull, the other only five. Caught by two bubble pulses of explosive shock and gas, U-32 tumbled and shook. The twin shocks tore equipment loose from its mountings, bounced the crew off the bulkheads, and even deformed the pressure hull. She lost half her batteries and her AIP engine shut down – badly damaged. Even her fire control system went dead in a shower of sparks and fused circuit boards.

Chatham, cued by the hovering Lynx, heeled over – coming round in a tight, high-speed turn to attack the crippled German submarine. Her active sonar found and fixed U-32 at almost point-blank range. A Stingray torpedo plunged into the water.

Inside U-32, the crew worked desperately to restore her propulsion and her fire control systems. But the British frigate's sonar pulses were already deafening and growing louder.

Screee.

Panicked faces turned aft, toward the new noise in the water.

'Torpedo! Bearing two four five!' The sonarman's shouted report was redundant.

Ritter ran his eyes over the plot one last time and then looked at his haggard men. They were finished. U-32's damage was too great, and the British ships were too close. There were only twenty-three men in U-32's crew, but they were as close as brothers. He would save what he could by surrendering. 'Blow all tanks! Emergency surface!'

Chatham's Stingray barely had time to steady up before its active sonar found U-32. The submarine, unable to dodge, lay right in its path.

The British torpedo slammed into the U-32 just as her conning tower broke the surface. The Stingray's shaped-charge warhead, intended to kill much larger vessels, hit aft and exploded, obliterating the sub's engineering compartment. With her hull ripped open, U-32's ballast tanks could not keep her afloat. Only five of her crew, all sailors stationed in the conning tower, managed to scramble out before she slid downward in a maelstrom of bubbling foam, Oil, and wreckage – joining her victims at the bottom of the estuary.

MINISTRY OF DEFENSE, LONDON

In a reluctant concession to the war raging across the Channel, the soldiers stationed around London's famous public buildings and government offices wore combat gear instead of their colorful, full dress uniforms. Bearskin caps and scarlet coats had given way to Kevlar helmets and camouflaged body armor.

Adm. Jack Ward strode out into the Defense Ministry's inner courtyard between sentries who snapped to attention. Lieutenant Harada, his flag secretary, followed right behind. Their ride out to Heathrow, a tiny British Army Air Corps Gazelle helicopter, sat on the pavement with its rotor already slowly turning. A U.S. Navy Grumman COD – carrier onboard delivery plane – was waiting on the tarmac at the airport, ready to take them back to sea.

He bent low to clear the Gazelle's rotor blades and hauled himself inside, taking a seat on a narrow folding bench behind its two crewmen. Harada squeezed in beside him and pulled the helicopter's side door shut.

The admiral leaned forward to speak to the warrant officer piloting the help. 'Anytime you're ready, mister.'

'Yes, sir. We'll just be half a tic.' The sandy-haired warrant officer grinned round at him. 'We're only waiting for our clearance from those Nervous Nellies in Air Defense Command. Right, Tony?'

His copilot looked up from flicking switches and nodded. 'The bloody Frogs and Jerries are at it again, Admiral. Over Southampton this time. It's a right mess, they say.'

Ward grimaced and sat back impatiently. He couldn't afford to get stuck ashore under enemy air attack – not now. Events were moving too fast.

The sudden surge in French and German attacks against British airfields and harbors had come as a very unpleasant, though not wholly unexpected, development. Stymied in every attempt to sink Ward's juggernauts, his three carrier battle groups, the EurCon high command had apparently decided to concentrate their air and naval resources against the weakest link in the sea line of communications to Poland – the United Kingdom itself.

Cost-cutting and the end of the cold war had slowed the U.K.'s efforts to rebuild its long-neglected air defenses. The RAF's E-3 Sentries, a few, overworked squadrons of Tornado interceptors, and Patriot missile batteries could knock down some of the attacking aircraft, but they couldn't stop every incoming raid – not when EurCon planes based in France were only minutes' flying time from targets in southern England. There were too many potential targets and too few fighters and SAM batteries available to protect them.

As a result, Ward knew, EurCon's first attacks had been disturbingly effective. The Mirage raid on Brize Norton had killed nearly one hundred soldiers and airmen. Hundreds more were wounded, many seriously. Later raids on other bases had inflicted similar losses. The initial enemy air and submarine attacks had also destroyed a number of transport planes and cargo ships that were worth their weight in gold.

EurCon's leaders must be hoping that expanding the war to British soil would throw the United States and its allies off balance. Certainly the losses they'd inflicted would slow the movement of British troops to Poland. And they probably hoped the Combined Forces air commanders would strengthen the U.K.'s defenses by diverting some of the American F-15 and F-16 squadrons now bombing installations inside France and Germany.

Of course, by demonstrating just how vulnerable the United Kingdom was to any enemy attack, the EurCon raids had helped spur Washington and London into approving drastic retaliatory and preemptive measures. The men in both Paris and Berlin were about to relearn the law of unintended consequences, Ward thought dourly.

He had been summoned to London from midocean late the night before – forced to endure a bumpy, low-altitude COD flight to arrive in time for this morning's meeting hosted by the Combined Chiefs of Staff. Although it had cost him a badly needed night's sleep, a stiff neck, and a bruised backside, the show had proved well worth the price of admission.

For all his three stars, the admiral had soon realized he was a small fry in a very select group. Aside from a number of very silent junior officers present as aides, the active participants had included Britain's Prime Minister, the heads of the British Army, the Royal Air Force and Royal Navy, the U.S. Navy's chief of naval operations, and the U.S. Air Force general who served as vice-chairman of the Joint Chiefs.

The Prime Minister's first words had ended any idle speculation that they were there for a simple update or get-acquainted meeting. 'I've just come from a secure-line conference call with the President and the Norwegian Prime Minister, gentlemen. You now have a new mission – one you will accord an equal priority with our resupply and reinforcement operations for Poland. Beginning immediately, you will exert every effort to eliminate the French tactical and strategic nuclear arsenal.'

Ward could still remember the sudden, startled murmur that had greeted the Prime Minister's soft-spoken, matter-of-fact announcement. Going after French nukes was a serious upping of the ante. Despite the warning order he'd received from Washington indicating that such a move might be in the works, he'd never actually expected the politicians to show enough guts.

'So far, thank God, there is no indication that our enemies intend to use nuclear weapons against the United Kingdom or Norway itself, but their willingness to use them at all is rather unsettling.'

Ward shook his head, still bemused by the Prime Minister's classic British understatement. Seeing that hideously beautiful fireball blossom near his ships had been daunting enough. The prospect of more nuclear weapons going off, this time over cities and towns, was too horrible to contemplate.

'If we win this war, and we shall do our utmost to win, Paris could well find itself with its back against a wall,' the Prime Minister had continued. 'We cannot predict the actions of desperate men.

Accordingly, while we know this will take substantial resources, it is vital that our national territories be protected against a last-ditch nuclear strike.'

Some of the steps the Prime Minister detailed were familiar to Ward. After all, he'd helped plan them. Other precautionary measures raised hairs on the back of his neck. Commanders aboard several of America's *Ohio*-class SSBNs had been ordered to retarget their missiles – aiming them at France and, to a lesser extent, at Germany. French nuclear-capable forces were the primary targets, along with the command centers of both countries' armed forces.

The Royal Navy's own SSBNs were engaged in the same doomsday process. More ominously still, the RAF's tactical nuclear weapons were being dispersed from its heavily guarded stockpiles to operational bases – ready for immediate use if need be. Selected American subs and surface ships were being rearmed with nuclear land attack Tomahawk cruise missiles and deployed into firing positions off the French coastline.

Although the Combined Forces would not initiate the use of nuclear weapons against populated areas, they were absolutely determined to make the French realize who would win and who would lose if the gloves came off.

The Gazelle pilot's voice broke in on his grim thoughts. 'Understood, Lionheart. Safe corridor is direct to Heathrow. Two six two degrees at five hundred feet.' He twisted around in his seat. 'Buckle up if you please, gents. We're on our way.'

'That was your okay?' Ward asked, complying with the tactfully disguised order.

The pilot nodded. 'ADC reports the Frogs are outbound from Southampton. Our assigned flight path is clear.'

Lieutenant Harada snapped his own seat belt and shoulder harness in place. 'What happens if we stray outside that corridor?'

The sandy-haired warrant officer grinned abruptly. 'Then we're fair game for any trigger-happy bugger with a gun or missile.' He faced front again and pulled up on the collective while rotating the throttle to full power.

The Gazelle lifted off in a shaking, teeth-rattling roar, sliding slowly toward the far end of the ministry's courtyard as it climbed. Five hundred feet above the ground it spun left and dipped its nose slightly, transitioning to forward flight.

Ward stared down out the side window, fascinated by this close-up view of London from low altitude. It had still been dark when they'd arrived early this morning. Now he could see the vast city stretching out on all sides – mile after mile of public buildings, residences, and office blocks, some elegant and some drab, tall church spires, and lush, green parks.

They flew low over the landscaped splendor of St. James's Park and past the imposing walls of Buckingham Palace. Heads on the streets below turned upward in alarm. Londoners had long-held memories of danger from the skies, and the steady stream of emergency BBC news bulletins since dawn had rekindled those memories.

Sirens howled, off in the distance at first and then closer in – audible even over the Gazelle's clattering roar.

'Shit.' The pilot spun the helicopter right and dove, picking up speed. A broad expanse of trees, grass, and paths opened up before them. Sunlight glinted off a mile-long lake, Hyde Park's Serpentine.

Ward and Harada heard his shouted explanation over their intercom earphones. 'ADC just set Warning Red! There's another raid inbound – heading for London this time. I've been ordered to set down and set down fast. When I say go, both of you hop out and run like hell for the nearest cover!'

The Gazelle swooped low over the park and flared out near a stand of trees. Its landing skids bounced lightly once and then settled firmly onto the ground. New-mown grass whirled above the cockpit, caught in the rotor wash.

'Go! Go! Go!'

Harada flipped open his seat belt and slammed the helicopter's side door open. He dropped outside, followed a second later by Ward. Air currents whipped by the whirring rotor blades tugged and tore at their uniforms.

Crouched low to clear the rotor, both Americans raced for the trees – a clump of tall, spreading oaks. This far away from the helicopter, they could hear the air raid sirens still wailing across the city.

As he ran, Ward eyed the buildings visible to the north and south, weighing their chances of reaching a shelter in time. Then he shook his head. Hyde Park was nearly a thousand yards across at this point, and they'd come down almost smack-dab in the middle. They would have to ride out whatever was coming right here.

Once they had the Gazelle's engine shut down, the two British crewmen scrambled out of the cockpit themselves and sprinted across the open ground, heading for the same grove. The helicopter stood deserted behind them with its doors wide open.

Ward slid to a stop beside one of the oaks and dropped prone, breathing hard. The others joined him just in time.

Bright lights streaked into the sky, moving south and east at incredible speed – missiles rising on columns of white smoke and fire. Several British-manned Patriot batteries were deployed near key installations around London. Now they were firing at attackers who were still well beyond visual range.

Seconds passed. Ward caught one blinding flash low on the southern horizon. Then nothing.

Whummp. Whummp. Whummp. A series of muffled explosions rumbled across the park. More smoke, black this time, stained the sky to the east beyond the city center's soaring modern office towers.

The helicopter's copilot shaded his eyes against the sun, studying the billowing cloud. 'That's oil burning. The bastards must be hitting the docks.'

They nodded. The freighters and oil tankers tied up along the Thames were prime targets. They were also sitting ducks.

Ward squinted, trying to estimate the damage inflicted by the lightning-fast French air raid. One hell of a lot of smoke, he thought. More than one ship must be on fire downriver. He tried to remember if there were petroleum storage tanks near the docks. Something moved on the edge of his vision, silhouetted against the rising pall – a tiny dot growing larger very fast.

'There!' He pointed.

An arrowhead shape screamed overhead, barely over the treetops but climbing steeply as it turned. The four men on the ground caught just a split-second glimpse of a delta-shaped wing, gray and light blue camouflage paint, and tricolor roundels on the fuselage. It was a Mirage exiting the battle area!

Ward turned, following the French attack aircraft as it climbed. He suddenly realised this was the first time he'd actually seen one of his enemies with his own eyes. He'd watched every other battle in the sterile, artificially calm confines of a CIC, tracking different-shaped blips on radar screens and computer-generated displays. But this was real.

'Admiral! Look!' Harada gestured back the way the French warplane had come. A new jet, larger and with swing wings, came into view – higher up but closing rapidly. A Tornado. But whose? German or British?

The tan-colored 'hemp' camouflage gave him his answer. It was an RAF interceptor!

The Tornado flashed past, turning to match the Mirage. For several seconds, the two jets kept turning and climbing – visibly slowing as their maneuvers bled airspeed and energy. Then, for one brief instant, they came nose-to-nose. Both fired and veered away, each pursued by a heat-seeking missile.

Ward tracked the Mirage as it twisted and turned, vainly trying to shake off the pursuing Sidewinder. Flares tumbled through the sky in its wake, each briefly brighter than the sun. None of them worked. The proximity-fused Sidewinder detonated only yards away, sending a hail of incendiary fragments slashing through the French jet's fuel tanks.

The Mirage exploded. It arced across the sky as a rolling, tumbling ball of flame. Burning pieces of wreckage cascaded down across the rooftops and city streets below.

'Oh, Christ,' someone muttered behind him.

Ward turned and saw a stricken look on the Gazelle pilot's face. The sandy-haired Englishman had been watching the RAF Tornado. It had been hit, too.

Trailing smoke, the British fighter turned south, wobbling from side to side. Orange and red flames licked under its fuselage. They were growing brighter as they fed on leaking fuel.

'Get out. Get out.' The warrant officer's hands balled into fists. 'Come on, mate. Eject!'

But the Tornado crew stayed with their dying aircraft. They were nursing it toward the Thames, Ward realized, riding the burning plane down to make sure that it didn't come down on top of houses full of women and children.

Ward and the others watched in silence until the Tornado vanished beyond the buildings lining the southern edge of Hyde Park.

USS *BOSTON*, OFF THE FRENCH ATLANTIC COAST

Boston's short, black-haired skipper was as Irish as his sub's namesake city, and he had the temper to go with it. Right now Comdr. Pete Conroy fought to control his natural impatience, following orders that went against his instincts and years of training. *Boston* and two other *Los Angeles*-class subs were hunting a French ballistic missile submarine, and they were doing it exactly the wrong way.

Boston was in the center of a line of three submarines, spaced three miles apart. He felt very vulnerable steering a straight course at five knots just below the thermocline, the sound-reflecting boundary between layers of warmer and colder water. These were French waters with French airspace overhead. Even though CINCCOMBFLT had promised fighter cover to drive off any enemy ASW aircraft on patrol, things could still go wrong. What if the Frogs escorted their Atlantiques with a strong fighter force of their own? The last thing Conroy wanted to hear was an air-dropped homing torpedo whining right up his sub's ass.

Worse still, he and his crew probably wouldn't find a damn thing. Commander in Chief, Combined Fleet's staff had reason to believe that these waters were an SSBN patrol area. That was an educated guess they'd pulled together from several different things: French ASW patrol plane patterns, the water depth and conditions, and a few intelligence sources they wouldn't even describe. Based on those clues, they were betting that one of France's few ballistic missile submarines was close by – creeping along in silence, waiting for an order to launch her sixteen MIRVed warhead missiles.

The only problem was that SSBNs, 'boomers,' don't like to fight. Their whole mission depends on staying hidden. To accomplish that, they carry very sensitive sonars to let them detect a prowling enemy boat long before it can hear them. At the first whiff of an enemy ship or sub coming after them, SSBNs just quietly run away.

Conroy frowned. Although his *Los Angeles*-class SSN didn't make much noise at five knots, it made a little, and that would probably be enough to give the hunt away.

Worse yet, there were three subs looking. In submarine warfare, there is no safety in numbers. Stealth and surprise are strength – not numerical superiority. Once he detected the first American sub, the Frenchman would probably spot the other two quickly. The SSN sweep probably covered one entire side of the enemy's patrol zone, but that left the SSBN's skipper plenty of room to run. If pushed hard enough, he'd even leave his patrol area.

No, Conroy, thought, he and *Boston* received the wrong end of this deal. Even if they did detect another sub, they would have to positively identify it before firing. With so many friendlies operating so close to one another, throwing torpedoes out against an unidentified contact was a good way to commit fratricide. For the same reason, all three American

SSNs had to follow a precisely laid-out path . . .

'Conn, sonar. Contact bearing one three five, almost directly ahead of us.'

Conroy almost sprinted to the sonar shack, but controlled the impulse enough to slow to a fast walk. It only took seconds, in any case. Poking his head into the crowded space, he asked softly, 'What's it look like?'

The chief sonarman, standing behind the two seated operators, replied. 'Single transient, sir. Loud and broadband. Depression angle says it's deep.'

Conroy realized that the chief was letting him make his own evaluation. The description only fit one thing. 'An explosion?'

'I concur, Captain.' The chief shrugged. 'No way to tell who fired or what hit what, if it hit anything at all. Damn far off, though.'

Both operators sat up. One of them tapped his screen. 'Same thing again, Chief. Two of them this time, closely spaced. Torpedoes, most likely.'

Both Conroy and the chief studied the display, which showed two sudden, broad pulses of light. More explosions off in the distance. Somebody was dying out there. But who?

They could only wait and listen and hope.

Five minutes later, a new signal appeared on the sonar display. It was a coded sonar pulse, the kind sent out by a communications sonobuoy. Dropped by a friendly ASW aircraft, the transmission ordered all three SSNs to radio depth. It took several more minutes to carefully come up and signal they were in position.

The SSBN hunt was over. A controlling P-3 Orion passed the word. A fourth *Los Angeles*-class boat, *Louisville*, hunter to their hounds, had just sent a *Le Triomphant*-class missile sub to the bottom. While Boston and her companions came in from one side of the French patrol area, *Louisville* had crept in from the other direction – almost drifting with the current more than using her single screw for propulsion.

Once inside the patrol area, she had positioned herself along the SSBN's most likely escape route.

When the French boat moved to avoid *Boston* and its companions, it had become slightly more detectable itself. That was when it had fallen prey to *Louisville*. Only one of the first two torpedoes it fired had hit, but a second salvo finished the wounded boat. Sixteen missiles carrying ninety-six 150-kiloton nuclear warheads were lost to the French cause. So were 135 crewmen.

The Orion's brief report was followed by new orders. They were going hunting for the second French boomer reported at sea. Any celebration would have to wait until they returned to port. Damn *Louisville*'s luck, Conroy thought. Maybe he would get his chance for a kill next time.

JUNE 26 – IRBM COMPLEX, PLATEAU D'ALBION, FRANCE

The Plateau d'Albion lay east of the southern French city of Avignon, in the Haute-Provence. On one side of the plateau, the ground rose sharply, climbing to meet the first foothills of the Alps. To the west, it fell away into the vineyard-laced Rhone Valley.

The plateau was home to the silos housing eighteen intermediate-range ballistic missiles – the land-based component of the French strategic nuclear forces. Organized in two squadrons of nine missiles, each S3 IRBM carried a single 1.2-megaton warhead and had a range of nearly 2,200 miles. One hit could turn a city the size of Moscow or London into a charred, radioactive ruin. Determined to preserve their nation's strategic independence and status as a world power, successive French governments had spent billions of francs building, maintaining, and periodically upgrading its 'force of last resort.'

They spent hundreds of millions more protecting their investment from ground or air attack. Bunkers and minefields ringed the missile complex, manned by soldiers wearing the large midnight-blue berets of the 27th Mountain Division. Batteries of Roland and Improved Hawk surface-to-air missile launchers were deployed to provide a last-ditch defense against enemy air raids. But the IRBMs' main protection came from the underground silos themselves – layer after layer of heavily reinforced concrete hardened against nuclear attack.

BATTERY A, 5TH AIR DEFENSE REGIMENT

Battery A's electronics van was parked under camouflage netting a short distance away from its trailer-mounted target acquisition radar. Its crew had the van's door open to catch the remnants of a gentle night breeze tinged with the aromatic smell of pine and eucalyptus. Three triple-rail Hawk launchers surrounded the van and radar trailer.

'There they are again, sir,' the sergeant manning the SAM battery's radar console announced with some reluctance. 'The same bearing as before, but closer.'

Capt. Claude Jussey sighed and set the technical manual he'd been studying aside. By rights, the tall, lantern-jawed officer thought wearily, he should be in bed, not sitting inside this crowded van watching men watching blank radar screens. Unfortunately, ever since the Americans and British began bombing targets in northern France and Germany, periodic drills and false alarms had been cutting into his sleep time. He rolled his chair closer to the console. 'Where?'

'It's gone again.' The sergeant sounded frustrated. He was a man who liked dealing in certainties and right now he seemed to be seeing ghosts. 'I can't seem to get a solid return, just faint sparkles that fade to nothing in the next second.'

He sat up suddenly. 'There! You see them?'

Jussey blinked, not sure whether he had or not. The radar traces had flickered out so fast – literally from one second to the next. Was there a glitch in the target acquisition program? Or was there really something out there? Something able to absorb or deflect the radar pulses striking it? Would the Americans risk their precious stealth aircraft this far from England?

Irritation turned to unease. He lifted the direct line link to the central Air Defense Command center.

* * *

Outside the van, a bomb fell through the night sky. Seconds from impact, the Paveway III sensor rigged on the bomb's nose 'saw' the laser light illuminating its target and fed a series of guidance commands to fins at the back. The 2,000-pound GBU-24 veered, settling onto a slightly different course while still falling.

'Command Center.'

Jussey kept his eyes on the glowing radar display, noticing the faint sparkles again. 'A Battery here, we have a possible air contact bearing . . .'

The electronics van exploded – torn apart by a massive blast that threw fragments over a wide area and left the mangled wreck ablaze. Jussey, his sergeant, and the five other men inside died instantly.

Within seconds, the 5th Air Defense Regiment's other SAM batteries met the same fate – obliterated by a perfectly timed and perfectly aimed salvo of laser-guided bombs.

Six miles away and six thousand feet above the plateau, twelve very odd-looking aircraft banked north. Black against a pitch-black sky, they were extremely hard to see with the naked eye. More important, the U.S. Air Force 45th Tactical Fighter Wing's F-117A stealth fighters were practically invisible to enemy radar.

Radar-absorbent materials and mesh screens over their engine intakes helped reduce each jet's radar signature, but the real stealth secret lay in its strangely shaped fuselage and wings. Each F-117 was made up of a series of small flat surfaces, or facets, angled in different directions. Radar pulses striking each plane could only bounce back from those few sections aimed straight at the radar set itself. In flight, no facet would ever point toward a given radar for very long. So the aircraft would literally 'appear and disappear' in seconds – confusing search radar crews and making it almost impossible for SAM and antiaircraft gun fire control sets to lock on.

In 1991 America's stealth technology had proved itself in the skies over Iraq. Now, seven years later, it was proving itself over France.

With their mission accomplished, the twelve F-117As headed home for a base in southern England. Behind them, the door to the Plateau d'Albion missile complex lay wide open and unguarded.

RINGMASTER, CIRCUS STRIKE, OVER FRANCE

If the men aboard the big, lumbering E-3 Sentry AWACS plane were nervous about being so far inside French airspace, they were hiding it well, Brig. Gen. Robert Keller decided. The voices coming through his headphones were remarkably steady.

He looked up from the radar repeater display at his command station. Rows of equipment consoles crammed the converted 707's interior, each manned by a U.S. Air Force officer or enlisted man. From time to time, their hands moved, adjusting settings or fine-tuning controls, but mostly the operators stayed still – keeping their eyes glued to the glowing displays in front of them. All told, they were responsible for coordinating the movements of more than eighty U.S. aircraft.

One of his strike controllers came over the intercom circuit. 'Lion Tamer exiting the target area. The SAMs are down.'

Here we go, Keller thought, tensing. The stealth fighters had done their work. Now it was up to the rest of his strike force to finish the job. Reports began pouring over the intercom in a rapid, precise sequence:

'SpaceCom confirms Keyhole will be up in five.' The general nodded to himself. One of America's KH-11 spy satellites would be coming over the target area horizon in five minutes – ready to transmit high-resolution pictures back to the photo interpreters in Washington. For this strike, real-time BDA, bomb damage assessment, was critical. They couldn't afford to leave any undamaged missiles behind.

'Pile Driver, Strongman, High Wire, and Freak Show are all in position.' The strike's attack aircraft, fighter escorts, SIGINT, and jammer support planes were ready.

Keller clicked the transmit button on his throat mike. 'All Circus units, this is Ringmaster. Initiate attack!'

The cluster of blips on the radar display representing his strike force surged ahead. The general watched carefully, alert for any last-second hitch or unexpected enemy move. But his eyes kept straying to the second hand sweeping around a clock mounted next to the display. Since no one knew how the French National Command Authority would react to the threatened destruction of its precious missile force, no one could rule out a French decision to launch their nuclear missiles under attack.

If Paris gave its commanders the order to fire, Keller's planes would have just two hundred seconds to destroy the silos before the first S3 IRBMs roared aloft.

PILE DRIVER LEADER, OVER THE PLATEAU D'ALBION

Col. Neil Campos watched the darkened landscape roll away beneath his F-15E Strike Eagle. The chain of fires marking destroyed French Hawk batteries flashed past and vanished astern. 'Got anything yet, Mac?'

His back seater, Jeff McRae, spoke up. 'Nope. But the computer says we're still on course.'

The thirty-six F-15Es under the colonel's command were converging on the French IRBM complex at high speed – racing through a radar and radio jamming corridor created by two EF-111 electronic warfare aircraft. Two squadrons of F-16s followed behind, ready to jump any French fighters that tried to interfere.

The Strike Eagles carried drop tanks on their wing hardpoints and two LANTIRN infrared pods on special hardpoints – one for targeting, the other for navigation. Sparrow radar-guided missiles mounted next to their drop tanks provided air-to-air combat capability. Each of the two-seater attack aircraft also carried one massive GBU-28 laser-guided bomb on its centerline pylon.

The 4,700-pound GBU-28 was an extraordinarily powerful weapon developed under extraordinary circumstances. During Desert Storm, several of the first U.S. attacks on Baghdad's hardened command and control bunkers failed when 2,000-pound bombs bounced off or failed to pierce multiple layers of reinforced concrete. Frantic requests for more potent air ordnance resulted in the GBU-28 penetrator, commonly called Deep Throat. Designed, built, and shipped to the combat zone in seventy-two hours, the weapon was a miracle of ingenuity and improvisation.

The Deep Throat was also as ugly as hell. To manufacture it, U.S. arms experts had snagged surplus eight-inch gun barrels, machined them out, and buried them upright in the ground. Then bucket gangs of men wearing protective suits took turns pouring molten explosive right into the open barrels. Once the explosives cooled, specialists fitted a delay fuse and laser guidance system to the front and control fins to the back. The whole result looked very much like a giant, homemade pipe bomb.

But it was incredibly effective. When dropped on Iraqi targets, the GBU-28 had vividly demonstrated that it could punch through more than twenty-two feet of reinforced concrete or more than one hundred feet of packed earth before exploding. Now America's war planners were betting the same weapons could rip open the French missile silos.

Campos hoped they were right. The penalties for failure were too terrible to contemplate.

The colonel checked one last time, making sure his wingman was still back there – ready to attack immediately after he and McRae rolled off the target. The Eagles were attacking in pairs. Their orders were clear: even if the first bomb scores what looks like a solid hit, dump the second Deep Throat in right after it. When attacking heavily protected weapons that could kill millions if they got off the ground, air force doctrine was explicit – bounce the rubble.

'Bingo!' McRae had spotted their assigned missile silo several miles ahead and several thousand feet below.

A new steering cue appeared on the F-15E's HUD.

In the Strike Eagle's backseat, McRae stared hard at the LANTIRN display. Despite the darkness, the surrounding barbed-wire fence and an adjacent radio mast showed up clearly in infrared. He looked for the flat concrete slab that covered the silo itself and found it. His hand settled on the laser designator, switched it on, and held the beam right in the middle of the slab. 'Anytime you're ready, Neil.'

Campos nosed over into a gentle dive and held the Strike Eagle on course so he wouldn't pull the laser off target. Sure that he had the right parameters, he thumbed the weapon release on his stick.

The GBU-28 dropped away from the F-15 and fell toward the French missile silo.

SILO 5, 1ST SQUADRON, FRENCH STRATEGIC MISSILE FORCE

Guided by McRae's laser, the bomb slammed nose-first into the thick silo cover. Still moving at more than six hundred miles an hour, it smashed through layers of steel and concrete and exploded inside the silo itself – just meters away from the forty-five-foot-tall S3 ballistic missile.

White-hot fragments shattered the delicate mechanism of the missile's nuclear warhead, turning the deadly device into useless junk. Others ruptured the missile casing and plowed into tons of packed-solid fuel propellant.

The propellant ignited.

The whole concrete cover bulged and then blew off – tossed to one side by what looked like the world's biggest Roman candle. A blinding plume of fire and flaming gas rocketed hundreds of meters into the air, turning night into day across the Plateau d'Albion.

JOINT DEFENSE SPACE COMMUNICATIONS FACILITY, WOOMERA AIR STATION, AUSTRALIA

The picture being transmitted from a point 22,300 miles above the earth's equator showed a darkened globe fringed with sunlight spilling along its eastern horizon.

For more than twenty years, data from American DSP early warning satellites in geosynchronous orbit over the Indian Ocean had been routinely processed at the Woomera facility, code-named Casino, before being transmitted to the United States. But nothing about this morning was routine for the air force officers crowding around the monitoring station. They were watching for the first pulses of light that would signal French missiles roaring up and out of their silos.

Even though the Circus strike had been timed so that one of the two operational G-PALS constellations was over northern Europe, no one knew how effective the system would be against a real missile attack. And no one really wanted to find out. The space-based defense system's Brilliant Pebbles had proved they could knock down satellites following predictable orbits. Detecting and intercepting ballistic missiles arcing up from the atmosphere was likely to prove considerably more difficult.

Bright white lights blossomed suddenly across a small section of southern France.

One of the watching officers, a colonel, turned ashen. 'Flash message to the NCA! Possible IRBM launches from the Albion complex!'

Another man, this one monitoring satellite-relayed radio transmissions from the strike controller, interrupted him. 'Negative! Negative! Ringmaster radar shows no missile tracks! Repeat, no missile tracks! Those plumes are secondary explosions.'

Some of the men closest to the screen whistled softly in admiration. All of the eighteen white-hot tongues of fire bathing the Haute-Provence in an eerie glow had appeared within seconds of each other. General Keller's F-15 crews had achieved an almost perfect time-on-target attack.

France no longer possessed a land-based strategic nuclear deterrent.

JUTERBOG AIR BASE, GERMANY

Pairs of Mirage FlEs soared off the long, concrete runway, climbing fast into the gray, predawn sky. In itself there was nothing unusual about that. The interceptors and fighter-bombers based at Juterbog had been flying sorties over the Polish front since the war began. But these planes were flying west – back to France.

Col. Manfred Witz stood near the windows of the base control tower with his hands on hips and an angry expression on his face. The small, spare Luftwaffe officer scowled down at the frantic scene unfolding on his flight line.

French ground crewmen in greasy coveralls scurried back and forth between aircraft shelters, ordnance bunkers, and maintenance workshops. They were loading gear aboard a long line of canvas-sided trucks guarded by French military police. Other crews were mustering beside a camouflaged C-130 Hercules transport.

Despite heated German protests, the French Air Force squadron at Juterbog was pulling out – under orders from Paris. Witz knew they weren't the only ones going. He'd seen message traffic recalling at least two other air units and several SAM batteries. With U.S. and British planes apparently roving over France at will, the French were desperately trying to strengthen their own air defenses.

The colonel grimaced. Transferring so many aircraft away from the Polish front was madness – especially right now. Caught between their own combat losses and the steady tide of U.S. reinforcements flying into Poland, the Luftwaffe and the French Air Force were already increasingly unable to control the air over the battlefield. This latest move would only make the situation worse.

He turned abruptly and stomped away from the window. The tower's junior officers and enlisted personnel saw him coming and hastily bent to their work. When the colonel was in one of his rages, it was safest to stay out of his way.

These French idiots have opened a hornet's nest and now they're clutching at straws, Witz thought bitterly. The Combined Forces were stripping away French and German military capabilities one at a time. Round-the-clock air raids and cruise missile attacks had sunk most of the Confederation's naval units. Those few ships and submarines still afloat were being bottled up in port by enemy minefields. Now the Americans and British were going after French nuclear forces. And once they were finished with that, he knew only too well whose air bases would be next on the target list.

CHAPTER 27
Annunciation

JUNE 26 – MOSCOW

Diplomats stationed in Russia's capital city, especially those from the world's wealthier nations, had a range of perks and special privileges beyond the common Muscovite's wildest dreams. Those perks included unrestricted access to fresh produce and other foodstuffs. While average citizens made do with ration coupons that allowed them meat and other luxuries only two or three times a month, a foreigner with rubles in his pocket could still buy whatever he could pay for. That was one of the few concessions the military-controlled bureaucracy was willing to make to the free market.

So the three-man FIS surveillance team stationed outside the U.S. Embassy wasn't especially surprised when a delivery van from the Kuskovo Commercial Food Collective pulled up to the enclave just before first light. After all, everybody knew how particular the Americans were – especially when it came to their precious stomachs.

'Whew! Take a look at that!' Pavel Voronzov, the youngest and least experienced of the three, had their tripod-mounted binoculars focused on the van as it drove around the big, red brick chancery building and parked near a side door.

'Take a look at what, Pasha?' A second team member pushed back the earphones he was wearing and looked up from a bank of reel-to-reel recorders. So far this morning their directional microphones hadn't picked up anything worth listening to. Just the usual obscenity-sprinkled complaints from the Russian militiamen on duty outside the compound and incomprehensible sports chatter from the U.S. Marines guarding the main gate.

'Fresh sausages! Crates of vegetables.' The young man could feel his mouth watering as he watched workers in coveralls unloading the van. 'My God, they've even got two sides of beef. And a box of oranges!'

'Oh for Christ's sake, shut up! And look at something else!' the senior watch officer snapped in irritation. 'We're hunting for spies, not greengrocers!' Not even the special ration coupons issued to state officials under martial law stretched far enough – not this close to the end of the month. His dinner the night before had consisted of weak tea, stale bread, a very thin pat of butter, and some suspiciously spotted cabbage. The older FIS man turned back to the reports he was filling out, determined to ignore the growling noises coming from his stomach.

Properly chastened, Voronzov swung his binoculars back to the chancery. Only a few lights were on, all on the floor where the Americans maintained a round-the-clock duty station and communications watch. Whoever was awake over there was probably as bored as he was, he decided. But they probably had food right at hand. Chocolate bars, perhaps. Or maybe even a Big Mac. He sighed.

Without really meaning to, he found his gaze drawn back to the delivery van. No, it was no good. The Kuskovo Collective's workers had finished unloading and were leaving. Lucky bastards. They probably got to squirrel away a few delicious odds and ends from every shipment. He looked away, losing interest. The edible objects of his desire were inside the embassy's kitchens, not inside an empty truck.

It never occurred to him that the van might not be empty – that other items and even people might have been slipped in while the food was being taken out.

The van from the Kuskovo Commercial Food Collective, a wholly owned subsidiary of the New Kiev Trading Company and the CIA, turned left out the main gate and accelerated.

Swaying with the van's movement, Erin McKenna finished unzipping her workman's coveralls and shrugged them off. The baggy cloth cap hiding her auburn hair came off next. Underneath the rough disguise she wore a plain, dark blue sweatshirt, shorts, and running shoes. Nothing fancy. Nothing eye-catching.

She glanced up and saw Alex Banich watching her with a carefully blank face. She knew that he still didn't approve of this rendezvous with Colonel Soloviev – that he thought it was too risky. In the end it had taken a direct order from Len Kutner, backed by Langley itself, to break down his resistance. And even then he'd insisted on taking every precaution he could think of.

Like the wire she was wearing under her clothes.

Whenever Erin shifted positions she could feel the tiny microphone taped just below her throat. She could also feet the hair-thin connecting cable running down between her breasts to a miniaturized battery pack, microrecorder, and transmitter taped to the small of her back. Since the system was fully self-contained, she shouldn't have to fiddle with it while running. 'Just don't sweat,' Banich had said with a faint grin. Faint or not, that was the first time he had smiled since the Russian colonel made his covert approach.

Wearing the wire was a calculated risk. If Soloviev's request *was* a trap, the fact that she was wired for sound could be used as evidence that she was an espionage agent. On the other hand, wearing it would let Banich and Mike Hennessy listen in on the meeting from start to finish. If anything went wrong, that might give them enough of a head start to pluck her out of trouble. Maybe.

'You know what to do if you see something odd or if you start getting a bad feeling about the way the conversation's heading?' Banich asked.

Erin nodded silently. She'd spent several hours the night before memorizing a short list of innocuous-sounding emergency phrases that would trigger action by Banich and Hennessy. At his insistence, she'd even read a brief rundown on escape-and-evasion techniques. She had also learned the location of one of the CIA's Moscow safe houses.

'Remember to let Soloviev do most of the talking. Stick to generalities wherever you can. Got it?'

She nodded again, half-angry at being treated like a small child or hapless nitwit and half-amused by the evidence of the depth of Banich's concern for her safety. He knew that she had the contact procedures down cold, but he couldn't stop himself from going over them one last time. For someone other embassy staffers called the Ice Man, Alex Banich had a bad case of the jitters.

If she called him on it, he'd only claim he was worried that she might blow their cover here in Russia. She knew better. Shared work, shared meals, and a growing appreciation of each other's intelligence and sense of humor had brought them closer and closer together – whether or not they were willing to admit it yet. The van slowed and came to a stop. 'We're here, Alex. The Novodevichy Convent's just up ahead, on the right,' Hennessy announced from the driver's seat, his voice muffled by the partition.

'No signs of a tail?' Banich asked.

'Nope. And Alcott and Teppler say we're clean, too.' The second pair of CIA operatives were in a chase car that had followed them at a distance, hoping to spot anyone else tracking the delivery van.

'That's good, isn't it?' Erin asked.

'Possibly.' Banich looked unconvinced. 'But maybe the FIS isn't tailing us because they're here already, waiting.'

He sighed. 'This is your last chance to back out, McKenna. Nobody could blame you for not wanting to stick your head into a buzz saw.'

'No.' Erin shook her head fiercely, fighting the doubts and fears that were starting to creep in. What if the Russians *were* out there waiting for her? Images of arrest, torture, and imprisonment flashed through her mind. She could feel her heartbeat starting to speed up.

'All right,' Banich said flatly. He swung away from her and opened the blinds covering one of the van's rear windows just long enough for a quick look outside. 'It's still clear. So let's do it.'

Moving fast now, he popped the doors open, dropped lightly onto the street, and turned to help her down. Erin suspected the sudden burst of speed came because he wanted to hurry things along before he changed his own mind about letting her do this.

The CIA agent checked his watch. 'It's five fifty-eight. Remember, if Soloviev doesn't show by five after, come right back here. No hanging around. Clear?'

She didn't answer him. Instead, acting on a long-restrained impulse, she leaned forward and kissed him. Then she turned and loped away, running toward the convent.

Alex Banich stood watching her leave with a stunned expression on his face.

* * *

The Novodevichy Convent, the New Convent of the Virgin, loomed ahead of her – a massive, imposing complex surrounded by a crenelated wall and twelve towers. Buildings, some topped by golden Russian Orthodox domes and crosses, lofted above the walls. 'Whatever you do, don't go inside the convent,' Banich had told her. 'We'd lose contact right away.'

Now Erin could see why he'd been so insistent. Radio signals from her wire wouldn't stand a chance of penetrating walls built to withstand cannon shot and siege engines. The exterior of the convent, which was founded in 1524, looked more like a fortress or prison than a place of worship. Some of the tsars had used it as a kind of gilded prison, she knew, a cage to hold noblewomen they considered too dangerous or too influential. She only hoped that wasn't a bad omen for her.

Water sparkled close by, lit by the sun rising behind her. After looping around a collection of stadiums, arenas, and swimming pools originally expanded for the 1980 Summer Olympics, the Moscow River flowed north past the convent grounds.

Erin found Valentin Soloviev standing near the main entrance – an arched passageway flanked by thick columns. Dressed in running shorts and a sweatshirt himself, the Russian colonel looked subtly different than he had in uniform, less rigid and slightly less imposing. He seemed to be watching a pair of bearded, somewhat bedraggled artists at work. Or were they plainclothes security men only pretending to be artists? Her steps faltered in sudden doubt.

She knew that the Novodevichy was a favorite subject and gathering place for Moscow's street painters, but the gates were still shut this early in the morning. She slowed to a walk and drew closer. From what she could see of their easels, the two men were working on twin watercolors of the convent at sunrise. Their brushes moved in swift, sure strokes, laying down pale colors across white emptiness.

Erin felt a surge of relief as her first fears faded. Either the FIS had agents who were also gifted artists, or these guys were exactly what they appeared to be – starving students trying to squeeze out a few extra rubles by painting one of Moscow's most famous landmarks.

Soloviev heard her footsteps and looked round. He smiled, but she noticed the smile didn't quite reach his eyes. They were still wary. When he spoke, he spoke in Russian. 'You made it! I'm glad.'

She answered in the same language, consciously trying to damp down her American accent. 'You sound surprised. Why?'

The colonel shrugged. 'I thought you might be busy. I'm sure you have a great deal of work to do these days.' He glanced toward the two artists and nodded toward the street behind her. 'Shall we run, then?'

She noticed he was being careful not to use any names. 'Certainly. If you think you can keep up with me, that is.'

Soloviev smiled again, for real this time. He led the way out of the arched passage and turned right, heading toward the river. She matched his stride easily.

They ran in silence for a few minutes before swinging onto a street that paralleled the river. The pale brown towers of the Ukraina Hotel rose in the distance. There were very few cars or trucks on the road. Gasoline rationing and restrictions on private use saw to that.

At last Erin couldn't contain her curiosity any longer. 'Well, Colonel? You're calling the shots here. Why did you want to see me?'

Soloviev turned his head toward her and she could see amusement dancing in his gray eyes. He arched an eyebrow. 'Do I need a reason, Miss McKenna? Beyond the simple desire for your company?'

'Yes, you do.' Erin knew that many men considered her attractive, but she couldn't see a man like Soloviev risking his career for lust, or even for love. Besides, she suspected the handsome, aristocratic colonel didn't have any trouble finding suitably beautiful Russian women to meet his needs – women who were considerably safer to pursue.

'Fair enough.' He nodded and his face grew more serious. 'Very well, I have such a reason.'

She waited for him to go on, running steadily by his side.

Finally Soloviev seemed to come to a decision. Still running, he changed direction, turning into a small park below the convent's western wall. A gravel path wound around two fishponds and a fragrant garden. He stopped beside a park bench and pivoted to face her squarely. 'I know you have shown great trust in coming here this morning, Miss McKenna. After all, I could easily be some kind of *agent provocateur*, correct?'

'The thought had crossed my mind,' Erin admitted.

'That is understandable.' The Russian officer shrugged. 'Some of my countrymen have a deserved reputation for such trickery. *I* do not.'

He looked closely at her. 'But you must also understand how dangerous this is for me. If one word of what I tell you reaches the wrong ears . . . *whiitt*.' He pulled one hand across his throat in a fast, slashing motion. His eyes were suddenly bleak. 'This is not melodrama. I know that such things happen. I know it all too well.'

Erin felt her brain kick into overdrive. Smells, sights, and sounds were all magnified as her senses came fully alive. It was a familiar sensation – one she always felt whenever the critical clue to a particularly complicated puzzle came within her grasp. Oh, her fears were still there, she realized. Everything Soloviev was saying might still be window dressing, part of a plan orchestrated by Russian counterintelligence to entrap her. But her instincts said that was less and less likely.

She spread her hands. 'I can only promise to do my best, Colonel.'

Some of the bleakness faded. 'I can only accept that.' He sat down on the bench, facing the river.

Erin did the same thing, noticing the faint white blob that was Banich's delivery van parked several blocks down the street. She hoped the wire was still working.

'The French want us to intervene against Poland,' Soloviev said abruptly. 'They've sent a high-ranking delegation to negotiate directly with Marshal Kaminov and the rest of our Military Council.'

Erin shivered suddenly. Despite the sunlight, the day felt colder. Russian involvement in the war had been one of Washington's nightmare scenarios from day one. Neither the United States or Great Britain could possibly ship troops into Poland fast enough to fend off the Franco-German attack from the west and a Russian avalanche from the east. She took a deep breath and asked, 'Have Kaminov and the others agreed to this proposal?'

He shook his head. 'Not yet. They want more than the French are offering to pay.' He sounded contemptuous of their mercenary motives.

'And what are the French offering?'

'Financial aid and technology transfers worth several billions of your dollars,' Soloviev told her.

'But that's not enough?'

He shrugged. 'No.' He hunched his shoulders and explained. 'Kaminov knows that the longer he waits, the more important our aid becomes to Paris. In any event, it will take several days to move the additional forces we would need through Belarus and into position on the Polish border.'

Erin nodded. 'So what does he want?'

'More money. More access to advanced military technologies. Co-equal status with France and Germany as a member of the Confederation.' The Russian colonel saved the worst news for last. 'And a free hand against Ukraine, the Baltic States, Kazakhstan, and the other republics.'

His mouth tightened to a grim line as he spoke. 'Many men of high rank in my country have never accepted the dismemberment of the old Soviet state, Miss McKenna. They long for the old days of empire.' His gaze turned inward, 'No matter what price others must pay for *their* glory and *their* power. And the people would follow them. My countrymen are tired of hunger and tired of insignificance. They long for prosperity and our place on the world stage.'

Erin sat numbed. The specter of a Europe held captive by France and Germany was awful enough. The prospect of that *plus* a reunited and aggressive Russian empire was even worse.

She twisted her ponytail around and around her fingers, thinking hard. Something Soloviev had said, or rather had not said, seemed significant. 'You keep mentioning the French. What about the Germans? Are they part of this?'

The colonel shook his head. 'I don't believe so. All the negotiators I've seen are Frenchmen and all the meetings are being held under the strictest security – at a dacha outside the city.' He smiled thinly. 'I doubt the Germans have the faintest idea of what their "allies" are up to.'

Interesting. That also made sense. The Germans were unlikely to welcome the notion of a resurgent Russia. But the French willingness to cut their supposed partner out of such an important effort spoke volumes about French arrogance or French desperation. Maybe a little bit of both, she decided.

A truck rumbled by on the street, calling Erin out of her reverie. Time was passing and Moscow was waking up. They'd have to go their separate ways soon or become uncomfortably noticeable. Few Russians had the leisure time to sit companionably on park benches during the workweek. 'Do you have any proof of all of this?'

Soloviev frowned. 'No, Miss McKenna, I do not. As I said, these negotiations have been closely guarded and very discreet.'

She frowned back. Without concrete evidence to back up its claims, the United States could not go public with its knowledge of these secret Franco-Russian talks. Both countries would simply indignantly deny the story, Soloviev would disappear into a shallow grave or reopened gulag, and the talks would proceed on schedule. She looked up from her fingers. 'Can you get proof?'

Soloviev stared back at her for what seemed a very long time. Then he nodded slowly. 'Perhaps . . . though it will be difficult.'

'When?'

He shrugged. 'I don't know. Slipping anything in writing or on tape past security will take thorough planning . . . and a great deal of luck. The planning I can guarantee, the luck I cannot.'

'It is important, Colonel. Vitally important.'

Soloviev nodded. 'I understand.' He checked his watch and stood up. 'I think we've stayed here long enough.'

Erin looked up at him. 'How can I contact you again?'

He shook his head decisively. 'You can't. The FIS is growing stronger all the time. By now they must be monitoring all incoming and outgoing Defense Ministry calls.'

Erin made a decision. Banich had reluctantly given her a secure telephone number she could pass on to Soloviev *if* the Russian proved trustworthy. 'Okay, Colonel. Then you call me to arrange another meeting – if you can find an untapped phone. Use this number only: two, fifty-three, twenty-four, sixty-two.'

He repeated the numbers back to her once, perfectly. Then he smiled, a brief sunburst across a somber face. 'For a simple commercial attaché, Miss McKenna, you are astonishingly resourceful.'

Despite her best efforts at self-control, she blushed.

'Until our next meeting, then.' He took her hand, kissed it gallantly, and swung away.

'Colonel!'

Soloviev turned back.

'One more question.' Erin got up and walked toward him. 'Why are you doing this?'

'I am a patriot, Miss McKenna.' He donned a sardonic grin. ' "My loyalties to Mother Russia supersede those to any individual." Or so Marshal Kaminov told my President when he took power and began this madness. If his own reasons now turn against him as dogs against their master, so much the better.'

JUNE 27 – ON THE BREST-SMOLENSK HIGHWAY, NEAR STOLBTSY, BELARUS

The main highway linking the Russian city of Smolensk with the Belarussian border city of Brest passed right through the upper reaches of the wide Niemen River valley. Quiet, shadowed woods and green meadows stretched peacefully to the north. To the south, a wall of thick, yellowish dust shrouded the countryside, kicked up by the military traffic clogging the highway.

Militiamen and military police squads stood guard at intersections along the route, turning civilian cars and trucks off onto smaller, unpaved side roads. To save road space and time, the three divisions moving west were using both sides of the highway. Giant tank transporters carrying canvas-shrouded T-80s and BMP-2s mingled with trucks and wheeled BTR-80 APCs carrying troops and supplies. All told, two thousand vehicles and sixty thousand men were heading for the Polish frontier in a march column that stretched for more than seventy kilometers. Freight trains crammed with fuel and ammunition paralleled the column.

While the subordinates haggled with the French, Marshal Yuri Kaminov was massing his forces.

PARIS

Nicolas Desaix eyed the man and woman sitting in front of him with a mixture of scorn and irritation. The two Belgians were a thoroughly unimpressive pair. How could anyone take a female defense minister seriously? Especially one who looked more like a plump, white-haired housewife than a senior government official. Nor did the thick waist and heavy jowls of the Belgian Army's chief of staff inspire much confidence. The only point in their favor was that they at least had the wit to know who really wielded power inside the Confederation.

He shook his head. 'I cannot agree to this request for special treatment, Madame Defense Minister. Being asked to commit a mere two brigades of mechanized troops for noncombat duties hardly strikes me as particularly taxing.'

'But those brigades represent half of our regular army, monsieur!' the Defense Minister protested. 'Worse, deploying them would violate my government's solemn pledge to the voters that our conscripts won't be asked to serve outside our own national boundaries!'

Desaix glowered back at her. It had been his idea to requisition Belgian troops in the first place. Reports from Moscow made it painfully clear that it would take longer than he had hoped to bribe the Russians into the war. In the meantime, the French and German forces in Poland urgently needed more men and more tanks to revive their stalled offensive. Using Belgian soldiers to guard the Confederation's lines of communication was one way to free up units for frontline duty. He was not prepared to see those plans undone by pigheaded Belgian politicians.

'Your government's solemn pledges to the Confederation outweigh trivial domestic considerations, madame. If you have any doubts of that, I suggest you reread the relevant treaties.' Desaix didn't see any point in mincing his words. These people represented a small and vulnerable nation flanked by both France and Germany. They should remember that. Besides, by showing a firm hand now, he could stop their reluctance from sliding into outright resistance.

He leaned forward. 'The orders from the Defense Secretariat are final and we expect full and prompt compliance. I suggest you both begin issuing the necessary instructions to your commanders.'

With that, he looked away, ignoring the stunned, strained look of disbelief on their faces. By the time his aides ushered the two appalled Belgian officials out of his office, Nicolas Desaix's mind was already busy grappling with other, far more important matters.

CHAPTER 28
Bridgehead

JUNE 27 – HEADQUARTERS, 19TH PANZERGRENADIER BRIGADE, SOUTH OF BYDGOSZCZ, POLAND

Signs of war littered Poland's roads and fields. Two burned-out T-72s stood off to one side of Highway 5. They had been destroyed while trying to delay the advancing EurCon army. Blackened grass and melted steel and rubber surrounded the wrecks, and the faint, sickening stench of smoke, burned diesel, and burned flesh lingered in the air – a disturbing contrast to the ordinary Polish countryside smells of sunbaked earth, horses, and cattle.

Lt. Col. Willi von Seelow waited by the other side of the road, watching the long column of his brigade's Marder APCs and Leopard 2 tanks grind past on their way north. Thousands of fighting vehicles and guns were on the move, their passage marked by drifting clouds of dust. After five days spent in reserve, resting and absorbing replacements, the EurCon II Corps was going into battle again – led as usual by the 7th Panzer Division.

Clumps of silent, morose-looking infantrymen rode atop the Marders. Most had scarves pulled up over their mouths and noses to ward off the thick, gritty dust churned up by speeding tracks. Oil and diesel fumes and the scorching heat trapped by their armor made staying inside the APCs' crowded troop compartments unbearable.

Some of the soldiers crowded atop the APCs were familiar faces. Far too many were men he didn't know. Although some of the brigade's losses had been made good by lightly wounded troops returning to duty, most of their replacements were Territorial Army soldiers hastily drafted into regular service.

The rough equivalent of the U.S. National Guard, Germany's territorial forces were supposed to be used for home defense, not aggressive war, but unexpectedly heavy casualties had forced a change in official policy. Nobody was happy about that. Not the commanders who were being asked to make do with troops who were older, less physically fit, and less prepared for combat. Certainly not the Territorials themselves. Most were businessmen, shopkeepers, and factory workers who had only signed up to defend their own homes against a Soviet invasion. Angry at being ordered into battle on foreign soil, many had refused to report for duty. Others had come prepared with convenient medical reports that excused them from active service. All told, barely half of those called up had joined the German divisions fighting inside Poland.

Willi watched the glum, depressed faces sliding by and sighed. Though on paper his brigade was back to almost full strength, it was still a far cry from the polished, powerful combat formation that had crossed the Neisse twenty-two days before.

A Marder turned out of the column and pulled up beside von Seelow's own command vehicle. Numbers and letters chalked on the APC's armored flanks identified it as belonging to Lt. Col. Klaus von Olden, the 192nd Panzergrenadier Battalion's commanding officer. He noted with some amusement that the brightly painted heraldic crest that had once served the same function was gone. Apparently common sense and a fine nose for battlefield survival had overridden the man's pride in his noble Prussian ancestors. Von Olden, a middling-tall, grim-faced officer, climbed out of the APC and dropped lightly onto the grass.

Willi strode forward to meet him, trying hard to keep a neutral expression on his face. Arrogant, obnoxious, and ambitious, the 192nd's CO had been a thorn in his side ever since he'd joined the brigade. Von Olden despised 'ossies', East Germans like von Seelow – especially ossies who were ahead of him on the promotion ladder. But, like it or not, Willi knew, he had to work with this man.

If anything, his jump to brigade commander had intensified their mutual dislike. Von Olden made no secret of the fact that he considered himself far more competent and deserving than 'a jumped-up East German refugee.' Willi suspected that several members of the 7th Panzer and II Corps staffs harbored the same sentiments.

Willi shrugged inwardly. He'd assumed command under the most difficult circumstances imaginable and performed well. At least this war had forced the army's internal politics to one side in favor of basic competence.

Von Olden stood in front of him with his hands on his hips and his chin jutting out. 'You wanted to see me?'

Everything about the battalion commander, from his sarcastic tone and sour expression to the rakish tilt of his dark green beret, seemed designed to show contempt.

Von Seelow waited coldly, saying nothing. Insolence and insubordination were both grounds for disciplinary charges – even against senior officers. If the 192nd's troublesome CO wanted to push matters that far, he would be happy to oblige him.

Gradually the man's self-assurance wilted in the face of his continued silence. Still scowling, von Olden straightened to a semblance of attention and asked again, 'You wanted to see me, *sir*?' The last word slipped out through clenched teeth.

Von Seelow nodded calmly. 'We've been given a new objective, and I'm assigning it to you and your troops.'

He turned on his heel and strode briskly toward the M577 command vehicle where Major Thiessen was waiting to brief them. Von Olden didn't have any choice but to tag along behind.

Surprised by the Polish counterattack that had checked II Corps south of Poznan, the EurCon high command had been forced to send its jealously guarded reserves into action. For two days, the V Corps' two fresh panzer divisions had ground forward against the battered Poles – locked in a bloody slugging match to clear the city's eastern and western approaches. At last, faced with flanking maneuvers that threatened to isolate Poznan entirely, the Poles evacuated and resumed their delaying fight – trading space for time while waiting for reinforcements from the east and from the Combined Forces.

Two of the six Polish divisions on line withdrew toward Warsaw, screening the roads to the Polish capital in case the French and Germans turned that way. The rest were falling back on Gdansk. Every kilometer they retreated brought them closer to better defensive terrain and to the port facilities where the American and British troops already at sea would have to land.

EurCon's invasion armies had turned north in pursuit. Now they had a new strategic objective, their third in a little over three weeks: seize Gdansk and shut off the flow of enemy reinforcements and war supplies. Then, with the Poles isolated and reeling, Paris and Berlin could make new peace overtures from a strong battlefield position.

Von Seelow studied the map thoughtfully. Gdansk should have been their objective right from the start. The first Franco-German attacks toward Wroclaw and Poznan had gained ground and nothing else. Taking the Polish port city offered real hope that this idiotic war could be won – or at least brought to a close on honorable terms.

Unfortunately, capturing Gdansk before the Americans could land their heavy armor and mechanized units would take some doing. During the three days of nonstop pursuit since Poznan fell, EurCon's forces had advanced more than eighty kilometers. Now they were closing in on the sprawling industrial city of Bydgoszcz. But the port was still another 150 kilometers beyond that, and Bydgoszcz itself could prove a tough nut to crack.

Anyone trying to advance through or around the city first had to cross the Notec River and then penetrate a fairly thick band of forest. Swinging wide to the west would be difficult at best, impossible at worst. The Pomeranian Lakelands began there – a vast marshland of more than a thousand lakes and tree-lined, winding waterways. Moving east was also impractical. The broad Vistula River looped north there, blocking easy flanking moves.

Willi frowned. Terrain and the road net were both combining to funnel EurCon's advancing army into a frontal attack against Bydgoszcz. If their enemies were looking for a good place to turn and fight, this was it.

The Notec River, though not as wide as the Vistula, was still a formidable tactical barrier. Given enough time, the Poles could dig in solidly behind the river line – barring the main road to Gdansk.

II Corps headquarters wanted the 19th Panzergrenadier Brigade to seize a bridgehead across the Notec, and soon. But where?

Major Thiessen answered his question by leaning across the map and pointing to a village several kilometers up the road from their present position. 'There, Herr Oberstleutnant. The highway bridge at Rynarzewo.'

Willi nodded, feeling cold inside. II Corps wanted them to attack straight up the middle. If the Poles were still retreating, they'd only blow the bridge right in his face. If they were deploying to hold the river line in strength, the 192nd's assault could easily run headfirst into a ready-made killing ground.

From the troubled look on Klaus von Olden's face he had come to the same conclusion. The corners of his thin-lipped mouth turned down. 'What kind of support can I count on, Major?'

Thiessen looked apologetic. 'Very little, I'm afraid, Herr Oberstleutnant.'

Von Olden stabbed a finger down on the woods shown just north of the bridge. It offered perfect concealment for any Polish tanks and infantry lurking in ambush. 'What about an air strike here? Using napalm or cluster munitions, if possible.'

The major shook his head. 'No air support is available, sir.'

Not particularly surprising, Willi thought numbly. The focus of the air war had shifted west, into France and Germany. The small numbers of exhausted fighter and fighter-bomber squadrons left to both sides were being used solely for air defense or for raids on vital installations. Neither side could claim any measure of air superiority over the battlefield.

Von Olden rocked back on his heels. 'And my artillery support? What guns will I have on call?'

'Our brigade guns and mortars only, Herr Oberstleutnant. Apparently all corps and divisional artillery is being committed to other operations,' Thiessen replied.

Willi's suspicions hardened into near certainty. General Montagne, the II Corps commander, had something else up his sleeve. Nobody could seriously expect a single brigade to capture the bridge at Rynarzewo without more support. Clearly he and his men were being asked to fight and die as part of a feint. While the Poles concentrated their forces to butcher the 19th Panzergrenadier, Montagne must be hoping that other units would be able to cross the river elsewhere against lighter opposition.

Anger gripped him. It was bad enough to be sacrificed so callously. The French general's apparent willingness to keep them in the dark was worse. Did Montagne think his German troops wouldn't fight hard enough if they knew the truth?

For an instant von Seelow considered refusing the attack order. Then reality flooded back in. In the abstract, his defiance would be a fine thing. In practical terms, it would achieve nothing. Montagne and General Leibnitz would only replace him with von Olden or someone similar.

He peered down at the map, aware that both Thiessen and von Olden were watching him carefully, waiting for their instructions. For a moment, his mind stayed obstinately blank. Then, suddenly, the beginnings of an idea tugged at his consciousness. If you couldn't bypass a strong enemy position or spend the time needed to pulverize it with superior firepower, there was just one real option left. Speed was life, the fighter pilots said. Well, the same often applied to land warfare. Rapid maneuver was the key to seizing the initiative and disrupting enemy plans. It also lay at the heart of German tactical doctrine.

Willi looked up at the 192nd's commander. 'When can you attack, Colonel?'

'An hour? Perhaps two?' Von Olden shrugged. 'Once we've closed up on the river, I'll need time to deploy my companies, scout the ground, and brief my officers. I'll want tank support from the 194th, too.'

'No.' Von Seelow shook his head. He nodded toward the northern horizon. 'The more time we use up now, the more time we give those Poles to finish digging in.'

He turned back to von Olden. 'So don't mess about, Colonel! Hit them as hard and as fast as you can before they've got time to get set! Swing right out of your march column into the attack! I'll feed the other battalions into the fight as fast as they arrive. Clear?'

The 192nd's aristocratic commander nodded reluctantly, clearly unenthusiastic about the whole idea. For all his aggressive posturing, Klaus von Olden was a cautious man at heart.

Willi ignored his subordinate's uncertainty. He glanced at Thiessen. 'Get on the radio to Captain Brandt. Tell him I want the approaches to that damned village cleared as quickly as he can!'

The major nodded and hurried away. Gunther Brandt commanded the brigade's advance guard – a battle group made up of the captain's Luchs scout cars and a Leopard company attached from the 194th Panzer for added striking power. Brandt and his men had been skirmishing with retreating Polish armor and infantry units all morning, engaging at long range and maneuvering off the highway to outflank the Poles whenever they turned to fight. It was the kind of fighting designed to minimize casualties while still gaining ground, but it was time-consuming. Von Seelow's new orders would change that.

Whatever Montagne and his French staff officers expected, the 19th Panzergrenadier Brigade would do its damnedest to seize the Rynarzewo bridge intact.

C COMPANY, POLISH 421ST MECHANIZED INFANTRY BATTALION, RYNARZEWO GARRISON

Rynarzewo, a tiny cluster of brick and wood-frame houses split in two by the highway, lay on the south side of the Notec River. Two buildings dominated the little village – an old red brick church and a two-story, concrete-block building that served as a combination post office, library, and town hall. Outside the village, fields, pastures, isolated farmhouses, and apple orchards stretched almost as far as the eye could see. Woods stood dark in the distance. A narrow ribbon of blue, one of the Notec's tributary streams, snaked through the green and brown landscape before cutting in front of the village and under the highway.

Two kilometers west of Rynarzewo, the twisted remains of a railway bridge lay half in and half out of the river. French jets had dropped the steel-girder span with laser-guided bombs several days before as part of the effort to keep Polish reinforcements from reaching Poznan.

But the highway bridge was still up. Troop carriers, supply trucks, and other vehicles fleeing the approaching EurCon Army lumbered across in a never-ending stream. They were the tail end of a withdrawing army and it showed. Though never beaten decisively in a stand-up fight, three weeks of almost continuous retreat were starting to take a toll on Polish morale. Heads turned apprehensively toward the south whenever sounds of gunfire crackled above the roar of traffic. Although friendly troops were still screening the retreat, everyone knew the French and Germans couldn't be far away.

Combat engineers swarmed over the span, dodging APCs and trucks as they frantically wired it for demolition. Several hung over the sides, dangling from climbing ropes while they placed charges against the concrete piers supporting the roadway itself.

Two hundred meters from the southern end of the bridge, a short, brown-haired Polish officer hurried from house to house on the village outskirts, checking his defenses. Capt. Konrad Polinski commanded the mechanized infantry company ordered to hold Rynarzewo while the engineers finished their work.

As an experienced soldier, Polinski was not happy with his company's tactical situation. He didn't like fighting with a river at his back – especially when the only way across was liable to go up in smoke at any minute. His small detachment was not strong enough to defend the village against a determined EurCon attack. Detailed at the last minute, C Company hadn't had time to lay mines and barbed wire, or to dig holes with good overhead protection.

There were supposed to be T-72s stationed in the forest across the river, but that was really too far away to do much good. Rynarzewo's buildings would also block much of their field of fire. Even the best tank gunners in the world couldn't hit targets they couldn't see. He couldn't even count on reinforcements. The 421st's other mechanized infantry companies were several kilometers beyond the river, reorganizing and refitting before coming back to form a defensive line.

The captain stopped behind a garden wall and raised his binoculars. There, at the very edge of his vision, pillars of black smoke billowed skyward. Half-hidden beneath a thick brown mustache, his mouth turned down in a sudden grimace. That was a full-fledged battle raging out there, something far more serious than the usual isolated sniping. EurCon's leading elements must be trying to smash through the covering force guarding the retreat.

His radioman, a skinny, eighteen-year-old corporal, confirmed that. 'Sir! Tango Foxtrot reports contact with a strong German unit near Kolaczkowo! Tanks and APCs both!'

Polinski swore inwardly. Kolaczkowo was the closest village – a tiny hamlet barely four kilometers down the highway. If the enemy advance guard was already there, they could be on top of him in minutes. 'Order all platoons to stand to!'

'Yes, sir.'

The Polish captain spun around to look back at the vehicle-choked bridge behind him. The engineers were still hard at work. How much more time did they need? More important, how much more time would the Germans give them?

A COMPANY, 194TH PANZER BATTALION, NEAR KOLACZKOWO

Smoke from burning buildings, burning vehicles, and turret-mounted grenade launchers had turned the battlefield outside Kolaczkowo into a gray, hazy, nightmarish swirl of deadly, split-second encounters.

'Veer right! Right!' Lt. Werner Gerhardt screamed, already hoarse from yelling orders above the deafening noise all around. He tightened his grip on the hatch coaming as his mammoth Leopard 2 roared out of its own smoke screen and swung sharply to avoid a wrecked vehicle dead ahead. Fifty-five tons of steel moving at high speed clipped the burning Luchs scout car, sending it tumbling out of the way in a high-pitched, grinding shriek of tearing metal.

Another tank, a Polish T-72, appeared almost directly ahead, trundling backward in a tangle of flapping camouflage netting as it reversed out from behind a farmhouse. Its 125mm cannon still pointed away from the German lieutenant's Leopard.

'Gunner! Target at one o'clock!' Gerhardt squeezed the turret override, guiding the Leopard's main gun around himself.

'Sabot up!'

'Fire!'

Hit point-blank, the T-72 slid sideways and exploded. Steel splinters thrown by the blast spanged off the Leopard's own armor and screamed over Gerhardt's head. He ducked and then stood higher, looking from side to side for new dangers.

More German tanks emerged from the smoke, strung out in a long fighting line. The lieutenant tallied them rapidly while still searching for signs of the enemy. Counting his own Leopard, ten of A Company's twelve vehicles had survived the tank duel.

As the smoke cleared, he could see that the Polish rear guard and Captain Brandt's scout company had been far less fortunate. Destroyed T-72s, BMPs, and German Luchs scout cars covered the fields on both sides of the highway, facing in every direction in mute testimony to the confused, savage nature of the short battle. Only his own tanks were still moving.

Gerhardt switched his radio to the brigade frequency. 'Top Cat One, this is Falconer One.'

'Go ahead, Falconer.' Major Thiessen's voice sounded distorted, wavering in and out between bursts of static. The 19th's headquarters unit must be on the move.

Gerhardt released the transmit button on his mike. 'We've cleared the first village. Now proceeding toward the river.'

'Acknowledged, Falconer. Where is Prowler One?'

The lieutenant stared out across the battlefield and swallowed hard. He looked away. 'Captain Brandt and his men are dead, Top Cat. All of them are dead.'

Von Seelow's own calm, determined voice came on line. There was no time now to mourn Brandt and his men. Controlling his emotions, he said, 'Understood, Lieutenant. Can you continue the attack?'

Gerhardt gripped the turret ring, regaining his own control. 'Yes, sir.'

'Good.' Von Seelow's voice took on a sharper edge. 'Keep moving, Falconer. Press them hard. Don't let them regroup! Predator One is right behind you.'

Gerhardt stared down the highway. The colonel was correct. He could already see the 192nd Panzergrenadier Battalion's infantry-filled Marders pouring into Kolaczkowo in column. He signed off and relayed the necessary orders to his crews.

Alpha Company's ten surviving Leopard 2s rumbled north toward the bridge at Rynarzewo.

C COMPANY, RYNARZEWO GARRISON

Polinski breathed a faint sigh of relief. The last canvas-sided trucks, BMPs, and GAZ jeeps were finally inching their way toward the Rynarzewo bridge, and the black ribbon of highway stretched away empty to the south. Even the sounds of firing had stopped. Captain Kubiak's covering force must have stopped the German probes cold. Good. The engineers still hadn't finished wiring the bridge and every extra minute counted.

He glanced at the radioman hovering nervously beside him. 'Contact Tango Foxtrot. Ask them how much longer they can hold before handing off to us.'

'Yes, Captain.'

Polinski lifted his binoculars again. Plumes of bluish-black exhaust appeared behind a low rise roughly a kilometer away. There were tanks moving out there, diesel engines straining even on the shallow uphill grade. He frowned. Why hadn't Kubiak's T-72s reported in before falling back so far?

'Sir! I can't raise Tango Foxtrot!' the radioman stammered, aghast.

'Jesus Christ.' Polinski saw a line of armored vehicles appear like magic along the crest of the rise he'd been scanning. Large, angular turrets and dark green, brown, and black camouflage schemes identified them as enemy Leopards – not Polish T-72s. His mouth dropped open in shock. They were under attack!

The German tanks fired, opening up in one long, rippling salvo that sent shell after shell screaming low overhead. Trucks crowding the bridge approaches on both sides of the river began going up in flames. The Leopards were methodically working their way from front to back – gutting trapped vehicles with high-explosive rounds.

Horrified, Polinski let the field glasses fall down around his neck. He whirled and grabbed the corporal's arm. 'Come on!' he roared, tugging the young soldier toward the concrete-block building serving as the company's command post. 'Back to the CP!'

They raced down the street, running hard past blazing trucks and jeeps. Torn bodies, jagged, blast-warped shards of metal, and shredded truck tires littered the pavement in front of them.

Polinski threw himself through the post office door and took the stairs up two at a time. He skidded into the second-floor library room serving as his company headquarters unit. Maps and a longer-range radio sat on one of the reading tables. The sandbags, bookcases, and books piled across its windows offered a measure of protection against small-arms fire and shell fragments.

A worried-looking lieutenant, his second-in-command, looked up from the radio with evident relief. 'Captain! Battalion's on the line!'

The captain grabbed the headset. 'Polinski here!'

'This is Major Korytzki, Captain. What the hell is happening over there?'

Polinski scowled. He loathed the major, and he knew the feeling was mutual. A born staff man, Zbigniew Korytzki had taken charge when the battalion's old commander was killed near Poznan. Since then his combat troops and line officers had scarcely ever seen the man. He always seemed to lead from far to the rear, preferably from inside an armored command vehicle. 'We're being fired on by at least one company of enemy armor, Major! I request reinforcements.'

'Impossible,' Korytzki said crisply. 'You have antitank weapons. I suggest you use them. In any event, you must hold your position until the engineers have completed their work. Remember your duty, Captain! And keep me informed. Korytzki, out.'

Polinski ripped the headset off and tossed it back to his executive officer. He mastered his temper with difficulty. 'See if you can raise the CO of that tank outfit across the bridge. Tell him we need help to claw a few Leopards off our backs.'

The lieutenant nodded and turned to obey him.

'Sir!' The shout came from a sergeant watching out one of the windows. 'Enemy infantry carriers approaching – many of them!'

Polinski peered out through a slit they'd left in their makeshift barricades. German Marder fighting vehicles were visible now, rolling down off the same low rise held by their own tanks. Twenty at least. Probably more. Wonderful. They were being hit by a battalion-plus of panzergrenadiers. He whirled toward his radioman. 'All platoons! Open fire!'

The Marders roared closer, charging across the open fields. They fanned out while rolling forward. The captain swore out loud, suddenly realizing the Germans were deploying from column into line right in front of his face. Cocky bastards!

Three TOW missiles leapt toward the Marders. Two hit their targets and exploded. Further along the line, Polish BMP-ls opened up with 73mm cannon, pumping HEAT – high-explosive antitank – rounds out at the rate of eight per minute. More German troop carriers slewed sideways and began burning.

Retaliation came swiftly.

In quick succession, accurate fire from the overwatching Leopards and

25mm rounds spray-fired from the Marders fireballed two of C Company's three TOW-Humvees and smashed a third of its BMPs into smoking ruin. More shells slammed into several of the houses on Rynarzewo's outskirts. Rubble spilled out into the narrow village streets.

Polinski stared out through the firing slit, straining to see the enemy assault wave through all the smoke and dust. Were they going to try driving right through his defenses? No! The surviving Marders were stopping in whatever cover they could find – behind farmhouses and gentle knolls, inside orchards, and behind their own destroyed comrades. Soldiers tumbled out of each fighting vehicle. Now that most of the Germans were within four hundred meters of his line, they were continuing their attack dismounted.

The Polish captain's eyes focused on the stretch of relatively open ground the enemy infantry would have to cover. He bared his teeth and turned to his second-in-command. 'Contact the artillery, Jozef! Tell them we have a fire mission!'

192ND PANZERGRENADIER BATTALION, OUTSIDE RYNARZEWO

Lt. Col. Willi von Seelow hung on grimly as the Marder he was riding in swerved suddenly, dropped into a ditch, and bounced out – all without slowing down.

Whammm! A near miss rocked the speeding vehicle. Fragments and pieces of shattered rock rattled against its side armor. Even with the Marder's hatches closed, the noise was ear-shattering, almost maddening in its intensity.

Von Seelow spoke into the Marder's intercom. 'How much further, Gerd?' Another close explosion punctuated his query.

'Not far, Herr Oberstleutnant!' the vehicle's commander shouted. 'I've got Predator One in sight!'

'Good. Take us right up next to him.'

The Marder jolted through another drainage ditch, bumped over what felt like a low wall, and braked to a stop. Without the engine turning over at full power, the drumming roar of the Polish barrage was even louder and more menacing.

Moving rapidly now, von Seelow unbuckled his safety belt and got out crouching to clear the low armored ceiling. He pulled a G3 assault rifle out of the clips beside his seat. Captain Meyer, one of his aides, and Private Neumann, his radioman, imitated him, checking their own gear and personal weapons. Both tugged at their Kevlar body armor, assuring themselves that the flak jackets were securely fastened.

Willi put his hand on the button that would drop the Marder's rear ramp and took a last look around the troop compartment. 'Ready, gentlemen?'

They nodded.

'All right. Remember, spread out right away, don't bunch up. Then run like hell for von Olden's vehicle! Understand?'

'Yes, sir.' Despite the standard and expected response, Meyer sounded uncertain. Sweat beaded his high pale forehead. 'But I must ask you once more to remain here . . . in relative safety. Let me bring Lieutenant Colonel von Olden to you instead.'

'No.' Willi shook his head firmly. There were times when a leader had to put himself at risk to get results. This was one of those times. He took several quick breaths and punched the release button. 'Go!'

The ramp clanged open.

They were in a farmyard. Waist-high stone walls enclosed a dilapidated wooden barn and the wreckage of a small, wood-frame house blown apart by a Polish artillery shell. Flames danced eerily in the ruins, licking up the two walls still standing. Near the barn, an old tractor lay toppled on its side. A sow and her piglets lay dead inside a muddy sty.

Beyond the farmyard, gently rolling fields planted in oats and rye stretched toward Rynarzewo. Burning German vehicles dotted the fields. Hundreds of men wearing helmets and camouflage battle dress lay prone among the standing grain, cowering as shells rained down all around them. The Polish barrage had pinned the 192nd Panzergrenadier Battalion in place.

Klaus von Olden's command Marder lay just a few meters away, partially veiled by the smoke. Willi headed in that direction, running flat out.

Another salvo arced out of the sky with a freight-train roar.

'Incoming!' Willi shouted. He threw himself flat next to von Olden's vehicle.

Whammm! Whammm! Whammm! The ground rocked, bounced, and rolled as shell after shell slammed to earth just outside the farmyard and exploded in a hail of flame and deadly steel splinters.

With his ears still ringing, Willi spat to clear the taste in his mouth and got to his feet. He used the butt of his rifle to hammer on the Marder's armored flank. 'Open up!'

The command vehicle's ramp fell open, exposing an interior compartment already crowded with two fold-down map tables, a radio set, and three haggard-looking men – von Olden, his battalion operations chief, and a sergeant who manned their communications gear. Willi, Neumann, and Meyer ducked inside.

The ramp closed right behind them, cutting off some of the noise outside. He squeezed over to where the 192nd's CO sat. 'I need a situation report, Colonel.'

Von Olden glared up at him. 'Can't you tell?' His hands clenched and unclenched repeatedly. 'My men are being murdered by Polish artillery! We can't go forward and we can't go back! It's impossible!'

Willi frowned. From the quiver in his voice, von Olden was riding right on the edge.

The communications sergeant interrupted. 'Striker One is on line, Herr Oberstleutnant. His guns are deployed.'

That was good news. The eighteen 155mm self-propelled howitzers of the brigade's artillery battalion were finally ready to fire.

'Can he hit the Polish batteries?' Willi asked.

'No, sir. They're out of range.'

Willi nodded. He'd expected as much. Content to hold the river line, the Poles had placed their artillery far enough back to avoid German counterbattery fire. Too bad. Victory in war usually went to the side that made the fewest mistakes, and Poland's field commanders weren't making enough mistakes.

'Then tell him I need smoke to cover my withdrawal!' von Olden demanded suddenly. He glanced at his operations chief. 'Order all companies to fall back immediately. We'll regroup near Kolaczkowo.'

'Hold it, Major.' Willis flat tone stopped the man dead. He looked hard at the 192nd's commander. 'No one withdraws. We're not scuttling off with our tails between our legs. Not when we're this close to that damned bridge! Get your troops moving again and use the artillery to screen your attack.'

Von Olden flushed. 'I will not ask my men to commit suicide, von Seelow. They're fought out!'

'Oh? And how do you know that?' Willi waved a hand around the crowded compartment. 'Can you see through steel?' He didn't bother hiding his contempt. Von Olden should have been outside kicking, cajoling, and inspiring his troops to press on – not sitting safe inside this armored box jabbering over the radio! He hardened his voice. 'My orders stand. I suggest you implement them.'

'Go to hell!' the other man barked, stung to fury by von Seelow's scorn. 'I don't have to obey a damned traitor, a whining, bootlicking ossie!'

Willi's own temper flared. 'Then you're relieved!' He turned to the stunned operations chief. 'I'm taking tactical command of this battalion, Major. Pass the word to all company commanders and order them to advance on my signal.'

Von Olden stood for several seconds with his mouth open, shocked speechless. When he recovered enough to talk, he stammered out, 'You can't do this! I'll fight you all the way up the line!'

Willi nodded brusquely. 'Protest all you want. But do it somewhere else. Captain Meyer!'

'Sir!'

'Wait for a break in the shelling, then escort this officer to my vehicle and arrange his safe passage to the rear area.'

'Yes, sir.' Meyer sat down across from the dumbfounded former commander of the 192nd Panzergrenadier. His hand rested casually on the pistol holstered at his side.

Willi turned away, focusing wholly on the task at hand.

'Sergeant, raise the artillery again. Starting now, I want them to dump as much smoke as they can between here and the village. So much that I could walk on the stuff!'

The sergeant hurried to obey.

Satisfied that his instructions were being carried out, he picked up his rifle and dropped the Marder's troop compartment ramp. 'All right, Private Neumann. Let's go.'

'Wait!'

Willi turned to find Klaus von Olden, sagging and suddenly looking much older, clutching the door frame.

'Where are you going?'

Von Seelow's answer was brutally frank. 'To do *your* job, Colonel.' He spun away and headed toward the fields where the 192nd lay pinned down. Neumann, bent low under the weight of his radio gear, trotted along behind.

More Polish artillery rounds landed ahead and to either side.

Willi scrambled over the farmyard's low stone wall and pulled the radioman over after him. Dead and wounded men were scattered all around – cut down by the enemy barrage or by machine-gun fire from the village in front of them. He paused, scanning the fields for the telltale whip antenna of a manpack radio that would mark a command group.

There. He spotted one waving above a small group clustered near a wrecked Marder. He and Neumann sprinted across the open ground – ducking whenever enemy shells exploded.

But now German guns were answering the Polish barrage, firing salvos of smoke blossomed wherever the shells exploded, mingling to form a thick, gray-white cloud drifting slowly downwind.

Near the smoldering Marder, a dark-haired man wearing the three light gray pips of a captain on his shoulder straps saw von Seelow and Neumann and waved them on. 'Faster! Faster! Hurry up, you goddamned fools! You want to get killed?'

Willi reached the little group of soldiers and dropped into their midst, breathing heavily. Their eyes widened when they saw his rank and recognized him. He grinned. 'Good afternoon, gentlemen.'

The captain stammered an apology, but von Seelow shook his head. 'There's no need for that. You were quite right. Clearly anybody stuck out here in this field is a goddamned fool.'

A few men chuckled nervously. The rest flinched as another Polish salvo landed only a couple of hundred meters away. German artillery rounds howled overhead in an eerie counterpoint.

Willi watched the smoke screen billowing higher and higher above the peaked roofs of Rynarzewo and nodded in satisfaction. It seemed dense enough now to blind any Polish artillery spotters stationed there. Once he got these men out of the killing zone and closer to the enemy's own positions, the Poles would have a hard time adjusting their fire to hit them again.

He looked at the young officer who had yelled at him. 'What's your outfit, Captain?'

'B Company, Herr Oberstleutnant.'

Willi studied the frightened faces turning his way. Words alone would not be enough to move these men forward into enemy fire. Stunned by heavy casualties and the incessant shelling, they were too near the breaking point. They needed an example – his example.

So be it. Rank should not confer immunity from risk. He climbed to his feet and stood motionless for several moments, ignoring the explosions plowing the earth all around. He wanted them all to see him. Then he raised his voice to carry above the barrage. 'All right, B Company! On your feet! Up! Up! Up!'

Led by their captain, soldiers began scrambling upright. In ones and twos at first. Then in larger numbers as the force of example spread. Officers and NCOs in the battalion's two other companies saw what was going on and started urging their own men up, too.

Von Seelow held up his rifle and pointed toward the Polish village, now all but invisible through the dense, man-made haze. 'We're going forward,' he shouted. 'We're going into that town. And we're going to take that damned bridge. Now follow me!'

Without waiting for a response, he swung into a fast walk and headed for Rynarzewo. Neumann fell in at his side, pacing him. Only Willi could hear the diminutive radioman muttering a simple childhood prayer over and over. He found his own lips forming the same heartfelt words. 'Oh, God, keep me safe. Oh, God, make me strong.' Another, older part of him added, 'And give these men the courage they need to come after me.'

His prayers were answered. With a ragged cheer, the soldiers of the 192nd Panzergrenadier Battalion surged forward, passed him, and plunged into the smoke.

COMMAND POST, RYNARZEWO GARRISON

Half the village was on fire. Columns of thick black smoke from burning buildings blended with the lighter gray mists spawned by the German artillery shells. Wrecked vehicles dotted the streets. Some were surrounded by sprawled corpses. Others seemed undamaged but were abandoned.

From his vantage point at one of the post office building's barricaded windows, Capt. Konrad Polinski caught signs of movement down by the river and stared intently through the drifting haze. There! The wind tore a small hole in the smoke, and he saw German soldiers dashing from one house to the next, firing from the hip. The Germans were inside Rynarzewo! Worse, he and the rest of his troops were cut off from their only way back across the Notec River.

Sick at heart, he turned to his radioman. 'Get that engineer CO now!'

'Major Beck, sir.' The corporal passed him the headset.

'What do you want, Captain?' Beck asked. The commander of the combat engineers sounded understandably worried. If the Germans broke through Polinski's defenses, his men would be dangerously exposed to enemy fire.

'Are your charges laid yet?'

'Almost. We need another five minutes.'

A German machine gun opened up somewhere outside the post office, sending rounds tearing through the windows. Polinski dropped behind a solid oak reading table, seeking cover. He kept his grip on the headset. 'Hell, Major, you may not have five minutes!'

INSIDE RYNARZEWO

Willi von Seelow crouched beside a second-story window in a ruined house on the river. He could see the span perfectly from here. He could also see the Polish engineers busy rigging the bridge for demolition. More and more of them were peeling away, running toward the north end and safety as they finished their work.

He and his troops were too late. Although they were just two hundred meters from their objective, they might as well be on the far side of the moon. The Poles were going to blow the Rynarzewo bridge, and there wasn't a damned thing he could do to stop them.

The radio on Neumann's back caught his eye. He still had one desperate card left to play. 'Contact Striker One,' he ordered.

When the brigade artillery commander's voice came on line, von Seelow took the mike Neumann offered him. 'Striker One, this is Top Cat. I have a priority fire mission.'

'Go ahead, Top Cat. My guns are standing by.'

Willi keyed the mike. 'Target location is the center span of the Rynarzewo highway bridge. Troops moving in the open.'

'Understood, Top Cat. Wait one.'

Von Seelow crouched by the window, watching the Polish combat engineers working with mounting impatience. Come on, come on, he silently urged his distant gunners. We're running out of time.

The radio crackled again. 'Shot, over.'

A single shell, a spotting round, howled overhead and exploded in an open field just across the Notec.

Willi clicked the transmit button and yelled, 'Shot, out. Drop one hundred meters and fire for effect!'

HEADQUARTERS BMP, 421ST MECHANIZED INFANTRY, ACROSS THE NOTEC RIVER

'Oh, my God.' Major Zbigniew Korytzki stared fixedly at the bridge, watching in horror as five German artillery shells fused to burst in midair exploded just above the unprotected engineers.

Thousands of razor-sharp fragments whirred outward from each explosion, striking bridge concrete, the water, and human flesh with murderous impartiality. Men who survived the first salvo were cut down by a second and then a third. When the shelling finally stopped, corpses lay heaped one on top of another across the span. Many of the dead combat engineers were so shredded and torn that they looked more like piles of bloody rags than human beings.

The major felt his hands starting to shake. He didn't want to be here. He didn't want to see this kind of butchery. Acid-tasting bile rose in his throat. His long-held beliefs were being proved right. Being so close to the battlefield only clouded a commander's judgment and made logical decision-making almost impossible.

With an effort he pulled his gaze away. German soldiers were visible along the riverbank now, sprinting from building to building as they drew closer to the bridge approaches. Polish machine guns and assault rifles crackled in the distance. Korytzki shook his head sadly. A few of C Company's isolated squads were still fighting, but they were doomed by the enemy's superior numbers and firepower.

He swept his binoculars through an arc. Movement just beyond the burning village caught his attention. German Leopards were advancing, rolling forward through the lingering smoke. Forward toward the bridge. Forward toward *him*.

Korytzki froze for several precious seconds, unable to think past the possibility of his own death.

When he could move again, he whirled around, leaning far out over the side of his BMP to see where the commander of the slaughtered combat engineers knelt. His eyes focused on the gray metal detonator box beside the man. 'Major Beck!'

When the tall, bespectacled engineer officer looked up, Korytzki could see tears staining his cheeks.

'Blow the bridge!'

Beck stared back at him as though he'd gone mad. 'But what about your men, Major? What about your troops across the river?'

'My men are dead, Major. Just like yours,' Korytzki snarled. He jabbed a finger toward the river. 'Now, blow that fucking bridge!'

Slowly, almost as though he were moving against his own will, the engineer reached out, took hold of the detonator box, and turned the key.

192ND PANZERGRENADIER BATTALION

The Rynarzewo highway bridge disappeared in a rippling series of explosions that raced the length of the span. A dense smoke pall cloaked the scene, lit from within by several more bright white blasts as secondary charges went off.

Von Seelow sagged back from the window in dismay. It was all for nothing, he thought wearily. I've thrown away my soldiers' lives for nothing.

'Herr Oberstleutnant! Look!' Neumann's startled yell snapped his head up.

The bridge was still up. Badly battered, buckled in places, and punctured by several huge holes and deep, jagged craters, yes, but very definitely still standing.

Willi's eyes widened in astonishment. The artillery fire he'd walked in on top of the Polish engineers must also have cut some of their detonator wires, he realized. Not all of them, obviously – just enough to keep the span largely intact.

Tanks and other heavy armored vehicles couldn't make it across – not until his own engineers had time to make hasty repairs – but foot soldiers could use it now. Right now. He grabbed the radio mike. 'All Predator companies, this is Top Cat! Cross the bridge! Repeat, cross the bridge!'

Obeying his orders, small bands of panzergrenadiers broke from cover and stormed onto the span. Ignoring sporadic shooting from Polish die-hards still holding several positions along the river, the German infantrymen raced north toward the opposite bank. A few of them fell dying, shot in the back by rifle and machine-gun fire. The rest pressed on, fanning out across the countryside to seize and hold a bridgehead.

Willi could see several Polish T-72s and a few scattered BMPs pulling out, retreating north along the highway at high speed. They were fleeing from infantry? Why, he wondered?

The sudden roar of powerful diesel engines and the full-throated bark of tank cannon gave him the reason.

Lieutenant Gerhardt had brought his Leopards right down to the water's edge. Now they were busy pummeling the retreating Poles – keeping them on the run while the 192nd's survivors dug in around the bridge.

More vehicles pulled up beside the Leopards, Marders from the 191st. Willi breathed a quick sigh of relief. Now that the leading elements of his brigade's other fighting battalions were beginning to arrive, he should have enough men and firepower on hand to root out the Poles still holed up inside Rynarzewo. Once that was accomplished, he could start funneling more troops across the highway bridge to expand the 19th's foothold on the north bank of the Notec. Tanks and other heavy equipment would have to wait until the engineers repaired the bridge and laid temporary pontoon spans to handle even more traffic.

Still planning his next moves, von Seelow turned away from the window and headed outside to confer with his battalion and company commanders. He felt an odd mixture of elation and sorrow. Against all the odds but at a painfully high human cost, his soldiers had won a stunning victory. The 19th Panzergrenadier Brigade had cracked the Notec River line before the Poles had time to form a cohesive defense.

EurCon's II Corps had its bridgehead on the main road to Gdansk.

3RD BRIGADE HEADQUARTERS, 101ST AIRBORNE DIVISION (AIR ASSAULT), IN THE TOWN HALL, GDANSK

Several dozen American officers wearing battle dress and their web gear sat in rows inside the Gdansk Town Hall's main council chamber – the Red Room. Their warlike, woodland camouflage pattern uniforms were a stark contrast with the chamber's ornate, sixteenth-century decor and its colorful Baroque ceiling and wall paintings. The Poles were letting the U.S. Army use the room for a briefing theater. Easels covered with large-scale maps and charts occupied one side of the chamber, surrounded by the brigade staff.

The assembled line officers were edgy, aware that something big was in the works. They'd been summoned to this emergency brief by the 3rd Brigade's commander, Colonel Gunnar Iverson. Outside the building, Gdansk's city streets were jammed with Polish and American military vehicles heading south. The armed sentries stationed outside the Red Room doors were another sign of impending trouble.

Sitting at the back with the other company commanders, Capt. Mike Reynolds stifled a yawn. He'd had only four hours' sleep in the past twenty-four, and that small amount had come in even smaller pieces. Unfortunately sleep deprivation was becoming a pattern. Their first day in Poland had passed in a jet-lagged confusion of unfamiliar streets and hurried procedures as the brigade first found, then took possession of, its equipment. None of the four days since then had been much more restful. Or less frustrating.

After all the rush to get them to Poland in the first place, it had seemed strange that the 101st and its constituent brigades were still sitting on their collective butts only a few klicks from the Gdansk Airport. To many of the airborne troopers, the delay seemed just another typical army snafu, a standard case of 'hurry up and wait.' But Reynolds was pretty sure there had been a lot more to it than that.

The scuttlebutt at brigade HQ was that the 101st and parts of the 82nd Airborne were being held as a 'strategic reserve' – as an American trip-wire force to deter the Russians from jumping in on the EurCon side. The rumors had gained powerful credibility when all of the division's operations and intelligence officers were summoned to a special briefing on last-ditch defensive positions around Warsaw – defensive positions facing east. Just the possibility of Russian intervention sent chills down the captain's spine. Getting caught in a land war against the French, the Germans, and the Russians seemed like a surefire prescription for a short fight and a long stretch as a POW – or an eternity as a dead man.

Reynolds shifted uneasily in his chair. Whatever the reason, the five-day delay had not been wasted. Although they'd been ready to go into combat within hours of touching down from the States, the extra time had given the division a much-needed chance to sort itself out. During the emergency deployment to Poland, their weapons and vehicles had been packed 'administratively,' meaning tightly, to make the most efficient use of the valuable space aboard the USAF's cargo planes. Once in Gdansk, the 101st's forward staging base, everything had to be assembled and checked out, before being readied for helicopter deployment to the front. With that done, the division's brigade and battalion commanders had run their units through an intensive series of combat drills and physical training, honing the 101's already sharp edge even sharper.

Well, it looked like their mini-Phony War was finally coming to an end.

'Attention!'

Boots slammed onto the floor as the brisk command brought Reynolds and the others to their feet. Accompanied by a single aide, Colonel Iverson marched to the front of the room and stood facing them.

'Take your seats, gentlemen.' Iverson waved them down impatiently. 'I'll keep it short and sweet. This is no drill. We're going into the line against EurCon.' He ignored the stir that caused and turned to his S-2, the brigade intelligence officer. 'Start your dog-and-pony show, John. I want this outfit on the move before dark.'

Reynolds nodded to himself. There'd be no fancy speeches from this officer. Iverson had a reputation for being quick, to the point of brusqueness. If you weren't ready to say something useful when you went in to see him, you didn't bother going.

The S-2 moved to center stage. His presentation was what everyone had been waiting for. It touched on the real reason for their being there: the enemy's latest moves.

He pointed to the largest easel-mounted map as he talked. Eurcon's first two pincer attacks against the Polish Army had failed. Now the French and Germans had turned north and were driving on Gdansk. And the most recent reports from the battle front said EurCon troops were across the Notec River. Their armored spearheads were already closing in on Bydgoszcz, an important road and rail junction just 150 kilometers south of Gdansk's vital port facilities.

That might seem like a lot, but every American soldier on Polish soil had heard stories about just how quickly the EurCon Army, especially its German components, could move. The rear-area types, always nervous about their own skins, were convinced that French and German tanks might show up at the Renaissance High Gate any second, blasting their way into the city.

Reynolds and his men held a combat soldier's contempt for anyone stationed safely outside artillery range, but the tales hit a nerve anyway. Light soldiers do not think of themselves as mobile, in spite of their helicopters. Tough, yes, but they still walked on the battlefield. In a mobile battle they could be quickly cut off and destroyed in detail, and this was a fast-moving war.

Now they would find that out at first hand. Worn down by three weeks of gallant resistance against superior numbers, the Polish Army was starting to crack. Positions that should have been held for days were falling in hours. And Russian threat or no Russian threat, the Combined Forces couldn't let EurCon capture Gdansk.

'*Attention!*' Iverson's call startled the intelligence officer, intent on his task. Reynolds and the others leapt to their feet a second time as Maj. Gen. Robert J. 'Butch' Thompson strode into the chamber. Thompson was the Big Dog from Hell, the top soldier in the whole 101st Air Assault.

At a distance, the division commander looked like a man of average height. But nobody held on to that impression once they'd seen him up close or in close company with other men. He actually stood half a head taller than Mike's own six feet. The general wore his gray-streaked blond hair cut very close over a powerful, square-jawed face and ice-cold blue eyes. Thompson had led the 101st for over a year, and during that time he'd imparted his characteristic drive to the entire division.

The general took position in front of the S-2's maps and charts. 'First, I want to compliment this brigade on the job you've done getting over here and getting ready to fight.'

He glanced at the maps behind him, but returned his gaze to the assembled officers almost immediately. 'I know everyone here wants to get in and mix it up with the bad guys. Some of you have fought before, but for many this is going to be your first time in combat. You may be worried about how you'll do. That's natural. All I ask is that you remember your training and that you remember your men. You have the best of both – the best in the world.

'Now, we're not out to defeat EurCon all by ourselves. People have been calling us a fire brigade. That's not quite right. We're not here to put out the fire, just to keep it from spreading.

'My intention is to delay the enemy, slowing him by any means possible, while conserving our own strength. We all want to die in bed, but more important, this division will be the only significant help the Poles can expect for some time to come. So our mission is to wear EurCon down until our own heavy units can arrive in strength.'

Thompson paused, letting that sink in. 'That won't be easy. Make no mistake, we're in for a hard fight, but I've got the hard fighters to do it. And by the time we're through with 'em, these EurCon bastards are gonna be mighty sorry they ever tangled with the Screaming Eagles.' He nodded to them. 'That's all, gentlemen. Good luck and may God bless you all. Air Assault!'

After the division commander left, the rest of the 3rd Brigade's staff officers finished filling them in on the hundreds of details they needed to move and fight in a foreign land. For Mike Reynolds, their rapid-fire dissertations on movement routes and maintenance, fueling, and rearming points passed in something of a blur – subordinated to a single, overwhelming reality. This briefing was in deadly earnest. All of his years at West Point and in the army since, all the years of learning, training, and preparing, were coming to fruition. He was going to lead his troops into battle.

When the staff finished, Colonel Iverson stepped forward for his own laconic version of the pep talk. 'Send 'em to hell. Dismissed.'

CHAPTER 29
Inside Straight

JUNE 27 – THE WHITE HOUSE, WASHINGTON, D.C.

Ross Huntington paced moodily back and forth, practically wearing a furrow in the carpet while paging through the latest batch of top-secret NSA signals intercepts delivered by special courier. When he'd first suggested to the President the idea of looking for weak points in the EurCon coalition, he'd been confident the research might actually lead somewhere. Now the job just seemed more like meaningless make-work than ever.

Physically he looked and felt better than he had in months. Nearly two weeks under the no-nonsense care provided by the President's personal doctor had worked wonders. His chest pains, shortness of breath, and other danger signs had all faded or vanished entirely. After constant monitoring even his heart rate seemed relatively steady. But with every passing day, he grew more restless. Oh, the White House guest quarters he'd been assigned were comfortable, even luxurious, but he was tired of comfort and bored with bed rest. Although Dr. Pardolesi and the other medicos kept warning him that much of the improvement he sensed was illusory or fragile, Huntington felt fine – perfectly ready to go back to work.

After all, while he idled the hours away as a semi-invalid, events were passing him by. Twelve days were an eternity in a world on the edge of global war, and he desperately wanted to get back in synch before it was too late.

At least he wasn't completely out of the loop. The President looked in on him from time to time for a quick chat and a rundown on major developments. And he still had access to the NSC's classified daily intelligence summaries.

Huntington sighed. Taken together, those intelligence reports painted a grim picture of the military and political situation facing the United States and its allies. Despite recent victories in the air and at sea, they were still behind the power curve in eastern Europe. In the north, EurCon's armies were deep inside Poland – advancing against defenders who were rapidly running out of men, machines, and endurance. Several British and American 'heavy' divisions were on their way, but even the closest convoys were still days away from Gdansk. To the south, half of

Hungary lay under French and German occupation. In the center, the Czechs and Slovaks were hanging on by their fingernails – too hard-pressed themselves to send much aid elsewhere.

Even if Poland and the other countries could hold out long enough for aid to arrive, the Combined Forces faced the likely prospect of a prolonged and bloody ground campaign to roll EurCon back to its prewar borders. Tens of thousands were already dead on both sides, Huntington knew. How many more would have to die before the madmen in Paris and Berlin came to their senses?

Against that backdrop, yesterday's Flash message from the CIA's Moscow Station took on an even bleaker aspect. News of the secret Franco-Russian military talks had hit the President and his closest advisors like a sledgehammer right between the eyes. With good reason, too. Russian intervention would irretrievably tip the scales against the Combined Forces in eastern and central Europe. Even in her weakened state, Russia could throw nearly half a million soldiers into the field. Her navy was still the second most powerful in the world, and her slimmed-down air force included large numbers of sophisticated, highly capable fighters and fighter-bombers. More ominously, Russia retained a sizable stockpile of tactical and strategic nuclear weapons. If she joined the fighting, the world would again face the specter of uncontrolled escalation to thermonuclear war.

Ever since the first closely guarded reports sent shock waves through official circles, both the NSC and the British War Cabinet had been meeting in almost continuous session, searching frantically for some way to break up the secret talks and keep Russia on the sidelines. So far, they'd had scant success. If the CIA's initial reports were accurate, the French were offering Kaminov and his fellow marshals military, economic, and political concessions that Washington and London could not possibly hope to match. Not without reawakening a monster that had prowled round the free world's doors for nearly five decades, forever trying to claw and pry its way inside. Containing the old Soviet state's imperial ambitions had cost the West many lives and trillions of dollars. Nobody in power now wanted to risk repeating the experience at the dawn of the twenty-first century.

Huntington's watch beeped, reminding him it was time to take the next dose of the medication Pardolesi had prescribed. He stopped pacing long enough to down one of the orange-colored pills from the bottle he carried in his pants pocket. Even a short acquaintance with the President's doctor had soon convinced him that strict compliance with any reasonable orders would be his quickest ticket out of this gilded cage.

He thrust the medicine bottle back into his pocket and made an effort to concentrate on the job at hand. In dealing with the Russians, the President could count on advice from hundreds of better-qualified experts. His job right now was to keep searching for ways to unravel the European Confederation from the inside.

He skimmed through the collection of signals intercepts in growing frustration.

After two weeks spent scanning hundreds of bits and pieces of intelligence, his whole grand notion seemed more like a dead end than a road to victory. It wasn't that the smaller member states were happy with their de facto masters – far from it. The airwaves and land lines back and forth between Paris and their national capitals were full of complaints of French arrogance. But bellyaching, bitching, and moaning were a far cry from action, and Huntington hadn't yet been able to find a single opening worth exploiting. Few of the European governments had many illusions left about their position inside the Confederation, but none wanted to risk French or German wrath by openly breaking their signed agreements – especially when this war's outcome still hung in the balance. Most seemed hopeful they could just hunker down, stay uninvolved in any combat, and let the whole unpleasant business pass them by. With their hands full in eastern Europe, EurCon's ruling circles had seemed perfectly willing to accept that attitude.

Until now.

Huntington froze, staring down at the document he'd just read. If the National Security Agency's analysts were right, he was looking at the transcript of a conversation between Belgium's Prime Minister and Minister of Defense.

Every day, the dozens of NSA-managed satellites and listening posts scattered around the world routinely intercepted huge volumes of radio, radiotelephone, telephone, telex, and fax transmissions. Ironically, evaluating this enormous flow of information was far more difficult than collecting it in the first place. Messages or conversations in the clear were stored and sorted by supercomputers programmed to hunt for hundreds of key words or phrases. Transmissions that were scrambled or coded in some fashion were automatically bucked up to special teams equipped with their own code-breaking computers. Nevertheless, although automation helped eliminate much of the preliminary 'grunt work,' the thousands of human intelligence experts behind the machines were always swamped. Their work was often tedious, but sometimes they struck gold.

Huntington read the transcript again, this time more carefully, testing his first impressions. His eyebrows rose as his imagination added inflections and hidden meanings to the plain, black-and-white typescript in front of him. His every instinct sensed an opportunity here.

COMINT INTERCEPT – NSOC EURCON WORKING GROUP

Intercept Station: USAF Electronic Security Command Detachment, RAF Chicksands, England
Time: 121627 Jun
Transmission Method: Microwave relay, scrambled

Belgian Minister of Defense (MOD): I am afraid I have very bad news, Mr. Prime Minister. Desaix has completely refused to

consider our concerns about the use of our troops. He . . .
Belgian Prime Minister (PM): What? He dismissed our request? Out of hand?
MOD: Yes, sir. Not only that, but he reiterated the Defense Secretariat's warning order. We have just seventy-two hours to begin moving both the 1st and 4th mechanized brigades.
PM: But not into combat, I hope?
MOD: No, Prime Minister. At least not directly. I've been assured that our soldiers will only be used to man key logistics centers – one at Metz and the other in Germany, just outside Munich. They won't be on the front lines.
PM: But these supply depots are still targets for American bombs, true?
(Note: Pause timed at 6.5 seconds.)
MOD: Yes, Prime Minister. That is true.
PM: Very well, Madeleine. When do you return?
MOD: Immediately, sir. General Leman and I see no point in staying here any longer.
(Note: Leman identified as Gen. Alexandre Leman, chief of staff of the Belgian armed forces.)
PM: I understand. In that case, I shall convene an emergency cabinet meeting as soon as you arrive.
MOD: Of course, Prime Minister. Though I fear we have no choice but to comply with this directive.
PM: Yes . . . you are undoubtedly correct. Still, I would prefer to go over *all* our options. I wish you a safe journey, Madeleine.
MOD: Thank you, Gerard.
LINE DISCONNECT

Identification Confidence Factor: High. Voice patterns for both participants match patterns already on file.

Huntington nodded to himself, convinced he was right. As the head of his own firm, he'd visited Belgium many times back when Brussels was the administrative center of the old EC. He knew many of the tiny country's leading industrialists, financiers, and politicians personally. With a little pressure in the right places, this new display of French arrogance could be turned into one of the EurCon fault lines he'd been seeking. But could the United States and its allies move quickly enough to capitalize on it?

He laid the rest of the SIGINT data aside and picked up the phone. 'This is Ross Huntington, I need to speak to the President . . . Yes, right away.'

THE OVAL OFFICE

An hour later, Ross Huntington sat in a chair facing the President's imposing desk. Both Gen. Reid Galloway and Walter Quinn flanked him, one on either side. After hearing his close friend and advisor's plan through once by himself, the President had asked the chairman of the Joint Chiefs and the CIA director to sit in while Huntington walked them through his supporting evidence, his deductions based on that evidence, and the high-stakes gamble he proposed. Harris Thurman hadn't been invited, and the ultracautious, fence-sitting Secretary of State was conspicuous by his absence.

'Well, gentlemen?' the President asked after Huntington had finished laying out his case. 'What do you think?'

Galloway stirred, looking up from his big, capable hands. 'From a military point of view, what Ross suggests is perfectly feasible. It'll play merry hell with our bombing schedule for a couple of days, but we've definitely got the aircraft and weapons in-theater to do the job and to do it damn thoroughly.' His voice trailed off.

'But?' the President pressed him.

'Frankly, sir, it's what comes next that worries me.' The general nodded toward Huntington. 'Sending any civilian, especially someone as high up as Ross, so deep into enemy territory strikes me as taking one hell of a big chance. I'm not sure the game's worth the candle.'

Huntington spoke up. 'Technically we're not at war with Belgium, General.' He held up a hand to forestall any protest. 'Oh, I know the Belgians are part of EurCon, but we've never recognized EurCon – not as a legitimate government. And we've never received a declaration of war from Brussels. So, legally, I can travel wherever I want – with a valid passport and visa.'

Galloway snorted. 'Yeah. But we already know the French don't give a damn about legality. If they get wind of what you're up to, you can bet the DGSE will close in hard and fast, visa or no visa.'

Huntington nodded. 'That's why this whole affair has to be handled carefully and by me personally. Our embassy staff over there can't do it. They're probably tagged by French or German intelligence wherever they go. But I know the right people to contact – people I can trust to keep quiet.'

Galloway looked unconvinced. But then he shrugged. Debating imponderables wasn't the general's style. He preferred dealing in facts.

The President glanced at Quinn. 'What about you, Walt? Any thoughts on this?'

'Yes, sir. I say it's worth trying, risks and all.' The rotund CIA director surprised them all with his certainty. He explained. 'So far we've been playing catch-up to the French and Germans, Mr. President. They shut off Poland's oil and gas. We ship new supplies. They blow up a tanker. We provide naval escorts. They attack. We defend.'

Quinn leaned forward. 'I think it's high time we made the enemy dance to our tune. What Ross has in mind might just do the trick. If not, we haven't lost much – just a little time and maybe some diplomatic face.'

The President nodded slowly and rocked back in his own big, leather chair, thinking over what he'd been told. When he looked up, his gaze fastened on his old friend's face. 'How about it, Ross? You're sure you're up to this?'

'I feel fine, Mr. President,' Huntington said with as much conviction as he could muster. He was determined not to let ill-health or fear sideline him again. Though he didn't harbor any illusions about being irreplaceable, he was pretty sure that none of the State Department's bright-eyed boys had the inside knowledge and official anonymity that would be needed to pull this thing off successfully.

The faint trace of a smile flashed across the President's weary face. 'Could you get a doctor's note to prove that, Ross?'

Huntington shrugged noncommittally. 'Given enough time, I could. But do you really want me to go doc-hunting? Now?'

The President laughed softly. 'No, I guess not.' His smile faded, replaced by the firm-jawed, determined look that signaled his mind was made up. 'Okay, gentlemen, I'm sold.'

He turned to Galloway. 'Issue the necessary orders, General. I want the military side of this operation in gear within thirty-six hours.'

'Yes, sir.'

The President swiveled his chair to one side and punched the intercom button on his black phone. 'Marla? I need you to make some arrangements for me. Ready? First, rustle up an air force flight for Mr. Huntington. Where? To London. After you've done that, get on the horn to Number 10 Downing Street. Fix up a time this afternoon our time for a secure-channel videoconference with the Prime Minister.' He looked at Huntington over the phone. 'Better get packed, Ross. You'll be on your way just as soon as I hang up.'

Huntington grinned. 'Yes, Mr. President.' He stood up, amazed by the sudden surge of energy coursing through his body. In some strange way, the prospect of another important mission made him feel ten years younger. After months of watching Paris and Berlin wreak havoc on America's friends and allies, he was going to get the chance to wreak a little havoc of his own.

JUNE 29 – EURCON LOGISTICS CENTER, METZ, FRANCE

Metz lies almost two hundred miles east of Paris, close to the border with Germany and Luxembourg. Nestled in the Moselle River valley, the town stands on the northern edge of Lorraine – a countryside of rustic farmland and rusting heavy industry, a land marked by more than a thousand years of war. Down through the centuries, knights in surcoats and chain mail, the Sun King's proud musketeers, Napoleon's grumbling foot soldiers and dashing cavalrymen, the Kaiser's spike-helmeted infantry, Hitler's grim, merciless panzers, and the GIs of George Patton's Third Army had fought and bled from one end of the province to the other. Metz had seen its share of those battles.

Now a web of military installations, headquarters, and supply depots sprawled in an untidy arc around the town's western suburbs. Among others, Metz was the permanent headquarters site for the First French Army and France's northeast military defense region.

Although most of EurCon's combat troops were fighting in Poland, Hungary, or the Czech Republic, Metz was still swarming with military activity. Its storehouses and repair facilities bustled as French soldiers and civilian contractors labored overtime – shipping the munitions, spare parts, and other supplies needed by their comrades in the field.

Their jobs had little to do with direct combat, but they knew how important their work was. Without supplies and maintenance, any but the most primitive army would grind to a halt in days. So the men who manned the Metz logistics centers thanked their lucky stars that they had an important job to do – especially one that did not routinely involve getting shot at.

Of course, there were air raids. Since the air war over France escalated, Metz had been hit twice by American bombers. But the damage and casualties inflicted by both raids had been relatively light – certainly nothing compared to the carnage at the front. No, most of the French soldiers were happy with their assignment, even if it meant toiling in round-the-clock shifts. Few of them were glad to hear they were about to be freed for combat duty by units of the Belgian Army. Camp rumors said the Belgians would arrive within the next twenty-four hours, and for once the camp rumors were right.

But America's airmen got there first.

It was just before dawn when air raid sirens sounded across the city. Even as crews ran to man their missile and gun batteries, explosions split the darkness, silhouetting weapons and men. A few defenders caught angular outlines against the sky, and recognized F-117 stealth fighters.

Almost before the sirens finished wailing, the black jets were gone. Only the air defenses had been attacked, but they had been thoroughly and systematically pulverized. The Americans had used laser-guided bombs and cluster weapons to smash each battery's weapons, early warning radars, control bunkers, and ammunition storage sites.

American bombs had also flattened the fire department, leaving nothing but piles of broken concrete and shredded metal. Understanding the implications, the French general commanding the base tried desperately to rebuild his shattered defenses. He wasn't given enough time.

Moments after the F-117s disappeared, forty B-1B Lancers roared overhead, hugging the earth. With the air defenses destroyed, there could be no warning. Anyone caught out in the open could only throw himself flat and hope to be spared.

The huge, swept-wing bombers laid patterns of death across the military compounds outside Metz. Each plane carried fifty-six 500-pound bombs, and from two hundred feet, they might as well have been placed by hand. Deadly accurate, devastating in their numbers, the Lancers disappeared as suddenly as they came. Behind them, warehouses, freight yards, and repair facilities lay in ruins.

Even as the smoke still boiled out of the bombs' explosions, the stunned French troops turned in horror to see more bombers flying toward them. These were not the sculpted shapes of B-1s, but thin-winged, slab-sided B-52s. More explosions rippled across the military compounds – leveling almost any building larger than a guardhouse. Even the water and sewage treatment plants were a shambles.

Those few surviving SAM and antiaircraft batteries that did try to attack the bombers were quickly smothered by Wild Weasels and other escorting planes. Two squadrons of F-15s kept close watch on the operation, while further out, U.S. Navy Tomcats made free-ranging sweeps – hunting down the few EurCon interceptors that tried to interfere.

When the B-52s turned for home, the sun was still not completely over the horizon. Battered survivors pulled themselves from the wreckage. Some turned back to help those who were still trapped. Others, driven mad by the noise and confusion, wandered at random through a sea of smoke and fire.

About an hour later, with most of the explosion-churned dust blown away and some of the fires burned out, the sirens wailed again. Too exhausted to run, the survivors were spared an attack this time. Instead, a lone American reconnaissance aircraft, heavily escorted, swept overhead, photographing the devastated logistics complex. Those on the ground breathed a small sigh of relief, even as they cursed the enemy plane. This poststrike reconnaissance flight should be the final note in a deadly song.

Four squadrons of U.S. Navy attack aircraft, escorted by another four fighter squadrons, hit Metz again just around noon. Soldiers, already battered and stressed by a morning of terror, collapsed or cried or fled. Their comrades dragged them to shelters if they had the strength.

With measured aggression, the Navy Intruders and Hornets carefully blasted every remaining structure with a shred of value. Only the hospital and civilian housing tracts were again spared. By the time the strike was over, half an hour later, they stood alone in a Hiroshima landscape.

The skies were barely clear when another formation appeared. The exhausted defenders could only cower, as straight and level, and completely unmolested, U.S. Air Force F-15E Strike Eagles streaked overhead and released their own payloads. As if sowing a freshly plowed field, they scattered mines and delayed-action bomblets everywhere. The lethal devices would drastically slow down any attempt to rebuild, or even clear the wreckage.

USS *GEORGE WASHINGTON*, IN THE NORTH SEA

Adm. Jack Ward stood above the flight deck in an open gallery on *George Washington*'s island, watching the last of the second wave land. Standing at the railing, enduring noise so loud he could feel it in his teeth, it was satisfying to see a jet slam into the deck on landing. Each one was a little piece of good news, a happy ending for some pilot's mission. He'd counted the planes as they landed, and felt some of his anxiety lift with each successful recovery.

They'd been lucky. His strike force had only lost two planes, both to ground fire. A Hornet pilot had been hit while suppressing an antiaircraft gun, and, according to his wingman, had simply continued his dive and smashed into the ground. French gunners had also nicked an A-6 Intruder, but her two crewmen had nursed the stricken attack jet back out over the North Sea before ejecting. And both men were already on their way home to the carrier after being scooped up by a waiting search-and-rescue helicopter.

Just as the last plane, an S-3 Viking serving as an in-flight tanker, caught the wire, Ward felt the wind shift. *Washington* and *Roosevelt* were turning north, bending on as much speed as their massive engines could produce.

Metz lay well inland, almost two hundred miles south of the coast, almost at the limit of a carrier plane's effective range. To give his pilots more time over the target, Ward had ordered the carriers to move in, close to the coast. The fast nighttime run, followed by a dawn launch, had cost him a sleepless night, but it was worth the risk. Several of his pilots had made it back low on fuel. If he hadn't ordered his ships in, his aircraft losses might have been far higher.

Ward gripped the railing tighter. But why had he been forced to run the risk at all? So far inland, Metz was in air force territory, and Ward would have been perfectly happy to let them have it. Land-based B-1s or B-2s could reach it easily. In fact, a strike by just the heavy bombers would have disrupted the base for a week.

So why had Washington specifically ordered him to use the combined strengths of two aircraft carriers against Metz, as part of the most destructive raid he had ever seen? From a strictly military point of view, the orders didn't make much sense.

Metz was an important French Army base, and obliterating it certainly hurt the EurCon cause. The forces that had been concentrated on it, though, could have smashed a dozen targets. Normally planes operating off his carriers in the North Sea hit three, four, or even five targets each, every single day, systematically working their way down a carefully planned list. Organizing this grand air extravaganza had thrown a day-long monkey wrench into his bombing campaign.

What was happening along the rest of the North Sea and Baltic coasts while they pounded this one army base? True, they'd already neutralized the entire network of EurCon bases and ports, but without constant pressure, EurCon's naval and air forces would start to recover.

Ward shook his head impatiently. EurCon was getting a twenty-four-hour respite, thanks to direct orders from Washington. He just hoped that the annihilation of Metz was worth that price.

OVER THE NORTH SEA

Backlit by the late afternoon sun, two Puma helicopters in civilian markings clattered low over the rolling, gray-green waters of the North Sea. Only one of the two helicopters carried passengers. The second was a backup transport equipped with a diver and rescue hoist in case the first had to ditch.

Inside the lead helicopter, Ross Huntington finished studying the poststrike recon photos he'd been handed just before takeoff and slid them back into his briefcase. He glanced up and saw a look of horrified fascination on the face of one of the two Secret Service agents assigned to escort him on this mission.

'Christ' – the agent leaned closer, shouting over the Puma's engine noise – 'I've heard of bombing places back to the Stone Age . . . I didn't know you could go back any further!'

Huntington nodded somberly. He'd never before been directly responsible for instigating so much death and destruction, and he didn't like the feeling. His whole life had been spent building things up, not tearing them down.

A new voice crackled over his earphones. 'Puma Lead, this is Guardian. Four bogies bearing zero nine five, forty miles and closing.'

The helicopter's pilot, a uniformed Royal Army Air Corps warrant officer, acknowledged the orbiting E-3 Sentry's transmission, then glanced over his shoulder at Huntington. 'Here we go, sir. If the Belgians are playing it straight, that's our escort through the no-fire corridor for their SAMs. If not . . .' He shrugged. 'It's a long swim back to England.'

Three minutes later, four F-16 Falcons in Belgian Air Force markings streaked toward them from over the horizon, flashed overhead, and circled back – visibly slowing as they slid in beside the helicopters to make a visual identification.

Huntington stared out the side window at the nearest fighter, noting the pilot's head turned toward him, faceless behind a visored helmet. The Puma's copilot flashed the helicopter's navigation lights on and off in Morse code. This close to French airspace, nobody wanted to make any radio transmissions that weren't strictly necessary.

Apparently satisfied, the F-16s accelerated back to their normal cruising speed and took station above and behind them, weaving back and forth to keep pace with the slower British helicopters. They flew east toward the distant Belgian coast, gray and featureless beneath a growing cloud bank.

DE HAAN, BELGIUM

The Pumas crossed the coast at high speed, skimmed low over a wide, firm, sandy beach, and climbed to clear the rows of brightly painted villas that made De Haan a favorite holiday resort during peacetime. For a minute, they flew inland, still escorted by the F-16s – flying above a flat, open countryside crisscrossed by narrow, tree-lined canals. A gray stone chateau loomed ahead, surrounded by a vast expanse of open, green lawns.

Huntington craned his neck, trying to get a better view of their destination. He and his family had once spent a very pleasant two weeks at that chateau as the guests of a Belgian industrialist. Isolated and easily guarded, the estate should make a perfect covert meeting place.

Flying slower now, the British helicopters lost altitude again, flared out, and touched down next to the main building. Soldiers wearing the camouflage battle dress and maroon berets of Belgium's elite Para-Commando Regiment surrounded both Pumas, wary but not openly hostile.

Huntington took a deep breath to calm himself, slid the helicopter's side door open, and stepped down onto Belgian soil. A small band of civilians stood waiting for him. With a small flutter of relief, he recognized an old friend, Emile Demblon, an official in the Belgian Ministry of Trade, among them.

Demblon hurried forward. 'Ross! I am glad to see you safe and well!'

'Thanks, Emile.' Huntington shook the smaller man's outstretched hand. 'We're set?'

Demblon nodded. 'Yes. Everything is in readiness.'

Heart pounding, Huntington followed his friend across the lawn and into the chateau. The U.S. Secret Service agents, Belgian soldiers, and other civilians trailed them at a discreet distance.

Demblon came to a sturdy oak door and opened it with a flourish, revealing a small, elegantly appointed study. 'In here, my friend.'

With a sudden surge of excitement, Huntington recognized the trim, dapper man waiting inside. Belgium's Prime Minister had come to the rendezvous himself. The first cracks in EurCon were starting to widen.

CHAPTER 30
Alarms

JUNE 29 – FRANCO-RUSSIAN CONFERENCE DACHA, OUTSIDE MOSCOW

The sprawling, timbered dacha serving as the conference site lay deep in the heart of a pine forest fifteen kilometers outside the city. Once reserved for top-level Communist Party officials, it now belonged to Marshal Yuri Kaminov. To ensure privacy, the estate could only be reached by an unmarked access road leading off the Moscow-Yalta highway. All vehicles heading for the dacha were stopped and searched at a military checkpoint several hundred meters down the twisting, narrow road. Army and FIS troops patrolled the rest of the wooded enclave.

Inside the dacha's main hall, two sets of high-ranking soldiers and civilians sat facing each other across a large rectangular table. Each man had a blotter, notepad, and a pitcher of ice water set out in front of him. Translators were seated behind the negotiators, providing a whispered, running commentary on what was being said.

Maj. Paul Duroc stood against a wall with the other junior members of the French negotiating team. After several hours on his feet listening to the same trivial issues being debated by the same droning voices, he was bored out of his skull, tired, and increasingly irritated. He shifted awkwardly, feeling the sweat trickling down his back beneath his jacket. Even with the drapes closed against the summer afternoon sun, the room was uncomfortably warm.

How much longer today would these idiots babble on? he wondered. This negotiating session had already run well over its allotted time without any apparent progress. Both Desaix's handpicked representative, Ambassador Sauret, and Kaminov seemed perfectly willing to talk each other to death before coming to any agreement.

Duroc grimaced. He could understand that in the Russian. Kaminov, for all his rank and power, was still a peasant at heart. You could find his kind in any rural French village – the surly, suspicious old man who couldn't buy a horse without counting its teeth and poking and prodding the poor beast to distraction, complaining all the while about the seller's obvious villainy. But Sauret was supposed to be an educated gentleman, the product of Europe's most sophisticated society. His participation in this haggling seemed both ignoble and foolish.

If France truly needed Russia's assistance to win this war, then why not promise Kaminov and his followers anything they wanted? To Duroc, promises, especially those made by diplomats, were made to be broken – or at the very least carefully ignored. Besides, what difference did a few billion francs really make? If the Confederation won, the extra money could always be squeezed out of its smaller members or the defeated Poles, Czechs, and Hungarians. If the Confederation lost, Russia wouldn't be in any position to press its financial demands anyway.

Weary of watching the negotiators fumble with their papers or sip their water, the major found his gaze wandering over the Russian soldiers and civilians lining the opposite wall – his counterparts in boredom. Most wore the same practiced look of long-suffering patience and forced interest, an expression common to subordinates of all kinds in boardrooms, government ministries, and military posts around the world. But there was one exception. One officer, a tall, handsome, fair-haired colonel, seemed uneasy. While Duroc discreetly inspected him, the Russian glanced down at his watch and looked up in evident dismay. He did it again just thirty seconds later. And again a few seconds after that. Interesting.

Duroc mentally sorted through the intelligence files he'd studied before coming to Moscow, trying to put a name to the aristocratic face in front of him. If nothing else, the effort was a useful exercise – a way to stave off the meeting's tedium for a few moments. Memory and vision merged successfully in short order. The Russian was one Col. Valentin Alexievich Soloviev, one of Marshal Kaminov's top military aides.

Key sections of the file on Soloviev came bubbling to the surface along with his name. A decorated veteran of the Afghan War with a reputation for daring and tactical skill. In politics, a hard-liner, firmly wedded to Kaminov's policies and person. The colonel was also reported to be one of the prime movers behind the Russian Army's ongoing purge of officers with democratic connections or suspect 'ethnic' ties. Overall, the analysis prepared by the DGSE's Moscow Section presented the picture of a cool, calm, resourceful officer.

The Frenchman pursed his lips, increasingly interested in what he was seeing. If the reports he'd read were accurate, the nervous tension so readily apparent in this Colonel Soloviev was almost wholly out of character. And in his experience, men did not break long-established patterns of thought and action without good reason. So why was this ice-cold Russian soldier so jumpy?

During a brief pause while the French translators struggled to catch up with one of Kaminov's long-winded pronouncements, Soloviev leaned forward to whisper something in the marshal's ear. Without really listening, the older, stockier man nodded impatiently, flicking his hand toward the exit.

Clearly relieved, the colonel straightened up and headed for the conference room door. Several of his fellows looked surprised to see him leaving.

Intensely curious now, Duroc made his own muttered excuses and left the room close on Soloviev's heels. The Russian colonel was moving faster, hastening down the hall toward the dacha's main entrance. That erased the last, faint trace of doubt from the French security agent's mind. The other man wasn't simply seeking a washroom. He was leaving the compound – unexpectedly and in a tearing hurry.

Why? What did Soloviev consider more important than these negotiations? And important enough to risk angering his notoriously short-tempered superior? Duroc frowned. Whatever was going on, he wanted to know more about it. He'd had enough surprises in Hungary and they'd almost wrecked his career.

He stepped out onto the mansion's enclosed front porch in time to see the Russian sliding behind the steering wheel of a staff car, a black Volga. Plainly, wherever the man was headed, he was headed alone.

Not so fast, Colonel, Duroc thought coldly. He clattered down the front steps and strode toward a group of men standing idle around their own vehicles, smoking cigarettes and chatting softly while waiting for their masters to emerge.

Against Duroc's advice, the French special ambassador and his staff always traveled out to the conference site from the embassy in several armored limousines flanked by chase cars manned by members of his security team. Although the practice had seemed unnecessarily showy and indiscreet to the DGSE officer, at least it gave him manpower on the scene now.

'Foret! Verdier!' He motioned the two closest agents over. Both were experienced, veterans of several covert operations.

Obviously surprised to see him, they hurriedly stubbed out their cigarettes. 'Yes, Major?'

Duroc nodded toward the black Volga slowly backing out of its parking place. 'I want you to follow the Russian officer in that car. Carefully, so that he doesn't know you're there. I don't want him spooked. Find out where he goes, and who, if anybody, he meets. You have a camera?'

Foret, a tiny, rat-faced man, nodded. 'Yes, sir.'

'Good. Then get pictures if you can.'

Verdier, bigger and better-looking than Foret, jerked his head toward the woods and the access road. 'What do we tell the soldiers at that checkpoint when they ask us why we're leaving early?'

Duroc shrugged. 'Tell them the ambassador wants to make sure his steward has the right wines ready for dinner tonight. You shouldn't have any trouble making them believe that.'

Both men smiled and nodded. Ambassador Sauret's devotion to his stomach and his fussiness were already a source of secret amusement for his underlings and their Russian counterparts.

'Any more questions?' Duroc asked. 'No? Then get going.' Soloviev's car was already halfway down the drive to the woods.

While Foret and Verdier hustled to obey, he turned back to the dacha, pondering his next move. If nothing else, tailing this fellow Soloviev would help keep his own men on their toes. But he felt sure his orders would achieve far more than that.

To the major, the intelligence game was only a variation on the age-old hunt – a quest for facts in the midst of uncertainty, instead of food in the midst of the wilderness. He knew that no man's conscious mind could possibly pick up more than a fraction of the sensory and other cues flooding in from all sides. The rest had to be processed by the subconscious – emerging as sudden flashes of insight and inspiration. Although his decision to put the Russian colonel under surveillance had been largely instinctive, Paul Duroc had long ago learned to trust his instincts.

ARBAT STREET, MOSCOW

During the early part of the twentieth century, Arbat Street was one of Moscow's most fashionable shopping districts. Under communist rule, it had fallen on hard times as a symbol of 'capitalist exploitation.' Now, as the twentieth century came to a close, the area had come full circle. Private renovations, foreign investment, and government preservation orders had spruced the Arbat up, creating a cobblestone-paved pedestrian district crowded with gift shops, art galleries, and theaters.

Even under the harsh austerity program imposed by Kaminov's martial law government, the Arbat still had life and color. As the capital city's ministries and businesses closed for the day, shoppers and theatergoers swarmed into the area seeking bargains and entertainment. Many were in uniform – officers on headquarters duty in the vast concrete bulk of Russia's Ministry of Defense right down the street.

Erin McKenna moved with the throngs, pretending to window-shop while she kept her eyes peeled for Col. Valentin Soloviev. She was growing edgy, conscious of the time flashing past. The Russian officer was late, and if he didn't show up in the next couple of minutes, she would have to abort this rendezvous. Where the hell was he? Simply caught in traffic? Or under arrest for treason? Uncertainty gnawed at her, only partially allayed by the knowledge that Alex Banich was somewhere reasonably close by, keeping watch over her.

She moved to the next window, simulating an interest in a display of beautifully carved chessmen. Other pedestrians brushed past without a second glance, intent on their own errands or pleasure. How odd, Erin thought, to feel so alone surrounded by so many other people. Alex had been right when he said that crowds conferred their own special measure of anonymity.

A familiar reflection appeared over her shoulder, this time in full uniform. Her gaze flickered toward the man standing at her side and then back to the chess pieces. 'Nice of you to show up, Colonel.'

'My apologies, Miss McKenna.' Soloviev sounded just the slightest bit out of breath. He explained, 'The conference dragged on longer than I had anticipated. As it was, I had to leave before the session ended.'

'Was that wise?'

He shrugged uncertainly. 'Perhaps not, But I had no time to contact you to arrange a new meeting.'

Erin nodded her understanding. If Soloviev had missed this rendezvous, she doubted that Banich and Len Kutner would ever have allowed her to schedule another. The risk that the Russian had been caught and turned would have been too high for them to accept. When you were engaged in espionage in a hostile capital, paranoia was a survival trait.

They moved down the Arbat to stand in front of another shop, close enough to speak softly and fairly privately but far enough apart to seem separate – two chance passersby animated only by similar tastes and interests.

'What's happening out there?' Erin asked bluntly. They didn't have time for small talk. Two strangers could companionably converse for a few minutes. Anything longer might draw unwanted attention.

Soloviev was equally blunt. 'Nothing good. Despite their bickering, Kaminov and the Frenchman are very close to reaching an agreement. And our military buildup is well under way. We already have eight divisions massed inside Belarus, with another three en route to the border. Several more are on alert – ready to move once the roads and railroads are clear.' He frowned. 'In fact, I think the marshal is only waiting for this latest EurCon attack to bog down before making a firm commitment to intervene. He's a hard bargainer, that one. He knows the less certain the French are of victory, the more they will pay for our help.'

Erin nodded again. From what she knew of Kaminov's character, Soloviev's assessment made sense. She moved on to the next item on Alex Banich's list. 'And what about the hard evidence we need, Colonel? Do you have anything for me?' She glanced down at the open shopping bag resting on the ground between them. She had brought the bag with her as a cover and also as a means of carrying away any documents the Russian could provide.

Soloviev shook his head. 'Unfortunately, no.'

'Colonel, you know how important . . .'

He held up a hand to stop her. 'My dear Miss McKenna, I am a man of many talents. But I am not a miracle worker.' The Russian officer grimaced. 'My countrymen may not be able to build a decent automobile or grow enough food to feed themselves, but they are masters of the art of secrecy.'

Still frowning, he elaborated. 'Every document used in these talks is numbered and can only be signed out by the most senior members of each delegation. Any photocopying required, even something as simple as an agenda or a lunch menu, can only be done under observation by security officers from both countries. Although there may be a way around these precautions, I haven't found it yet.' He shrugged. 'Tell your superiors that I am still trying, Miss McKenna. But remind them that it won't help any of us if I am caught for the sake of a single scrap of paper.'

'All right.' Erin heard the strain in his voice and realized the pressure the Russian must be under. If *she* were arrested, she could at least hope to be exchanged one day. If the FIS captured Soloviev . . . she shuddered inwardly. In one instance, the old KGB had reportedly fed a 'traitor' into a furnace alive. They'd even filmed the execution as an example to other would-be Western 'moles.' She turned toward him. 'Believe me, Colonel, we appreciate everything you've done so far.'

'Do you?'

She looked up at him. 'Yes, I do.'

He smiled, showing a brief flash of the devil-may-care attitude she'd found so attractive when they'd first met at the embassy dance. 'Then that is enough for me.' His smile turned wistful. 'For now, though, I think we must go our separate ways.'

Erin nodded. They were out of time and in public. 'When can I expect your next call?'

'Tomorrow.'

'That soon?'

Soloviev nodded grimly. 'Events are moving faster, Miss McKenna. By tomorrow or the next day, your country and mine could very easily be at war.'

Neither spotted the small, rat-faced man just a hundred meters further up Arbat Street, quietly taking pictures of them using a telephoto lens.

CHAPTER 31

Gdansk Is the Key

JUNE 29 – ALPHA COMPANY, 3/187TH INFANTRY, 101ST AIRBORNE DIVISION (AIR ASSAULT), SWIECIE, POLAND

The improvised convoy carrying the eight hundred men of the '3rd of the 187th' pulled up outside brigade headquarters in the rural town. Capt. Mike Reynolds shifted in his cramped seat, glad the trip was finally over. He stood gratefully, gathered his gear, and stepped off the hastily camouflaged school bus.

They'd left from Gdansk at six that morning, despite the risks of daylight travel. Speed was more urgent than anything else, and headquarters had reassured them that there would be continuous fighter patrols over the convoy. Well, Reynolds hadn't seen any aircraft from either side, but at least they'd arrived intact. Part of his relief over the end of the journey was his joy at getting out of what his trained eye told him was a conspicuous, barely mobile, and horribly vulnerable four-wheeled target. As an infantryman in a combat zone full of tanks, artillery pieces, and laser-guided munitions, Reynolds was only really comfortable in cover and on his own two feet.

It had taken them four hours to cover the 125 kilometers between Gdansk and the small town of Swiecie. He was sure many tourists had taken the same trip. Highway 5 paralleled the Vistula River, past historic buildings and hundreds of small farms. It would have been a scenic drive if not for the bedraggled refugees clogging the road. Although Gdansk had shown all the signs of war, the morning's trip had given Reynolds a real sense of the struggle. Those people on the road had not left their homes because of some abstract threat. Armies were on the move.

All along the route, bombed-out buildings had provided evidence of EurCon power. Polish demolition teams were also busy. At first, Reynolds had thought the wrecked bridges and cratered roads were more results of EurCon air raids, but then they had driven past a party of engineers actually blowing the bridge over the Vistula at Grudziadz.

'They don't have a lot of confidence in us, do they?' he thought, but he remembered Thompson's speech. The Poles were realists. He and his troops were all too likely to be coming back over this road again, heading in the other direction.

The relatively short trip also brought home to Reynolds just how close the French and German divisions were to their goal. Even at twenty-mph convoy speeds, he and his troops had covered the distance in a single morning. If the 101st didn't slow EurCon down, and quickly, Gdansk would fall.

The closer they got to Swiecie, the fewer civilians they saw, and the more military activity. He was relieved to see a group of AH-64 Apache attack helicopters half-hidden in a copse of woods, and, as they drove into the town itself, he spotted a battery of Hawk missiles guarding the gunships.

Swiecie was the forward support base for the 3rd Brigade and its three infantry battalions, and drab green-gray vehicles lined its narrow streets. The Piast Hotel, the only one in town, had been taken over as the brigade's headquarters. Reynolds guessed that Americans now outnumbered Poles in this village, especially with so many of the original inhabitants in flight.

As he watched his men debark, all stretching and yawning, a private came up and saluted. 'Battalion brief in the hotel, sir, right away.'

Reynolds acknowledged his salute, gathered up his assembling platoon leaders, and headed for the hotel.

The Piast was a stone and brick building, shabby enough to be 'rustic' but really just spartan and old. The dining room on the main floor was quickly filling with the 3rd Battalion's officers, all silent as they waited for the final details of their assignment. Tables and chairs had been pushed to one side, while easels in the center held maps and status boards.

Reynolds spotted his battalion commander, Lt. Col. Jeff Colby, conferring with the brigade's civil affairs officer. The S-5's responsibilities included the civilian evacuation plan, and while their convoy hadn't been horribly delayed by the refugees streaming north, the main road was supposed to have been kept clear. Reynolds was sure the hapless captain was receiving some pithy, pungent feedback from the colonel.

Reynolds liked Colby. A flamboyant, energetic commander, he had passed on some of that energy to his battalion – to some extent compensating for Colonel Iverson's restrained style. Sometimes, though, he seemed too flamboyant, too 'hell-for-leather,' to be real. The colonel had the 'army look,' a lean frame with a long, tanned face and close-cropped hair, in this case brown. He was also a Desert Storm veteran, though not as a battalion commander.

Reynolds sighed. The real issues weren't with Colby, but with himself, and with the entire battalion. Would they hang together? Would this complex machine built of men and weapons work right? The shooting was still too far away for him to feel any personal fear, but he'd admitted to himself that he was terribly afraid of screwing up.

Colby finished his conversation, straightened up, and looked around. Only a few of the battalion's thirty-odd officers were absent, and he said, in a powerful carrying voice army wags said was only issued to lieutenant colonels and above, 'All right, let's get it done.'

Even as he spoke, an enlisted man passed out copies of the battalion operations order. Reynolds quickly scanned its cramped, coded, familiar format:

Task Organization
TF 3-187

A/3-187	TM BASTARD	TM CHOP	TM WOLFPACK
	B/3-187	C/3-187	D/3-187 (-)
	5/D/3-187	3/3/C/326 EN	1/3/C/326 EN
			COLT TM HHB/ 3-320

TF CONTROL
Scouts
81mm Mortars
3/C/326 EN (OPCON)
3-320 FA (DS) (105mm)
213 Polish FA BN (155mm)
A/1/101 AVN (DS)

1. Situation
a. Enemy Forces. II EurCon Corps is expected to continue offensive operations, driving on Gdansk. In our sector we can expect to see reinforced brigade and division-sized attacks, supported by air and artillery. They are at 75% to 90% strength, and their morale is good.
b. Friendly Forces. To our front is the Polish 314th Mechanized Regiment. To our left (across the Vistula River, division and corps boundary) is the Polish 9th Mechanized Division. On our right we tie in with 2-187th. To our rear is Gdansk. 3rd BDE's mission is to defend in sector to allow passage of the Polish 11th Mech Div and destroy enemy first echelon units. On order withdraw to subsequent battle positions near Laskowice.
c. Attachments and detachments. None.
2. Mission. TF 3-187 conducts defense NLT 2400 29 Jun to destroy enemy in sector VIC Swiecie. Assist the rearward passage of the Polish 314th Mech Rgmt. On order withdraw . . .

The rest of the order was amplification and explanation, but Reynolds instantly understood his task. Their battalion had its left flank anchored on the Vistula River, and would deploy its three infantry companies, with their attachments, on a line. Bravo Company, 'Team Bastard,' had the left flank, west of the highway, then 'The Choppers,' Charlie Company, then Reynolds' Alpha Company. Engineers and TOW missiles were attached to every company but his. He might have been disappointed by that, but at least it meant that his men weren't expected to take the heat.

He'd still see plenty of action, though. Third Brigade guarded the most direct route between the EurCon II Corps and Gdansk. EurCon would want that road, real bad.

Out in front of them, the Polish 314th Mechanized Regiment clung to a battle line north of Bydgoszcz. At its present strength of just forty tanks and APCs, it should have been withdrawn from the line and reequipped, but Poland had no reserves left. The 314th would have to hold the enemy for as long as it could, blooding and delaying them.

After falling back through the 101st, the battered Polish regiment and its parent division would form a mobile reserve, resting and refitting. Meanwhile, the Screaming Eagles, and Reynolds' 'Angels from Hell,' would be responsible for keeping the advancing French and Germans at bay.

It took Alpha Company's soldiers thirty minutes of hard marching to reach their section of the new line, minutes Reynolds was already ticking off against a dawn deadline. He and his troops had what seemed like a million things to do before then.

Standard operating procedure saved him. His troops knew what they had to do as soon as they arrived. While that still left a lot of work and planning for the officers and noncoms, the routine items were already part of the plan.

Reynolds quickly walked the ground with his platoon commanders. He forced himself to take the time to do it right, to do it by the book, because the book wouldn't let him forget anything important. To hold his section of the line, he had three platoons of infantry of about thirty men each, armed with automatic rifles and machine guns. The company's heavier firepower came from two 60mm mortars, useful for laying smoke or harassing unprotected troops but not much else, and six Javelin antitank missile launchers.

He took strength from the familiar routine, even in an unfamiliar landscape. But behind the quiet, calm front, dozens of troubling questions filled his mind. Would his men hold up under enemy fire? Would he? Had he forgotten anything – anything that might get his soldiers killed unnecessarily? At last, he shrugged inwardly. There was no way he could answer questions like that. Not until tomorrow.

The sun lay low on the western horizon by the time Alpha Company broke for dinner. Reynolds squatted on the grass near the other men in his company headquarters, chewing reflectively on the rubbery Swedish meatballs in his mess tin. His troops had accomplished a lot, he decided. Ammunition was still a problem, but their communications nets, both radio and landline were in place, and battalion had promised him engineer support to help build obstacles and lay minefields . . .

'Movement to the front!' The sudden shout snapped everyone's eyes around, and those few men who did not have their weapons immediately to hand cursed their error and raced to get them.

Even as he was moving to cover, Reynolds spotted a Humvee roaring up a dirt road from the southwest. The driver seemed to be doing his best to keep the utility truck airborne as much as possible, and Alpha Company's commander carefully checked to make sure there wasn't an enemy in hot pursuit.

As the wheeled vehicle roared closer, Reynolds recognized Colby in the passenger seat, along with Captain Marino, the battalion's intelligence officer, or S-2. Another lieutenant colonel, a stranger, drove. The Humvee was heading for a stone barn serving as the company CP, and Reynolds hurried back, making it there just as the dust cleared and the riders disembarked.

Colby had on his best outgoing, cheerful manner. 'Can you take three more for dinner, Mike?'

'No problem, Colonel,' Reynolds answered, glad that he had successfully arranged a hot meal for this evening. With combat imminent, it might be their last for some time.

The battalion commander introduced the other lieutenant colonel. 'Captain, meet Ferd Irizarri, liaison with the Polish 11th Mech. You may remember him. We were at Irwin together.'

Reynolds nodded. He remembered Irizarri very well. Of middling height, the dark-haired liaison officer seemed to pack enough energy into his frame for a much taller man. He wore Polish battle dress, but with American rank insignia, and he carried an American-made Ingram submachine gun. While Colby's and Marino's gear looked neat and fresh, Irizarri's was worn – not slovenly, but he'd definitely been in the field for a long time.

The last time Mike Reynolds had seen Ferdinand Irizarri up close, the man had been serving as the executive officer of the OPFOR battalion at Fort Irwin, the army's National Training Center. The OPFOR unit specialized in using Soviet gear and Soviet-style tactics against regular battalions like the 3/187th rotating in for advanced tactical training. They were good, very good. Low-powered lasers, blanks, and small explosive charges used as artillery simulators took the place of real bullets and shells, but everything else was kept as close to real combat as possible. Harsh experience in Korea and Vietnam had taught the American military to train hard and train often. Combat leaders and troops were supposed to make their basic mistakes in front of Fort Irwin's unforgiving evaluators – not in a real war.

He led them toward the chow line. 'So now you're working with the Poles, Colonel?'

Irizarri nodded. 'I've been here for two months, getting the 11th ready for the transition to U.S. tactics and equipment. The war caught us just a few months short of trading in the Soviet gear. Now I'm the link between their fighting style and ours.'

Colby and Marino had brought Irizarri back to coordinate the withdrawal of the 314th. Its escape route, once the EurCon pressure grew too great, lay right through the middle of Alpha Company's position. The movement of one unit through another, called a passage of lines, was always dangerous. First, because it could be tough to identify the incoming unit as friend or foe, and second, because there was always a risk that the two formations would get tangled up in each other, so that instead of two combat-ready units, you wound up with one disordered mess.

'We've been up ahead getting the exact picture,' Colby announced as they ate. 'I wish I could send all the battalion's officers up there, but there's no time. I'll tell you this, though.' He leaned forward a little, emphasizing his point. 'You are going to see some beat-down soldiers come through here tomorrow morning. They need us.'

After finishing the quick meal and briefly touring Alpha Company's defenses, Colby was done. He had two more companies to visit before it got too dark to see. But before climbing back into his Humvee, the 3/187th's dapper commanding officer clapped Reynolds on the shoulder. 'I like what I see, Mike. You're on track. What'll we do tomorrow when they come at us?'

Reynolds smiled. 'Give 'em hell, sir.'

19TH PANZERGRENADIER BRIGADE, NEAR BYDGOSZCZ

Lt. Col. Willi von Seelow looked up from the map at the circle of tired, confident faces in front of him. 'That's it, then, gentlemen. Are there any questions?'

'No, Herr Oberstleutnant.' His battalion commanders and senior staff officers shook their heads in unison.

'Good.' Von Seelow slowly straightened to his full height, aware that the top of his head almost brushed against the shelter tent his headquarters troops had rigged between the brigade's command vehicles. 'Remember this: when we attack, we attack hard. Push your companies forward on a narrow front, using heavy smoke as a shield. Then find the Poles, fix them with firepower, and grind them under!'

They nodded, stiffened to attention, and then filed out, heading for their own command tanks and Marders.

Willi followed them outside and stood looking out across the darkened landscape in front of him. He was taking a big risk with this attack. Trying to conduct offensive operations at night invariably spawned serious command and control problems. Unable to see clearly, units got lost or blundered into each other. Friendly-fire incidents multiplied. As the surrounding darkness magnified fears and confused the senses, attacks could bog down without even encountering significant enemy resistance. Given all of that, he knew that many of his counterparts would have waited longer, at least until first light.

But von Seelow had his eyes on the clock, not on tactical perfection.

For the EurCon forces inside Poland, time was as much an enemy as the opposing soldiers waiting up the highway. Every day – no, every hour – they were delayed gave the Americans and British more time to land troops, tanks, artillery pieces, and combat helicopters at Gdansk. The first big seaborne convoys could only be days away at most.

Willi gritted his teeth. They should be closer to the port city than they were. Much closer. But routing the Poles out of the factories, chemical storage areas, and housing tracts around Bydgoszcz had taken far longer than it should have – thanks largely to what seemed the typical French reluctance to take casualties. He shook his head angrily. Again and again, Germany's 'allies' had relied on time-consuming artillery barrages and tiny, halfhearted attacks to drive the city's defenders from their positions. They had gained ground, but slowly, so slowly. Twenty kilometers in two days! At that rate, the whole American army could reach Poland before he and his men caught even a glimpse of Gdansk's skyline!

So, von Seelow thought bitterly, it was up to the 19th Panzergrenadier to kick the attack into high gear. As always. Well, he was getting tired of asking his soldiers to fight and die just to correct French mistakes.

He swallowed the anger, knowing it was unproductive now. They were committed. Instead, he ran over his attack plan one more time, looking for weaknesses or problems he'd overlooked earlier. He couldn't find any. If the Polish defenses were as thin as his scouts reported, this sudden, sharp blow under the cover of darkness should break them wide open.

Willi squared his shoulders. Very well. He would shatter the Poles, regroup and refuel through the night, and push on through the gap at sunup. The brief pause should give his troops time to sort themselves after the inevitable confusion of a night battle without giving the Poles enough time to rebuild their defensive line.

Only one nagging worry remained. Where exactly were the Americans? Reliable reports said they had the better part of two divisions in Poland – the lightly armed 82nd and the 101st – but where in Poland? Without their photo recon and SIGINT satellites, France and Germany lacked any real ability to collect strategic intelligence. Even their air reconnaissance was spotty at best. As more and more U.S. and British warplanes joined the battle, fewer and fewer EurCon air recon missions were getting through to their targets.

As a result, educated guesses about enemy dispositions were all EurCon intelligence officers had to offer. And right now, their situation maps showed both American outfits still deployed around Gdansk and Gdynia, defending the area's ports and airfields against a possible surprise attack by French or German airmobile units.

He hoped they were right about that. Of course, light infantry units were no real match for his Leopard and Marder-armed battalions, but they could slow him down.

Willi von Seelow stared out into the blackness ahead. Without firm intelligence, he and his brigade were fighting blind in more than one way.

ALPHA COMPANY, 3/187TH INFANTRY

Thunder roused Mike Reynolds from an uneasy sleep, the kind of hammering rumble that you get on the flat Texas plain during a summer storm. Then he remembered that he wasn't in Texas.

'Heavy artillery fire to the southwest, Captain!' Corporal Adams shouted from the cluster of radios and telephones that kept them in touch with the rest of the battalion and brigade. 'And heavy-duty jamming on all radio frequencies!'

Southwest. That was the Poles getting pummeled, then. Reynolds scrambled to his feet.

'First Platoon reports movement to their front!'

'On my way!' Reynolds sprinted out of the old stone barn they were using as a company CP, heading for the front. The sounds were changing – shifting from a distant rumbling to a staccato series of higher-pitched bursts. Tank fire. The Poles were under attack.

First Sergeant Ford was there ahead of him, waiting in a foxhole with 2nd Lt. John Caruso, the 1st Platoon's young and inexperienced leader. Both men were scanning the ground ahead, using night-vision gear. Repeated flashes lit the horizon.

'What have you got?' Reynolds fought to keep his voice under control. Fear was always contagious.

'Six-plus tracks, advancing,' Ford answered, pointing out into the darkness.

One of the vehicles was moving a lot faster than the others, bouncing and rolling across the uneven ground with its headlights on. It had to be a friendly. Didn't it? Reynolds snapped out an order. 'Pass the word to all platoons: hold fire!'

He didn't want to start his war by killing allied soldiers by mistake.

The vehicle slowed and stopped just outside Alpha Company's perimeter. It was a Humvee. One man slid out from behind the wheel and came forward with his hands up to show he was unarmed. Guided by 1st Platoon soldiers who kept their guns on him just in case, Lt. Col. Ferdinand Irizarri made his way to the foxhole where Reynolds and the others were waiting.

'Those are Polish tracks out there, Colonel?' Reynolds asked.

'Yes.' Irizarri's mouth tightened as he filled them in. Hit first by heavy artillery and then by at least a brigade-sized attack on a battalion-sized frontage, the Polish outfit he'd been attached to had never stood a chance. Some parts of their defensive line had simply disappeared – deluged by German armor. The rest had either fled or died in place.

Jesus, Reynolds realized, we're next. He shivered, suddenly cold.

'Look, Mike. I've got wounded in the Humvee. And more coming. You can expect stragglers coming in across your whole line,' Irizarri said, grim-faced. 'They'll be showing green chem lights.'

Reynolds nodded, hearing Ford and Caruso already organizing ground guides and safe lanes through the company's defenses. 'We'll bring your people through, Colonel.'

Within minutes, small clumps of armored fighting vehicles were crawling through Alpha Company's fighting positions. Wounded men were piled on top of each tank and APC. The smell of diesel fuel hung in the air, along with the smell of burned metal and rubber.

The last Polish survivors were still coming in when the 3/187th's battalion commander arrived. Colby looked worried.

Reynolds could understand that. Without the Polish armor as a mobile reserve, the battalion was going to be left dangling pretty much on its own. Colby didn't waste any time before outlining Alpha Company's new orders.

Along with an attached TOW platoon, he wanted Reynolds and his men to set up one thousand meters out in front of the rest of the line. They were expected to delay the next German attack for as long as possible, taking over the 314th's job of blooding and slowing the oncoming enemy.

Reynolds whistled softly in dismay. The mission was important, but it was also the kind of assignment that could go suddenly, disastrously wrong.

'One last thing, Mike,' Colby said. 'What will your team's call sign be?'

A company with attachments was called a team, and one centered on Alpha Company would normally be 'Alpha Team,' but no self-respecting grunt would settle for something so tame-sounding. Reynolds knew that, considering where they were going, there was really only one choice. 'How about "Hell Team," sir?'

Colby nodded. 'Go brief your people, Captain.'

19TH PANZERGRENADIER BRIGADE, NORTH OF BYDGOSZCZ

The short summer night was coming to an end as the cloud-covered darkness overhead slowly gave way to a gray, pink-tinged glow in the east.

Willi von Seelow sipped cautiously at the scalding-hot coffee in his mug, feeling the caffeine washing away fatigue and infusing new energy. Then he looked up from the mug, surveying the rutted field around him. The brigade's forward command post – a small, battered collection of Marders, American-made M577 command tracks, trucks, and jeeps – occupied what had been the Polish main position. Shell craters and burning wreckage scattered all around testified to the power and stunning ferocity of the German attack.

'Herr Oberstleutnant!'

Von Seelow turned around. Major Thiessen's head poked out of a roof hatch on the M577 serving as the brigade's TOC, its tactical operations center.

'All battalions report they are ready to resume the advance, sir!'

Willi dumped his coffee out on the flattened grass and whirled toward his own APC's open ramp, already snapping out new orders. 'Radio all units to push forward up the highway. We'll exploit this breach toward Swiecie. Our objective is Gdansk!'

HELL TEAM POSITION

Reynolds both hated and welcomed the first brightening of the eastern sky. On the one hand, the morning light gave him his first real chance to see the ground he would be defending. On the other, dawn meant that the Germans would be coming soon.

He yawned uncontrollably, hoping that the coming daylight would fool his body into wakefulness. So much for the battalion's sleep plan, he thought. He had a sneaking suspicion that it was only the first of many that would go astray.

Nobody had slept last night, or wanted to – not knowing they were almost sure to be attacked the next morning. While he frantically set up artillery target points and designated fields of fire, his men dug in and camouflaged their new positions – doing everything they could to turn the ground they occupied into a small fortress.

Irizarri's help had been invaluable. He had thrown himself into organizing Hell Team's defense, almost adopting Reynolds and his company as his own. Reynolds remembered the colonel's training background at Fort Irwin, and was grateful for his assistance on this 'final exam.'

All of the setup had to be done in near-absolute dark, and with absolute security. If Alpha Company's battle positions were discovered too soon, its mission would fail before it even began. Battalion's scouts had been right about the woods being clear of Germans. He could only hope they had kept the enemy scouts at bay as well.

Hell Team held a thin line of woods on the edge of a dilapidated farm. The trees were old, well-established growth, originally planted next to a low stone wall that had fallen into disrepair. Brush had grown up along the treeline, and the three-hundred-meter-long grove had widened over the years until there was plenty of cover for a reinforced company. The woodland's only flaw was the difficulty of digging in its root-tangled earth.

The trees also created a mix of problems and opportunities for the team's antitank missile operators. To hide both themselves and the backblast when they fired their TOWs and Javelins, they wanted to be as far back inside the treeline as possible. Too far back, though, and they would risk tangling the TOW's missile guidance wires on branches when they fired. It had taken them much of the night just to position all their weapons to Reynolds' satisfaction.

A two-lane asphalt road ran through their front, angling in from the right and cutting through their line. About fifty meters back, it curved east and eventually joined with the motorway. To their front, rolling fields extended another two thousand meters up to a low wooded crest, the graveyard of the 314th and now held by the Germans.

Reynolds had spent part of the night studying the crest, looking for clues to the enemy's deployment or strength, but even in the thermal sight, there was nothing for him to see. The Germans were staying well out of sight.

They were there, though.

Two early morning Polish air raids on the 314th Regiment's old positions had drawn ground fire – a lot of ground fire. About midnight, and again at three, jets shrieked past overhead, darting south toward the German-held hill. Seconds later, bright explosions had billowed out from the trees. More significantly, sparkling tracers had climbed into the night from dozens of separate points – most spraying the sky at random, but a few converging on the fast-moving attack planes as they circled away.

Reynolds couldn't tell if the Polish pilots had hit anything during their brief forays over the battlefield. The few hot spots he'd found using the thermal sights never moved. In the gray, predawn light they were also marked by column of thin black smoke. Were there German tanks at the base of those flames, or just burning leaves?

He lowered the sight and turned his head toward Sgt. Andy Ford. 'All right, Sergeant. Have the men stand to.' They were as ready as they'd ever be.

Most of Hell Team were already at their posts, with their weapons ready, so there was no noise, no bustle – just an increase in alertness, and tension.

Irizarri had left an hour ago with two more Polish stragglers who had wandered in. Both the Poles had insisted on staying and helping Hell Team until the last possible minute, and one, wounded in the leg, had to be near-dragged to Irizarri's waiting Humvee. The man had wanted a weapon.

Reynolds' fingers drummed steadily against the butt of the M16 assault rifle lying next to him. Despite all their hard work through the night, Hell Team's present location was a poor match for their previous position. The company CP was nothing more than a few shallow holes dug in the middle of a tiny cluster of trees, with the spoil piled in front to provide more cover. It was euphemistically called a 'hasty position,' as opposed to the 'prepared positions' they had reluctantly abandoned yesterday evening. Knowing all of that, Alpha Company's commander felt insecure, exposed. Why don't those bastards come ahead and get it over with? he wondered.

He forced himself to wait, to sit quietly. Every minute EurCon delayed was a win for his side. If he had his druthers, he'd sit here until Christmas, while the German tanks rusted. But that wouldn't happen.

The field phone buzzed. Corporal Adams answered it. 'It's the OP, sir.'

Reynolds took the handset offered him by the tall, gangling soldier. He had placed two of his men, Corp. Ted Brown and Pvt. Gene Webster, on a small rise a kilometer in front of Hell Team's position, halfway to the enemy. Thoroughly dug in and camouflaged, they were there to give him a few minutes' extra warning.

'We can see 'em, sir. Dozens of tanks!' Brown's voice mixed eagerness and excitement with fear. He'd finally seen the enemy, in the flesh, arrayed for battle. 'They're still back in the trees, but they're moving up.'

'How many? What are they doing?' Reynolds spoke sharply, feeling his own pulse rate climbing. This was it. 'Come on, Ted. Use SALUTE.' The acronym was a memory aid, designed to help observers report what they saw clearly – even in the noise and confusion of battle. Including size, activity, location, unit, time, and equipment in any contact report usually covered all the essentials.

'Oh, yeah. Sorry, sir.' There was a small pause. 'Size – six armored vehicles. They're wheeled. I think they're Luchs armored cars.'

Reynolds scribbled the information down. 'Roger.' He didn't ask what happened to the 'dozens' Brown had seen moments ago.

'Activity, moving up to the edge of the woodline.'

Once he remembered the much-practiced drill, Brown quickly passed the rest of the information. It sounded like the reconnaissance element of a German armored division, getting ready to move forward. Reynolds nodded to himself. That made sense. The Germans would certainly throw a line of scout vehicles out ahead of their advancing tanks. Alternatively they could be using the recon unit's movements as a feint while the panzer division launched its real attack in some other sector. Which was this?

Reynolds scanned the area with his own binoculars. Nothing. The enemy scout cars Brown and Webster had spotted were still too far away. He asked the observer, 'Can you see any other movement? Tanks or APCs?'

'No, sir. Just the recce vehicles. It looks like they're getting ready to move out.' The concern in Brown's voice hinted at his real message: 'Can we leave now?'

At normal rates of advance, the enemy would take three to four minutes to reach the OP. And it would take two men, sprinting with their gear, longer than that to reach the safety of Hell Team's position. In other words, they had to bug out the second that the Germans started to move.

Reynolds had no intention of sacrificing his two men unnecessarily, but he wasn't going to let them leave a second early, either. His only reply was 'Stay low and keep your eyes peeled.'

He passed the sighting report back to battalion, then to his three platoon leaders. Their waiting was almost over.

A few minutes later, the OP called in again, with a new report. They could now see tanks, at least ten, and the armored cars were moving forward. This time Corporal Brown wasn't shy about it. 'Sir, we'd like to get out of here.'

'Get back here, fast.'

Reynolds alerted his platoon leaders, then searched the woods ahead again. At two kilometers, the small, gray-green vehicles would be hard to see, even if the ground had been perfectly flat. This wasn't Texas, though, and the rise and fall of the terrain would give him only glimpses of the enemy scouts.

The German scouts were playing a deadly game, daring the Americans to shoot at them, thus revealing their positions. They trusted to their own luck or their enemy's poor shooting for survival. It was a dare Reynolds couldn't pass up. If he left the scouts unmolested, depending purely on concealment, they might get close enough to see the battalion's positions as well as his own. No camouflage was ever perfect – especially against expert observers with their own thermal imaging equipment.

Instead, he was going to let the Germans close until they were well inside Javelin range, then open up and try to kill several at once. He had time, a few minutes yet.

Alpha Company's first victory came without firing a shot. One of the scout cars, angling off to Reynolds' left, hit a mine laid by the engineers last night. *Whummp*. The sudden, powerful explosion tossed the Luchs into the air and then over onto its side. No one crawled out of the smoking, twisted vehicle.

The captain smiled grimly. That minefield wasn't very wide or very dense, but it would take the Germans a while to find that out.

Meanwhile, one of their six reconnaissance vehicles lay wrecked out in the open.

Reynolds studied the surviving scout cars through his binoculars, taking care to keep the lenses out of the sunlight. Each Luchs was a long, eight-wheeled thing. Angular, lightly armored, and capped with a small turret holding a 20mm gun, they were 'easy meat' for an Ml Abrams or even a Bradley, but to Reynolds and his men, they could be a real threat – if they got close enough. Except he didn't plan to let them live that long.

Three of the five Luchs rumbled up and over the low rise occupied by the now-abandoned OP. They were within seven hundred meters. Now. He lifted the field phone. 'Shoot!'

He heard several, muffled *whumphs*, followed by a thin, rippling whistle of missiles in flight. One TOW and four of the Javelins fired – the smaller missiles double-teaming their targets.

Reynolds lowered his field glasses, trying to follow one of the Javelins, no more than a small black dot moving incredibly fast. As the gunner made course corrections, it darted a little from side to side, then arced up and flew above one of the Luchs.

Whammm. The anti-tank missile exploded into a round gray-black ball right over the German scout car. Puffs of dust or smoke danced on its engine deck and turret top, and sparks flew as if it were being struck by dozens of small hammers. He never saw the second missile aimed at the Luchs. Luckily, one hit was enough.

The armored car slewed right and stopped, with greasy black smoke pouring out of the engine compartment, in the rear. The jagged fragments spewed by the Javelin's warhead not only pierced armor – they were also white-hot.

Through the binoculars, Reynolds saw two men stumble out of the Luchs, quickly scrambling out of sight. They were at the ragged edge of small-arms range, but his well-disciplined company held their fire. With two of their comrades dead and their vehicle wrecked, the German scouts were no longer a threat.

More explosions echoed across the countryside. Two more vehicles were also hit. The leftmost, targeted by the TOW, was a mass of flame. The TOW's larger warhead must have detonated its on-board ammunition. The third, hit by two Javelins, sat motionless – wreathed in dust and smoke. Reynolds nodded somberly. Hell Team had just announced its existence to the EurCon commanders.

The first steps in the dance had been his, but he knew what had to come next, and so did the rest of his men. He'd exercised with the Germans as a young platoon leader, and they were good.

'Incoming! Take cover!' Sergeant Ford's shouted warning rose above the shrill whistle of the first enemy shell arcing in.

Whammm. Christ! As tight as he'd been hugging the earth before, Reynolds buried himself in it now. The explosion tore a chunk out of the ground a hundred meters away, still about ten meters out from the copse of trees they were holding, thank God.

It was as close as Reynolds had ever been to a real live artillery shell fired at him, and it awed and frightened him. In exercises, they used artillery simulators, 'devices' that exploded with about the same force as an old M80 firecracker. You really had to use your imagination to turn a bunch of those into an artillery barrage.

He wouldn't need to use his imagination ever again, he thought grimly. He'd remember this for the rest of his life. Probably a 155mm, the professional part of his mind speculated – a ranging shot. More to come.

There were, and for the next few minutes the earth and air blended in a thunderous roar as HE rounds hammered the area around Alpha Company's positions. Reynolds' stomach turned to water every time a round landed nearby, and he buried his face in the dirt, in genuine fear for his life. He risked a glance to his right. Adams was curled up into an impossibly small ball, tucked into the space between two trees.

After the first few blasts didn't kill him, his sense of duty took over. How were his men doing? Their foxholes would protect them from near misses, but they had little overhead cover. Even more important, he knew what he'd be doing, if he were the enemy commander.

He risked raising his head, buffeted by the pressure wave from an explosion in the middle distance. Raising his glasses and bracing them on the mound of dirt piled in front of his hole, Reynolds saw tanks, formed up in neat rows, advancing out of the distant woods.

He studied them for a minute, then reached over, lightly punching Adams in the side. The corporal looked up, and Reynolds shouted, 'Get the arty. We need a fire mission, SADARM, ref point seven one. Got it?'

Adams nodded. He scuttled over to the field phone. Hugging the instrument close, the corporal passed on his captain's message – screaming to be heard over the shells still howling in and exploding all around.

The important thing was to keep busy, Reynolds realized. Action helped suppress fear. He concentrated on his next move. One of the first tactical lessons any junior officer ever learned was the importance of retaining the initiative. You couldn't let the enemy force you into reacting the way he wanted you to. Well, right now the Germans wanted him to keep his head down. He studied the advancing line, ignoring the shells still raining down all around.

The German batteries were firing blind, he decided – flinging shells out toward unseen map coordinates. With their forward scouting parties either dead or in flight, they couldn't possibly have an observer close enough to adjust their rounds directly onto his positions. So the enemy gunners were just firing among the trees, not concentrating their barrage anywhere, or even aiming it accurately. Of course, there was still dumb luck, he thought as a near miss rattled his teeth. He spat out dirt.

Adams shouted in his ear, 'Done, sir.' The 3/187th had a battery of Polish-manned 155s in direct support, with a full artillery battalion on call if they needed it.

'Great!' Reynolds ate dirt again as another 155mm round exploded close by. Fragments screamed overhead, tearing leaves and lethal splinters off the trees above the CP. He lifted his head again. 'Have all the platoons check in.'

The corporal nodded, more intent on his task now.

The reports came back quickly, and they were encouraging. So far Hell Team had been lucky. A few men had been wounded by shell fragments or splinters of wood, but no one was dead. Not yet. Reynolds relaxed minutely, relieved that the moment had not yet arrived when he would have to deal with losing any of his men. But he couldn't fool himself. Once the Germans started concentrating their artillery fire, his casualty count would skyrocket.

'Captain! Hewitt wants to open up!'

Sergeant Hewitt commanded the team's attached TOW antitank platoon. The German Leopards were well inside effective range, and at the rate that they were moving, the sergeant and his ATGM gunners would only get a few shots in before they'd have to displace or be overrun. Reynolds understood that, but he had his own ideas. 'Tell him we're sticking to the original plan.'

Now, where the hell was that fire mission?

Reynolds steeled himself, studying the approaching tanks, counting them, checking their formations, trying to be all business. He could feel his insides starting to liquefy again. They were less than a thousand meters from his positions! He opened his mouth, just about ready to have the TOW missiles fire anyway, when the American artillery arrived, whistling past on its way toward the oncoming German tank company.

He raised his binoculars, looking above the armored formation.

The German barrage stopped suddenly, having done about as much as could be expected with unobserved fire. Besides, this far inside Poland, artillery ammunition was undoubtedly at a premium. Reynolds noticed the cessation only when he realized that he hadn't flinched for a good minute.

A clump of small parachutes blossomed almost directly above the German Leopards. More followed in short order, popping into existence faster than the eye could follow.

Old-style HE barrages were rarely effective against armored units. Unless a round scored an incredibly lucky direct hit or knocked a track loose, tanks could roll right through the artillery fire, ignoring the man-killing fragments rattling off their armor. SADARM was an advanced form of artillery ammunition designed to give U.S. guns a way to kill enemy tanks.

Each of the tiny parachutes drifting toward German armored vehicles carried a small, sophisticated submunition. As the chute spiraled down, a millimeter-wavelength radar constantly scanned the ground in a slowly widening cone. The instant the seeker detected the characteristic radar profile of a tank, it would fire – sending a sharp-edged fragment lancing down through the tank's thin top armor.

Puffs of smoke appeared beneath the chutes, each connected by a straight, glowing white line with a Leopard below. Three German tanks veered out of line and halted. Two were on fire.

In the same instant, Hell Team's TOW and Javelin gunners fired another volley of antitank missiles. More Leopards died – hit before they could realise they were under attack from more than one direction.

A second ATGM volley was on its way before the Germans twigged to what was going on, and even then, the word didn't get out to all their tanks in time. Only a handful popped smoke, triggering grenade launchers mounted on the turret sides. Those that did were suddenly covered in a dome of opaque whiteness, and Reynolds knew the smoke was multispectral, just as opaque to his team's thermal imagers. Shit!

Three Leopards, the remnants of a platoon, surged out of their own smoke, swinging wide to flank the American-held treeline. One after the other, they stumbled into one of Hell Team's minefields and stopped – immobilized by thunderous blasts that ripped tracks off road wheels and smashed through their weaker bottom armor.

Reynolds bared his teeth in a tight, tense grin. It had been relatively simple, given the range at which he'd planned to engage the Germans, to guess which way any tanks trapped in his kill zone would try to dodge.

Some of the tanks opened up, pumping 120mm rounds and long-range machine gun fire into the trees ahead of them. Since the Germans could have only a general idea of where the American positions were, their shooting was wildly inaccurate, but the shells roaring overhead were impressive and terrifying, a new kind of fear for him to face.

All of the surviving Leopards were using smoke now, and weaving back and forth in violent evasive maneuvers. Reynolds was amazed at the agility of the fifty-five-ton monsters dancing over the ground at near-highway speeds. They were not advancing, though. Instead, the German vehicles started to disappear, hiding in folds in the ground or other cover. Good, thought Reynolds. Hooray for our side.

'Hewitt says he can't see through the smoke,' Adams reported. The antitank section commander's message was expected. Reynolds acknowledged, then told the corporal to pass the word: stand by for more artillery.

He craned his head, studying the wreck-strewn field in front of him. Hell Team had seriously dinged the German tank company, inflicting far more losses than he'd expected. He guessed the Leopard commanders hadn't expected to meet any opposition this far forward. The company, though, was only the lead element for a tank battalion, and the battalion for an armored or mechanized brigade. God alone knew what was backing that up.

Reynolds shook his head. He couldn't stop them all, and he wasn't about to play Fort Apache. Instead, he was presenting the Germans with a tactical problem, one that could be solved – but solving it would eat up precious time.

The book said that you didn't charge dug-in troops with tanks. The book said that to push enemy foot soldiers out of the woods, you suppress them with artillery, then send in your own dismounted infantry to clear it, man-to-man.

He searched the German-held woods, two kilometers away. Past the wisps of clearing smoke, he could see a line of boxy, angled troop carriers pouring out of the trees. This time there really were dozens of them, with more Leopards coming right behind. They were just dots at this range, but he worked out the math: The Marders could cover that first kilometer in just three minutes. From that point, the panzergrenadiers they carried would dismount and cover the next thousand meters on foot. He had roughly ten minutes before they'd be close enough to engage.

It was time to skedaddle. 'Pass the word to the platoon leaders. Get the wounded ready to move. Start packing up. First and 3rd platoons will move in five minutes.'

And then the German artillery opened up again, flaying the woods held by Hell Team with high explosive.

Reynolds heard the wailing freight-train roar and dove back to the bottom of the CP, seeking cover just as the first shells went off.

Whammm. Whammm. Whammm. The ground shuddered, rocked, and bucked. Trees toppled – sheared off by direct hits.

Reynolds crouched helpless in his hole, trying to breathe air that contained more dust and smoke than oxygen. This was worse than the first barrage. Now that German forward observers could see where their rounds were falling, they could concentrate their fire, systematically walking the barrage up and down the small patch of woodland. Reynolds and his men were also more than a mere nuisance, and thus worthy of more attention. The Germans were using more guns this time, a lot more. Maybe a full battalion.

A nearby burst picked him up and slammed him into the ground, then another rolled him over before he could get his grip again.

Reynolds heard someone screaming and realized his men were being hit, maybe killed. Hatred flared. He was suddenly glad about the German tanks and crews they'd killed.

But it was still time to leave.

The barrage shifted slightly. Now most of the enemy shells were dropping to their front, about a hundred meters or so out. And the Germans were firing smoke, not explosives.

Uh-oh. With a smoke screen in place, the Marders could advance under its cover to almost point-blank range before dismounting their troops. Well, he knew the correct tactical solution to this problem, too. Bug out now.

His 1st and 3rd platoons, as planned, were already moving out. Reynolds took the field phone from Adams, amazed to find that the lines were still open. Speaking rapidly, he passed the word for all but the rear guard to get out.

He also had to phone his boss. 'German infantry battalion advancing under smoke cover. They're about a klick out,' Reynolds reported.

'Good job, Mike.' Colby paused, and then confirmed the decision he had already made. 'Get your boys back now.'

Reynolds hung up and turned to check the progress of their retreat.

More foot soldiers ducked past him, sprinting north, away from the oncoming Germans. He looked around quickly, peering through the drifting smoke. He couldn't see anybody else. And the engine noises from inside the enemy smoke screen were growing louder fast. Time to go.

He turned to the sergeant commanding his seven-man rear guard and shouted, 'Okay, Robbins! We're clear! Fall back!'

Staying low in case the German smoke screen thinned, they ran back, careful to take the same path followed by the rest of the company. The engineers who had laid the minefields in front of Hell Team's positions had also mined areas behind the patch of woods. With a little luck, a few German tank crews might find that out the hard way.

The pickup zone was five hundred meters back, in a low spot well out of the German line of sight. Reynolds ran like he'd never run before, the distance seeming to stretch ahead of him forever.

The whine of turbines grew louder when he burst over the small rise that shielded the pickup zone.

Drab-green UH-60 Blackhawk troop carriers waited in the hollow, rotors already turning. Soldiers scrambled aboard by squads while other helicopters, already loaded, lifted off – streaming away to the northeast. One of the 1st Platoon's rifle squads covered the area, lying prone in a line with their weapons pointed outward.

A howling roar snapped Reynolds' head around in time to see two waves of four AH-64 Apache gunships flash past just a dozen meters off the ground. One of the machines flew past close enough so that he could see the gunner in the front seat, bent over his sight. When the pilot, seated higher up and further back, looked in his direction and waved, the 30mm gun mounted below its belly eerily tracked with the man's gaze.

Then they were gone, climbing over the low rise and spreading out into fighting pairs as they clattered south. Reynolds stood at the top of the hollow watching them vanish into the smoke and dust. He felt a sense of grim anticipation. Those Apaches carried enough firepower to tear a bloody chunk out of the German attack.

'Captain. Last chopper's ready to roll.' Andy Ford's calm voice called him back to his own responsibilities. Adams and the last men from 1st Platoon were just crowding into the helo's troop compartment.

'Okay, Andy.' Reynolds followed Ford downhill, ducked under the rotors, and pulled himself inside.

As soon as he was aboard, the big helicopter lifted off, turbine engines screaming with effort. The deck surged up beneath him and they were off – sliding low over the landscape at nearly 150 miles an hour. This close to the ground, the sensation of speed was overwhelming,

With the speed flowed relief. They'd made it. His company had done its job. Combat was a known quantity now, to his men and to himself. They'd paid a blood price for their success, though, and now the war had turned personal. It was no longer just a professional exercise in tactics.

FORWARD HEADQUARTERS, 19TH PANZERGRENADIER BRIGADE

Despite the periodic, hissing waves of static generated by American jamming, the increasingly desperate voices crackling over Willi von Seelow's headphones came in clearly – mirroring the state of the battle raging in front of Swiecie.

'Can you get forward, Jurgen?'

Von Seelow heard the major commanding the 191st Panzergrenadier Battalion talking to an infantry company commander trying to push into the village itself.

'No, Herr Major!' the unknown captain shouted. 'The damned Amis have us pinned down short of the farmhouse . . . shit!' The staccato, ripping sound of high-velocity cannon fire echoed over the radio circuit. 'Another fucking gunship just made a pass. Oh, Jesus. Sammi's Marder is hit. It's burning!'

Willi was listening in to the radio frequencies allocated to his combat battalions and support units, trying to extract as much information from sketchy reports and snatches of panicked dialogue as he could. Frustrated, he tore the headset off and poked his head out through one of the command Marder's rear roof hatches.

Smoke, white from artillery smoke rounds, and black from blazing tanks and APCs, stained the northern skyline. Flashes rippled through the smoke pall. Tank guns, exploding shells, and infantry small arms all blended in one hammering, thumping, discordant roar.

Von Seelow's eyes narrowed. His attack was falling apart – broken up by the unsuspected American defensive line behind the Polish positions he'd overrun the night before. He scowled, furious with the 19th's new recon unit – two Luchs platoons he'd cobbled together with replacements and attached Territorial Army units – and with himself. Poorly motivated, poorly led, and made overconfident by their easy victory over the Poles, his scouts had sat on their asses through the night instead of probing ahead. That was bad. Even worse was the fact that he'd let them get away with it.

Willi closed his eyes, shutting out the sight of the fighting up ahead. Men, his own soldiers, were dying because he'd neglected one of his responsibilities. The pain he felt was almost physical, like a bayonet tearing at his guts.

'Sir!'

Private Neumann's cry pulled him back down inside the Marder. 'Yes? What is it?'

'Major Feist is on the division frequency, Herr Oberstleutnant. He wants to speak with you.'

Willi put his radio headset back on. What did the 7th Panzer Division's assistant operations chief want now? 'Von Seelow here.'

'Good,' Feist said coldly. He was one of the division staff officers who had sided with von Olden before he was relieved and sent home to Germany in disgrace. The little mustachioed major was a charter member of the 'I hate ossies' club. 'We have new orders from II Corps, Herr Oberstleutnant. The 19th Panzergrenadier is to disengage and fall back on Gruczno.'

'What? Why?' Von Seelow didn't bother hiding his astonishment. The tiny hamlet of Gruczno had been the jump-off point for his night attack.

'We've identified a new enemy formation in line – the American 101st Division.'

'Tell me something I don't know!' Willi snarled. 'That's all the more reason to push ahead and break through now! Before the Amis can dig in any deeper!'

'Negative, Herr Oberstleutnant. General Montagne's orders are explicit,' Feist sniffed. 'Units from the French 5th Armored and the III Corps have also run into stronger opposition than expected. Corps believes we must regroup and rethink our plan of operations in light of these new developments.'

Von Seelow saw red. The one thing the enemy needed was time, and now Montagne and those other idiots were handing it to them on a silver platter. 'Tell corps to stuff its "developments" up its ass . . .'

'I suggest you comply with your orders, Herr Oberstleutnant,' the major said coolly, apparently unmoved by his outburst. 'You have thirty minutes to begin withdrawing. If not, I'm sure we can find someone else to command your brigade. Feist, out.'

Willi stood staring at the appalled faces of his staff for several seconds before growling out the string of orders that would put the 19th Panzergrenadier's drive toward Gdansk on hold.

11/34TH FIGHTER REGIMENT, GDYNIA AIR BASE, POLAND

Maj. Tad Wojcik climbed down from his F-15 Eagle feeling like he'd run a marathon and then boxed a few barefisted rounds with a gorilla. Flying combat missions all day and doing paperwork all night was bleeding away his last carefully hoarded stores of endurance and energy. Even now, after a hectic air-to-air combat mission, his work wasn't done. One of the squadron staff, Sgt. Jerzy Palubin, was waiting, both with information about the rest of the regiment and with questions about the mission he'd just finished flying.

His new slot as 1st Squadron's operations officer, and the promotion that came with it, had come quickly – but holes in the composite fighter regiment's organization had to be filled as soon as they opened up. Major Wolnoski had died an airman's death, crashing trying to land a crippled Eagle. Tad had taken over his job and rank the same afternoon. He was one of the last of the squadron's original pilots. Wolnoski had been another.

Now, just a few days later, it felt like he'd been doing the job forever. He'd been ready for it, having proven himself a survivor as well as a skilled pilot. He'd kept flying, of course – just like his predecessor. There just weren't enough pilots.

In spite of his fatigue, Tad was pleased. The morning's mission had been a good one, the first in a long while. Ten Eagles had managed to intercept a EurCon raid near Stargard that morning, well before they could reach the rail yards there. For once, French and German fighter cover had been light, and they'd torn into the enemy attack aircraft, downing at least a quarter of the thirty-plane raid.

His own flight of four planes, about all that was left of 1st Squadron in flyable condition, had accounted for five Mirages all by themselves.

'It's just too bad none of them were Germans. I really wanted to kill a few more Krauts on this hop,' he remarked grimly to Palubin, as they walked back to the ops building.

The older noncom glanced back at him, obviously puzzled and a little disgusted by the disappointment in his voice. 'Who cares whether they're German or not? They're all the enemy, aren't they?'

Evidently reminded of the disparity between their ranks by Tad's shocked look, Palubin quickly apologized for his outburst, but Tad waved it off. 'Never mind, Jerzy. You're right anyway. It doesn't matter.'

He followed the sergeant back to the ops building in a pensive mood. He had spoken reflexively, but maybe it was stupid to count Germans apart, as if they were some sort of evil breed. After all, France was at least as much to blame for this war.

He wondered how his parents were faring. A brief message passed through official channels had told him that they were alive and safe in Warsaw. Make that relatively safe, he decided. There were too many rumors that the Russians could come pouring across the border at any moment. If that happened . . . Tad felt cold. If the Russians sided with EurCon, then all their sacrifices would be in vain. Poland would fall. He pushed the depressing thought away, focusing his worries instead on his mother and father.

The fragmentary message hadn't said where exactly his parents were living in Warsaw. Probably in one of the sprawling, dirty refugee tent cities that were springing up on the capital's outskirts. Did they have enough food to eat? Probably not. The war had badly disrupted Poland's own food distribution systems, and the limited supplies coming in by sea went to the armed forces first. While their nation was under threat, civilians would have to fend for themselves. Tad grimaced. Maybe it wouldn't be so hard to hate the French, after all.

But did he have to hate to do his job? That was worth thinking harder about.

When they got to the operations building, the 1st Squadron's commander, Lieutenant Colonel Lyskawa, congratulated him on his two kills. They raised Tad's score to nineteen.

Then Wojcik saw him smile for the first time in a week.

'We're getting some new aircraft, Major. Eight 'C' models will be delivered tomorrow, along with three new pilots. Our two oldest planes get sent to England, for rework.'

Tad's mind raced. New planes and pilots? They were the first in weeks – the first tangible signs that Poland's American and British allies were winning their battle to open the sea and air corridors to his adopted country. They already had more pilots than F-15s, so the reinforcements would almost double the squadron's available aircraft. As operations officer, it would be his job to assign missions to the squadron's planes. Suddenly his options had grown, and he felt as if there was a chance. They weren't overstrength enough to pull any pilots out of the line, but they'd be able to stand a few down for a day's rest.

It gave him a small measure of hope. Maybe not for him personally, but for Poland, at least.

CHAPTER 32
Knife Edge

JUNE 30 – COMMUNICATIONS CENTER, 25TH TANK DIVISION, IN THE BIALOWIEZA FOREST, ON THE POLISH-BELARUSSIAN BORDER

For hundreds of years, the vast primeval forest of Bialowieza had served as a kind of sanctuary – a refuge for the endangered European bison during times of peace and for Polish and Russian partisans during times of war. Now a new armed force laired beneath the forest's thick leafy canopy, seeking shelter from American spy satellites orbiting hundreds of miles above the earth.

As sunlight filtered through to the forest floor, the sound of thousands of murmuring voices, the clanking noises of metal and machinery, and the smell of thousands of small cook fires all wafted skyward. The soldiers of Russia's 25th Tank Division were stirring to life after another night spent camped beneath the camouflage netting covering their T-80 tanks and BMP-2s.

Near the center of the sprawling encampment, alert sentries, tents, and a circle of parked command vehicles signaled the presence of the division headquarters. Inside the headquarters itself, the telephone wire strung from tree to tree to tent identified the main communications center – a canvas roof covering two eight-wheeled BTR-80 APCs, a radio van, and tables piled high with radios, field phones, cryptographic gear, and scrambling equipment. A portable electric generator thumped noisily in one corner, supplying power to save valuable batteries.

A tall, black-haired man stood near one of the tables, talking into a secure field phone. The ragged scar running diagonally from his forehead down across his nose and left cheek ruined what would otherwise have been a handsome face. Years before, while serving as a battalion commander during the Afghan War, Maj. Gen. Sergei Rostopchin had been seriously wounded – badly disfigured by fragments from a mujaheddin mortar shell. 'Yes, Colonel. I understand completely. You may tell the general staff that the 25th will be ready to move on time.'

Rostopchin was young for his post as a division commander, especially in Kaminov's purged and restructured Russian Army. The marshal, an old man himself, had a notorious penchant for equating age with competence. Rostopchin had earned his command, in spite of his age, through a varied set of converging circumstances – his family's long record of military service, his own exemplary war record, and, perhaps most important of all, a complete lack of interest in politics. The leader of the 25th Tank Division adhered to one, unswerving principle: he obeyed orders from those above him without question, without exception, and without reservation. That made him valuable in a time when loyalties seemed to change with every shift in the political wind.

Now Rostopchin hung up and turned to find his chief of staff waiting anxiously close by. 'That was Colonel Soloviev, Mikhail. We can expect the authorization to launch our attack sometime in the next twenty-four to thirty-six hours.'

The colonel nodded abruptly, ready for further instructions.

'Contact all regimental commanders,' Rostopchin continued. 'I want them here for a final briefing by 1600 hours. And move the division supply trains forward. I want all our vehicles fully topped off with fuel before sunset.'

'Yes, sir.'

Rostopchin left the communications tent, striding briskly toward his personal trailer. He had competent subordinates who were perfectly able to handle the purely mechanical, last-minute details involved in readying the division for combat. Instead, he wanted to spend the next several hours going over his plans one more time.

Not that he expected much trouble when the time came. Far from it.

With eight divisions already on the border and another four en route, Russia's invasion army should crush the lone Polish division facing them in a matter of hours. Rostopchin shrugged. Given the existing correlation of forces in the region, the campaign against Poland and its allies would be more a maneuver exercise than a real war.

HEADQUARTERS, FIRST AVIATION ARMY, GRODNO AIR BASE, BELARUS

Col. Gen. Vasiliy Uvarov, commander of the First Aviation Army, looked down from Grodno's central tower with undisguised satisfaction and a growing sense of fierce anticipation. Thousands of hours of staff work and intricate preparation were paying off as the last elements of Russia's aerial strike force touched down.

The shelters lining the air base's runways were already crowded with newly arrived aircraft, and other planes were still flying in from bases further back in Russia. Long-range, swing-wing Su-24 Fencer strike aircraft taxied past pairs of smaller, more heavily armored Su-25 Frogfoots – the counterparts of America's A-10 Thunderbolt tank-killers – parked between the massive concrete structures.

All across the giant base, flight crews and maintenance technicians hurried to their posts, dodging trolleys hauling bombs, air-launched missiles, and gun ammunition to the flight line and aircraft shelters. In the distance, barely visible among low hills and stands of trees, weapons crews worked feverishly to ready the SA-10 and SA-15 SAM batteries deployed along the base perimeter.

Uvarov knew the scenes he was watching were being duplicated at dozens of other air bases along the frontier. Whole regiments of strike aircraft and MiG-29 and MiG-23 fighters, held back to deceive Western spy satellites for as long as possible, were flying in – marrying up with ground support personnel deployed days ago by truck and by train. Once Marshal Kaminov reached agreement with the French, the First Aviation Army would be ready to hurl nearly a thousand warplanes into the skies over Poland.

The colonel general nodded, pleased by the prospect. As a pilot and then a commander in the Soviet Air Forces, he had spent his adult life preparing for a war that was lost without ever being fought. Now, by serving under the Russian tricolor, a flag that was both new and old at the same time, he and his pilots would have a welcome opportunity to show the world their power and their skills.

COMMAND CENTER, TEYKOVO MISSILE FIELD, RUSSIA

Several hundred feet beneath the earth's surface, Gen. Viktor Grechko watched the status lights on his missile control boards change color, moving from amber to green as individual SS-24 crews reported full readiness. After years spent in a kind of politically imposed stasis, his solid-fueled ICBMs were being brought back to operational status. Originally slated for deployment aboard special, mobile rail launchers, the SS-24s under his command had instead been fitted inside fixed silos first built for much older SS-11s. In his view, that was a mistake. Silo-based missiles were vulnerable missiles. The U.S. air strike against the French weapons on the Plateau d'Albion proved that beyond all doubt. Nevertheless, each of his ICBMs had a range of more than five thousand nautical miles and carried ten highly accurate 550-kiloton nuclear warheads. And this far inside Russia, even in their silos, they would be vulnerable to American attack only if the Americans fired their missiles first.

When the last lights turned green, the general picked up his direct line to Moscow. 'This is General Grechko. The Teykovo field is active. Our systems checks are complete. All crews are on alert. All enable and launch code lists and launch keys have been distributed. Standing by.'

If the United States or Great Britain tried to fend off Russia's move into Poland with nuclear threats or nuclear weapons, Russia would be ready to respond in kind.

BORNHOLM ISLAND, DENMARK, IN THE BALTIC SEA

Ten-year-old Christian Petersen stood on a low, grassy hill, peering out to sea – transfixed by the sight of the long, silent parade of gray ships steaming east past Bornholm. His schoolbooks lay tumbled at his feet, forgotten in his sudden excitement. A brisk wind ruffled the small boy's fair hair and tugged at the blue and yellow windbreaker his mother always made him wear to ward against the early morning chill.

Ten. Twelve. Fifteen. Christian's eyes widened as he counted aloud.

There were dozens of ships out there! More vessels than he had ever seen at one time, and all of them bigger than the interisland ferries that usually plied these waters. Most were rust-streaked freighters, massive oil tankers, or big new container ships, but he could see smaller, antenna-studded warships prowling beyond the merchantmen.

Gray-painted helicopters, with the sunlight flashing off their rotors, probed ahead and behind the enormous formation. High overhead, tiny specks orbited – U.S., British, and Norwegian fighters ready to fend off any EurCon air attack.

The Danish schoolboy didn't know it, but he was watching the first convoy carrying substantial reinforcements from the United States to Poland. The ships carrying the tanks, APCs, and artillery pieces belonging to the U.S. 24th Mechanized and 1st Armored divisions were just two hundred miles from Gdansk.

DGSE SECURE SECTION, FRENCH EMBASSY, MOSCOW

Maj. Paul Duroc leaned over a desk in one of the DGSE's windowless, electro-magnetically shielded offices, studying the photographs his surveillance team had taken of Col. Valentin Soloviev talking with a striking auburn-haired woman. He looked up at tall, powerfully built Michel Woerner. 'Foret and Verdier are sure this was a rendezvous and not just a chance encounter?'

The big man nodded. 'Very sure. The Russian left his car in the Defense Ministry parking lot, went straight to this part of the Arbat, encountered this woman, and then went straight back to the ministry.'

'Yes . . .' Duroc's fingers drummed briefly on the desk while he considered that assessment. He nodded to himself. His operatives were right. Soloviev's behavior fit the classical pattern of a man making a clandestine contact. But with whom? He looked up at Woerner again. 'And we still have no identification of this woman?'

'No, Major.' The other man shook his head. 'We've run her picture through the files both here and over the satellite link to Paris. They weren't able to make any matches with any known intelligence agent of any country.'

'I'm not terribly surprised,' Duroc said caustically. After years on the operational side of the French intelligence service, he had very little respect left for those in the administrative and analytical sections – men he considered little better than glorified file clerks.

He studied the woman shown standing next to Soloviev again. Who the devil was she? She didn't look Russian, but then who could really tell? Even with the old Soviet Union's outlying provinces stripped away, this damned country was still a polyglot mishmash of different ethnic groups. Still, everything about her – the shape of her face, her clothes, her posture – shouted 'foreigner' to him. But a foreigner from which country? Britain? America? Germany?

'Perhaps we should ask the Russians,' Woerner offered. 'The FIS might have a file on her.'

Duroc snorted. 'Them? Not likely.' His eyes narrowed in thought. 'In any case, Michel, running to the FIS could prove a huge mistake. What if this Soloviev's actions are sanctioned by Kaminov himself? What if that old Russian bastard is playing a double game with us, eh? Bargaining with us and with the British and Americans at the same time?'

'Then should we alert Paris?' Woerner asked.

'No.' Duroc scowled. He tapped the photos. 'Not until we have something more conclusive than these.' He doubted that his unimaginative higher-ups would see anything very wrong or suspicious in a Russian colonel meeting publicly with a beautiful woman. If anything, a cable to Paris at this point would probably only earn him another reprimand for straining at the procedural leash they'd looped around his neck.

No, he would need a lot more than unsubstantiated supposition to convince his superiors that something was very wrong in Moscow. He would need hard proof of Soloviev's treachery – evidence that would either prompt the Russians to move against the colonel themselves or expose Kaminov's own duplicity.

Duroc stood up straight and shoved the surveillance photos aside. From what he could see, the negotiations with the marshal and his fellow hard-liners were at a critical stage. Ambassador Sauret expected a major breakthrough sometime in the next several hours. And, with time at a premium, there was only one sure and certain way to break Soloviev's clandestine link and obtain the necessary proof before it was too late. Direct action. Violent action.

GORKY PARK

Moscow's citizens were out in full force – enjoying the last few hours of a warm summer day. Couples strolled through the park hand in hand or sat on benches soaking up the welcome sunshine. Stripped to their shirt sleeves in the heat, bureaucrats and businessmen paused on their way home to play chess, to skim the afternoon editions of the government-controlled newspapers, or to down vodka or beer with friends and colleagues at one of Gorky's cafés. Others stood in groups shouting encouragement to the schoolchildren booting soccer balls up and down the park's sports grounds. A few madcap youths wearing in-line roller skates imported from the West raced each other down the winding paths, narrowly dodging slower-moving pedestrians. Halfhearted curses and shaken fists trailed after the grinning teens.

Erin McKenna stepped lithely aside from one howling, laughing pack, and paused in the shade of one of Gorky Park's two giant Ferris wheels. She swore a few times herself, but not at the skaters. Her curses were directed at Kaminov, the French, the Germans, and all the other idiots who were leading the world into another general war.

She'd just come from another hastily arranged meeting with Valentin Soloviev, and none of the news she was carrying back to Alex Banich and the others was good. According to the Russian colonel, his masters were within inches of reaching agreement with the French envoys. Kaminov had already issued preliminary war orders to the army and air force units poised on the Polish border, and even Russia's remaining ICBMs were on a higher state of alert.

Erin closed her eyes briefly, feeling the beginning of a tension headache knotting her temples. War and the threat of nuclear war between the United States and Russia, for God's sake! It was like reliving her worst childhood nightmares all over again. So much for the shortsighted, protectionist politicians who had bought votes by appealing to isolationism, raising barriers to foreign trade, and slashing defense and foreign aid, she thought angrily. They and the other opportunists like them around the globe had sown a bitter harvest – one that millions of innocents caught in the fighting were reaping now.

After the last of the long-haired roller skaters swooped past, she stepped back out onto the walking path and headed for the gray delivery van parked near the tall, towered Museum of Paleontology at the park's southern end. She knew that Banich, Hennessy, and the other CIA field agents covering her would want to report back to the embassy as soon as possible.

The footpath joined the sidewalk paralleling Kaluga Road a hundred meters short of Banich's van. There were even more people there, flowing into Gorky Park from the offices and high-rise apartments lining the other side of the busy street. Erin brushed past the small crowd watching a street performer juggling three balls and a kitchen knife and lengthened her stride. She was almost safe.

Two plain black sedans veered out of traffic and pulled up right beside her, brakes squealing sharply. Their rear doors popped open before they even stopped moving. Two men jumped out and rushed toward her – hard-faced, expressionless men wearing dark, look-alike suits.

Erin froze, horrified.

Before she could recover, they grabbed her, shoving her toward one of the waiting sedans.

A big, brutal-looking man standing near the second car motioned impatiently. '*Vite! Vite!*'

They were French! The realization shook Erin awake. Her diplomatic immunity might offer some small measure of protection against the Russians, but it offered none against kidnapping by French intelligence agents. Instincts honed by years of life in a big city and by the self-defense courses she'd taken came fully alive.

Now! She tore her arms loose from their grip, slammed an elbow into one man's stomach, then pivoted and drove her heel down hard on the other Frenchman's instep. They fell away. Momentarily free, she whirled and ran, angling away from the street – heading deeper into the wooded park.

'*Merde!*' Maj. Paul Duroc swore violently. He leaned out the window of the first car, motioning toward the fleeing woman. 'Woerner! Foret! Verdier! Chase her down!'

Humiliated by their first failure, the three men nodded abruptly and ran in pursuit.

Duroc pulled his head back inside the sedan, still seething. He'd counted on surprise and their semiofficial appearance to cow the woman long enough to get her inside and out of public view. It should have been both quick and reasonably discreet. Now everything was about to get a whole lot messier. He leaned forward and rapped on the clear partition separating him from the driver in the front seat. 'Head south and turn right past the museum. Then take the Pushkin Quay north. She can't stay in the goddamned trees forever.'

'Yes, Major.' The sedan pulled out into traffic and accelerated.

Intent on their prey, neither man noticed the delivery van pulling out right behind them.

Erin ran blindly onward, dodging people coming the other way or moving too slowly in the direction she was going. She could hear feet pounding after her and startled shouts as the people who'd stopped to stare were shoved out of the way. The French weren't giving up, but she couldn't risk glancing behind to see how close they were.

Beneath her mounting terror, she realized she'd made a fundamental mistake by running *away* from Banich's security team. Damn it, she thought, I'm supposed to be smarter than that. She'd let panic lead her down the path of least resistance. Now it was too late to try doubling back. She had to keep heading for the Moscow River – looking for a chance to shake her pursuers and reach one of the Agency's safe houses or find some other kind of help.

She flashed past a group of laughing children skipping rocks across the still waters of a weed-choked pond, hurtled through a cluster of their wide-eyed, astonished mothers, and plunged into the stand of trees beyond them. She heard a splash and shriek as a child went into the water. But nobody made a move to intervene.

Maybe that wasn't really very surprising. Decades of life under dictatorship had taught Muscovites when to look the other way. Especially when they saw a foreign-looking woman being chased by men who were obviously Chekists, secret policemen of some kind.

Erin lengthened her stride again, running faster now as she neared the river. Should she turn north or south once she reached the quay? South would take her closer to where she'd last seen Banich and the others. But north would take her back toward the bulk of Gorky Park, the Crimea Bridge, the giant Hotel Warsaw, and, most important of all, a Metro stop. That cinched it. She would go north. Moscow's intricate subway system offered her the best chance to evade pursuit and make her way to safety.

Still sprinting at top speed, she broke out of the woods and saw the sunlight sparkling on the river. Tall apartment buildings, the Frunze Quay housing complex, lined the opposite shore. She slanted north, flying down a gentle grassy slope to the edge of the road. An angry shout, more a bull roar than a human cry, told her that the three Frenchmen, breathing hard now, were falling behind.

She was outrunning them!

Her own labored breathing steadied as new energy surged through her body – the same burst of strength and endurance she'd always relied on to win distance races. As she opened the gap, pulling away from her pursuers, Erin felt the exhilaration she always experienced in victory.

And then her euphoria turned to despair.

A black sedan zoomed past her, braked wildly, and skidded sideways to a stop right in her path.

Erin tried to twist away, but she was running too fast and the car was just too close. Her ankle gave way when she tried to turn. She stumbled, lost her balance, and slammed into the side of the sedan while still moving flat out.

Pain flared red and the world went away for several seconds.

When the pain receded slightly, she found herself firmly held, her arms pinioned behind her back. Her captor, a short, narrow-faced man with pale blue eyes and a reptilian gaze, wasn't taking any chances. From the sound of the short-tempered orders he snapped out to the three sheepish men who'd been chasing her on foot, he was in charge of this whole operation.

Operation, Erin thought numbly. Now, *there* was a ridiculously neutral term to describe her own kidnapping. Her escape attempt had failed. She was a French prisoner.

The sound of another engine snapped her head back up in time to see a battered gray delivery van pull up beside the black sedan. The van's side door slid open and Alex Banich jumped down onto the grass, his face carefully blank. Hennessy and another CIA agent named Phil Teppler appeared over his shoulder.

Banich stepped forward, addressing the man who held her in slurred, uneducated, working-class Russian. 'Is there a problem here, friend? Don't you think you should let go of that poor lady's arms?'

Duroc watched the three men climb down out of the van with increasing irritation. First that ridiculous, comic-opera chase through the park, and now this interference by a few grubby Russian passersby – workmen by the look of their filthy coveralls. He scowled. What should have been a smooth, professional snatch was rapidly deteriorating into a bloody farce.

The first one out of the van, a short, brown-haired man about his own height, said something in Russian – something that sounded hard-edged and menacing despite his soft tone.

'He wants you to let the lady go, Major,' rat-faced Foret translated.

'Does he now?' Duroc sneered. Then he shook his head angrily. They didn't have time for this chivalrous nonsense. By now, even Moscow's sleepy militia must be on their way here.

The DGSE agent transferred his grip to the woman's neck, reached inside his jacket, and pulled the 9mm Makarov automatic out of his shoulder holster. Then he pointed the pistol at the man, sighting on his midriff. 'Tell this goddamned peasant to back off, Foret. Tell him this is official business.'

Incredibly, despite the warning and the pistol pointing in his direction, the man took another step forward. His hands hovered near his side.

Exasperated, Duroc flipped the Makarov's safety catch off and raised his aim. Maybe the sight of death staring him right in the face would knock some sense into this pig-ignorant Russian's thick skull. 'He's got three seconds to live, Foret. One . . . two . . .'

Suddenly the red-haired woman writhed out of his grasp, trying desperately to grab his gun hand.

'Bitch!' Furious, Duroc yanked her back by the hair and then cuffed her out of the way with a single backhanded blow.

'Look out, Major!' big Michel Woerner shouted suddenly.

Alarmed, Duroc whirled around.

Too late. He felt something cold and sharp lancing into his own stomach, ripping up under his ribs. Then the pain hit, a tearing, flaming wall of agony, that darkened the whole world around him. His lungs were on fire. Maj. Paul Duroc stared down in appalled astonishment as the brown-haired man stepped back a pace, still holding a wide-bladed workman's knife stained red to the hilt.

Knife held ready to strike again if the Frenchman tried to use his pistol, Alex Banich watched the man he'd stabbed sag, slump to his knees, and then pitch over onto his side. The DGSE agent twitched a few times, coughed wetly, and died. Rich, red, arterial blood pooled on the grass beneath his gaping, slack-jawed mouth. The pistol fell out of his unclenched hand and lay at Banich's feet.

Without thinking further, he knelt down and scooped the Makarov up. Just in time.

The tallest of the four surviving Frenchmen snarled something guttural and ugly, clawing for his own holstered weapon. Banich saw the pistol come clear and turn toward him.

'Alex!' Erin screamed.

Damn it. He squeezed the trigger three times in rapid succession, firing at point-blank range. The first 9mm round caught the Frenchman in the chest and threw him backward. The second blew the top of the man's head off. The third missed.

Banich swiveled rapidly, bringing the rest of the DGSE operatives into his sights. Stunned by the sudden carnage and their leaders' deaths, they paled and carefully raised empty hands.

'Watch 'em!' At his command, Hennessy and Teppler moved closer to frisk the captive Frenchmen, holding their own unsheathed knives at the ready. Their choice of weapons made sense for agents working under cover. If they were stopped and searched by the Moscow militia or security services, carrying firearms would sign their death warrants, but many Russian workers carried knives.

The French, all fight beaten out of them by the unexpected turn of events, willingly submitted to being searched. One by one, three more pistols were found and confiscated.

'That's it, they're clean,' Hennessy said over his shoulder.

Banich nodded. 'Good. Okay, here's what we'll do . . .'

'Hold it! Hands up! Get your hands up!' The shout came from higher up the slope, near the edge of the woods.

Banich turned slowly and saw a group of very young-looking Russian militiamen cautiously advancing toward them – emerging from the trees with their weapons out and aimed. Red and blue lights flashed in the distance. Militia squad cars were closing in from both sides of the quay, sealing off any hope of escape.

'Do as they say,' Banich said quietly. He dropped the pistol and raised his hands in surrender. He saw the horrified look on Erin McKenna's face and felt sick. He'd killed two men to save her from captivity and he'd still failed. Now he couldn't save any of them.

CHAPTER 33
Preemptive Strike

JULY 1 – MILITIA HEADQUARTERS, MOSCOW

Moscow's militia, the city's police force, had its main headquarters in a large yellow-brick building on Petrovka Street, several blocks north of the Kremlin and the Bolshoi Theater. The six floors aboveground contained offices for the militia's investigators and administrators, forensic labs, an armory, and evidence storage rooms. Drunks and other petty criminals were dealt with by the district stations scattered across the capital and its outlying suburbs, but dangerous or politically important prisoners awaiting interrogation or trial were held in small cells buried deep in the building's subbasement, below an underground parking garage.

Bone-weary after a sleepless night, Alex Banich sat hunched over on his cell's only piece of furniture – an iron-frame cot inadequately cushioned by a single, folded wool blanket. He closed his eyes against the painful glare coming from the single, unshielded light bulb above his head. The light had been left on all night.

All night . . . Banich straightened up slightly. Since the guards had stripped him of his watch before they'd thrown him inside this cell, he couldn't be sure of the exact time. But the exact time didn't especially matter. What mattered was that it had to be close to dawn outside. That meant he and the others had been in militia custody for at least ten hours. So where were the FIS interrogators? He, Hennessy, and Teppler were all operating with false identification papers, but Erin and those French bastards certainly weren't. Any case involving foreigners was clearly the province of the FIS – not the Moscow militia. Then why this delay in handing them over to the counterintelligence agency? Bureaucratic infighting? Some kind of clerical glitch or other administrative foul-up? Or something else, something more significant?

And what about the three DGSE agents who had survived that bloody encounter in the park? Had they already been released? He'd heard cell doors clanging open and muffled voices down the corridor some time ago. He nodded grimly to himself. For all practical purposes, France and Russia were already allies. Kaminov's security chiefs might have some pointed questions about what the French had been up to, but they weren't likely to jeopardize their leader's hard-won ties with Paris just to have them answered. Not when they had four other captives to quiz.

Banich found himself running through different scenarios and options using his knowledge of the Russian agencies and personalities in play. Realistically he knew the effort was probably a meaningless mental exercise – akin to asking a blindfolded man to find one particular person in a crowded football stadium. Still, it helped him fend off his fears for Erin, his men, and himself for a little while longer.

Not that he had many illusions about his likely fate. Murder convictions under martial law carried one sentence – death. If the FIS broke his Ushenko cover story and identified him as a CIA agent, the sentence would be the same. Only the method of carrying it out would change – a secret death after prolonged interrogation and torture instead of swift public execution. The French were bound to insist on at least that much as compensation for their two dead spies.

Faced with the evidence against him, he doubted Langley would want to make much of a fuss over his 'disappearance.' Senior Agency field operatives were not supposed to kill rival intelligence agents – especially in broad daylight in an ostensibly neutral capital. They certainly weren't supposed to get caught.

And what about Erin and the others? Despite the close, confined, muggy air in his cell, Banich felt suddenly cold. He knew how Kaminov and those who toadied to him thought. Four 'disappearances' were as easy to explain as one. Maybe even easier, since there would be no one left alive to dispute whatever story the marshal's military junta concocted.

Boots rang on the bare concrete floor of the corridor beyond his cell, coming closer. They stopped right outside the cell door. A key grated in the lock, and he barely had time to stand up before the door slammed open. Four militiamen waited outside, a flabby, middle-aged sergeant and three leaner, fitter privates. All had their pistols drawn. Through the rising tide of his despair, Banich found a moment's pale amusement in that. Clearly these Russians at least regarded him as a very dangerous fellow indeed.

'You! Come out of there.' The sergeant jerked his head back down the corridor. 'You're wanted upstairs for a little chat.'

Banich sighed. This was it, then. The Russian counterintelligence agency had finally shaken off its curious bureaucratic lethargy and come to inspect its prizes. He thought about squaring his shoulders, but then decided that a stoop-shouldered, dejected look would be more in character for a bewildered, hard working Ukrainian merchant caught up in events through no fault of his own. Although he doubted his cover identity would hold up for very long under determined investigation, he planned to play it out for as long as possible. Every hour that passed gave Len Kutner that much more time to find out what had happened to the four of them. If nothing else, he might be able to buy enough time for the rest of his field team to get clear.

He stepped warily out into the corridor. The militiamen closed in around him, with the sergeant and one private in back, and two more ahead.

'Move!' Banich felt a pistol barrel grind painfully into his back, just above his left kidney, prodding him onward. He stumbled into motion, trying to mask a sudden flash of anger beneath a properly submissive, frightened expression. Nikolai Ushenko was a man of money, not a man of action.

They marched him down the narrow basement corridor at a brisk pace, past rows of other locked cell doors. The clipboards hanging beside each bore only a number – never any names. Russia's new military rulers hadn't abandoned their old and ugly penchant for dehumanizing those who crossed them, he thought scornfully.

Banich's guards led him up two flights of stairs and out into an empty hallway toward the rear of the militia headquarters. The marble floor, faded photographs and paintings of senior officials, and crowded notice boards told him they were somewhere in the more public areas of the building. This early in the morning there were very few militia officers or civilian clerical workers in evidence. Occupied offices were indicated only by a light under the door, and occasionally by the soft rattle of keys on a word processor or the low, whooshing hum of a photocopier in operation. The Petrovka Street headquarters, like the rest of Moscow, was just starting to come to life.

Despite his fatigue, Banich noticed that all of his senses were fully alert and finely tuned. Sights, sounds, and smells were all magnified as the animal side of his brain sensed danger ahead and began reacting – preparing to fight or flee. The world, even this small, sterile portion of it, seemed clearer and sharper than ever before.

The sergeant stopped outside a solid-looking, wood-paneled door and pushed it open. 'Inside.'

Still in character, Banich turned toward the NCO with a pleading whine on his face and in his voice. 'Please, Sergeant, I swear that I am an honest man, not a criminal . . .'

The sergeant snorted, 'Of course.' He shoved Banich through the doorway. 'Inside, pig!'

They pulled the door shut behind him.

The room was not what he'd expected. Instead of a drab interrogation chamber, he was alone in a handsomely appointed conference room – complete with dark wood paneling, carpet, a long, polished table, and upholstered armchairs. He sniffed the air, caught the scent of fresh, hot tea, and turned.

Tall glasses in metal holders stood on a sideboard next to a samovar. A nearby tray held slices of lemon, spoons, and a dish of fruit jelly. Banich arched an eyebrow in surprise. What the hell was all of this? A ploy to soften him up before the gloves came off? Was the tea drugged? he wondered.

He stood uncertainly for a few moments, then shrugged and moved toward the sideboard. He had to react as Nikolai Ushenko, not as a professionally suspicious American intelligence officer. The Ukrainian commodities trader he'd created would never pass up the chance for a free cup of tea. Even if it was drugged, at least pouring his own would give him some control over the dosage.

'I've always thought that you led a very interesting life for a simple merchant, Mr. Ushenko. Now I see I was right.'

Banich replaced the glass he'd selected and turned toward the familiar voice. Col. Valentin Soloviev stood poised in the doorway, holding a dossier in one hand. As always, the Russian soldier's dress uniform looked freshly pressed. He was suddenly conscious of his own bedraggled, unshaven appearance.

Soloviev came in and closed the door.

'I don't see why I'm being held prisoner like this, Colonel,' Banich protested automatically, thinking fast. What was Soloviev doing here? 'All I did was help a poor woman who was being mugged.'

'Killing two French security agents in the process.' The Russian seemed amused. 'And the woman turns out to be an American diplomat who is also suspected of being a spy. A curious coincidence, indeed. Almost impossible to believe, in fact.' His voice turned harsher. 'But not so hard when one realizes exactly how you came to be in that particular place at that particular time.

'Let's be honest with each other. There was no good reason for a man named Nikolai Ushenko to be in Gorky Park yesterday afternoon, or for such a man to interfere in what must have looked very much like an official arrest – not a "mugging." ' Soloviev smiled thinly. 'But we *both* know there was a very good reason for an American CIA officer to be there, don't we, Mr. Banich?'

Shit. He tried to brazen it out. 'Who?'

'Don't play games with me. Neither of us has any time to waste.' Soloviev opened the dossier he was carrying and tossed two black-and-white surveillance photos onto the table.

Banich looked down at them. Both showed him in a suit and tie, holding a drink in one hand. They must have been taken at one of the innumerable trade conferences he'd attended shortly after arriving in Moscow. Damn it.

Soloviev nodded. 'Unless you just happen to have an exact double stationed at the American embassy, those pictures identify you as Alexander Banich – ostensibly a somewhat simpleminded deputy assistant economic attaché.'

The colonel shook his head in mock disappointment. 'It seems that my secret-police colleagues at the FIS have been rather sloppy, Mr. Banich. Their file describes you as "a nonentity, an Ivy League drone, and a borderline alcoholic." ' He shrugged. 'I must admit that your work has been brilliant. I suspected that the man I knew as Ushenko might be feeding confidential information back to Ukraine. But I never dreamed you were an American espionage agent.'

Banich felt dizzy. He looked up sharply, suddenly tired of Soloviev's cat-and-mouse game. 'If you're so goddamned sure of that, Colonel, where's the FIS? Why aren't they here to haul me away?'

The other man eyed him grimly. 'For two very good reasons, Mr. Banich. First, they don't know what I know about your identity. And second, they don't yet know anything about what happened in Gorky Park yesterday afternoon.'

'What?' Banich couldn't conceal his surprise. 'Why not?'

'Because I am not the only Russian of rank opposed to this illegal regime and its insane policies, Mr. Banich. General Pikhoia is another.'

The American whistled silently. Maj. Gen. Konstantin Pikhoia commanded the whole Moscow militia force. No wonder the word about Gorky Park hadn't leaked yet. He found himself reappraising Soloviev. Allies that highly placed put the colonel in a very different context. Not as a lone wolf, after all, but instead as the point man for an opposition movement operating covertly inside Kaminov's martial law government itself. Was such a thing possible?

Yes, he judged. The marshal's purges had been directed primarily at the most outspoken supporters of democratic ideals in the military and the ministries. Officers and officials who were more discreet or more farsighted could easily have clung to their posts with an outward show of loyalty to Russia's new rulers. Men like Soloviev.

Banich nodded. Playing that kind of double game must be familiar to those who had risen in rank during the old Soviet Union's last days. For the first time he began to see a way out of the deadly box he'd put Erin and the others inside. Soloviev, Pikhoia, and their compatriots would have every incentive to hush this whole affair up. But then an unpleasant thought struck him. 'What about the French? By now they must be back in their embassy screaming at the top of their lungs to anyone who'll listen. And once the FIS starts asking pointed questions, both you and the general are going to be sitting pretty far out on a damned thin limb.'

Soloviev's pale blue eyes grew cold. 'I can assure you that those three gentlemen of the DGSE will not be shouting to anyone . . . ever.'

Oh. Banich's estimation of the man in front of him as one ruthless bastard went up another notch. He gave in to a sudden impulse to needle the other man. 'You don't fool around very much, do you, Colonel? Someone gets in your way and *bang*, they're dead.'

'Perhaps.' The Russian's thin-lipped mouth tightened. 'But then the same could probably be said of you, couldn't it, Mr. Banich?'

Maybe so, Banich admitted to himself, remembering the two men he'd killed while trying to rescue Erin.

Soloviev shook his head in abrupt exasperation. 'All of this is beside the point, however. We face much larger problems, you and I.' He pulled a chair out from the table and waved Banich toward another.

Somehow the Russian colonel looked older and wearier off his feet. 'I've just come from an all-night negotiating session, Mr. Banich.' He leaned forward and lowered his voice. 'Kaminov has reached a final agreement with the French. Once he issues the go-ahead orders, my nation's armed forces will cross into Poland. And our two countries will find themselves at war with each other within hours after that.'

This bad news, though expected, still hit Banich with sledgehammer force. If they were caught between two fires, the U.S., British, and Polish troops fighting in Poland were doomed. Russian intervention in the war would leave the U.S. policymakers with just two unpalatable options. Accept defeat and a Europe forcibly united under a hostile banner. Or prepare for a prolonged war that would make World War II look like a child's tea party.

Banich swallowed hard, staring blindly down at the table in front of him. 'It'll be a goddamned bloodbath.'

Soloviev nodded somberly. 'Yes, it will be. *If* we allow it to happen.'

Puzzled, Banich stared back at him. 'What exactly do you mean by that, Colonel?'

The Russian's eyes grew even colder. 'The orders that will commit my country to this conflict have not yet been issued. In fact, they cannot be issued until Marshal Kaminov and the other members of the Military Council arrive back in Moscow and regain their access to the Defense Ministry's secure-communications channels. Therefore, I believe the equation is simple: if we stop those orders from being given, we can stop this war before it escalates.'

Prevent Kaminov from contacting his field commanders? How on earth did Soloviev propose . . . The answer flashed into his mind. In that instant, the whole world seemed to narrow down to the Russian colonel's grim face. 'Are you serious?'

Soloviev nodded. When he spoke, his voice was flat, utterly without emotion. 'Deadly serious, Mr. Banich.'

MILITIA HEADQUARTERS

Flanked by armed guards, Erin McKenna followed the paunchy militia sergeant who had ushered her out of her cell. She kept her head held high. She didn't want to give these people the satisfaction of seeing her frightened or distressed in any way. But she couldn't stop the panic welling up inside as she contemplated the next few hours. Alex Banich had said she wasn't ready to take prolonged torture and interrogation, and he was right. Oddly enough, though, she found the prospect of being forced to betray Soloviev and her friends and colleagues far more horrifying than the physical pain and mental anguish she expected to suffer.

Her guards came to a heavy metal door at the end of the hallway and halted, waiting while the sergeant fumbled with his keys and unlocked it. When the door swung open, a sickly-sweet stench waited inside – the smell of diesel exhaust mixed with rotting garbage. Erin gasped softly. The door opened out onto the back of the headquarters building, into a narrow alley crowded with overflowing trash bins. Where were they taking her?

Several men wearing Russian Army uniforms were busy hurriedly loading an odd assortment of long crates and boxes onto a pair of canvas-sided URAL trucks parked just down the alley. Two officers, one tall and slender, the other somewhat shorter, stood with their backs to her, supervising the loading process. Another man, much younger and wearing civilian clothes, waited beside a black ZIL sedan – an official staff car of some kind. Five shapes swathed in drab-green army blankets lay on stretchers lining one side of the alley. When two soldiers picked up the first stretcher and carried it toward a truck, an arm fell out from under the blanket – dangling lifelessly until one of the men shoved it back out of sight. To her horror, she realized the blanket-shrouded shapes were corpses.

She hesitated in the doorway, unwilling to go further. Fears that until then had been largely abstract, the product of her own imagination, were rapidly becoming real.

'Let's go, Little Miss Precious,' the sergeant grumbled. He grabbed her arm and hustled her down the small set of steps. She briefly considered resisting but decided against it. Fighting back would only give the odious twerp another excuse to paw her body.

Still gripping her arm, the militia noncom marched her up behind the tall army officer, stamped his feet as he came to attention, and loudly announced, 'The female prisoner you wanted, Colonel!'

Erin had to stifle another astonished gasp when the soldier turned around.

Col. Valentin Soloviev stared down at her without a hint of recognition. 'An attractive specimen, Sergeant. You've enjoyed having her in your custody, eh?'

'Yes, Colonel.' The middle-aged jailer smirked. 'Makes a nice change from the usual riffraff we get. A real tasty morsel.'

'Yes.' Soloviev pulled his eyes away from Erin to study the militia NCO. A look that mingled disdain and anger flickered across his face before he nodded toward the door in polite dismissal. 'Thank you, Sergeant. That will be all. I'll take charge of this prisoner now.' His voice hardened. 'But you can be sure I will remember everything you have done.'

The words were pleasant enough, but something about the way he said them sent a shiver down Erin's spine and wiped the self-satisfied smile off the militiaman's pudgy face. Suddenly pale, her jailer hurried back into the headquarters building.

After the door swung shut behind him, Soloviev swung back to face her. 'My dear Miss McKenna. I sincerely hope you're all right?'

Speechless with relief, she could only nod.

'Good.' The Russian smiled then. He inclined his head toward where the other man wearing an army officer's uniform stood, still with his back to them. 'I would introduce you to my new aide-de-camp, but I believe you already know each other.'

He raised his voice. 'Captain Banich?'

Erin could scarcely believe her eyes when Alex Banich spun lightly around to face her.

He grinned faintly. 'Hello, McKenna.'

'Alex!' The knowledge that he was safe and free brought feelings she'd been holding back for months to the surface in a torrent. All the game-playing, teasing, and tiptoeing around real emotion disappeared in the abrupt realization that she was in love with this quiet man. Without thinking, she was in his arms.

Neither of them saw the fleeting look of sadness and disappointment cross Soloviev's normally impassive face. It disappeared as suddenly as it had come.

Reminded of where they were by a discreet cough from the Russian, Erin pulled away slightly from Banich. She fingered the thick cloth of his uniform tunic and looked closely at him. 'How on earth did you . . .'

'Not me. Him.' Banich nodded toward Soloviev. Talking fast, he filled her in on the events of the past several hours. When he came to the marshal's decision to intervene on EurCon's behalf, he slowed down and looked away as he continued, 'The colonel has a plan to stop Kaminov in his tracks, but he needs our help to pull it off.'

'Our . . .' For the first time, Erin noticed Mike Hennessy and Phil Teppler among the Russian enlisted men loading the two trucks. Both saw her looking at them and grinned back. She turned her gaze on Soloviev. 'Am I included in this plan of yours, Colonel?'

'Regrettably no, Miss McKenna. Mr. Banich and the others have weapons skills we will need. You do not.' The Russian sounded relieved more then regretful. He pointed to the young man waiting next to the ZIL sedan. 'Plekhanov there will escort you back to your embassy instead. Taking you where we must go would only expose you to grave danger without purpose.'

Banich seconded that. 'He's right. Besides, somebody has to fill Washington in on what's happened already and what may yet happen if we fail.'

Erin looked again at the uniform he was wearing. 'Then at least tell me what you're going to try to do.'

He shook his head sadly. 'I can't.'

'Why not?' she demanded. Fear for him made her tone sharper than she'd intended. 'Don't you trust me?'

'You know I do.' Banich put his hands on her shoulders and looked deeply into her eyes. His voice grew quieter. 'But we're about to do something that's absolutely illegal. If we fail, I'll probably be dead. Even if we succeed, I could still be crucified by the Agency, the Congress, or the courts. Whatever happens, I don't want you dragged down with me. Keeping you at least partly in the dark is the only way I can make sure that doesn't happen. Can you understand that?'

'Yes,' Erin whispered softly, fighting back tears. Crying now wouldn't help either of them. She wiped her eyes and forced a smile. 'But you'd better not get yourself killed, Alex Banich. I look pretty awful in black.'

He grinned tightly himself, appreciating the effort she was making to keep her sorrow at bay. 'Understood, McKenna.' Then he leaned forward and kissed her.

Soloviev's voice broke in on them. 'It's time we were on our way, Mr. Banich. The trucks are loaded.'

'Coming, Colonel.' Banich gently disengaged himself from her embrace. He kissed her again, softly this time. 'I'll be back.' Then he stepped back.

The Russian moved in front of him. 'I will say my good-byes here, Miss McKenna. Whatever happens, I do not believe that we will see each other again.' The tall colonel bowed slightly, then straightened up. He smiled gravely. 'You know, you really are a most remarkable woman.'

Erin had the strange feeling that the man wanted to say more and couldn't.

Abruptly Soloviev turned away, striding toward the waiting trucks. Banich fell in beside him. One after the other, the two men swung themselves up into the cab of the lead truck.

As soon as they were inside, powerful diesel engines coughed to life and the trucks lurched forward. She lifted her hand briefly in a silent farewell, then stood watching as they rolled out of the alley onto Petrovka Street and disappeared from her sight.

OUTSIDE MOSCOW, ON THE YALTA HIGHWAY

The two canvas-sided trucks rumbled down the highway, rolling south at a steady sixty kilometers per hour, well within the legal speed limit. None of the men crowded aboard each vehicle wanted to attract any unnecessary attention to themselves or their cargo.

Inside the lead truck, Soloviev leaned forward, peering out through the windshield while studying the forest off to the right side of the highway. He nodded to himself and turned to their driver, a young Russian lieutenant wearing a private's uniform. 'The access road is just ahead, Pasha. You'll see it when we come around the next bend.'

The lieutenant bobbed his head nervously. 'Yes, Colonel.' He tightened his grip on the big URAL's steering wheel.

Soloviev glanced at the man sitting on his right. 'The checkpoint is only a few hundred meters up the access road. You know what to do?'

Alex Banich nodded. 'Yes.' He checked the automatic lying in his lap one last time, making sure the silencer screwed on its barrel was secure and that he had a full clip. Then he slipped the pistol back inside his uniform jacket and settled back, trying to fight off the doubts crowding in on him.

What had seemed so necessary and so possible back in the militia headquarters conference room seemed more and more insane the closer they got to the isolated, wooded enclave surrounding Kaminov's dacha. If this wild-eyed scheme of Soloviev's backfired in any way, he thought, Russia would have a perfect excuse to act against the United States – a ready-made *casus belli* handed them by yours truly.

Banich shook his head grimly. Now, *there* was an unpleasant thought.

The truck wheeled off the main highway and turned onto a narrow, winding road heading west. Pine trees lined both sides, and the overarching branches broke the track ahead of them into a dappled stretch of alternating sunlight and shadow. Birds, frightened by their growling engines, took flight – screeching and wheeling through the clear air above the forest before fluttering away.

'There it is, Colonel.'

Banich looked up at the driver's muttered warning to Soloviev. He squinted through the dust-streaked windshield.

The checkpoint was just ahead.

A wood barricade dotted with reflectors and painted a bright orange and white closed off the road, but a set of tire spikes pulled across the road behind the barricade was the real vehicle stopper. Two soldiers with AK-74 assault rifles lounged near a wooden sentry box on the left. Blue shoulder patches marked with a sword and shield identified them as uniformed members of an FIS security unit. Four more FIS troopers manned two sandbagged machine-gun nests – one sited on each side of the access road. An officer wearing a peaked cap was just stepping out of the sentry box, yawning and adjusting his pistol belt.

Banich frowned. This was going to be tricky. They were facing seven men with only six – Soloviev, Banich himself, Hennessy, Teppler, and the two young Russian Army officers the colonel had been able to round up at short notice. The trouble with the democratic conspiracy inside Kaminov's government, the Russian colonel had remarked wryly, was that it had far too many chiefs and far too few Indians. Ostensibly, that was why he'd jumped at the chance to recruit Banich's team. In the back of his mind, the CIA agent also had the sneaking suspicion the Russian planned to use the Americans as fall guys if anything went wrong. Soloviev struck him as a survivor, not a martyr.

The truck slowed and came to a complete stop within meters of the barricade. Their second vehicle stopped right behind them. The FIS officer, a captain, stepped forward smartly. 'Your papers, please.' He recognized Soloviev sitting in the middle and started. 'Colonel Soloviev? What are you doing there? Where's your staff car?'

The Russian colonel shrugged. 'Broken down about five kilometers back up the highway, Vorisov. Whichever idiot checked it last missed something pretty big. I must have been leaking oil since leaving Moscow.' He laughed sourly. 'If I hadn't been escorting these boys here, I'd have had to hitchhike.'

'Damned mechanics.' The FIS captain shook his head in sympathy. Then his eyes narrowed slightly. 'But why are you here now, sir? Didn't they tell you? These big hush-hush meetings are over. Everyone's supposed to be heading back to the city any moment now.'

Soloviev chuckled. 'So I hear. But you know the high brass. The marshal asked me to bring down some extra "supplies." Cases of them.' He winked and tossed off an imaginary glass of vodka. 'Seems they're having themselves quite a party.'

Banich clamped down on a grin. Marshal Kaminov was an old-fashioned Russian – the kind of man who would insist on celebrating the birth of this new Franco-Russian military partnership with a liberally poured vodka baptism. And, from the look on the guard captain's face, Soloviev's story had struck a receptive chord.

'Supplies, eh?' the man said slowly. He rubbed his jaw, obviously debating with himself. But with temptation and duty both on the same side for once, the struggle was over quickly. 'I suppose I should inspect those cases before I pass you through . . . just to be safe.'

Soloviev showed his teeth. 'Ivan Andreivich, I wouldn't have it any other way. I'll even help you.' He glanced at Banich. 'In the meantime, Ushenko here and his boys can have a little stretch or take a leak. Right, Captain?'

Banich nodded briefly, hiding his relief. If the FIS officer hadn't taken their vodka bait, things could have gotten messy fast. But Soloviev had been reasonably confident the ploy would work. Despite years of official antidrinking campaigns, alcoholism was still a major killer among Russian men. Even more important, underlings in rigid hierarchies take their cues from their superiors – and Kaminov and the men around him were all hard drinkers.

The American climbed down out of the truck cab and signaled Hennessy and the others in the second truck. 'Everybody out! We're taking a short break. Move it!'

Out the corner of his eye, he saw Soloviev leading the FIS officer around to the back of that second truck. His pulse accelerated. Any second now.

Banich began walking toward one of the machine-gun positions, stretching and twisting as though he were shaking loose the knots wound up by an uncomfortable journey. Fear, not fatigue, made him yawn once and then again, deeper and longer. With an effort, he shut his mouth and moved closer.

The two FIS guards manning the PK machine gun ignored him. Like their commander, they were more interested in the contents of the trucks. He saw one of them nudge the other and grin. Maybe they thought this Captain Vorisov would share the results of his 'inspection' with them.

Phut. Phut. The sound of Soloviev's two silenced shots spurred Banich into action. His right hand darted inside his uniform jacket and came back out holding his own silenced automatic. Everything around him slowed as adrenaline altered his time sense.

One of the startled gunners saw the weapon in his hand and opened his mouth to yell a warning. Banich squeezed the trigger – firing again and again. Hit by two or three rounds apiece, both FIS men crumpled. One screamed and fell forward over the machine gun with a huge, red-rimmed hole in his back. He shuddered once and then lay still. Struck in the stomach and head, the second guard sprawled back against the sandbags, staring up at the sky with unblinking eyes.

The American turned rapidly, scanning for new targets. There weren't any. The other checkpoint guards were already down and dead or dying. He tugged the partly empty magazine out of the Makarov and snapped in a fresh clip. Hennessy, Teppler, and Soloviev's two Russian officers were doing the same thing with their own silenced weapons.

Soloviev himself came around the side of the truck, dragging the dead FIS captain by his arms. 'Don't stand there! Move! Haul those corpses off into the trees! We haven't much time.' He dumped the guard officer out of sight and turned around, looking for the lieutenant who had driven the first truck. 'Pasha! Clear those vehicles off to the side of the road. Hurry up!'

It took several minutes of frantic effort to restore the checkpoint to a semblance of normal order. While Banich and the others hauled the bodies of the guards they'd killed out of sight, Soloviev scrambled up into the lead truck's cargo bay and began unloading the long, narrow boxes he'd commandeered from the militia headquarters armory – boxes containing RPG-16 antitank rocket launchers, ammunition, and more AK-74 assault rifles. As each man came back from his grisly task, the colonel handed him a weapon and a pair of gloves.

All of them started when the sentry box phone rang – shrill in the eerie silence hanging over the checkpoint. Soloviev jumped to answer it. He listened briefly, answered in a gruff voice, and then poked his head back out through the open door. 'Get ready! The French delegation is leaving now. Kaminov and the rest will follow shortly.'

Three big black official sedans came barreling around a bend just minutes later. Tiny French flags fluttered from the hood of each car. The cars braked, waiting just long enough for them to pull the tire spikes off the road and shoulder the barricade aside. Then they accelerated again, whizzing past the checkpoint without stopping. With a treaty signed, sealed, and in hand, Ambassador Sauret and the rest of his negotiators were evidently in a tearing hurry to get back to Paris.

Once the last French limousine disappeared around another curve, Soloviev, Banich, and the others exploded into action. Hennessy, Teppler, and the two junior Russian officers replaced the barricade and tire barrier, grabbed loaded assault rifles, and trotted up the access road toward the dacha. Banich and the colonel both scooped up an RPG-16 launcher and a pack containing extra rounds and followed their men – staying well inside the trees lining the road.

They'd gone only a hundred meters or so when they heard the sound of several engines rumbling closer, but that was far enough to lose sight of the deserted checkpoint past a curve in the winding road.

At a hand signal from Soloviev, the rifle-armed men faded back into cover, hunkering down in the shadows under the trees. Their two leaders did the same. The Russian glanced at Banich. 'The first vehicle, understand?'

Banich nodded impatiently. 'I know.' He settled the RPG on his shoulder after making sure he'd remembered to remove the safety pin from its antitank warhead.

'Just checking.' Soloviev surprised him by grinning. 'Take away the trees and this could be Afghanistan all over again . . . only I would be on the other side, of course.' He clapped the American on the shoulder. 'Don't miss!'

Then the Russian was gone, cradling his own rocket launcher as he hurried forward – dodging tree trunks and patches of sunlight. The engine noises grew louder.

Banich stayed absolutely still as the first vehicles came into view. The convoy was organized exactly the way Soloviev had said it would be. A GAZ-69 jeep with a light machine gun in a pintle mount was in the lead. The driver, machine gunner, and two passengers, both officers, all wore the blue shoulder flash of the FIS. Three armored limousines came next – each an identical black and with tinted windows that hid their occupants from public view. He tensed. Kaminov, the high-ranking officers who were his closest subordinates, and their personal bodyguards were riding inside those three vehicles.

An eight-wheeled BTR-80 armored personnel carrier with a turret-mounted heavy machine gun brought up the rear. Like the four-wheel-drive Blazers the U.S. Secret Service used as 'war wagons' to carry extra agents, commo gear, and heavy weapons, the BTR was a formidable fighting machine. The FIS troops it carried rode up top, helmeted heads poking through open fighting hatches on the BTR's deck. One man near the rear carried a shoulder-launched SA-16 for protection against air attack.

God. Banich blinked away the sweat trickling into his eyes. Odds that had sounded awfully high when Soloviev first outlined his hastily formulated plan now seemed insurmountable. This was not going to work. His hands started to tremble. Oh, Erin . . .

The jeep leading the convoy rolled past his position. Now! Banich stood up, all fear buried beneath the overriding need to make his shot count. He squinted through the rocket launcher's sight, steadied on target, and fired.

Whummph. The RPG round flashed across the intervening distance, slammed into the dashboard on the driver's side, and detonated. Five pounds of high explosive tore the open-topped vehicle apart in a searing ball of flame. It flipped over and landed sideways across the road.

Through the smoke, Banich saw Soloviev rise, take careful aim, and fire a HEAT round directly into the BTR-80's thinly armored flank. The APC exploded. Sheets of bright red fire flared out through every open hatch, fed by fuel and ammunition stored aboard. Pieces of burned bodies arced out from the exploding vehicle.

In that single horrifying instant, all hell broke loose.

Caught traveling just meters behind the jeep Banich's warhead had mangled, the lead armored limousine roared ahead and crashed into the flaming wreckage at thirty kilometers an hour. The massive grinding impact threw both vehicles across the road and into the trees in a shower of sparks and shrieking metal. When they stopped spinning, both were locked together – completely blocking the access road.

The second black sedan skidded wildly, sliding sideways as it braked, narrowly avoiding the collision just ahead. But then the driver of the last car, less alert or maybe distracted by the blinding flash in his rearview mirror, smashed head-on into the side of the fishtailing vehicle. Broken glass, crumpled metal, and torn rubber flew outward from the impact point.

The world seemed to stand still for a moment – frozen at a lone point in time. Both ends of the narrow road were barred. Kaminov's convoy was cut off – unable to go forward and unable to go back.

Car doors popped open, shattering the stasis. Dazed-looking men began scrambling out of the wrecked limousines, clawing their way past others who couldn't move because they were too badly stunned or injured. A few, younger than the rest, clutched snub-nosed AKR assault carbines – staring wildly in all directions at the woods around them. Kaminov's bodyguards, Banich realized.

He knelt down, pawing through the satchel in front of him for another RPG round.

With their targets out in the open now, Mike Hennessy, Teppler, and the Russian lieutenants opened up from the treeline, firing on full automatic. Men jerked wildly, spun around and ripped apart by the dozens of hollow-point bullets hammering the area around the wrecked cars. Panicked screams rose above the gunfire and then faded away.

Those few who survived the first murderous fusillade turned and tried to run, stumbling away into the trees. They didn't get far.

Hennessy and the others stalked across the road and went after them, firing aimed three-round bursts on the move. When the firing stopped, silence fell over the ambush site – a silence broken only by the crackling flames consuming the destroyed jeep and APC.

Soloviev stepped out onto the corpse-strewn road, still carrying the rocket launcher he had used. 'Pasha! Take Vanya and bring that second truck up here! The one with the dead Frenchmen inside. We'll leave them here, by our weapons.'

The young lieutenant nodded sharply, slung his rifle, and signaled his counterpart. Both took off down the access road at a run. At the same time, Hennessy and Teppler came back from their hunt looking pale. They understood the need to make sure no one survived the ambush, but that didn't mean they enjoyed butchering men who weren't even trying to fight back.

Banich came out of the trees to join Soloviev by the second smashed limousine. He grimaced, trying to control his nausea as he surveyed the carnage. 'Why waste time planting Duroc and his men, Colonel? No investigator in his right mind would tie them into this!'

The Russian looked up at the smoke billowing above the trees before glancing down at him. 'We still have ten minutes or so before the first patrols will arrive here, Mr. Banich. As far as any investigation is concerned . . .' He shrugged. 'In America, the truth may be of paramount importance, but in Russia, the truth is *always* what is convenient for those in power. And once the dust settles from this day, it will be very convenient to blame the French for this butchery.'

He shrugged again. 'It makes a compelling story, you understand. Outraged by the heroic Marshal Kaminov's refusal to stab Poland in the back, renegade French security agents took their revenge here and then fled in panic – leaving a few of their fallen comrades behind.' Soloviev nodded toward one of the corpses lying at Banich's feet. 'An old and tired story of foreign treachery, I agree – but one familiar to many of my older countrymen. It will make that man's death easier for them to understand and accept.'

'I see.' Banich stared down at the corpse in front of him. The bulletproof vest the old man had been wearing hadn't been good enough to stop high-velocity rounds fired at point-blank range. A faint breeze eddied across the road, stirring the thin wisps of white hair above a strong, square-jawed face now smeared with blood. He looked up. 'So that's Kaminov?'

The Russian nodded grimly. 'Yes. That *was* Marshal Yuri Kaminov.' He turned away from the body of his former leader. 'You and your men had better head back to the city now, Banich. Take one of the trucks, but leave the other for us. Those identity cards and uniforms should serve you long enough to find shelter or make your own way back to your embassy.'

'What about you, Colonel? What will you do now?'

Soloviev glanced dispassionately at the mass of burning wreckage and tangled corpses. Then he looked back at the American. 'I have more work ahead, Mr. Banich. This was only a beginning.'

CHAPTER 34

Razor's Edge

JULY 1 – SPECIAL GUARD DETACHMENT, THE PRESIDENTIAL DACHA, OUTSIDE MOSCOW

'Major!'

Irritated by the shouted summons, Maj. Pavel Zubchenko of the FIS tossed his newspaper aside. He fastened his tunic collar and stepped out onto the dacha's front porch. 'Yes, Sergeant? What the devil is it now?'

The hatchet-faced noncom who had yelled for him pointed toward the forest. 'That smoke's still rising, sir. And they've got helicopters out now.'

'What?' Zubchenko came to the railing and squinted into the distance, shading his eyes against the bright noontime sun. He frowned. The man was right. There, ten or fifteen kilometers to the west, several plumes of dark black smoke were still visible, climbing into a cloudless blue sky. And those small specks orbiting slowly around the rising smoke were definitely helicopters.

He chewed his lower lip, suddenly worried. The first time the sergeant had called his attention to the smoke curling up from an area near Kaminov's country house, he'd dismissed it as unimportant. Foresters burning deadwood. Or maybe the old marshal's overzealous security detail conducting yet another exercise or realistic drill. Now he wasn't so sure.

Zubchenko turned on his heel and went back inside. Russia's civilian President, kept isolated and under virtual house arrest with his family, had the run of the dacha's second floor, but his FIS 'protectors' had commandeered the whole first floor for their own offices and living quarters.

Moving faster now that his men couldn't see him, the major went straight to his desk and picked up the direct phone line to Moscow. Nothing. He jiggled the receiver hook impatiently. Still nothing.

Zubchenko turned pale. The line was dead.

'Sir!' Another shout from the front porch brought him outside in a hurry.

He was just in time to see a column of armored vehicles – eleven wheeled BTR-80s – turning onto the long gravel drive leading to the dacha. He could see helmeted soldiers riding with the hatches open.

There were regular army troops aboard those APCs, a full-strength motor rifle company at least. The major swallowed hard. 'Call out the guard, Sergeant. But no one opens fire without my direct order, understand? These men may be reinforcements for us.'

'Yes, Major.' The noncom sounded unconvinced. He turned and began bellowing orders that brought the thirty-man security detachment onto the porch or into position at the dacha's doors and windows. Most of them were only half-dressed, roused from their off-shift slumber by the surprise alert.

By the time the last yawning FIS trooper stumbled outside, the BTRs were practically right on top of the building.

A tall, fair-haired colonel jumped down out of the lead vehicle and strode arrogantly toward the porch. To his astonishment, Zubchenko recognized the man. He was Kaminov's personal aide. Colonel . . . Soloviev. Yes, that was it.

Zubchenko came down the front steps to meet him halfway. 'What the bloody hell is going on, Colonel?'

Soloviev's pale blue eyes stared right through him. 'I'm afraid I have terrible news, Major. Marshal Kaminov and all the senior members of the Military Council are dead.'

Stunned by what he'd just heard, the FIS man felt his mouth fall open. 'What? How?'

'They were ambushed. Shot to pieces on the compound road. No one survived.' Soloviev grimaced. 'I've just come from there.'

Zubchenko believed that. He could smell the smoke and sweat on the man. 'Ambushed?' he repeated. 'By who?'

The colonel shrugged. 'We don't know . . . yet. But we found several dead men near the scene – apparently killed by the marshal's bodyguards. One of them was the head of the French security force.'

'Mother of God!' After that first shocked outburst, the FIS man stammered, 'But I thought the French . . .' His voice trailed off. 'Then why are you here, Colonel?'

Soloviev arched an eyebrow in mock surprise. 'I would have thought that was obvious, Major. I've come to escort the President back to Moscow.'

Although he'd been half expecting that, the announcement still rocked Zubchenko back on his heels. He cleared his throat, unsure of what he should do next. He desperately wished he could contact someone at his own agency's headquarters. 'By whose authority?'

'Authority? With Marshal Kaminov dead, our nation is leaderless and on the brink of war. Just whose authority do you think I need?' Soloviev asked flatly. He stared down at the FIS man in contempt. 'Which are you, Major? A lawyer? Or a patriot?'

Zubchenko stiffened. 'I know my duty, Colonel. I cannot allow the President to leave this compound without written orders from someone in legitimate authority!'

'The President himself is the *only* legitimate authority we have left!' Soloviev growled. He stepped closer, speaking lower so that only the FIS man could hear him. 'Think carefully, Major. Are you really prepared to fight the first battle of a new civil war right here and now? A battle you *will* lose?'

Zubchenko felt cold. By training and temperament, he was more a policeman than a professional military officer, but he knew how to count rifles. More important, he could read the iron determination in Soloviev's voice and eyes. If he tried to resist this man and his soldiers, he would only be signing his own death warrant. He looked away from the colonel's steady, unnerving gaze, turned to his sergeant, and said through gritted teeth, 'Let them through.'

Soloviev pushed past the ashen-faced security officer, marched into the dacha, and took the stairs to the second floor. Russia's tall, barrel-chested President came down to meet him before he was halfway up. Ironically, eight months of enforced seclusion seemed to have restored the man's vigor. He looked rested and even a little younger than he had in the days before the generals forced him to declare martial law.

The President stopped on the staircase, looking down with a tight, controlled smile. 'Is this a state visit, Colonel Soloviev? Or a firing squad?'

'Neither, sir. Marshal Kaminov and his subordinates are dead.' Soloviev said it bluntly. 'My men and I have come to escort you back to Moscow.'

'Back to power?'

Soloviev nodded. 'Yes, sir. By the time we reach the city, it should be reasonably secure. Generals Pikhoia and Baratov and their troops are busy now disarming certain FIS and military units . . . until their loyalties can be "determined." '

The older man seemed strangely unsurprised. 'I see.' He straightened up, somehow gaining apparent height and size. 'Very well, Colonel. Let's be about it. I suspect that time is at a premium.'

'Yes, sir.' For the first time Soloviev hesitated. 'Our forces on the Polish border . . .'

'Are about to invade,' the President finished for him. When he saw the younger man's surprise, he laughed harshly. 'Marshal Kaminov was "kind" enough to keep me informed about what he was doing with the nation I was elected to lead.' He shook his massive head. 'The thought of Russian soldiers acting as paid mercenaries for the French! What insanity! I'll soon put a stop to that nonsense.'

Soloviev nodded, relieved.

When they turned to go downstairs together, the President laid a hand on Soloviev's shoulder. He lowered his voice. 'One thing more, Colonel. I know how much you and your comrades have risked to restore our democracy. I only wish our people could know how much they owe you.'

Soloviev shook his head slowly. 'We merely did our duty, Mr. President – to you and to the Constitution. Nothing more is necessary.'

'Or wise . . .'

'Or wise,' Soloviev agreed. 'Kaminov and his closest followers are dead, but there are many more like them scattered throughout our military and the ministries. For now they are confused, adrift and rudderless. But that will change as time passes.' His mouth thinned to a grim line. 'Who knows? You may have need of us again someday.'

Slowly, sadly, Russia's President nodded. Both men walked out toward the waiting vehicles in silence.

SITUATION ROOM, THE WHITE HOUSE, WASHINGTON, D.C.

The high-ranking soldiers and civilians gathered in the Situation Room sat clustered at one end of the rectangular table. They faced an array of video cameras and a giant wall screen which showed their British opposite numbers meeting in the Cabinet Room at Number 10 Downing Street. As the war escalated, these satellite teleconferences between the allied military and political leaders were becoming a daily routine. However, the scattered news reports coming out of Moscow made this morning's top-level conclave anything but routine.

Electronic display maps visible to the men and women on both sides of the Atlantic showed the current status and deployment of all Combined Forces naval, air, and ground units. Other symbols, highlighted in red, depicted the latest intelligence regarding EurCon's military forces. At the moment, the Russian divisions detected on Poland's eastern frontier were lit up in white. With Kaminov apparently dead, no one really knew which way they would jump now.

The President leaned forward, eager to get straight to the point. The letters *ENG* glowing next to the symbol for America's 101st Air Assault Division showed that elements of the division were in combat against French and German forces. It was a constant and useful reminder that American soldiers were dying while they deliberated. He rapped on the table, stilling all conversation in both widely separated chambers. 'Okay, ladies and gentlemen, you've all heard the tape of my conversation with Russia's President. He says his troops and aircraft are standing down. The question is, do we believe him?'

The director of Central Intelligence spoke up first. 'Yes, sir, I think we should.' Quinn went on with specifics, 'The real-time pictures from our most recent satellite pass over the border area showed several troop units on the move in Belarus. They were moving east – not west. Moscow's orders for a pullback were also mentioned in several tactical communications between Russian field commanders picked up by our Vortex SIGINT satellite over eastern Europe.'

The President eyed his portly CIA chief narrowly. He suspected the man had other reasons to believe what the Russians were saying – reasons he didn't want to go into here. Not in front of the British. Just before they'd made the satellite hookup to London, Quinn had been called out of the room to receive an urgent signal from his agency's Moscow Station. When the director returned, he'd looked stunned at first – almost poleaxed by what he'd been told. The President made a mental note to shake the story out of the man after the meeting. To make sound decisions he needed every scrap of information he could lay his hands on.

He turned to Gen. Reid Galloway. 'Is there any other hard evidence of a Russian withdrawal, General?'

Galloway, the chairman of the Joint Chiefs, nodded firmly. 'Yes, Mr. President. Our AWACS plane flying over eastern Poland has detected large numbers of Russian combat aircraft heading back to their old bases. They're not making any effort to avoid our radar coverage or hide their movements. Those are not the actions of a country still preparing a sneak attack.' The U.S. and Royal Air Force officers seated around both tables muttered their agreement.

'Very well.' The President looked into the video camera feeding his image to London. 'What do you think, Mr. Prime Minister?'

The Englishman's eyes gleamed behind his thick glasses. 'I think, Mr. President, we should redouble our efforts to bring this war to a speedy and victorious close.'

'I agree.' The President breathed out in relief, feeling a tiny part of the strain he'd been under dissipate. War with France and Germany was bad enough. The prospect of war with Russia as well had been almost too terrible to contemplate.

His gaze settled on the map display showing friendly naval forces and convoys in the North Sea. If the Russians were really going to stay out of the conflict, it was time to take more decisive measures against the enemies they already had. Time to roll the dice. He set his jaw. 'That's why I'm convinced we should approve "Haymaker" immediately, Mr. Prime Minister.'

The other man sat forward. 'You've heard from Ross, then?'

The President nodded. 'Very late last night. Everything's set on his end. But apparently our newfound friends are waiting on us before giving the final go-ahead for their own forces.' He glanced at his own advisors, knowing some of them were still very leery of what they considered essentially a political gambit – one that could carry an extremely high military price tag if any one of a dozen things went wrong. 'I know there are risks in this operation, but I believe the risks are worth taking.'

Britain's leader glanced at his cabinet colleagues for a moment. Then he nodded decisively. 'Speaking for Her Majesty's Government, Mr. President, I agree. We must strike, and strike now.'

'Then Haymaker is a go.' The President turned to General Galloway.

The chairman of the Joint Chiefs grinned. 'Yes, sir.' He turned to the other British and American service chiefs.

While the military men took over the meeting, the President motioned one of his aides over. 'Put a scrambled call through to our Netherlands embassy. I want to speak to Ross Huntington, pronto.'

ABOARD USS *JOHN HANCOCK*, TASK GROUP 24.1, IN THE NORTH SEA, NEAR THE SKAGERRAK

Even closed up against enemy air or submarine attack, the second major reinforcement convoy destined for Poland sprawled over a vast area. Dozens of merchant ships plowed through the North Sea swells at fifteen knots. Together they carried the M1A2 tanks, M2 APCs, guns, and other gear of two U.S. 'heavy' divisions – the 1st Cavalry and the 4th Infantry.

Thirty nautical miles ahead of the main formation, USS *John Hancock* steamed east with her towed sonar array deployed. Although she was the command ship for the U.S., British, and Norwegian warships escorting the convoy, her position that far out in front made good military sense. No captain hunting for ultraquiet diesel submarines wanted to be any closer to the convoy's thrashing propellers – the 'thundering herd' – than was absolutely necessary.

Tensions on the *Spruance*-class destroyer's bridge and inside her combat information center were rising. They were just hours away from entering the narrow, confined waters of the Skagerrak – the preferred hunting grounds for Germany's surviving U-boats. Although this was *John Hancock*'s first trip through the deadly passage navy pessimists had already dubbed Ironbottom Sound North, every man aboard knew the score. Too many good ships and good crews were missing from the navy roster – sent to the bottom by German torpedoes.

Inside the destroyer's CIC, Capt. Tom Weygandt, the convoy's short, redheaded commander, leaned over a plot table, watching his tactical action officer, or TAO, lay out a new search pattern for the P-3 Orions assigned to shepherd them across this patch of the North Sea. He frowned inwardly, knowing he wouldn't have control over the aircraft for very much longer. The P-3s would have to turn back before the convoy entered the Skagerrak. Even with heavy fighter escort, the big, lumbering turboprops were just too slow and too vulnerable to operate that close to EurCon airspace.

'Sir, we have Oboe traffic from CINCLANT.'

His concentration broken by the radioman's quiet announcement, Weygandt looked up from the chart. 'Oboe' was navy slang for an operational priority message – only one category down from the Flash level reserved for enemy contact reports and other emergency traffic. What was up?

He took the message flimsy and scanned it. After the usual routing remarks, its content was short and utterly astonishing. When he looked up again, he hoped like hell the command 'poker face' he'd been working on since his years at Annapolis could hide his surprise from his subordinates. U.S. Navy commanders were not supposed to let new orders shake their composure – no matter how unexpected they were.

Commander Avery, *Hancock*'s skipper, moved closer. 'Trouble, sir?'

Weygandt shook his head. 'Not exactly, Rich.' He moved to the plot table again, staring down at the sea approaches to the Skagerrak. 'But we've got a new destination. Signal all ships that we're changing course in half an hour.' He leaned over the table, took the ruler, and traced a new line out from *Hancock*'s current indicated position. The line led southwest – away from the Skagerrak and away from Gdansk.

ABOARD USS *INCHON*, AMPHIBIOUS GROUP, IN THE NORTH SEA

Two hundred miles to the southwest, ten U.S. Navy amphibious assault ships crammed full of marines, landing craft, stores, and helicopters steamed inside a protective ring of five escorting warships – a *Ticonderoga*-class Aegis cruiser, two *Spruance*-class destroyers, and two *Perry*-class frigates. The vessels the warships screened ranged in size and capabilities all the way from the thousand-foot-long assault carrier *Wasp* down to smaller amphibious landing ships and attack transports. *Inchon*, a twenty-thousand-ton *Iwo Jima*-class helicopter assault ship, served as the Amphibious Group's command vessel.

Adm. Jack Ward waited uneasily on *Inchon*'s six-hundred-foot flight deck. There wasn't much that could make him nervous, not after all he'd seen, but mysterious visitors with 'presidential authority' were on that short list. Especially a mysterious visitor arriving by air from The Hague, the capital of the supposedly neutral Netherlands.

At CINCLANT's instructions, Ward had transferred his flag to *Inchon* from *George Washington* the day before – presumably in preparation for this meeting.

The message he'd received had said simply that the man he was waiting for carried 'orders,' presumably orders that were too secret to be entrusted to anyone else or to regular communications channels. But orders to do what? Ward hated cloak-and-dagger operations. He'd seen enough of that stuff in the movies, and to his way of thinking that was where it belonged.

Inchon's radars had been tracking the inbound aircraft – a Marine Corps V-22 Osprey – for several minutes. Now the admiral and several 'requested' members of his staff, most of them amphibious warfare experts, waited to meet their uninvited guest. Although he apparently had no official rank, Ward had already decided that anyone with the President's ear was going to get special attention.

If this gent really had that much pull, Ward planned to seize the chance to get a little information of his own. He had a lot of questions he wanted answered. For example, why had the ten-thousand-man Marine Expeditionary Brigade aboard *Inchon* and its consorts been ordered to stay in the North Sea instead of proceeding on to Gdansk? More important, why were the second group of heavy divisions, even more badly needed in Poland, sailing southwest to link up with this amphibious group instead? And why were Pentagon brass hats suddenly meddling in his bombing target lists? Some targets were added, some deleted – all without explanation. He grimaced. His staff officers were having almost daily go-rounds with Washington and London about the unexplained 'micromanagement.'

He had the plane in sight now. The big Osprey slowed, its outline changing as the wings tilted from horizontal to the vertical. Hovering now, the aircraft settled smoothly onto the assault carrier's deck.

Now comes the interesting part, thought Ward. Arriving VIPs were usually accorded some sort of honors, but how many sideboys would a 'special representative' expect? Formal shipboard etiquette was not often a critical question – not unless you screwed it up.

After some debate, his staff had recommended an honor guard of marines. The platoon, in battle dress and armed, sprinted across the flight deck and fell in next to a door in the Osprey's mottled green side.

When the door swung open, a sergeant bellowed 'Attention on deck!' and twelve men came to ramrod-straight attention. Ward studied the marines, hoping they would satisfy this visitor. They looked good anyway, trim, fit, and ready for combat.

Not so their mystery VIP. The first man down the steps was so tall that he seemed bent double coming out the aircraft door, and he straightened slowly. His charcoal-gray suit and briefcase looked out of place among all the military colors. Thin and gray-haired, he looked distinguished, but also worn down – as though he'd once been a much bigger, more vibrant man.

He moved carefully down the steps, alert eyes taking in the scene, including the line of marines. Even from across the deck, Ward could see the man's eyes brighten. He carefully straightened to his full height, walked over to the platoon leader who saluted, and shook the young man's outstretched hand.

He turned to Ward, waiting a few steps away. 'Admiral, thanks for the welcome. I'm Ross Huntington.'

Ward shook hands, immediately liking the man. This Huntington character looked refreshingly down-to-earth, not at all the kind of stuck-up Washington prig he'd been half expecting and half dreading. The admiral suspected that he and Huntington were about the same age, but the President's man looked somewhat older, and strained. Just who was he, that they needed him this badly?

RECON FLIGHT, NEAR GDANSK

Two delta-winged jets, French Mirage IIIR recon planes, flashed across the Polish coastal town of Sopot at low altitude and turned south, heading for the distant cranes marking the Gdansk waterfront. At six hundred knots, Sopot's beachfront houses and hotels blurred into a rippling kaleidoscope of rooftops, chimneys, and stretches of sand. To the east, the Baltic stretched off to the horizon.

The pilot of the lead Mirage, Capt. Charles Bertaud, put his thumb over the camera button on his stick. He and Lieutenant Simonin, his wingman, were only seconds away from their mission objective. Amazing. Even though headquarters had promised heavy air raids on other targets to lure the defending Polish and American interceptors away, it still seemed impossible that they could get this close to Gdansk without being jumped.

It was.

'Missile! Missile! At my six . . .' Simonin's sudden panicked radio warning ended abruptly in a muffled bang and then crackling static. The trailing Mirage vanished in a ball of fire.

Bertaud reacted instantly, throwing his aircraft into a series of wild evasive maneuvers that took him out over the sea. A tiny arrowhead shape trailing smoke and flame raced across the sky in front of him and exploded. He jinked again, desperately trying to catch sight of the enemy fighter that had fired at him.

Nothing. Nothing. There. The French pilot caught a brief glimpse of a large, twin-tailed jet behind him. An F-15! Suddenly the pursuing fighter's silhouette began changing rapidly – showing more wing and fuselage. It was turning away!

For a split second Bertaud's aggressive instincts took over. Although it was configured for reconnaissance, his Mirage mounted heat-seeking air-to-air missiles for self-defense. Why not turn after the apparently fleeing Eagle and take revenge for poor Simonin? Common sense pushed the thought away.

The F-15 pilot would never have abandoned his chase without good reason. He must be right on the edge of the SAM envelope surrounding Gdansk harbor – inside the zone where all incoming aircraft were automatically treated as hostile and fair game for the Hawk and Patriot batteries ringing the city. Bertaud pulled hard on the stick, bringing the Mirage around to the south again. Gdansk's waterfront cranes were closer now – only kilometers away.

Beep-beep-beep. His threat receiver went off and he dove for the deck, seeking cover from the enemy fire control radar hunting for him.

Flying just meters above the waves now, the Mirage shuddered, bucked, and rolled as it punched through layers of choppy air. Grimly determined now, Bertaud gripped the stick tighter, guiding his aircraft through the turbulence and toward the Polish port.

A SAM rose from the coast right ahead of him, climbing on a pillar of smoke and fire. He tensed, knowing he didn't have the time or altitude to try evading the incoming missile. All he could do was hold his course and pray. With luck, the American-made radar wouldn't be able to hold its lock on him this low.

His luck was in. The SAM streaked overhead and exploded far above and behind him. Before the enemy battery could fire again, he was over the city itself.

Bertaud eased back on his stick, climbing to clear the warehouses, shops, and homes lining the waterfront. His thumb settled back over the camera button on his stick. Any second now . . .

Still moving at high speed, the Mirage thundered over one last row of buildings and came out over the ship-crowded harbor. Now! He stabbed the camera button and leveled off.

Spewing flares to decoy away any hand-held SAMs fired from the merchant vessels below, Bertaud made one lightning-quick pass over the harbor area – racing above at least a dozen large transports and freighters tied up along the docks, uniformed men scattering for cover, and hundreds of camouflaged armored vehicles parked nose-to-tail on the quay. My God.

He keyed his radio. 'Scout Control, this is Scout Leader! The Americans are landing their heavy equipment. Repeat, the Americans are already landing their heavy equipment.'

With his mission completed, Bertaud turned away, heading for safety at full military power.

He never saw the radar-guided surface-to-air missile speeding after him. The Hawk's powerful warhead went off right behind the recon jet's starboard wing and ripped it off. Cloaked in flame, the Mirage III cartwheeled into the water and exploded.

PALAIS ROYAL, PARIS

The first reports of Captain Bertaud's radioed warning reached Paris well after dark.

In private conference with the head of the DGSE and the Minister of Defense, Nicolas Desaix sat staring down at his desk with his shoulders hunched as he absorbed this latest piece of horribly bad news. All the exhilaration of the morning generated by Ambassador Sauret's report that the Russians would join the war had turned to ashes in his mouth.

He grimaced. The news from Moscow was still very sketchy, but it was clear that Marshal Kaminov and his followers were dead – and with them any hope of a Franco-Russian treaty. Even worse, it appeared that Russia's civilian President had regained power. The man was notoriously pro-American. How had this happened? Who had betrayed them? He looked up at Morin. 'You still haven't been able to make contact with Duroc?'

The intelligence director shook his head, looking very worried. 'No, Minister. And no one at our embassy has seen the major or his surveillance team for more than twenty-four hours.'

'Impossible!'

Michel Guichy stirred in his chair. 'Impossible or not, Nicolas, they are missing.' The Defense Minister shrugged. 'Perhaps they are dead. Or held prisoner. What difference does it really make in the greater scheme of things? We face far more pressing problems.'

The big Norman leaned forward. 'Without the Russians on our side, we have just one chance left for victory. We *must* seize Gdansk before more American reinforcements arrive.'

'Tell me something I don't already know, Guichy!' Growing despair stripped away Desaix's thin veneer of politeness. Then, with an effort, he regained a measure of self-control. 'You've spoken with our field commanders?'

Guichy nodded. 'They say it is still possible.'

'How?' For the first time in hours, Desaix felt a measure of hope. Perhaps the war was not lost, after all.

'These armored units our reconnaissance pilot spotted were still unloading. Meanwhile the American and Polish divisions deployed near Bydgoszcz are still very weak and spread too thinly over too wide an area,' the Defense Minister said. 'General Montagne and the other commanders are convinced that once our tanks and troops punch a hole in those defenses and pour through, the enemy won't be able to stop us short of the port.'

'When do we attack again?' Desaix asked eagerly.

'Tomorrow, at first light.'

CHAPTER 35

Cataclysm

JULY 2 – HEADQUARTERS, 19TH PANZERGRENADIER BRIGADE, NEAR GRUCZNO

Lt. Col. Willi von Seelow was still refining his plans, trying to find some combination of moves that would give his brigade an extra edge when it went into battle. He could not change geography or the clock. Unless they broke through soon, today, and kept moving, they would never make it to Gdansk in time.

He knew what the Americans were capable of. Back when he'd reluctantly served East Germany's dying regime, he had trained against the 'NATO threat.' After the reunification, he'd trained with the Americans as new allies. He cursed them now. If not for the infantry division dug in to his front, his brigade would be halfway to Gdansk by now. Worse, the stubborn resistance his brigade had encountered in its first attack against Swiecie was only the barest taste of what lay ahead.

Right now, ships loaded with Abrams tanks and Bradley fighting vehicles, trucks, and supplies crowded the docks at the Polish port. Commercial passenger jets were shuttling soldiers in around the clock. It would take some time to restore the collection of machines and men into fighting units. That interval measured how long he had to get there.

Tasked by II Corps with conducting the breakthrough, General Leibnitz, the 7th Panzer Division's commander, had left von Seelow and his 'Bloody 19th' in the lead. Willi was grateful for the general's show of confidence in his abilities, but putting the 19th Panzergrenadier first also made good military sense. As the division's sole infantry-heavy formation, the brigade was the best suited to fighting through the difficult terrain in front of them, opening a path for the panzer brigades behind them.

At last, he laid down his pen and stood back – satisfied that the attack plan he'd drawn up was the best one possible under the circumstances. He looked up at his operations chief. 'See anything I've missed, Major?'

Thiessen shook his head. 'No, Herr Oberstleutnant.'

Around them, the headquarters bustled with final preparations for the new attack. For the better part of two days now, the 7th Panzer Division had been feinting at a strongly defended part of the American line, near Bladzim. It was good tank country, and a logical route of attack. An understrength battalion from one of the 7th's other brigades had been ordered to look like a division, and had done a good job of it.

Meanwhile, Willi von Seelow's troops had another target.

A stir outside the command vehicle attracted his attention, and he stepped out to see Leibnitz arriving, along with a French brigadier general whose narrow face seemed locked in a disdainful sneer. Willi scowled, but only inside, not where the Frenchman could see it. He recognized the man: Cambon, operations officer for the II Corps.

After exchanging salutes, Leibnitz asked him. 'Any last-minute problems, Willi?'

Von Seelow shook his head. 'No, sir. Everything is in order. My battalions are moving toward their start lines now.'

'I hope you understand the importance of this attack, Colonel,' urged Cambon. Addressing both officers, the Frenchman continued, 'I will be candid. General Montagne had grave concerns about allowing this unit to play such a critical role after its earlier failures.'

Willi fought down an urge of his own – an urge to smash the French staff officer in the face. Clearly the rear-echelon drones at corps had never forgiven him for threatening to turn his guns against the fleeing French 5th Armored back at the Warta or for short-circuiting their elaborate plans to cross the Notec by grabbing his own bridge at Rynarzewo.

Leibnitz must have seen the anger on Willi's face because he broke in before he could reply. 'I have reviewed Colonel von Seelow's plan and it is a very good one. The colonel's grasp of tactics is excellent, and it is his right to lead this attack.'

'As you wish, General.' Cambon turned away, apparently utterly uninterested in discussing the matter any further. He sauntered toward a group of officers clustered around a map.

Von Seelow's eyes narrowed. If II Corps was so worried about this attack succeeding, Montagne should have met more of his requests for fire support. Instead, outside of a few scraps, this was an all-German operation. Given that, it seemed obvious that the French corps commander planned to let his German 'allies' pay the blood price necessary to rip a hole in the American lines. Then, if they succeeded, the rest of II Corps stood ready to pour through the gap. The French would take Gdansk, and all the credit with it.

Leibnitz moved after the Frenchman.

Willi sighed, but again only on the inside. Having the division CO looking over your shoulder was a mixed blessing. You knew you were the *Schwerpunkt*, the spearhead, but the old man got to see your every move, right and wrong. And what about the Frenchman? What kind of report was he going to make? And to whom?

Von Seelow shrugged, suddenly too fatalistic to give a damn. This was a make-or-break attack. Enemy resources were stretched to the limit, and this time he was sure there was no second defensive line. A breach would lead into an empty rear.

If his plan worked, the 7th Panzer had a chance to reach Gdansk itself, shut off the flow of reinforcements, and end the war in victory. If the attack failed, what Leibnitz or the French thought of him wouldn't matter, because they wouldn't be able to win at all.

ALPHA COMPANY

They heard the artillery first, a dull booming off in the distance. Without a word spoken, Reynolds ran for the CP. Around them Polish and American soldiers raced to take up their firing positions or man their vehicles.

The Poles were the remnants of the 314th Mechanized Regiment, assigned to brigade reserve along with Alpha Company. Commanded by Maj. Miroslaw Prazmo, the twenty-odd armored vehicles were a poor match for the armored corps bearing down on them. It was all the armor they had.

Sgt. Andy Ford and Prazmo were already at the CP, just hanging up the field phone. 'No news from Brigade. They're checking up the line to Division.'

The Polish major cocked his head, listening for a moment. The barrage continued, sounding like thunder, but far too even, too steady. 'That is not a skirmish, Captain. I must see to my men.' The short, dark-haired tanker hurried away.

The company CP was in a small equipment shed on the outskirts of town, facing south. Biala, a small farming hamlet about ten kilometers north-northeast of Swiecie, had been their home for almost two days now. The front had been quiet for all that time, crashing against the 101st, then ebbing back, and gathering strength. The word was that the enemy would try again soon. The question was where.

Reynolds, Ford, and Corporal Adams, his radioman, moved to the doorway, scanning the landscape to the west. Silently they listened to the pounding artillery fire, literally trying to pull information out of the air.

Ford, speculating, said, 'It sounds like they're hitting Bladzim.'

Reynolds nodded absentmindedly as he studied his map. 'If the Germans punch through there, we'll have to move fast or we might be cut off.' The problem was, of course, that Colby and the men above him would be the ones who decided when Alpha Company moved. The idea that his fate was not in his own hands was something that Reynolds accepted, but he didn't have to like it.

He fidgeted, wanting to do something, but no real action was required. Someone else was taking the heat this time, and he resigned himself to a long morning of waiting and listening – trying to sort out what was happening from confusing and fragmentary radio and telephone messages.

Whummp. Whummp. Whummp. A new set of explosions hammered the Polish countryside, but this time close, so close that for a moment his surprised mind chided the Germans for being so far off target. A fraction of a second later, he realized his men *were* the targets. Then he heard the high-pitched scream of jet aircraft howling overhead. This wasn't artillery!

He rushed outside in time to see pointed shapes curving around to the west, and billowing brown-black smoke clouds roiling over Biala, some of them over his own troops' positions.

Seconds after seeing the planes, Reynolds heard the now-familiar sound of incoming artillery – big stuff. He dove to the ground, hugging the outside of the shed.

A rippling chain of explosions seemed to tear apart the ground itself, but trailed off after a few volleys. Reynolds raised himself to his knees, scanning the area. Now Maj. Prazmo's Poles were being hit, he judged. He hoped they were all under armor.

He could hear more artillery, too, distant, but not that distant. What was going on? This didn't fit in with an attack on Bladzim.

He scrambled back inside the CP. Ford's face was grim, and said more than the words did. He seemed reluctant to speak.

'Report,' ordered Reynolds.

'Second Platoon's been hit hard, Captain.' The sergeant's clipped tone was heavy with loss. 'Those were cluster bombs, and a stick landed square on top of 'em. Three killed, about ten wounded. Lieutenant Riley is dead. Two of the wounded need immediate medevac. And one of the Humvees is a total write-off, along with the antitank missiles it carried.'

Reynolds's chest suddenly felt tight and ice-cold. That one German air strike had just killed or wounded more of his men than he'd lost in the whole of Alpha Company's first battle. What could he have done differently? Probably nothing, but he wasn't sure he believed it. What should he do now? Deaths were a part of combat, but these were his men. He tried to push the questions to the back of his mind. There were still things to do.

When they called to organize the medevac, they got the word: the brigade was being hit, hard. Armored vehicles were pouring out of the woods to their front, while a storm of artillery and air strikes pounded their positions. Radars and radios were jammed. There was no question. The Germans were going to try again, harder and faster than before.

Ford had to spend considerable time calming the corporal on the other end of the phone, who from the sound of things was ready to bolt that moment for Gdansk. The sergeant finally hung up and turned to face Reynolds. 'They're coming at us full tilt, Captain. With everything, including the kitchen sink.'

Prazmo ran in, one sleeve bloody, but apparently none of it his. Reynolds gave him a quick summary of the situation, but Prazmo barely let him finish before he declared, 'We have to move, Captain. Your men, mine. All of us. The Germans move fast. Damned fast. Your general may not understand this.'

Reynolds started to protest, but the Pole cut him off, pointing to a spot on the map about two kilometers east of Biala. An irregular clump of woods, several kilometers across, lay over Highway 5 as it headed north.

'We must defend here. When the Germans break through, they will try to take this place. Look,' he urged, moving his finger north along the road. 'It is the last big block. Once past this, their tanks will be out in open country.' Reynolds gauged the terrain carefully, trying to think carefully in spite of the Pole's urging. As brigade reserve, they were responsible for a sector almost ten kilometers across. It would take time to move there, more time to set up, and if he was wrong, they'd be out of position, helplessly watching the enemy onslaught go by them.

But blocking the highway made the most sense. Other roads led off in the wrong direction or went through tighter, more constricted terrain.

Reynolds agreed, and told Ford to have the company prepare to move. They couldn't stay here anyway, he thought. The enemy obviously knew where they were and could hit them again. This harassing fire was bad enough.

He'd be damned if he'd move without brigade's permission, though. Adams reached the brigade TOC, but Colonel Iverson was gone – up at one of the battalion command posts. The S-3 okayed Reynolds' recommendation, though. 'Get in those woods and watch out,' he warned. His voice took on a desperate note. 'The Germans aren't maneuvering at all. They're coming on at full speed.'

The sound of diesel engines outside drowned out the still-falling shells. Reynolds ran out in time to see T-72 tanks and BMP fighting vehicles lumbering by. As planned, most of Alpha Company clung to the sides of the tanks or rode on top, while the Polish soldiers rode inside. Prazmo's command tank halted long enough for Reynolds, Sergeant Ford, and Corporal Adams to climb aboard, then shot off to the east.

The ride was not gentle, although Reynolds thanked God the ground was relatively flat. Prazmo's driver was heading pell-mell for the woodline, now a little over a kilometer away. He looked back to Biala. There was no further sign of falling artillery. Was their departure noted, then? Were they being tracked right now?

A louder-pitched whine over their heads made him look up. A flight of four AH-64 Apache gunships flashed by, low, and at top speed. A few moments later another and then another appeared. Reynolds was both heartened and concerned. That many attack birds would give the Germans something to worry about, but if they were committing the division reserve this early, just what was hitting them?

As his eye tracked the southbound helicopters, following them out of sight, more movement attracted his eye. This time he saw fighter aircraft, distant but still recognizable, and as they banked, turning toward the battlefield, he identified them as F-4 Phantom fighters, American-made, but flown by Germans. Wonderful. The Apaches would not have a free ride this time.

Suddenly he felt very exposed. He wanted to get under the trees or some sort of cover, out from under the open sky. The steel shell of the tank beneath him was hard, as unyielding as a stone. It would make a fine anvil if the Germans provided the right hammer.

Reynolds tried to organize his thoughts. Looking back and to the right, he saw the land between the woodline and Swiecie. On the northern side of town, the buildings thinned out rapidly, replaced by farmland, half-fallow, the rest planted with wheat, now half-grown.

Swiecie itself was almost smothered by masses of black and gray and white smoke. The sounds of battle were fainter and confused, but he could pick out tank guns and the crash of artillery shells. The T-72's engine slowed as they neared the woodline, and he could hear the pop of small-arms fire as well.

The edge of the woods was sharply defined. It was an old forest, carefully tended, with little undergrowth. The trees were well spaced, mostly evergreens with a few others mixed in. Thick enough to provide cover for the infantry, they were still spaced widely enough to allow armored vehicles to pass.

Highway 5, a four-lane asphalt road, entered the woods from the southwest and came out about five hundred meters to the northeast. Beyond the road and forest, open, boggy ground sloped down to the Vistula River.

Prazmo's tanks stopped just outside the trees to allow the American infantrymen to jump off.

Reynolds grabbed Ford's shoulder after they'd both scrambled down off the T-72. 'Okay, Andy, first thing is local security. Get a squad from 1st Platoon deployed so we don't get bushwhacked while we're setting up. I'll reconnoiter the area so we can site the Javelins, then . . .'

Prazmo arrived, and Reynolds noticed that Ford looked uneasy. 'Sir, I don't know if we'll be able . . .'

A sound grew from nothing into a howling scream and everyone dove for cover as a jet roared overhead. The delta-winged shape of a Phantom flashed by, the German Maltese crosses seeming out of place on the American-built plane. Although it did not attack, they all knew they'd been spotted.

Reynolds turned back to Ford, still snapping out instructions. He had to concentrate to hear himself speak, because Prazmo was also issuing orders in rapid-fire Polish. A small cluster of senior noncoms and officers nodded at the major's staccato sentences. They ran off, and the Pole turned back, impatiently waiting for the younger American to finish.

Ford looked stubborn. 'Skipper, we may not have time for all this. From what I heard on the horn, the goddamned Krauts are already rolling right through the rest of the brigade.'

Prazmo suddenly shouted, pointing to the south. He shouted something in Polish, his excited tone also carrying a warning. Then he repeated the call in English. 'Tanks! German tanks to the south. In Swiecie!'

Oh, Christ. Reynolds used his own binoculars. Among the buildings, he picked out low square shapes moving and firing as 120mm HE shells turned American-held houses into heaps of smoldering rubble. Machine guns chattered over the crack of tank cannon.

He fought a rising sense of panic. There was so much to do. They weren't ready. He needed more time, but even as he wished for it, he knew he wasn't going to get it. The Germans were too close and coming on too fast.

He let the binoculars fall back around his neck and turned to Ford. 'Get everyone under cover, at least forty meters in from the edge. If they shell the woodline, we don't want to be caught. Get going, I'll be there in a second.'

Guided by a young crewman on foot, Prazmo's driver was already working the T-72 deeper into the woods. Reynolds studied the area once more, then proposed, 'What if I take everything east from this spot, and your tanks and APCs cover from here west, back toward Biala?'

Prazmo nodded quickly. 'I agree, and have already given the orders to my men.' He pointed south. 'Move quickly, my friend. We have about five minutes, then they will be on us.' He hurried off.

'So much for step-by-step deployment,' Reynolds thought as he mentally tossed FM100-5 over his shoulder. Trotting into the forest, he tried to decide what was important, what was not. The army said it was all important, not to miss any step.

Screw that. What was going to count was getting firepower onto the enemy. The rest of it could wait. Calling 'Orders group!' he quickly organized the company. He split up the Javelin launchers, two to each platoon, and told them to deploy in a line, one platoon east of the highway, two platoons to the west. The outfit he'd deployed to the east, the 1st Platoon, hopefully steadied by Sergeant Ford's calm presence, was somewhat isolated, but the clump had to be occupied or the Germans would just stick to that side of the road and roll right around him. His CP would be with his hard-hit 2nd Platoon. With Lieutenant Riley dead, they needed all the encouragement he could give them.

As the platoon leaders ran off to deploy their men, a whistling howl announced the start of another German artillery barrage.

As expected, the first volley landed short, out in the open, and the thick trees all around them gave Reynolds a feeling of protection, like an awning in a rainstorm. He knew that was deceptive, though, and he could only hope that his men were all back from the treeline. More shells exploded, battering the edge of the woods.

Adams was busy setting up the radio and frantically digging in. Reynolds ordered, 'Quit that and get me Brigade.'

The corporal nodded and reached for the equipment, but warned, 'Jamming's heavy, sir. I already tried to do a check once.' He had to shout to make himself heard over the artillery fire.

'Do it again, and do it until you get through. I need contact bad.'

Adams nodded and picked up the handset.

Braving the shells still screaming in, Reynolds darted from tree to tree, locating each of his platoon leaders. Together, they picked spots for the antitank missile launchers. The Javelins were the only long-range weapon he had, and he wanted them well sited. All six had to cover the highway. Each squad also had AT-4 missile launchers, shorter-range and with a lighter punch. They had to hit a tank from the rear or flank to have any chance of killing it.

'Here they come!' A Javelin gunner pointed toward the open fields separating them from smoke-shrouded Swiecie. Camouflaged vehicles were visible now, emerging from the haze and moving northeast on either side of the highway – right toward them.

The enemy movement caught Reynolds while he was conferring with Ford and Lieutenant Caruso, the 1st Platoon's leader. He dashed back across the highway at full speed, heading for his CP. His men were still trying to sort themselves out. Half were clearing brush or other obstacles for the antitank missile crews while the rest dug 'hasty positions,' scrapes in the ground that barely hid your body. Soldiers often called them 'shallow graves.'

Adams looked up as he skidded through the thin screen of brush surrounding the CP and dropped prone. 'I got Brigade, Captain, and I've told them where we and the Poles are.'

'Great! Good work.' The corporal had also scraped out holes for both of them, and Reynolds rolled into his, frantically opening his map. He studied it, marking points and noting the coordinates. 'Get me brigade again.'

A first muffled *whumph* told him his Javelins were firing. The first wave of Germans must be just under two thousand meters away. Adams handed him the radio.

'I have an urgent fire mission, tanks in the open, coordinates one seven nine, two five six.' He raised himself up high enough to see, scanning the area with binoculars. 'Target is forty-plus tanks and APCs, more stuff in the distance.'

Even as he counted the German vehicles, a small cloud puffed over one and it exploded – ignited by a Javelin missile. More missiles flashed across the open ground, but with only six launchers, they could only kill a few of the enemy at a time.

The German Leopards and Marders kept coming – thundering across the fields at full speed. Reynolds swore. This wasn't a careful advance by bounds. This was close to an old-fashioned cavalry charge. And against his ill-prepared infantry and Prazmo's too-few tanks, it just might work, too.

Smoothbore 125mm guns barked from his right. The Poles were shooting now. The deep crack of tank fire was much more rapid than his own missile fire, but the tanks were hitting the Leopard 2s head-on, where their advanced armor was thickest. Prazmo's BMP infantry fighting vehicles carried wire-guided antitank missiles, but they were an older type that couldn't penetrate the front armor on the German tanks.

Few of the German tanks were firing yet. They could see little among the trees, even with thermal sights, and they were at maximum range for their 120mm guns, even with a stabilized turret.

Burning Leopards dotted the wheat fields now – maybe eight or ten of them. That was good shooting. But not good enough. The first elements of the German advance had closed to within a thousand meters. Marders packed with infantry followed right behind.

Polish T-72s and BMPs began going up in flames – hit by return fire from the Leopards. Machine guns and 25mm cannon mounted on the Marders chattered, tearing limbs, bark, and leaves off the trees. Reynolds flattened himself inside his shallow foxhole. The enemy APCs were trying to suppress his missile teams.

Whammm. Whammm. Whammm. Dirt fountained skyward among the advancing Germans. Reynolds grabbed the mike again. 'On target! On target! Fire for effect!'

More shells fell, exploding about five hundred meters to his front. The barrage wouldn't kill many tanks, but it might slow them down. Even better, the deadly hail of fragments whining outward from each blast ought to keep the panzer commanders buttoned up and half-blind. The artillery fire should also pin the German panzergrenadiers inside their Marders until they, too, were in among the trees and shadows.

While the battle raged ahead, Reynolds continued to work with the map, passing new coordinates back to brigade – walking the barrage north in time with the advancing Germans. Several more Leopards and Marders were hit and wrecked, but it was clear that the attackers would reach the woods with a sizable force. That was bad. What was worse was that it was already too late for Alpha Company to retreat.

When the first Leopards were just two hundred meters away, the enemy artillery fire slackened. Fearful of hitting their own men, the German gunners had stopped flaying the woods. At this range, the tanks were immense and he felt an urge to run building inside him, but knew that would be suicidal. More important, he would be letting his men down. Men who were counting on him to bring them safely home.

Suddenly the Germans were inside the woods.

'Cover!' A burst of fire scythed the air right over his head and the *crack-boom* of a close explosion shoved him into the ground.

Spitting out blood and dirt, Reynolds looked up from his hole at a German Marder only fifty meters away. The APC was pointed off to their left.

The tracked vehicle was steeply sloped in the front, but boxy and high in the rear where it carried its squad of infantry. A clumsy-looking turret on the top held a 25mm cannon, a launcher for antitank missiles, and a thermal imager.

The Marder's turret was slewed in their direction, but aimed over their heads. The gunner must have fired a suppressive burst in their direction on general principles, but now the barrel moved slightly from side to side as he searched for real targets. Its rear ramp fell open and German soldiers in camouflage gear poured outside. Some were already firing their assault rifles from the hip, pumping rounds into 2nd Platoon's positions.

Still prone, Reynolds grabbed his M16 and opened up. Adams did the same thing, firing in short, aimed bursts. Although that turret pointing their way was intimidating, the shot was too good to pass up. Besides, the panzergrenadiers would spot them at any moment.

One man went down instantly – knocked off his feet by two or three hits. Another screamed and slid backward against the Marder, clutching a face that had been torn apart. The rest went to ground, flattening themselves behind tree trunks or in the tall grass beside the APC.

The instant the Germans disappeared, Reynolds and Adams also dove for cover – just in time. A 25mm burst rippled overhead and exploded behind them, showering them with dirt and bits of wood. The autocannon dipped lower, still firing.

Whoosh. An antitank missile visible only as a streak of light from the left hit the Marder in the side. Sparks flew out from the point of impact, and part of the explosion inside vented out through the vehicle's open troop compartment. Moments later, a ball of gray-white smoke cloaked the APC – luridly lit from inside by the flames consuming its fuel and ammunition.

A few more German troops appeared, bailing out of the vehicle – trying to get clear of the flames. Reynolds and his RTO shot at them, but their targets vanished in the smoke, apparently unscathed.

Firing surrounded them on all sides, mixed with sounds of diesel engines. Clouds of exhaust, woodsmoke, and dust cut visibility to almost nothing, allowing only glimpses of the combat. Inside the smoke, bright flashes of light marked a weapon firing or a vehicle being hit. Forms moved through the trees, firing, running, falling.

A storm of gunfire from their left drew the two men, and crouching almost double, they ran in the direction of 2nd Platoon's positions. A crashing roar from the right turned into a German tank, breaking through a thicket of small trees. They threw themselves back behind a tree, watching helplessly as the armored behemoth passed close by and then rumbled into the murk.

'Shit!' Reynolds whipped around as bullets snapped past his face. There were five German infantrymen following the Leopard. Muzzle flashes stabbed out of the smoke. He snapped his M16 up and squeezed off a long burst, but recoil pulled the barrel up, and his shots went wild. The bolt clicked on an empty chamber.

He rolled right, trying to get behind the tree while frantically fumbling for a new magazine. Too late, his mind screamed. The Germans would be on top of him in a fraction of a second.

Adams popped up beside him and lobbed an egg-shaped fragmentation grenade into their midst.

The grenade went off with an earsplitting *whummp*. Two of the Germans went down, bleeding and dead or unconscious. The others, stunned, stopped moving long enough for Reynolds to slam his new magazine home and fire.

Hit several times each, the panzergrenadiers stumbled backward and fell in a heap. Still holding his aim, Reynolds moved out from cover. One good look told him they were dead. He nodded his thanks to the tall, skinny corporal and then scanned the scarred woods around them, desperately trying to reorient himself. He still felt the urge to run, but just to 2nd Platoon. He had to regain control of this battle.

Sprinting, pausing, ducking occasionally, Reynolds and Adams worked their way toward 2nd Platoon's fighting positions. At times the smoke and trees cut off all view, so that they were surrounded by a gray-green wall. The sounds of firing were no help, either, as omnipresent as the smoke.

They kept working their way east, meters seeming like miles and seconds like days. Finally Reynolds spotted Sergeant Robbins, crouched with two other soldiers. With Riley gone, the short, dark-featured sergeant was now in charge of 2nd Platoon.

Robbins spotted the captain and corporal as they ran up. 'They're past us, sir!' Frustration and fatigue filled his voice as well as his face. 'We've knocked out ten tracks, maybe more, but they just keep coming.' The crack of cannon fire to the south announced the arrival of more enemy tanks.

'What are your casualties?' Reynolds demanded.

'Three dead I know of, probably more. Eight – no, nine wounded.'

Reynolds grimaced. Even out of a full-strength platoon of thirty-eight men, that would have been a heavy toll. But 2nd Platoon was badly understrength when the battle started, and the battle was far from over. On the other hand, his troops had already destroyed a lot of enemy armor. Was it worth the cost, though?

He couldn't tell. From what little he could see, they'd blunted and disorganized the first wave of the German attack. The woods were full of burning vehicles and German stragglers, either tangled up with Alpha Company or pressing on to the northeast, and he was sure there were follow-on forces moving up. Alpha Company couldn't stop them anymore. He needed more firepower.

Reynolds leaned over, speaking carefully to Adams. 'Get Brigade. Tell them to shift the arty.' As the corporal picked up the handset, he pulled out the map he'd marked earlier. 'New reference point is seven four, time on target, airburst. I want everything they've got for five minutes.'

Sergeant Robbins, standing next to him, looked at the marked spot and paled. He grabbed the two kneeling privates by the shoulders and spoke urgently. 'Find the 1st and 3rd platoons. Tell them there's incoming mail, airburst. Everyone go to ground. Move!'

The two soldiers disappeared, one to the east, one west. Robbins moved off himself, passing the word down his shattered line while Reynolds and his radioman took cover under a wrecked Leopard 2. Two privates also arrived to share the space, and all four of them kept scanning the woods.

The sounds of tank guns and light cannon mixed with machine-gun and rifle fire. They spotted men running to the southeast, but Reynolds stopped the others from firing. It was impossible to tell which side those shadowy forms belonged to.

The freight-train roar of heavy artillery suddenly drowned out the gunfire around them and the woods exploded in fire and smoke.

This was no ranging shot, no ragged one-battery barrage. The shells cascading into the narrow band of forest had been carefully timed to arrive on target almost simultaneously.

The air itself exploded, suddenly filled with millions of lethal fragments. Crouched beneath the tank, Reynolds was stunned by the ferocity he'd unleashed. This was more than the brigade artillery battalion firing. Guns from the division, maybe even the corps, must be in on the act.

Tree after tree went down with their tops blown off.

The American shells were detonating ten to twenty meters off the ground, sleeting the air with fragments and shredding anyone caught in their path. Pieces of leaves and pine needles poured down, thick enough to cover the ground like a rug.

As fragments *ping*ed off the German tank's steel hull, Reynolds tried to imagine being exposed in that hurricane of fire, and failed. At least his troops had been warned. The Germans, though, should have been caught by surprise. Most people killed by artillery die in the first thirty seconds. That's about as long as it takes trained soldiers to find decent cover. So by now, everyone caught inside the barrage was either dead or cowering in some kind of shelter. Most important of all, the Germans weren't moving.

When the artillery stopped, the silence it left behind was almost absolute. In that silence, Reynolds could hear a new noise, the bass roar of dozens of diesel engines. He crawled out from under the wreck and moved toward the edge of the woods with Adams at his side. There, grabbing his binoculars, he peered through the clearing smoke and dust to the south.

A new formation of Leopard 2s swept across the open fields, headed straight for them. He stared in horror. Neatly grouped by platoons and companies, the panzer battalion moving up could almost have been on parade. A second rank of Marder APCs followed close on their treads, and Reynolds bet that behind them was a third. Probably with more tanks in reserve.

While the first German outfit had blown open the breach, weakening itself in the process, this new enemy brigade had run through the open. Fresh, unbloodied, and moving fast, it would slam into the woods in a few minutes, and they didn't have a prayer of stopping it.

Sergeant Robbins ran over and dropped prone beside him. 'My guys are scattered all over hell, Captain. We've got five more dead, another six or seven wounded. Both M60s are manned, but both Javelin crews are gone, wounded or missing. We only had two missiles left anyway. I'm rallying the men now.'

Rallying what? Reynolds wondered numbly. Second Platoon couldn't have very many men left in fighting shape. Probably fewer than a dozen. Were the other platoons in any better shape? For the first time in minutes he wondered how Major Prazmo's Poles had fared. He glanced off to the right, toward the sector the major's men and tanks had been holding. Columns of black smoke spiraled upward from the tangle of splintered trees.

He grimaced. He had to regain control of his scattered company. They might have some fight left, but they had to recover. It took time to reorganize and treat the wounded – time the Germans were not going to let him have.

Even as he started to pass orders, the *whumph* of an antitank missile told him Alpha Company was in the fight again. The sound came from the left, and through the trees he saw part of the enemy tank formation turn tightly while one of their number fired its gun, presumably back toward the launcher.

From the direction the Leopards were pointing, it looked like 1st Platoon had fired. At least one of the two Javelin teams he'd assigned to Caruso's men was still intact and had missiles to fire. He felt proud that his men still had fight left in them after all they'd been through. But stacking one or two antitank teams up against an intact enemy tank formation was asking too damned much. Even David had only had to fight *one* Goliath.

Another missile leapt out toward the Germans. Then another, and another, and another flashed out from under the tree – seeking targets. His pride turned to puzzlement. Altogether, almost a dozen missiles were fired, and half found marks, some far beyond Javelin range. Where the hell were those missiles coming from?

Boots crashed through the undergrowth and he heard Andy Ford's voice calling. He answered the hail, and the noncom came running up with a stranger in tow – an American lieutenant colonel. The man wore armor insignia on his collar tab, and a 1st Armored Division patch on his shoulder. The pair stopped and dropped to one knee next to Reynolds.

'I'm Jim Kelly, 1st of the 37th, 3rd Brigade. I've got forty-two M-1s coming in on the highway. I need ground guides and places to put them, fast.'

Reynolds found himself staring at the colonel and closed his mouth with an effort. He pointed east and asked. 'Then those missiles from the other side of the highway . . . ?'

'Seventh Battalion of the 6th, mech infantry with Bradleys,' Kelly hurriedly explained. 'My battalion will deploy west of the road.' He grabbed Reynolds' shoulder. 'If the Bradleys are already firing, we don't have much time.'

'But how . . . ?'

Kelly grinned. 'Thought you boys might need some help, so our guys worked all last night to get their gear unpacked and then marched like bats out of hell to get here on time. But we're it for now. The rest of the division's still back on the docks.'

Still scarcely able to believe it, Reynolds quickly passed the word, sending runners from his 2nd and 3rd platoons back to bring Kelly's tanks forward. Within minutes, the Alpha Company soldiers reappeared, four-tank platoons following behind like monstrous pets. Reynolds spent the time keeping his people clear of the lumbering machines, at the same time deploying riflemen and machine-gun teams into the gaps between the tank platoons. There weren't many of them left. Fewer than half the soldiers he'd taken into battle were still on their feet.

Out in the open, he watched as German tanks and APCs maneuvered, dodging the near-continuous missile fire. Their once-neat formations were now spotted with burning vehicles, while smoke grenades popped, obscuring parts of the attacking brigade with puffs of gray-white vapor.

Around him, dozens of M1A2 tanks took position in an uneven line. The high, thin whine of their turbine engines filled the woods. There was so much commotion that Reynolds was worried that the Germans might spot them, but experience told him otherwise. The trees would conceal the American tanks, at least until they fired. After that it wouldn't matter.

Reynolds was standing near one company commander's tank, trying to hurriedly coordinate a fire plan, when the officer straightened up in his turret hatch. He listened to a voice in his headphones and replied, 'Estimate seven hundred. We haven't lased.' After another pause, he acknowledged the order he'd received with a quick 'Roger.'

'They aren't waiting for the rest!' he called down to Reynolds. 'Are your people clear?'

Reynolds nodded. 'They'd better be—'

An ear-splitting *crash* interrupted him, the sound of a tank battalion firing en masse. Pressure waves from the guns on either side buffeted him, plucking at his clothing and throwing dust and leaves in his face. The smell of gun smoke was literally rammed down his nose.

Out in the track-torn wheat fields, the oncoming brigade suddenly blossomed with gray-black flowers. Where the shells found their mark, and at least two-thirds had, German armor burned.

He barely had time to recover from the first blast when a second followed, almost in unison. The shock waves were knocking him off balance, and he dropped prone rather than get slammed off his feet.

The third volley was much more ragged as faster loaders and better-coordinated crews outpaced their counterparts. By the fourth, the firing had become a continuous roar.

Caught at short range in the open, the Germans, who had been expecting the woods to be clear, instead ran into a hail of tank-killing fire. At half a klick, the Abrams' 120mm shells had more than enough killing power to rip through a Leopard 2 tank, or literally dismantle a thin-skinned Marder. While the Americans were in firing positions that allowed them to see and shoot out, all the Germans had to shoot at were half-concealed shapes. They had only three options: kill the enemy, find cover, or die.

A few of the Leopards tried to return fire – sending sabot rounds crashing through the trees in front of them. Most missed, and few of the German tanks had time for a second shot. Almost as soon as it started, though, the volume of fire fell away. The Leopards and Marders died or went to ground.

Reynolds raised his head, still in shock. Three minutes of firing had been enough to stop the German brigade cold. Through his binoculars, he counted thirty dead tanks and as many APCs – slewed crazily at all angles amid the flattened wheat. There were no signs of life or movement. EurCon's grand attack had been stopped.

No, he thought coldly, more than stopped. The Germans who'd come storming across those fields so boldly had been butchered. It would be a long time before the bastards recovered from this disastrous attack.

Alpha Company had held just long enough.

Half-deafened, Reynolds stood slowly and shook himself, like a man coming out of the water. Voices and engine noises replaced the silence, and he slowly began to realize that nobody was going to shoot at him in the immediate future.

As he gathered what was left of his company and set about finding out what Brigade wanted him to do, the roar of jet engines through the sky brought fear back up his throat again. A glance upward, though, showed them to be American and Polish planes, loaded with bombs and headed southwest. Flight after flight screamed overhead, hugging the earth on the way to their targets.

EurCon had reached its high-water mark. Now the tide was turning.

HEADQUARTERS, 19TH PANZERGRENADIER BRIGADE

The steady flood of damaged tanks and horribly wounded men filtering back from Swiecie told its own story of defeat and despair, but radioed reports confirmed the worst.

Von Seelow put down the handset and looked at Leibnitz. His face was pale. 'That was Major Schisser. Colonel Baum is dead, along with most of the 21st Panzer. The highway north is blocked by large numbers of tanks and missile vehicles. Our men came under intense fire just short of the woods.' He swallowed hard. 'Casualties are very heavy – at least forty percent, probably much more.'

Leibnitz's face was a mask of shock and repressed sorrow. Willi knew that the division commander and Baum had been friends for a long time. More telling than that was the destruction of the 21st Panzer Brigade – the follow-on force for his own decimated command. Minutes before, Baum's Leopards and Marders had been the leading edge of the German breakthrough, actually passing through the breach and headed full speed up the highway. Near full strength and unengaged, they should have been able to crush anything the Americans or the Poles could throw in their path. Instead, they were strewn across the open countryside – wrecked and on fire.

Beside the 7th Panzer's stricken leader, General Cambon exclaimed, 'Those woods were supposed to be clear!' He turned to face von Seelow. 'Your brigade reported overrunning the American infantry there. Obviously your incompetent fools missed something.'

Sneering openly now, he challenged the two Germans. 'Well, what will you do now?'

Willi set his teeth.

Leibnitz asked, 'Is General Montagne willing to commit the exploitation force? We can keep the breach open . . .'

'Down!' Major Thiessen screamed.

The staff officer's warning barely preceded the roar of enemy aircraft streaking low overhead. Bombs and cluster munitions tumbled off wing racks. Explosions rippled through the brigade area. Thick, choking smoke billowed over von Seelow and the others as they hugged the grass.

A few moments later, the jets vanished as quickly as they had come, having brought the battle back with them to brigade headquarters. Screams and low, pain-filled moans rose from those who had been wounded.

Willi, Leibnitz, and the Frenchman picked themselves up, brushing off the dirt and grass. As the men around them tried to regain control of the battle, Cambon declared, 'We will not commit the 5th Armored without knowing more about the enemy positions north of Swiecie. It would be suicide to send more units into the same ambush.'

The Frenchman pointed to the map. 'Here. Take your 20th Brigade and probe northward. Once you've pinpointed the enemy concentrations, we will decide whether to attack or bypass them.'

Leibnitz stiffened. 'Impossible. The 20th is only at half-strength. That's why we didn't use it in the attack. It's out of position as well.' His voice rose to a challenge. 'Why waste precious hours shifting my last brigade when you have a full-strength French division, ready and waiting, with their motors running. Send it through the gap.'

Cambon sniffed. 'Ridiculous. The corps' plan is quite clear, General Leibnitz. "The exploitation force will be committed only after the 7th Panzer has secured the breach," ' he quoted. 'It's clear your men were not up to the task. I told the general that you Germans were fit only for garrison troops.'

That did it. Willi von Seelow's eyes flashed and he nodded.

'True. In the last war we garrisoned Paris, Lyons, Cherbourg . . .'

Astonishingly, Leibnitz grinned.

'I won't stand here and listen to this!' Cambon spluttered.

'Then leave,' replied Leibnitz calmly. 'We've fought hard, and taken the losses to prove it. Those losses were justified only if the attack succeeded.' He stood close to the Frenchman, almost nose-to-nose. 'And it won't succeed now, not without help that you French bastards are unwilling to give. If that is true, then this battle, this war, is not worth the loss of another German soldier.'

Evidently shocked by the sudden turn of events, Cambon strode off. Once the Frenchman was out of earshot, Leibnitz turned to face von Seelow, his anger already sliding back to sadness. 'Pull your troops back to the start line, Willi, and pass the order to Major Schisser as well. There's good defensive terrain. We'll reorganize there, and begin planning a fighting retreat, all the way back to Germany if need be.'

In one part of Poland at least, the Franco-German alliance was dead.

CHAPTER 36
Pressure Points

JULY 2 – PARIS

Unwilling to believe what he'd just read, Nicolas Desaix stared down at the message form he held crumpled in his hand. He looked up at Michel Guichy. 'Montagne is sure of this?'

'Yes, very sure,' the Defense Minister growled. 'This man Leibnitz and his subordinates have refused all of II Corps' orders to renew the attack. They've even abandoned all the ground gained this morning. They may be preparing to fall back further.'

'*Boche* bastards!' The coarse epithet felt so good rolling off Desaix's tongue that he repeated it. He tossed the message form aside. 'Does Berlin know anything about this situation yet?'

Guichy shrugged. 'Who knows? II Corps controls all landline communications access to the 7th Panzer, but the Germans do have radios.'

'Damn.' By rights, the German Chancellor and his cabinet ministers should be equally appalled by their panzer division's refusal to obey EurCon orders. Unfortunately Desaix was no longer sure he could predict Heinz Schraeder's reactions. Russia's state television had begun broadcasting reports of Kaminov's secret negotiations with France. Since then, Berlin's willingness to accept French political and military advice had perceptibly diminished. And in recent telephone conversations, Schraeder's tone had grown notably tepid, even cold.

Another troubling thought struck him. 'What about Montagne's own German staff officers? Who controls them?'

'Unimportant, Nicolas.' The Defense Minister shook his head. 'Our people already have General Wismar and his subordinates in "precautionary custody." '

Desaix relaxed minutely. Though somewhat high-handed, General Montagne's prompt action had at least blocked one path by which the 7th Panzer's mutiny might have spread. Once this 'insurrection' was snuffed out, apologies, compensation, and perhaps even a judicious promotion or two should soothe any ruffled German feathers.

He pursed his lips. 'Very well. What other measures have been taken to isolate this Leibnitz and his soldiers?'

Guichy rattled them off in quick succession. 'Troops from General

Belliard's 5th Armored are posted on all roads leading into the 7th Panzer's sector. And all supply deliveries have been halted.' He smiled grimly. 'After all, if these German cowards won't attack, they certainly don't need any fuel or ammunition. Or food.'

Desaix nodded his approval. 'Good. Good.' Then he frowned. Isolation alone would not solve this problem. Not in time. With more and more American and British troops pouring into Poland, EurCon could not afford to wait long enough to starve the 7th Panzer Division into submission. He said as much to Guichy.

The other man spread his hands. 'Then what do you propose we do?'

What indeed? Desaix found himself wishing his enemies would end this mutiny for him. U.S. and British commandos and Polish guerrillas were already making life hell for other German and French outposts scattered across occupied Poland. So why couldn't they hit Leibnitz and his rebels, too? An idea dawned. A bold scheme – one whose rewards might well be outweighed by its risks. Or so a more cautious man might say. But, with other, far more carefully laid schemes collapsing around his ears, Nicolas Desaix was in a mood to gamble.

He leaned forward and bluntly outlined his plan to bring the mutinous German troops to heel. Army units in any semblance of order were always rigidly hierarchical. The junior officers, the sergeants, and the common soldiers were all schooled in obedience. If Montagne could lop off the 7th Panzer's upper echelons quickly enough, those who were left should fall in line.

Guichy heard him out in stunned silence. When he'd finished, the big Defense Minister breathed out, dismayed. 'My God, Nicolas. If anything went wrong . . . or if anybody talked . . .' He shook his head. 'The effects could be catastrophic.'

'Exactly.' Desaix hardened his voice. 'That is precisely why we must not fail and why no one can be left in a position to talk. You understand?'

The Defense Minister nodded, still shaken.

'Then I suggest you transmit the appropriate orders to General Montagne. And that will be that.' Desaix tossed the message form into a wastebasket – the one his aides emptied into a shredder and then an incinerator at the end of each working day.

After Guichy left, he sat back, mulling over the rest of the war situation. His mouth turned downward. At every turn, his best efforts had been thwarted by bad luck or incompetent subordinates. First Duroc's bumbled attempt to crush the Hungarian resistance. Then the overconfident generals who had promised complete victory in Poland in days – not weeks of futile warfare. Admiral Gibierge's wasted nuclear strike. The destruction of his nation's precious nuclear deterrent force. The catastrophe in Moscow. And now this failed attack on Gdansk.

Abruptly Desaix slammed his fist down. Idiots! Fools! He glared at the map laid out across one side of his desk. Seizing the Polish port was still the only way to end this war on a victorious note. He could see that, even if the military men could not.

His intelligence experts still insisted there were only two Combined Forces armored divisions in Poland. A new offensive, one backed by fresh EurCon troops, might still succeed in reaching the city. But where could he find those fresh troops?

Not from Germany. Schraeder's government had only a few Territorial battalions and one panzergrenadier division left to guard its own borders and military installations. A month of war had bled the once-mighty German Army dry. A thin, humorless smile flitted across Desaix's face. At least the fighting had brought one positive result.

France was in better shape. She still had her fifty-thousand-man-strong Force d'Action Rapide – the airmobile, marine, airborne, and light armored troops of her rapid deployment force. His smile faded. Those soldiers were needed to defend military posts against enemy commando raids. Unfortunately they were also needed to help hold down an increasingly restive French populace. As the fighting dragged on, there were more signs of trouble brewing in the big cities – Paris, Lyons, Lille, and the rest. And the gendarmes were again showing a reluctance to suppress civil disorder.

Desaix moodily contemplated the map. Perhaps they would have to abandon the territory won in Hungary in order to send part of General Fabvier's IV Corps north. He scowled, detesting the thought of giving the Hungarian rebels a propaganda victory they would undoubtedly trumpet from the rooftops.

His eye fell on Belgium. Where the hell were those two combat brigades the Belgians had been ordered to provide? Those troops were desperately needed to free French soldiers for frontline service. Never mind the delays imposed by American air strikes on the German and French rail net, the damned Belgians could have walked to their new posts by now! He made a mental note to raise the issue with Belgium's ineffectual ambassador and moved on.

JULY 3 – HEADQUARTERS, 7TH PANZER DIVISION, NEAR BYDGOSZCZ, POLAND

The sultry July morning seemed to last forever. General Karl Leibnitz, Willi von Seelow, and the other two brigade commanders sat sweltering in the meager shade provided by a tree overlooking a cleared patch of grazing land. After two sleepless nights, they were hot and tired and dirty.

The lack of any breeze seemed symbolic, as well as uncomfortable. Nothing moved. Although they could have set up the division headquarters in the open, the trees were much safer. The unit was actually spread across one edge of a large clump of woods, tucked back inside about fifty meters or so.

The division's four M577 headquarters tracks were parked back-to-back in a cross, with a camouflaged awning spread on poles between them. Around that were the other trucks and tents of the headquarters, all carefully concealed, and in turn surrounded by fighting positions and foxholes for the headquarters troops. A few Marder APCs were deployed around the perimeter for added firepower.

Willi glanced down at his watch again. Only a few minutes had passed since he'd last checked the time. The man they were waiting for was late. As usual.

During the twenty-four hours since they'd sent that French cretin Cambon packing, Leibnitz and the other officers of the 7th Panzer had already ignored one peremptory order to advance, and another directing them all to report to II Corps headquarters for an 'urgent conference.'

II Corps' latest message was more promising. It had requested a meeting, to resolve 'difficulties in the command structure.' To do that, General Montagne himself would come to the 7th Panzer's headquarters.

Now they waited for the French corps commander's helicopter, due to arrive momentarily. They still had no idea what Montagne would say, but his willingness to talk at all was heartening. 'First intelligent thing the French have done,' Leibnitz had muttered.

Willi nodded to himself. That was true enough. Certainly the other actions the French had taken were less reassuring. The supply cutoff had left the division with just enough gas and ammunition for one defensive battle. Now scouting parties were reporting heavy roadblocks across all major roads, and most of the secondary roads. In the circumstances, it seemed clear that any major German movement might trigger a new conflict, this time between erstwhile allies. In the field, in front of a hostile army, that would be worse than disastrous, and Willi's military training rebelled at the idea.

He grimaced. This situation had to be resolved quickly. Food and fuel were incidentals compared to the strategic issues.

So far, the Americans had not counterattacked. Nobody knew how much of the 'mutiny' was known on the other side, but both the French and German participants were doing their best to keep it quiet. Like family members with a grievance, they still argued in whispers, lest the neighbors overhear.

A shout from an enlisted man brought them to their feet. A gray-and-green-camouflaged Puma helicopter, moving low and slow, was in full view, coming in for a landing in the clearing in front of the headquarters.

Willi glanced left and right. Soldiers in nearby foxholes tracked the helicopter, an indication of just how far relations with their 'allies' had deteriorated.

The Puma settled to the ground in a cloud of dust and dried grass, its rotors seeming to take forever to slow. Finally, as the blades spun down to a stop, the side hatch slid open.

Suddenly Willi heard the crash of an explosion behind him, and the rattle of small-arms fire from somewhere further back among the trees. He spun round, looking for the source. The shooting continued, doubling in intensity.

New rifles crackled, from closer now. The soldiers near him were firing at the grounded Puma. Instead of French generals, two squads of French troops in full combat gear were pouring out, shooting on the move. Rounds whined over his head and smacked into the trees close by.

Christ. He knelt down, unslinging the MP5 submachine gun he'd been carrying. Leibnitz and the other brigade commanders were already prone. They all kept weapons close to hand. Nobody wanted to follow Bremer's fate.

Just beyond the clearing, a French Gazelle attack helicopter popped into view over the trees, followed closely by another. Hugging the ground, the two gunships swept toward the woods, searching for targets. A puff of smoke appeared under one machine, and a missile leapt away, flashing into the trees.

One of the Marders, parked a few dozen meters away, fireballed – hit broadside by a warhead designed to kill tanks. A powerful, ringing explosion blew the APC's 25mm gun and turret high into the air.

But German Marders also carried portable Milan antitank missile launchers. Even as the French HOT missile struck, the rest of the APC's crew avenged its destruction. A Milan streaked upward from a nearby foxhole toward the Gazelle. Flying too low and slow to evade, the helicopter took a direct hit – just under its rotor transmission. The blades and part of its engine broke clear, spinning out of sight, while the rest of the airframe, burning brightly, slammed into the ground.

In response, the other Gazelle gunned the treeline, almost casually lacing it with 20mm shells. Von Seelow could hear men screaming as the cannon rounds ripped through their foxholes.

Killing them took time, though – time enough for a second Marder, still concealed by camouflage netting, to slew its own 25mm turret around and fire. One long, clattering burst seemed to pin the French helicopter in place. Armor-piercing rounds tore off pieces of the Gazelle until what was left was no longer fit to fly. It dropped to the ground, a mass of burning metal.

The Marder fired again, this time aiming for the French Puma. More than a dozen explosive shells hit the helicopter hard enough to knock it over and set it ablaze. The commandos it had carried, now pinned down in the open, fired back, but they had lost surprise, as well as their supporting firepower. Several were already dead or badly wounded. The rest wouldn't last much longer, Willi thought grimly.

Gunfire and grenade explosions still rattled and thumped in the woods behind him. The French were launching a two-pronged attack, he realized. One force had infiltrated through the trees to hit the headquarters from behind, while the Puma brought in this second unit to cut off any attempted retreat.

Leibnitz scrambled up. 'Our men need help, gentlemen. He jerked his head toward the sound of firing. 'Come.'

Willi nodded and gripped his submachine gun tighter. Personal weapons out and ready, the four senior officers scuttled away from the clearing, moving deeper into the woods. They were only twenty meters short of their command trucks, when a long, searing burst of fire drove them to ground.

Jansen, commander of the 20th Panzer Brigade, screamed once and then fell silent. He'd been shot through the head.

Dead soldiers, both French and German, sprawled everywhere. Heart pounding now, von Seelow lay still, scanning the surrounding area for signs of living enemies. Where had those shots come from?

They'd hit the dirt close to a burning truck, but the choking smoke and flames forced them to edge away from the cover it provided. The closest trees, spaced meters apart, were no help. They only made it more difficult to see. The sounds of firing still surrounded them, spasmodic, but almost constant overall, and the flames crackling noisily nearby further confused the picture.

Suddenly a pair of French soldiers burst into view, running hard toward some point off to Willi's right. They spotted the prone Germans at almost the same instant and skidded to a stop, swinging their assault rifles around. They were too late.

Von Seelow pulled the trigger on his submachine gun, spraying the two Frenchmen with several short, deadly bursts. Hit repeatedly, both men went down in a tangled heap.

The firing had attracted attention, though. Out the corner of one eye, Willi caught a flicker of movement as a second pair of commandos appeared and then went prone, diving into some brush a short distance away. Desperately he swung the MP5 around, already knowing he was too late.

Two grenades sailed toward the German officers.

'Down!' he shouted, burying his face in the dirt.

One landed too far to the right and exploded harmlessly, but the other landed a bare two meters away.

Whummp. A wall of hot air, almost a solid thing, buffeted Willi, threatening to lift him off the ground. He clung desperately, knowing that hundreds of steel fragments were embedded in that mass, sleeting out from a point only a man's height away. The howling sound of their passage, though, was masked by the explosion itself, and by the time von Seelow wondered whether any would hit him, they were past, and he was still alive.

His training told him what must come next, and he fought with his body, trying to shake off the dizziness and to raise his weapon. It seemed to weigh a ton, and his arms would not point it in the right direction. He was half-blind, too, with the dust blown in his eyes and not enough time to wipe it out.

Finally, still prone, he levered the submachine gun over and fired a long burst toward the enemy. It was not a well-aimed burst, but it was fast, and it worked.

He didn't hit anything, but the two French soldiers, rising to follow their grenades in on the heels of the blast, were caught by surprise. They dove back into cover.

Now, Leibnitz and Schisser, the 21st's acting commander, both pumped short accurate bursts from their own submachine guns, one after another, into the brush. They were rewarded by screams and a low, gurgling moan that slowly died away.

When they stopped shooting, the woods were quiet, the stillness unnerving after the deafening din just moments before. With his ears still ringing, Willi kept swiveling his weapon from side to side. Did the trees hide more armed enemies, waiting for them to move? Or were the French defeated, his freedom proof of their failure? In the first case, lying still and waiting was the key to survival, in the other it just made him feel a little silly.

'Herr General!' It was Major Feist's voice. Von Seelow started at the sound, suddenly realizing how tense he was. Leibnitz called back. The danger was over, only minutes after it appeared.

Willi stood slowly, shaking off the last of the grenade's effects. He walked over to the little clump of brush where they had just poured so much fire.

Two bodies lay at odd angles.

He pushed one corpse with the toe of his boot, rolling the man over, studying his uniform. A badge with a silver wing and sword on the dead man's red beret identified him as a member of the 13th Airmobile Dragoons, an elite outfit like Germany's own Long-Range Scout Troops or the American Special Forces. And yet they had been beaten. Willi nodded grimly. Not bad for a bunch of headquarters troops. He had to give Leibnitz a lot of the credit, though. Like Willi himself, the 7th Panzer's commander had learned a hard lesson from the Polish raid that had killed Georg Bremer. The older man had taken special pains to strengthen his division's headquarters security.

He turned away from the dead men.

Feist, panting, had arrived and was almost frantically reporting to Leibnitz. 'No, Herr General, there were no reports of any other attacks, either by the Poles or the French. I've counted at least twenty French bodies so far. We're trying to see how they infiltrated in, but it must have taken them a long time, almost all night.'

Leibnitz growled, almost an animal sound. The French never meant to negotiate. Looking at the German wounded and dead lying all around, he said, 'It appears we have another enemy.'

Willi, ignoring rank, countered, 'No, only one.'

The immediacy of combat had prevented him from fully appreciating Montagne's treachery, but he could feel the anger burning inside. Before, the French had been self-serving fools. Now they were criminals.

The general nodded. He turned back to Feist. 'Pass the order to all units. Tell them to fire on any Frenchmen they see.' He paused. 'Then get me a secure channel. I need to talk to Berlin.'

JULY 4 – ABOARD USS *INCHON*, AMPHIBIOUS GROUP, OFF THE BELGIAN COAST

Inchon's darkened bridge was not a good place to pace. Too many people and too much equipment filled the space, and the near-total darkness just increased the chance of a collision. Adm. Jack Ward still tried, though, like a nervous father in a 1930s comedy, burning off adrenaline as best he could while they waited and waited. Half an hour seemed like an eternity.

He picked up the glasses and stepped out onto the bridge wing again. The cool North Sea night air, stiffened by a fifteen-knot formation speed, made him glad for the khaki jacket.

The Belgian coast was a dark line, invisible except for the uneven horizon it gave the water. A few scattered lights marked small towns, while a larger smear of brightness showed where the port of Ostend lay. It was a dark, quiet scene, with only a thin sliver of moon and almost no wind to stir the sea.

The darkness could hide a lot, like the blacked-out Task Force or the amphibious craft moving toward the beach. The first wave of LCACs – high-speed, air-cushion landing craft – had been launched fifteen minutes ago.

The coast seemed distant, but he knew better than anyone that they had been standing into danger since midnight. They were out of artillery range, but coastal missile batteries were mobile and hard to find.

Ward and his captains had been lucky so far. Taking advantage of Combined Forces naval superiority, he'd risked a daylight move the day before, and a short nighttime run, to put the assault force in position for a night landing. Now the darkness was on their side, and with luck the first wave would be ashore and well established by dawn.

Still, he fretted. No detections and good weather had given them a good start, but the element of surprise could be lost to one fisherman with a radio or a beachcomber with sharp eyes. Stealth was everything in a landing like this.

Virtually every aircraft in the Combined Forces was overhead, providing air cover, knocking out nearby radars and communications stations, or hitting nearby shore bases. Raids on Dunkerque, Calais, and Lille should keep the French occupied, until it was too late.

If they were caught this close to land, with boats and helicopters deployed, even the weakened EurCon air and naval forces would have a field day. They were all taking a terrible chance.

He glanced down at *Inchon*'s flight deck. A row of Ospreys sat waiting, with men seated in neat groups near each VTOL aircraft. Within minutes of the word, they would be airborne, along with similar contingents from the other ships in the force. Aircraft were the quickest way to get men ashore, but vulnerable. Seaborne troops would make the initial landing.

Ward walked over to the dark figure sitting in the admiral's chair. Motionless, the man appeared asleep, and by rights should have been at this hour. Ward knew differently. 'We'll know soon, Ross.'

'How fast do those LCACs move, Admiral?' Huntington asked quietly.

'About forty knots, loaded like they are. It'll take them about half an hour to make the run to the beach. During World War II, it used to take twice that long with the ships much closer in.'

'What could be longer than forever?' Huntington asked half-jokingly.

CHARLIE COMPANY, 3RD MARINE BATTALION, FIFTH MARINE EXPEDITIONARY BRIGADE

Braving the cold forty-knot wind and clinging tightly against the LCAC's rough ride, Capt. Charlie Gates, USMC, peered out over the bow ramp. 'As if I could see anything,' he muttered. Even with his night-vision gear, they were still too far off the coast. The darkness could hide an army, he knew, and by the time he saw the flashes of hostile fire it would be too late for him, and for his men.

If he couldn't see anything, anyone waiting on the beach couldn't, either, unless they had night-vision gear, which these days was no trick. But they wouldn't shoot now, he knew. They'd wait until the LCAC had beached itself and the ramp was down. Then they'd . . .'

Cut that shit out, he thought to himself. He had his orders, and intelligence said there'd be no fire from the beach. Right.

Gates turned to check his men. In the dimness he could only make out forms, but they were all where he had last seen them, standing or sitting, waiting out the thirty-minute ride to the beach. Loaded down with weapons and equipment, there was no really comfortable way to rest, but his marines managed as best they could.

They were close now. He turned to the corner where his lieutenants were clustered and pumped a fist up and down. With a deceptive carelessness, he watched his officers find their sergeants, motion spreading through the company as his men took their places.

He knew what should be waiting. A nice, smooth, shallow grade led to a low seawall capped by a frontage road. The far side was lined by warehouses and light industry, perfect cover for enemy tanks or infantry – if they were there.

The roar of the LCAC's turbines changed pitch as it slowed. They didn't want to plow into the beach at forty knots, after all. Even at the lower note, the LCAC's engines produced a deafening howl. He felt like it would have been quieter riding a steam calliope. If there were hostiles here, they didn't need to see him. They must have been able to hear the marines coming for miles around.

'Captain Gates, I can see them.' The LCAC operator's voice in his headphones almost made him jump. Gates looked over to the glassed-in cab where the craft's 'driver' sat. The petty officer was pointing, not that you needed his guidance to see the cluster of lights on the beach.

Dead ahead, he spotted a cluster of three lights: red, white, and blue. To the right, he saw another group of lights – right where they were supposed to be. No tracers, no other signs of life even through the night-vision goggles. All right. 'It's a go,' he answered in his microphone, and instantly the LCAC's running lights flashed to life, almost blinding in the darkness.

The hovercraft lumbered up onto the beach, throwing spray and pebbles in all directions even as its giant fans wound down.

When the bow ramp dropped, Gates almost sprinted down it, anxious to get off the vulnerable landing craft. The rocky, pebble-covered beach didn't provide the best footing, especially in the dark, but a little of the tension left him when he felt his boots slam down on solid ground again. The worst was over.

As planned, Charlie Company fanned out, providing security for the rest of the wave, only minutes behind him. He trotted toward the lights, followed by his radio telephone operator and a squad from 1st Platoon.

A small party stood next to the metal framework holding the three spot-lights. First silhouetted, then illuminated as Gates changed direction, were three men in camouflage battle dress, but wearing berets, not helmets.

The marine captain slowed to a fast walk, slinging his M16 and unconsciously straightening his gear. Two of the men stepped forward to meet him. In the darkness, the marine could see a tall, long-faced officer with a black, bristling mustache and another shorter, clean-shaven man, but their unfamiliar rank insignia baffled him. Given the situation, it was a silly thing to worry about, but old reflexes die hard.

The tall man saved him the trouble, saluting first and announcing in clipped English accent, 'Major Vandendries, Belgian Army.' He nodded toward his shorter companion. 'And this is Colonel Luiten of the Dutch Royal Army.' He smiled. 'Welcome to Belgium.'

Gates quickly returned the salute, answering, 'Captain Gates, United States Marines, and I'm damned glad to see you, sir.'

Turning to his radiotelephone operator, he ordered, 'Send "Bayonet." '

ABOARD USS *INCHON*

'Message from the first wave, sir.' The intercom's message stilled all other activity on *Inchon*'s bridge. 'Bayonet!'

Ward exhaled and grinned, suddenly not caring how it looked if the Old Man looked like an idiot. He wanted to dance. *Inchon's* bridge crew was too professional to shout or cheer, but he saw the smiles matching his own.

'Bayonet' meant the marines had made peaceful contact with the Belgian armed forces. 'Dagger' would have signaled a peaceful landing but no contact, and 'Sword' had been the code word for a hostile reception – for utter and abject failure.

Ward realized that everyone on the bridge was looking to him, and that Captain March was standing nearby, waiting patiently. Harry was smiling, he noted, but was also impatient.

'Order the second wave in, and pass the word to all forces: we're among friends.'

March turned and hurried away.

By the time the admiral had walked over to the bridge wing again, the Ospreys' rotors were turning and the last of the marines were aboard. He wondered how they felt, suddenly finding out that there would be no shooting, no 'opposed landing.' Instead of invading an enemy, they were reinforcing a friend.

Down below on the flight deck, rotors spun faster, the sound made by eight 6,000-horsepower engines growing to a roar. When the noise reached a peak, the four Ospreys lifted off, one after another, and smoothly curved toward the now-friendly shore. Their marines would be on the ground in minutes, and by dawn the battalion *Inchon* carried would be in place, along with the rest of the Marine Expeditionary Brigade loaded aboard the rest of the Amphibious Group.

Once it was light enough, the rest of the freighters – those carrying the armor, guns, and supplies belonging to the 1st Cavalry and 4th

Infantry – would steam into Belgian and Dutch ports. They would debark their load at harbor piers, instead of across a conquered beach. What might have cost lives, and almost as important, time, would now be an 'administrative landing.'

Ward suddenly remembered Huntington, still sitting in his chair, and went over to congratulate him. As he approached the man, though, he turned away. He'd do it later, when the presidential advisor woke up.

PARIS

Ignoring the clock, Desaix had worked into the early morning hours at his desk, trying to cope with the results of the army's latest failure. Intelligence reports and other documents lay neatly piled on one corner, while the remains of a late supper covered a map. He'd given up studying the data. He knew the problems France faced, and no piece of paper could solve them for him.

Montagne's commando raid against the mutinous leaders of the 7th Panzer had failed utterly. And now this General Leibnitz had gone from being merely intransigent to openly hostile.

Desaix grimaced. He already faced the unpleasant prospect of a mutinous German division and a stalled offensive. The potential was far worse.

Schraeder's government, now informed of the 7th's refusal to obey orders, appeared oddly reluctant to relieve Leibnitz of his command or issue its own orders for his arrest. With thousands of its own soldiers refusing lawful directives, Berlin seemed completely paralyzed.

Now, until the issue was resolved, he couldn't depend on any German unit – whether in Poland or outside the invaded country. The whole EurCon offensive had come to a screeching halt. No one could expect the alliance's French divisions to fight effectively – not when they had to watch their backs as well as their front. Worse, since the army's supply lines ran through Germany on the way back to France, they were now horribly vulnerable. What if the railroad workers or German soldiers guarding those supply lines decided to follow the 7th Panzer's bad example?

And what would happen when the Americans learned about this mutiny? How long would they wait before pouring into the gap that created in the EurCon lines? Desaix closed his eyes against the glare from his desk lamp, wishing the pain surging through his head would go away. He was rapidly running out of options.

'Minister.' One of his duty aides, Radet, stood in the doorway, tentatively addressing him and even more tentatively offering him a single sheet of paper. The younger man seemed pale.

He took the document, and before he could even ask what it was about, the unwilling messenger fled. Bad news, then, Desaix thought resignedly. What have the Germans done now?

It took a moment for his overtaxed mind to focus on the information, and he had to start reading again at the beginning before he understood that this wasn't about Germany.

Belgium's border was closed to all ground and air traffic. A communications blackout had thwarted all attempts to establish any reason for the closure. Phones and data lines were dead, and all television and radio stations were off the air. Even radio communications were affected, because of Combined Forces jamming in connection with heavy air raids now pounding northeastern France.

His subordinates at the Foreign Ministry could not reach their embassy in Brussels or any of the other French consulates.

Desaix felt cold as he read further. Whatever was happening involved more than just Belgium. DGSE monitoring stations reported that all television and radio stations inside the neutral Netherlands were interrupting their normal programming to order Dutch reservists to their wartime posts. And now the embassy in The Hague had signaled that it had been asked to stand by to receive an official message 'of vital importance' from the Dutch government.

For a moment, he wondered if this was a hoax, some diabolical deception by the British and American spy services, but the scale of the action made that impossible. Questions whirled through his head. Is this tied in with the German crisis? But how?

Desaix scooped the phone off his desk and punched in the special code for Morin. He needed input from the head of the DGSE fast.

'Director's office.' The voice on the other end sounded nervous.

'This is Desaix. Put me through to Morin immediately!'

There was an audible pause. 'I'm very sorry, Minister, but I regret to inform you that the director is unavailable at the moment.'

Desaix saw red. 'I don't give a damn whether he's in the bathroom, sleeping, or with his mistress! You find him and bring him to the phone! Understand?'

Strangely his anger seemed to stiffen the other man's spine. 'I'm afraid that is impossible, Minister. I will pass your message on and have him contact you as soon as he is free.'

The line went dead.

Nicolas Desaix stared down at the softly crackling phone in dismay. It appeared that the first rats were beginning to desert his sinking ship.

HEADQUARTERS, 7TH PANZER DIVISION

Willi von Seelow started from an uneasy sleep. Someone was shouting 'Movement!' and men were running to their battle stations. A flash of panic filled him. Were the French attacking again, in real strength this time, or were the Poles and Americans ready to exact their revenge? He rolled out of his cot, grabbed the MP5 next to it, and stumbled out into the predawn gray. General Leibnitz and Schisser were awake, too, with the same worried expressions on their faces.

They ran toward the shouts, and were relieved to see a muddy and tired German lieutenant climbing off a civilian motorcycle.

When he spotted the men coming toward him, all fatigue left the young officer. Bracing and saluting, he reported, 'Oberleutnant Meyer, Headquarters, 2nd Panzergrenadier, sir.'

Willi's ears pricked up at that. The 2nd Panzergrenadier was their sister division in the II Corps. Within hours of the raid on the division's headquarters, the French had begun jamming all their radio channels, blocking any communications with their fellow German units. And none of the couriers they'd sent out in all directions with the real story had returned yet.

Leibnitz returned the salute carefully. 'At ease, Lieutenant.'

Meyer relaxed slightly, but remained at attention. 'Sir, General Berg sends his greetings and a message,' he recited.

'Continue,' prompted Leibnitz. Every ear in range listened closely. If the man carried the message in oral form, that meant it was too sensitive to commit to paper.

'We've heard about the French attack on your headquarters, and your casualties,' the lieutenant recited. 'We are with you, and the last Frenchman we saw was given an extremely hot reception. I am passing word of this crime to every other German unit I can reach.' Meyer stopped, drew a breath, and relaxed a little more. 'That's all, sir. I can take a reply back right now, or act as a runner if you want me to stay.' Someone handed him a cup of coffee, and he took a grateful sip.

'Stay, then,' Leibnitz ordered. 'Have you had any word from Berlin?'

'No, sir, our command nets are being jammed now, too, the landlines as well. The only message we received said to stand by.'

Leibnitz nodded somberly. 'Then that's what we'll do.'

Willi and the other officers muttered their agreement. Just sitting did serious damage to the EurCon cause.

USS *INCHON*

Adm. Jack Ward sat in *Inchon*'s flag plot, watching the inland air battle on radar. France had thrown every plane in its waning arsenal against his formations. It hadn't been enough. The attacks had been piecemeal, almost hurried, and strangely enough, no German units had participated. The intelligence people were still trying to piece the story together, but they confirmed the basic fact. The Luftwaffe was not flying.

Left hanging out in the open by their allies, the incoming French aircraft had met a fire-tipped wall of F-14s and F-18s from the two carriers supporting the landing, F-15 and Tornado interceptors from England, and gratifyingly, Dutch and Belgian F-16s. It hadn't been a 'fair fight,' but then a well-planned battle never was.

To the north, the tanks, trucks, and guns of the 4th Infantry were coming ashore at Rotterdam and Amsterdam. Flown in from Britain by air, its forward elements were already probing toward the German frontier. Here in Belgium, the 5th Marine Expeditionary Brigade was now completely ashore and moving west. And the U.S. 1st Cavalry Division would be unloaded by noon, and on the road shortly thereafter, a sword at France's throat.

'Jack.' Ward turned around to see Ross Huntington towering over him, accompanied by another much shorter, much younger civilian. 'Can you spare a few minutes? I think I've got something you'd like to see.'

Huntington and the other man followed Ward out of CIC, down a ladder, and through a short passageway to his stateroom. 'Admiral's Country' was a well-appointed, if not luxurious, combination of bedroom, office, and meeting room. As they settled themselves, Ward studied the contrast between the Huntington of last night and the one sitting in front of him now.

Refreshed, almost eager, the President's close friend and advisor no longer seemed frail or tired, but full of energy. You couldn't get that from eight hours' sleep, especially when half of it was in a bridge chair, he thought. Ward always got a crick in his neck the next day.

A mess steward served coffee and laid out a silver tray with fresh-baked sweet rolls, then quickly disappeared.

Huntington introduced the stranger as an analyst from the National Security Agency. Even that mention of the shadowy agency seemed to make the young man uncomfortable. Ward knew that Huntington received regular intelligence updates by special courier. He'd never shared any of the information in them, until now.

Motioning to the courier, Huntington remarked, 'Paul here has spent the early morning hours in the backseat of an F-14, from Washington to London to *George Washington*. And by helicopter to here.

'This stuff is new, less than six hours old in some cases.' He leaned forward, rubbing his hands. 'And it's hot. It looks like about half the German Army is on strike. Attacks on the Polish front have virtually stopped, and in a very uncoordinated manner. Despite some heavy-duty jamming, we've also picked up plain-language radio transmissions that talk about the French as if they were the adversary, not us or the Poles.'

Ward whistled. No wonder the Luftwaffe hadn't shown itself anywhere near Belgian or Dutch airspace. 'What do we do about it?'

Huntington smiled. 'If you can show me to your radio room, I've got a few ideas to put in front of the President.'

ALPHA COMPANY, 3/187TH INFANTRY, NEAR SWIECIE, POLAND

Alpha Company had almost recovered from its last battle, at least as recovered as any outfit could be with nearly half its soldiers dead or wounded. Still, Mike Reynolds counted himself lucky. The rest of the battalion had taken the brunt of the German offensive. Some squads had disappeared altogether, and some platoons could barely scrape together a fire team. Total casualties throughout the division were said to be more than a thousand men. He shook his head. One or two more battles like that and they wouldn't have a division left – not as an effective fighting force anyway.

Now, though, the Germans were not attacking at all. Even their recon units had stopped probing. And Division and Corps had used the time, to strengthen their defensive positions and to build up desperately needed supplies and reinforcements. Better still, more battalions from the 1st Armored and the 24th Mech were arriving from Gdansk – feeding into a powerful mobile reserve held right behind the battle line.

Reynolds couldn't understand why the Germans had stopped. Exhaustion? Some brilliant tactical maneuver? Whatever the reason, when EurCon tried to attack again, they'd find a very different enemy.

Alpha Company had taken over part of 2nd Battalion's position, just east of Swiecie. He remembered his men as they had moved forward. The company had been proud of their fight, bragging about it to each other. They'd stopped bragging when they saw the shattered remnants of the town.

Adams trotted up. 'Officer's call, sir. Platoon and company leaders. In the hotel.'

The Piast Hotel was little more than a shell, with its upper floors collapsed, and the stone walls scorched by fire. It was a recognizable landmark, though, and still partially intact. Colby had chosen to remain there. Habitable buildings were in short supply.

Colby almost matched his headquarters. He'd been caught on the edge of the bomb blast that had shattered the hotel, and he'd been lucky to escape with some first-degree burns, singed hair, and a lot of lacerations. He looked like hell.

He was still upbeat, though, almost cheerful with the front quiet. 'New orders, sports fans, new ROEs.'

The officers and noncoms looked at him expectantly, more than a little puzzled. They were already in a full-fledged shooting war. Why would the brass issue new rules of engagement now?

Colby went on. 'Unless the Germans shoot at us, we don't shoot at them.'

He waved down the startled chorus of questions and protests. The 3/187th was a disciplined group, but this was different. Was the war over? What the hell was Division thinking about?

'This didn't come from Division,' Colby countered. 'This is diplomatic stuff, all the way up to the C-in-C level.'

Reynolds stepped out of the group. With his men's lives on the line, he wanted the orders he would have to fight under crystal-clear. 'What do we do if they come at us?'

'Report to me. If they're close enough to shoot, shoot first and we'll sort it out later. But if you just spot 'em, don't shoot. The idea is to leave them alone, so no patrolling, no harassing fire with artillery, no air strikes. We watch, and we wait.'

'What about the French?' Reynolds asked.

'If you can ID a target as French, give it everything you've got.'

CHAPTER 37
Collapse

JULY 5 – ADVANCE ELEMENTS, 1ST CAVALRY DIVISION, NEAR MONS, BELGIUM

Deployed in a wedge formation, nineteen M3 Bradley fighting vehicles rolled southwest. They were moving through a flat, drab countryside dotted by beet fields, small orchards, and gray slag heaps. Tiny helicopters flitted ahead of them, climbing only to clear power lines – OH-58 Kiowas probing for the first signs of any EurCon force. Behind the scouts, shark-nosed Apache gunships flew even lower, ready to pop up and unleash salvos of deadly, laser-guided Hellfire antitank missiles. The Belgian border with France lay just twenty kilometers up the highway.

Hundreds of M1 tanks and M2 infantry fighting vehicles, the rest of the U.S. 1st Cavalry Division, were further back, moving in columns behind the advance guard. Their presence was signaled by billowing dust clouds and a low, deep, grinding, growling, clanking roar. More dust clouds along the western horizon revealed units of the Belgian Army advancing alongside the Americans.

Riding with his turret hatch open, Lt. Col. John Chandler, the commander of the U.S. division's cavalry squadron, studied his surroundings intently. Eighty-four years before, during one of the World War I's opening battles, Britain's khaki-clad riflemen and the Kaiser's spike-helmeted infantry had clashed at Mons. Thousands had died on both sides. Now, as the century drew to a close, it seemed bitterly ironic that men were still prepared to fight and die across the same bleak, polluted landscape.

Chandler shook his head somberly, listening to the steady stream of reports crackling through his headphones. The French and Germans had started this insane war. If they were foolish enough to fight on against overwhelming odds, he and his troopers would certainly oblige them.

JULY 6 – CHANCELLOR'S OFFICE, THE REICHSTAG, BERLIN

Like a stone and glass phoenix, Germany's resurrected Reichstag – its Parliament Building – stood almost alone in the vast, darkened expanse of the Platz der Republik. Inside a corner office in the building's east wing, Chancellor Heinz Schraeder turned away from his inspection of Berlin's blacked-out skyline. He glanced at the clock on his desk. It was just past midnight. How appropriate, he thought wryly.

He looked up from the clock toward the five grim, determined men standing on the other side of his desk. Germany's Defense Minister, her Foreign Minister, and the three uniformed service chiefs stood motionless, waiting for his permission to speak. Even in the face of certain defeat, certain formalities had to be observed. 'Well, gentlemen?'

'The strategic situation is hopeless, Chancellor.' Jurgen Lettow, the Minister of Defense, never minced words. 'Belgium's defection and the Dutch declaration of war against the Confederation have finished us.'

Schraeder nodded. Together, the Americans, the British, and their new Dutch and Belgian allies now had well over 150,000 troops and nearly two thousand tanks massed within striking distance of Germany's virtually unguarded industrial heartland. With most of its army tied down in Poland and refusing any orders from higher headquarters, Germany had almost nothing left to throw in their path. Little more than a corporal's guard of reservists and a single panzergrenadier division. It was not enough.

He cleared his throat. 'Then what do you suggest, Herr Lettow?'

'That we seek a separate peace while we still can,' Lettow replied. His companions muttered their agreement. The Defense Minister's eyes flashed. 'We owe the French nothing.'

That much was certainly true, Schraeder thought angrily. Entranced by the man's vision of a Europe united under French and German influence, he'd backed Nicolas Desaix down the line – only to have his trust betrayed at every turn. The secret negotiations with the Russians had demonstrated only too clearly that France was perfectly willing to sacrifice Germany's vital strategic interests for its own short-term gain. And the murderous French attack on the 7th Panzer's headquarters only confirmed what many Germans already suspected: France viewed its ally not as an equal partner, but instead as a puppet to be used, bled white, and then contemptuously discarded.

Still he hesitated. Too much of his own political prestige and power was bound up in the French alliance. Could he afford to walk away from Desaix so lightly?

Lettow leaned across the desk. 'I speak for the rest of the cabinet and for the armed forces, Chancellor. Abandon this absurd alliance and this lost war before it is too late.'

Again, heads nodded their agreement. Every man in the room knew only too well the horrible price Germany had paid for her last military defeat.

Schraeder slumped back in his chair. 'Very well.' His shoulders bowed. 'What must I do?'

'Sign these orders.' Lettow began laying documents in front of him.

Suddenly weary beyond his years, the Chancellor paged through them. The first formally notified Paris that Germany was withdrawing from all its treaty obligations as a member of the European Confederation. The second authorized the Foreign Minister to open immediate peace talks with the Combined Forces. The third and final document instructed the country's two railway systems – the Deutsche Bundesbahn and the Deutsche Reichsbahn – to halt all supply shipments to French forces in Germany or eastern Europe.

Moving slowly, almost unwillingly, Schraeder uncapped his fountain pen and scrawled his signature across the bottom of each page.

Before he'd put his pen down, one of the waiting officers picked the orders up and hurried out of the room. Lettow tossed another piece of paper onto the desk. His voice turned ice-cold. 'You have one more document to sign, Chancellor.'

Schraeder stared down at it. 'What is this?'

'Your resignation.'

ALPHA COMPANY, 3/187TH INFANTRY, NEAR SWIECIE, POLAND

'Movement to the front!'

The shout woke Capt. Mike Reynolds from an after-lunch siesta. Two days of relative peace and quiet made the sudden warning almost as startling as it would have been during his first days in Poland, but his reflexes were still solid. In seconds he was out the CP's door, weapon in hand.

The rest of Alpha Company's soldiers were just as fast. They dove into foxholes and readied their weapons, all the while scanning the ground to their front for signs of the approaching enemy. Or was 'enemy' still the right word? The scuttlebutt filtering up from the rear areas said that EurCon was breaking up.

Was the war really over? Reynolds wasn't sure, but with the practical cynicism of a combat soldier, he'd decided he wouldn't let down his guard until he had definite proof.

The CP was fifty meters back from the center of Alpha Company's sector. Reynolds covered the distance in what seemed like three strides.

Sergeant Robbins reported as he slid into position, 'We've got a single Marder cruising up the road, Captain. Nothing else.' He managed to shrug, even while tracking the vehicle on binoculars.

Reynolds lifted his own field glasses. The German APC was roughly five hundred meters away and still closing. 'Tell the company to stand to. No chances.'

The Marder was just coming into Javelin range. Whatever the bastards inside wanted, if they made trouble, they'd have a short life and a violent death.

He studied the vehicle, as if its steel sides could tell him the intentions of the people inside. In a way, they could, because as the Marder drew near, he saw that its turret and 25mm cannon were reversed.

'Pass the word to Battalion. I think they want to talk.' Now Reynolds was almost sure the Germans had peaceful intentions. Either that or they had a strong death wish.

The Marder stopped well short of their positions, about a hundred meters out. Two officers in German battle dress got out, carefully walking down the lowered rear ramp. One was tall and thin, but looked fit. He wore the green beret of armored infantry. The second German was shorter and older. His beret was black, indicating a tank unit. Although they appeared to be unarmed, both men were wearing standard-issue flak vests.

They strode forward confidently, heading straight for the 2nd Platoon's positions. Fighting his instincts, but convinced he was right, Reynolds climbed out of the foxhole. Accompanied by Sergeant Robbins, he walked out to meet them. He kept his own M16 cradled casually under his arm. During Alpha Company's two bloody encounters with the Germans there had been winners and there had been losers. He wanted to make sure they knew which was which.

He stopped a few paces away and regarded the two Germans carefully. A few years back he would have been saluting these guys as senior officers in an allied army. A few days ago he might have shot them on sight.

The taller man spoke first, in hard-edged, accented English. 'Good afternoon, Captain. I am Lieutenant Colonel Wilhelm von Seelow, commanding officer of the 19th Panzergrenadier Brigade. This is General Karl Leibnitz, commanding officer of the 7th Panzer Division. We would like to speak with your division commander. We are here to arrange a temporary cessation of hostilities while our respective governments negotiate a more permanent peace.'

Reynolds stared back, scarcely able to believe what he'd just heard. For once, the rumors were true.

JULY 7 – CNN HEADLINE NEWS

On the edge of London's Piccadilly Circus, CNN's lead political correspondent stood against a backdrop of revelry. 'Like a gigantic block party, the celebration in Piccadilly continues nonstop. As EurCon collapses like a house of cards, the news of each country's defection provides new energy and new celebrants.'

The image changed to show an overhead view of the crowd.

They filled the square, with the statue of Eros rising like a maypole in their midst. A close-up showed exultant Londoners in every kind of dress, waving and cheering, dancing either to the music from nearby radios or to no music at all.

The picture switched back to the reporter. 'Right now, the crowd is celebrating news of Austria's decision to withdraw from EurCon. The Austrian move was expected last night, but apparently it required what a government spokesman termed "a change in internal political alignments." Others might call it a coup d'état.'

A map of Europe appeared with EurCon's prewar member states colored red. 'Starting with Belgium three days ago, nation after nation has withdrawn from the French-dominated European Confederation.

'Belgium's decision to switch sides rocked the continent.' Belgium flashed from red to blue. 'But then Germany dealt the Confederation a body blow.' It changed color as well, leaving only France and a scattering of small red blots across the map.

'Since then, all the smaller states, either yielding to internal pressures or free of EurCon restraints, have jumped on the Combined Forces bandwagon.' As he spoke, countries turned blue in sequence, until only France was left, alone.

JULY 8 – NEAR TATABANYA, HUNGARY

Col. Zoltan Hradetsky and Oskar Kiraly drove slowly up the designated road. It led through a forest just north of Tatabanya, a city roughly sixty kilometers west of Budapest. Presumably the area was crawling with French soldiers, but none were visible. Though neither said anything, that made them wary. Despite French assurances, weeks of war had made the two men suspicious and bitter. Even so, with EurCon destroyed, Hungary was on the brink of victory.

Obeying Berlin's stringent orders, the remaining German troops inside Hungary were withdrawing peacefully – guaranteed safe conduct and assistance in leaving the country. Eager to see the last of them, Hungarian military police units were even providing traffic control for the 10th Panzer's vehicles as they headed west.

The German retreat left the EurCon IV Corps' two small French divisions alone and isolated. Austria's defection left them unsupplied.

Hradetsky permitted himself a small smile. The French had their backs right against a cliff. Now it was time to push them off.

'Halt!' French soldiers emerged from the woods and waved them to a stop. They left their own vehicle in a clearing and rode the rest of the way in a jeep, accompanied by a grim-faced French lieutenant. More troops mounted in an AMX-10 APC pulled onto the road and followed the jeep.

Hradetsky suspected that this was all part of an attempt to intimidate them. Knowing what he knew, it didn't work. He looked over at Kiraly. The broad-shouldered blond man was smiling, almost gleeful.

IV Corps headquarters was a textbook model of efficiency. Carved out of the forest, fully camouflaged, and heavily defended, it looked like an important and busy place. It impressed Hradetsky, and Kiraly, with his army background, nodded approvingly, but there was still the hint of a smile on his lips.

The jeep stopped, and they were escorted to a tent in the center of the compound.

Gen. Claude Fabvier waited for them, seated at a folding table. The short, lean man's camouflage battle dress was neatly creased. As he rose to greet them, Hradetsky saw the briefest of scowls pass over the Frenchman's face, but that was quickly replaced by an expression of studied indifference.

Fabvier seemed a little impatient. 'All right, gentlemen. As you can see, we are all here. Now, what is it that you wish to discuss?'

'Your surrender,' Hradetsky shot back. There was anger in his voice, more than he had intended to reveal. Fabvier had led the invasion of his country. Apart from Nicolas Desaix, this French general was the man most responsible for Hungary's pain.

Fabvier flushed beneath his dark tan. He silently motioned the Hungarians to seats at the other side of the table.

As the three men sat, the Frenchman set his jaw. 'It was my understanding that this meeting was to arrange my corps's withdrawal from Hungary.' A little of his own anger crept into his voice.

Hradetsky shook his head. 'Not quite, General. Our message requested a meeting to discuss "the peaceful departure of the troops remaining on Hungarian soil." That is not quite the same thing. Certainly you didn't think you'd be allowed to leave so easily – not after invading our country.'

Fabvier's eyes narrowed. 'I am prepared to withdraw unmolested. I am not prepared to surrender. We can cut our way out through your precious land if need be,' he warned.

Oskar Kiraly shrugged, speaking for the first time. 'A brave sentiment. But we know your supply status. You've got less than twenty thousand liters of fuel, barely enough ammunition for one short battle, and you're already forced to send foraging parties out to scour the countryside for any food they can find.' His smile reappeared.

Fabvier sat, impassive and silent, showing neither agreement nor disagreement with Kiraly's figures.

Hradetsky leaned forward a little, pressing home the point. 'You've got just enough gas for an uncontested road march to the Austrian border. But what then? The Austrians have turned against you, too. Besides, you know you'd never make it that far.'

Kiraly nodded. 'We have two motorized rifle divisions, also fresh and rested, dug in along the roads east of here. More Hungarian and Slovak units are moving into striking range. You are already outnumbered. Within hours, you will also be completely surrounded.'

Fabvier sat silent, his head bowed.

'Here are our terms, General.' Hradetsky removed a document from his jacket pocket. 'Your troops will disarm and assemble in areas we designate. They will turn over all their equipment intact, down to the last radio and pistol. Only personal gear – clothing, bedding, and the like – is exempt. Your tanks and guns will be partial compensation for what you've destroyed here.

'In return, we will transport you and your men to the Austrian border. We will also grant all French soldiers immunity from prosecution under Hungarian law.'

'What?' Fabvier exploded. 'How dare you threaten us with prison! We are at war—'

Kiraly interrupted him. 'Many of your men have committed what could be considered war crimes, General. Your own hands aren't clean, either. Summary execution of hostages, demolition of homes by the occupying forces . . .'

'Make up any charges you want. That's the right of the winning side,' Fabvier snarled.

Hradetsky ignored the dig. 'What will it be, General?' he demanded.

'Will you yield or will you throw your men's lives away to save your own pride?'

'Your soldiers will die, too.'

'We're used to it,' Hradetsky said coldly.

Fabvier looked at the two implacable Hungarians, then away from them as though a solution to the dilemma they posed might lie off to one side. It didn't. 'Very well, we will disarm,' he said, refusing to face them.

Six hours later, 25,000 French troops marched into temporary captivity. Tens of thousands more left stranded in Germany and Poland met the same fate before nightfall.

JULY 9 – PARIS

Abandoned by his closest associates and subordinates, Nicolas Desaix sat alone in his private office. Ever the opportunist, Morin had vanished as soon as the news of Germany's defection reached his desk. Guichy was dead. Shamed by failure and fearful of the future, the Defense Minister had shot himself after learning that all French units in Germany and eastern Europe had capitulated.

Desaix grimaced. Both the DGSE chief and the Defense Minister had chosen a coward's way out. He had not yielded so easily. For hours he had worked frantically, trying his best to restore order – to salvage something for France from the wreckage of his ambitious schemes. He had failed.

His orders were ignored. His telephone calls went unanswered. France was tired of Nicolas Desaix and all his works.

Not that there was very much he could have done anyway, he reflected sourly. Spread thin from the Mediterranean to the Channel ports, the tattered remnants of the French Army and Air Force were no match for the armies arrayed against them. At last report, U.S., British, and Belgian troops were already past Cambrai, advancing cautiously toward Paris against pitiful resistance. Most Frenchmen seemed content to sit at home waiting for a change of government – whether imposed from the outside or altered from within.

Cloaked in his own despair, Desaix barely noticed the four tough-looking men file in from his outer office. Even wearing civilian clothes they couldn't hide the air of complacent authority common to policemen or special security agents.

'You are M. Nicolas Desaix?' one of the men asked in a bored, unhurried voice.

Desaix glanced up sharply. Idiots! Who else would he be? His fingers drummed sharply on his desk. 'I am.'

'Then I must inform you that you are under arrest.'

Something of his old fire flashed through Desaix. He drew himself up haughtily. 'I am a minister of the republic! By whose authority do you arrest me?'

In answer, the senior plainclothesman handed him a sealed warrant. Signed by all his cabinet colleagues except for Guichy and Morin, it also bore the signature of the President. Desaix stared down in utter astonishment. Having at last nerved themselves to act against him, the little worms had even roused Bonnard from his senile torpor long enough to plant this dagger in his back. Determined to save themselves, the President and the others were throwing him to the wolves.

Numbed by constant disaster, Nicolas Desaix allowed his captors to lead him out to a waiting unmarked car.

His downfall preceded the complete collapse of the French Fifth Republic by only a matter of hours.

CHAPTER 38
New Beginnings

JULY 15 – THE WHITE HOUSE, WASHINGTON, D.C.

The President's smiling face was the first thing Ross Huntington saw when he walked into the Oval Office. It was hard to recognize him as the same coldly determined leader who had sent him off to Europe to break EurCon to pieces. 'Ross! Come on in and take a pew.'

Huntington dropped lightly into a chair, amazed to find himself feeling better than he had in years. Considering how he'd spent the past few weeks, that was strange: First the sleepless days and nights at sea off an enemy coast. Then the twenty-hour days he'd spent shuttling between European capitals to patch together a temporary armistice. And finally the long, red-eye flight home. By any rational measure, he should be dead on his feet. Maybe even dead, period – given his prior medical history. But victory and the prospect of a lasting peace seemed to be a better tonic than bed rest.

He said as much to the President.

The other man nodded, still grinning. 'Damn right. I feel like a kid again myself.'

That wasn't quite true, Huntington thought, studying his longtime friend carefully. New lines and creases on what had once been a boyish face showed where the strains and stresses of war had taken a permanent toll.

Still, the President's essential optimism remained intact. It came roaring to the surface as the two men talked about what came next. 'At least now we've got a real chance to put the world back on the right track! A real window of opportunity.'

Huntington nodded. Thoroughly discredited by the war, the apostles of ultranationalism and protectionism were in retreat around the globe. Shocked by the sight of so many new blood-soaked battlefields, politicians and peoples alike seemed ready to lay aside old hatreds and misguided ambitions. But how long would that last? 'That window could slam shut pretty damn fast, Mr. President,' he warned.

'I know.' The President's gaze turned inward. 'We've paid a high price for *this* peace. I don't intend to see it thrown away. Not this time.'

Huntington knew what he meant by that. Transfixed by domestic squabbles after the cold war ended, the world's industrial nations had turned inward and against each other. Recessions had bred resentment – resentment against 'foreigners' and 'foreign'-made products. And cynical politicians had made use of those resentments for their own gain. Protective tariffs had spawned more tariffs and more trade restrictions in a vicious cycle of retaliation and counterretaliation. The trade wars and festering racial and ethnic hatreds had all been part of a long, ugly, melancholy slide toward real war – wars between neighbors and between nations.

He asked, 'What exactly do you have in mind?'

'A new alliance among nations. An alliance based on four firm principles: free trade, free enterprise, free markets, and free governments. An alliance that isn't limited to a single continent or a single ocean.' The President laughed self-consciously. 'Not much to ask, is it?' He turned serious. 'It's the only real way I know to promote peace, Ross. Prosperous democracies don't make war on one another. All the treaties and solemn pledges in the world don't mean anything unless they're backed by goodwill and shared interests.'

Huntington nodded. 'Building something like that won't be easy.'

'Nope. It sure won't,' the President agreed. 'But since this is the third time we've picked up the pieces in Europe this century, the United States has a lot of moral authority and practical power right now. And I plan to use every last bit of it.' He glanced toward the phone on his desk. 'I just finished talking with the British, and we've agreed to jointly sponsor talks in London beginning as soon as possible.'

'Who's invited?'

The President smiled. 'Since we plan to start small, just Europe, Canada, Mexico, and the United States for now. Eventually? Say in a few months? The whole world. It'll take a hell of a lot of hard work and some fancy footwork – especially from whoever gets the unenviable task of shepherding the conference through to completion.' The President's smile grew wider as it became clear that Huntington was his choice for the job.

Huntington felt the first flicker of alarm.

'So, what do you say, Ross? Have any other urgent plans? Golf? Tennis? A summer by the shore?'

He shifted awkwardly in his chair. 'But . . . you can't be serious, Mr. President. I'm not a statesman.'

'I'm perfectly serious,' the President said firmly. 'You're honest. You're intelligent. You don't put up with bullshit. And that's exactly the kind of statesman the world needs right now.' He got up from behind his desk and laid a hand on Huntington's shoulder. 'You've served your country in the shadows long enough, Ross. It's time to step out into the light.'

JULY 16 – BUDAPEST AIRPORT, HUNGARY

Feeling stiff and awkward in his new dress uniform, Zoltan Hradetsky stood among a host of other dignitaries on the tarmac – waiting impatiently while the British Airways jetliner from Paris taxied off the runway and turned toward them. The twin silver stars on each shoulder board that proclaimed him a major general seemed to weigh a ton apiece.

Give me enough time, he thought, and I will become accustomed to them. The rank bothered him. The job that went with the stars did not.

As the new commander of Hungary's National Police, Hradetsky was charged with reforming and reorganizing his country's law enforcement organizations. It was a mission he'd been preparing for all his adult life. He was already seeking organizational and training aid from the American FBI and Britain's CID. For once he could be sure of getting foreign advisors who would come bringing sound counsel, not seeking covert control.

The passenger jet rolled to a stop in front of the assembled crowds, and airport workers rushed a mobile staircase into place against its forward cabin door. When the door swung open, an army honor guard came to attention. Drums rolled softly as a band began playing the national anthem.

Hradetsky held his breath, waiting until Vladimir Kusin, tall and unbowed by his captivity, walked out into the afternoon sunlight. Hungary's new President had come safely home.

JULY 17 – PREFECTURE OF POLICE, PARIS

Nicolas Desaix paced angrily back and forth through the darkness. He'd been penned up inside this special holding cell for days – held incommunicado while the newly formed Sixth Republic prepared to try him for crimes against the French people and against humanity. Aside from the prosecutors building the case against him, he'd been visited only by two doctors who had warned him against high blood pressure and prescribed medications that he'd immediately thrown back in their faces. He snorted in contempt. How absurd this false concern for his health was! Clearly the government only wanted to make sure he lived long enough to serve as a scapegoat.

He scowled. Perhaps Guichy had chosen the best path, after all. A bullet in the brain might be preferable to this prolonged mockery of justice.

Desaix shrugged the thought away. He would not surrender so tamely. The years he'd spent in the upper echelons of the intelligence service and the French government had given him access to many secrets – secrets that could prove highly embarrassing to a number of important officials. If bargaining failed, he could always use a public trial to drag others down with him. That, at least, would be a kind of pleasure.

A key rattled in his cell door. He turned in surprise. More visitors? This late?

The door flew open and three men crowded inside. Desaix recognized one of them, Philippe Gille, the head of the DGSE's Action Service – its covert operations wing. The other two were mere thugs, the kind of petty criminals the Action Service often employed for deniable missions.

Desaix's alarm turned to panic when he saw the surgical gloves on their hands. He opened his mouth, trying to scream. It was too late.

Something cold and sharp pricked his forearm. Pain flared in his chest, and he spiraled down into blackness and then oblivion.

Several hours later, an elderly police doctor rose awkwardly from beside the contorted body. He sighed, taking the stethoscope out of his ears.

'Well?' The chief prosecutor looked thoroughly irked. Desaix's testimony would have been an invaluable aid in the new French government's efforts to reform and reorder the various intelligence agencies. This death would complicate matters. Still, it showed that his probes were hitting nerves in certain, secretive quarters.

'I am sorry, Monsieur Prosecutor. It appears that the minister died sometime late last night of a massive heart attack. As I feared would happen.' The doctor, a short, thin white-haired man named Arnault, shrugged nervously. 'It is a great pity.'

'I see. A very convenient heart attack for some, wouldn't you say, Doctor?' The prosecutor studied him for another few moments, as though waiting for more. When the doctor stayed silent, his mouth tightened. He turned and signaled through the door. Two more men moved into the holding cell. Both carried medical bags of their own.

The prosecutor turned back to a now visibly worried Arnault. 'I'm sure you understand that I must have my own experts verify your findings.' He glanced at the two waiting men. 'Check for anything unusual. Needle marks, bruising, you know the sort of thing.'

They nodded somberly.

The police doctor began trembling slightly but noticeably. The DGSE men had promised him protection from this grim, implacable official. Now Arnault was beginning to suspect that the intelligence agents had overestimated their remaining authority and underestimated the determination of their new superiors to make a clean sweep. 'On reflection, Monsieur Prosecutor, I must confess that I noticed certain things that are perhaps inconsistent with my earlier, *preliminary* diagnosis.'

'Oh?' The prosecutor turned his head slowly. 'How very interesting, Dr. Arnault.' He laid a firm hand on the older man's shoulder. 'Then why don't we go to my office and discuss exactly what else and who else you are beginning to remember?'

AUGUST 1 – THE WHITE HOUSE

Erin McKenna sat in the antechamber outside the Oval Office. Unable to stop herself, she checked her watch again, wishing she weren't so nervous. Still, how many people in the United States were ever invited to a private meeting with the President? She glanced to her right, comforted by the sight of Alex Banich sitting at her side. He smiled back.

Despite their best intentions, they hadn't had much time together since returning from Moscow. Len Kutner, appalled by the risks they'd run and elated by their success, had shipped them back to Washington as soon as he safely could. Since then, Erin and Alex had both been kept hopping – briefing what seemed like every section head and file clerk in the CIA on the situation inside Russia. But, under explicit orders from the director of Central Intelligence himself, never, never, *never* mentioning their own role in Marshal Kaminov's assassination.

'Ms. McKenna? Mr. Banich?'

They looked up.

A secretary motioned them toward the door. 'The President can see you now.'

Heart pounding, Erin rose and followed Alex into the Oval Office.

The President himself was waiting for them, standing alone by the windows overlooking the White House Rose Garden. He smiled broadly when they came in and stepped forward to greet them both with a firm, friendly handshake. 'Ms. McKenna and Mr. Banich! I'm very glad to finally meet you.'

He looked older than he did on television, but also more human. She could see real warmth in his eyes. The next few moments passed in a whirl of polite conversation.

Suddenly the President's manner became far more formal. He gathered two small boxes off his desk and flipped them open. Each contained a medal and a length of ribbon to hold it. 'Erin McKenna and Alexander Banich, it is my great privilege to award you each with the Medal of Freedom – the highest civilian honor a grateful nation can bestow.'

Blushing now, Erin and Alex bent their heads one after the other, allowing him to slip the medals over their necks.

Then, amazingly enough, the President seemed embarrassed himself. 'Of course, I have to ask for them back before you leave.' He grinned, shamefaced. 'Since we don't exactly want the whole world to know just how that old bastard Kaminov met his very timely end, your awards are classified Top Secret!'

Erin couldn't help it. She had to laugh. Giving you a medal you couldn't talk about or show off was just so typical of the way the government worked.

The President laughed with her. He stopped her when she tried to apologize. 'No need for that, Ms. McKenna! You're absolutely right. I only hope you'll let me offer you something more concrete. Not exactly a reward, though. Just another chance to do more hard work for your country.'

She nodded. 'Of course, Mr. President.'

'Good. I'd like to send you to Great Britain. To work as a senior staffer on the U.S. delegation to the London Conference.' He sounded pleased. 'Ross Huntington needs a trade expert – especially someone skilled at stripping away phony numbers and deceptive claims.'

The President arched a skeptical eyebrow. 'The world may be singing songs of goodwill and fellowship right now, but neither Ross nor I believe we've reached the Millennium. There are still going to be people and countries out there who bear close watching.'

Erin and Alex both nodded. There was plenty of proof of that everywhere you looked. Still, progress was being made. Right now, for example, the newspapers and television news programs were full of revelations from Paris. Even killing Desaix to shut him up hadn't saved the hard-line elements of the French secret services. If anything, his murder seemed to have energized the Sixth Republic's investigations. Every passing day saw new details of the old French government's unsavory, often illegal, doings come to light. Dozens of high- and middle-ranking DGSE officials were either under arrest or in forced retirement. For the first time in decades, it appeared that France might actually gain control over its shadowy 'government within a government.'

The President looked toward Banich. 'As for you, Mr. Banich, I think we'd both agree that your days as a field agent are numbered.'

The CIA officer nodded slowly. He'd known that ever since Soloviev penetrated his cover, but it was still hard to accept that he'd been locked out of the covert game forever.

The President watched him carefully. 'How would you like a posting as a chief of station?'

Erin's heart sank. She knew this was a big step for Alex – one he richly deserved. But it also meant he would soon be stationed at another embassy far away from her and far too busy for close contact. Slowly, inexorably, they would drift apart over time – each consumed by his or her own work. She turned away, unwilling to influence his decision by letting him see her sadness. She didn't really have a claim on him – not yet.

Then the President went on with just the faintest suggestion of a twinkle in his eyes. 'I understand you're a skilled linguist, Mr. Banich. That you're fluent in Russian, Ukrainian, and several other languages?'

'Yes, sir.'

The President nodded. 'Thought so. That's why I think it's high time you polished up your English skills.' He grinned. 'Walt Quinn and I want you to take over the London Station at the end of this month. I hope you'll accept.'

Banich grinned back. 'You can count on it, Mr. President!'

Erin turned toward him, her own eyes sparkling. London was one of the CIA's most important and prestigious posts. Better yet, it meant that they would be together, after all.

SEPTEMBER 3 – NORFOLK, VIRGINIA

Jack Ward sighed and looked around his new office. Although his retirement was still three months away, he'd decided to rent an office as soon as he was transferred to shore duty. It had just enough paneling and thick-enough carpets to be comfortable without appearing ostentatious. Compared to the steel bulkheads of a navy warship, it was luxurious.

He sat behind the desk, studying the still-empty walls and empty in-basket. There wasn't much to do yet, but he enjoyed the idleness. After running the biggest U.S. naval force since World War II and seeing too many men and ships die, he could appreciate a little boredom.

Many of his friends were still surprised that he'd decided to retire. If he'd stayed in the navy, he would have been a shoo-in for the next chief of naval staff, the highest-ranking job in the fleet. But the CNS slot was a thankless task, an administrator's job with no command function at all.

Ward knew he was an 'operator,' and being a wartime fleet commander was as high as he could ever want to rise. It was time to get out while he was still ahead.

There was still a lot to do. There were the obligatory memoirs. Writing those would take a year or two. There was that cabin on the Carolina shore that he'd promised Elizabeth and himself. Navy men spent far too much time away from their families, and now he was going to take some of that time back.

The phone rang, startling him a little. Just installed, few people had the number. Probably his wife.

It rang a second time. Ward picked it up, expecting to hear Elizabeth's voice.

'Admiral, it's Ross Huntington. Your wife said I could reach you here.'

'That's right,' Ward answered, surprised. The admiral was still only vaguely aware of Huntington's role during the war, except that he was very close to the President. Since the war, though, the papers had been full of stories about the London Conference and its organizer. He was delighted to hear from Huntington, and a little flattered. His friend's voice was strong and full of energy, which also pleased Ward.

They chatted for a while, exchanging news about their families and postwar celebrations. After a few minutes of small talk, Ward congratulated Huntington on his appointment and asked how preparations were going. It was the opening the other man had been waiting for. 'It's going well, Jack. We're getting a lot of support from all over Europe. The French and Germans are jumping at the chance to attend. They need all the goodwill they can get. I've got one problem, though.'

'What's that?' asked Ward.

'I've got a hole on my team, Jack. I don't have a military advisor. Defense plays a big role in all of Europe's economies, and if I don't have someone who can handle that part of the equation, I'm bound for disaster. Will you take it on?'

Even as Huntington continued, thoughts whirled to the front of Ward's mind. Dealing with dozens of European countries.

'I'd need you for at least a year.'

Trying to build up an accurate military picture of postwar Europe.

'I can't lie to you. The work load would be awful.'

Defining a new pattern of security relationships for the postwar world.

'I'll do it,' Ward said. Idleness be damned. His memoirs could wait. He wanted to add a few more chapters.

SEPTEMBER 10 – WROCLAW, 11TH FIGHTER REGIMENT

Glumly Maj. Tadeusz Wojcik reviewed his plans for the next series of tactics lectures. It was his unenviable task to make sure they folded smoothly and logically into the regiment's existing training plan.

He'd been transferred to the training command after the war. It was a rest, they said. He should relax, they said. You need the administrative experience, they said.

Tad missed flying. He maintained proficiency with once-a-week hops, but milk runs weren't the same as flying with an operational squadron. Sometimes, sitting there at his desk, he could almost hear his arteries hardening.

He heard a rapping and looked up to see one of his staff knocking on the open door. 'Major, there's someone here to see you.' The corporal's stunned expression did not match his prosaic words. The noncom looked so surprised, in fact, that Tad wondered if the air force's inspector general had dropped by to rake him over the coals for misfiling some bureaucratic form or another.

The corporal stepped aside, replaced by a man in ill-fitting civilian clothes. He spoke in accented English, which threw Tad off for a moment. He didn't speak English that much anymore.

The stranger reached forward and enthusiastically pumped Tad's hand as he rose behind the desk. 'Major Wojcik. I am very glad to meet you.' He paused for a moment and smiled. 'I am sorry. I am glad to see you *again*.' The smile got bigger.

Tad was at a complete loss. The stranger had longish black hair and blue eyes. He was reasonably fit, and seemed just a little younger than Tad himself. They'd met before? When? Where? Who was this guy?

'I'm sorry, I'm afraid . . .'

The grin widened some more. 'Of course.' The man suddenly snapped to attention. 'I am Leutnant Dieter Kurtz of the Deutsche Luftwaffe, with Jagdgeschwader Three.'

A German? Tad's face mirrored his puzzlement. But he'd never met . . .

Kurtz continued. 'I was in a MiG-29 on June 8, near the German-Polish border.'

Recognition dawned on Wojcik's face. 'You tangled with two F-15s. I was in one of them.'

The German nodded. 'And you shot me down.'

An image of the dogfight flashed through Tad's memory. A night intercept that had resulted in a classic two-versus-two engagement, with the maneuvers as clean and well executed as a game between chess champions.

It had not ended quickly, though. Move had followed countermove until Tad had finally taken a chance snapshot with his cannon and scored on the German. It had been his sixth kill and it had firmly cemented his reputation as an ace with the regiment.

Tad remembered the MiG, sparkling in the darkness as his cannon shells struck, then spiraling down into the night, one wing gone and on fire.

At the time, he hadn't even thought about the other pilot, hadn't felt anything except a grim joy at the victory. He compared that feeling with the affable stranger standing before him.

Remembering himself, he offered Kurtz a chair, and then sat down himself. 'You ejected?' Tad asked.

'*Ja*, and my back was badly twisted.' The German motioned to show his posture as the ejection seat fired, but winced and quickly straightened himself out.

Wojcik nodded knowingly. Back injuries were almost certain if a pilot's spine wasn't perfectly straight when he ejected. It was a common problem, but compared to being a thin red smear on the landscape . . .

'Unfortunately I landed in Poland. Where your soldiers found me and took me to hospital. Where they put me in a damned big cast. As much to keep me away from the beautiful Polish nurses as to help me, I think.' Kurtz smiled, swinging his arms to show his freedom. 'Now that the war is over, they have released me. And I am on my way home.' He paused. 'But in the hospital I asked who had shot me down. Natural curiosity, I think.' The German grinned again. 'Imagine my surprise when they were actually able to find out. But I was not so surprised to hear that I was downed by an ace – a hot pilot.'

Tad remembered the fierce engagement. 'You were pretty good yourself,' he countered.

The German leaned forward. 'When you fired your cannon, it was a lucky shot?'

Tad nodded emphatically. 'Yes. On your last turn, you slid further down than I expected, and I was pulling up . . .' His hands automatically came up to show the relative positions of the two fighters, elbows cocked as they moved.

Kurtz interrupted. 'I was trying to force you to overshoot. My speed brakes were open and I had cut my throttles.'

'I did overshoot,' Tad agreed. 'But only after my snapshot.'

He looked at the work on his desk, then at his watch. It was only two o'clock, but he wanted to know more, about that dogfight and this German pilot, so like himself. He stood up abruptly and picked up his uniform cap. 'Come on, let's get out of here and go over to the O Club. I'm buying.'

The two pilots left, hands already raised as they walked, Eagle and MiG maneuvering once more.

SEPTEMBER 19 – BERLIN

His suit had been carefully chosen to give him the 'banker' look. Solid, respectable, not a man to take risks. The only splash of color was a fashionable tie, but Willi von Seelow had needed help with that. Like most soldiers, his civilian clothes were usually badly out of style, because they rarely wore out.

Now Willi, along with his rapidly growing assemblage of aides, supporters, and staffers, stood watching the large-screen television set up along one of the hotel ballroom's walls.

Their 'victory party' had started early, right after the polls closed. Food, beer, and music helped make the interminable waiting more bearable. Although Willi was confident, he believed the outcome was far from certain. His supporters, whose futures depended on his rising star, were of course sure of his victory.

And in the end, they were right. A newsreader, with grave formality, announced, 'In the election returns from Berlin, our projections now show that Wilhelm von Seelow of the New Democratic Party has defeated his opponent, Ernst Kettering of the Social Democrats, with fifty-five percent of the vote.'

The ballroom erupted in cheers, and in midsong the band suddenly switched to a stirring march. As probable as victory had been, the new party, formed in the weeks since Schraeder's resignation, was only now meeting its first test, special postwar elections called to form a new, untainted government.

As suddenly as the cheers erupted, everyone hushed. A videotape of von Seelow speaking at an earlier political rally had flashed on the screen.

In it, Willi stood behind a podium, against a map of the Berlin district he was running to represent. The video clip cut in near the end of his speech. 'Let there be no doubt. Germany will be a great power in Europe – and in the world. But that power must be used more wisely than in the past. I left the army, not because I was ashamed of my service, but because the army only serves those elected to office. And those who have never seen battle with their own eyes or heard the wounded crying for help with their own ears are often far more ready for war than the soldiers they would send. Germany's brave men and brave women must never again be asked to shed their blood for a shameful cause – for aggression against our neighbors. Never again!'

Standing in the spotlights, his aristocratic bearing perfectly captured by the camera, Willi epitomized the good sense and decency the German people now knew had been lacking in Schraeder's mob. Combined with a political platform that emphasized open markets, lower taxes, and a firm commitment to the new, brighter future being hammered out in London, his election had been more certain than he would have ever admitted.

Some of his supporters had wanted him to become party chairman. In their view the New Democrats needed a national spokesman and Willi was the perfect choice. He had turned that down, though. He had no political experience, and he wanted to act – not just to give speeches.

No, for now, the Bundestag was the place for him, although people were already speculating about what might come next. A few terms in the legislature for seasoning, then perhaps a cabinet post. After that, who could say?

SEPTEMBER 24 – GDANSK

Capt. Mike Reynolds watched Alpha Company's soldiers file into the belly of a C-141 Starlifter transport plane. He was sorry to leave Poland, but most of his men couldn't have been happier. The hard work involved in rebuilding a nation ravaged by war had made them restless and eager to get home.

Reynolds was sure he would have felt the same, if he'd had a family waiting, too, but there was precious little in West Texas or Fort Campbell for him. Poland was far more interesting.

Nevertheless, the army said it was time to go. The speeches and ceremonies were over. The 3/187th's battalion colors bore a new battle honor. Those who had fallen in combat were at rest – buried in a new cemetery outside Swiecie. And those who had lived had been decorated, feted by town after town on their march north, and generally given a hero's farewell.

Reynolds straightened up, feeling the box containing the Silver Star he'd been awarded shift inside one of his pockets. He was proud of what that medal represented – proud of what he and his men had accomplished. Right now, though, he felt mostly sorrow for the men he couldn't bring back with him, for the Poles who had died beside them, and, oddly enough, even for the French and Germans.

The line of soldiers shuffled ahead. Now it was his turn. The last Alpha Company soldier to leave Polish soil, he stepped onto the C-141's ramp. Even this late in September, the dim interior of the plane was stifling in the afternoon heat, but that would change as soon as they were airborne.

Tomorrow they would be back at Fort Campbell, and in his mind Mike Reynolds was already starting to organize his thoughts around a peacetime schedule. The war was over. Now it was time to immerse himself again in the army routine – in training and more training, and, through it all, the continuous struggle to stay ready.

Until the next time.

GLOSSARY

ADC – British Air Defense Command, responsible for defending the U.K. against air attack.

Aegis cruiser (Leyte Gulf) – Technically called *Ticonderoga*-class cruisers, these ships are more commonly referred to by the name of their Aegis air defense system. This powerful combination of missiles, radars, and computers makes the 'Ticos' the most powerful surface warships in the world.

AH-64 Apache – A sophisticated, first-line gunship, the Apache carries laser-guided Hellfire antitank missiles, unguided rockets, and a 30mm cannon, along with an array of sensors so that it can fight at night as well as day. It is heavily armored.

AIM-7 Sparrow – A medium-range (about 20 to 25 miles) radar-guided air-to-air missile, the Sparrow can be carried by most American and many other Western-built fighters. It is moderately effective but is beginning to show its age. One problem is that the firing plane must keep its nose pointed at the missile's target. Even though the Sparrow is fast, Mach 4, those seconds are too long to fly straight in air combat. Sparrow is being replaced by the more modern AMRAAM.

AIM-9 Sidewinder – Almost legendary for its reliability and simplicity, the Sidewinder has appeared in dozens of versions and has been carried by scores of different aircraft. It has also been extensively copied. The missile's guidance package, or seeker, homes in on a heat source, usually a jet exhaust, but later versions can even detect the hot skin of a fast-moving aircraft. It has a relatively short range, about ten miles, less for earlier versions.

AIM-54 Phoenix – The longest-range air-to-air missile ever built, the Phoenix is carried only by the U.S. Navy's F-14 Tomcat. Combined with the Tomcat's weapons system, the Phoenix can attack targets over 100 miles away. It is a big missile, and not very maneuverable, but it flies over five times the speed of sound.

AIM-120 AMRAAM – The replacement for the Sparrow, the long-overdue advanced medium-range air-to-air missile will allow a plane to maneuver freely after launch, since the missile has its own active radar-seeker in the nose. The missile can also receive updates on its target's position from the launching plane. The French Mica, also in development, is similar. The AMRAAM's range is slightly better than the Sparrow's, about 30 miles.

Airmobile – The term 'airmobile' refers to a U.S. Army unit's ability to be moved quickly from one place to another by air, either by cargo plane or by helicopter. It does not refer to its mobility on the battlefield. *See* Light infantry.

AK-74/AKR – A replacement for the famous AK-47, the newer AK-74 is the standard Russian Army weapon and has been widely exported. It uses a smaller 5.45mm round and a 30-round magazine. The AK-74 weighs eight pounds without a magazine. The AKR is a smaller, carbine version of the AK-74 with a folding stock and a short barrel.

AKM – A modernized, refined version of the AK-47 assault rifle, it uses the same 7.62mm round and has the same performance. It weighs nine and a half pounds and has a 30-round magazine.

AMX-1OP – A boxy tracked vehicle with a steeply sloped front plate, this French APC can carry eight infantrymen and a crew of three. The vehicle's power-operated turret mounts a 20mm autocannon and a 7.62mm machine gun, but like other armored personnel carriers, the AMX-1OP is only lightly armored.

AMX-10RC – A six-wheeled French armored car, the AMX-10RC carries a 105mm gun equipped with a sophisticated fire control computer and ranging system. Although only lightly armored, it packs a powerful punch and is a useful scout vehicle.

An-26 – Called Curl by NATO, this light twin-engine turboprop is similar in size and role to the F-27 Fokker transports seen at many American airports. It cruises at 270 mph and can carry a load of six tons or 40 passengers.

ANL/ANS – The successor to the famous French Exocet, the ANS (surface-launched) and ANL (air-launched) will be longer-range (100+ miles), stealthy, and supersonic. These will present a difficult target for even the most sophisticated air defense weapons. They are due to enter service in the late 1990s.

APC – armored personnel carrier.

Arleigh Burke-class destroyer (**John Barry**) – These general-purpose ships carry a smaller version of the Aegis system and a moderate number of missiles. They also have good sonars and carry surface-to-surface missiles. Their only flaw is that they do not carry a helicopter. They have a pad on the fantail, but no hangar.

ARM – anti-radiation missile. This class of air-launched missiles homes in on the signal given off by an emitting radar. They can be set to attack a particular type of radar set. Once they reach the signals source, they explode and destroy the radar. The American HARM and French ARMAT are both ARMs.

ASMP – A French nuclear-armed missile, it is launched from a plane in flight and flies at three times the speed of sound. It carries a 150 kiloton warhead.

AT-4 – A Swedish-designed, shoulder-fired antitank rocket purchased for the U.S. Army, it weighs just over 13 pounds, and the rocket has a range of 300 meters.

ATGM – antitank guided missile.

AWACS – Airborne Warning and Control System. Often used as a nickname for the E-3 Sentry.

B-1B Lancer – Originally designed as a strategic nuclear bomber, the Lancer operates at low altitudes and high speed. The plane is now being adapted to a conventional role and can carry dozens of high-explosive bombs. It may also be able to carry a large number of laser-guided or optically guided bombs.

B-52 Stratofortress – Originally designed as a high-altitude, subsonic bomber, the B-52's long lifetime has seen it in many roles. It is equally capable of dropping both nuclear and conventional bombs.

Battalion – Consisting of three to five companies, a battalion generally contains between 800 and 1,200 men – with 50 or so tanks or APCs if the unit is armored or mechanized. Battalions are usually commanded by a lieutenant colonel, who will have a major as his executive officer. Several battalions make up a brigade.

Battery – a group of four to eight artillery pieces. They will usually all fire at the same target. Several batteries make up an artillery battalion.

BfV – Bundesamt für Verfassungsschutz, the Federal Office for the Protection of the Constitution. Roughly the German equivalent of the American FBI.

BRDM – A small, lightly armored, four-wheeled Russian reconnaissance car, it can carry a heavy machine gun or antitank missiles. It has been widely exported.

Brigade – Made up of three to four battalions, and smaller, specialized units, a brigade is commanded by a colonel or brigadier general. Several brigades make up a division.

BTR-80 – A Russian-designed, eight-wheeled troop carrier, it has light armor and only a heavy machine gun for armament. It can carry 14 troops.

CAP – combat air patrol. Fighters, armed and aloft, patrolling against sudden enemy air attack.

CIA – The Central Intelligence Agency is tasked to provide information on threats to the United States outside her own borders. For this purpose, the CIA has personnel assigned to foreign embassies around the world. The individual in charge is the 'chief of station.' CIA officers may operate openly, or they may have cover identities, e.g., 'assistant trade attaché.'

CIC – combat information center. A space on a warship where information from all the ship's sensors (radar, sonar, etc.) is collected, displayed, analyzed, and acted on. The ship's captain will 'fight his ship' from here, not from the bridge.

Company – A group of three to four platoons, totaling 100 to 200 men, a company is commanded by a captain. Tank companies contain ten to fifteen armored vehicles. Several companies make up a battalion.

Corps – A group of two to four divisions, a corps is commanded by a lieutenant general. A corps will usually contain roughly 40,000 soldiers and more than 1,000 tanks and APCs.

CP – command post.

DCI – director of Central Intelligence. The head of the CIA, besides running his own organization, is tasked with collecting and presenting information from all the U.S. intelligence agencies to the President. These include the Defense Intelligence Agency, the National Security Agency, and probably some outfits nobody's ever heard of.

DGSE – Direction Générale de Sécurité Extérieur. The General Directorate of External Security is the French security service, equivalent to the American CIA.

Division – In Western armies, divisions are made up of several brigades. In armies modeled on the Soviet pattern, divisions consist of several regiments. In both cases, divisions are commanded by major generals.

Durandal – A French-made weapon, the Durandal is a rocket-boosted, armor-piercing bomb dropped from a low-flying aircraft. The Durandal is designed to 'crater' runways so that they cannot be used by airplanes.

E-2C Hawkeye – The Hawkeye is a twin-turboprop airplane launched from aircraft carriers. It is unarmed, but it carries the APS-145 radar in a huge saucer on its back. Carrying a crew of radar operators and fighter controllers, the E-2C can spot air and surface contacts up to 250 miles away.

E-3 Sentry – An ultrasophisticated AWACS, the E-3 is built into a converted Boeing 707 airframe. Like the E-2C Hawkeye, the E-3 mounts a huge radar in a saucer on top. Its radar can spot sea surface and air targets 360 miles away, and vector fighters to intercept them.

EA-6B Prowler – An adaptation of the Intruder attack jet, the Prowler has a crew of four and is usually unarmed. Instead of carrying ordnance, it uses a suite of powerful jammers to scramble enemy radars and radio circuits.

ECM – electronic countermeasures. This term is technically defined as a range of measures designed to deny the enemy the use of radar or radio but is used colloquially to mean radar or radio jamming.

EMCON – Emission control is the technique of shutting down radars and radios so that the enemy will not detect their emissions and learn of your presence. 'Radio silence' is a common part of EMCON, but to be effective it must include radars and even active sonar emissions as well.

ESM – electronic support measures. This meaningless term describes equipment used to detect enemy radars. All radars send out energy and 'listen' for 'echoes' bouncing back from solid surfaces. The energy they emit can be detected by another radar receiver, and, depending on the signal's characteristics, it can give the listener the direction and type of enemy unit.

F-14 Tomcat – A huge, carrier-launched fighter, the F-14 is designed exclusively to engage enemy aircraft at long range with Phoenix and Sparrow radar-guided missiles. It is also fairly maneuverable and carries Sidewinders and a 20mm cannon for close-in work. The Tomcat has two engines and a crew of two.

F-15 Eagle – First appearing in the 1970s, the Eagle is an outstanding air-to-air fighter, equipped with the powerful APG-70 radar and up to eight air-to-air missiles, as well as a 20mm rotary cannon. It has a long range, is very maneuverable, but is a little on the large side.

F-15E Strike Eagle – This two-seat version of the F-15 can still carry air-to-air missiles, but it is intended for long-range, low-altitude attack missions, hitting enemy targets well back from the front lines.

F-22 Lightning II – The newest generation of U.S. Air Force fighter, the Lightning is meant to replace the Eagle. It is incredibly maneuverable, and stealthy, armed with advanced missiles like the AMRAAM and a rotary cannon. It will enter service in the very late 1990s.

F-117A – The famous, oddly angled 'Black Jet' is used by the U.S. Air Force to destroy vital, heavily defended targets. Alternately it can attack the defenses themselves, clearing the way for more conventional aircraft to attack safely. A combination of flat surfaces and special materials makes the plane virtually invisible to radar. Its official name is Nighthawk, but it is called the Black Jet by its crews.

F/A-18 Hornet – A twin-engine, single-seat jet designed to replace the A-7 Corsair II, the F-18 is a multirole aircraft designed to be equally adept as either an attack aircraft or an air-superiority fighter. It is very maneuverable and is designed to be launched from carriers.

FA MAS – One of the most compact assault rifles ever designed, the FA MAS is the French Army's standard infantry weapon. It uses a 'bullpup' configuration with the trigger group in front of a 25-round magazine. Its unique appearance has earned it the nickname Le Clarion (the Bugle).

Fire team – The smallest unit of tactical firepower. A fire team contains three or four men led by a corporal or junior sergeant. For instance, it might have three riflemen, one of whom also has a grenade launcher, and a man with a light machine gun. Two or three fire teams make up a squad.

FIS – Federal Investigative Service, the Russian agency that has assumed the old KGB's internal security and counterintelligence functions.

FLIR – forward-looking infrared. A heat-sensitive TV camera used by aircraft that displays a magnified image on a video screen. It is very effective, in both day and night.

Fuchs – A German armored personnel carrier, it has six wheels, light armor, and can carry 14 troops. It is often used for specialized purposes, such as carrying surveillance radars, supplies, or as a command vehicle.

G3A3 – The standard German infantry weapon, it fires a large 7.62mm round and weighs almost ten pounds. It has a 20-shot magazine. It has been widely exported.

G11 – The planned standard weapon for the German Army, this futuristic-looking rifle is expected to enter service around the turn of the century. It fires a 4.7mm caseless round from a 50-round magazine and weighs just over eight pounds. It has an extremely high rate of fire and will be very accurate.

Gazelle – This French-made light helicopter has been widely exported. It can carry two men and a light load of antitank missiles or an autocannon. It is usually used for scouting.

G-PALS – Global Protection Against Limited Strikes. The name currently used to describe a planned strategic defense system that would destroy enemy ballistic missiles before they could reach their targets. As currently envisioned, the system would include ground-based interceptors in the continental U.S., mobile ground-based interceptors to accompany U.S. military units overseas, and several 'constellations' of advanced space-based interceptors in low earth orbit.

HELIOS – a French surveillance satellite.

HOT – A Franco-German antitank missile, it has a long range (4,000 meters) and a large warhead, and is in the same class as the American TOW.

HUD – heads-up display. Projects important information onto a piece of glass mounted directly in front of the pilot's eyes, making it possible to avoid going 'heads down' to look at cockpit instruments. The HUD is a vital aid during fast-moving air combat. The data displayed includes speed, altitude, weapons status, g-forces, target data, and fuel status.

Humvee – Actually HMMWV, but pronounced '*humm*-vee,' this light utility truck replaced the U.S. Army's jeep, which was proving too small to carry many loads. The jeep's gasoline engine was also a drawback, and the HMMWV uses a diesel.

IFF – Identification, Friend or Foe. In this method of identifying unknown aircraft, an air-search radar uses a special attachment to send out coded radar pulses. A transponder (receiver-transmitter) on the plane checks the code, and if it is correct, responds with a signal identifying the aircraft. Unfriendly aircraft do not respond to the signal – appearing only as a radar blip.

IR – Infrared. This refers to the heat emitted by objects. This heat can be detected, and even used as a light source.

IR homing – Some air-to-air missiles home in on the heat generated by an aircraft. The first IR seekers, built in the 1950s, had to be looking almost directly up a jet engine's tailpipe. They were also easily deceived by flares or the sun. Current-generation IR seekers can 'see' the hot metal on the leading edge of a plane's wing, as well as its exhaust, and over a much larger field of view. They are also very hard to decoy. The

American Sidewinder, French Magic, and Russian Archer AAMs all use IR homing.

Iwo Jima-class assault carrier (**Inchon**) – Although these ships look like aircraft carriers, they do not carry jet aircraft. Instead they carry large helicopters and up to a battalion of marines.

Javelin – A replacement for the near-worthless Dragon, the Javelin antitank missile has a range of 2,000 meters and can either attack the thin top armor of a main battle tank or the side armor of a lightly armored vehicle. Unlike its predecessor, it does not use a wire, but carries its own 'fire and forget' homing system. It takes a team of three men to carry the launcher and reload missiles. Javelin will enter U.S. Army service in the mid-1990s.

Kormoran 2 – A German-built antiship missile, the Kormoran has a relatively short range (just over 30 miles) but flies at sea-skimming altitude. This makes it a difficult target for many antiaircraft weapons. It carries a 480-pound warhead.

Leahy-class cruiser (**Dale**) – These large ships were purpose-built to escort an aircraft carrier and protect it from air attack. They also carry some antisubmarine and antisurface weapons, but their 'main battery' is a pair of twin-railed surface-to-air missile launchers, one forward, one aft.

LeClerc – An advanced French battle tank, the LeClerc will replace the aging AMX-30s in the mid-1990s. It uses composite layered armor and is fitted with a 120mm gun and an auto loader. It is in the same class as the U.S. M1A2 Abrams and the German Leopard 2.

Leopard 1 – The first German tank built after World War II, it appeared in the 1960s. Combining a low silhouette with high speed and a 105mm gun, the Leopard was more than a match for its expected adversary, the T-55, and even its successor, the T-62. It was replaced in front line service in the late 1970s by the Leopard 2.

Leopard 2 – Larger and heavier than the Leopard 1, the Leopard 2 is the equal of the M1A2 Abrams but appeared several years earlier. It carries a 120mm gun, a sophisticated fire control system, and is fitted with advanced armor, which greatly increases its protection against tank-killing missiles.

Light infantry – Several types of infantry units, airborne, airmobile, and Rangers among them, class themselves as 'light' infantry. They do not have many armored vehicles, if any, or in most cases even trucks. This makes them less than mobile on a modern battlefield, but in proper terrain, they can cause the enemy a great deal of trouble. Because they are 'light,' they are easily transported and are often the first units present in a conflict.

LNG – liquefied natural gas.

Los Angeles-class submarine (**Boston**) – The principal U.S. attack sub class, the *Los Angeles* boats carry a powerful sonar suite and four torpedo tubes. Almost twenty years after entering service, they are still among the most effective subs in existence.

Luchs – An eight-wheeled armored car, the Luchs carries a 20mm gun in a small turret. It is lightly armored but is very useful for scouting.

M1A2 Abrams – The American main battle tank, the latest versions of which carry a 120mm gun and layered armor. A very fast, well-armored vehicle with a sophisticated fire control system, the Abrams is a match for any other tank now in production.

M2 Bradley – Designed to carry infantry, the Bradley is classed as an 'infantry fighting vehicle,' because it also mounts a 25mm gun and a TOW antitank missile launcher.

M16 – The standard U.S. Army infantry weapon, it is much lighter and smaller than its predecessor, the M14 rifle. The M16 weighs eight and a half pounds.

M113 – One of the first armored personnel carriers, the M113 has been produced in huge numbers, and has seen service all over the world. Nothing more than a lightly armored box on a tracked chassis, it can carry 11 troops.

M577 – A variant of the M113 personnel carrier, it is fitted out with radios and map tables for use as a command vehicle.

MAD – Magnetic anomaly detector. A sensitive instrument used to detect the minute bending in the earth's magnetic field caused by large masses of metal (like submarine hulls). It has a very short range.

Marder – A German infantry fighting vehicle, it currently mounts a 20mm cannon and an antitank missile launcher in a small turret. The German Army plans to upgrade its existing Marders with a new 25mm cannon during the 1990s.

Mica – A new French air-to-air missile in the same class as the American AMRAAM, the Mica will be launched from the Mirage 2000 and the Rafale. It can be fitted with either a radar or heat-seeking head, and has a range of 30 miles.

MiG-29 Fulcrum – An advanced Russian air-superiority fighter, the Fulcrum is in the same class as the American F/A-18 Hornet and the French Mirage 2000. It carries both radar-guided and heat-seeking missiles and carries a 30mm cannon. It is fitted with the Slot Back radar.

Milan – A wire-guided Franco-German antitank missile in the same class as the American Dragon but much more effective, it has a range of 2,000 meters and is used by many countries.

Mirage 2000 – A French delta-winged air superiority fighter, it is designed to carry air-to-air missiles, but it can also carry air-to-surface and antiship missiles.

Mirage F1 – An older French fighter, the swept-wing F1 can carry the Super 530 air-to-air missile and a light load of bombs or missiles.

MP5 – Built in many different versions, the MP5 is a submachine gun firing a 9mm round from a 15- or 30-shot magazine. It weighs about five pounds and is carried by armored vehicle crews and other troops whose duties prevent them from carrying a rifle.

Nimitz-class carrier **(George Washington, Vinson, Theodore Roosevelt)** – These nuclear-powered aircraft carriers displace almost 100,000 tons and are over 1,000 feet long. They can carry 80 to 90 aircraft and crews of more than 6,000.

O. H. Perry-class frigate **(Simpson, Klakring)** – Designed to escort other ships, *Perry*-class frigates have a good mix of antisubmarine, antiaircraft, and antisurface weapons, but their relatively small size prevents them from carrying a heavy armament.

Ossie – a derogatory term in German used to describe former East Germans, from the German *ost*, for 'east.' Ossies are regarded as lazy and without ambition, as well as potentially disloyal.

PAH-2 – A heavily armored Franco-German attack helicopter, it will carry a mix of advanced antitank missiles and 30mm cannon. It has a crew of two and is in the same class as the American Apache and the Russian Havoc.

Panzer – the term used to describe German units primarily made up of tanks.

Panzergrenadiers – German armored infantry, or infantry riding in armored troop carriers.

Phalanx – An automated close-in defense weapon against antiship missiles, it combines a 20mm Gatling cannon and a high-frequency radar. Firing a stream of depleted uranium projectiles, it is very accurate.

Platoon – a group of three or four squads, led by a first or second lieutenant, with about 30 to 40 troops. Tank platoons contain three to five armored vehicles. Several platoons make up a company.

Proximity fuse – A small device used primarily against aircraft, it detonates a shell or missile warhead when it passes near the plane. Proximity fuses use radar, laser, or infrared seekers to measure the distance to a target.

Puma – A French-designed troop-carrying helicopter, it can carry 16 infantrymen and has been widely exported.

R.550 Magic 2 – A heat-seeking missile designed and exported by the French, it is in the same class as later models of the American Sidewinder. It has a range of about ten miles.

Rafale – An advanced air superiority fighter, its only match is the American F-22 Lightning. A computer-controlled flight system and fully movable canards will make the Rafale extremely maneuverable. Designed to be 'low observable,' it will be difficult to spot by radar or IR, although not a full stealth design.

Regiment – In the Russian pattern, three to four battalions make up a regiment. Commanded by a colonel, four regiments make up a Russian-style division.

Regimental system – All U.S. army formations are based on regiments of three battalions. Some of these regiments have histories going back to the Revolutionary War, and soldiers identify themselves with their assigned regiment. Battalions from the regiment will be assigned on a long-term basis to various divisions. For example, the 3rd Brigade of the 101st Airborne Division is made up of all three battalions of the 187th Infantry Regiment.

RPG, RPG-16 – rocket propelled grenade. These Russian one-man antitank weapons use a shaped charge to penetrate a tank's side or rear armor, at short ranges, usually 50 to 500 meters. The latest model is the RPG-16, which carries one rocket in a disposable tube.

RWR – radar warning receiver. A special detector on board an aircraft that warns of enemy weapons radars locked on the plane.

Sabot (pronounced '*say*-bo') – A solid tungsten dart launched from a tank cannon, it penetrates enemy armor by sheer punch.

SAM – surface-to-air missile.

Seahawk – The Sikorsky SH-60B Seahawk is carried by many U.S. Navy ships. It can be used to hunt subs or serve as a scout with its wide variety of sensors.

Section – a group of two artillery pieces, missile launchers, or other special vehicles that operate as a team on the battlefield. It is equivalent to an infantry fire team. Two or three sections make up a platoon or a battery.

SIS – Secret Intelligence Service. The United Kingdom's primary intelligence organization.

Spruance-class destroyer – A general-purpose warship that began entering service in the mid-1970s, it is a very effective antisubmarine vessel and can also attack surface targets. The same hull is used for the Aegis cruisers.

SPY-1 – The SPY radar is the heart of the Aegis air defense system and the *Ticonderoga*-class cruisers. Based on four huge nonrotating radar antennas, a sophisticated computer electronically steers the beams. It can detect aircraft and surface targets. The radar has a range of about 200 miles.

Squad – Led by a sergeant, a squad has two or three fire teams, totaling 10 to 14 men. Several squads make up a platoon.

Staff abbreviations – Battalion and brigade commanders (and larger organizations) have staffs to assist them. U.S. Army staffs are organized on uniform lines. The S-1 is in charge of personnel, S-2 is intelligence, S-3 is operations, S-4 is supply, and S-5 is civil affairs.

Standard missile series – The U.S. Navy's long-range antiaircraft missile, it is used by itself as a medium-range weapon (SMIMR) or with a booster for extended range (SMIER). A newer version of the missile, introduced in the early 1980s, is the Standard 2, which is also used in two versions, called SM2MR and SM2ER.

Stealth technology – A relatively new technology, stealth involves designing aircraft so that they are hidden from radar, infrared, and even sound detection. A plane may be completely stealthy, which can be very expensive, or it may just have its 'signature' reduced. Stealth not only reduces the chance of original detection but also prevents enemy weapons from locking onto the plane.

T-55 – A 1950s-vintage tank, this Russian-designed vehicle mounts a 100mm gun. Badly outclassed by almost any Western design, its only virtue is a low silhouette.

T-72 – A 1970s-era tank, the T-72 mounts a 125mm gun fitted with a laser range finder and an automatic loader. It is outclassed by the Ml Abrams, the German Leopard 2, and the French LeClerc. Like the T-55, it has been widely exported.

T-80 – The present-day Russian main battle tank, the T-80 mounts a 125mm gun coupled to an advanced fire control system. It is fitted with both layered and reactive armor. In addition to a shell, the gun can also fire a laser-guided antitank missile with a range of several kilometers. In general ability, the T-80 is at worst half a notch below the M1A2.

Thermal imager – A heat-sensitive TV camera, it displays a black-and-white image where objects can be viewed clearly in day or night. In addition to darkness, thermal imagers can 'see' through dust and some types of smoke. They are blocked by fog, rain, and special types of smoke. Thermal imagers are widely used for battlefield surveillance and as weapons sights.

TOC – tactical operations center. A battalion command post, usually consisting of several specialized command vehicles.

Tomahawk – A ship- and sub-launched long-range cruise missile, different variants can be launched against ships and land targets. There is also a nuclear version, presently removed from service. The Tomahawk carries a large high-explosive warhead or submunitions. It is very accurate, with new versions adding improved guidance features and stealth.

TOW – tube-launched, optically tracked, wire-guided missile. A long-range 'heavyweight' antitank missile, the TOW has undergone several improvements and is still an effective missile. It is fired from a ground-mounted tripod or from vehicles.

UH-60 Blackhawk – The standard U.S. Army troop-carrying helicopter, the Blackhawk can carry 11 troops and has many features designed to improve its survivability on the battlefield.

V-22 Osprey – A proposed replacement for the U.S. Navy CH-46 Sea Knight, the V-22 uses 'tilt-rotor' technology. Starting out as helicopter rotors, the plane's huge propellers are rotated forward after takeoff for normal forward flight. It is an excellent performer, but there are questions about its cost, and bureaucratic resistance to its development.

Vampires – radio shorthand for antiship cruise missiles.

Wessie – a German term, derogatory slang for West Germans. Ex-East Germans regard Westerners as arrogant and exploitative, trying to take advantage of their present economic distress.

ZSU-23-4 Shilka – A track-mounted antiaircraft vehicle, it carries a turret with four radar-guided 23mm autocannon. Although it appeared in the 1960s, it is still an effective weapon.